EX LIBRIS

VINTAGE **CLASSICS**

IRIS MURDOCH

Iris Murdoch was born in Dublin in 1919. She read Classics at Somerville College, Oxford, and after working in the Treasury and abroad, was awarded a research studentship in Philosophy at Newnham College, Cambridge. In 1948 she returned to Oxford as fellow and tutor at St Anne's College and later taught at the Royal College of Art. Until her death in 1999, she lived in Oxford with her husband, the academic and critic John Bayley. She was made a Dame of the British Empire in 1987 and in the 1997 PEN Awards received the Gold Pen for Distinguished Service to Literature.

Iris Murdoch made her writing debut in 1954 with *Under the Net*. Her twenty-six novels include the Booker prize-winning *The Sea, The Sea* (1978), the James Tait Black Memorial prize-winning *The Black Prince* (1973) and the Whitbread prize-winning *The Sacred and Profane Love Machine* (1974). Her philosophy includes *Sartre: Romantic Rationalist* (1953) and *Metaphysics as a Guide to Morals* (1992); other philosophical writings, including 'The Sovereignty of Good' (1970), are collected in *Existentialists and Mystics* (1997).

ALSO BY IRIS MURDOCH

Fiction

Non-Fiction

IRIS MURDOCH

The Sea, The Sea

WITH AN INTRODUCTION BY

Daisy Johnson

VINTAGE

2 4 6 8 10 9 7 5 3 1

Vintage
20 Vauxhall Bridge Road,
London SW1V 2SA

Vintage Classics is part of the Penguin Random House group of companies
whose addresses can be found at global.penguinrandomhouse.com.

Penguin
Random House
UK

This edition reissued in Vintage in 2019
First published in Vintage in 1999
First published in Great Britain in 1978 by Chatto & Windus

www.vintage-books.co.uk

A CIP catalogue record for this book is available from the British Library

ISBN 9781784875190

Typeset in 10.75/13.25 pt Perpetua
by Integra Software Services Pvt. Ltd, Pondicherry

Printed and bound in Great Britain by Clays Ltd, Elcograf S.p.A.

Penguin Random House is committed to a sustainable future for
our business, our readers and our planet. This book is made
from Forest Stewardship Council® certified paper.

Contents

To Rosemary Cramp

INTRODUCTION

I first encountered Iris Murdoch not through her writing but in the book *Elegy for Iris*, which her husband, John Bayley, wrote about living with her when she had Alzheimer's disease. I was working on a novel, later titled *Everything Under*, which was in part about a woman living with her mother who had a degenerative disease. It was not something I had personal experience of, and I was nervous about writing about it. I read *Still Alice* by Lisa Genova and *The Almost Moon* by Alice Sebold and then discovered *Elegy for Iris*. It is not an easy book to read. Bayley writes: 'Inside marriage, one ceases to be observant because observation has become automatic, its object at once absorbing and taken for granted.'[1] The book is not only about what it was like to care for Murdoch but what it was like to love her. He describes the slow degeneration of her logic and language, watching *Teletubbies* together in the mornings, calming her anxiety and agitation which often came around language and her own understanding of it. It felt unfair of me to encounter her this way first, without having read the work which she presented to the world. Murdoch was, as she describes in an interview in the

---

[1] *Elegy for Iris* by John Bayley (Picador, 1999), p. 213

Paris Review, a great planner, writing 'one piece of imagination leads to another'.[2] So often as writers we throw our work ahead of us, our carefully chosen sentences like nets to protect us from scrutiny. Nets made, as she says, of these pieces of imagination.

Still, I did not read her then either. I had studied English literature at university and come away from the experience saturated with the canon, these books a person should or must have read. For a long time I read only contemporary novels, mulishly, as a reaction to those years of enforced Charles Dickens and James Joyce. I have never liked being told what to read. It is only now that I am, tentatively, coming back to all the books I have missed through my stubbornness.

When I was asked to write this introduction, I came to the task with trepidation. Everyone said good things about *The Sea, The Sea* but for years people had told me I would love specific books which I had then gone on not to enjoy. I think often of the story of *The Emperor's New Clothes* in which two weavers promise an emperor the finest outfit around, so fine that it is invisible to anyone who is unfit to see it. I began reading *The Sea, The Sea* and immediately wished I had read it sooner. I was prepared to write an introduction out of necessity, with a critical eye, but I was unprepared to love *The Sea, The Sea* as much as I did. I hope that you love it too.

The novel comes to us in the form of a journal – an almost-maybe memoir – narrated by Charles Arrowby, an ageing actor who has moved from the city to a house by the sea. He writes, to begin with, ramblingly, often distracted. His days are long and glorious, he swims and describes in detail simple – but very specific – meals, he talks about

---

[2] *Paris Review*, https://www.theparisreview.org/interviews/2313/iris-murdoch-the-art-of-fiction-no-117-iris-murdoch

how glad he is that he has made the move. The descriptions of these meals are some of my favourite moments in the book: 'spaghetti with a little butter and dried basil. (Basil is of course the king of herbs.) Then spring cabbage cooked slowly with dill. Boiled onions served with bran, herbs, soya oil and tomatoes, with one egg beaten in. With these a slice or two of cold tinned corned beef.' He is unreliable – one of the great unreliable narrators – but we do not know that yet. The journal format means that Charles is entirely in charge; we know as little or as much about him as he wants us to.

Later in the book Charles is less rambling and the peace in the house on the cliff is destroyed. Often I read with my teeth gritted and my hand ready to cover my eyes. Murdoch's plotting is pitch-perfect, her sense of how a person reads a book exquisite. We watch Charles slowly and irrevocably ruin his life and the lives of those around him. At times we laugh out loud or gasp, often we hate him and sometimes we pity him, and a lot of the time we understand him despite everything.

Throughout the book water runs like a spell or a curse. The sea of the title is not just a background or vista, it is a character. At times it seems to reflect Charles's moods, his unhealthy obsessions, his bouts of serenity. The rope Charles has tied to a rock to haul himself from the water after swims is swept away again and again; the sea is sometimes docile and at others raging, storm-swept. The tides come and go just as the journal sometimes seems to do, dragging us along different routes and funnels, forever changing direction. The sea takes everything, and this book sometimes appears as warning as well as yarn. We can try but the tide will always bring the water back.

In a time when fiction seems to be growing resolutely weirder, bending and breaking the boundaries between genres, reaching for the strange and the uncanny to better understand the world we live in, Iris Murdoch is the perfect companion. Her writing inhabits an underbelly of darkness that we dip in and out of, always watchful of. The sea broils with monsters, there are ghosts or poltergeists or intruders. The home here is not homely or safe. Bedrooms become prisons, rooms in the city are piled high with abandoned furniture, doors do not keep anyone out. If ghost stories are about what comes back, what returns, what will not stay down, then *The Sea, The Sea* is a ghost story with the same fierce, growing momentum that horror has.

Weirdness, here, wins out. We long for a succinct ending, a conclusion in which to draw together the story. The novel falls into fragmentation, language betrays Charles and us; the journal cannot continue forever.

The Sea, The Sea seems, in part, to be about what it is to grow older and look back on a life both well and badly lived. Again and again Charles professes that marriage is a cage, demeans his friendships and familial relationships. He tries to escape to the coast, but everything he has ever known (first and last loves, betrayed friends, misunderstood relatives) follows him there, sometimes in weird, almost ridiculous moments of coincidence. The house by the sea could almost be seen as some underworld place of judgement where everything we have done is paraded before us, all of our decisions gone over again and again. Charles is offered, if not retribution, then an opportunity to make better decisions. Of this he is incapable. He is like Estragon and Vladimir, waiting for a character who never comes and never comes again and again and again.

Iris Murdoch was shortlisted for the Booker Prize six times, eventually winning with *The Sea, The Sea* in 1978. It is not a book of our times although it does, still, feel relevant to our discussion of toxic masculinity. Charles's litany of former lovers almost all reappear and have something to say for themselves, but it is Charles who narrates the story and we are carefully reminded of this throughout. One of the great joys of the book is to see beyond the things that Charles tells us, to observe the overwhelming dominance in the way he uses language, how he wields love like a weapon. In the end, perhaps, we understand that he is the ghost who moves through the house and through his own life, futile in his misunderstanding. The women who he has hurt often get their revenge because they are happy or content or simply living in a way that he does not seem to be able to do. In one scene a woman crouches on the cliffs and throws rocks at the carful of men until the windscreen cracks and the vehicle has to be abandoned. The life Charles has tried to build by the sea is riven and we are, in the end, glad of it.

The narrative style of the novel meant that often I expected to look up and see Charles (or Iris) sitting across the table drinking retsina and eating canned fruit, eyeing me with both suspicion and greed, glad of a good listener. I tried out some of Charles's meals and at times, after I had put the book down for the day, felt as if I could still hear him, offering observations about the river outside the house, the state of the rooms in which I live.

I live in Oxford, the same city where Iris and her husband lived for a long time. One sunny Saturday in February I walk along the river and canal to Iris's street. It is possible to walk almost entirely from my house to hers without leaving the water. The house is hidden by trees and I skulk around, trying to get a good view. It is difficult to know what I went there to find. Her ghost or some slither of the inspiration she found to write such a book. Curtains in the houses opposite flicker. Down the end of the road the heat haze looks almost like a sea monster, there and then gone, rising from the concrete water. My partner crosses the street and takes a photo of me standing on the pavement outside the house. I had not expected to feel anything — had already earmarked a pub to make the trip worthwhile — but standing there there's a flutter of something, momentous, tingling. We hang around for as long as we can without seeming suspicious and then walk back down to the water, stop for a drink. I tell my partner about Iris and what I have come to love about her work. I relate a story I discovered in the *Guardian* about Iris and John losing a large and expensive pork pie in the wild, beautiful untidiness of their house.[3]

I think about getting lost in the library at my university when I was younger. I spent a lot of time crouched in the stacks, searching for particular books or simply searching, picking things at random or because I liked the spines, the sound of the names. There were automatic lights which went off if you kept still too long and sometimes tiny birds got in and flew around above the shelves. I was not a discerning reader, found it difficult to tell which books I liked and which I enjoyed because I'd been told I should. Still, I began in those lonely days, to create a canon not from the books I was expected to read but from the ones which meant something to me, whose writing moved me in some way. Now, later, hopefully a better reader, I think of the importance of creating a canon without limitations, with authors who do not all look or sound the same, created because of the writing we love not the writing we should love. Everyone's canon will, of course, look different but *The Sea, The Sea* holds a steady position in mine. It is a joy to think not of the language Murdoch eventually lost, but of the language she gave us.

Daisy Johnson, 2019

---

[3] https://www.theguardian.com/books/2001/mar/18/biography.irismurdoch

PREHISTORY

THE sea which lies before me as I write glows rather than sparkles in the bland May sunshine. With the tide turning, it leans quietly against the land, almost unflecked by ripples or by foam. Near to the horizon it is a luxurious purple, spotted with regular lines of emerald green. At the horizon it is indigo. Near to the shore, where my view is framed by rising heaps of humpy yellow rock, there is a band of lighter green, icy and pure, less radiant, opaque however, not transparent. We are in the north, and the bright sunshine cannot penetrate the sea. Where the gentle water taps the rocks there is still a surface skin of colour. The cloudless sky is very pale at the indigo horizon which it lightly pencils in with silver. Its blue gains towards the zenith and vibrates there. But the sky looks cold, even the sun looks cold.

I had written the above, destined to be the opening paragraph of my memoirs, when something happened which was so extraordinary and so horrible that I cannot bring myself to describe it even now after an interval of time and although a possible, though not totally reassuring, explanation has occurred to me. Perhaps I shall feel calmer and more clear-headed after yet another interval.

I spoke of a memoir. Is that what this chronicle will prove to be? Time will show. At this moment, a page old, it feels more like a diary than a memoir. Well, let it be a diary then. How I regret that I did not keep one earlier, what a record that would have been! But now the main events of my life are over and there is to be nothing but 'recollection in tranquillity'. To repent of a life of egoism? Not exactly, yet something of the sort. Of course I never said this to the ladies and gentlemen of the theatre. They would never have stopped laughing.

The theatre is certainly a place for learning about the brevity of human glory: oh all those wonderful glittering absolutely vanished pantomimes! Now I shall abjure magic and become a hermit: put myself in a situation where I can honestly say that I have nothing else to do but to learn to be good. The end of life is rightly thought of as a period of meditation. Will I be sorry that I did not begin it sooner?

It is necessary to write, that much is clear, and to write in a way quite unlike any way which I have employed before. What I wrote before was written in water and deliberately so. This is for permanence, something which cannot help hoping to endure. Yes, already I personify the object, the little book, the *libellus,* this creature to which I am giving life and which seems at once to have a will of its own. It wants to live, it wants to survive.

I have considered writing a journal, not of happenings for there will be none, but as a record of mingled thoughts and daily observations: 'my philosophy', my *pensées* against a background of simple descriptions of the weather and other natural phenomena. This now seems to me again to be a good idea. The sea. I could fill a volume simply with my word-pictures of it. I would certainly like to write some sustained account of my surroundings, its flora and fauna. This could be of some interest, if I persevered, even though I am no White of Selborne. From my sea-facing window at this moment I can see three different kinds of gulls, swallows, a cormorant, innumerable butterflies drifting about over the flowers which grow miraculously upon my yellow rocks ...

I must make no attempt at 'fine writing' however, that would be to spoil my enterprise. Besides, I should merely make a fool of myself.

Oh blessed northern sea, a real sea with clean merciful tides, not like the stinking soupy Mediterranean!

They say there are seals here, but I have seen none yet.

Of course there is no need to separate 'memoir' from 'diary' or 'philosophical journal'. I can tell you, reader, about my past life and about my 'world-view' also, as I ramble along. Why not? It can all come out naturally as I reflect. Thus unanxiously (for am I not now leaving anxiety behind?) I shall discover my 'literary form'. In any case, why decide now? Later, if I please, I can regard these ramblings as rough notes for a more coherent account. Who knows indeed how interesting I shall find my past life when I begin to tell it? Perhaps I shall bring the story gradually up to date and as it were float my present upon my past?

To repent of egoism: is autobiography the best method? Well, being no philosopher I can only reflect about the world through reflecting about my own adventures in it. And I feel that it is time to *think* about myself at last. It may seem odd that one who has been described in the popular press as a 'tyrant', a 'tartar', and (if I recall) a 'power-crazed monster' should feel that he has not hitherto done so! But this is the case. I have in fact very little sense of identity.

It is indeed only lately that I have felt this need to write something that is both personal and reflective. In the days when I wrote in water I imagined that the only book I would ever publish would be a cookery book!

I might now introduce myself – to myself, first and foremost, it occurs to me. What an odd discipline autobiography turns out to be. To others, if these words are printed in the not too distant future, there will be in a superficial sense 'no need of an introduction', as they say at meetings. How long does mortal fame endure? My kind of fame not very long, but long enough. Yes, yes, I am Charles Arrowby and, as I write this, I am, shall we say, over sixty years of age. I am wifeless, childless, brotherless, sisterless, I am my well-known self, made glittering and brittle by fame. I determined long ago that I would retire from the theatre when I had passed sixty. ('You will *never* retire,' Wilfred told me. 'You will be *unable* to.' He was wrong.) In fact I am tired of the theatre, I have had enough. This is what no one who knew me well, not Sidney nor Peregrine nor Fritzie, not Wilfred nor Clement when they were alive, could either foresee or imagine. And it is not just a matter of sagely departing 'on the crest of the wave'. (How many actors and directors pathetically overstay their welcome.) I am tired of it all. There has been a moral change.

'All right, go,' they said, 'but don't imagine that you can come back.' I don't want to come back, thank you! 'If you stop working and live alone you will go quietly mad.' (This was Sidney's contribution.) On the contrary, I feel completely sane and free and happy for the first time in my life!

It is not that I ever came to 'disapprove' of the theatre, as my mother, for instance, never ceased to do. I just knew that if I stayed in it any longer I would begin to wilt spiritually, would lose something which had travelled with me patiently so far, but might go away if I did not attend to it at last: something not belonging to the preoccupations of my work, but preciously separate from it. I remember James saying something about people who end their lives in caves. Well, this, here, is my cave. And I have reached it bearing the precious thing that has come with me, as if it were a talisman which I can now unwrap. How grand and pompous this sounds! And yet I confess I scarcely know what I mean. Let us break off these rather ponderous reflections for a while.

The above observations have been written on a sequence of different days, wonderful empty solitary days, such as I remember yearning for, and never quite believing that I wanted so much that I would finally obtain them.

I went swimming again but still cannot discover quite the right place. This morning I simply dived into deep water off the rocks nearest to the house, where they descend almost sheer, yet with folds and ledges enough to make a precarious stairway. My 'cliff' I call it, though it is barely twenty feet high at low tide. Of course the water is very cold, but after a few seconds it seems to coat the body in a kind of warm silvery skin, as if one had acquired the scales of a merman. The challenged blood rejoices with a new strength. Yes, this is my natural element. How strange to think that I never saw the sea until I was fourteen.

I am a skilful fearless swimmer and I am not afraid of rough water. Today the sea was gentle compared with antipodean oceans where I have sported like a dolphin. My problem was almost a technical one. Even though the swell was fairly mild I had a ridiculous amount of difficulty getting back onto the rocks again. The 'cliff' was a little too steep, the ledges a little too narrow. The gentle waves teased me, lifting me up towards the rock face, then plucking me away. My fingers, questing for a crevice, were again and again pulled off. Becoming tired, I swam around trying other places where the sea was running restlessly in and out, but the difficulty was greater since there was deep water below me and even if the rocks were less sheer they were smoother or slippery with weed and I could not hold on. At last I managed to climb up my cliff, clinging with fingers and toes, then kneeling sideways upon a ledge. When I reached the top and lay panting in the sun I found that my hands and knees were bleeding.

Since my arrival I have had the pleasure of swimming naked. This rocky coast attracts, thank God, no trippers with their 'kiddies'. There is not a vestige of beastly sand anywhere. I have heard it called an ugly coast. Long may it be deemed so. The rocks, which stretch away in both directions, are not in fact picturesque. They are sandy yellow in colour, covered with crystalline flecks, and are folded into large ungainly incoherent heaps. Below the tide line they are festooned with growths of glistening blistery dark brown seaweed which has a rather unpleasant smell. Up above however, and at close quarters, they afford the clamberer a surprising number of secret joys. There are many V-shaped ravines containing small pools or screes of extremely varied and pretty stones. There are also flowers which contrive somehow to root themselves in crannies: pink thrift and mauve mallow, a sort of white spreading sea campion, a blue-green plant with cabbage-like leaves, and a tiny saxifrage thing with leaves and flowers so small as almost to defeat the naked eye. I must find my magnifying glass and inspect it properly.

A feature of the coastline is that here and there the water has worn the rocks into holes, which I would not dignify with the name of caves, but which, from the swimmer's-eye-view, present a striking and slightly sinister appearance. At one point, near to my house, the sea has actually composed an arched bridge of rock under which it roars into a deep open steep-sided enclosure beyond. It affords me a curious pleasure to stand upon this bridge and watch the violent forces which the churning waves, advancing or retreating, generate within the confined space of the rocky hole.

Another day has passed since I wrote the above. The weather continues almost perfect. I have received no letters since my arrival, and this does seem rather odd. My ex-secretary, Miss Kaufman, kindly detains the diminishing flow of business mail in London. Well, whom do I want to hear from after all, except Lizzie, and she is probably away on tour?

I have continued to explore the rocks in the direction of my tower. Yes, I am now the owner not only of a house and a lot of rocks, but of a ruined 'martello' tower! It is alas only a shell. I would like to restore it and build a spiral staircase and a lofty study room, only contrary to what is commonly believed about me I am not rich. My sea-house took most of my savings. However I have a good pension, thanks to darling Clement's business sense long ago. I must save up. Near to the tower I found a pleasing piece of archaeology, which is also evidence that I am not the only person to have discovered it difficult to get out of this sea. In a little secret inlet below the tower, and invisible except from directly above, some steps have been cut in the side of the rock, descending into the water, and surmounted with an iron banister. Unfortunately the lower part of the banister is broken away, and the rock face being smooth, the slippery steps are useless, except at high tide, if there is any strong swell. The waves simply pluck one off. It is remarkable how quietly firmly powerful my sportive sea can be! But the idea is clearly excellent. I must have the banister extended; and it occurs to me that a few iron stanchions, let into the face of my 'cliff', would provide quite enough hand and foot holds for the climb, in any state of the tide. I must enquire in the village about workmen.

I swam from the 'tower steps' at high tide and then lay naked on the grass beside the tower, feeling exceedingly relaxed and happy. The tower, I regret to say, does attract the occasional tourist; but I am loath to put up a notice saying *Private*. This little lawn is the only piece of grass which I own, except for a small patch directly behind the house. This grass, tormented no doubt by the sea wind, is extremely short, its blades spread out in little circular mats of an almost cactus-like toughness. Pink and white valerian grows round the base of the tower, and a kind of purple flowering thyme mingles with the grass and perches here and there among the rocks on the landward side. I examined this, and also the tiny saxifrage, through my magnifying glass. I wanted to be a botanist when I was ten. My father loved plants, though ignorantly, and we looked at many things together. I wonder what I would have done with my life if I had not been theatre-mad?

Walking back I looked into my various pools. What a remarkable amount of beautiful and curious life they contain. I must buy some books about these matters if I am to become, even to my own modest satisfaction, the Gilbert White of this area. I also picked up a number of pretty stones and carried them to my other lawn. They are smooth, elliptical, lovely to handle. One, a mottled pink, elaborately crossed with white lines, lies before me as I write. My father would have loved this place – I still think of him and miss him.

It is after lunch and I shall now describe the house. For lunch, I may say, I ate and greatly enjoyed the following: anchovy paste on hot buttered toast, then baked beans and kidney beans with chopped celery, tomatoes, lemon juice and olive oil. (Really good olive oil is essential, the kind with a taste, I have brought a supply from London.) Green peppers would have been a happy addition only the village shop (about two miles pleasant walk) could not provide them. (No one delivers to far-off Shruff End, so I fetch everything, including milk, from the village.) Then bananas and cream with white sugar. (Bananas should be cut, *never* mashed, and the cream should be thin.) Then hard water-biscuits with New Zealand butter and Wensleydale cheese. Of course I never touch foreign cheeses. Our cheeses are the best in the world. With this feast I drank most of a bottle of Muscadet out of my modest 'cellar'. I ate and drank slowly as one should (cook fast, eat slowly) and without distractions such as (thank heavens) conversation or reading. Indeed eating is so pleasant one should even try to suppress thought. Of course reading and thinking are important but, my God, food is important too. How fortunate we are to be food-consuming animals. Every meal should be a treat and one ought to bless every day which brings with it a good digestion and the precious gift of hunger.

I wonder if I shall ever write my *Charles Arrowby Four Minute Cookbook*? The 'four minutes' of course refer to the active time of preparation, and do not include unsupervised cooking time. I have looked at several so-called 'short order' cookery books, but these works tend to deceive, their 'fifteen minutes' really in practice means thirty, and they contain instructions such as 'make a light batter'. The sturdy honest persons to whom my book would be addressed would not necessarily be able to make a light batter or even to know what it was. But they would be hedonists. In food and drink, as in many (not all) other matters, simple joys are best, as any intelligent self-lover knows. Sidney Ashe once offered to initiate me into the pleasures of vintage wine. I refused with scorn. Sidney hates ordinary wine and is unhappy unless he is drinking some expensive stuff with a date on it. Why wantonly destroy one's palate for cheap wine? (And by that I do not of course mean the brew that tastes of bananas.) One of the secrets of a happy life is continuous small treats, and if some of these can be inexpensive and quickly procured so much the better. Life in the theatre often precluded serious meals and I have not always in the past been able to eat slowly, but I have certainly learnt how to cook quickly. Of course my methods (especially a liberal use of the tin opener) may scandalize fools, and the various people (mainly the girls: Jeanne, Doris, Rosemary, Lizzie) who urged me to publish my recipes did so with an air of amused condescension. Your name will sell the book, they tactlessly insisted. 'Charles's meals are just picnics,' Rita Gibbons once remarked. Yes, good, even great, picnics. And let me say here that *of course* my guests *always* sit squarely at tables, never balance plates on their knees, and *always* have proper table napkins, *never* paper ones.

Food is a profound subject and one, incidentally, about which no writer lies. I wonder whence I derived my felicitous gastronomic intelligence? A thrifty childhood gave me a horror of wasted food. I thoroughly enjoyed the modest fare we had at home. My mother was a 'good plain cook', but she lacked the inspired simplicity which is for me the essence of good eating. I think my illumination came, like that of Saint Augustine, from a disgust with excesses. When I was a young director I was idiotic and conventional enough to think that I had to entertain people at well-known restaurants. It gradually became clear to me that guzzling large quantities of expensive, pretentious, often mediocre food in public places was not only immoral, unhealthy and unaesthetic, but also unpleasurable. Later my guests were offered simple joys *chez moi*. What is more delicious than fresh hot buttered toast, with or without the addition of bloater paste? Or plain boiled onions with a little cold corned beef if desired? And well-made porridge with brown sugar and cream is a dish fit for a king. Even then some people, so sadly corrupt was their taste, took my intelligent hedonism for an affected eccentricity, a mere gimmick. (*Wind in the Willows* food a journalist called it.) And some were actually offended.

However, it may be that what really made me see through the false mythology of *haute cuisine* was not so much restaurants as dinner parties. I have long, and usually vainly, tried to persuade my friends not to cook grandly. The waste of time alone is an absurdity; though I suppose it is true that some unfortunate women have nothing to do but cook. There is also the illusion that very elaborate cooking is more 'creative' than simple cooking. Of course (let me make it clear) I am not a barbarian. French country food, such as one can still occasionally find in that blessed land, is very good; but its goodness belongs to a tradition and an instinct which cannot be aped. The pretentious English hostess not only mistakes elaboration and ritual for virtue; she is also very often exercising her deluded art for the benefit of those who, though they would certainly not admit it, do not really enjoy food at all. Most of my friends in the theatre were usually so sozzled when they came to eat a serious meal that they had no appetite and in any case scarcely knew what was set before them. Why spend nearly all day preparing food for people who eat it (or rather toy with it and leave it) in this condition? A serious eater is a moderate drinker. Food is also spoilt at dinner parties by enforced conversation. One's best hope is to get into one of those 'holes' where one's two neighbours are eagerly engaged elsewhere, so that one can concentrate upon one's plate. No, I am no friend to these 'formal' scenes which often have more to do with vanity and prestige and a mistaken sense of social 'propriety' than with the true instincts of hospitality. *Haute cuisine* even inhibits hospitality, since those who cannot or will not practise it hesitate to invite its devotees for fear of seeming rude or a failure. Food is best eaten among friends who are unmoved by such 'social considerations', or of course best of all alone. I hate the falsity of 'grand' dinner parties where, amid much kissing, there is the appearance of intimacy where there is really none.

After this tirade it looks as if the description of the house will have to wait until another day. I might add here that (as will already be evident) I am not a vegetarian. In fact I eat very little meat, and hold in horror the 'steak house carnivore'. But there are certain items (such as anchovy paste, liver, sausages, fish) which hold as it were strategic positions in my diet, and which I should be sorry to do without; here hedonism triumphs over a peevish baffled moral sense. Perhaps I ought to give up eating meat, but by now, when the argument has gone on so long, I doubt if I ever will.

I will *now* describe the house. It is called Shruff End. End, yes: it is perched upon a small promontory, not exactly a peninsula, and stands indeed upon the very rocks themselves. What madman built it? The date would be perhaps nineteen ten. But why 'Shruff'? I have asked two of my (so far) very few local informants, the shop lady and the landlord of the village pub, and they both said, but could give no further account of the matter, that 'shruff' means 'black'. (Shruff: *schwarz*? most unlikely.) I cannot yet discover anything about the history of the house. I never met the person, described as an old lady, a Mrs Chorney, from whom I bought it. The price was not low, and I was also compelled to purchase the almost worthless furniture and fittings. Considered as a *house* Shruff End has obvious disadvantages which I was not slow to point out to the house agent. It is mysteriously damp and the situation is exposed and isolated. There is running water and main drainage, thank God (I have lived without these in America), but no electricity and no heating system. Cooking is by Calor gas. There are also some oddities of construction which I will describe in due course. The agent, smiling, could see I loved the place and the disadvantages meant nothing. 'It is unique, sir,' he said. Yes it is.

The position is inspiring, though as my village 'neighbours' take pleasure in telling me, it will be cold and stormy in wintertime. Little do they realize how ardently I look forward to those storms, when the wild waves will beat at my very door! Since I have been here (now a matter of a few weeks) the weather has been quite distressingly calm. Yesterday the sea was so motionlessly smooth that it supported a whole flotilla of blue flies which seemed actually to crawl upon the surface tension. From the upper seaward windows (where I am sitting at this moment) the view is total sea, unless one peers down to glimpse the rocks below. From the lower windows, however, the sea is invisible and one sees only the coastal rocks, elephantine in size and shape, which surround the house. From the back door, which is the door of the kitchen, one emerges onto the little rock-surrounded 'lawn' of cactus-grass and thyme. This I shall leave to nature. I am in any case no gardener. (This is the first land which I have ever owned.) Nature, I note, has here provided me with a rocky seat, upon which I put cushions, and a rocky trough beside it, into which I put the pretty stones which I am collecting; so that one can sit upon the seat and examine the stones. From the front of the house a path leads along a steep-sided rocky causeway, a sort of natural drawbridge, to what is dignified by the name of 'the coast road'. It is a tarmac road, but the kind where grass tends to grow in the middle. It is, even in May, little frequented by motor cars. I may add here that one of the secrets of my happy life is that I have never made the mistake of learning to drive a car. I have never lacked people, usually women, longing to drive me whithersoever I wanted. Why keep bitches and bark yourself? Below the causeway, on either side, there is a wilderness of small rocks, piled higgledy-piggledy by nature, and not accessible to the sea. This is a less attractive scene and not without a few rusty tins and broken bottles which I must one day climb down and remove. Beyond the road the humpy yellow rocks, some of them extremely large, appear again, here set in wiry springy grass and among innumerable flaring gorse bushes. There are also (placed there by man or nature?) quite a lot of skinny fuchsias and dense veronicas, all in flower, and some kind of rather attractive grey-leaved sage. Beyond this 'shrubbery' there is a more barren heathland, covered with gorse and heather, and containing treacherous boggy pools, evil-smelling and full of a virulent green and reddish moss. I have not yet explored this inland country. I am not a 'great walker', and I am absorbed and contented by my seaside paradise. Upon this heath, incidentally, and about a mile and a half from Shruff End, is the nearest dwelling, a place called Amorne Farm. From my upstairs front windows I can see their lights at night.

The coast road, if followed to the right, curves round into the next bay, which is invisible from Shruff End territory, except at the tower which stands on the promontory. Here, at a distance of three or four miles, is an establishment called the Raven Hotel about which I have mixed feelings since it is a place of some pretension which attracts tourists. The bay itself is very beautiful, being fringed by rather remarkable, almost spherical boulders. It is known locally as 'Raven Bay' after the hotel, though it has some other name, something like 'Shahore' in the local dialect. (Shore Bay? Why?) If followed to the left from Shruff End, the coast road passes through a curious narrow defile, which I have nicknamed 'the Khyber Pass', where the way has been cut through a big outcrop of rock, which here invades the land to a considerable distance. Beyond this there is a very small stony beach; this is the only beach in the area, since elsewhere, a feature which originally attracted me to this coastline, there is deepish water up against the rocks at any state of the tide. Beyond the beach a footpath leads diagonally to the village which is set a little inland, but if one continues to follow the road one reaches a very pretty little harbour with a magnificently built crooked stone quay, all silted up and entirely abandoned. There used to be fishing boats here, I gather, but these now operate only from further north: I sometimes see them upon my otherwise remarkably empty tract of sea. Beyond the harbour a long and quite broad shelving slope has been cut in the rock to form what is known as 'the ladies' bathing place'. I have seen no ladies there, only occasionally a few boys. (The local people hardly ever swim; they seem to regard the activity as a form of madness.) In fact 'the ladies' bathing place' is now so overgrown with slippery brown weed and so strewn with boulders tossed in by the sea that it is scarcely 'safer' than anywhere else. The coast road here becomes a track (unfortunately suitable for motor cars) which climbs up into a wild region, which I have not yet had time to explore, where my yellow rocks turn into handsome and quite sizeable cliffs. The tarmac road turns inland to the village and beyond.

The village is called Narrowdean. The old form of the name was *Nerodene,* and a handsome milestone upon the coast road retains this spelling. The little place consists of a few streets of stone-built cottages, some hillside bungalows and one general shop. I cannot get *The Times,* or any batteries for my exhausted transistor radio, but this does not worry me too much, nor am I dismayed by the total absence of a butcher's shop. There is one pub, the Black Lion. The cottages are charming, solidly built in the yellowish local stone, but the only building of any special architectural interest is the church, a fine eighteenth-century structure with a gallery. I am of course not a churchgoer, but I was glad to find that there are services, though only once a month. The church is well kept and regularly provided with flowers. The distant sound of bells which I sometimes hear comes I think from an equally tiny village lying inland beyond Amorne Farm, where the country is gentler and there is grazing for sheep. There is no rectory or manor house in Narrowdean; not that it was ever part of my plan to hobnob with the parson and the squire! I am also glad to intuit that the place is not infested with 'intellectuals', a hazard everywhere nowadays. To return to the church, there is a most attractive *cimetière marin,* which evidences a more spacious past than one would expect this 'one horse' village to possess. Many of the tombstones carry carvings of sailing ships, decorative anchors and strangely eloquent whales. Could men have gone whaling from here? One stone in particular attracts me. It bears a beautiful 'foul anchor' and the simple inscription: *Dummy 1879–1918*. This puzzled me until I realized that 'Dummy' must have been a deaf and dumb sailor who never managed to achieve any other identity. Poor chap.

Let us now come back again to Shruff End. The façade which looks onto the road is, I suppose, not in itself remarkable, but in its lonely situation is strangely incongruous. The house is a brick-built 'double-fronted' villa with bay windows on the ground floor and two

peaks to the roof. The bricks are dark red. It would scarcely attract
notice in a Birmingham suburb, but all alone upon that wild coast it
certainly looks odd. The back has been horribly 'pebble-dashed', no
doubt against the weather. An expert could probably date the house from
the pale buff-coloured blinds which survive in almost every room, in
excellent condition, with glossy wooden toggles on strings, silk tassels,
and a lace fringe at the bottom. When these blinds (expressive word)
are drawn down, Shruff End, seen from the road, has a weird air of
complacent mystery. While within, the yellow light of the 'blinded'
room somehow and sadly recalls my childhood, perhaps the atmosphere
of my grandfather's house in Lincolnshire.

The two bay-window rooms I have christened the bookroom (where
I have put my crates of books, still not unpacked) and the dining room,
where I store my wine. But I live entirely on the seaward side of the
house, upstairs in my bedroom and what I am determined to call my
drawing room, and downstairs in the kitchen and a small den next to
it which I call 'the little red room'. Here there is a good fireplace,
with traces of a wood fire, and also a decent bamboo table and bamboo
armchair. The walls have white wooden panels on the lower part, above
which they are painted tomato red, an exotic touch not matched elsewhere in the house. The kitchen, with the Calor gas stove, is paved with
the most enormous slate flags I have ever seen. There is of course no
refrigerator, which is dismaying to a fish-eating man. There is a large
larder full of woodlice. All the downstairs woodwork tends to be damp.
I prised up some linoleum in the hall, and replaced it with a shudder.
There was a salty smell. Is it conceivable that the sea could be rising
up through a hidden channel under the house? I suppose I ought to
have had a surveyor's report, but I was in too much of a hurry. There
is an old-fashioned mechanical front doorbell with a brass handle and
a long wire. It rings in the kitchen.

The chief peculiarity of the house, and one for which I can produce no rational explanation, is that on the ground floor and on the first floor there is an *inner room*. By this I mean that there is, between the front room and the back room, a room which has no external window, but is lit by an internal window giving onto the adjacent seaward room (the drawing room upstairs, the kitchen downstairs). These two funny inner rooms are extremely dark, and entirely empty, except for a large sagging sofa in the downstairs one, and a small table in the upstairs one, where there is also a remarkable decorative cast-iron lamp bracket, the only one in the house. I shall certainly not occupy these rooms; later on, by the removal of walls, they shall enlarge the drawing room and the dining room. The whole house is indeed sparsely furnished. I have introduced very little of my own. (There is only one bed; I am not expecting visitors!) This emptiness suits me; unlike James I am not a collector or clutterer. I am even becoming fond of some of the stuff which I complained so much about having to buy. I am especially attached to a large oval mirror in the hall. Mrs Chorney's things seem to 'belong'; it is my own, few in fact, possessions which look out of place. I sold a great many things when I left the big flat in Barnes, and removed most of the remainder to a tiny *pied-à-terre* in Shepherd's Bush where I pushed them in anyhow and locked the door. I rather dread going back there. I cannot now think why I bothered to keep a London base at all; my friends told me I 'must' have one.

I say 'my friends': but how few, as I take stock, they really are after a lifetime in the theatre. How friendly and 'warm-hearted' the theatre can seem, what a desolation it can be. The great ones have gone from me: Clement Makin dead, Wilfred Dunning dead, Sidney Ashe gone to Stratford, Ontario, Fritzie Eitel successful and done for in California. A handful remain: Perry, Al, Marcus, Gilbert, what's left of the girls ... I am beginning to ramble. It is evening. The sea is golden, speckled with white points of light, lapping with a sort of mechanical self-satisfaction under a pale green sky. How huge it is, how empty, this great space for which I have been longing all my life.

Still no letters.

The sea is noisier today and the seagulls are crying. I do not really like silence except in the theatre. The sea is agitated, a very dark blue with white crests.

I went out looking for driftwood as far as the little stony beach. The tide was low, so I could not swim off the tower steps, and until I can get some handholds fixed I think I shall shun my 'cliff' except in calm weather. I swam at the beach but it was not a success. The pebbles hurt my feet and I had great difficulty in getting out, since the beach shelves and the waves kept tumbling the pebbles down against me. I came back really cold and disgruntled, and forgot the wood which I had collected.

I have now had lunch (lentil soup, followed by chipolata sausages served with boiled onions and apples stewed in tea, then dried apricots and shortcake biscuits: a light Beaujolais) and I feel better. (Fresh apricots are best of course, but the dried kind, soaked for twenty-four hours and then well drained, make a heavenly accompaniment for any sort of mildly sweet biscuit or cake. They are especially good with anything made of almonds, and thus consort happily with red wine. I am not a great friend of your peach, but I suspect the apricot is the king of fruit.)

I shall now go and have an afternoon rest.

It is night. Two oil lamps, purring very faintly, shed a calm creamy light upon the scratched and stained surface of what was once a fine rosewood table, the erstwhile property of Mrs Chorney. This is my working table, at the window of the drawing room, though I also use the little folding table, which I have brought in from the 'inner room', to lay out books and papers. I have had to shut the window against the moths, huge ones with beige and orange wings, who have been coming in like little helicopters. The lamps, there are four in all, and in good working order, are also Chorneyana. They are handsome old-fashioned things, rather heavy, made of brass with graceful opaque glass shades. I learnt to master oil lamps in the USA, in that hut with Fritzie. Two paraffin heaters downstairs remain, however, a mystery. I must get new ones before chillier nights arrive. Last night was chilly enough. I attempted to light a driftwood fire in the little red room, but the wood was too damp and the chimney smoked.

I think that in winter I shall live downstairs. How I look forward to it. The drawing room is still more of a lookout point than a room. It is dominated by a tall black-painted wooden chimney piece, with a lot of little shelves with little mirrors above them. A collector's item, no doubt, but it looks a little too like the altar of some weird sect. (It has that oriental vegetable look.)

Before I lit the lamps tonight I spent some time simply gazing out at the moonlight, always an astonishment and a joy to the town-dweller. It is so bright now over the rocks that I could read by it. Only, oddly enough, I note that I have had no impulse to read since I have been here. *A good sign.* Writing seems to have replaced reading. Yet also, I seem to be constantly putting off the moment when I begin to give a formal account of myself. ('I was born at the turn of the century in the town of ———' or whatever.) There will be time and motive enough to prose on about my life when I shall have generated as it were a sufficient cloud of reflection. I am still almost shy of my emotions, shy of the terrible strength of certain memories. Simply the tale of my years with Clement could fill a volume.

I am very conscious of the house existing quietly round about me. Parts of it I have colonised, other parts remain obstinately alien and dim. The entrance hall is dark and pointless, except for the presence of the large oval mirror aforementioned. (This handsome object seems to glow with its own light.) I do not altogether like the stairs. (Spirits from the past linger on stairs.) These lead half way up, via a narrow branching stairway, to a surprisingly large bathroom which faces the road, and from which, behind an odd little door, more steps lead to the attics. The bathroom has some good original tiles representing swans and sinuous lilies. There is a huge much-stained bath on lions' paws, with excellent enormous brass taps. (There is no system for heating the water however! A hip bath in a downstairs cupboard represents, I suspect, the reality of the situation.) There is also a notice in a continental hand giving useful instructions about how to make the lavatory work. The main staircase turns inward to reach the space of the upper landing. I call this a 'space' because it is a rather odd area with an atmosphere all its own. It has the expectant air of a stage set. Sometimes I feel as if I must have seen it long ago in a dream. It is a big windowless oblong, lit during the day through open doors, and adorned, just opposite the 'inner room', by a solid oak stand upon which there is a large remarkably hideous green vase, with a thick neck and a scalloped rim and pink roses blistering its bulging sides. I have become very attached to this gross object. Beyond it there is a shallow alcove which looks as if it should contain a statue, but empty resembles a door. After this comes the most fascinating feature of the landing: an archway containing a *bead curtain*. This curtain is not unlike those which exclude flies from shops in Mediterranean countries. The beads are of wood, painted yellow and black, and they click lightly together as one passes through. After the archway come the doors of my bedroom and drawing room.

It is time for bed. Behind me is the long horizontal window, several feet up in the wall, which gives onto the 'inner room'. As I rise I am impelled to look towards it, seeing my face reflected in the black glass as in a mirror. I have never suffered from night fears. I was never, that I can recall, afraid of the dark as a child. My mother early impressed upon me that fear of the dark was a superstition from which God-trusting people did not suffer. I hardly needed God to protect me. My parents were an absolute defence against every terror. It is not that I find Shruff End in any way 'creepy'. It is just that, as it now suddenly occurs to me, this is the first time in my life that I have been really alone at night. My childhood home, theatrical digs in the provinces, London flats, hotels, rented apartments in capital cities: I have always lived in hives, surrounded by human presences behind walls. And even when I lived in that hut (with Fritzie) I was never alone. This is the first house which I have owned and the first genuine solitude which I have inhabited. Is this not what I wanted? Of course the house is full of little creaking straining noises, even on a windless night, any elderly house is, and draughts blow through it from gappy window frames and ill-fitting doors. So it is that I can imagine, as I lie in bed at night, that I hear soft footsteps in the attics above me or that the bead curtain on the landing is quietly clicking because someone has passed furtively through it.

Perhaps this is a foolish moment, so late at night, to choose to approach the subject, but it has come suddenly and vividly into my head. The reader, if there is one, may wonder why I have not referred again to a 'horrible experience' which I suffered here beside the sea but could not bring myself to describe. It might seem by now that I had 'forgotten' it; and indeed in an odd way I think I had forgotten it: a tendency which is evidence, perhaps, for one possible view of the phenomenon. Let me now describe what happened.

I was sitting, with this notebook beside me, upon the rocks just above my 'cliff', and looking out over the water. The sun was shining, the sea was calm. (As I have described it in the first paragraph of this notebook.) Shortly before this I had been looking intently into a rock pool and watching a remarkably long reddish faintly bristly sea-worm which had wreathed itself into curious coils prior to disappearing into a hole. I sat up, then settled myself facing seaward, blinking in the sun. Then, not at once, but after about two minutes, as my eyes became accustomed to the glare, *I saw a monster rising from the waves.*

I can describe this in no other way. Out of a perfectly calm empty sea, at a distance of perhaps a quarter of a mile (or less), I saw an immense creature break the surface and arch itself upward. At first it looked like a black snake, then a long thickening body with a ridgy spiny back followed the elongated neck. There was something which might have been a flipper or perhaps a fin. I could not see the whole of the creature, but the remainder of its body, or perhaps a long tail, disturbed the foaming water round the base of what had now risen from the sea to a height of (as it seemed) twenty or thirty feet. The creature then *coiled* itself so that the long neck circled twice, bringing the now conspicuous head low down above the surface of the sea. *I could see the sky through the coils.* I could also see the head with remarkable clarity, a kind of crested snake's head, green-eyed, the mouth opening to show teeth and a pink interior. The head and neck glistened with a blue sheen. Then in a moment the whole thing collapsed, the coils fell, the undulating back still broke the water, and then there was nothing but a great foaming swirling pool where the creature had vanished.

The shock and the horror of it were so great that for some time I could not move. I wanted to run away, I feared beyond anything that the animal would reappear closer to land, perhaps rising up at my very feet. But my legs would not function and my heart was beating so violently that any further exertion might have rendered me unconscious. The sea had become calm again and nothing further happened. At last I got up and walked slowly back to the house. I went up the stairs and into the drawing room where I sat for some time just breathing carefully and holding my heart. I could not bear to take my usual place at the window, so I sat at the little table against the wall of the inner room, leaning my head against the wall, and about half an hour later I was able to write down what now appears as the second paragraph in this notebook.

During that time, as I held on to myself and breathed and trembled, I managed gradually to *think* about what had occurred. Thought, rational thought, which had been utterly routed, returned gradually to my rescue. Something had happened and happenings have explanations. Several possible explanations came before me, and as I began to number and classify and relate them some relief came, and the awful uncon-ceptualized terror receded. It was possible that I had 'simply' imagined what I saw. But of course one does not 'simply' imagine anything so detailed and dreadful. It later struck me as significant that the creature had appeared at once as utterly frightful, rather than as very surprising or even interesting. I was *excessively* frightened. I am a moderate drinker and certainly not an unbalanced or crazily 'imaginative' person. Another possibility was that I had, again 'simply', seen a monster unknown to science. Well, that was just possible. Or: was what I had seen an absolutely enormous eel? Could there be such an eel? Did eels ever rise up out of the sea and wreathe themselves into coils and balance themselves high in the air? I could not think that the thing was an eel, this was impossible. It had a substantial body, I had seen its *back*. I was quite sure too that I could not have seen a mere eel, however large, as this coiling monstrosity through which I had looked at the sky.

How far off had the animal been and how high above the water had it risen? On further reflection I was not so certain of my first impressions, though I remained sure that I had seen something abso-lutely remarkable. Explanations in terms of floating seaweed or bobbing driftwood were not to be considered. I explored another possibility.

Just before I saw my huge monster I had been closely inspecting, in the rock pool, a little monster, the red bristling worm, whose five or six inches of wriggling body appeared big in the confined space of the pool. Was it possible that through some purely optical mechanism, some unusual trick of the retina, I had 'thrown' the image of the worm out onto the surface of the sea? This was an interesting idea but totally implausible, since the red worm bore no resemblance to the bluish-blackish monster, except in so far as both of them had wreathed into coils. Besides, I had never heard of any such retinal 'cinematography'. I was struck, on reflection, by the fact that I recalled the creature with extreme clarity, the visual impression remained extremely detailed, while at the same time I felt more and more vague about its exact distance away from me.

The solution which I now think to be the most probable, though whether I shall continue to think so remains to be seen, is this, and I record it with a little shame. I am neither a drunkard nor a drug addict. I scarcely ever drink spirits. I have smoked 'hash' occasionally in America. However, on one occasion, several years ago, I was idiot enough to take a dose of LSD. (I did it to please a woman.) I had what is known as a 'bad trip'. It was a very bad trip. I shall not attempt to describe what I experienced on that dreadful and rather shameful occasion. (I will only add: it concerned entrails.) In fact it would be extremely hard, even impossible, to put it properly into words. It was something morally, spiritually horrible, as if one's stinking inside had emerged and become the universe: a surging emanation of dark half-formed spiritual evil, something never ever to be escaped from. 'Undetachable,' I remember, was a word which somehow 'came along' with the impression of it. In fact the visual images involved were dreadfully clear and, as it were, authoritative ones and they are rising up in front of me at this moment, and I will not write about them. Of course I never took LSD again.

I had no further after-effects, and after a while I began mercifully to forget the experience in the quite special way in which one forgets a dream. However: it is possible, perhaps plausible, to conjecture that the sea monster which I 'saw' was a hallucination which was also caused by my one foolish experiment with that awful drug.

It is true that the rising coiling monster did not really resemble what I saw on the first occasion, any more than it resembled the red worm in the pool. But the feeling of horror was similar in quality, or at any rate began to seem so very soon after the experience itself. Also, the quality of the tendency to forget also now seems to me to be similar in the two cases. A bad trip can recur in this way, I am told: readers, be warned. However, it must be admitted that as I reflect about it all at this moment, the strongest evidence for this explanation is the total implausibility of all the others.

My heart is beating violently again. I must go to bed. Perhaps I should have waited until tomorrow morning to tell this story. I shall take a sleeping pill.

Two days have passed since I wrote the above. I slept well after writing about my monster and I still think my explanation is the right one. Anyway he recedes and the horror has gone away. Perhaps it did me good to write it all down. I have decided that the 'footsteps' in the attics are rats. Another sunny day. Still no letters.

I swam again at the little stony beach and although the sea was fairly calm I had the same irritating difficulty getting out of it. I had to climb a steep bank of tumbling shifting pebbles while each successive wave was submerging me from behind. Swallowed a lot of water and cut my foot. Found my abandoned pile of driftwood and carried it home. Felt very chilled but too tired to organize hip bath, which seems to be made of cast iron. Not worth carrying hot water up to bathroom.

It has occurred to me that if I attached a rope to the iron banister at the tower steps I could use the steps even in rough weather; and if I could find anything to tie it to I could dangle a rope over my 'cliff' to help me out of the water there. I must see if the village shop sells rope. I must also find out where I can get more cylinders of Calor gas.

My paternal grandfather was a market gardener in Lincolnshire. (There, quite suddenly I have started to write my autobiography, and what a splendid opening sentence! I knew it would happen if I just waited.) He lived in a house called Shaxton. I thought it was very distinguished to have a house with a name. I do not know what my maternal grandfather did, he died when I was a small child. I think he 'worked in an office', as indeed my father did too. Doubtless he was some sort of clerk; as indeed my father was too I suppose, though we never used the word 'clerk' at home. My paternal grandfather had two sons, Adam and Abel. He never seemed to me to be an imaginative man, but there was some touch of poetry in those names. It was early evident to me that my uncle (Abel) was more loved and more fortunate than my father (Adam). How does a child perceive such things, or rather how is it that they are so perceptible, so obvious, to a child, who perhaps, like a dog, reads signs which have become invisible amid the conventions of the grown-up world, and are thus overlooked in the adult campaign of deceit? I knew that my father, who was slightly the elder of the two, was some sort of luckless failure before I knew what 'failure' meant, before I knew anything about money, status, power, fame or any of those coveted prizes whose myriad forms have led me throughout my life that dervish dance which is now, I trust, over. And of course when I say that my dear father was a failure I mean it only in the grossest worldly sense. He was an intelligent good man, pure in heart.

My maternal grandparents lived in Carlisle and I scarcely knew them. My mother's sisters figured as two pale 'aunties', also in Carlisle. My paternal grandmother died young, and in my memories of Shaxton she appears as a photograph. Indeed my grandfather, whom I disliked and feared, appears to me now only as Wellington boots and a loud voice. Adam and Abel crowded my childhood world, dominating it like twin gods. My mother was a separate force, always separate. And then of course there was my cousin James who, like me, was an only child.

The ways of the brothers parted. My father drifted into Warwickshire and worked in 'local government'. Drifted: I see him on a raft. Uncle Abel became a successful barrister in Lincoln and lived in a house in the country called Ramsdens: another distinguished place with a name. Ramsdens was larger than Shaxton. I still see both those houses in my dreams. Later on the Uncle Abels moved to London, but kept Ramsdens as what they called their 'country cottage'. Uncle Abel married a rich pretty American girl called Estelle. I remember her being referred to by my mother as an 'heiress'. My father married my mother who was working as a secretary on a farm. Her name was Marian. He called her 'Maid Marian'. She was a strict evangelical Christian. My father was a Christian too of course, so was I, so was Uncle Abel until Aunt Estelle took him away into the world of light. I cannot see my mother as a lovely girl, as the Maid Marian of the Warwickshire lanes. I see her face, in my earliest memories, as a mask of anxiety. She was the strong one. My father and I loved and obeyed and comforted each other in secret. Well, we all three loved and comforted each other. We were poorish and lonely and awkward together.

I was utterly horrified in the kitchen this morning to see what I took to be a grotesquely huge fat fleshy spider emerging from the larder. It turned out to be a most engaging toad. I caught him easily and carried him across the wood to the mossy boggy pools beyond the rocks. Here he ambled away. How can such gentle defenceless animals survive? I lingered for a little while after the toad had gone, and looked at the red-tufted mosses and the flowers, mare's tails which I remember from my youth, and that weird yellow flower that catches flies. Heather grows upon the higher ground inland, towards Amorne Farm. I was told by the house agent that there are orchids in the vicinity, but I have seen none. Perhaps they are as legendary as the seals.

Later on I went into the village to buy deep-freeze kipper fillets (the poor man's smoked salmon). Of course it is quite impossible to buy fresh fish here, as all the villagers tell me with pride. I also made some rather inconclusive enquiries about a laundry. So far I have washed everything myself, including the sheets which I lay out to dry upon the lawn. Perhaps I will continue to do this; there is a remarkable satisfaction in the performance of these simple tasks. I forgot to record that I have found a second shop in the village, a sort of ironmonger's, in the row of cottages behind the pub. It calls itself the Fishermen's Stores and no doubt did once sell gear to the fishermen. This place, I discovered this morning, supplies paraffin and Calor gas. I also purchased from them some candles, a new oil lamp and a length of rope. Carrying these trophies I dropped into the Black Lion on the way home. The bar there falls silent when I enter and bursts into raucous chatter when I leave, but I propose to make a habit of coming nonetheless. The mild hostility of the villagers does not worry me. Of course, thanks to television, they know who I am. But they have been at pains to exhibit indifference, and indeed, in all their worthy simplicity, they may even be indifferent. For them I am perhaps something 'unreal', touched by the unreality of the medium itself. No one, thank God, has attempted to befriend me.

For lunch I ate the kipper fillets rapidly unfrozen in boiling water (the sun had done most of the work) garnished with lemon juice, oil, and a light sprinkling of dry herbs. Kipper fillets are arguably better than smoked salmon unless the latter is very good. With these, fried tinned new potatoes. (No real new potatoes yet.) Potatoes are for me a treat dish, not a dull everyday chaperon. Then Welsh rarebit and hot beetroot. The shop sliced bread is less than great, but all right toasted, with good salty New Zealand butter. Fortunately I like a wide variety of those crackly Scandinavian biscuits which are supposed to make you thin. (Of course they do not. If you are destined to be fat, food makes you fat. But I have never had a weight problem.) Now that I own land I must have a herb garden. A supply of fresh herbs has always been a problem of my life as an enlightened eater. (Of course the notion of growing herbs never entered my head as a child in my parents' garden: I suspect children cannot understand food.) But where am I to put it? I hesitate to dig up either of my little lawns, and anyway they are rather too close to the sea. If I were to make myself a secret allotment on the other side of the road, would some peasant or animal rob it? I must reflect on these things: happy and innocent reflections, so unlike the agonizings of the past!

After lunch I cut off a length of my rope and tied it onto the iron banister at the tower steps, and now it trails handily into the sea, moving darkened in the waves. I have knotted the seaward end for easier grasp. I have had less success with the 'cliff' for the simple reason that there is nothing here to attach the rope to. The rocks are too humpy and smooth, and the rope is not long enough to reach the house. Buy a longer piece and attach it to the kitchen door or to the post at the bottom of the stairs, and haul the long wet end into the kitchen every night? These problems too are not without interest. The rope itself is beautiful stuff, lightly burnished and smelling like retsina. I am told it is made locally.

I spent part of the afternoon lying upon my rock 'bridge', between the house and the tower, and watching the waves coming flying through beneath me and killing themselves in fits of rage in the deep enclosed rocky area on the inland side. The sight of the rushing foaming water made me feel, after a while, almost light-headed, as if I might have become giddy and fallen in. Most enjoyable. I am a bit dismayed however to find, from studying the picture postcards in the shop, that my bridge and its whirlpool are well-known local features. Fortunately the cards seemed rather old and crumpled, and I bought up the entire stock for less than a pound. I want no trippers here seeking for a 'beauty spot'. In fact the 'bridge' is nothing much, just a hump of rock with a hole in it and an open pit beyond. At certain states of the tide the water, forcing itself through, produces a loud hollow report; I hope this does not draw attention to the place. I learnt from the cards that the enclosed whirlpool is called 'Minn's cauldron'. I asked the shop lady who Minn was, but she did not know.

Statements made by distant church bells remind me it is Sunday. Today the sky has become cloudy. I have been watching the clouds and it occurs to me that I have never done this in my life before, simply sit and watch clouds. As a child I would have been far too anxious to 'waste time' in this way. And my mother would have stopped me. As I write this I am sitting on my plot of grass behind the house where I have put a chair, cushions, rugs. It is evening. Thick lumpy slate-blue clouds, their bulges lit up to a lighter blue, move slowly across a sky of muddy and yet brilliant gold, a sort of dulled gilt effect. At the horizon there is a light glittering slightly jagged silver line, like modern jewellery. Beneath it the sea is a live choppy lyrical goldeny-brown, jumping with white flecks. The air is warm. Another happy day. ('Whatever will you *do* down there?' they asked.)

In a quiet surreptitious way I am feeling *very pleased with myself.*

Another day. I have decided not to put dates as they break up the sense of a continuous meditation. I have been rereading the opening pages of my autobiography! How full, for me at any rate, of frightful resonance those statements are which I have made, with such an odd and sudden air of authority, about my childhood. I had never thought of myself as being that much interested. I had intended to write about Clement. Do I really want to describe my childhood?

I have not swum today. I went to the tower steps in the afternoon intending to swim but found to my annoyance that the rope which I had fixed to the banister had somehow become untied and floated away. I am not very good at knots. In any case, that rope is perhaps too thick to knot easily. It occurs to me that a long piece of nylon cloth might be more serviceable.

Felt a little depressed but was cheered up by supper: spaghetti with a little butter and dried basil. (Basil is of course the king of herbs.) Then spring cabbage cooked slowly with dill. Boiled onions served with bran, herbs, soya oil and tomatoes, with one egg beaten in. With these a slice or two of cold tinned corned beef. (Meat is really just an excuse for eating vegetables.) I drank a bottle of retsina in honour of the undeserving rope.

It is now late at night and I am sitting upstairs, with one of my old oil lamps and the new lamp. The new one gives a less beautiful light but it is easier to carry. I must get more of these lamps, though I suppose I shall never be able to dispense with candles. Mrs Chorney left me about a dozen candlesticks, handy though not things of beauty, and I have placed these, complete with candles and matches, at strategic positions throughout the house. The smell of the new lamp reminds me of Fritzie. I shall now continue my autobiography.

I was born at Stratford-upon-Avon. Or to be exact, near it, or to be more exact, in the Forest of Arden. I grew up in leafy central England, as far as it is possible to be in this island from the sea. I did not *see* the sea until I was fourteen. Of course I owe my whole life to Shakespeare.

If I had not lived close to a great theatre, indeed close to *that* great theatre, I would never have managed to see any plays. My parents never went to the theatre, my mother positively disapproved of it. There was little enough spare money for 'going out' anywhere, and we never went out. I did not go to a restaurant until after I left school. I did not enter a hotel till later still. For holidays we went to Shaxton, or to Ramsdens or to the farm where my mother had worked as a secretary. I would never have gone to a theatre at all if it had not been that Shakespeare was 'work'. A master at the school was Shakespeare-mad. That man too made my life. His name was Mr McDowell. We went to the plays often, we saw everything. Sometimes Mr McDowell paid for me. And of course we acted plays too. Mr McDowell was stage-struck, an actor *manqué*. I became his stage-struck pet. (It was he who took me and some other boys to the sea in Wales for a week. I think this was one of the most important and happy weeks I have ever spent. 'Happy' hardly expresses it. I was nearly insane with joy the whole time.) My mother accepted the theatre-going because it was 'part of my school work'. I even cunningly pretended that I did not really enjoy it: it was just necessary for my exam. Wicked lying little boy. I was in heaven. My father knew, but we would never have confessed to each other that we were deceiving my mother.

My father was a quiet bookish man and somehow the gentlest being I have ever encountered. I do not mean he was timid, though I suppose he *was* timid. He had a positive moral quality of gentleness. I can picture him now so clearly, bending down with his perpetual nervous smile to pick up a spider on a piece of paper and put it carefully out of the window or into some corner of the house where it would not be disturbed. I was his comrade, his reading companion, possibly the only person with whom he ever had a serious conversation. I always felt that we were in the same boat, adventuring along together. We read the same books and discussed them: children's books, adventure stories, then novels, history, biography, poetry, Shakespeare. We enjoyed and craved for each other's company. What a test that is: more than devotion, admiration, passion. If you long and long for someone's company you love them. I remember feeling in later life that no one else ever knew how *good* my father was; I doubt if even my mother knew. Of course I loved my mother too, but she had a hard line in her where my father had none. She believed in a just God. Perhaps this belief supported her through what may have proved a somewhat disappointing life.

The trouble with my parents, at least from my point of view, was that they did not want to go anywhere or do anything. My mother disapproved of going anywhere or doing anything, partly because this involved spending money, and partly because of the worldly vanities which any such removal might lead us to encounter. My father did not want to go anywhere or do anything, partly because my mother was against it, and partly because of his timidity and a certain indolence of character. I may have made it sound as if my father was a sad man but this was not so. He understood the pleasures of the simple life and how to look forward to little treats. He did his dull office work diligently I am sure, and did odd jobs about the house with zeal. He enjoyed his reading which, when he was not partaking in my education, tended to be novels and adventure stories. I can remember him, when he was fatally ill, reading *Treasure Island* with a magnifying glass. He loved and cherished my mother and me. And there his world ended. He was not interested in politics or travel or any form of entertainment, or even any form of art other than literature. He had no friends (except me). It may be mentioned that he liked his brother Abel, though just how much I was never sure. He never entirely got on with my cousin James because he saw him as a rival to me. Aunt Estelle embarrassed him. My mother detested the lot of them, but behaved very well in spite of it.

I went into the theatre of course because of Shakespeare. Those who knew me in later years as a Shakespeare director often did not realize how absolutely this god had directed me from the very first. I had of course other motives. From the guileless simplicity of my parents' life, from the immobility and quietness of my home, I fled to the trickery and magic of art. I craved glitter, movement, acrobatics, noise. I became an expert on flying machines, I arranged fights, I always took, as my critics said, an almost childish, almost excessive delight in the technical trickery of the theatre. I also took up acting, and was conscious of this too from the beginning, because I wanted to have fun myself and to procure some for my father. I doubt if he possessed the concept, or ever managed to acquire it later under my eager guidance. In having fun myself I have throughout my life been fairly consistently successful. I was much less successful in persuading my parents to enjoy themselves. Eventually I took them to Paris, to Venice, to Athens. They were always thoroughly uneasy and longing to get home, though I think it may later have given them some satisfaction to think that they *had been* to these places. They really wanted to remain always in their own house and their own garden. There are such people.

I was a docile quiet loving child; but I knew that a great fight was coming and I wanted to win it, and win it quickly. I did both. When I was seventeen my father wanted me to go to the university. My mother did too, though she feared the expense. Instead I went to an acting school in London. (I obtained a scholarship. Mr McDowell had not laboured in vain.) One of the saddest things in my life was crossing my dear father in this. But I could not wait. My mother was appalled. She thought that the theatre was an abode of sin. (She was right.) And she thought that I would never succeed and would return home starving. (She despised people who could not earn their living.) Here she was not right; and at least, as the years went by, she could not help respecting

my ability to make money. The theatre then and thenceforth became
my *home;* I even spent the war acting, since a patch on the lung, which
cleared up soon after, kept me out of the armed forces. I was rather
sorry about this later on.

'Mr Arkwright, do you ever see any very large eels in this vicinity?'

Direct speech. I record what I said this morning in the Black Lion,
where I was buying some of the local cider. The cider is unfortunately
too sweet; and I shall before long have exhausted the modest supply
of wine which I brought with me. The Black Lion has of course never
heard of wine; but the intelligent shop lady tells me that the Raven
Hotel sells 'real wine'.

The Black Lion landlord's name, Arkwright, disturbs me with memories of a chauffeur of that name whom I once had when I was a
grandee, and who regarded me with rancorous hatred. The relation
between the chauffeur and the chauffeured can be curiously intense.
Black Lion Arkwright is in fact fairly disturbing in his own right. He
is a big fellow with long black hair and black whiskers, like a sort of
Victorian cad. He leads the bar in the game of embarrassing me. He
now analyses my question. Eels? Large? Very large? Vicinity? 'Do you
mean on land?' he asks. 'He means worms,' says one of the clients. The
clients are almost always the same, retired farm labourers I imagine.
No women of course. 'I mean eels in the sea.' All shake their heads
gloomily. 'Wouldn't see them in the sea, would you, they'd be under
water,' someone offers. Someone else adds darkly, 'Eels is no good.'
The question drops. I return home carrying pointless cider purchased
out of politeness.

I have had one success however. The little upstairs room facing the
road (on the 'inner room' and drawing room side) sported a pair of stout
cotton curtains. (I should add that the corresponding front window on

the other side is that of the bathroom.) I have cut one of these curtains down the middle, knotted the two ends, and tied this 'rope' onto the iron banister at the steps, thereby enabling myself to have an excellent swim this morning at low tide, even though the sea was choppy. Lunch: frankfurters with scrambled eggs, grilled tomatoes and a slight touch of garlic, then shop treacle tart squeezed with lemon juice and covered with yoghurt and thick cream. I drank some of the cider just to spite it. After lunch I started to make a border round my lawn with the pretty stones which I have collected. I cannot decide whether or not it looks ridiculous. A rather cloudy day and a cool breeze, with a strange coffee-coloured light over the sea. Towards evening, the usual cloud-show. Great cliffs and headlands of light golden-brown cloud build up to majestic heights, with a froth of pure gold clinging to their huge sides. I tried to light a fire of driftwood in the little red room but the chimney smoked again.

I have been cleaning and tidying up the house. What an extraordinary satisfaction there is in cleaning things! (Does the satisfaction depend on ownership? I suspect so.) I swept the hall and stairs. I washed the big slate flagstones in the kitchen (very rewarding). I also dusted the big ugly vase on the landing and polished the battered rosewood table (it was grateful). I started to dust the drawing room chimney piece but some spirit that dwelt therein resisted me. And I have now been polishing the big oval mirror in the hall (which I think I mentioned before). This fine thing (date eighteen ninety?) is perhaps the best 'piece' in the house. The glass is bevelled and somewhat spotted but remarkably luminous and silvery, so that the mirror seems like a source of light. The frame is made of a dullish grey metal (pewter?) and represents a sort of swirling garland of leaves and branches and berries. Metal polish brought a little more luminosity and detail into this metal vegetation. A lot of dirt certainly came off on the cloth. Since I have just spent a little while gazing at myself in this mirror it is perhaps time to attempt to describe my appearance.

This may seem superfluous. Yes, of course, I have been a much photographed man. But the camera has never been entirely my friend. (How fortunate that I never wanted to be a film star.) Let me describe the real me. I am slim and of medium build. I have an oval face with a short straight nose and thin lips and a uniformly fair fine complexion which is given to blushing. If annoyed or affronted I blush scarlet. This habit, which used to worry me, later became a kind of trade mark; and when I became known in my profession as a 'tartar' it was inadvertently useful in frightening people. My eyes are a rather pale chilly blue; I wear small oval rimless spectacles for reading. I have light rather colourless straight fair hair, not worn long. This, never brilliant, fades and dims, but does not go grey. I have decided not to dye it. (A few years ago when my hair began to recede I enlisted the aid of science, with entirely satisfactory results.) I should say that what the camera fails to catch is the fine almost girlish texture of my, of course clean shaven, face, and its somewhat ironical and wily expression. (Not to beat about the bush, it is a clever face.) Photographers can too easily make one look a fool. I often think I resemble my father, and yet he looked both gentle and simple, whereas I look neither. To bed early with a hot water bottle. Very tired.

I think it is not going to be too easy to write about the theatre. Perhaps my reflections on that vast subject will make another book. I had better get straight on to Clement Makin. After all, it is for Clement that I am here. This was her country, she grew up on this lonely coast. We never visited it. Was I superstitious? Her Ultima Thule bided its hour.

Clement was my first mistress. When we met I was twenty, she was thirty-nine (or said she was). Partly because of someone I had loved and lost, and partly because of my puritan upbringing, I remained virgin until Clement swooped like an eagle. Was she a great actress? Yes, I think so. Of course women act all the time. It is easier to judge a man. (Wilfred for instance.) I shall have to talk a bit about the theatre simply to give Clement her context, to dress the scene for her to sweep upon. She was not like what people thought; neither her fans nor her foes did her justice and she had her lion's share of both. She always fought mercilessly for those she loved, and then she became totally immoral; she lied and cheated for them, she trampled upon rights and upon hearts. She loved me and I am quite prepared to admit that as it happened she made me; though I would have made myself anyway. God rest her restless soul.

Emotions really exist at the bottom of the personality or at the top. In the middle they are acted. This is why all the world is a stage, and why the theatre is always popular and indeed why it exists: why it is like life, and it is like life even though it is also the most vulgar and outrageously factitious of all the arts. Even a middling novelist can tell quite a lot of truth. His humble medium is on the side of truth. Whereas the theatre, even at its most 'realistic', is connected with the level at which, and the methods by which, we tell our everyday lies. This is the sense in which 'ordinary' theatre resembles life, and dramatists are disgraceful liars unless they are very good. On the other hand, in a purely formal sense the theatre is the nearest to poetry of all the arts. I used to think that if I could have been a poet I would never have bothered with the theatre at all, but of course this was nonsense. What I needed with all my starved and silent soul was just that particular way of shouting back at the world. The theatre is an attack on mankind carried on by magic: to victimize an audience every night, to make them laugh and cry and suffer and miss their trains. Of course actors regard audiences as enemies, to be deceived, drugged, incarcerated, stupefied. This is partly because the audience is also a court against which there is no appeal. Art's relation with its client is here at its closest and most immediate. In other arts we can blame the client: he is stupid, unsophisticated, inattentive, dull. But the theatre must, if need be, stoop – and stoop – until it attains that direct, that universal communication which other artists can afford to seek more deviously and at their ease. Hence the assault, the noise, the characteristic impatience. All this was part of my revenge.

How vulgar, how almost cruel it all was; I gloatingly savour now that I am absolutely out of it at last, now that I can sit in the sun and look at the calm quiet sea. This solitude and quiet after all that babble, after all that garish row, a deep undynamic stillness so unlike the fine dramatic silences of the theatre: *Tempest* scene two, or the entry of Peter Pan. So unlike too the strange familiar and yet exciting hush of an empty theatre. Actors are cave dwellers in a rich darkness which they love and hate. How I enjoyed rending expectant silences with noise, noise as structure, noise as colour. (I once directed a thriller which began with a long silence and then a scream. That sound became famous.) Yet, or perhaps consequently, I do not care greatly for music. Noise yes, music no. I admire the intricate and essentially silent musical drama of ballet, but opera I detest. Clement used to say this was a case of envy. I must admit I envy Wagner.

The theatre is a place of obsession. It is not a soft dreamland. Unemployment, poverty, disappointment, racking indecision (take this now and miss that later) grind reality into one's face; and, as in family life, one soon learns the narrow limitations of the human soul. Yet obsession is what it is all about. All good dramatists and directors and most (not all) good actors are obsessed men. Only geniuses like Shakespeare conceal the fact, or rather change it into something spiritual. And obsession drives to hard work. I myself have always worked (and worked others) like a demon. My mother's training made me a compulsive worker. She was never idle and she did not tolerate idleness in others. My father enjoyed a certain amount of fixing and mending, but he would have liked to sit sometimes quite vacantly and watch the world drift by, only he was never allowed to. My mother was not ambitious for him in a worldly sense – she scorned the successful world of Uncle Abel and Aunt Estelle, though I think that the prospect of it always hurt her in some obscure way. She simply wanted my father to be always usefully employed. (Fortunately discussing books with me counted as useful.) She did not profess to understand his office work, she showed no curiosity about it and I suspect she had no idea what he did. She organized him at home. She also organized me, but this was easy because I was only too ready to be obsessively industrious. Journalists have often asked me how it was that I first started to write plays. I did not, as has been unkindly suggested, turn to writing out of disappointment with my career as an actor. I started to write when I was still quite young because I could not bear to waste time when I was unemployed. I early saw the demoralization of so many of my out-of-work companions. 'Resting' is one of the least restful periods of an actor's life. Those times were also, of course, my university. I read and I wrote and I taught myself my trade.

Since there has been quite a lot of uninformed and not always unmalicious speculation on the subject let me now say something about my plays. They were always intended to be ephemeral, rather like pantomimes in fact; and they existed only in my direction of them. I never let anyone else touch them. Unless one is very talented indeed there is no resting place between the naïve and the ironic; and the nemesis of irony is absurdity. I knew my limitations. The plays were also said to be only vehicles for Wilfred Dunning. Why 'only'? Wilfred was a great actor. They do not make them like Wilfred any more. He started his career in the old Music Hall in the Edgware Road. He could stand motionless, not moving an eyelid, and make a theatre rock with prolonged laughter. Then he would blink and set them off again. Such power can be almost uncanny: the mystery of the human body, the human face. Wilfred had a face which glowed with spirit; he also had, with the possible exception of Peregrine Arbelow, the largest face I have ever seen. It is true that he was in a sense the only begetter of my work as a dramatist, and when he died I stopped writing. I can say without regret that my plays belong to the past and I bequeath them to no one. They were magical delusions, fireworks. Only this which I write now is, or foreshadows, what I wish to leave behind me as a lasting memorial. Someone once said that I ought to have been a choreographer and I understood the comment. People were surprised that I was so popular in Japan. But I knew why, and the Japanese knew.

Though described as an 'experimentalist' I am a firm friend of the proscenium arch. I am in favour of illusion, not of alienation. I detest the endless fidgeting on the surrounded stage which dissolves the clarity of events. Equally I abhor the nonsense of 'audience participation'. Riots and other communal activities may have their value but must not be confused with dramatic art. Drama must create a factitious spell-binding present moment and imprison the spectator in it. The theatre apes the profound truth that we are extended beings who yet can only exist in the present. It is a factitious present because it lacks the free aura of personal reflection and contains its own secret limits and conclusions. Thus life is comic, but though it may be terrible it is not tragic: tragedy belongs to the cunning of the stage. Of course most theatre is gross ephemeral rot; and only plays by great poets can be *read,* except as directors' notes. I say 'great poets' but I suppose I really mean Shakespeare. It is a paradox that the most essentially frivolous and rootless of all the serious arts has produced the greatest of all writers. That Shakespeare was *quite different* from the others, not just *primus inter pares* but totally different in quality, was something which I discovered entirely by myself when I was still at school; and on this secret was I nourished. There are no other plays on paper, unless one counts the Greek plays. I cannot read Greek, and James tells me these are untranslatable. After looking at a number of translations I am sure he is right.

Of course the theatre is essentially a place of hopes and disappointments and in its cyclical life one lives out in a more vivid way the cyclical patterns of the ordinary world. The thrill of a new play, the shock of a flop, the weariness of a long run, the homeless feeling when it ends: perpetual construction followed by perpetual destruction. It is to do with endings, with partings, with packings up and dismantlings and the disbanding of family groups. All this makes theatre people into nomads, or rather into the separated members of some sort of monastic order where certain natural feelings (the desire for permanence for instance) have to be suppressed. We have the 'heartlessness' of monks; and in this respect we suffer the changes characteristic of ordinary life with a difference, in a sublimated symbolic way. As actor, director and playwright I have of course had my full share of disappointments, of lost time and lost ways. My 'successful' career contains many failures, many dead ends. All my plays flopped on Broadway for instance. I failed as an actor, I ceased as a playwright. Only my fame as a director has covered up these facts.

If absolute power corrupts absolutely then I must be the most corrupt of men. A theatre director is a dictator. (If he is not, he is not doing his job.) I fostered my reputation for ruthlessness, it was extremely useful. Actors expected tears and nervous prostration when I was around. Most of them loved it; they are masochists as well as narcissists. I well remember Gilbert Opian hysterical and enjoying every moment. Of course the girls wept all the time. (When, advanced in my career, I directed Clement, we both wept. My God, how we fought!) I was always merciless to drunks, and this did strain my relations with Peregrine Arbelow, even before the Rosina business. Perry is an Irish drunk, the worst kind. Wilfred drank like a fish, but it never showed on stage. Christ, I miss him.

I liked that handy picture of myself as a 'tartar'. Other publicized conceptions of me have been uglier and more misleading. I never used my power to haul girls into bed. Of course the theatre is all that my mother thought and a great deal that the poor dear could not have conceived of. Yet also it must be remembered that the theatre is a profession and many perfectly 'typical' actors are middle-aged men who are regularly supplied with work and who live faithfully with wives and families in suburbs. Such persons are the backbone of the trade. Of course the theatre is sex, sex, sex, but how much does the subject-matter affect the professional? My mother was upset at the thought of my 'acting bad people', because she thought this would corrupt me. (In fact, except in school plays, she hardly ever saw me act.) I wonder if such corruption ever occurs? The question is worth asking. To some extent one has to 'identify' with villains in order to portray them, but there are limits to this identification partly because wickedness is so specialized. (Every actor has a level at which he cannot portray character. He may operate above it or below it.) And we are masked figures; ideally the masks barely touch us. (Such is my view, with which some fools will differ.) I recall a story of an old actor asked to portray an old man, who said with dismay, 'But I've never played an old man!' That was professionalism.

But to return to myself. I daresay an unfashionable thing to say nowadays, I am not 'very highly sexed'. I can live perfectly well without 'sexual relations'. Some observers have even thought I must be homosexual because I did not have perpetual mistresses! I hate *mess*. Perhaps my morally hygienic mother somehow taught me to. And I have never liked the complicit male world of foulmouthed talk and bawdy. Of course I have had not a few love affairs. But I never bribed a woman into bed. Someone (Rosina) once said, 'You care about the theatre more than you care about women' and it was true. I never (except for once when I was young) seriously considered marriage. I loved once (the same once) absolutely. Then there was Clement, eternal wonderful unclassifiable Clement. And I have been 'madly infatuated'. And there have been, oh such sweet girls. But I am not a womanizer. I have always been a dedicated professional. I was in this respect harsh with myself as well as with others. Silly messy love affairs, especially within a closed group, interfere with serious work. I am very prone to jealousy myself, and I have mixed with very jealous people. Envy has always troubled me less. Crippling envy can be a terrible disability in the theatre, and I early realized that to overcome it was a prerequisite of success.

Was I sorry that I never became a first-rate actor? How often I have been asked that question! Well, of course. Directors always envy actors and I suspect that almost every great director would secretly prefer to be a great actor. Some people held the view that a more successful acting career awaited me in films and television and they tried to lure me in; but in spite of many amusing excursions I never cared much for these media. I always felt real drama belonged to the live theatre. I had my ambitions, especially of course in Shakespeare; but I always funked Lear and the less said about my Hamlet the better. I think I was a good Prospero, that time when Lizzie was Ariel. That was my last great part, and now so long ago. After that I laid a certain vanity aside. Vanity receives such a battering in the theatre, one would imagine that it would tend to vanish, but most actors manage to retain theirs: not only as an occupational ailment, but perhaps actually as a necessary instrument of survival. Genuine generous admiration, and there is plenty of it, always helps and heals. I looked at the good actors and the great actors, at Wilfred, at Sidney Ashe, at Marcus Henty (also one of Clement's lovers), at Fabian Ginsberg, even at Perry, even at Al. And, as an actor, I quietly took a backseat. This was easier to do by then as I was fully absorbed in directing. I amused myself and the public by playing tiny parts in my own productions and once nearly stole the show as Jacob in *The Seagull*.

Well, well, I seem to be writing everything down all at once in a sort of jumble. Perhaps I should indeed regard this diary as rough notes. I shall resist, for the present at any rate, the temptation to reminisce about my productions. I am known as a Shakespeare man but of course I have tried my hand at everything; you name it, I did it. And so – enough of boasting. These ramblings were to introduce Clement Makin. But poor Clement can wait, indeed she cannot choose but wait. That great battle of wills is finished forever. And I sit here and wonder at myself. Have I abjured that magic, drowned my book? Forgiven my enemies? The surrender of power, the final change of magic into spirit? Time will show.

Something rather odd and distressing has just occurred. I wrote the above sitting outside on my lawn on my stone seat beside my trough of stones. As the morning sun became hot I decided to go inside and fetch my sun hat. I have a slight headache, possibly I need new glasses. I went into the house and up the stairs, blinking in the comparative gloom, and when I reached the upper landing I was at once aware that something had *happened*, although I could not understand what. Then I realized that my lovely big ugly vase was gone from its pedestal. It had fallen onto the floor and was broken into a great many pieces. But how? The pedestal is perfectly steady and has not moved. There has been no wind, the bead curtain is motionless. Perhaps I shifted the vase very slightly when I dusted it yesterday? Or has there been an earth tremor? I am reluctant to think that I am to blame and I am sure I am not. I liked the poor ugly thing, it was like an old dog. I picked up the pieces thinking vaguely of mending it, but of course that would be impossible. How can it have jumped off its stand? I am totally puzzled.

'But all your letters are in the dog kennel, Mr Arrowby.'

I had broken down at last and asked at the Post Office. I say broken down, not so much because I was thereby losing face with the village (though that too was in my mind) as because I was losing face with myself. Why should I now need letters or miss them or pine for them or be surprised if nobody wrote to me? I had already arranged with Miss Kaufman for business letters to be kept in London. Only letters from friends were to be sent on. And as I was explaining to myself, really I have no friends. But there was one letter which I was interested in having, which at least I was expecting. However, let us return for the moment to this dog kennel.

'*Dog kennel?*' I said to the Post Office lady. (She is the sister of the shop lady, the Post Office being part of the shop.)

'Yes, the stone dog kennel just before you go across to your house. Mrs Chorney always had her letters put in there.'

This object, at the road end of the causeway, pointed out to me by the house agent as the boundary of my land, I had of course noticed but not investigated. It was quite big and had indeed the form of a dog kennel, but one which in my opinion would be suitable only for a stone dog. I imagine it had originally had some other purpose, though I cannot think what.

I protested. How was I to know? Was I supposed to guess? Why had someone not told me? Why did the postman not notice that no letters had been picked up? What happened when it rained? And so on.

The Post Office lady repeated with dignity that Mrs Chorney had always had her mail in the dog kennel, that it saved the postman a walk, that he could not be expected to peer inside to see if letters had gone, and anyhow I might be away. And so on.

I bought some frozen coley (much better than cod) and hurried home. Yes, the letter I was waiting for, together with various other missives, was in the dog kennel (which would be swimming with water in rainy weather) and I carried the lot into the house.

The letter I wanted was from Lizzie Scherer, and when I transcribe it it will become clear in what respect I have been less than frank with this diary. In fact I have been disinclined to discuss Lizzie earlier because I was not sure what I felt about something which I had recently done about her. Not that I was upset or anxious. When I came here I decided that I would never be anxious any more about personal relations; such anxiety is too often a form of vanity. What I had done was to send Lizzie a letter which constituted a – what? – a sort of test, or game, or gamble. A serious game. I had always played serious games with Lizzie. Did I regret sending the letter? Do I, will I, regret it? Well, a word first perhaps about the girl herself.

Clement Makin was, or was nearly, a great actress. Lizzie Scherer is, at the other end of the scale, very nearly not an actress at all. In so far as Lizzie was ever successful I made her so. I stretched her beyond her limits; and I may as well confess now that I took trouble with Lizzie because, in a way, I loved her. I say 'in a way' not only because I have only really loved once (and Lizzie was not it), but also because I found it surprisingly easy to leave her when the time came. I was never 'mad' about Lizzie, as I have occasionally been about other women (Rosina, Jeanne). I cared for her in a quiet rather dreamy way which was perhaps unique in my life. But I left her. She loved me far more intensely. For Lizzie I was it.

Lizzie is Scottish, half Sephardi Jew. Although she has the most adorable breasts of any woman I ever made love to, she is not really beautiful, and never was even when she was young, but she has charm. This 'fetching' charm, and her youth while it lasted, took her a little way in the theatre. She was a hard worker and had a kind of steady Scottish reliability which always helped. Her appearance is not easy to describe. She has a large wide brow and a strong attractive profile. (One can fall in love with a profile.) The line of her brow runs down in a smooth fine curve into a smallish pretty nose which speeds forward at the world without quite turning up. Then there is a straight line to a firm chin wherein there is the faintest dimple. Her lips are firm too, not full but well moulded and sensitively textured. (How different individual lips are.) Nature not art has painted them an attractive terracotta-pink. Her upper lip is long and beautifully indented. (Is there any language in which there is a word for that tender runnel that joins the mouth and the nose?) One would call hers a clever face if it were not for a kind of childish timidity which hangs about it. I suspect that this gentle pleading diffidence *is* Lizzie's charm. Her eyes are a light dewy brown; when I kissed her how those pale eyes flashed! She is short-sighted and tends to peer. (As Peregrine once said, very few pretty women can see anything, since vanity precludes glasses.) She has almost invisible orange eyebrows which she never, under my regime, tampered with. Her complexion is healthy, rosy, rather shiny. She wears very little make-up and lacks (perhaps makes a point of lacking) the wonderful artificiality of many theatre ladies, their enamelled lacquered surfaces. This artificiality of course attracts. It attracted me. I like art in a woman's looks, though I do not necessarily want to see all the working. Lizzie's hair, now tinted, is a cinnamon brown, of the hyacinthine variety and copious. (It is a bit fuzzy and grows more in screwy tendrils than in curls.) When she is happy her face is conspicuously radiant and merry. (At her best on the stage, her face could make audiences *sigh* with pleasure.) She is still quite good-looking, though she has allowed herself to become untidy and out of condition. Any drama school teaches physical discipline; acting is a physical discipline. The ladies of the theatre tend to keep themselves sleek and youthful, and this Lizzie has failed to do. Nor was she ever smart. (I am not indifferent to the unique pleasure afforded by a smart woman.) And with advancing years she has, not to put too fine a point upon it, got fat. My God, she must now be getting on for fifty. Well, here, retrieved from the dog kennel, is Lizzie's letter, which will be to some extent self-explanatory.

My dear, your beautiful generous letter has come, but I don't understand it. Perhaps I don't want to understand it. It is enough to have it. When I saw your writing I felt faint with joy and fear. But why fear? What have I ever done to you, except love you? When I read your letter I cried and cried. I wonder if you know how long it is since you wrote me anything better than a postcard? I almost feel as if I simply want to be happy ever after because you have written to me, and not to have to *think* about your letter or to answer it. For now I am falling into anxiety and dread.

What do you want, Charles? Oh, you are so present to my mind as I write. But you have always been present to my mind ever since I first loved you, you live in my mind. Something about your letter that made me especially glad is that you do not doubt that I still love you. 'Still' hardly has meaning here. My love for you exists in a sort of eternal present, it almost is the meaning of time. I don't protest too much. Such love can live with despair, with quietness, with resignation, with ordinariness and tiredness and silence. I love you, Charles, and I will love you till I die, and you can put that away in your heart and be utterly certain of it.

Your letter is so cool, purposely cool and full of jokes. (All that about wanting a 'nurse'!) All right, you would like to see me, why not, we are old friends. But these two particular old friends cannot just say 'hello', at least this one cannot. I look at your letter and I try to read between the lines. *What* is between the lines? I feel I am supposed to guess your mood. Oh God, your *mood*. Do you want me to drop in for a short love affair? Please excuse these awful words, but you have put me in an awful situation. Perhaps your letter means very little and I am imagining things. Perhaps you yourself do not know what you mean, and don't care. That would be like you too. Forgive me.

Listen, Charles. I have said I am grateful and I am. For years and years, as you know, I would have married you if you had crooked your finger. And I proposed to you every day when we were together! I know this letter of yours now is *of course* not about marriage. But what is it about? A weekend visit? You don't say that you love me. Do you want to experiment now that you have time on your hands? Charles, I want to live, I want to survive, I don't want to be driven mad a second time. When I consider it all now I'm just afraid to come near you. You would have to convince me and I suspect you can't. You once said yourself, how much A loves B shows, like your slip showing. We haven't met for more than a year, the last time was that luncheon for Sidney Ashe and how intensely I looked forward to it and you scarcely spoke to me! Then I wanted to leave with you in that taxi and you suddenly asked Nell Pickering to come too. (You've probably forgotten.) You haven't communicated with me since. You haven't telephoned or sent a line although you know I would be wild with joy to hear from you. You don't even know where I live, you had to send the letter care of my agent! All this is evidence,

Charles. And now suddenly, you write this funny ambiguous letter. It's just an *idea* you've had, there's something sort of abstract about it. You've probably thought better of it already.

If I came to see you like you want, just coming because you feel in the mood to see me, to sort of try my company again, I would fall straight back into the old madness. I don't mean that I ever really got over it, but I've lived, I've managed, I've even put some sort of order into my life at last. I've had long enough, after all, since you left me! You never fully knew how mad I was in those days. I didn't want to hurt you by showing you my pain by way of revenge. All the time we were together I knew every minute, every second, that it would end. You told me often enough! But somehow (I was that mad) I embraced the suffering, if I could have suffered more I would have suffered more. I wonder if you've ever loved anyone like that? Maybe you only understood it on the stage. (I think I fell in love with you when you were shouting at Romeo and Juliet, 'Don't touch each other!') You kept saying there was this great love when you were young, but I think that was just to console me for your not loving me enough. Anyway you didn't love me enough, and now – I don't believe in miracles.

Charles, I've been in hell and I've come out of it and I don't want to go there again. Jealousy is hell and I'm not cured. Suppose I come to you, with all that old love – and you smile and stroll away? You're free, your letter made that clear all right. Forgive me, but you know how people talk, everybody tells everybody everything, and I still keep meeting girls I didn't even know you knew who say they've had romances with you, they may be lying of course. You know you can't keep your hands off women, and I'm not young and beautiful any more, and you like chasing what isn't easy to get, you don't want to stay with anyone, in the end you drop everyone! You once said getting married was like buying a doll, which shows what you think of marriage. And I don't believe you've really retired, Gilbert said it was like God retiring, you're too *restless*. You made me act, you made everyone act, you're like a very good dancer, you make other people dance but it's got to be *with you*. You don't respect people as people, you don't *see* them, you're not really a teacher, you're a sort of rapacious magician. How can I imagine that all this could stop? Do you want me as a sort of patient friend, a chaperon with knitting, a calm wise older woman, a sort of retired senior wife to whom you can complain about the others? It wouldn't work, Charles. I'm not calm and wise. I'd want everything. You could still have children. I remember you saying more than once how much you wanted a son. You could still have a son, only I couldn't bear him. Oh Charles, Charles, why didn't you marry me long ago, I loved you so much. I love you so much – only I can't put my head into that noose. My love for you is quiet at last. I don't want it to become a roaring furnace.

And there is something else I must tell you. I am living with Gilbert Opian. You obviously didn't know or you'd have mentioned it in the letter. I know you made me promise to let you know if I ever settled down permanently with anyone. (I was so hurt when Rita Gibbons told me you'd made her promise that too. I didn't tell her about my promise. She says she doesn't regard hers as binding because it was given under duress.) I didn't tell you about Gilbert because I'm not living *like that* with him, I mean we're not lovers, of course not, Gilbert hasn't suddenly become heterosexual. We just love each other and care for each other and we share a house and, Charles, I have been happy for the first time in my life. This is the most creative thing I've ever done, far more than acting. I was living like this when we met at Sidney's lunch and I would have told you then if you'd shown any interest and really asked! And, Charles, I've left the theatre and I feel so much better. Honestly the theatre was always a torment for me. I only shone for you, and when you left me I faded! (I was never much good anyhow!) When I look back and see what a miserable stupid anxious messy existence I led over years and years I can't think how I tolerated it. I was perfectly capable of being happy but somehow I always managed not to be! Men were always being beastly to me. Gilbert is so different. Don't sneer at this. I've been bullied by bloody men all my life. Now I have a decent orderly cheerful existence. I'm even useful! I work part-time in a hospital office. I'm learning to paint and I write children's stories (none published yet). You may think this sounds pathetic, but for me it's happiness and freedom. And Gilbert is happy too. He's stopped fretting about being unsuccessful and not being a star. He can get some small parts and he works a bit on TV. We're not rich, but we can earn money and look after each other. Tenderness and absolute trust and communication and truth: these things matter more and more as one grows older. Gilbert's given up 'hunting', he says all he ever wanted was love and he's got mine. It's all somehow suddenly simple and innocent. (It seems to me now we were all brainwashed about 'sex'!) Please understand, dear dear Charles, and do not be angry. You know (and I won't go on about this because it used to annoy you) how much Gilbert loves you too. Really he worships you. But he's so frightened now. He says you'll come with a troika and carry me off to the gipsies. (I suppose that's a quotation, you always said I read nothing but Shakespeare and then only my own part!) He is frightened of you still, and so am I. The habit of obeying you is strong in both of us! Don't use your power to hurt us. You could put the most terrible pressure on us, only don't do it. Be generous, dear heart. You could drive us both mad. We've come a long road to solving our problems, and if some people think it's a funny solution that's just because they lack imagination and intelligence. And you lack neither.

Charles, I don't want to see you now, yet. I'd simply succumb. I've got to recover from your letter. *Please write and say you are not angry.* When I am calmer let's meet, and you must come here and see Gilbert too. There must be a way. Your letter has made an aching emptiness and a need and I shall not be the same. But I am happy here and Gilbert needs me and we have this house (it's half a house actually) which we have *made* together, and if I left him it would be a terrible smash-up for both of us, we'd be in pieces. (Anyway I don't know what you want – and whatever it was you may not want it now. Oh *God*.) Gilbert says you must in the end receive us as if we were your children. Oh Charles, I am amazed at the strength of those forces which I commanded to sleep. It is all there still, all my old love for you. Somehow, let us not waste love, it is rare enough. You have thought of me, you have written to me, so sweetly, so generously. Can we not love each other and see each other at last in freedom, without awful possessiveness and violence and fear, now that we are growing old? I do so want us to love each other, but not in a way that would destroy me. I've felt so sad for years about you. My love for you has always had a sad face. Oh the weakness of the power of love ! You feel you can compel the beloved, but it's an illusion! I am crying as I write this. Please write at once, and say that we can meet later, in a little while, and that you won't stop loving me. Somehow don't lose that love, the love, whatever it may be, that made you write that letter. And we will look at each other.

Always yours –

Lizzie.

I have been sitting for some time in the little red room, where I have at last lit a successful fire. The chimney seems to have got over its smoking fit. Perhaps it was just that the wood was too wet?

I have read Lizzie's letter through twice. Of course it is a silly inconsistent woman's letter, half saying the opposite of what it is trying to say. Lizzie cannot quite refrain from offering herself. And of course she does, in answer to my deliberately cool missive, protest too much. A cleverer woman might have replied coolly and let *me* read between the lines. A cleverer woman, or a less sincere one. Lizzie's letter has its own little attempts at ambiguity, but they are transparent. Poor Lizzie. I cannot take the stuff about Gilbert Opian too seriously, though I do feel cross with her for not having told me, and I feel she has broken her promise. Besides, what are their relations? Lizzie's proximity is surely enough, even now, to convert any man to heterosexuality. (Her breasts are enough.) Do they drink cocoa together in their dressing gowns? The whole thing is rather horrid. Of course Gilbert is nothing, he is a man of twigs, I could crush him with one hand and take Lizzie with the other. I certainly cannot envisage any platonic love trio. From the date of Lizzie's letter it appears to have been in the dog kennel for well over a week. On reflection this seems to be no bad thing. If I had received it at once I might have been tempted to write an ill-tempered or facetious reply by return of post. As it is, she has had a silence to reflect upon. It may be best to prolong the silence.

However, to repeat Lizzie's own perfectly reasonable question, what do I want? Oh why do women take everything so intensely and make such a fuss! Why do they always demand definitions, explanations! There are in fact some quite shrewd guesses in her letter, and the quiet outburst of resentment has not escaped me. Those wounding and not wholly unjust observations have doubtless been stored up for a long time! Perhaps I do want a sort of retired part-time 'senior wife' figure, like an ageing ex-concubine in a harem who has become a friend: a companion who is taken for granted, to whom one is close, but not committed except by bonds of friendship? (This need not preclude occasional love-making. In fact the harem situation would suit me down to the ground.) Why can't Lizzie be intelligent enough to understand? My letter said nothing about time and space, I simply thought of her and wanted to see her. But then she will start asking absolute questions. An 'experiment'? Yes, why not? She knows how I hate exhibitions of emotion, but she pours it all out all the same. She 'wants everything', does she. Well, she can't have it; and that doubtless is that.

I feel no jealousy of Gilbert, but I feel a sort of envy of him! *He* is the clever one. He has got simple Lizzie as his sweet affectionate housekeeper; and meanwhile I very much doubt whether he has given up 'hunting'. I must confess I still have feelings of ownership about Lizzie. She has 'lasted' in my mind. Yet, she is quite right, loving shows like one's slip showing, as I once said to her when her slip was showing! (How these girls do treasure up one's words.) I have neglected her, I have even been cruel, though that could be called a sign of love and the neglect a sign of trust. I do in fact recall the business of the taxi after Sidney's luncheon. I saw that Lizzie was scheming to leave with me. But at the last moment I quite deliberately brought Nell Pickering along too. Nell is the new musical comedy star, with whom I had been flirting all through lunch. Nell is twenty-two. (I wouldn't mind having her in my harem.) Poor Lizzie. What made me suddenly write that teasing semi-serious letter to her I wonder? Some fear of loneliness and death which has come to me out of the sea?

Since the subject of Lizzie Scherer has come up I may as well give some further account of her. I began to love Lizzie after I realized how much she loved me. As does sometimes happen, her love impressed me, then attracted me. I was directing a season of Shakespeare. She fell in love with me during *Romeo and Juliet,* she revealed her love during *Twelfth Night,* we got to know each other during *A Midsummer Night's Dream.* Then (but that was later) I began to love her during *The Tempest,* and (but that was later still) I left her during *Measure for Measure* (when Aloysius Bull was playing the Duke). I recall very clearly that occasion when I first realized that Lizzie loved me. She was playing Viola. (This was during Lizzie's brief 'shining period', her *annus mirabilis.*) It was the production in which Wilfred Dunning, who usually played Sir Toby Belch, suddenly insisted on playing Malvolio. At least, he did not insist, I let him. It was a marvel but it wrecked the production. Lizzie and I were alone in a rather draughty church hall which for some reason was all we could get at that moment to rehearse in. It was a winter's evening and I remember the place as being lit with gas. Lizzie (now in Act two, Scene four) got as far as 'she never told her love'. Then she stopped and seemed to choke and uttered no more. I thought at first that this was her own extremely effective idea of how to speak the speech, and I waited for her to go on. She gazed at me. Then huge glistening tears rose into her eyes. When I realized what the matter was I began to laugh and laugh and laugh, and after a bit Lizzie laughed, laughing and crying helplessly. And I loved her for that laughter too. She was a good girl. She is a good girl.

I somehow always picture Lizzie in breeches. She first won a little fame as principal boy in small provincial pantomimes. She was very slim in those days and rather boyish in appearance and used to stride around in boots and cut her hair very short. Her great ambition, never realized, was to play Peter Pan. She was (briefly) quite serviceable as Shakespeare's transvestite girls. (Sidney later directed her as Rosalind.) I made her into an adorable Viola, but her greatest success in that historic season was as Puck. (In *Romeo and Juliet* she was a mute lady. I forget who played Juliet, except that she was no good.) I was touched by her love and by her superb obedience, but I was tied up with Rosina at the time and I saw Lizzie as a wispish enchanting rather infantile sprite. Every time I met her I laughed and then she laughed too. We used to laugh at each other across restaurants and suddenly and mysteriously during rehearsals. I did not need to be told how much she loved me, though she never, even on the first occasion, said anything about it. I thought that was stylish of her. Throughout the *Dream* her radiant gaze rested on me, her will touched my will and trembled. She understood and obeyed, and although (as she told me later) she knew about Rosina, she existed in a sort of heaven of suffering which I must confess gave me some gratification. Perhaps this gratification was a prophetic gleam from the love I was later to feel for her. And by then I was getting thoroughly tired of Rosina. In that production of the *Dream* Al Bull (a most uneven actor) played Oberon rather boorishly, and I regretted not taking the part myself. Lizzie's cup would then have been full and running over! It was at the end of that season that I went to America, and there followed the horrible interlude in Hollywood and the first debacle with Fritzie Eitel. I think I went to Hollywood partly to escape from Rosina: in any case I escaped. Rosina thought I left her because of Lizzie, but this was not so.

When I came back to England again there was suddenly an interval of peace and an atmosphere of restored innocence and joy. It was summer. I was on good terms with Clement who had one of her silly young men at the time. I felt, after the horrors of California, free and happy. I wanted to get back to Shakespeare after the muck I had been wading through in America. A fly-by-night American director called

Isaiah Mommsen let me play Prospero. It was the last substantial part I ever played. Lizzie was Ariel. She was the most spiritual, most curiously *accurate* Ariel I ever saw. Her love for me made her so, and in the midst of all that magic made me love her. Oddly, I felt then, and the feeling remains with me, that I loved her as if she were my son. She often called herself my page. She had a pretty little singing voice and I can still hear the thin true tone of her *Full Fathom Five*. How now, after all these years, my tricksy spirit. I remember that she once played Cherubino in an amateur production of *Figaro,* and I think this tiny success was one of the things she valued most. Damn, it has just occurred to me that Gilbert Opian probably regards her as a boy!

My love for Lizzie was somehow an innocent love. (God, what messes I got into with Rita and Rosina and Jeanne and Doris and the rest.) The innocence was Lizzie's pure gift. Her love was so scrupulous, so intelligent. She never used her power to lay upon me the lightest of moral bonds. The reader will say, but the bonds were there! Well, yes, and yet some grace born of Lizzie's selflessness seemed almost to abolish them and we lived in the golden world. Of course she never reproached me. It was as if she positively did not want me to feel any sense of duty towards her, but wanted me simply to use her for my happiness. Written so, this sounds crude. But as we lived it, it was the profoundest humblest tact on her part, and on mine a love that was composed of gentle gratitude. We were gentle with each other.

And yet of course it was also at the same time a scene of carnage. (Why do I so much enjoy writing this down?) I told her from the start that I had no conception of marrying her. Was it blind stupid hope nevertheless which made her so infinitely kind to me? An ungrateful thought: I am sure she had no hope. I told her that the affair was temporary, that my love for her was temporary, and doubtless her love for me was temporary. I spoke of mortality and the fragile and shadowy nature of human arrangements and the jumbled unreality of human minds, while her large light brown eyes spoke to me of the eternal. She said, I want to be perfect for you so that you can leave me without pain, and this perfect expression of love simply irritated me. She said, I will wait forever, although I know ... I am not ... waiting for ... anything. What a love duet, and how much I enjoyed it although in her suffering I suffered a little too. Certainly she concealed her pain as much as she could; but towards the end it was impossible. She cried before me with wide open eyes, not staunching the tears. Her tears fell on my sleeve, on my hand like storm rain. And when at last I told her to go she went like a shadow, with silent swift obedience. After that I went on my second visit to Japan. The taste of *sake* still makes me remember Lizzie's tears.

She never prospered in the theatre after I went away. (All the ladies went downhill after I left them, except Rosina. Clement of course I never really left, even when we both had other lovers, which was rather horrid for the other lovers.) Two years after Lizzie's apotheosis as Ariel they were asking, whatever happened to Lizzie Scherer? I was so grateful to her, and this alone has made her 'last' in my mind. The dear girl never made me feel guilty! A light of courage and truth shines on her in my memory. She is possibly the only woman (with one exception) who never lied to me. And the remembrance of her sufferings often filled me with a kind of tender joy, whereas when I think of the sufferings of other women I tend to feel indifference, even annoyance.

I wanted a wife once when I was young, but the girl fled. Since then I have never really seriously thought of marriage. My observation of the state never made me fancy it. The only happily married couples I know at all well are my Cambridge friends Victor and Julia Banstead, and, in the theatre, Sidney and Rosemary Ashe; and even they, who knows ...

People are so secretive. I might also count Will and Adelaide Boase, but they only survive because she gives in all the time, which I suppose is one method. What suits me best is the drama of separation, of looking forward to assignations and rendezvous. I cannot prefer the awful eternal presence of marriage to the magic of meetings and partings. I do not even care for sharing a bed, and I rarely want to spend the whole night with a woman I have made love to. In the morning she looks to me like a whore. Marriage is a sort of brainwashing which breaks the mind into the acceptance of so many horrors. How untidy and ugly and charmless married people often let themselves become without even noticing it. I sometimes reflect on these horrors simply in order to delight myself by thinking how I have escaped them!

In this respect Clement understood me perfectly, perhaps because she was always so excessively conscious of being 'old enough to be my mother'. How often, glowing with that famous beauty and charm which she retained for so long, she battered me with that phrase! We knew that we would never marry and we knew that we would make each other suffer, yet we schemed for our happiness, we really used our joint intelligence on that problem. Of course in a way it was a hopeless case, but it was a hopeless case which marvellously lasted for the rest of Clement's life, so I did not do too badly by that wonderful maddening woman. Was I a little cruel to her, never quite saying how much I loved her, always trying to keep her 'on the hop', puzzled, baffled, at a disadvantage? Perhaps. I was afraid of being 'swallowed'. I went away, I came back, I went away again. She was not alone either. She was always beset. I was never terribly jealous, except perhaps for a short while of Marcus, because I had such a close connection with Clement, just as if (though I never used these words to her) she were indeed my mother! She became very irritable and possessive in the last years; and she went on so touchingly trying to please me. She could not stop flirting. When she was ill she became rather hideous towards the end and had to be lied to about her appearance. She lost her figure and went about in corduroy trousers and a baggy jacket. She looked like an old bachelor with drink stains and snuff all down her clothes. Yet still she would spend an hour a day 'doing her face'. Perhaps that is the last pleasure which a woman leaves. No, I never considered marriage. That first girl made all the rest seem shoddy. Or perhaps it was just the comparison with Shakespeare's heroines.

I am writing this after dinner. For dinner I had an egg poached in hot scrambled egg, then the coley braised with onions and lightly dusted with curry powder, and served with a little tomato ketchup and mustard. (Only a fool despises tomato ketchup.) Then a heavenly rice pudding. It is fairly easy to make very good rice pudding, but how often do you meet one? I drank half a bottle of Meursault to salute the coley. I am running out of wine.

Lizzie, yes. She has stayed the course. I have felt more passion with less comfort elsewhere: the mysterious deep half-blind preferences of human beings for each other, the quick probing tentacles that seek in the dark, why one inexplicably and yet certainly loves A and is indifferent to B. I was at ease with Lizzie, her gentle clever teasing made me feel free. Yes, the final question is, how much does one crave for someone's company; that is more radical, it matters more than passion or admiration or 'love'. And am I wondering who will cherish me when I am old and frightened? On the whole I am rather relieved that her letter can be taken as a simple negative. No more anxieties and decisions. I shall let the matter drift. As for Gilbert, that water fly, he is not near my conscience. I rather wonder at Lizzie's touching belief in him. It is true that I could put a most terrible pressure upon both of them, but of course I shall not. No doubt I have done enough damage by simply reminding poor Lizzie of my existence!

'Do you know what a *poltergeist* is, Mr Arkwright?'

Mr Arkwright allows a scornful interval to pass, while he slowly mops the counter. His silence does not connote hesitation. 'Yes, sir.' The 'sir' is sarcastic, not respectful.

'Did you ever hear that there was one at Shruff End?'

'No, sir.'

'A what? What did he say?' asks one of the clients.

'*A poltergeist*,' says Mr Arkwright. 'It's a – sort of a –'

He cannot quite say, so I come in. 'It's a kind of a ghost that breaks things.'

'A ghost –?' There is a significant silence.

'You never heard tell that Shruff End was haunted?'

'Any house might be haunted,' someone volunteers.

'Mrs Chorney haunted it,' someone else says.

'She looked like a – like a –' The simile remains elusive. I leave the matter there.

My question to Mr Arkwright was not prompted solely by the fate of my ugly vase. Something rather frightful happened last night. I was wakened at about five-thirty, as it turned out, by a most fearful shattering crash down below. It was already daylight, but the hall and stairs are dark so I lit a candle. I went down, thoroughly frightened, I must confess, and found that the big oval mirror in the hall had fallen to the ground. The glass was shattered into tiny pieces. What is odd is that both the wire at the back of the mirror and the nail, which remained in the wall, appeared to be intact. I was so appalled and upset I did not stop to investigate properly, and I was afraid that my candle would go out. There was a surprisingly strong draught. I returned promptly to bed.

This morning I rather stupidly pulled the nail out of the wall and threw it away without inspecting it properly. Of course the nail must have been gradually bent by the weight of the mirror until the wire slipped over the end. I feel curiously unwilling to reflect about the matter in detail. I am very sorry about the mirror. The frame is undamaged and it can be reglazed, but the original glass was mysteriously silvery and beautiful. It took me some time to get to sleep after the crash, and I left my candle burning in the dawn light. When at last I fell asleep I dreamt that Mrs Chorney had come out through a door in the alcove to ask me what I was doing in her house. She looked like a –

Searching for a place to plant my herb garden I have found some clumps of excellent young nettles on the other side of the road. I also managed to buy some fresh home-made scones in the village this morning. Some splendid local lady occasionally sells these through the shop. I am told she makes bread too, and I have ordered some. For lunch I ate rashers of cold sugared bacon and poached egg on nettles. (Cook the nettles like spinach. I usually make them into a sort of purée with lentils.) After that I feasted on the scones with butter and raspberry jam. I drank the local cider and tried to like it. The wine problem is still on the horizon.

I have found a few more letters in my dog kennel. They seem to arrive rather irregularly, and I have never yet seen the postman. No word from Lizzie. There is a missive from my cousin James which I shall record. It is characteristic.

My dear Charles,

I understand that you have purchased a house by the seaside. Does this mean that you have given up your theatrical activities? If so it must be a relief no longer to have to do hurried work with a 'deadline' in mind. I trust, in any case, that you are having a well-earned rest in your marine abode, that your 'things' have found satisfactory perches, and that you have a pleasant kitchen wherein to practise your brand of gastronomic mysticism! Have you retained your London flat? I confess I set you down as a dedicated Londoner, so this defection is surprising. I wonder if you have a sea view? The sea is always a refreshment to the spirit, it is good to see the horizon as a clean line. I could do with some 'ozone' myself. The weather in London is intolerably hot and the temperature seems to increase the traffic noise. Perhaps there is some physical cause for this connected with sound waves? I expect you are doing a lot of bathing. I always think of you as a fanatical swimming man. Pray let me hear from you in due course and if you are in town we might have a drink. I hope you are happily 'settled in' and on good terms with your house. I was interested in its curious name. With usual cordial wishes.

Yours,

James.

James's letters to me contrive to be slightly patronizing, as if he were an elder brother, not a younger cousin; indeed they sometimes achieve that well-meaning almost parental stiffness which makes one's own doings seem so puerile. At the same time, these letters, of which I regularly receive two or three a year, always seem to me to combine a dull formality with the faintest touch of madness.

Perhaps at this point I had better offer some longer and more frank account of my cousin. It is not that James has ever been much of an actor in my life, nor do I anticipate that he will ever now become one. We have steadily seen less of each other over the last twenty years, and lately, although he has been stationed in London, we have scarcely met at all. The reference in his letter to 'having a drink' is of course just an empty *politesse*. I have rarely introduced James to my friends (I always kept him well away from the girls), nor has he introduced me to his, if he has any. (I wonder how he heard about my 'seaside house'? That too must be in the newspapers, alas. Is publicity to plague me even here?) No, cousin James has never been an important or active figure in the ordinary transactions of my life. His importance lies entirely in my mind.

We rarely meet, but when we do we tread upon a ground which is deep and old. We are both only children, the sons of brothers close in age (Uncle Abel was slightly younger than my father) who had no other siblings. Though we rarely reminisce, the fact remains that our childhood memories are a common stock which we share with no one else. There are those who, even if valued, remain *sinister* witnesses from the past. James is for me such a witness. It is not even clear whether we like each other. If I were told today that James was dead my first emotion might be pleasurable; though how much does this prove? *Cousinage, dangereux voisinage* had a quite special meaning in our case. I see I have used the past tense; and really, when I reflect, I see how much all this now belongs to the past: only the deeper parts of the mind have so little sense of time. As the years have rolled I have had less and less difficulty in resisting an image of James as a menacing figure. One day a friend (it was Wilfred), meeting him by accident, said, 'What a disappointed man your cousin seems to be.' A light broke, and I felt better at once.

When I was young I could never decide whether James was real and I was unreal, or vice versa. Somehow it was clear we could not both be real; one of us must inhabit the real world, the other one the world of shadows. James always had a sort of beastly invulnerability. Well, it goes right back to the start. As I have explained, I was early aware, through the sort of psychological osmosis of which children are so capable, that Uncle Abel had made a more 'advantageous' marriage than my father, and that in the mysterious pecking-order hierarchy of life the Abel Arrowbys ranked above the Adam Arrowbys. My mother was very conscious of this, and I am certain struggled in the depths of her religious soul 'not to mind'. (She had a special way of emphasizing the word 'heiress' when she spoke of Aunt Estelle.) My father, I really believe, did not mind at all, except for my sake. I remember his once saying, in such an odd almost humble sort of voice, 'I'm so sorry you can't have a pony, like James ...' I loved my father so intensely at that moment and was at the same time conscious (I was ten, twelve?) that I could not express my love, and that perhaps he did not know of it, how much it was. Did he ever know?

As far as the material things of life were concerned the families certainly had different fates. James was the proud possessor of the above-mentioned pony, indeed of a series of such animals, and generally lived in what I thought of as a pony-owning style. And how I suffered from those bloody ponies! When I visited Ramsdens James sometimes offered me a ride, and Uncle Abel (also a horseman) wanted to take me out on a leading rein. Although passionately anxious to ride I always, out of pride and with a feigned indifference, refused; and to this day I have never sat on a horse. A perhaps more important, though not more burning, occasion of envy was continental travel. The Abel Arrowbys went abroad almost every school holiday. They drove all over Europe. (We of course had no car.) They went to America to stay with Aunt Estelle's 'folks', about whom I was careful to know as little as possible. I did not leave England until I went to Paris with Clement after the war. It was not only their ponies and their wide-ranging motor cars that I envied here, it was their enterprise. Uncle Abel was an arranger, an adventurer, an inventor, even a hedonist. My dear good father was none of these things. My uncle and aunt never invited me to join them on those wonderful journeys. It only much later occurred to me, and the idea entered my mind like a dart (I daresay it is still sticking in there somewhere), that they did not ask me because James vetoed it!

As I said, the situation worried my father, I think, only on my behalf. It worried me on my behalf too, but also and quite separately on his. I resented, for him, his deprived status. I felt, for him, the chagrin which his generous and sweet nature did not feel for himself. And in doing this I was aware, even as a child, that I thereby showed myself to be his moral inferior. Although I had such a happy home and such loving parents, I could not help bitterly coveting things which at the same time, as I looked at my father, I despised. I could not help regarding Uncle Abel and Aunt Estelle as glamorous almost godlike beings in comparison with whom my own parents seemed insignificant and dull. I could not help seeing them, in that comparison, as failures. While at the same time I also knew that my father was a virtuous and unworldly man, whereas Uncle Abel, who was so stylish, was an ordinary average completely selfish person. I do not of course imply that my uncle was a 'cad' or a 'bounder', he certainly was not. He loved his beautiful wife and, as far as I know, was faithful to her. He was, as far as I know, an affectionate and responsible father. I am sure he was honest and conscientious in his work and in his finances, in fact a model citizen. But he was an ordinary self-centred go-getter, an ordinary sensualist. Whereas my father, although perhaps nobody ever knew this except my mother and me, was something quite else, something special.

None of this stopped me from rather worshipping Uncle Abel and dancing around him like a pleased dog. At least I did so when I was a young child. Later, because of James, I was slightly more dignified and aloof. Was my father sometimes hurt because I found Uncle Abel so picturesque? Perhaps. This thought saddens me now as I write with a special piercing sadness. He did not care about the worldly goods, but, though he never showed it, he might have felt sorry, again for my sake, that he was so much less of a 'figure'. My mother may have intuited some such regret in him (or perhaps to her he expressed it) and this may have contributed to the irritability which she could not always suppress when the Abel Arrowbys were mentioned, or especially when they had lately been with us on a visit. They did not in fact visit us very often, since my mother felt that we could not 'entertain' them in sufficient style, and would embarrass them, when they did come, with aggressive apologies concerning our humbler way of life. We, I should add, lived upon a housing estate where loneliness was combined with lack of privacy. My visits to stone-built tree-surrounded Ramsdens were usually made alone, because of my mother's horror of being under her brother-in-law's roof, and my father's horror of being under any roof except his own.

I must now, in mentioning my mother, speak of Aunt Estelle. She was, as I have said, an American, though where exactly she hailed from I do not remember to have discovered; America was a big vague concept to me then. Nor do I know where or how my uncle met her. She certainly represented to me some general idea of America: freedom, gaiety, noise. Where Aunt Estelle was there was laughter, jazz music, and (how shocking) alcohol. This again might give the wrong impression. I am speaking of a child's dream. Aunt Estelle was no 'drinker' and her 'wildness' was the merest good spirits: health, youth, beauty, money. She had the instinctive generosity of the thoroughly lucky person. She was, in a vague way, demonstratively affectionate to me when I was a child. My undemonstrative mother watched these perhaps meaningless effusions coldly, but they moved me. Aunt Estelle had a pretty little singing voice and used to chant the songs of the first war and the latest romantic song-hits. (*Roses of Picardy, Tiptoe through the Tulips, Oh So Blue, Me and Jane in a Plane*, and other classics of that sort.) I remember once when she came one night at Ramsdens to 'settle me down', her singing a song to the effect that *there ain't no sense sitting on the fence all by yourself in the moonlight.* I found this very droll and made the mistake of trying to amuse my parents by repeating it. (*It ain't no fun sitting 'neath the trees, giving yourself a hug and giving yourself a squeeze.*) It is probably in some way because of Aunt Estelle that the human voice singing has always upset me with a deep and almost frightening emotion. There is something strange and awful about the distorted open mouths of singers, especially women, the wet white teeth, the moist red interior. Altogether my aunt was for me a symbolic figure, a modern figure, even a futuristic figure, a sort of prophetic lure into my own future. She lived in a land which I was determined to find and to conquer for myself. And in a way I did, but by the time I was king there she was already dead; and it seems strange to think that we never really knew each other, never really talked to each other at all. How easily, later on, we could have bridged the years and how much we would have enjoyed each other's company. I mentioned her occasionally to Clement who said she was the only one of my relations she would have liked to meet. (My parents of course never met Clement, since it would have made them very unhappy to know that I was living openly with a woman twice my age; but I could have introduced her to my aunt.) When Aunt Estelle was killed in a motor accident when I was sixteen I was less upset than I expected. I had other troubles by then. But it is sad to think that, although she was so kind to me in her absent-minded way, she probably never thought of me except as James's awkward boorish undistinguished little cousin. She was a marvel to me, a portent. Sorting out oddments at Shruff End two days ago I came across a photograph of her. I could not find one of my mother.

My mother did not exactly dislike Aunt Estelle, nor violently disapprove of her, though she shuddered at the noise and the drink; and she was not exactly envious because she did not want the worldly things that pleased Aunt Estelle. She was just thoroughly depressed by her existence and cast into the gloom and irritation which I mentioned earlier by her visits. It may be that my uncle and aunt thought that my upbringing was too strict. Outsiders who see rules and not the love that runs through them are often too ready to label other people as 'prisoners'. It is conceivable that clever Uncle Abel and liberated Aunt Estelle actually pitied my father and myself, and blamed my mother for what they regarded as a repressive regime. If my mother suspected the existence of such judgments she must have felt pain and resentment; and this resentment may even have had the effect of making her still stricter with us. It is also possible that, divining my childish fantasies concerning that 'America' which Aunt Estelle represented to me, she felt jealous. Much later I wondered if she imagined that my father was attracted by his vivacious sister-in-law. In fact I am sure that he had no deep feelings of any sort about Aunt Estelle, except again in relation to me, and that my mother must have known this. (How egoistic I sound as I describe myself as the centre of my parents' world. But I was the centre of their world.) In the end I ceased looking forward to Aunt Estelle's visits, although they always excited me when they happened, because they made my mother so depressed and cross. Our house was always somehow *spoilt* by these visits, and took a little time to recover. As the Abel Arrowby Rolls-Royce was finally waved away down the street, my mother would fall silent, answer in monosyllables, while my father and I tiptoed about, avoiding each other's eyes.

I was happy at school, but there were no close friendships, no dramas there, no dearly beloved schoolmasters, though some influential ones, such as Mr McDowell. My aunt and uncle loomed as large significant romantic figures, focuses of obscure emotion, in a childhood which was in a way curiously empty. Yet also they were remote, a little hazy, a little cloudy, partly of course because they were only marginally interested in *me*. I never felt that they really saw me or even looked at me much. With cousin James it was far otherwise. Silently, James and I, from earliest moments, were acutely, suspiciously, constantly aware of each other. We watched each other; and by a mute instinct kept this close mutual attention largely secret from our parents. I cannot say that we feared each other; the fear was all mine, and was a fear not exactly of James but of something that James stood for. (This something was I suppose my prophetic veiled conception of my own life as a failure, as a total disaster.) But we lived, in relation to each other, in a cloud of discomfort and anxiety. All this of course in silence. We never spoke of this strange tension between us; perhaps we would not have been able to find words for it. And I doubt if our parents had any idea of it. Even my father, who knew that I envied James, had no conception of *this*.

As I have indicated, part of my unease about my cousin consisted in a fear that he would succeed in life and I would fail. That, on top of the ponies, would have been too much. It is scarcely possible to say how far my 'will to power' was inspired by a deep original intent to outshine James and to impress him. I do not think that James felt any special desire to impress me, or perhaps he knew that he did not have to try. He had all the advantages. He received, and this is where I really began to grind my teeth, a better education than I did. I went to the local grammar school (a dull decent school, now defunct), James went to Winchester. (Perhaps this was a mixed blessing. In a way he never recovered. They say they rarely do.) I got myself a reasonably sound education, and especially I got Shakespeare. But James, it seemed to me then, was learning everything. He knew Latin and Greek and several modern languages, I had only a little French and less Latin. He knew about painting and regularly visited art galleries in Europe and America. He chatted familiarly of foreign places. He was good at mathematics, he won prizes for history. He wrote poetry which was published in the school magazine. He *shone*; and although he was not at all boastful, I increasingly felt myself, and was made to feel, a provincial barbarian when I was with James. I felt a gap between us widen, and that gap, as I more intelligently surveyed it, began to fill me with despair. Clearly, my cousin was destined for success and I for failure. I wonder how much my father understood of all this?

Rereading these paragraphs I feel again that I am giving the wrong impression. What a difficult form autobiography is proving to be! The chagrin, the ferocious ambition which James, I am sure quite unconsciously, prompted in me was something which came about gradually and raged intermittently. When we were younger, and even when we were older, James and I played together as ordinary boys play. I had few friends, partly because my mother did not want to invite other children to the house. (I did not mind. I did not like other children very much.) And if James had friends he kept them away from me. So we played alone with each other, watching each other, but not always as crammed with consciousness as the above description might seem to imply. Even in ordinary play however some effortless superiority of James's would tend to emerge. He knew far more than I did about birds and flowers, and was very good at climbing trees. (As a small child I remember his most seriously attempting to learn to fly!) He could find his way across country like a fox. He had a sort of uncanny instinct about things and places. When the ball got lost it was always James who found it; and he once instantly recovered an old toy aeroplane of mine simply on the basis of my having told him I had lost it.

When I was causing misery to my parents by learning the histrionic arts in London, James was being a golden boy at Oxford where he studied history. At this time I lost touch with him; I did not crave

further news of his triumphs and quite positively did not want to know
what cousin James was up to. Whatever it was he never finished it
because the war arrived. He joined something called the Rifle Corps,
later called the Green Jackets, and thus began, though I think he did
not realize it at the time, a lifetime as a soldier. Indeed it is now hard
for me to think of James at all except as a soldier. He had quite an
interesting war, while I was going round in buses playing Shakespeare
to coal-miners. After a while I heard he was in India, at Dehra Dun.
I had my own problems, notably first love and its after-effects, then the
opening skirmishes in my long war with Clement. I heard the outlines
of James's adventures later. He climbed various mountains. He became
interested in Tibet, learnt Tibetan, and was constantly disappearing
over the border on his pony. (All that early training must have come
in useful.) Then he was sent on some embassy or embassies to some
nearby Tibetan ruler about something to do with German prisoners
of war. He had a picturesque time, but I think he never saw any real
action. I was always afraid of hearing he had won the VC. Of course I
have never doubted that he is, in a sense in which I am not, a brave man.

My parents were very surprised when it turned out after the war
that James had decided to become a professional soldier. They said that
Uncle Abel was disappointed by the decision. Uncle Abel saw James
as prime minister. (Aunt Estelle was dead by then.) I felt obscurely
cheered because I intuited that James had taken a wrong turning. I was
by then just beginning to do well in the theatre, my 'will to power' was
bringing in results, and Clement was in my life like a sort of travelling
carnival. So cousin James was to be a soldier. Uncle Abel said that it
was only temporary and he was doing it so as to have more time to
write poetry. My mother said that Uncle Abel was whistling in the
dark. It did not seem to occur to any of us then that the army too is,
and traditionally, a road to power and glory.

I saw a little of James after the war in that rather moving time of the reunion of survivors, but then he vanished again. He was always vanishing. He came back from India and was posted to Germany. Then he was in England again at the Staff College, then back to India. Someone told me later that he was sent on a secret mission into Tibet to investigate Soviet activity there. Of course James never told me anything about his work. I knew minimally of his travels because, with increasing regularity, he sent me picture postcards at Christmas and on my birthday. I paid him no such attentions, but if he wrote me a letter I always sent a brief reply. His letters were usually dull, always uninformative. Then he turned up in London just after the Chinese invasion of Tibet. I never saw him, before or since, display so much emotion. This was clearly for him a personal tragedy. He exclaimed bitterly about the stupidity of those who had failed to see that China, not Russia, was the real menace. But what grieved him was not this ignoring of (perhaps his own) good advice so much as the destruction of something he loved. This emotion was soon muted and he never spoke of the matter to me again.

The next postcard I received was from Singapore, and the next letter, also from Singapore, was a condolence on my father's death. (I wonder how he knew?) After that I lost sight of James because for a time I lost sight of everything, the lights went out in my life. I mourned long and miserably for my father. The loss of that dear good man touches me deeply still. And, as if in sympathy, everything else was wrong. I had left Clement and was wretchedly involved with some other ladies; and my professional career had crashed into what appeared to be irrevocable ruin. My mother's death not long after seemed less an individual event than a sort of doomed extension of the loss of my father. A little later Uncle Abel died. I had long ago stopped caring about him or even thinking about him. I recall that I intended

to write to James, but I never wrote. I recall too that I wondered only
then how James had felt when his marvellous mother died when he
was a boy. I was deep in my own early sorrows at that time, and was
not greatly affected by Aunt Estelle's fate. I somehow never reflected
what it might have done to James.

I mentioned just now, and should have named him (his name is
Toby Ellesmere), a man who told me about James's 'secret missions' in
Tibet. This man, not remarkable in any other way, sometimes brought
me news of my cousin. They had been together at school and also in
the Green Jackets. Ellesmere became a stockbroker, then a publisher,
and also dabbled in theatre matters as an investor and in this context
I came across him. Some time just after my 'bad patch' we met at a
first night party and Ellesmere said, 'I suppose you know your cousin
has become a Buddhist?' I was fascinated and amazed by this news. I
had never connected James with religion. We had both of us acquired
that vague English Christianity which disappears in adolescence. My
mother, I should say here, did not force her particular evangelical beliefs
upon my father and me. Perhaps she realized that 'it would not do'.
However she took it for granted that we were Christians. We attended
an Anglican church. Naturally James and I did not discuss religion. If I
had considered the matter when we were young I think I would have
said that the basic spiritual principle of James's life was an avoidance of
vulgarity. Religion as 'good form'? One could do worse. I would never
have imagined him as an enthusiast in pursuit of the exotic mysteries
of the East. How extremely *odd*!

My surprise soon wore off. What did it mean after all? Obviously
James could not believe in the transmigration of souls. When I met my
cousin again it was somehow another era in our lives. My father's death,
my period of professional despair, my misadventures in Hollywood,
these things were now behind me. I had made peace with Clement.

(We were in Japan together.) I was by now a very successful man, in Aunt Estelle's country a king indeed. I said to James, 'So you're a Buddhist, I hear?' He smiled and said 'Oh yes!' in a tone which could mean either 'Yes' or 'What nonsense!' I dropped the subject. Later on he came to live more permanently in London and to work in the Ministry of Defence, as he still does. His flat in Pimlico is full of Buddhas, but then it is full of all sorts of eastern trash, some of it I daresay Hindu.

James is now a general of course, I forget what kind. I suppose he too has been in a way a successful man. My own feeling that I have 'won the game' comes partly from a sense that he has been disappointed by life, whereas I have not.

'A man would drown there in a second.'

'Three seconds.'

'A second.'

'Three seconds.'

Example of Black Lion conversation and level of debate. The clientele seem to resent the fact that I go swimming in a sea whose killer propensities they are so proud of. Conversations of this sort arise as soon as I appear, not of course addressed to me.

I join in. 'I'm a strong swimmer.'

'It's them that drowns.'

'You swim bare,' someone adds.

'Bare?'

'You swim bare.'

'Oh – you mean naked.' So I am watched.

They look at me with dull silent hostility.

'Seen any seals?' Mr Arkwright asks brightly.

'No, not yet.'

I was sorry to observe, visiting the tower steps this morning, that my curtain 'rope' had also somehow come undone and vanished. I swam nevertheless. I think that my muscles are stronger and I am becoming more skilful at climbing out. I always manage to scrape or cut myself however. The yellow rocks, which look so smooth from a distance, have a rough scratchy surface, as if they were closely covered over with millions of tiny sharp broken-off limpet shells. Yesterday I dived from Shruff End 'cliff' at high tide and managed to get out all right, though a little anxiety spoilt the swim. I am certainly not going to lose face at the Black Lion by going along to the 'ladies' bathing place'!

Today there is a pleasant very light haze over the whole sky, and the sea has a misleadingly docile silvered look, as if the substantial wavelets were determined to stroke the rocks as hard as they could without showing any trace of foam. It is a compact radiant complacent sort of sea, very beautiful. There *ought* to be seals, the waves themselves are almost seals today, but still I scan the water in vain with my long-distance glasses. Enormous yellow-beaked gulls perch on the rocks and stare at me with brilliant glass eyes. A shadow-cormorant skims the glycerine sea. The rocks are thronged with butterflies. The temperature remains high. I wash my clothes and dry them on the lawn. I have been swimming every day and feel very fit and salty. Still no move from Lizzie, but I am not worried. I feel happy in my silence. If the gods have some treat in store for Lizzie and me, good. If not, also good. I feel innocent and free. Perhaps it is all that swimming.

How high-flown, almost pompous, I am becoming, now that I am a prose-writer! I know many playwrights who regard continuous prose as a sort of alien language which they could not dream of mastering. I think I may have felt like this myself at one time. And yet look at all the pages I have already covered! I have been looking back over my little sketch of James and it is quite stylish. Is it true however? Well, it is not totally misleading, but it is far too short and 'smart'. How can one describe real people? James looks, in my description of him, so complete, so hard. I have omitted to say that he has little square teeth and an inane childish grin. Sometimes his mouth hangs vacantly open. He has a hooked nose and a dark complexion. Aunt Estelle was rather dark too. Perhaps she had Red Indian blood?

I must work harder on these portraits. Perhaps that is what this book will turn out to be, simply my life told in a series of portraits of the people I have known. What a funny heterogeneous crew: Clement, Rosina, Wilfred, Sidney, Peregrine, Rita, Fritzie, Jeanne, Al Bull ... I must write about Clement. She is the main theme. How mad and bad she became at the end when she had lost her beauty and was losing her wits. And what a bitchy old bore she was, telling the same scandalous obscene stories over and over again. That terrible atmosphere in her flat, the smell of drink, the smell of tears and hysterics. Her deep sonorous drunken voice droned on in endless recrimination. Did I face it well? I think I did. Forgiveness and mercy were so ready to hand as soon as I knew that she was doomed. That sounds cynical. I always loved her; and we were rewarded. At the very end we were both perfect. Poor Clement. That is a dreadful land, old age. I shall soon be entering it myself. Is that why I feel I need Lizzie?

I am writing this the next morning. I was sitting writing the above late last night in my drawing room when something very disconcerting happened. I looked up and was for a moment *perfectly sure* that I saw a face looking at me through the glass of the inner room. I sat absolutely still, paralysed by sheer terror. The vision was only momentary but, although I cannot now describe the face, very definite. Perhaps it is significant that I cannot *remember* the face? After an interval of course I got up to investigate. The new oil lamp is easy to carry so I was not reduced to peering about with a candle. And of course there was nothing to be seen. I even walked round the house. I felt, I must confess, very odd. I went, with a sort of deliberate slowness, up the stairs to bed and took a sleeping pill. I thought I heard the bead curtain clinking in the night, but that is a natural phenomenon. A little wind has arisen today and the sea is blue and white again.

I have considered two possible explanations of my apparition. One is that it was simply a reflection of my own face in the blackness of the glass. But (unless I had unconsciously risen?) I was sitting well below the level at which I could have been thus mirrored. Also, the face appeared rather high up in the window, and so (a further thought) must have belonged to a very tall person or to someone standing on something. (Only there is nothing to stand on, since I have moved the folding table in here.) Another theory I shall check tonight. The window that gives onto the sea was uncurtained and there was an almost full moon. Could I have seen the moon reflected in the inner glass?

'Everything is full of gods,' cousin James once said, quoting somebody. Perhaps I have been surrounded by little gods and spirits all my life, only the magic of the theatre exorcized or absorbed them? Theatre people are notoriously superstitious. Now we are all alone together! Well, I have never gone in for persecution mania and do not propose to start now.

I must soon go over to the Raven Hotel to get some more wine. I think I will stop talking about ghosts and monsters in the Black Lion.

Decided not to swim today.

I have been out shopping. The shop keeps promising lettuce but so far has had none. No fresh fish of course. I found some more letters in my stone dog kennel. Nothing from Lizzie. A communication from Peregrine Arbelow however. For lunch made my heavenly vegetarian stew of onions, carrots, tomatoes, bran, lentils, pearl barley, vegetable protein, brown sugar and olive oil. (The vegetable protein I brought with me from London.) I add a little lemon juice just before eating. With that (it is very light) a baked potato with cream cheese. Then Battenberg roll and prunes. (Carefully cooked prunes are delicious. Drain and add lemon juice or a dash of orange flower water, never cream.) If anyone wonders at the absence of 'eating' apples from my diet let me explain that this is one case where I have spoilt my palate with an aristocratic taste. I can eat only Cox's Orange Pippins, and am in mourning applewise from April to October.

I will transcribe as an introduction to him, Peregrine's letter.

Charles, how are you getting on? We are all consumed with curiosity. No one admits to having been invited. But don't you miss us terribly? Perhaps you have sneaked back to live secretly in your new flat, not answering the phone and going out at night? Someone said your house was on a lonely wave-washed promontory but that can't be true. I see you in a cosy marine bungalow on the sea front. After all, how could you live without your liquidizer? I couldn't bear it if you had really changed your life. That is something which I have always wanted to do but never could and never will. I shall die with my boots off, the bastard I have ever been. I have been drinking for a week after returning from hell, alias Belfast. Civilization is terrible, but don't imagine that *you* can ever escape it, Charles. I want to know what you are doing. And don't imagine that you can ever hide from *me,* I am your *shadow.* I think I shall come down and see you at Whitsun. (Someone dared me to and you know I can't resist dares.) Various people would send their love if they knew I was writing, but of course it isn't love, it's insolent curiosity. Few are worthy of you,

Charles. Is the undersigned one? Time will show. Shall I come and bring my swimming trunks? I haven't swum since our epic days in Santa Monica. Another theory is that you are not in England at all but gone to Spain with a girl. To disprove which you must write. Your shadow salutes you.

Peregrine.

It is after lunch (it is perfectly true that I miss my liquidizer) and I am sitting at my upstairs seaward window. It is cloudy and the sea is a choppy dark blue-grey, an aggressive and unpleasant colour. The seagulls are holding a wake. The house feels damp. Perhaps I am still depressed by last night's experience, which was of course a simple visual illusion. (However I will check about the moon.) And at least I can write 'depressed' and not 'afraid'. There is nothing to be afraid of.

Perhaps I shall make some notes for a character sketch of Peregrine. This will involve writing something about Rosina, and I would rather forget that lady. Well, autobiography cannot be self-indulgent fun all of the time.

Peregrine (he detests being called 'Perry' as much as I detest being called 'Charlie'; only people who do not know me call me 'Charlie') is one of those who have a strong concept of the life they want to lead and the role they want to play and lead it and play it at the expense of everyone, especially their nearest and dearest. And the odd thing is that such people can in a sense be wrong, can as it were miscast themselves, and yet battle on successfully to the end, partly because their 'victims' prefer a definite simple impression to the pains of critical thought. Peregrine, although in many ways a gentle kind man, has cast himself as a noisy bear. This 'role-playing' makes him stupidly careless of making enemies. Whereas I think it shows a lack of professional skill to make unnecessary enemies in the theatre, or indeed in life.

Peregrine is always blundering along. He lacks the meticulous quality of the true artist. I always had to terrorize him to get him onto the stage sober. He has the makings of a fine actor, only he is too damn conceited and casual, there is a sort of slapdash Irishry about him, he has too many off-days.

Peregrine is an Ulster Catholic who started out as a medical student at Queen's University, Belfast, and then ran away to the Gate Theatre in Dublin. He hates Ireland as only the Irish can hate it. He early abandoned religion for Marxism, then abandoned Marxism. I first saw him as the Playboy (he was slim in those far-off days) and coveted his talents at once. He is now, since he parted professional company with me some years ago, going to seed as a fat charming television villain. He knows what I think of his career. But we remain friends; and this in spite of the fact that I stole his wife. He has married again, equally disastrously, an ex-actress called Pamela Hackett, who has a little daughter by her earlier awful marriage to 'Ginger' Godwin. (Ah, where is he now?) Why do people ever marry?

Yes, well, I shall have to talk about Rosina and maybe it will do me some good to write it all down. Not that I could write it *all* down if I wrote volumes. Rosina was a huge phenomenon. She was already married to Perry when I first encountered her. They met in America in some interval after I had first spotted him at the Gate. I was still fairly young though becoming known as a playwright and as a director. Some further time must then have passed (how I wish I had kept a diary), since I started to pursue Rosina after a period when I had again been living with Clement. What a lot of energy in my life I have spent escaping from women. Rita Gibbons comes into that story too, so perhaps it was later still. Clement tolerated Rita and Lizzie and Jeanne but she detested Rosina. Of course I lied to Clement (she lied to me) but various people made a point of keeping her informed.

Rosina is of course Rosina Vamburgh, and is probably the most famous person in this book, after me. Her real name, which she keeps secret, is Jones (or Davis or Williams or Rees or something) and she is Welsh, with a French Canadian grandmother. I was never 'in love' with Rosina. I would like to reserve that phrase to describe the one single occasion when I loved a woman absolutely. (Not dear Clement of course.) But I was certainly mad about Rosina. (Moreover, when a beautiful witty woman is passionate about you you cannot but feel that she has the root of the matter in her.) I am not sure whether she was 'in love' with me. A furious mutual desire for possession dominated the whole affair while it lasted. At one stage she certainly wanted to marry me, whereas I never had the slightest intention of marrying her. I simply wanted her, and the satisfaction of this want involved detaching her permanently from her husband. Clement, when younger, was probably the most beautiful woman I ever knew. But Rosina is the most stylish, the most gorgeously adorably artificial. There was something factitious and brittle and thereby utterly feminine about her charm which made me want to crush her, even to *crunch* her. She has a slight cast in one eye which gives her gaze a strange concentrated intensity. Her eyes sparkle, almost as if they were actually emitting sparks. She is electric. And she could run faster in very high-heeled shoes than any girl I ever met.

She was (and is) a good actress and a very intelligent woman. (These qualities do not always go together.) She had a mixture of Celtic and Gallic good looks, with blue eyes and wiry dark hair and a big moist sensual mouth. God, how different kisses are. Lizzie's kisses were dry and chaste yet clinging. Rosina's kisses were those of a tigress. Rosina had the fierce charm of the rather nasty girl in the fairy-tale who fails to get the prince, but is more interesting than the girl who does, and has better lines too. She was a good comic actress and excelled in

rubbishy Restoration Comedy, a genre I have never cared for. She made
a memorable Hedda Gabler, and a rather touching Natalia Petrovna in
A Month in the Country. Unfortunately she was never able to play Honor
Klein. When I worked with her I used to cast her against her type; I
often did this successfully with actors. She was surprisingly good as *La
Présidente* in Sidney's adaptation of *Liaisons Dangereuses.* I never let her
play Lady Macbeth but Isaiah Mommsen did much later on and it was a
disaster. After I left her Rosina lost her way for some time in silly films
and television. I was glad. After I left her I no longer wanted to see
her name in lights in Shaftesbury Avenue, nor did I care to know who
directed her. *La jalousie naît avec l'amour, mais ne meurt pas toujours avec lui.*

The interval between possession and hell was short though I admit
it was wonderful. Rosina was one of those women who believe that
'a good row clears the air'. In my experience a good row not only
does not clear the air but can land you with a lifelong enemy. Rows
in the theatre can be terrible and I avoided them. Rosina more than
once called me a coward for this. She liked rows, any rows, and she
believed in loving by rowing. I began to grow tired. The golden bridge
for the departing lover I have always, I hope, provided when it became
necessary. Rosina, when she saw me cooling, had no such merciful
contraption ready. She clung closer and closer and screamed louder
and louder. She was always insanely given to jealousy, even more than
I was. How very much jealousy, the spectacle of it, the suffering of
it, has been a feature of my whole life. I think now of something so
different but equally awful, my mother's silence after the departures
of Aunt Estelle.

In the end we both became half mad. I remember my cousin James
quoting some philosopher as saying that 'it is not contrary to reason to
prefer the destruction of the world to the scratching of one's finger'.
Rosina and I reached a state (though I would not have described it as

a rational one) where we definitely preferred the former. I remember
Rosina once hurling herself downstairs in a fit of rage. On several
occasions I was quite ready for her to jump out of an upstairs window
and rather hoped that she would. I came to feel, perhaps I always
felt, again in the words of some Frenchman: *elle n'a qu'une faute, elle
est insupportable.* Sometimes even now I wake up in the middle of the
night and think, at any rate thank God that woman has gone out of
my life. Of course when I left her she never went back to Peregrine.

I was intensely grateful to Perry, and indeed admired him, for the
way he behaved. Cynics said he was glad to have Rosina taken off his
hands. I knew better, he suffered. I am sure that he and Rosina had
lived in a perpetual state of war, but many not unhappy couples do so.
I think he loved her, though he probably came, as I did, to find her
simply impossible. So there may well have been an element of profound relief in having the problem removed without his will. Later, he
went out of his way to make quite a show of masculine solidarity. He
remains very attached to me, and I value this. One result of his truly
remarkable generosity and kindness was that although I saw objectively
that I had behaved badly, I felt practically no guilt. This was *because*
Perry never reproached me. Just as, on the other hand, I have always
felt guilty about my chauffeur Freddie Arkwright *because* he once flew
at me, and not because I had occasioned his resentment by keeping him
waiting hungry for hours while I was guzzling at the Connaught Hotel.
Guilt feelings so often arise from accusations rather than from crimes.

I have been out picking flowers upon my rocks! I collected a fine mixed
bunch of valerian and thrift and white sea campion. The campion has a
very strong sweet smell. I cannot stop collecting stones, and the trough
is overflowing even though I have put some of the best ones into my
lawn border. This border looks a little 'quaint', I will have to see how

I like it when it is finished. It is a good way to display the stones, but will the earth discolour their undersides?

This morning I swam in the rain from the stony beach. The beach is about a mile from the house on the village side, so I took bathing trunks, but did not don them as there was no one there. The rain had a quieting effect on the sea, making it smooth and pitted, almost oily. I had no difficulty getting out. I collected more stones. Then I went home and sat naked in the warmish rain on Minn's bridge and watched the glossy water running into the deep enclosure. Even on a calm day it runs in and out like a tidal wave.

I was unable last night to check my theory that my ghostly 'face' was a reflection of the moon, since the sky was cloudy. But I feel sure now that it was an optical illusion and needs no further explanation. I occupied the little red room in the evening and lit the fire there. The chimney smoked again, perhaps because of the direction of the wind. As I rescued a spider running upon a half-burning piece of wood I remembered my father. Since I came here I have lived with naked flames for the first time for some years. Clement always loved an open fire. What a strange process burning is. How utterly and sort of calmly it transforms things, it is so clean, as clean as death. (Shall I be cremated? Who will arrange it? Let me not think of death.) So far I have been keeping my wood in the larder, only there is not enough space and the floor is curiously damp. I might make the downstairs inner room into a fuel store. The driftwood is so beautiful, smoothed by the sea and blanched to a pale grey colour, it seems a shame to burn it. I set several pieces aside and admired the grain. Perhaps I shall make a collection of driftwood 'sculpture'.

It is after tea and I am sitting at the drawing-room window watching the rain falling steadily into the sea. There is a terrible grim simplicity about this grey scene. Apart from an iron-dark line at the horizon the sea and the sky are much the same colour, a muted faintly radiant grey, and expectant as if waiting for something to happen. As it might be flashes of lightning or monsters rising from the waves. Thank heavens I have had no more such hallucinations, and the extent to which I have forgotten what I saw persuades me that it was indeed an after-effect of that drug which I so foolishly took. Or did I really 'see' anything which needs even this much of an explanation? I keep a careful watch upon the flattened rainy sea but no great coiling form comes rising up! (No seals either.) It did, oddly enough, occur to me afterwards to reflect upon what the Black Lion yokels said about 'worms'. 'Worm' is an old word for dragon. Well, this is getting a little too picturesque: dragons, poltergeists, faces at windows! And how restless this rain makes me feel.

I reread my pieces about James and Peregrine and was quite moved by them. Of course they are just sketches and need to be written in more detail before they become really truthful and 'lifelike'. It has only just now occurred to me that really I could write all sorts of fantastic nonsense about my life in these memoirs and everybody would believe it! Such is human credulity, the power of the printed word, and of any well-known 'name' or 'show business personality'. Even if readers claim that they 'take it all with a grain of salt', they do not really. They yearn to believe, and they believe, because believing is easier than disbelieving, and because anything which is written down is likely to be 'true in a way'. I trust this passing reflection will not lead anyone to doubt the truth of any part of this story! When I come to describe my life with Clement Makin credulity will be strained but will I hope not fail!

Since I started writing this 'book' or whatever it is I have felt as if I were walking about in a dark cavern where there are various 'lights', made perhaps by shafts or apertures which reach the outside world.

(What a gloomy image of my mind, but I do not mean it in a gloomy sense.) There is among those lights one great light towards which I have been half consciously wending my way. It may be a great 'mouth' opening to the daylight, or it may be a hole through which fires emerge from the centre of the earth. And am I still unsure which it is, and must I now approach in order to find out? This image has come to me so suddenly, I am not sure what to make of it.

When I decided to write about myself of course the question arose: am I then to write about Hartley? Of course, I thought, I must write about Hartley, since that is the most important thing in my life. And yet how can I, what style can I adopt or master worthy of such a sacred tale, and would not the attempt to relive those events upset me to some intolerable degree? Or would it be simply a sacrilege? Or suppose I were to get the wrong tone, making the marvellous merely grotesque? It might be better to tell my life *without* mentioning Hartley, even though this omission would amount to a gross lie. Can one, in such a self-portrait, omit something which affected one's whole being and which one has thought of every day of one's life? 'Every day' exaggerates, but not much. I do not need to 'recall' Hartley, she is here. She is my end and my beginning, she is alpha and omega.

I thought it better to draw a veil over this question, which was starting to worry me too much. I decided simply to write and to see if I could somehow approach, or find that I had approached, the vast subject of Hartley. And, just as I found myself unexpectedly and spontaneously writing 'My paternal grandfather was a market gardener in Lincolnshire', so now I find that, wandering in my cavern, I have in fact come near to the great light-source and am ready to speak about my first love. But what can I say? I feel just as suddenly tongue-tied. My first love, and also my only love. All the best, even Clement, have been shadows by comparison. The necessity of this seems, in my own case, so great that I find it hard to imagine that it is not so with everyone. *On n'aime qu'une fois, la premiere.*

Her name was Mary Hartley Smith. How quickly, readily I write it down. Yet my heart beats fast too. Oh my God. Mary Hartley Smith.

That is the heading of the story then. But really I cannot tell the story. I will write some notes for the story and perhaps never tell it. Or indeed it may be untellable, since there are hardly any 'events' in it, only feelings, the feelings of a child, of a youth, of a young man, nebulous and holy and stronger than anything in the whole of life. I can scarcely remember a time when I did not know Hartley. I went to a school for boys only, but the girls' school was nearby next door and we saw the girls all the time. As there were a lot of Marys around in those days she was always known as 'Hartley' and that was somehow very much her name. We paired off early on, but merrily, childishly, and without any deep shaking emotions, as far as I can remember, in those earliest days. When we were about twelve the emotions began. They puzzled us, amazed us. They shook us as terriers shake rats. To say we were 'in love', that vague weakened phrase, cannot express it. We loved each other, we lived in each other, through each other, by each other. We were each other. Why was it such pure unadulterated pain?

It is odd that I now write down (and will not change) the word 'pain', for of course what it was was pure joy. Perhaps the point is that whatever it was it was extreme and pure. (I am told that a blind-folded man cannot distinguish severe burning from severe freezing.) Or perhaps at that age emotions tend to be felt as pains because they are not lightened by reflection. Everything becomes dread and fear, and the more wonderful and the more joyful, the more dread and the more fear. But let me repeat that this was not reflection, not thought. I did not harbour intelligent doubts about whether Hartley would go on loving me, naturally I knew that she was mine forever. But as we closed our eyes upon tears of joy there was cosmic dread.

Of course, and instinctively, we kept it all a secret. Our school-fellows had got used to our playful friendship. Now we lay low, we were casual, we had secret meeting places. All this, as I say, was instinctive, never discussed or decided. We had to hide the precious thing in case it was hurt, derided, damaged or offended in some way. My parents vaguely knew Hartley of course, but she hardly ever came to the house, because of their almost morbid dislike of visitors, and also because I never suggested it. They did not suspect my special interest in her because they regarded me then as much too young to have special interests. Her parents, equally vaguely aware of me, were equally uninterested, except that I think they rather disliked me. She had an elder brother who despised us both. Our world was sealed and secret. Parents would be duly informed later on when we got married; for of course we were going to marry when we were eighteen. (We were the same age.) There were many caresses, but we did not make love. Remember, this was long ago.

I must try to describe Hartley. Oh, my darling, how clearly I can see you now. Surely this is perception, not imagination. The light in the cavern is daylight, not fire. Perhaps it is the only true light in my life, the light that reveals the truth. No wonder I feared to lose the light and to be left in the darkness forever. All a child's blind fear was there, the fear that my mother so early inspired in me: the kiss withheld, the candle taken. Hartley, my Hartley. Yes, I see her clearly, jumping over a rope, higher and higher it was raised, Hartley still flew over, the watchers sighing each time with sympathetic relief; and I hugging my heart in secret pride. She was the champion jumper of the school, of many schools, the champion runner, Hartley always first, and I cheering with the rest and laughing with secret joy. Hartley, in a breathless stillness, crouched upon a parallel bar, her bare thighs gleaming. The games master spoke of the Olympics.

Come, Holy Ghost, our souls inspire, and lighten with celestial fire ... We went up for confirmation together, to receive the divine blessing upon our love. I remember Hartley singing in church, her bright innocent lovely face raised up to the light, to God, towards the joy which belonged to her and which she must have. We talked a lot about religion (we talked a lot about everything), and we felt that we were dedicated people who would be protected by love. We experienced our innocence and we did not think it would be difficult to be good. I can remember Hartley's marvellous laugh, but not that we teased each other much or were always making jokes. Ours was a solemn holy happiness, and we shunned the coarser talk of our schoolfellows. I think we had little curiosity about sex. We were one, and only that mattered. We lived in paradise. We fled on bicycles to lie in buttercup fields, beside railway bridges, near canals, in wasteland awaiting housing estates. Ours was already a suburban countryside, but it was as lovely and significant to us as the Garden of Eden. She was not an intellectual or bookish girl, she had the wisdom of the innocents and we conversed as angels. She was at home in time and space.

I can see her smiling at me now. She was beautiful but with a secret beauty. She was not one of the 'pretty girls' of the school. Sometimes her face looked heavy, almost dour, and when she cried she looked like the pig-baby in *Alice*. She was very pale, and people sometimes thought she looked ill, although she was so strong and so healthy. Her face was rather round and white and her eyes gazed out with such a fey puzzled look, like a young savage. She had dark blue eyes which seemed to be violet when you were not looking at them. Her pupils were often dilated so that her eyes became almost black. She had very fine straight fair hair in a long bob. Her lips were pale and always cold; and when, with my eyes closing, I touched them so childishly with mine, a cold force pierced me like a spear, such as a pilgrim might feel when he knelt and touched some holy life-renewing stone. Her body was passive to my embraces, but her spirit glowed to me with a cold fire. Her beautiful shoulders, her long legs, were pale too and seemed cold. I never saw her entirely undressed. She was slim, very slim, leggy and clean, and so strong. She never hugged me, but sometimes, rigidly, she held my arms, leaving great bruises. Her secret violet eyes did not close when I moved to kiss her. They stared with that strange puzzlement which was at the same time passion. Those quiet, silent, almost stiff embraces were the most passionate that I ever knew. And we were chaste, and respected each other absolutely and worshipped each other chastely. And that was passion and that was love of a purity which can never come again and which I am sure rarely exists in the world at all. Those memories are more radiant to me than any work of art, more vivid and precious than Shakespeare or Piero della Francesca. There is a deep foundation of my being which knows not of time and change and is still and ever with Hartley, in that good place where we once were.

Having written this much what can I say now? I could go on and on simply describing Hartley. But it is becoming too painful. I lost her, the jewel of the world. And it remains a mystery to me to this day how that came about: a mystery concerning a young girl's soul and her life-vision. I feared so many things, that she would die, or I would die, that we would be somehow cursed for being too happy; but I did not, at any rate in a conscious way, fear and envisage that which actually happened. Or were all my fears really of that, only that was too terrible to bring to consciousness? Extreme love must bring terror with it, and great terror, like some kinds of prayer which lean upon the omniscience of the Almighty, has a vast unlimited all-embracing compass. So perhaps I did fear that too. I must have cried in my incoherent heart: and *that*, let not that happen either, even though that seemed inconceivable.

Let me try and put it down simply, and it is of course very simple. Hartley decided, when the time came, that she did not want to marry me. It was impossible to find out exactly why. I was too smashed by misery to think clearly, to question intelligently. She was confused, evasive, perhaps out of some desire to spare me pain, perhaps simply because of her own misery, perhaps because of some indecision which I stupidly failed to discern. She said certain terribly memorable things. But were these the 'reasons'? Everything she said she seemed to efface afterwards in a fit of crying. We had said long ago that we would marry when we were eighteen, when we were grown up. How passionately, amid those mysterious, evasive, effacing tears, I cried out to her that I would wait, I would never hurry her. Was it a young girl's fear? I would respect it, she should do as she would so long as she left us our precious future, with which we had lived for so long. Our marriage was a fixed and certain mark, and I only feared that I might die before I reached it. I went to London to the drama school with this fixed mark before me. We had still not told our parents. Perhaps this was my mistake? I was afraid of my mother's disapproval, of her opposition. She might say we were too young. I did not want, yet, to mar our happiness with parental rows, though we had so often said that we would outface any row. But if our parents had known and had agreed, or if we had done battle for our love, the very publicity of the plan would have made it more binding, more real. It would certainly have changed the atmosphere of our little paradise. Did I fear just this change, and did I lose her because I was a coward? Oh, what mistake did I make? What happened when I went to London, what went on in her mind? She had agreed, she had understood. Of course there was a separation, but I wrote every day. I came for weekends, she seemed unchanged. Then one day she told me ...

We had bicycled down to the canal, a way we often went. Our bicycles lay embraced together, as they always did, in the long grass beside the towing path. We walked on, looking at familiar things, dear things which we had made our own. It was autumn time. There were a lot of butterflies. Butterflies still remind me of those terrible minutes. She started to cry. 'I can't go on, I can't go on, I can't marry you.' 'We wouldn't make each other happy.' 'You wouldn't stay with me, you'd go away, you wouldn't be faithful.' 'Yes, I love you but I can't trust, I can't see.' We were both demented with grief, and we cried out to each other in our grief. In despair, in death-fear, I raved, 'At least we'll be friends, forever, we can't leave each other, we can't lose each other, it's impossible, I should die.' She shook her head, weeping, 'You know we can't be friends now.' I can see her eyes glaring, her mouth, wet with her tears, jerking. I never understood how she was able to be so strong. Did she mean what she said or did the words conceal other words which she dared not say? Why had she changed her mind? I asked her and asked her, why did she think I would not be faithful, why did she think we would not be happy, why could she no longer trust the future? 'I can't go on with it, I just can't.' Had someone lied about me? Surely she could not be jealous about my life in London where I did nothing but think about her! (Clement of course was hidden in the future.) Had she met someone else? No, no, no, she said, and then she just repeated her terrible incomprehensible words. Yes, she was very strong. And she escaped.

I had to go back to London. After a day of two I could not believe in the possibility of anything so dreadful. I wrote to her commandingly, understanding, confidently. I cancelled everything and ran back. I saw her again, and there was the same scene, and again. Then suddenly she

was gone. I called at her house. Her parents, her brother, looked at me
with hostility. She had gone to stay with friends, they did not know the
address. I called again the next week. Then I got a letter from her mother
saying that Hartley did not want to see me and asking me not to pester
them. I searched, I asked, I watched. How in the twentieth century
can people just *vanish*, why is there not a register one can consult, a
department one can write to? I spent my holidays on detective work.
None of our school friends knew where she was. I put a notice in the
local paper. I visited every place she had mentioned, everyone who had
known her well. I wrote dozens of letters. Much later of course it was
clear to me that she could only have escaped by running, by vanishing.

Some time during this period her parents left the district, then I
got a curt letter from her mother, giving no address, and saying that
Hartley was married. I did not believe her. The parents were liars, a
sinister influence, they hated me because Hartley loved me. I went on
searching, I went on waiting. I felt that there must be some particular
special cause for her flight, and that time would remove the cause and
make things as they were. I conducted myself in such a wild crazy
manner that quite a lot of people came to know about my love, and I
became quite famous as a mad lover. By then I wanted to advertise my
plight, since someone might then bring me news. And someone did. Mr
McDowell wrote to me and said that it was true, Hartley was married.
I believed him. He gave no details (perhaps he feared I might commit
some act of violence) and I asked for none. He said in his letter, 'You
must simply accept that she does not want you, that she loves someone
else. With this no man can argue.'

Of course I 'recovered' in a sense. I worked. I met Clement Makin
and let her kidnap me. I told her the whole story, I think the first time
I met her. I never told my parents, and I believe they never knew. They

were such simple unsuspicious people and they never met anybody. Clement nursed me, she nursed my jealousy, it was a great 'topic' between us for a while. She rather enjoyed it all, she felt she was curing me and I let her think so, but she was mistaken. The wound was too deep and now it was infected by the raging bitterness of jealousy. That awful leprosy came into my life when I read Mr McDowell's letter, and has never left it since. 'She does not want you, she loves someone else.' When I was searching for her I was bemused by hope. I constantly forgave her in my heart, and this constantly renewed act of forgiveness brought me comfort. I felt that she must somehow know how I suffered, and that the antennae of my thought must touch her. But I always thought of her as alone. After I really understood that she was married I did not hate her, but the demon of jealousy befouled the past and left my mind no place to rest. Jealousy is perhaps the most involuntary of all strong emotions. It steals consciousness, it lies deeper than thought. It is always there, like a blackness in the eye, it discolours the world.

Hartley made a permanent metaphysical crisis of my life by refusing me for moral reasons. Did this lead me to make immorality my mask? Such pompous speculations are of course a kind of nonsense and I surprise myself by writing them down. What were Hartley's 'reasons'? I shall never know. It is possible that some demonic sense of a surrender of innocence entered into my affair with Clement, as if I were saying to Hartley: You did not trust me. Well, I will show you, now and forever after, how right you were! Perhaps all my love affairs have been vicious attempts to show Hartley that she was right after all. But she was only right because she left me. You die at heart from a withdrawal of love. My mother's threats of such a withdrawal made me utterly vulnerable to Hartley's crime. Hartley destroyed my innocence, she and the demon of jealousy. She made me faithless. But with her I would have been faithful, with her my whole life would have been different, less rootless, less empty. Do I then think my life has been empty, *my* life? A ridiculous judgment! Could Hartley really have thought the youth that I then was was 'a worldly man'? If so she was more like my mother than I ever suspected. She made me a worldly man by rejecting me, that failure ruined me morally. Did she think I would be 'lost' in the theatre? She never said that. It was her rejection that made me lose my way. Would I have been faithful? How could I not have been, if she had lived with me, sewed for me, cooked for me. We would have become one, and the holiness of marriage would have been our safety and our home forever. She was a part, an evidence, of some pure uncracked unfissured confidence in the good which was never there for me again.

Much later on it was a little as if the past had recovered. The past can recover. I saw again, far away like a dulled yet glowing painting of Adam and Eve upon an old fresco, two innocent beings bathed in a clear light. She became my Beatrice. As I went on, all the goodness of my life seemed to reside there with her. Goodness – or was it just a very special blend of innocence and chaste passion? I have been able to write about her as she then was, and I am deeply glad to find that I can do it. There is that faint smell of fire and brimstone when something of the past comes tearing to the surface vivid and complete. Of course the whole of my life has been a tissue of memories of Hartley. But earlier on I think I could not have written these things down; or admitted that, in her despite and in mine, that ancient love is somehow still alive. Of course I never saw her again. In the years to come I thanked God that the demon of jealousy itself had warned me not to find out any details, the suffering would have been too great, and I never even knew her married name. I stopped searching; I did not want to know where she was dragging out her obscure existence. I did not want my circling thought to have names and places to feed upon. But it pleased me to think of her life as dull. And then when I became well known and my name was often in the papers, it pleased me to imagine that she felt terrible secret pangs of remorse and regret, and that a bitter worm gnawed her as painfully as it has gnawed me. She threw away her happiness when she threw away mine. I would have made her a queen in this world.

Ever since those terrible days I have feared the possibility of an over-whelmingly powerful pain-source in my life, and I have nursed myself so as not to suffer too much. Possibly this is the deep reason why I have not married. What a queer gamble our existence is. We decide to do A instead of B and then the two roads diverge utterly and may lead in the end to heaven and to hell. Only later one sees how much and how awfully the fates differ. Yet what were the reasons for the choice? They may have been forgotten. Did one know what one was choosing? Certainly not. There are such chasms of might-have-beens in any human life. When I was confirmed I was determined to be good forever, and I still feel a ghostly illusion that I could have been. The image of Hartley changed in my mind from fiery pain to sadness, but never became blank. And in a way I did keep on searching for her, only it was a different and quite involuntary kind of search, a sort of dream-search. It was as if in my persisting memory of her I seemed to 'body her forth', the ways she moved, the ways she walked, as if a physical scheme of her being kept me always company. And so, and especially as the pain faded, I kept 'seeing' her, seeing shadow forms of her imposed upon quite different women; her shoulders, her hair, her walk, her puzzled fey expression. I still sometimes see these shadows. I saw one lately upon an old woman in the village, a transient look of her head placed like a mask upon somebody entirely different. Once or twice in London, long ago, I even followed these ghosts, not because I thought they were she, but simply to torment myself, to punish myself for still remembering.

A little while ago the thought came to me that she was dead. That strange pallor, those dilated pupils: perhaps these were presages of disease, of some quiet killer biding its time? Perhaps really she had died long ago when I was still young? In a way I would be glad to know that she was dead. What would my love for her do then? Would it peacefully die too, or be transformed into something selfless and innocent? Would jealousy, the jealousy which has burned even in these pages, leave me at last, and the smell of fire and brimstone fade away?

Even now I shake and tremble as I write. Memory is too weak a name for this terrible evocation. Oh Hartley, Hartley, how timeless, how absolute love is. My love for you is unaware that I am old and you perhaps are dead.

I ate three oranges at eleven o'clock this morning. Oranges should be eaten in solitude and as a treat when one is feeling hungry. They are too messy and overwhelming to form part of an ordinary meal. I should say here that I am not a breakfast eater though I respect those who are. I breakfast on delicious Indian tea. Coffee and China tea are intolerable at breakfast time, and, for me, coffee unless it is very good and made by somebody else is pretty intolerable at any time. It seems to me an inconvenient and much overrated drink, but this I will admit to be a matter of personal taste. (Whereas other views which I hold on the subject of food approximate to absolute truths.) I do not normally eat at breakfast time since even half a slice of buttered toast can induce an inconvenient degree of hunger, and eating too much breakfast is a thoroughly bad start to the day. I am however not at all averse to elevenses which can come in great variety. There are, as indicated above, moments for oranges. There are also moments for chilled port and plum cake.

The orange feast did not dim my appetite for lunch, which consisted of fish cakes with hot Indian pickle and a salad of grated carrot, radishes, watercress and bean shoots. (I went through a period of grated carrot with everything, but recovered.) Then cherry cake with ice cream. I had mixed feelings about ice cream until I realized that it must always be eaten with a cake or tart, never with fruit alone. By itself it is of course pointless, even if stuffed with nuts or other rubbish. And by 'ice cream' I mean the creamy vanilla sort. 'Flavoured' ice cream is as repugnant to the purist as 'flavoured' yoghurt. Nor have I ever been able to see the *raison d'être* of the so-called 'water ice', which transforms itself offensively on the tongue from a searing lump of hard frozen material into a mouthful of equally tasteless water. I am grieved that my lack of a refrigerator involves me in a marginal waste of food. My refrigeratorless mother never wasted a crumb. Everything not consumed lived to fight another day. How we loved her bread puddings!

I have reread what I wrote about Hartley and feel moved simply by the fact that I was able to write it. It is but a shadowy tribute; if I can bear to write more on the subject I may try to improve it. How strange memory is. Since I wrote, so many more pictures of her, stored up in the dense darkness of my mind, have become available. Her long legs bicycling, her bare dusty feet in sandals. Her lithe movement from crouching to standing, balanced upon the parallel bar in the gym display. The feel of her strong hands through my shirt, holding on to my shoulders. We did not caress each other in an immodest way. Our burning youth was docile to the chivalry of a pure passion. We were prepared to wait. Alas and alas. Never so pure and gentle, never so intense did it come to me after, that absolute and holy yearning of one human body and soul for another. But reading my story I feel again the terrible mystery of it. When did she start to turn away? Did she deceive me? Oh why did it happen?

I have spent the afternoon tidying the house. I carried two dustbins to the end of the causeway – I note with displeasure that the dustmen last time let some rubbish fall down onto the rocks below. I have had to climb down and collect it. I cleaned the kitchen and washed the huge black slates of the floor. They arc worthy of a cathedral. A man came to deliver Calor gas cylinders, rather to my surprise. (I had mentioned the matter in the Fishermen's Stores.) I must remember to enquire if they can supply a Calor gas fridge. The remainder of the ice cream has melted. My larder is still damp. I have lit a fire in the little red room and left the downstairs doors open. I moved quite a lot of wood into the downstairs inner room where I hope it will get dry. I am getting used to the smell of woodsmoke which now pervades the house.

It has stopped raining and the sun is shining, but over most of the sea the sky is a thick leaden grey. The sunny golden rocks stand out against that dark background. What a paradise, I shall never tire of this sea and this sky. If I could only carry a chair and table over the rocks to the tower I could sit and write there with the view of Raven Bay. I must go out and study my rock pools while this intense light lasts. I think I am becoming more observant – I lately noticed a colony of delightful very small crabs, like little transparent yellow grapes, and some ferocious-looking tiny fish with whiskers which resemble miniature coelacanths.

I feel calmer now already about Hartley, as if the thought of her has been somehow mercifully absorbed into the sane open air of my home. This is indeed a test of my new environment. ('You'll go mad with loneliness and boredom,' they said!) All my instincts were right.

I would like to tell all these things to someone, perhaps to Lizzie. I left in store with that first love so much of my innocence and gentleness which I later destroyed and denied, and which is yet now perhaps at last available again. Can a woman's ghost, after so many years, open the doors of the heart?

HISTORY

ONE

I did not look at the crabs after all. I became obsessed with the idea of carrying a chair and table out to the tower, and I set off across the rocks with the little folding table which I had moved from the middle room to the drawing room. This object soon began to seem absurdly heavy, and I found to my annoyance that the smooth steep faces of the rocks were too difficult to climb while I was holding the table in one hand. Eventually I let the thing fall into a crevasse. I must try to pioneer some easier way to get to the tower.

I climbed onward and sat on a wet rock overlooking Raven Bay. The sun was still shining and the seaward sky was still grey. The smooth foamless sea was rising and falling against the rocks with a gentle inviting rhythm. The longer shadows made the big spherical stones of the bay stand out, half dark, half gleaming. The long quite pretty façade of the Raven Hotel showed very clear and detailed in the odd brilliant light.

I was just getting over my annoyance about the table when I noticed a man walking along the road in the direction of Shruff End, having just turned the corner from the bay side. He was dressed in a smart suit and a trilby hat, and looked in that vivid landscape like an incongruous figure in a surrealist picture. I surveyed his oddity. Walkers on that road were even rarer than cars. Then he began to look familiar. Then I recognized him. Gilbert Opian.

My first instinct was to hide, and in fact I moved into the moist salt-smelling interior of the tower, under the bright round of sky, feeling a small unpleasant shock. However I could not seriously regard Gilbert as a menacing figure and it then occurred to me that of course he was bringing Lizzie; so I hurried out again and began to scramble over the rocks in the direction of the road. By the time I reached the tarmac Gilbert had seen me and turned back. We met each other, he smiling.

Gilbert was wearing a lightweight black suit with a striped shirt and flowery tie. When he saw me he took off his hat. It was three or four years since I had seen Gilbert and he had aged a lot. The mysterious awful changes which alter the human face from youth to age may gently dally and delay, then act decisively all at once. Gilbert in young middle age looked rosy and boyish. Now he was all wrinkled and humorous and dry, with that faint air of quizzical cynicism which clever elderly people often instinctively put on, and which may be quite new to them, a final defence. When I last saw him he still wore a fresh unselfconscious air of childish conceit. Now his face was full of wary watchful anxiety masquerading as worldly detachment, as if he were cautiously trying out his new wrinkles as a mask. Though podgier, he still contrived to look handsome, and his white curly hair still had a jaunty look, had not learnt to seem old.

I was wearing jeans and a white shirt which had escaped from them. Seeing Gilbert's tie, his tie-pin, his (or was I mistaken?) discreet make-up, I felt a quick contemptuous pity for him, together with a sense of how fit I was, how hard. I could see Gilbert taking these things in, the pity, the fitness. His moist light-blue faintly pinkish eyes flickered anxiously between their dry layers of wrinkles.

'Darling, you look marvellous, so brown, so young – my God, your complexion' – Gilbert always speaks in a rich fruity ringing voice as if addressing the back of the stalls.

'Have you brought Lizzie?'

'No.'

'A letter, message?'

'Not exactly –'

'What, then?'

'Is that funny-looking house yours?'

'Yes.'

'I wouldn't mind a drink, guv'nor.'

'Why have you come?'

'Darling, it's about Lizzie –'

'Of course, but get on with it.'

'It's about Lizzie and me. Please, Charles, take it seriously and don't look like that or I shall cry! Something has really happened between us, I don't mean like that sort of thing, but like real love like, God, in this awful world one doesn't often have such divine luck, sex is the trouble of course, if people would only search for each other as souls –'

'Souls?'

'Like just *see* people and love them quietly and tenderly and seek for happiness together, well I suppose that's sex too but it's sort of cosmic sex and not just to do with organs –'

'Organs?'

'Lizzie and I are really connected, we're close, we're like brother and sister, we've stopped wandering, we're home. Till Lizzie came I was just waiting for the next drink, gin then milk, then gin then milk, you know how it used to go, I thought it would go on till I dropped.

Now everything's different, even the past is different, we've talked all our lives over together, every damn thing, we've talked it all out, we've sort of repossessed the past together and redeemed it —'

'How perfectly loathsome.'

'I mean we did it reverently, especially about you —'

'You discussed *me*?'

'Yes, how could we not, Charles, you're not invisible — oh, please don't be cross, you know how I've always felt about you, you know how we both feel about you —'

'You want me to join the family.'

'Exactly! Please don't be sort of dry and sarcastic and make a joke of it, please try to understand. You see, I believe in miracles, now, dear Charles, miracles of love. Love is a miracle, real love is. It's far above the sort of boundaries and limits we were always tripping over. Why define, why worry, why not just be simple and free and loving with other people? We aren't young any more —'

'Have you given up boys, no more dangerous adventures?'

Gilbert, who had been gazing at the open neck of my shirt all the time he was speaking, raised his eyes to mine. His eyes rolled and swung in an odd characteristic manner, perhaps the effect of drink, and he had a way of wrinkling his nose and pulling down the corners of his mouth which he had copied from Wilfred Dunning. He went through a sort of painful humorous grimace. How self-conscious these old actors' faces are. 'Listen, king of shadows, Lizzie has made me happy. I'm new, I'm changed like they say in religion. Of course I'm not a totally reformed character and I wouldn't mind a drink absolutely now. But listen, Lizzie won't give me up, you can't break this bond between us. If you think it's trivial or funny you haven't understood. All you can do is make both of us very unhappy by being violent and cruel. Oh yes, we're frightened of you, yes, like we always were. Or you can make us very happy and make yourself happy just by being gentle and kind and by loving us and letting us love you. Why ever not? And if you make us miserable you'll feel wretched yourself in the end. Why not opt for happiness all round? Christ, darling, can't you see, it's a choice between good and evil!'

Gilbert's tirade, which was rather longer and more mawkish and repetitive than what I have set down here, was of course absurd. But what really annoyed me was the idea of Gilbert and Lizzie analysing each other and discussing in God knows what beastly detail their relations with me. I should add here that as far as the theatre went, which in his case was most of the way, I had made Gilbert. He owed me everything. And now this puppet was talking back and positively threatening me with moral sanctions! However, I laughed. 'Gilbert, come back to reality. I am amused by your touching description of your relations with Lizzie, but really it won't do. You claim to be changed, but you didn't answer my question about boys. I am totally sceptical about your ménage and I don't see why I should respect it. Why come and bother me with all this drivel about brotherhood and cosmic sex? This matter concerns me and Lizzie. It is nothing to do with you, and I'm shocked that she even told you about it. Even if you are fond of each other, sisters don't have to get their brothers' permission for everything. I summoned her, not you. She and I will decide what to do, and you're not part of it. If you hang around here you'll simply get burnt.'

As I spoke I was becoming conscious of that old familiar possessive feeling, the desire to grab and hold, which had been somehow blessedly absent from my recent thoughts about Lizzie. Perhaps that was a miracle, or maybe just lack of imagination, the 'abstract idea' she had accused me of. This reflection increased my annoyance with Gilbert. He was making me coarsen and define an impulse which had been splendidly generous and vague. This bickering was mean and undignified, but now I could not stop.

'Charles, can't we go into your funny house and have a drink?'

'No.'

'Well, do you mind if I sit down?' Gilbert hitched his trousers and sat down carefully on a rock. He laid his hat on the grass and surveyed his well-polished mud-fringed shoes. 'Charles dear, let's be calm about this, shall we? Do you remember sometimes when it was all rather fraught and you were furious with us, you used suddenly to stop and say, "All right, this is the English, not the Turkish, court"?'

'Gilbert, just keep out of my way, will you? If Lizzie wants to come she'll come, if not not. You don't understand what this thing is all about, between Lizzie and me, how can you? I don't want it messed around with your dreams of miracles and perfect love. I don't believe in your set-up, I strongly suspect you're deceiving yourself and deceiving Lizzie too. I'm beginning to feel it may even be my duty to bust up your rotten arrangement. So don't provoke me. And take your bloody hand off my sleeve.'

'Darling, don't give way to anger, you frighten me so, you always did –'

'I don't think I frighten you enough.'

'You always had such a bloody bad temper and it didn't help any of us ever. I know you thought it did, but that was an illusion. There is a worse way and there is a better way here. God, didn't you read Lizzie's letter?'

'Did she show it to you?'

'No, but I know what she said.'

'Did she show you my letter?'

'Er – no –'

'All this makes me sick!'

'Charles, you can't take Lizzie away from me, don't be so conventional, what does ordinary sex matter here, you'd respect a marriage, well perhaps you wouldn't, but you must believe Lizzie and at least respect her, it's a sacred bond and she won't leave me, she's said so a thousand times —'

'A woman can lie a thousand times.'

'Lizzie's right, you despise women.'

'Did she say that?'

'Yes. And she thinks you're not serious. You can't take Lizzie away, but you can spoil things, you can make her mad with misery and regret, you can make her fall in love with you again in a rotten hopeless way, you can make both of us perfectly wretched —'

'Gilbert, stop. I'm not going to play your game or enter your muddle. You can muddle away and dream away by yourself. Why isn't Lizzie here to tell me what she thinks and wants? She's afraid to see me because she loves me.'

'Charles darling, you know I care for you very much, you could simply murder my peace of mind —'

'Oh damn your peace of mind —'

At that moment Lizzie appeared. She materialized as a dark blur in the corner of my eye, in the evening sunshine, and I knew it was she before I turned to look at her. And as soon as I saw her that old wicked possessive urge jumped inside me for joy and I knew that the battle was over. But of course I showed no feeling apart from a little air of annoyance.

Gilbert picked up his hat and crushed it onto his face. He said to Lizzie, 'You said you wouldn't, you said you didn't want to, oh why did I let you come —'

I took in Lizzie, but looked beyond her at the sea, which was so calm and blue and quiet after the stupid yapping of my argument with

Gilbert. I turned and walked along the road, and then leapt onto the rocks and began to make my way as fast as I could in the direction of the tower. At once I could hear the soft scrabbling pattering sound of Lizzie following me. She did well, considering I knew the rocks and she did not, and reached the grassy patch beside the tower very soon after I did, panting and with the strap of one sandal broken. As I turned round I saw Gilbert beginning to slip and slither on the rocks in his polished London shoes. He disappeared into a crevasse. There was a distant sound of lamenting and cursing.

I went on through the stone doorway into the interior of the tower. Lizzie followed and suddenly we were alone together in that strange greenish light, with the white round eye of the sky up above us, and cool grasses about our ankles. The moist atmosphere inside the tower had produced a quite different vegetation, longer lusher grass and dandelions and some white nettles which were just coming into flower.

Lizzie was wearing a very thin white cotton dress, straight like a shift, and she was holding her handbag close up against her breasts and shuddering a little. She looked slightly slimmer. Her abundant fuzzy cinnamon-brown hair was loose and tangled, and as the breeze blew it I could see the whiteness of her scalp. She was blushing extremely, but she stood very upright and stared at me, and her terracotta-pink mouth was firm and she looked brave, like a noble girl facing execution. She too looked older, older at any rate than the radiant teasing boyish creature I most remembered. But there was a contained canny shrewdness in her face which gave it form and still made it handsome: the strong brow and the sweeping line to the delicate almost retroussé nose. Her bright light-brown eyes were red-rimmed with recent tears. As I gazed at her I felt triumphant and delighted; but I looked grim.

Lizzie dropped her eyes, reached out one hand to the wall, balanced to shake her broken sandal off, and put her bare foot down into the grass. She said, 'Did you know that there was a table there among the rocks?'

'Yes, I put it there.'

'I thought the sea might have brought it in.'

I was silent, gazing at her.

In a moment, in a whisper, she said, 'Oh, I'm sorry – I'm sorry, I'm sorry –'

I said, 'So you discussed me with Gilbert?'

'I didn't tell him anything that mattered' – she was looking down at her bare foot, and gently touched a white nettle with her toes.

'Liar.'

'I didn't, I –'

'You lied to him, then?'

'Oh don't – don't –'

'Why didn't you want to see me?'

'I was afraid –'

'Afraid of love?'

'Yes.'

We were both standing very stiff, the wind coming in through the open door tugging at her skirt, and at my errant shirt.

I recalled her chaste dry clinging kisses and I desired them now. I wanted to seize her in my arms and shout with delighted triumphant laughter. But I did not, and when she made a slight movement towards me I forbade it with a quick gesture. 'You must go now – back to London with Gilbert.'

'Oh, please –'

'Please what? Dear Lizzie, I don't want to be unkind, but I want things to be clear, I always did. I don't know what we can do or be for each other now, but we can only find out if we both take the risk of being wholehearted. I want all your attention. I can't share you with someone else, I'm amazed that you ask it! If you want to see me you must get rid of Gilbert, and get rid of him properly. If you want to stay with Gilbert then you won't see me, and I mean that, we won't meet again. That seems fair enough. Let me know soon, will you? And now please go, your friend is waiting.'

Lizzie, once more hugging her bag and her breasts, started talking very quickly. 'I must have time – I can't just leave Gilbert like that, I can't, I can't hurt him so – I want you to understand – people don't understand and they've been beastly to us – but *you* must understand then you'll see –'

'Lizzie, don't be stupid, you were never stupid before – I don't want to "understand" your situation, it's your business. But you must either get out of it and come to me or stay in it and not come to me.'

'Oh – Charles – darling – darling –' She suddenly turned, the stiffness left her body and it was that of a dancer. She threw her handbag onto the grass and in a moment she would have been in my arms, only I stepped back and again forbade it. 'No, I don't want your hugs and kisses. You must go away and think.'

A few drops of rain fell and long dark stains appeared on her dress. She touched her blazing cheeks, and then with a continuation of her motion swooped and picked up her bag.

'Go now, Lizzie child, I don't want us to have a messy conversation or an argument. Goodbye.'

She gave a little wailing cry, then turned and fled out of the doorway.

I waited a moment or two and when I came out she had almost reached the road. A yellow Volkswagen was now parked on the grass, pointing towards Raven Bay. I saw Gilbert jump out and open the passenger door. Lizzie plunged into the car. Both doors slammed and the car leapt away round the corner. A couple of minutes later it reappeared on the road to the hotel – I watched until it had passed the hotel and vanished where the road turned inland. Then I went back into the tower and picked up Lizzie's broken sandal. She must have had a sore foot by the time she reached the road.

It is now two hours later and I am sitting in the little red room. I have just written out my account of Lizzie's visit as a story and it has somehow excited and pleased me to put it down in this way. If one had time to write the whole of one's life thus bit by bit as a novel how rewarding this would be. The pleasant parts would be doubly pleasant, the funny parts funnier, and sin and grief would be softened by a light of philosophic consolation.

I am moved by having seen Lizzie and am wondering whether I have been clever or foolish. Of course if I had taken poor Lizzie in my arms it would all have been over in a second. At the moment when she hurled her handbag away she was ready to give in, to make every concession, to utter every promise. And how much I wanted to seize her. This ghost embrace remains with me as a joy mislaid. (I must admit that, after having seen her, my ideas are a good deal less 'abstract'!) Yet perhaps it was wise, and I feel satisfied with my firmness. If I had taken Lizzie then, accepted her acceptance, there would still have remained the problem of Gilbert, and I would have had the task of getting rid of him. Much better to let Lizzie do this, and do it promptly under pressure of the fear of losing me. I want that situation cleared up and cleared away, and meanwhile I prefer not to think about it. I cannot attach much importance to Lizzie's other 'objection', expressed in her letter, her fear that I might break her heart! That risk will not deter her. And I think on reflection that this was just an excuse, an arguing point put in to gain time. She must have seen at once that she had to cashier Gilbert, and given his slimy tenacity this might have seemed a difficulty. Have I really been such a Don Juan? Compared with others, certainly not.

As for my stern policy with Lizzie, I really have nothing to lose. If she delays too long I shall go and fetch her. If she still tries to say no I shall not take it for an answer. My threats of 'never again' are empty of course, but she will not think so. If she really decides in the end not to come then that will prove she is not worthy of me. In spite of it all I can let Lizzie go. If she won't, she won't.

I think I shall now walk round the bay to the Raven Hotel and ask them about delivering some wine. If I like the menu I may even have dinner there. I am beginning to be hungry. I suddenly feel pleased as if all will be well.

Shortly after this something very disconcerting happened, and then ... But first ...

I walked to the Raven Hotel and asked for a delivery of wine and bought a bottle of some Spanish red stuff to take home. I looked at the rather unsatisfactory dinner menu, but was feeling so hungry that I attempted to enter the restaurant, only a waiter prevented me because I was not wearing a tie. I was tempted to tell them who I was, but did not; let them discover later. I caught a glimpse of myself in a mirror: I had tucked in my shirt tails, but I did look rather a tramp in stained jeans with jagged uncombed hair and an old cardigan on inside out. I set off again for home.

The walk to the hotel had been pleasant, but now it was colder and darker, and by the time I was nearing Shruff End the sun had set, though there was still a lot of light in the sky, now a radiant occluded azure and clear of clouds. The evening star was huge and brilliant over the sea, near to a pale lustreless moon, and faint dots of other stars were appearing. Some rather large bats were flitting around over the rocks. I could hear the sea booming into Minn's cauldron as I passed by. I approached the house by the causeway, carrying the bottle in one hand.

The house of course was dark within but stood out rather starkly in the brilliant twilight, its awkward tall thin shape appearing against the high horizon of the sea. When I was about half way across the causeway I thought I saw a movement at one of the downstairs windows. I stopped and stood perfectly still, staring at the house. It was difficult to look at it because of the vividness of the sky behind it, and my eyes kept jumping and refusing to focus. For a moment or two I could see nothing clearly, but I was now sure that I had seen that movement, something moving inside, in the book room. I moved very slowly forward, blinking and staring. Then I saw, momentarily but plainly, a dark figure standing inside the house, at the window, looking out. The figure dissolved into darkness and my eyes seemed blinded. I dropped the bottle and it slid down the steep side of the rock and quietly shattered below. I walked quickly back across the causeway to the road.

There was someone or something inside the house. What was I to do? I could now hear the soft grating sound of the waves, like a gentle scratching of fingers upon a soft surface. And I felt upon the empty darkening road a shuddering sense of my utter solitude, my vulnerability, among these silent rocks, beside this self-absorbed and alien sea. I thought of walking back to the Raven Hotel and staying the night. But this seemed absurd; and would they give me a room, with my wild appearance and no luggage? I then thought I might walk on to the village, to the Black Lion – but – and then? I had no friends in the village. A further more dreadful realization came to me. I would be afraid to walk anywhere now in this gathering dark along this awful empty road. There was nowhere else to go but into the house.

I began to walk slowly back across the causeway. I had left the back door open, but the front door was locked, so I would have to walk round to the kitchen. Then how quickly could I find matches, light a lamp? Supposing there was an intruder inside, he would hear me stumbling round to the back and would be waiting for me. How stupid it would be to be accidentally killed by a frightened burglar! I hesitated, but went on because by now my fear of the outside was as great as my fear of the inside, and most of all I feared my own fear and wanted desperately to end it or at least change it. Perhaps I had, in this funny light, imagined the whole thing, and would soon be laughing at myself and eating my supper.

I recalled where there was an electric torch on a shelf inside the kitchen door, and I pictured where the lamp was, and the matches near it. I got a last glimpse of the sky, full of subdued light, and then I began noisily fumbling with the handle of the door. I blundered in, leaving the door open, found the torch, then the lamp and the matches. I lit the lamp and turned it up. Silence. I called out 'Hello there.' The foolish frightened cry echoed in the hollow house. Silence.

I walked to the door, holding up the lamp, and looked into the hall. Nothing. I walked quickly to the front room where I had seen the 'figure'. It was empty. I searched the other downstairs rooms. Nothing. I tried the front door. Still locked. Then I began more slowly to mount the stairs. I had always somehow felt that if there was any-thing sinister in the house it was located on that long upper landing. As I was mounting the last few steps I heard a sudden and prolonged clicking sound. The bead curtain had been moved.

I stopped. Then went mechanically on, my mouth open, my eyes staring. As I stood at the end of the landing I lifted up the lamp again, and stared into the uncertain space before me, where the light of the lamp and the last outside twilight filtering through the open door of my bedroom made a dense foggy amalgam. I could make out the darkly shaded alcove, the outline of the archway, the dotted mass of the bead curtain. Then suddenly, I saw, beside the wall at the far end, between the curtain and the door of the inner room, the dark motionless figure of a woman. My first and clear thought was that I was seeing a ghost, the ghost of the house, at last! I gave a choked grunt of fear and wanted to run back down the stairs but could not move. I did not drop the lamp.

The figure moved, turned more fully towards me. It was a real woman, not a ghost. Then in a flash it looked familiar. Then I could see the face in the lamplight. It was Rosina Vamburgh.

'Good evening, Charles.'

I was still trembling and quickly digesting my fear. I felt intense relief mixed with rising anger. I wanted to curse aloud but I remained silent, controlling my breathing.

'Why, Charles, you're all of a tremble, what's the matter?' Rosina speaks, off the stage, if such a woman can ever be said to be off the stage, with an odd slight, I suppose Welsh, accent which is all her own.

The house felt terribly cold, and for a second I felt I hated it and it hated me.

'What are you doing here, why are you in my house?'

'Just paying a visit, Charles.'

'Let me see you off then.'

I went away down the stairs and on into the kitchen where I lit another lamp. I went into the little red room and lit the wood fire. Hunger, temporarily suspended by fear, returned. I came back into the kitchen and turned on the Calor gas stove to warm the room a little, and set out a glass, a plate, bread, butter and cheese and a bottle of wine. Rosina had followed me and was standing near the stove.

'Won't you give me a drink, Charles?'

'No. Go away. I don't like people who break into my house at night and play at ghosts. Just go, will you. I don't want to see you!'

'Don't you want to know why I've come, Charles?' Her repetition of my name was hypnotic and menacing.

'No.'

'You're surprised, you're curious.'

'I haven't seen or heard of you for two years, three years, and even then I think I only met you at a party. Now you suddenly turn up in this perfectly hateful manner. Or is it supposed to be funny? Am I expected to be glad to see you? You aren't part of my life. Just clear off, will you.'

'I *am* part of your life, you know. Yes, you *are* frightened, Charles. It's interesting, it's a revelation, it's so *easy* to frighten people, to bewilder them and persecute them and terrify them out of their wits and make their lives a misery. No wonder dictators flourish.'

I sat down, but I could not eat or drink in her presence. Rosina found herself a glass, poured out some wine, and sat down opposite to me at the table. I was still cold with anger and upset about my fear but now that I was a little less hungry I did feel a grain of curiosity about Rosina's strange manifestation of herself. Anyway, how could I get rid of her if she refused to go? It was wiser to placate her and persuade her to go of her own accord. I began to look at her. She was certainly, in her odd way, an extremely handsome woman.

'Dear Charles. You are recovering. I can see it. That's right, have a hearty supper, *bon appétit*.'

Rosina was wearing a sort of black tweedy cloak, with slits through which she had thrust her bare forearms. Her hands were covered with rings, her wrists with bracelets, which were glinting as she lightly tapped her fingers together. Her dark wiry hair, looking almost black in the lamplight, was pinned up in some sort of Grecian crown. She had either grown it longer or helped it out with false tresses. Her face was heavily made up, patterned with pinks and reds and blues and even greens, looking in the subdued localized light like an Indian mask. She looked handsomely grotesque. Her mouth, enlarged by lipstick, was huge and moist. Her squinting eyes sparkled at me with malign intensity. She was playing a part: putting on the controlled dramatic display of emotion which seems to the actor so moving, to the spectator often so unconvincing.

'You look a right clown,' I said.

'That's good, dear, that's like old times.'

'Do you want anything to eat?'

'No, I had high tea at my hotel.'

'Your hotel?'

'Yes. I'm staying at the Raven Hotel.'

'Oh. I was there this evening. They wouldn't let me into the dining room.'

'I'm not surprised, you look like a filthy student. Seaside life suits you. You look twenty. Well, thirty. I heard them discussing you in the bar. You seem to have annoyed everyone already.'

'I can't have done, I haven't met anyone –'

'I could have told you the country is the least peaceful and private place to live. The most peaceful and secluded place in the world is a flat in Kensington.'

'You mean the waiter turned me out even though he knew who I was?'

'Well, he may not have recognized you. You aren't all that famous. I'm far more famous than you.'

This was true. 'Stars are always more famous than those who create them. May I ask what you are doing at the Raven Hotel?'

'Visiting you.'

'How long have you been there?'

'Oh ages, a week, I don't know. I just wanted to keep an eye on you. I thought it might be rather fun to haunt you.'

'To *haunt* me? You mean –'

'Haven't you felt haunted? Not that I've done very much, no turnip lanterns, no dressing up in sheets –'

I wanted to shout with exasperation and relief. 'So it was you – you broke the vase and the mirror, and you've been creeping round at night and peering at me –'

'I broke the vase and the mirror, but I haven't been creeping round at night, I wouldn't come in here in the pitch dark. This house is creepy.'

'But you did, you looked at me through the glass of that inner room.'

'No, I didn't. I never did. That must have been some other ghost.'

'You did, someone did. How did you get in?'

'You leave your windows open downstairs. You shouldn't, you know.'

I suddenly then, as I was staring at her, saw a vision: it was as if her face vanished, became a *hole*, and through the hole I saw the snake-like head and teeth and pink opening mouth of my sea monster. This lasted a second. I suppose it was not really a vision but just a thought. My nerves were still terribly on edge. I could hear the sea again, louder. But as I could hardly suppose that Rosina had arranged for me to be haunted by a sea monster I decided not to mention it.

'But why did you persecute me in this way? And why did you decide to let me discover you now, if you did?'

'I saw Lizzie Scherer in the village today.'

'Yes, she was here, she's gone. But what has that got to do with it? I can't understand what this is all about.'

'Can't you, Charles? Have you forgotten? Let me remind you.' Rosina leaned across the table, laying her hands flat and pointing her long fingernails at me like little spears. The nails were painted a dark purple. The bracelets grated on the wooden table. 'Have you forgotten? You promised that if you ever married anybody you would marry me.'

Fear returned to me, a vista of cold dismay, the emergence in life of the unpredictable and dangerous. Rosina's unnervingly blue eyes were sparkling, her rings were glistening. What she said was perfectly true.

I said lightly, 'Did I? I can't remember. I must have been drunk. Anyway I'm not proposing to get married.'

'No? And you promised that if you ever settled permanently with anyone you would settle with me.'

This also was unfortunately true.

Rosina smiled. She has slightly irregular long, white teeth and a kind of 'smile' whereby she advances her lower teeth to meet her upper ones and draws back her lips. The effect is terrible. 'You were not drunk. And you remember, Charles.'

I was trying to think what line I had better adopt with this dangerous woman. I had certainly not expected her to reappear in my life. But now that she had done so I recognized and respected her style. The broken vase, the smashed mirror were not idle portents. Why these reminders now, what had set it all off? The reference to Lizzie was the clue, though unfortunately I had no time to reflect upon it. If that was her drift, suppose I told her that Lizzie's presence here meant nothing? This would only put off the crisis whose nature I was just beginning to grasp. Had I, in my recent thoughts, considered Lizzie in the hypothetical light of a permanent partner? Possibly. Had I thought seriously of marrying Lizzie? No. But Rosina's terrorism was intolerable, an impertinence. I decided it was better to be aggressively firm and direct straightaway.

'Look here, just stop this, will you. I forget what I said exactly but it was momentary emotional nonsense, as you perfectly well know. One can't bind oneself like that and I'm not bound. Those were just words, not a promise.'

'Promises are words. You are bound, Charles. *Bound.*' She repeated the word softly with an intense emphasis.

'Rosina, don't talk rubbish. People say all sorts of things during love affairs which they don't mean, you know that. Or if you prefer, all right I promised, but I shall break my promise just as soon as it suits me, like everybody else.'

'So you are going to marry her?'

'Who? What are you talking about? Do you mean Lizzie?'

'So it's true?'

'No, of course I'm not going to marry her.'

'So you're not going to marry her?'

'Rosina, will you leave me alone? Whatever put this idea into your head anyway?'

'Oh, as to that,' said Rosina, snapping her fingers, 'it's all over London. She had to crow. She's gone round telling everybody that you're plaguing her with proposals.'

I did not believe this of course.

Rosina went on, 'Gilbert Opian has rushed about trying to make up some sort of party against you. Everyone is very amused.'

Gilbert was the culprit.

'And I gather you didn't even know Lizzie was living with Gilbert. Surprise, surprise. Everybody knew that. If you aren't interested enough to know who she's living with you aren't interested enough in her to marry her.'

'I'm not going to marry her.'

'You've said that twice.'

'I mean — oh go away, Rosina. And they aren't lovers.'

'You believe that?'

'I mean I shall do what I want to do.'

'You've always known who I was living with.'

'You flatter yourself. I don't care what you do or who you're with so long as you keep away from me. Now clear off.'

Rosina did not move, except that she stretched out one hand across the table until the long pointed nail of her middle finger touched my shirt sleeve. Then I could feel the nail sticking into my arm. I sat rigid, not wincing. 'You have not understood,' she said. 'Why do you think I have come to you now? I did not enter your house and break things just to amuse myself and laugh with you afterwards. I want to tell you this. You may or you may not marry me, but I am not going to permit you to marry anybody else. I shall hold you to your promise.'

'You can't. You are living in a dream world.'

'Oh you can go through a marriage ceremony, or settle down with a lovebird of your choice, but you will not live happily ever after. If you set up with Lizzie I shall spoil your life as you spoilt mine. You will not be able to hide from me. I will be with you all the time, I will be in your mind day and night, I will be a demon in your life and in her life. Until she cries with misery because she ever met you. It is very easy to frighten people, Charles. I know, I have done it. It is easy to maim people and utterly destroy their peace of mind and cripple all their joy. I shall not tolerate your marriage, Charles. If you wed this wench, or if you keep her as your love, I shall dedicate my life to spoiling yours, and I shall find it *very easy*.'

She drew her hand back. A stain of blood appeared on the sleeve of my shirt. These were not the idle momentary ravings of a jealous woman. This was hatred, and hatred can destroy, it has its own magic. Rosina had the will and the power to do exactly what she threatened. And as I thought this I felt with a pang that this black will was, when it was otherwise directed, the very thing which had made me love her. She was smiling again, showing her white fishy teeth.

I took a reasonable tone, which did not deceive her, for she could feel my fear. 'Your threats are rather premature, but if you bother me for any reason I shall certainly retaliate. Why have a war on your hands, why waste your life and your time? This is hate not love. You're a rational woman. Forget it. Why make yourself miserable with these paroxysms of peevish jealousy?' These words were a bad mistake.

Rosina struck the table with the flat of her hand and her eyes sparkled with violence. 'You dare to talk of jealousy! As if I cared about that little lump you are running after! All right, you left me, *me*, to take up with her, and I haven't forgotten. I could have maimed her or maddened her, only I knew you'd get tired of her, and you did, you get tired of everybody. You wrecked my marriage, you prevented me from having children, for you I made a slaughter of all my friends. And when you'd begged me on your knees to leave my husband, and when I'd left him, you abandoned me for that baby-face. Do you not remember what our love was like? Have you forgotten why you uttered those words?'

'Mercifully one forgets one's love affairs as one forgets one's dreams.'

'You never had any imagination, no wonder you couldn't write plays. You are a cold child. You want women but you are never *interested* in the people you want, so you learn nothing. You've had love affairs but somehow you've stayed innocent, no not innocent, you are fundamentally vicious, but somehow immature. Your first mistress was your mother, Clement was baby-snatching. But don't you see that it has all been a mirage? Those women loved you for your power, your magic, yes, you have been a sorcerer. And now it's over – I am the only one who loved you for yourself and not your invincible locks.'

'This speech would be more impressive if you had uttered it earlier and not just because you've heard a rumour about Lizzie!'

'I was waiting to see if you would really give up the world, as you boasted you would. I wanted you stripped and alone. Then you might have been almost worthy of me. Well, what a fool I was to think that I would ever be able to admire you for anything except that facile sorcery! But the fact remains that you made that promise to me in a moment of truth, in an absolute of love such as few men are privileged to have in their lives ever. And that promise belongs to me, it is all I have got in exchange for my broken marriage and for the love which I poured out for you as I have never done for any man. I have got that promise and I will hold it and use it even if there is nothing I can do with it except make your life a desolation and a ruin.'

I got up suddenly, and she became tense and actually lifted up her glittering hands like clawed paws. She looked like a ballet dancer playing a cat.

'Listen, my cross-eyed beauty, it's late, just get along will you, go back to the Raven Hotel. I'm going to bed. And please don't creep around this house any more breaking things and peering through panes of glass. I have no plans for getting married or settling down with any female.'

'Do you swear that?'

'No arrangement exists. Lizzie is living with Gilbert. That's how it is. And of course I never proposed to her, that was just a crazy rumour. Now go, I'm exhausted, and you must be too after that long performance.'

She got up and pulled her cloak more closely around her, her arms emerging through the slits, gripping each other in front. She stood for a moment glaring at me. 'I will go. But tell me you believe what I have said.'

'I believe some of it.'

'Tell me you believe what I have said.'

'I believe it. Now for Christ's sake get out.'

I walked out with the lamp towards the front door and she followed. I opened the door. The light of the lamp revealed a mist which was waiting outside like a presence. It was impossible to discern the end of the causeway.

'I'll light you to the road,' I said, and I went back for the electric torch. 'But look, I'd better walk with you to the hotel. Oh *hell*.'

'You needn't,' she said in a dull lifeless tone. 'My car is near.'

I lighted her across the causeway with the torch. The mist was less thick on the road. 'Where is your car?'

'It's here, in this place behind the rock.'

We walked to it and she got in. I said, 'Goodnight.'

She said, *'Remember.'*

She switched on the headlights and I made out the form of a low red two-seater. She backed the car onto the road. As she turned it now and as it began to move in the direction of the hotel, a figure suddenly materialized, someone who had evidently been walking along the road. Rosina had stepped hard on the accelerator and the car leapt suddenly forward and the pedestrian was caught for a moment in the headlights, cowering back against the rock. The car swerved with a screech and then roared away down the road. I dropped my torch into the long grass and was left in darkness.

The pedestrian whom Rosina had almost run down was the old village woman who had so strangely reminded me of Hartley. Now in that moment of bright light, I saw. The old woman did not resemble Hartley. *She was Hartley.*

HISTORY

TWO

Now in London I am writing the story of Rosina's arrival and of what happened just after it. After Rosina's car raced away I stood quite still in a condition of total shock, the kind of shock which annihilates space and time and renders one almost contemplative. I was paralysed. I cannot think why I did not fall to the ground, the revelation was, in its initial impact, so terrible. I grasped it first, I do not quite know why, in this way, not as something unwelcome or horrible, but purely as the impossible come true, like what we cannot imagine about the end of the world. And indeed it was the end of the world. I remember then very slowly reaching out my hand so that I could support myself against the rock. By the time I was able to reach down to the ground and pick up the torch I somehow knew that Hartley must have gone, must have continued down the road and by now be far ahead, or that perhaps she was taking a short cut across the fields. I was in any case not sure which way she had been going when the car lights caught her. My mind was so shocked I could not make the simplest decision about what to do. I started off hurrying towards the village and then stopped. It did not occur to me to call out her name, that would have been *impossible*. I hardly indeed remembered her name, it would have emerged, as in a dream, as an incoherent bellow. I hurried back and stupidly shone the torch about, inspecting the place where I had seen her. The bright light revealed the marks of the car tyres, the trampled grass, the yellow pock-marked rock, the mist moving. At last slowly, and like a man returning from a funeral, I walked back across the causeway to the house. The lamps were still burning in the kitchen, the fire was alight in the little red room. It was all quiet and as it had been when, in a previous age of the world, I had been talking with Rosina.

I was trembling. Eating, drinking, were equally impossible. I went into the little red room and sat down by the fire. *Is she a widow?* This agonizing question had somehow, it seemed, formulated itself at once, in the very first awful moment of recognition. Awful, not because she had so almost completely changed, but because I knew that everything was in ruins about me, every old assumption was gone, every terrible possibility was open. That there could soon be dreadful pain did not then occur to me at all, I think. It was not envisaging pain that made me feel so shattered, it was just experience of the change itself. I felt a present anguish such as an insect must feel as it emerges from a chrysalis, or the crushed foetus as it batters its way into the world. It was not, either, a removal to the past. Memory seemed now almost irrelevant. It was a new condition of being.

I did eventually go to bed where I slept instantly like a dead thing. I had by then composed one or two more simple thoughts or questions. *Is she a widow?* was so pervasive as to be scarcely a question, it was the atmosphere I breathed. I wondered had she seen me in the village and if so had she recognized me? I had seen her distantly several times. Oh my God how *terrible*. I had seen her and not known her. But surely I, who was scarcely changed, must have been recognizable at once. Why then had she not spoken to me? Perhaps she had chanced not to see me, perhaps she was short-sighted, perhaps – what was she doing in the village anyway? Did she live here, or was she on holiday? Perhaps she would disappear tomorrow, never be seen again. Where was she going to along the misty sea road at night? The idea came to me that she might be working at the Raven Hotel. But she was over sixty, Hartley was over sixty. I had never put it to myself that Hartley too was growing old. Then I wondered if she had seen me in the dark, and if so had she realized that I had recognized her? Then I thought: she saw me with Rosina. What might she have overheard, what had we been saying? I could not remember. Then I decided she could not possibly have seen me as I was behind the headlights. And tomorrow: tomorrow I would search and search for her and find her and then ...

I woke up next morning to an instant sense of a changed world. The *awful* feeling was less, and there was a new extremely anxious excitement and a sheer plucking physical longing to be in her presence, the fierce indubitable magnetism of love. There was also a weird hovering joy, as if I had been changed in the night into a beneficent being powerful for good. I could produce, I could bestow, good. I was the king seeking the beggar maid. I had power to transform, to raise up, to heal, to bring undreamt-of happiness and joy. My God, I had come here, to this very place, and against all the chances I had found her at last! I had come here because of Clement, and I had found Hartley. But: *is she a widow?*

I was in the village before nine o'clock. It was a sunny morning promising heat. I walked quickly round the little streets. Then I went down to the harbour and back by a footpath which led up the hill to the bungalows. As soon as the two shops were open I visited both of them. I walked round again. Then I went into the church, which was empty, and sat for a while with my head in my hands. I found that I was able to pray and was indeed praying. This was odd since I did not believe in God and had not prayed since I was a child. I prayed: let me find Hartley and let her be alone and let her love me and be made happy by me forever. My being able to make Hartley happy had become the most desirable thing in the world, something the possession of which would crown my life and make it perfect. I went on praying and then in a strange way it was as if I had fallen asleep. I certainly had the experience of waking up and feeling panic in case I had lost Hartley, as my only chance to find her had come and gone while I was sleeping. Her holiday was over, she had gone home, she had run away, she had suddenly died. I jumped up and looked at my watch. It was only twenty past nine. I ran out of the church. And then at last I saw her.

I saw: a stout elderly woman in a shapeless brown tent-like dress, holding a shopping bag and working her way, very slowly as if in a dream, along the street, past the Black Lion in the direction of the shop. This figure, which I had so vaguely, idly, noticed before was now utterly changed in my eyes. The whole world was its background. And between me and it there hovered, perhaps for the last time, the vision of a slim long-legged girl with gleaming thighs. I ran.

I reached her, running up from behind, when she had just passed the pub, and as I came level with her I touched one of the wide brown sleeves of her dress. She stopped, I stopped. I could say nothing.

The familiar face turned to me, the pale round fey face with the secret-violet eyes, and with a sort of almost reflective movement of relief I thought: I can make sense of it, yes, it is the same person, and I can *see* it as the same person, after all.

Hartley's face, which now seemed absolutely white, expressed such an appalling terror that I would have felt terrified myself had I not been engaged in some urgent almost mechanical search for 'similarities', for ways to blend the present with the far past. Yes, that was Hartley's face, though it was haggard and curiously soft and dry. A sheaf of very fine sensitive wrinkles at the corner of the eye led upwards to the brow and down towards the chin, framing the face like a wreath. There were magisterial horizontal lines upon the forehead and long darkish hairs above the mouth. She was wearing a moist red lipstick and face powder which had caked here and there. Her hair was grey and neat and conventionally waved. But the shape of her face and head and the look of her eyes conveyed something untouched straight from the past into the present.

She started to murmur something. 'Oh – it's –' It was of course at once clear that she knew who I was. She mumbled 'Oh –' staring at me in a kind of blank terrified supplication.

I managed at last to say 'Come – come –' and pulled again at her sleeve and began to move back towards the church. I did not attempt to walk with her. She followed me a few feet behind and I kept looking back at her and stumbling. God knows who witnessed this encounter. Perhaps a dozen people, perhaps no one. I could not see anything except Hartley's terrified eyes.

I went into the church and held the big heavy door open for her. The place was still empty. The big windows of plain glass gave a bright cool light. I sat down in a nearby pew and she sat down close to me in the next row in front, so that she had to turn round to see me. In the damp musty atmosphere I could smell her face powder and feel the warmth of her body. She had dropped her bag and gripped the back of the pew with her two hands. The hands were red and wrinkled and in a moment she hid them again. She murmured 'I'm sorry –' and closed her eyes. I laid my brow on the polished wooden surface where her hands had been and said, 'Oh, Hartley – Hartley – Hartley –'

It occurred to me later that I never for a second doubted that her emotion was as strong as my own; although this could well have been otherwise. When I lifted my head she was dabbing her face with a handkerchief and breathing open-mouthed in a shuddering way, not looking at me.

'Hartley, I – oh, Hartley – oh, my dear – where do you live, do you live in the village?' I do not know why I asked this question first, perhaps just because it was easy to answer. Speech of any sort seemed the problem, as if we spoke different languages and must teach each other to talk.

'Yes.'

'You're not on holiday, you live here?'

'Yes.'

'So do I. I'm retired now. Where do you live?'

'Up on the hill.'

'In one of those bungalows?'

'Yes.' She added, 'There's a lovely view.' She too was babbling. Her handkerchief had smudged some lipstick onto her cheek.

'You got married, didn't you – are you still – I mean is your husband still – have you got a – husband – now –?'

'Yes, yes, oh yes. My husband is alive – he's with me, yes – we live – we live here.'

I was silent while a whole world of possibilities gradually folded themselves up, like some trick of stagecraft, quietly collapsing, folding, merging, becoming very small and vanishing. So that – was that – at any rate. And I would have to think, to invent, in a new way, to exist in this situation which was now, I realized, whatever was the case with Hartley, the continuing and only situation for me, the final state of affairs, the world centre.

'I'm sorry,' I said.

She shook her head slightly, jerked it with emotion, at this last awkward tribute. A short litany, a vast brief Amen.

I went on, 'I'm not married, I never married.'

She moved her head again, staring down at the reddened handkerchief. And we were silent for a moment together, as if surveying breathlessly a huge event which had just taken place. Then as in a crisis people will hurry on to talk at random, I said quickly, 'Did you see me before at all, did you see me in the street, perhaps you didn't recognize me?'

'Oh yes. I saw you nearly three weeks ago. I recognized you. You haven't changed.'

I could not bring myself to say 'You haven't changed', though later I cursed myself for not saying it. How much do women mind when they lose their looks, how much do they know? But I was instantly caught up and appalled by another thought. 'But then why didn't you speak to me?'

'I wasn't sure if you would want to know me. I thought perhaps you felt it would be better if we didn't recognize each other –'

'You mean you thought I'd recognized you and – and cut you – just ignored you? How *could* you think that?'

'I didn't know – I didn't know how you felt after all those years – whether you blamed me or had forgotten me. You are so grand and famous – you mightn't like me or want to know me –'

'Oh, Hartley, how can you, if you only knew – I've spent the years looking for you, I've never stopped loving you –' I touched the shoulder of the brown dress, taking the collar of it for a second between my fingers.

'Don't, don't,' she murmured, moving slightly away.

'Did you know that I saw you last night?'

'Yes.'

'I only recognized you then. I've been in a frenzy ever since. I wouldn't have pretended not to know you, what a terrible thing! How could you think I'd blame you or forget you! You are my love, you are still that, you are still what you were for me –'

She gave an odd little grimace like a smile and shook her head, still not looking at me.

I could not say more, I had to blunder on into the terrible things. 'You're still with the same – husband – the one you married–then?'

'Yes, the same one.'

'I never knew his name, I – I don't know your married name.'

'I'm Mrs Fitch. His name is Fitch, Benjamin Fitch.'

I bowed over this as over a stomach blow. There was now a name attached to this horror of her being married, this horror that I would have to live with somehow. An awful wave of self-pity overcame me and I wrinkled up my face with pain. 'Hartley – what does he do, I mean, what does he, does he work at?'

'He's disabled a bit, he went about in a car as a representative, did various jobs, like a salesman, he's retired now. We came here, we were in the Midlands, we came here, to the bungalow to live –'

'Oh isn't it strange, Hartley, we both came here to meet each other again, and we didn't know. It seems like fate, doesn't it?' But oh the pain of it.

Hartley said nothing. She looked at her watch.

'And – children – have you?'

'We have a son. He's eighteen. He's away just now.'

She spoke more calmly and with a sort of deliberation, as if getting some necessary task over.

'What's his name?'

She said after a moment, 'Titus.' She repeated, 'Titus – is his name.' Then she said, looking at her watch again, 'I must go, I must go to the shop, I shall be late.'

'Hartley, please, stay here please, I must go on talking to you, tell me – oh – tell me, what did your husband do, sell, before he retired?' I must just keep on asking questions.

'Fire extinguishers. He was in fire extinguishers.' She added, 'He was always so tired in the evenings.'

This sudden vista of her evenings, years and years of her evenings, led me on blunderingly to ask, 'And are you happily married, Hartley, have you had a good life?'

'Oh yes, yes, I've been very happy, a very happy marriage, yes.'

It was impossible to tell if she was sincere. Probably she was. A good life. What an odd phrase I had used. And had both our lives passed, and had they somehow been completed, since we last met? Hartley's voice, retaining the thin droning slightly monotonous, to me so immensely attractive, sound which it had always had, with the touch of the local accent, made me realize how much my own voice had changed.

I was suddenly breathless and put both of my hands onto the back of the pew. My little finger touched her dress and she moved slightly again. Something black seemed to threaten me from a little way above my head. She had been happy all these years, yes, why not, and yet I could not believe it, could not bear it. She had existed all these years and our lives were gone. I breathed quickly through my mouth and the darkness went away. I thought, I must be *ingenious,* and the word 'ingenious' seemed like a help to me. I must be ingenious and see to it that I do not suffer too much. I must look for some happiness, simply for some comfort, here, ingeniously.

I said, not knowing quite what I meant to say nor why, 'That woman in the car last night, she's a well-known actress, Rosina Vamburgh, she was just visiting me –'

'We hardly ever go to the theatre –'

'She was just visiting me on business –'

'I saw you on telly.'

'Did you, what was it –?'

'I forget. I must go now,' she repeated and got up and retrieved her shopping bag.

I felt panic. 'Hartley, don't go, you look – oh so tired –' This was not the best thing to say, but it expressed a sort of anguish of protectiveness and tenderness and pity and a kind of humility which I felt about her then as I saw her standing there before me in the guise of an old woman. She did look tired, tiredness was somehow the expression of her face, not sadness or suffering so much as a vast weariness as of one who has worked too hard for years and years.

'I'm very well, apart from endless tummy trouble. You look well, Charles, and so young. I must go.' She shuffled past me in the direction of the door.

I leapt up and followed her. 'But what shall we do?'

Hartley looked at me as if she was not sure what this question meant.

I repeated, 'What shall we do? I mean – oh, Hartley, Hartley, when shall I see you, can we meet after you've done your shopping, can we meet in the pub, or would you come down to my house –' Vistas of madness opened beyond these words.

Hartley opened the church door, pulling at it laboriously, and over her shoulder I could see Dummy's grave and the criss-cross iron gate and the village street with people in it and the far horizon line of the sea. I said wildly, 'Of course I'll call on you, I'd so much like to meet your husband, you must both come down to my funny house and have a drink, you know I live –'

'Yes, I know, thank you, but not just now, my husband is not too well –'

'But I'll see you, I must – what's your address, which bungalow?'

'It's called Nibletts, it's the last one, but don't – I'll let you know –'

'Please, Hartley, see me after you've done your shopping, let me help you –'

'No, no, I'm late. Don't come, you stay here. I'll see you later, I mean on another day, please don't do anything, I'll let you know. I must run now, I'll let you know. *Please* stay here. Goodbye.'

I had wanted to touch her, but somehow only with my fingertips as if she were a ghost which might dissolve, I had wanted to hold her dress between my fingers. Now I felt a more precise need to take her head and draw it quietly against me and hear her heart beating. Old desires were suddenly present. I saw her blue, blue eyes and the curious mad look of her round face which was so unchanged. And her lips which had been so white and so cold.

I started to say, 'I'm not on the telephone –'

She went quickly out of the church and closed the door carefully. Obeying her I stayed. I went back to the same place and sat down and once more put my hands where her hands had been.

What was I going to do, how was I going to *manage* myself for the rest of my life now that I had found Hartley again? Was I going to go round to 'Nibletts' once a week and have tea with Mr and Mrs Benjamin Fitch? Or entertain them to beans and sausages and claret at Shruff End? Take them up to London for a show? Take an interest in Titus's future? Look after them all? Leave Titus my money? My mind leapt wildly about, huge vistas opened, immense areas of the future were suddenly live and quick with possibilities, all of them terrible. Ingenious, I thought, I must be ingenious. I looked at my watch. It was ten-twenty. So much awful thought in so little time. I sat for a while until I reckoned that Hartley would have done her shopping and gone back up the hill, and then emerged from the church and sat on Dummy's grave, leaning against the gravestone which bore the image of the 'foul anchor'. From there I could see, over some trees, the roofs of the bungalows, including the last one, the residence of Mr and Mrs Fitch. A disabled travelling salesman. What was the matter with him? A cripple? I knew that I would have to go and take a look at Mr Benjamin Fitch, very soon.

Why had Hartley been so reluctant, why had she not said 'Yes, come and see us' or 'We'd love to come and see you'? Sanity demanded such gestures, whatever she felt. Politeness demanded them and by politeness one might, for the present at any rate, be saved. Or was the crippled husband really ill, suffering, peevish and bedridden perhaps? But oh what did Hartley feel, what made her seem so strained and anxious? Her reluctance to invite me to her house was perhaps understandable, indeed very understandable. 'You are so grand and famous.' She was perhaps a little bit ashamed of her house and her husband. That need not mean she did not love him. But did she love him? I had to know. Was she really happy? I had to know. And that old horrible sweetish thought now kept coming to me: she must regret it so much, that wrong choice. She must have spent her life regretting that she had not married me. 'I saw you on telly.' What was that like? What mean gnawing pains of remorse did she feel when she saw me as a 'celebrity'? How could she know that I was still just me and that I still missed her? And must she not think of me as surrounded by attractive women, as probably possessing a permanent mistress? She had seen Rosina, she might have seen Lizzie. Perhaps, it suddenly occurred to me, and this was so painful and so sweetish too, she is reluctant to see me precisely because of her regrets: remorse, jealousy, the waywardness of fruitless daydream. She does not want to know any more about what might have been. Oh God, those years, our whole life, that we might have spent together. She does not want ... to start to love me ... all over again ...

I already had enough instinct for dangerous thoughts to thrust this one aside. I was indeed, as I leaned back against the sun-warmed lichen-spotted surface of Dummy's laconic monument, sketching a kind of programme for survival. Roughly, the programme was like this. There was no doubt that I must now somehow contrive to devote the rest of my life to Hartley. (I quickly banished the idea that Mr Fitch was seriously ill and would shortly die.) This could only be done if I *accepted* their marriage and could successfully attempt to construct a friendship with her, and presumably with him. Hartley and I were not just revisiting each other as tourists, that was out of the question. At the least, the husband must tolerate me. Perhaps I could be allowable as a figure of fun? I did not quite care for this, but so quick is imagination that I already heard Hartley saying to her spouse, 'Why there's dear old Charles again, he can't keep away!' – while she *felt* – something a little different. Perhaps the husband might even be flattered that a 'show-business personality' admired his wife. However these were unsavoury or at any rate premature speculations.

What I must now concentrate upon was the possibility of love in the form of a pure deep affectionate mutual respect, a steady constant binding awareness. Of course it would be, it would have to be, love between us, but love purged of possessive madness, purged of self, disciplined by time and the irrevocability of our fates. We must find out how at last to be absolutes to each other, never to lose each other, without putting any foot wrong or spilling one drop of some brimming vessel of truth and history which was held up austerely between us. I will respect her, I will respect her, I kept saying to myself. I felt a tenderness for her that was deep and pure, a miracle of love preserved. How clear it flowed, that fountain from the far past. Yes, we must quietly collect our past, collect it up with tacit understanding, without any intensity or drama, blaming and exonerating ourselves with a difference. And how wonderfully possible it seemed, this silent process of redemption, as I rethought our passionate, yet gentle and divinely inept little conversation in the church. Was *that* what it was like, meeting the great love of one's life again after all those years? And had we not been for each other the shy direct innocent creatures we had once been? The nature of our converse had never been spoilt, and in that blundering conversation its note could unmistakably be heard again. Perhaps I would indeed, through her and through our old childish love, now irremediably chaste, be enabled to become what I had hoped to become when I came away to the sea, pure in heart.

The question: is she a widow? already seemed to belong to the remote past, to some vanished and entirely obsolete method of thinking. The question which was now, in spite of the programme for rational survival with which I was consoling myself, in danger of becoming agonizingly urgent, was: *is she happy?* To decide this it was necessary to inspect Mr Fitch. And moreover it was quite impossible to wait. As I walked slowly back to Shruff End I thought: I have got to see Mr Fitch today. I will call on them about six o'clock this evening.

It was not until I was actually ringing the bell at Nibletts that it occurred to me to wonder whether in all those years Hartley had ever actually told him anything about me at all!

Nibletts is a small square bungalow built of a red brick which has been partly and mercifully whitewashed. Without compromise it squats upon the hill, with a group of wind-tormented trees opposite to it, beside it the slope to the village, behind it the slope to the sea, beyond and above it, woodland. It has a firm solid air. Other houses might be built upon sand or even be made of sand, but not so Nibletts. The bricks are unchipped, sharp and uneroded at the corners. There is no moss upon the roof and one feels that none will ever grow there. An equally undimmed red-tiled path leads to the front door between beds of spiky little rose bushes in their first flowering. A fuzzy mass of white clematis, growing up one of the wooden posts of the porch, soothes with some grace the blue front door which is covered with very thick, very shiny paint. The door has an oval panel of opaque frosted glass which seems to creep before the eyes. Nibletts is not a charmless house, it is pretty and homey, with its discreet patchy whitewash and its bright flower-fringed door. Within there are four main rooms, the sitting room and kitchen-dining room being both at the back where a descending lawn is overwhelmed by the view of the sea. But I anticipate.

The day had become hot. The temperature had risen to eighty degrees in the afternoon and the air was still shimmering with heat.

From the hillside one could see the distant headlands of the bay couchant in a light-brownish heat haze. The vast bowl of the sea was glowing a very pale blue with silvery mirages and streaks of light. The crowded roses were hotly odorous. The bell, which I rang just as I suddenly thought that perhaps Mr Fitch was unaware that I knew his wife, and that this accounted for her panic, was penetratingly sweet, like a tuning fork struck for a choir of angels. Low voices were at once heard within. Then, after a moment, Hartley opened the door.

I got the shock again of her changed appearance, since in my intense and cherishing thought she had become young again, before I saw on her face a look of fear which instantly vanished. Then I could see nothing but her large eyes, seeming violet and somehow glazed and veiled as if they were looking beyond me. I could feel myself blushing, the accursed red wave surging up through my neck and face.

I had deliberately prepared nothing to say. I said, 'Oh excuse me, I was passing by, returning from a walk and I just thought I'd call in for a moment.'

I had time before she replied to think: I ought to have let her speak first! Then if she had indeed never told her husband about me she could pretend I was selling brushes. I was wearing my jeans with a clean white shirt and my faded but decent cotton jacket. I tried to look *into* her eyes but it was impossible, and the fear or whatever it was had gone.

She said nothing to me but turned to speak back into the house. It sounded like – 'It's him –' As she spoke she swung the door back, half closing it in my face, and for a moment I thought she was simply going to shut it.

There was the sound of an ejaculation within, perhaps just 'Oh.'

The door swung open again and Hartley was smiling at me. 'Do come in for a minute.'

I wiped my feet on the large clean bristly orange mat and stepped into the hall, blinded by the change of light.

All the way from Shruff End, and indeed all day since my resolve to call on Hartley, I had been feeling sick with excitement, sick with a blend of obscure bodily agitation and clarified fear, not unlike (only this was much worse) what I used to feel when I dived off very high boards in California to impress Fritzie. I could not now see Hartley properly in the sudden darkness of the interior, but I felt her presence as a violent diffused magnetism which somehow pervaded the whole house, as if Hartley were the house and as if I had been swept into a cavern where she embraced me and I could not touch her. Indeed the impossibility of touching her made my whole body shake with a kind of negative electricity. At the same time I was sickeningly conscious of the invisible husband. I had vividly imagined and reimagined beforehand the moment of arrival, ringing the bell, meeting Mr Fitch, and this had seemed in anticipation like a dive into the unknown, indeed into the irrevocable. Only now it was proving an agonizingly slow dive, as if the water towards which I was moving was receding, leaving me falling slowly through the air.

Hartley actually left me standing in the hall and went back into a room for a whispered consultation, almost closing the door. The hall was tiny. I was now conscious of an altar-like table with a rose bowl, and above it a large brown print of a mediaeval knight. Hartley emerged and threw open another door, ushering me into an empty room which proved to be the sitting room. She said, 'I'm so sorry, we're in the middle of our tea, we'll join you in a moment.' Then she left me again, closing the door.

I realized now how dangerously I had acted and how foolish I had been. Six o'clock for me meant drinks. I had imagined it would be a sensible and humane time to call. In fact I had interrupted their evening meal. To beguile the frightful interval I looked round the room. A large bow window with a big semicircular white-painted window ledge gave a partial view of the village and a full view of the harbour and the sea. A pair of expensive-looking field glasses lay on the ledge beside a massive bowl of roses. The sea was shining into the room like an enamelled mirror with its own especial clear light. This light excited and upset me, and dazzled me so that now I could scarcely see my surroundings. There was a thick carpet underfoot and the room was hot and stuffy and smelt excessively of roses.

Hartley came in followed by her husband. In my first dazzled view of him Fitch looked grossly boyish. He was rather short and thick-set and had a bullet-headed boy's look, with a thick neck and short mousy hair. He had very dark brown narrow eyes, a rather large clear-cut sensual mouth, and a prominent shiny nose with broad flaring nostrils. He was broad shouldered and powerful looking. If he was crippled it certainly did not show. He came in smiling. I beamed, blinking a little, and we spontaneously shook hands. 'Glad to meet you.' 'I hope you didn't mind my calling?' 'Not at all.'

Hartley, who had been wearing something blue, perhaps an overall, when she opened the door, was now revealed in a yellow cotton dress with a tight bodice and a big skirt. She moved nervously about, not looking at me. 'Oh dear, I must open a window. How stuffy this room is. Won't you sit down?'

I sat down in, or got stuck into, a tubby velvety low-slung armchair. Hartley said to Fitch, 'Shall we bring our meal in here?'

He said, 'Why not?'

Hartley went back into the kitchen where they had evidently been eating and returned with two plates, while Fitch pulled a gate-leg table out from the wall and set it up rather uncertainly upon the thick carpet. Hartley then handed the two plates to Fitch, who stood holding them while she fussed looking for table mats to put them on. The two plates, with their knives and forks upon them, were then put down, a plate of bread or something was fetched, upright chairs were pulled across the resistant carpet, and Hartley and Fitch sat down, their chairs half turned so as to accommodate me. They had been eating ham and salad, but it was now immediately clear that further eating had become impossible.

Hartley said to me, 'Would you like anything to eat?'

'Oh no thanks. I only called for a moment. I'm terribly sorry, I see I've interrupted your –'

'Not at all.'

Fitch said nothing but looked at me with his dark narrow eyes, flaring out his nostrils into two great holes. His big mouth in repose looked rather forbidding.

Surprise, or perhaps a flurried annoyance, seemed to have deprived them of the power of conversing, so I floundered quickly to get something going. I had decided to depart after the very briefest possible polite interchange.

'What a lovely view you have.'

'Yes, isn't it, we got the house for the view really.'

'My house just looks on the rocks and the sea. It's nice for swimming though. Do you swim much?'

"No, Ben can't swim.'

'I like your big window, you can see all round.'

'Yes, it's nice, isn't it.' She added, 'It's our dream house.'

'Have you got electricity?' asked Fitch, who had hitherto been silent.

I rated this as a definitely friendly remark. 'No. You have, haven't you, that must be a blessing. I get along with oil lamps and Calor gas.'

'Got a car?'

'No. Have you?'

'No. What brought you to this part of the world?'

'Well, no special reason, a friend of mine described it to me, she grew up near here, and I wanted to retire near the sea, and houses are cheaper here than –'

'They aren't all that cheap,' said Fitch.

All this while my visible surroundings were, now that I was accustomed to the light, imprinting themselves upon me with the sharpness and authority of a picture. I was conscious of my awkwardly outstretched legs, my still flushed face, my fast heartbeat, the stuffy rose-scented air to which the open window seemed to have made no difference, and the fact that I felt at a disadvantage in a low chair. I took in the brown and yellow floral design on the carpet, the light brown wallpaper, the shiny ochre tiles round the electric fire which was set in the wall. Two round brass bas-reliefs representing churches hung on either side of the fire. A funny-looking shaggy rug upon the carpet was making extra difficulties for one of the table legs. There was a large television set with more roses on top of it. No books. The room was very clean and tidy, so perhaps, except for watching television, life went on in the kitchen. The one sign of habitation was, on one of the chairs, a glossy mail order catalogue and an ashtray with a pipe in it.

At the table Hartley and Fitch were sitting stiff and upright, like a married pair rendered by a primitive painter. There was something especially primitive about the clear outlines and well-defined surfaces of

Fitch's eccentric and not altogether unpleasing face. Hartley's face was, perhaps just in my timid fugitive vision of it, hazier, restless, a soft moon of whiteness with hidden eyes. I was able to look only at her flowing yellow dress, round-necked, rather resembling a night-dress, and patterned all over with tiny brown flowers. Fitch was wearing a shabby light blue suit, jacket and trousers, with a thin brown stripe. Braces were visible through the unbuttoned jacket, which he had probably pulled on when I was announced. His blue shirt was clean. Hartley patted down, then plumped up, the waves of her grey hair. I felt sick with emotion and embarrassment and shame and a desire to get away and assess what all this was doing to me.

'Have you lived here long?'

'Two years,' said Fitch.

'Still settling in really,' said Hartley.

'We saw you on television,' said Fitch. 'Mary was thrilled, she remembered you.'

'Yes, of course, she remembered me from school, of course –'

'We don't know any celebrities, quite a thrill, eh?'

To get off this loathsome subject I said, 'Is your son still at school?'

'Our son?' said Fitch.

'No, he's left school,' said Hartley.

'He's adopted, you know,' said Fitch.

Earlier on they had been fiddling now and then with their forks, pretending to be about to eat. Now they had laid them down. They were looking, not at me, but at the carpet near my feet. Fitch shot an occasional glance at me. I decided it was time to go.

'Well, it's very kind of you to let me call. I must be off now. I'm so sorry I interrupted your – your meal. I do hope you'll come over and visit me soon. Are you on the telephone?'

'Yes, but it's out of order,' said Fitch.

Hartley had risen hastily. I got up and tripped over the shaggy rug. 'What a nice rug.'

'Yes,' said Hartley, 'it's a rag rug.'

'A —?'

'A rag rug. Ben makes them.' She opened the sitting-room door.

Fitch got up more slowly and as he now moved, standing aside to wave me out of the room, I saw that he limped. He said, 'You go first, I've got a gammy leg. Old war wound.'

I said, as I went through the dim hall towards the glaring brightness of the oval glass on the door, 'Well, we must be in touch, mustn't we, I do hope you'll both come over and have a drink and see my funny house and —'

Hartley swung the front door open.

'Goodbye, thanks for calling,' said Fitch.

I was on the red-tiled path and the door had closed. As soon as I was out of sight I began to run. I reached the village street panting and began to walk more slowly along the footpath which led to the coast road. As I walked I began to have a weird uncomfortable sensation in my back which, amid all the wild emotions and sensations which were rushing about inside me, I could identify as the sensation of being observed. I was about to turn round when it came to me that I was now well inside the span of the Nibletts view and within range of Fitch's powerful field glasses, should he care to sit on the window ledge and check on my departure. Parts of the village street were plainly visible from Nibletts, though the church and the churchyard were hidden by trees. So was that the explanation of Hartley's uneasiness, her thought that perhaps Fitch had actually seen me meet her and lead her away towards the church? She had, I remembered, walked behind me, not with me. How odd it must have looked though, with me as a crazed Orpheus and her as a dazed Eurydice. Yet why should she be afraid of being seen to meet somebody, even me, in the street? Resisting the present temptation to look back I walked smartly on and was soon among the stunted trees and gorse bushes and rocky outcrops near to the road, and out of sight from the hill. It was still very hot. I pulled off my jacket. It was soaked under the arms with dark stains of anxious perspiration and the dye had stained my shirt.

I then began to wonder many things, some very immediate, others vastly remote and metaphysical. First there was the question I had so belatedly asked myself when I was ringing the bell. Evidently Hartley had told her husband that she knew me, but when and how, and indeed why, had she told him? Years and years ago when she first met him? After they got married? When they 'saw me on telly'? Or even, when she got home this morning from our meeting in the street? 'Oh, I just met someone I used to know, such a surprise.' And she might then recall their having seen me on television. But no, this was too elaborate. She must have told him much earlier, after all why on earth not: did I *want* her to have kept me a secret? As indeed I had so devotedly kept her a secret ... Why had I done so? Because she was something holy which almost any speech would profane. In so far as I had ever mentioned Hartley to anyone I had always regretted it. No one understood, no one could understand. Better the austere sterility of silence. One of the horrors of marriage is that the partners are supposed to tell each other everything. 'It's him.' They had obviously been talking about me today. I just hated the idea that, through all those years, they could have chatted about me, dismissed me, demeaned it all, chewed it all up into some sort of digestible matrimonial pabulum. 'Your schoolboy admirer has done well for himself!' Fitch called her 'Mary'. Well, that was her name too. But 'Hartley' was her real name. In choosing to abandon it had she deliberately abandoned her past?

When I got home, although it was still very light outside, the house seemed dark and by contrast with the sunshine, cool and damp. I poured myself some sherry and bitters and took it out onto my little rock-surrounded lawn at the back and sat on the rug which I had placed upon the rock seat beside the trough where I put the stones. But it was at once intolerable not to see the water, so I climbed up a bit, gingerly holding my glass, and sat on top of a rock. The sea was now a bluish purple, the colour of Hartley's eyes. Oh God, what was I to make of it all? Whatever happened I must try not to suffer. But in order for me not to suffer two incompatible states of affairs had to exist: I had to achieve a steady permanent and somehow close relationship with Hartley, and I had to avoid entering a hell of jealousy. Also of course I must not disturb her marriage. And yet why 'of course'... ?

No, no, I could not, would not think of disturbing her marriage. It would be unthinkably immoral to try, and there was no reason to imagine that I would necessarily succeed if I did try! That way madness lay. I did not, looking at that pair, imagine that the glamour of a 'celebrity' would be much to conjure with. This made me think of how Hartley *looked*, that slightly vague fey look she had always had of looking past one. I had sometimes allowed myself the luxury of brooding upon her remorse. Perhaps she had felt remorse. But now – the person I had loved, and loved now, was not likely to be stupidly dazzled by a 'reputation'. So if I was searching for cracks in the fabric ... Well of course I was not doing that, I was just trying to understand. I could make little, on reflection, of *le mari*. I had expected, I now realized, an insignificant little man. I had doubtless required and wanted an insignificant little man. But Fitch was somehow, I could not quite think why, not insignificant. What *was* he like? What went on inside the sealed container of this marriage? And would I ever know? I could not help at least feeling rather pleased that Titus was adopted.

All this led me back to the now somehow central question: *is she happy?* Of course I knew enough about the mystery of marriage to be aware that this may be a frivolous question to ask about a married person. People may be settled into ways of life which preclude continued happiness, but which are satisfactory and far to be preferred to alternatives. A small number of married couples are increasingly pleased with each other and radiate happiness. Sidney and Rosemary Ashe radiated happiness. There was certainly no such radiation up at Nibletts; though of course I must take into account the unease caused by my sudden appearance. There had been an awkwardness the cause of which was obscure. And surely, if they *had* been very happy together, they would both instinctively have wanted to *show off* this happiness to the intruding outsider? A happy couple cannot help showing off. Sidney and Rosemary did it all the time. So did Victor and Julia. And yet this was inconclusive. What was plain, and this indeed was the thought which prevented the awful pain from beginning, was that I must soon see Hartley again, alone if possible, and get some clearer picture of the situation.

As the sun began to go down and the sea was turning gold under a very pale green sky I laid my empty glass in a cranny and crawled up to a higher rock from which I could get a view of the whole expanse of water. In the lurid yet uncertain light I found that I was now suddenly scanning the scene and watching it intently. What was I looking for? I was looking for that sea monster.

The next day before nine o'clock I was entering the church. I had reached it by a roundabout route, first climbing over the rocks on the other side of the road, then veering away through the gorse in the direction of the Raven Hotel, crossing the bog on the seaward side of Amorne Farm, going through three fields and three prickly hedges, and approaching Narrowdean from inland along the main road. By this method I did not at any point enter the Nibletts 'view'. I tried not to feel sure that Hartley would come to the church; in any case I decided that it was the only place where it was worth keeping a vigil, since it was more unlikely that she would walk out to Shruff End. Of course there was no one there, although someone had been in since yesterday and had put upon the altar a vast odorous bowl of white roses which disturbed me with all sorts of deep incoherent unconceptualized apprehensions. Time had suffered a profound disturbance, and I could feel all sorts of dark debris from the far past shifting and beginning to move up towards the surface. I sat feeling sick and reading the Ten Commandments which were almost illegibly inscribed upon a brown board behind the roses, and trying not to pay any special attention to the tenth and seventh and trying not at every moment to expect Hartley. The bright sun was blazing in through the tall rounded leaded faintly-greenish glass windows of the church and making the big room, for that after all was all that it was, feel weird and uneasy. There was a good deal of dust about, moving idly and airily in the sunlight, and the smell of the roses mingled with the dust and with some old musty woody smell, and the place seemed unused and very empty and a little mad. It seemed a suitable spot for a strange momentous interview. I felt frightened. Was I frightened of Fitch?

I waited in the church for more than an hour. I walked up and down. I read all the memorial tablets carefully. I smelt the roses. I read pieces of the horrible new prayer book (no wonder the churches are empty). I inspected the embroidered hassocks wrought by the local ladies. I climbed onto the pews and looked out of the windows. I thought of poor Dummy lying out there in the churchyard, scarcely more speechless now than he ever was. At about twenty past ten I decided that I had to get out into the air. It was all a great mistake, hiding in the church when Hartley might be walking openly about the streets. I wanted to see her so much that I was nearly moaning aloud. I ran out and went down through the iron gate and sat on a seat where I could see quite a lot of the little 'high street', but without being visible from the hillside. After a few minutes I saw a woman who looked like Hartley creeping along by the wall on the far side of the street, going in the direction of the shop. I say 'creeping along' because that was part of my first vision of her as an old woman, before I knew who she was, and it was this 'old woman' image that I was seeing now. I jumped up and set off after her. As she crossed the road she turned slightly and saw me and increased her pace. It was Hartley all right and she was running away from me! She did not go into the shop, but whisked round into what I called Fishermen's Stores Street. When I reached the corner running, she was nowhere to be seen. I went into the Fishermen's Stores, but she was not there. I wanted to howl with exasperation. I ran along to the end of the street where it petered out in a few derelict cottages and a five-barred gate and a large meadow fringed by trees. She could not have crossed that meadow. Had she gone into one of the houses? I ran back; then I saw a little alleyway leading off the street, a narrow sunless fissure between the blank sides of two houses. I ran down it, stumbled over a strewing of pebbles, and turned a sharp corner into a square enclosed space between the low whitewashed walls of backyards, where there were a number of overflowing dustbins and old cardboard boxes and an abandoned bicycle. And there, standing quite still in the middle of this scene, was Hartley. She was standing just behind a low outcrop of the sparkling yellow rock which surrounded my house. She looked at me out of a sort of resigned trance-like calm, staring and unsmiling, and yet I could see that inwardly she was trembling like a quarry. The dark shadow of a wall fell across the yard, dividing the rock and somehow composing the picture, covering Hartley's feet as she stood there holding a basket and her handbag. She was wearing a blue cotton dress today with a closely packed design of white daisies, and a loose baggy brown cardigan over it, although the day was already hot.

I ran up to her and seized hold not of her arm but of the handle of her shopping basket. This chase, this catch, had frightened us both. 'Oh Hartley, don't do it, don't run away from me, it's mad, thank God I found you, if I hadn't I'd have gone crazy! I must talk to you. Come to the church, please.'

I pulled at the handle of the basket and she walked in front of me down the narrow alley.

'You go to the church. I'll follow you after I've shopped. Yes, I promise.'

I went back to the church. After that chase, after that awful enclosed space with the dustbins and the rock and the bicycle, I too was trembling. She came in ten minutes. I went to take her heavy basket from her. I simply did not know how to behave to her, there was some profound awful barrier of what I felt as embarrassment, though it was also dread. If only some touch of grace could turn all this pain into communication and the gestures of love. But grace in every sense was lacking. I felt now a frantic desire to touch her, to hold her, but I could think of no way of achieving this, as if it would have been an amazing physical feat. We sat down where we had sat before, she in the pew in front, turning round to me.

'Why did you *hide*? I can't bear this. We must – we must somehow get a *grip* on this situation – I shall go mad –'

'Charles, please don't be so – and please don't call round unexpectedly like that –'

'I'm sorry – but I've got to see you – I still care about you. What do you expect me to do? At least we've got to be friends, now we've got this chance to – this chance – Of course I won't do anything you don't want – Please – look, couldn't you and your husband come round and see me, come round for drinks tomorrow at six, well at five, at seven, any time that suits you. Come to funny old Shruff End, I want you to see the house. Why not?'

Hartley was hunched up, her head shrunk into her neck, the rumpled collar of her blue dress cupping her hair. She was looking down, almost hidden by the pew. 'Please don't expect anything of us, I mean don't call on us or ask us to – we don't go to parties –'

'It's not a party!'

'It's not necessary for us to be like that just because – And please don't run after me in the street, people will notice.'

'But you ran away from me, you hid –'

'Where we live people don't sort of entertain because they're neighbours, they keep themselves to themselves.'

'But you already know me! And there needn't be any "entertaining" if you mean ridiculous formalities, I hate that anyway. Hartley, I won't put up with this. Can't you just *explain*?'

Hartley now looked at me properly. I noticed that today she was wearing no lipstick, and this helped me to read her, to read her young look into her old look. Her tired pale wrinkled soft round face now looked very sad, with a kind of resigned sadness, as I had never seen it then, even when she was leaving me. But her sadness was resolute, almost wary, and she was entirely attentive, the vivid eyes no longer vague. She revealed her red slightly swollen hands, and clawed ineffectually at her rumpled collar.

'What is there to explain, why should I –?'

'You mean I'm not behaving like a gentleman?'

'No, no – Look, I must go to the hairdressing lady.'

'I behaved like a gentleman then and look where it got me! I never pressed you. I believed you when you said you'd marry me. I loved you. I love you. All right, you said then that you couldn't trust me, you thought I'd be unfaithful and so on, oh God! Perhaps you feel something like that, that you couldn't trust me now – But believe me, there are no women, no one with me, I'm alone, really alone. I want you to know that.'

'There's no need to say, it doesn't matter –'

'Yes, don't misunderstand me. I just want you to know it's simply me, and I'm like I always was, so there's nothing to worry about.'

'I must go to the hairdresser.'

'Hartley, *please* – Oh all right, why indeed should you explain? Do you want me to go away now and never try to see you again?'

Of course I did not intend her to say yes, and she did not.

'No, I don't want that. I don't know what I want.'

The desolate sound of this, the sound of need at last, made me feel much happier and much more clear-headed. 'Hartley darling, you've got to talk to me, you know you have. After all there's so much to talk about, isn't there? I won't do you any harm. My love for you then was mixed up, with all sorts of conflicts which don't exist now, so it can all be better and we've sort of got it back again after all. Don't you see? We can be real friends. And I do want to get to know your husband.' I then felt bound to add, 'I did like him so much, by the way.' This rang false. Hartley had hunched herself up again behind the pew. 'Anyway we must talk. There's so much I want to tell you before it's too late. And I want to ask you hundreds of questions. I don't mean about what happened then. I mean about you and how you've lived and about – oh – Titus. I'd love to meet him. Perhaps I could help him.'

'*Help* him?'

'Yes, why not? Financially for instance, or – I know a lot about the world, Hartley – about some worlds, anyway. What does he want to do, what is he studying?'

Hartley gave a deep sigh, and then rubbed her cheeks with her red hands. She produced her handkerchief, still stained with lipstick. Tears had risen into her eyes.

'Hartley – dear –'

'He's gone, he ran away, he's lost, we don't know where he is. We haven't heard anything from him for nearly two years. He's gone away.'

'Oh God –' So cunning and vile is the human soul that I felt instantly glad that Hartley had this understandable cause of grief and had told me about it and was weeping about it in my presence. Suddenly there was sympathy, communication.

'I'm so sorry. But can't he be found, have you told the police? There are ways of finding people. I could help there.'

Hartley mopped her face, then took a mirror and powder compact out of her bag and dabbed powder round her eyes. I had seen so many women powder their faces. I was seeing Hartley perform this little ritual of vanity for the first time. She said, 'You can't help and please don't try to. Better to leave us alone and –'

'Hartley, I'm not going to leave you alone, so you must make up your mind to that and invent some humane way of dealing with me! Are you just afraid of falling in love with me again, is that it?'

She stood up, lifted her shopping basket, which was beside me, and dropped her handbag into it. I came round into her pew and put my arms firmly round her shoulders. It still felt like doing the impossible. For a moment she bowed her head and rolled her brow quickly to and fro against my shirt, and I felt the blazing warmth of her flesh against mine. Then she pushed past me and began to walk to the door. I followed.

'When shall I see you?'

'Please don't, you'll worry us, and please don't write.'

'Hartley, what is it? Let go. Let yourself love me a bit, there'll be no harm. Or do you think I'm such a grandee? I'm not, you know. I'm just your oldest friend.'

'Don't do anything, I'll write to you, later.'

'You *promise*?'

'Yes. I'll write. Only don't come.'

'Won't you explain?'

'There's nothing to explain. Stay here please.' And she went away.

Dearest Lizzie, I have been reflecting on what you said in your sweet and wise letter, and what you said also when we met at the tower. I have to ask your pardon. I think perhaps that you are right after all. I love you, but it may be that my rather (as you say) 'abstract' idea of our being together is not, for either of us, the best expression of that love. We might just create confusion and unhappiness for both. Your 'suspicions' of me may indeed be just, and you are not the first one to express such doubts! Perhaps I am by now too much of a restless Don Juan. So let us play it differently. This is not necessarily a sad conclusion, and we must both be realistic, especially as someone else's happiness is also at stake. I was very touched and impressed by the spectacle of your relationship with Gilbert. It is an achievement and must of course be respected. What does it matter what people exactly 'are' to each other, so long as they love and cherish each other and are *true* to each other? You were so right to emphasize that word. You doubted my capacity to be loyal and I am near enough to sharing your doubts to be anxious for us not to take the risk. It is just as well that we never defined what we expected. We are both fortunate in being happy as we are, and we can simply count our old affectionate friendship, now so happily revived, as a bonus. We don't want, do we, any more anguish or muddle. You are quite right. I shall respect your wisdom and your wishes and the rights of my old friend Gilbert! It is, as you said, important that we all three like each other; and let us, as you urged, enjoy a free and unpossessive mutual affection. So please forget my original foolish letter, to which you so bravely and rationally responded, and also my somewhat bullying tactics at our last meeting! I am lucky to have friends such as you and Gilbert and I intend to treasure them in a sensible and I hope generous way. I shall look forward to seeing you soon in London where I shall be arriving shortly. I will let you know. Accept, both of you, my affectionate best wishes and, if I may belatedly offer them, my congratulations. Be well, little Lizzie, and remember me.

    Your old friend,
      Charles.

This was the letter, partly disingenuous, partly sincere, which I wrote to Lizzie on the afternoon of the day when I saw Hartley in the church for the second time. I returned home in a frenzy of misery and indecision, and after a while spent fruitlessly wondering what to do next, I decided that one sensible thing at least which I could do to pass the time would be to get rid of Lizzie. This involved no mental struggle and no problem except the labour of writing a suitable letter and concentrating upon Lizzie long enough to complete it. How totally in every atom I had been changed was shown by the fact that my 'idea' about Lizzie now seemed to me an insane fancy from whose consequences I had been mercifully saved by Lizzie's own common sense; and for this I blessed her. A flame had licked out of the past and burnt up that structure of intentions completely. What had been made clear in the last two days (which seemed like months) was how far I had been right in thinking that there was only one real love in my life. It was as if I had in some spiritual sense actually married Hartley long ago and was simply not free to look elsewhere. Of course I had really known this all along. But on seeing her again the sense of absolute belongingness had been overwhelming; in the teeth of our fates' most exquisite cruelty, in the teeth of all the evidence, we belonged to each other.

I did in fact manage to think quite intensely about Lizzie while I was writing the letter, and to think of her with a kind of generous resigned affection. I saw her laughing radiant face as it had been when she was younger, when we used to laugh so much about her loving me. In spite of the incredible *gaucherie* of my 'idea' it was possible that I had, quite accidentally, acquired Lizzie as a friend whose affection and loyalty might even one day be of value. But now the decks must be cleared. There must be absolutely no problem, no 'interesting connection' involving discussions or letters or visits. I had no time and no strength for any such muddle and it would be criminal to risk one. My hint about coming to London was of course simply a ploy to keep Lizzie there. I could not have endured the arrival of an emotional Lizzie on my doorstep now. There had been a slaughter of all my other interests, and upon the strange white open scene of the future only one thing remained. So let little Lizzie remain safely in storage with Gilbert; I could now even feel benevolent towards him. Was this new detached generosity, I wondered in passing, a first symptom of that changed and purified form of being which the return of Hartley was going to create in me? Was Hartley, seen not touched, loved not possessed, destined to make me a saint? How strange and significant that I had come precisely *here* to repent of my egoism! Was this perhaps the final sense of my mystical marriage with my only love? It was an extreme idea, but it had its own deep logic, and flourished somewhat upon the absence of alternatives. There was, for me, surely no other move?

I was of course aware that one point of the 'extreme idea' was that it consoled me with an offer of happiness, though of an extremely refined and attenuated sort. Other prospects, more closely related to the horror of recent events, were less vague and less pleasing; and I had an urgent dark desire to *act* which was not illumined by my aspirations to sanctity. But what could I do? Start looking for Titus? My central question at least was now answered: Hartley was unhappy. But this brought forward a further central question. *Why was she unhappy?* Was it simply because her son had vanished or were there other reasons? Why would she not let me help her, why would she not let me *in*? Or was it naïve to expect confidences from a woman I had not seen for more than forty years? I had kept her being alive in me, but to her I might simply be a shadow, an almost forgotten schoolboy. I could not believe this. Was she perhaps on the contrary still so much in love with me that she dare not trust herself to see me? Did she imagine I had smart handsome mistresses of whom she would be miserably jealous? What had she been doing down on the sea road when Rosina's headlights suddenly revealed her to me? Had she come to spy, to find out?

She had promised to write, but would she write, and if she did would she 'explain'? Could I, was I capable of it, simply wait, and perhaps wait and wait, for that letter, and, obeying her, do nothing? I so intensely wanted to 'explain' myself, to pour out everything I felt and thought, and which in those miserable scrappy encounters I had not managed to say. Should I write her a long letter? If I did I would certainly not entrust it to the post. That brought me back again to *le mari*. Why was she unhappy? Was it because he was jealous, a tyrant, a bully, who never let anyone come near her? Was that it? And if so ... How my mind leapt forward at this thought, and how many lurid vistas and fiery hollows were suddenly opened up. At the same time

I knew that sanity, and a faithfulness to Hartley which must be kept untainted, forbade this kind of speculation.

I had no heart to cook lunch. I fried an egg but could not eat it. I drank some of the young Beaujolais which had been delivered from the Raven Hotel. (I found the wine, Beaujolais and some Spanish stuff, outside the door when I got back from the village.) Then I occupied myself by writing the letter to Lizzie which I have copied out above. After that I thought it might do my soul some good if I went swimming. The tide was in and the sea was very calm, and clearer than usual. Looking down from my cliff before I dived in I could see tall dark trees of seaweed gently waving and fishes swimming between them. I swam about quietly, looking at that special 'swimmer's view' of the sea, and feeling, for the time, possessing and possessed. The sea was a glassy slightly heaving plain, moving slowly past me, and as if it were shrugging reflectively as it absent-mindedly supported its devotee. Some large seagulls with the yellowest conceivable beaks gathered to watch me. I felt no anxiety about getting out, and when I swam back to my cliff face I was able quite easily to cling on to my handholds and footholds and pull myself up out of the water. In fact the little cliff is not in itself very hard to climb, it is just that, as I explained, if one is being constantly lifted up and abruptly dropped again by the movement of the waves, it is impossible to keep one's fingers and toes in place long enough to get a proper grip. When I was in the sea I thought to myself how little it mattered to me that Hartley was no longer beautiful. This seemed a good thought and I held on to it and it brought me, together with tenderness, a little calm.

After that I stupidly sat in the sun but it was too hot and my immersion had after all brought me little wisdom. Perhaps I had not been wrong in thinking of the sea as a source of peace, but it was an ineffective medicine thus taken in a gulp. It required a regime. I walked about, scorching my feet and looking into one or two of my pools but the pleasure had departed and I could no longer concentrate upon those brilliant lucid little civilizations, although in the strong light the coloured pebbles and the miniature seaweed trees looked like jewels by Fabergé. I watched a dance of prawns and the progress of a green transparent sea-slug, and saw again the long coiling red worm which had somehow reminded me of my sea serpent. Then I noticed to my annoyance some tourists from, I suppose, the Raven Hotel who were actually standing on my land and inspecting the tower. I went into the house with burning shoulders and a splitting headache.

It was now obvious that I would soon have to do something, to perform some ritual act which would relate to my situation and perhaps alter it. What I wanted to do, of course, was to run straight to Hartley. I had not even kissed her yet. How timid and feeble I had been this morning in the church. But I would have 'ingeniously' to find some substitute for this headlong rush. Like the deprived addict I found ordinary diversions useless. Everything I did now had to relate to the one world-centre. I decided, just in order to keep moving, to walk down to the village and post the letter to Lizzie. Of course I hoped to see Hartley, but I did not really imagine that I would. It was now late afternoon, the kind of vivid light which would have made me want to shout with joy a little while ago. When I had crossed the causeway I saw some letters lying in my dog kennel and I picked them up. One of them was from Lizzie. I tore it open and read it as I walked along.

My darling, of course the answer will have to be yes. My fears were foolish and unworthy, please forgive my confused response to your wonderful offer. I am your page, as I always was, and shall I not come to you if, even for a moment, you need me? I haven't said anything to Gilbert yet and I don't know how to.

When we meet will you please be gentle and help me about this? I can't just abandon him. There must be some way of not hurting him too much. Please understand. And let me see you *soon,* I want to say so many things. Shall I come to you, or will you be in London? I wish I could telephone you. (Don't ring here because of Gilbert.) By the way, I told Gilbert I was writing to you because he asked, and he says will you have dinner with us here Monday of next week if you're in town? I pass this on, but I imagine in the circumstances you won't want to.

    I love you so much.

      Lizzie.

    I am so frightened that you are angry with me. Please reassure me soon.

I sighed over this rather shifty missive, which gave me so little pleasure. What was this 'offer' I was supposed to have made her? She almost made it seem as if she was endeavouring to oblige me. I noted that she had not yet told Gilbert, and showed no signs of leaving him. But I felt no urge to reflect upon the state of Lizzie's mind, it did not matter now.

I hastened my steps and reached the Post Office just before it closed. I posted my letter to Lizzie and sent her a telegram which ran as follows. *Your first idea was right. See my letter which crossed with yours. In London soon and gratefully accept dine you and Gilbert. Love Charles.* That should make the situation sufficiently clear and also keep Lizzie in London. I had of course no intention of dining with them, and would send a cancellation at the last moment.

I emerged into the street where it was still sunny, and the evening light was making even the slates on the roofs cast little shadows, and the whitewashed walls were silver-gilt. I walked up to the church and looked inside. It was empty and already in shadow and full of the smell of the roses which were a white blur in the hazy dusty air. I came out into the light and spent some time looking at the various sailing ships on the tombstones which the slanting illumination had brought out in strong relief; walking back down the street it occurred to me that the Black Lion was open and I went in. There was the usual sudden hush.

'Seen any more ghosts?' said Arkwright, as he served me with cider.

'No.'

'Wasn't you asking about big eels,' said someone else, 'seen any?'

'No.'

'Seen any seals?'

'No.'

'He ain't seen nothing.'

A titter.

I was feeling hungry, so I ate a cheese sandwich and a horrible pork pie. I sat for a while and looked at the rest of my mail. I did not care a fig for the company and I did not mind if they knew it. The letters, sent on by Miss Kaufman, were all personal but of little interest. They included one which would formerly have pleased me from Sidney Ashe describing comical goings-on in Stratford, Ontario. There was also one from my physicist friend (previously mentioned I think) Victor Banstead of Cambridge. I crumpled all the letters up, including Lizzie's, and dropped them into a nearby basket, and then had to scrabble in it, under the amused gaze of the company, to get them out again. I crammed them in my pocket and said goodnight. No one answered. Once I had closed the door there was prolonged laughter.

I did not take the diagonal footpath but followed the road which led straight on towards the harbour. Once I was clear of the village I stopped and looked up at the hillside. The sun was low and a few lighted windows already shone here and there, weirdly pale. I am very long-sighted, and although I had needed my pince-nez to read the letters, I could see the bungalows quite clearly. There seemed to be a faint light in the sitting room at Nibletts. Supper would be over and they would be watching television. In silence? It occurred to me: I could not conceive of married life. How was such a state of affairs possible? I felt a very strong desire to go up the hill and knock on the door. Supposing I arrived with a bottle of champagne ... ? But I had now invented a device for getting through the next hours. There might very well be a letter from Hartley tomorrow morning. And if by any chance there was not ... I would ... decide what to do. Then I wondered, in that little house, how, where can she write a private letter? In the bathroom? He must go away sometimes. Would it *be* a private letter? Marriage was indeed a mystery.

I walked on down to the harbour where the calm, calm sea was just audibly lapping. The harbour was empty and quiet and darkish within the firm arm of its stone quay which seemed to be exuding the thick powdery light. As I loitered I could feel the warmth of the stone under my feet. A cormorant passed by, low over the waves, a black cross-shaped portent. Now there was a big pale crumbly moon and a brilliant evening star. Just beyond, in the ladies' bathing place, two boys were playing on the dark seaweed, but silently as if magicked by the hour. I walked slowly along the coast road in the direction of Shruff End, then on past it, and spent some time looking at Raven Bay with the hotel lights reflected in the water. The evening star changed from gold to silver and the moon diminished and gained a hard-edged brilliance. I walked back at last and as I turned onto the causeway I saw a curious flicker within the house as if a light were moving. I stopped and watched. There was a momentary clear flicker which ducked and then became hazy behind one of the front windows, then vanished. Someone inside was walking about carrying a candle. My first thought was that it was

Hartley. Then I thought it was more likely to be Rosina. I walked back along the road and sure enough, hidden behind the projecting rock where it had been before, was her horrible little red car.

I felt such intense annoyance that I actually kicked one of the wheels. I decided that I could not bear to see Rosina. Her unspeakable presence in my house was a sacrilege. The sight of her impertinent face would provoke me to unreasoning anger. The horror and vulgarity of a quarrel would be unbearable; and there would be no getting rid of her. I glided with long tip-toe strides along the causeway and round the side of the house onto the lawn. I could now see into the kitchen. Yes, there was Rosina, with two lighted candles on the kitchen table, trying unsuccessfully to light one of my lamps, and probably ruining the wick in the process. I saw her intent cross-eyed stare and the bad-tempered movements of her mouth as she twiddled the wick roughly up and down and poked it with the lighted match. The lamp flared up, then went out. She was wearing something black, with a white shirt, and her dark hair, which was hanging loose, was swinging almost into the candle flame. I receded quietly, picking up as I did so the rugs and cushions which were lying on the grass. It was just as well I had eaten something in the pub, otherwise hunger would have driven me into the house. I clambered over the rocks until the house was invisible and found, very close to the sea and just above it, a long shallow depression where I had sunbathed once or twice in the prehistoric days. The night was very warm, very still, and as I put my glasses in a place of safety and composed myself for sleep I wondered sadly why it had never occurred to me to sleep out here in the days when I was happy. It was so close to the sea which was gently slapping the rock just below, it was like being in a boat. And as my rocky bed sloped a little down towards the water, I could lie with my head on a cushion, looking straight out at the horizon, where the moon was making an almost but not quite motionless rift of silver. The first stars were already sharp and bright. More stars were coming, more, more. Lying on my back, wrapped in my rug, my hands clasped in front of me, I prayed that all might be well between me and Hartley, that somehow that lifelong faithful remembering, what I now thought of as my mystical marriage, might not be lost or wasted, but somehow come to good! And then, as if the spirit that I prayed to had admonished me in reply, I tried to put myself out of the picture and to pray only for Hartley: that she might be happy, that Titus might come home, that her husband might love her and she him. This was more difficult. In fact it was so difficult that the temptation of which I had been aware earlier, and which I had so firmly driven away, began to creep in again from the side, however hard I tried to think only good thoughts. Is her husband, Fitch, Ben, whatever his name is, a jealous tyrant, is he the cause of her unhappiness? If so then perhaps ...? I decided at last that if there was no letter from Hartley in the morning I would call at the bungalow and damn the consequences. Because ... I had to know ... the answer ... to that question.

Then I found that I was not thinking about Hartley any more, but about my mother. I saw her face covered with wrinkles of anxiety and disapproval and love. Then I was seeing Aunt Estelle, wearing a little round straw hat, sitting at the wheel of the white Rolls-Royce. I know that it excited my father to see her drive that big car. It excited Uncle Abel. It excited me. Aunt Estelle wearing a broad band round her head like a 'fillet', which we used to make such silly jokes about at school when we were translating Latin. She played tennis so well. They had a hard court at Ramsdens. How was it that she resembled James, she so pretty, so gay, he with his silences and his occluded lowering face? Some gauzy mask of similarity had been put over his head, like the Hartley-mask that so many women had worn for me through the years, even that funny old woman in the village who was so unlike her. But had I forgotten already, that funny old woman *was* Hartley! Then was James really Aunt Estelle? Now Aunt Estelle was dancing on a dark rotating gramophone record, dancing in the middle where the label was, and somehow she was the label, a face, with torn paper, torn paper, turning and turning with the record. And all this time I was keeping my eyes open, or trying to, only they kept closing, because I wanted to go on watching the stars, where the most extraordinary things were happening. A bright satellite, a man-made star, very slowly and somehow carefully crossed the sky in a great arc, from one side to the other, a close arc, one knew it was not far away, a friendly satellite slowly going about its business round and round the globe. And then, much much farther away, stars were quietly shooting and tumbling and disappearing, silently falling and being extinguished, lost utterly silent falling stars, falling from nowhere to nowhere into an unimaginable extinction. How many of them there were, as if the heavens were crumbling at last and being dismantled. And I wanted to show all these things to my father.

Later I knew that I had been asleep and I opened my eyes with wonder and the sky had utterly changed again and was no longer dark but bright, golden, gold-dust golden, as if curtain after curtain had been removed behind the stars I had seen before, and now I was looking into the vast interior of the universe, as if the universe were quietly turning itself inside out. Stars behind stars and stars behind stars behind stars until there was nothing between them, nothing beyond them, but dusty dim gold of stars and no space and no light but stars. The moon was gone. The water lapped higher, nearer, touching the rock so lightly it was audible only as a kind of vibration. The sea had fallen dark, in submission to the stars. And the stars seemed to move as if one could see the rotation of the heavens as a kind of vast crepitation, only now there were no more events, no shooting stars, no falling stars, which human senses could grasp or even conceive of. All was movement, all was change, and somehow this was visible and yet unimaginable. And I was no longer I but something pinned down as an atom, an atom of an atom, a necessary captive spectator, a tiny mirror into which it was all indifferently beamed, as it motionlessly seethed and boiled, gold behind gold behind gold.

Later still I awoke and it had all gone; and for a few moments I thought that I had seen all those stars only in a dream. There was a weird shocking sudden quiet, as at the cessation of a great symphony or of some immense prolonged indescribable din. Had the stars then been audible as well as visible and had I indeed heard the music of the spheres? The early dawn light hung over the rocks and over the sea, with an awful intent gripping silence, as if it had seized these faintly visible shapes and were very slowly drawing them out of a darkness in which they wanted to remain. Even the water was now totally silent, not a tap, not a vibration. The sky was a faintly lucid grey and the sea was a lightless grey, and the rocks were a dark fuzzy greyish brown. The sense of loneliness was far more intense than it had been under the stars. Then I had felt no fear. Now I felt fear. I discovered that I was feeling very stiff and rather cold. The rock beneath me was very hard and I felt bruised and aching. I was surprised to find my rugs and cushions were wet with dew. I got up stiffly and shook them. I looked around me. Mountainous piled-up rocks hid the house. And I saw myself as a dark figure in the midst of this empty awfully silent dawn, where light was scarcely yet light, and I was afraid of myself and quickly lay down again and settled my rug and closed my eyes, lying there stiffly and not imagining that I would sleep again.

But I did sleep and I dreamed that Hartley was a ballet dancer and was circling a huge stage *sur les points* dressed in a black tutu and a head-dress of sparkling diamonds and black feathers. Now and then she would leap, and I would say to myself, but she *stays* in the air, it's uncanny, it's

like levitation, she just *stays* there. And as I watched I said to myself in
a complacent way, isn't it wonderful that we're both so young and we
have all our lives before us. How can old people be happy? We're young
and we *know* that we're young, whereas most young people just take
it for granted. Then the stage was a forest and a prince also dressed
in black came and carried Hartley away, and her head hung back over
his shoulder as if her neck was broken. I stayed there still thinking,
how wonderful that I'm young; I had a bad dream and thought that I
was old. And I'm sure, I'm sure, that on the other side of those trees
there is a lake, or perhaps it is the sea. I woke up in the sunshine, and
whereas in my other wakings I had understood at once where I was,
this time I was very startled, and could still see Hartley's dead face,
her head hanging limply in that terrible way; and I felt a foreboding
and a horror which I had not felt in the dream. I pushed myself up
on my elbow and only gradually worked out why I was here, lying
on the rock, in the bright sunlight in front of a blue muttering sea. I
got up slowly, and then felt a pang of sadness as I remembered being
so pleased about being young in my dream. I looked at my watch. It
was six thirty. It was only then that I thought: if there is no letter this
morning I shall go to the bungalow. *That is settled.*

I felt very hungry. I wondered if Rosina had spent the night in the
house. I climbed over the rocks as far as the road and walked back
towards Shruff End. I looked into the rocky recess where she had left
her car. It was gone. I went on and across the causeway. Of course
there were no letters yet. When I got inside I made a thorough search
of the house. There were a lot of spent matches lying about, but my
bed showed no signs of having been slept in. I was glad about that. She
must have gone away late last night. She had opened a bottle of wine
and a tin of olives and had eaten some bread. She left no note, but
had left her mark by strewing the smashed remains of a rather pretty

teacup in the middle of the kitchen table. It could have been worse. I breakfasted, since I was so hungry, on tea and toast and the remainder of the olives. Then I just waited, and waited, and while I did so I tried to remember what I had felt when I looked at the stars, but already it was fading. Then I started making sorties to the dog kennel. About half past nine there were some letters, but none from Hartley. About ten I was walking around the village. At half past ten I was outside Nibletts.

I resisted the temptation to peer anxiously at the house as I walked up the path. I wanted to seem to blunder in, and the best way to do that was actually to blunder in. Down in the village I had felt sick with an anxious yearning sense of Hartley's proximity. Now the magnetism of her nearness produced a desperate audacity; I felt out of control, heavy, dangerous. I rang the sweet-sounding bell and its hollow angelic chime made a terrible vibration inside the house.

There was then a slight sound of scuffling, but no voices were audible. I realized that my head must be fuzzily visible through the frosted glass. Did they have many visitors?

Ben opened the door. He had by now become 'Ben' in my thoughts, so ardently had I been attempting to inhabit Hartley's mind. He was wearing a white cotton tee shirt which made him appear rather stout, and he looked unshaven. The parts of his face which were not grubbily bristled were greasy, and there were shiny lumps on his brow. As he tossed his head back with an animal gesture I saw the black interior of his wide nostrils.

I said, 'Good morning,' and smiled.

He said, 'What is it?' with an expression of surprise, genuine or assumed, which let him off smiling.

'Oh I was out for my morning constitutional and I thought I'd call. I felt it would be so nice to glimpse you and Hartley again, now we are neighbours. And I wanted to bring you something. May I come in for a moment?' I had planned this beforehand. I put my foot onto the step.

Ben glanced behind him; then he opened the door wider with one hand, while with the other he opened the door of one of the front rooms. Then he stood back with his arms extended so that he and the two doors made a screen or barrier to shepherd me harmlessly into the front room.

This was obviously the spare bedroom. It was rather small, containing a divan, a chair, a chest of drawers. Sunlight illumined bright red flowers upon the unlined curtains. The room smelt of furnishing fabric and furniture polish and dust and of not being used. The divan bed beneath a blue and white gingham cover had clearly not been made up. There was a framed colour photograph of a tabby cat. Ben came inside and shut the door and just for a second I felt afraid of him.

There was little space. He did not ask me to sit down, so we stood facing each other beside the divan. I had decided that to begin with I would keep on gaily chattering, and I had settled on an order of discourse which I hoped that I would now remember. There was much to be discovered, and perhaps a very short time to discover it in.

'How is Mary? I hope she is well?' I remembered to call her Mary. 'I hoped to catch a glimpse. I've got a little note here for you both.'

'She isn't here,' said Ben.

I felt sure this was a lie. 'Well, here it is, my little note.' I handed over a sealed envelope addressed to Mr and Mrs Fitch.

Ben took the envelope, gazed at it frowning, then gave me a blank stare. He said, 'Thank you,' and opened the door.

I said, 'Won't you read it please? It's just an invitation.' I smiled again.

Ben gave a sort of sigh of irritation and tore open the envelope. As he did so I saw over his shoulder through the open door that the door of the kitchen, which had been closed when I entered, was now ajar. The heavy smell of roses, dustier, more appallingly sad inside the house than outside, came through from the hall. I could see the 'altar' with the brown questing knight above it. Ben looked up, and closed the bedroom door again.

I said, waving my arm in an explanatory way towards the invitation, and trying with gestures of a simulated bonhomie to fill and dominate the little room and simulate a flow of mutual conversation, 'As you see, it's just a formal invitation, and, look, I've written on the back that I do so hope you and Mary will drop in. I've got one or two friends down from London,' this was untrue of course, but I thought it might sound less significantly alarming than a proposed *à trois,* 'and I wondered if you and your wife would be so good as to toddle over to Shruff End and have a drink on Friday, it's quite informal, no need to dress or anything, and you needn't stay long.' As this did not sound quite polite and as Ben was still frowning at the card, deciphering my kind message on the back, I added, 'Or of course if you would prefer it you could come over just the two of you on Thursday or Saturday or any time really, I'm not tied up. I do hope you will. Your house is so charming, so well done, I'm sure you could advise me about mine – I so wanted to ask you about various things – the village and – the locality and –'

'I don't think we can come,' said Ben. He added, 'I'm sorry.'

'Ah well, if you can't manage anything just now, I expect you're busy and it's not convenient, we could fix something a little later, perhaps, I could drop in next week, I often pass this way. I used to be such a busy person and now I have all the time in the world, do you find that now you've retired? Of course it's marvellous and one's so lucky, especially living in a place like this. Yes, I do like your house. Is that your pussy cat, isn't he charming?' I gestured towards the colour photograph of the cat which was hanging over the bed.

Ben turned towards the photo and for a second his brow and his mouth relaxed and his eyes lightened and widened. 'Yes. That's Tamburlaine. We called him Tambi. He's dead now.'

'What a splendid name. It's so important what you call a cat. Tabbies are top cats, don't you think? I've always been such a rolling stone I've never been able to keep an animal, such a pity. Have you got a cat now?'

Ben threw the invitation card and the crumpled envelope onto the bed. The brusque movement put an end to my chatter. He stood for a moment opening his mouth and showing his uneven teeth in some kind of indecision. He ruffled up his short thick mousy hair. He said, 'Listen.' There was a pause, he gulped breathlessly and my own breath was suspended. We stood together bulkily in the little room, I leaning a little over him. 'Listen, it's not on, sorry, we don't want to know you. Sorry to put it like that but you won't seem to take a hint. I mean, there's no point, is there. All right, you knew Mary a long time ago, but a long time ago is a long time ago. She doesn't want to know you now, and I don't want to start, see. You don't have to see people now because you saw them once or went to school with them or what. Things change and people have their own worlds and their own places. We aren't your sort, well, that's obvious, isn't it. We don't want to come to your parties and meet your friends and drink your drinks, it's not on. And we don't want you barging in here at all hours of the day either, sorry if this sounds rude, but it's better to get it understood once and for all. I don't know how you live with your friends in your world, but we don't live like that, we're quiet folk and we keep ourselves to ourselves. See? So as far as this stuff about "old school friends" or whatever goes, forget it. Of course we'll pass the time of day with you if we see you in the village, but we don't want to be on visiting terms, that's not our kind of thing. So – thank you for your invitation – but, well, there we are.' Here he fumbled loudly with the door handle, presumably to warn Hartley to be out of the way.

As he spoke, and as I listened to him, I had been looking down at the narrow scantily covered divan. That was certainly not Ben's bed; so they slept together. I listened to his rigmarole almost without any surprise, almost as if it were a cassette which I myself had invented. I felt at the same time angry, confused, and tormented by the certainty that Hartley was in the house, silent, hiding from me. *Why?*

One thing I had firmly decided beforehand was that however Ben reacted I was not going to lose my temper or display any emotion. It was certainly at this moment not easy to retain my mask of urbanity. Ben, after his speech, was standing stiffly, wrought up by his own words, frowning as if puzzled and staring at the photo of the cat. He had not raised his voice, indeed he had spoken in rather low though emphatic tones, and he had not yet opened the door. Doubtless he wanted, when he did so, to be sure of making a quick job of getting me out of the house.

I felt my accursed tendency to blush betraying me. My face and neck had changed colour, my cheeks were blazing. I said as coolly and airily as I could, 'Well, all right, but I hope you'll think it over. After all we are neighbours. And if you think I'm some sort of jet set grandee or something you're quite wrong. I'm a very simple person, as I hope you'll discover. I'll write to you again later on. I wonder if I could see Mary just for a moment before I go?'

'She isn't here.'

'I expect she's out shopping. Maybe she'll be back soon? I'd love to see her.'

'She isn't here!' Ben picked up the envelope and the invitation card from the bed and hurled them onto the floor. Then he threw the door wide open with a crash.

He was standing between me and the door, and there was an awkward moment. He backed a little and I made a concessive flourishing gesture with my hand, instinctively designed to dissipate the sudden aura of violence. I got past him into the hall and began to fumble with the front door. Ben, who had immediately followed me, began to open the door and our hands touched. I then had to sidestep again to get out of the house. I was not able to look back towards the kitchen, and was in any case blind with emotion. I saw with terrible clarity the glaring scarlet and orange of some extremely large roses growing beside the path. The door banged. I fumbled hastily with the complicated fastening of the gate and managed to get out onto the pavement. I walked fast down the hill. I did not run. I began to walk more slowly, more slowly, and by the time I reached the village I was strolling. Acute feelings of anger, fear and a sort of boiling shame gradually subsided. Had I scuttled out like a frightened dog? I decided that the answer to that question did not matter. I touched my burning cheeks and cooled them with the back of my hand.

And as the violent feelings became calmer another emotion, darker, deeper, came slowly up from below. Or rather there were two emotions closely, blackly, coiled together. I felt a piercing pain connected with the vision of that mean flimsily covered divan and with the inference that ... Hartley ... slept ... with that brutal ageing schoolboy. I knew that I felt this particular pain now not just because of the divan, but because, until I had made sure of what I had made sure of, I had been attempting to block out altogether certain reactions to the situation, certain pictures, certain terrible sensations. The other emotion which now, closely embraced with this one, rose dark and gleaming to the surface was: a kind of frightful *glee*. Ben was just as I had – feared – and hoped. He was a hateful tyrant. He was a thoroughly nasty man. And so ... And so ...

HISTORY

THREE

'EVERY persisting marriage is based on fear,' said Peregrine Arbelow. But let me explain. I am writing these pages, as I have written the previous ones (since page 100 in fact), in London, in my peculiar miserable derelict new flat. It has even occurred to me that if I wanted to live as a hermit retired from the world this would be a far better habitat! (Someone said something like this to me lately. Rosina?) So much has been happening, I thought I would write it as a continuous narrative without too many reversions to the present tense. So I am writing my life, after all, as a novel! Why not? It was a matter of finding a form, and somehow history, my history, has found the form for me. There will be plenty of time to reflect and remember as I go along, to digress and philosophize, to inhabit the far past or depict the scarcely formulated present; so my novel can still be a sort of memoir and a sort of diary. The past and the present are after all so close, so almost one, as if time were an artificial teasing out of a material which longs to join, to interpenetrate, and to become heavy and very small like some of those heavenly bodies scientists tell us of.

I arrived here two days ago and have spent most of the time writing. On the second evening, as I shall shortly recount, I visited Peregrine. Today I shall continue to write; it is oddly enough easier to write here, amid all this cramped chaos, than in the open spaces at Shruff End. I have been able to concentrate; and my God there is plenty to concentrate on. This evening I shall take the train back home. (Home? Home.) I have telephoned to the local taxi to meet me at the station. I am sitting at a rickety table up against a window, from which I can see the unutterably feathery tops of a very bland green plane tree and beyond its lilting leaves a jumble of walls and windows and chimneys, and backs of houses built out of the crusty dung-brown Victorian brick out of which this part of London seems to be constructed. I sold my big airy apartment in Barnes, so near the river, so near the railway, in a fever of haste when I was buying Shruff End. And this little flat was, almost in my intention, a sort of penitential chapel. I have not even yet had time to arrange the furniture. Beside me as I write is an armchair with a television set on top of it. (Thank God for the impossibility of television at Shruff End.) Beyond, a bookcase stands facing the wall, presenting to me its greyish back, draped with cobwebs and pitted with woodworm. Pictures, lamps, books, ornaments and rolled-up rugs cover the floor, together with a sinister scattering of pieces of broken glass and china. I hustled the removal men and they were not at their best. Crates of kitchen ware, not unpacked, fill the tiny kitchen. Even though I sold many things and put some in store (including several trunks full of theatre souvenirs) there is far too much stuff here. The two bedrooms are small, but have an attractive view down a mews where many plants and trees are growing outside the little houses. The kitchen, if you can get in, is satisfactory, with a good gas stove and a refrigerator. Yesterday I lunched on tinned macaroni cheese jazzed up with oil, garlic, basil, and more cheese, and a lovely dish of cold boiled courgettes. (Courgettes should never be fried, in my opinion.) I must remember to buy more courgettes and some green peppers to take back with me. And talking of food, I have just this moment remembered that last night (when I was with Perry) was the night when I was supposed to be dining with Lizzie and Gilbert, and I forgot to cancel it. They will have spent the whole day cooking for me. What brought me to London was the following. Fundamentally I suppose what brought me away was a sense of a very important interval in the problem of Hartley: an interval for reflection, planning and a certain necessary purging of intent. What more imme- diately brought me was Rosina and her horrible little red car. Rosina turned up again at Shruff End on the evening of the day when I had that informative encounter with Ben which I have just related; and I amazed her and also got rid of her by asking her if she would drive me to London, leaving early on the following morning. I wanted to come away, as I have said, to think. And I wanted, as I will explain, to find some old photos of Hartley which had been left in London. And the journey was incidentally a good way of brushing Rosina off me, at any rate for the moment. It was not just that this donation of my company and willingness to accept her services as a chauffeur (she drives very well) was likely to placate. I was also able over the journey to indicate half laughingly, and as if the idea had of course never been serious, that there was no question of anything between me and Lizzie. Rosina took this news, as I knew she would, coolly and with an air of wise gener- osity, which would have enraged me had I been telling her the whole truth. As it was I even hinted that she had helped to 'bring me to my senses'. Did she really believe that I had abandoned Lizzie and that her terrorist tactics had influenced me? Or did she suspect that there was something quite else afoot? It was hard to say. After all she is an actress.

We were both surprised at how pleasant the journey turned out to be. We spoke of nothing personal but chattered and gossiped all the way and, in that enclosed time, enjoyed each other's company as we used to do in the days before Rosina loved me and I was crazed by her. Tactfully she told me only what I wanted to hear about, failures and flops and bankruptcies and personal disaster. Fritzie's plan to film the *Odyssey* had run into money trouble, Marcus was suing Al over Nell's contract, Rita's third husband had run off with a male dancer, Fabian was back in a mental home. *Après moi le déluge.* While I amused her with descriptions of my misadventures at the Black Lion. And without seeming in the least preoccupied I managed to think about Hartley all the way to London. After all I am an actor. Rosina dropped me in Notting Hill. We parted with amicable vagueness. She was too intelligent to press me at this point, especially if she believed that she had won some sort of advantage by a successful exercise of power. I had no idea what she thought or what she wanted and I soon forgot her. I gave myself up to that not unpleasing slightly mad feeling that always comes over me when I enter London, the scattering anonymous feeling of returning into oneself in the great tragicomic metropolis when the bond of society, whether in train or car, is suddenly snapped. I walked to my flat (I would not let Rosina drive me there) and did some shopping on the way. I let myself in in a state of painful excitement. The alien jumbled rooms, still smelling of other lives, greeted me with hostility. I at once began searching for photographs of Hartley. I thought they might have got lost in the move, but all was well. I poured them from an envelope onto the table and spread them out, all brown and faded and curling at the edges. They were almost all snaps I had taken of her. Hartley always smiling or laughing, the wind blowing her hair and her skirt, posed upon a canal bridge, holding her bike, leaning against a five-barred gate, kneeling in buttercups and looking at me with a face blazing with love. I kept trying to trace the similarities, to build connections between the young face and the old, the old face and the new. But the images were too terrible, too agonizing, because of the overwhelming smell of youth and happiness which emanated from them. Prudent, careful of myself, I quickly gathered them all together and put them back into the envelope to take to Shruff End.

I then searched quickly for a picture of my mother, and soon found one, not anxious-looking but broad-faced and grinning with a jocund yet powerful expression that was terribly familiar to me. Her scraped-back hair revealed her bulky rounded brow, and her commanding wide-apart eyes gazed straight at the beholder. She would never have made an intellectual, but there were many careers in which she might have succeeded. She was often merry, but with a merriment almost ostentatiously derived from, or associated with, an ascetic simple blameless life. The jazz age passed my parents by. I also found, though I was not looking for it, a touching (too touching) picture of my father, very young, in the uniform of an infantry officer of the first war. How on earth had he survived that holocaust, and why had I never asked him really detailed questions about it? He too was looking at me, but unsmiling, diffident, with anxious eyes. How soft and young his mouth looked. However had that gentle timid being managed as a soldier? It was my mother who made decisions and argued with the tradesmen. Perhaps it was some of her northern toughness in me which had made me so browbeat the world as to accept me at my own valuation.

Then I saw, peeping out from under some horrible pictures of James on his pony (why ever had I kept those?), a photograph of Uncle Abel and Aunt Estelle dancing together. I pulled it out. They were in evening dress and holding each other rather far apart for what was obviously, from the way they were looking at each other, a moment only. The next moment they would be closely embraced. Tango? Waltz? Slow foxtrot? There was something in their attitude which announced not only their happiness but their mutual dependence, their absolutely satisfactory relationship: he so burly, so masterly, so elegant, so protective, she so frail, so graceful, so trustful and submissive, so confidently loving. So bloody beautiful. Poor lucky Aunt Estelle, she never lived to lose those charms. However had I got hold of that photo? I now quite suddenly recalled that I had *stolen* it from the family album at Ramsdens. I turned the stiff brown photo over, and saw the glue on the back and a little dark brownish fur of the thick page from which I had removed it.

As I had been bowling along the motorway with Rosina in the sunny early morning and chattering about California and the latest row in Equity, I had been composing a letter which I intended to write to Hartley as soon as I got to London. But after I arrived I felt, first of all, a more urgent need to clear my mind and somehow to steady and console myself by writing a full account of what had happened. Then I found other reasons for not, as yet, writing that letter. I was in fact in a terrible ferment, not exactly of indecision, but of anxious impatient frightened emotion. I was still struggling to hold off a frightful crippling mindless jealousy-pain which was waiting just round some corner in my distracted soul. I had to keep that away from me by *thinking*; and the fruit of my thought was somewhat as follows.

When I left Ben after that rather horrible interview, I felt dark feral glee because I realized that I was now free to detest him; and I was free to do more, oh ever so much more, than that. The crude summary of the matter was that I was now able to think in terms of *rescuing Hartley*. There was a kind of dreadful violent leaping ahead in this thought, as if I were being powerfully jerked by something which already existed in the far-off future. Hatred, jealousy, fear and fierce yearning love raged together in my mind. Oh my poor girl, oh my poor dear girl. I felt an agony of protective possessive love, and such a deep pain to think how I had failed to defend her from a lifetime of unhappiness. How I would cherish her, how console and perfectly love her now if only ... . But I still had just enough prudence left to go on *thinking*.

I reviewed the evidence and I had very little doubt about what it pointed to. Hartley loved me and had long regretted losing me. How could she not? She did not love her husband. How could she? He was mentally undistinguished; there was no wit or spiritual sweetness in that man. He was physically unattractive, with his big unshapely sensual mouth and his look of a cropped schoolboy. And he was, it seemed, a barbarian and a bully. He was a tyrant, probably a chronically jealous man, a dull resentful dog, a limited shut-in fellow with no sense of the joy of life. Hartley had been a captive all these years. She may, in the earlier times, have thought of escape; but gradually she fell, as so many bullied isolated women do, into a gradual despair. Better not to fight, not to hope. The shock of seeing me again must have been enormous. Of course she had digested some of it by the time I discovered her. Her frightened negative behaviour was easy to explain. She was probably afraid of her husband; but she was much more afraid of her old love for me, still alive, blazing away there like an underground oil fire: a love which, at the very least, could now utterly destroy her small despairing peace of mind.

About all this, and about how I could and would, if she wished it, take her away, I had intended to write to her in the letter, which I would of course deliver secretly. But reason and reflection, together with fear, suggested a delay. Fear said that if anything were to go terribly badly wrong now I should lose my mind. Reason said that the evidence was not conclusive and could be read in other ways. My anti-Ben persona was perhaps not a very reliable witness. *Had* Ben revealed himself as so very unpleasant in our meeting, given that my own conduct had been so exasperating? Well, he had, until the end, controlled himself; but I had felt, from the start, a fierce and unreasoning degree of hostility. Then there was the mystery of Titus. Why had he run away? Had he

turned out a problem child, perhaps a delinquent? Had the tragedy of
his departure, the shared grief, brought them closer together? The shared
grief, the shared bed. My thoughts had still to be kept on a leash, and
there were long dark passages down which they were straining to run.
And of course there was (and this was something huge) the possibility
that although he was ugly and charmless and brutal and dull she loved
him and had been reasonably contented with him. I had answered, to
my satisfaction, a series of questions. This one remained, and it was
the last. *Did she after all love him?* But it was impossible. And yet I must
find out. I must find out before I could proceed with the plans and
projects which were tugging and tugging at my attention and my will.
I must wait, everything must wait, until I had found out the answer
to that question.

But how? I dared not simply write and ask her, there was too much
at stake, and I realized as I thought carefully about it that her reply was
bound to be obscure. Then (and I am speaking of yesterday) I saw the
solution, the rather horrible but necessary solution to the problem.
And about this, I will write in due course. Meanwhile let there be an
interval of rest. In order to start resting I rang up Peregrine and went
round last night and got drunk with him, and what we talked about I
will now recount, since some of it is relevant to my situation. Indeed,
now I come to think of it, nearly everything in the world is relevant to
my situation. Of course I did not tell Peregrine anything about Hartley.
I have never mentioned her to him, though I may once have dropped
a hint about a 'first love'.

I did some more shopping and brought the ingredients of our supper
round to his flat in Hampstead. It has taken me a long time to persuade Perry that it is stupid and immoral to go to expensive crowded
restaurants to be served with bad food by contemptuous waiters and
turned out before one is ready to go. As it was we had a long relaxed

evening, ate a delicious curry (cooked by me, Perry cannot cook) with rice and a green salad, followed by an orgy of fresh fruit, with shortcake biscuits, and drank three bottles of Peregrine's excellent claret. (I am not a petty purist who refuses to drink wine with curry.) We then went on to coffee and whisky and Turkish delight. Thank God I have always had a good digestion. How sad for those who cannot enjoy what are after all prime pleasures of daily life, and perhaps for some the only ones, eating and drinking.

I confess I went to Peregrine not only for a drinking bout and a chat with an old friend, but for male company, sheer complicit male company: the complicity of males which is like, indeed is, a kind of complicity in crime, in chauvinism, in getting away with things, in just gluttonously enjoying the present even if hell is all around. In my case, I should however add, this did not include coarse and obscene conversation. I abhor artless bawdy. I had, long ago, to give some rather sharp lessons on this subject to Perry and to some others. Not Wilfred. He was never foul-mouthed.

So, having done my thinking and made my resolution, I had the relaxed sense of an interval, wherein I might rest and gather my strength. Hartley would wait. She would not run away. She *could not* run away.

'Every persisting marriage is based on fear,' said Peregrine. 'Fear is fundamental, you dig down in human nature and what's at the bottom? Mean spiteful cruel self-regarding fear, whether it makes you put the boot in or whether it makes you cower. As for marriage, people simply settle into positions of domination and submission. Of course they sometimes "grow together" or "achieve a harmony", since you have to deal rationally with a source of terror in your life. I suspect there are awfully few happy marriages really, only people conceal their misery and their disappointment. How many happy couples do we know? All

right, Sid and Rosemary, and they've got nice children, and they talk
to each other, they never stop chattering, it's a kind of miracle, but do
we *really* know, and how much longer will it last? I can't think of any
others, though I know several that look OK, only I happen to see behind
the scenes! God, Charles, you were a wise man never to get married.
You stayed free. Like Wilfred Dunning. Never put on a collar and chain.
Christ, I loathe women. But I can't get going on the other tack either.
And you needn't blush and look coy, I never fancied you. I know what
you got up to with Fritzie Eitel! No – but I'd have had old Wilfred if
he'd asked me. What did old Wilfred do for sex? No one ever knew.
Perhaps he didn't have any, and if so good on him. I still miss Wilfred.
He was a sweet man. And he was generous, he liked to be the cause
that wit is in other men. God, he inspired me. Getting drunk with old
Wilfred was like – hell, what was it like? Did you know Lizzie Scherer
was living with Gilbert Opian? I think that's smart of both of them.'

'I miss Wilfred too. Yes, I heard about Lizzie.' One of my minor
motives in going to see Peregrine had been to find out if there was
really any gossip going round about me and Lizzie, and if so to scotch
it. Apparently Perry had heard nothing. 'So you and Pamela –?'

'That's over, really. I mean, she still lives in the house, but we don't
communicate. That's hell, Charles, *hell,* like you don't know. To be tied
to someone where all the sources of speech are fouled up and poisoned.
Everything you say is wrong or vile. Christ, I'm a rotten picker. First
that bitch Rosina, then a friend like Pam. Seen Rosina lately?'

'No.'

'Nor have I, but every time I turn on the television there she is,
that's a bloody curse. I suppose I loved her once. Or it was just that
she made me feel like Mark Antony. *Penché sur elle l'ardent impérator* ...
All I saw in Rosina's eyes was a reflection of myself. Then I saw the
divorce court. The trouble with Rosina is she wants every man: Julius

Caesar, Jesus Christ, Leonardo, Mozart, Wilamowitz, Mr Gladstone, D. H. Lawrence, Jimmy Carter – you name him, she wants him. I suppose you wouldn't like to take Pam off my hands too, would you? No? Ah well, I can't convey to you what it's like, like a fight with knives, and really it's still going on – we haven't either of us got the sheer bloody strength to start arranging the divorce. Divorce proceedings are hell, you've got to think, you've got to decide, you've got to lie. I believe she's got another chap, I don't want to know. She goes away a lot, I only wish she didn't keep coming back, I suppose it's convenient. The sheer endless destructive bloody spitefulness, the wanton breaking of all the little tentacles of tenderness and joy, all the little spontaneous nonsenses that connect one human being with another. I do try to communicate with her sometimes, and she says the most hurtful thing she can think of in reply. One's soul becomes numb with the endless blows – and of course one becomes a sort of fiend oneself, that goes without saying, one becomes ingenious in evil. I've seen it in other cases, the spouse who feels guilty, even irrationally, is endlessly the victim of the whims of the other, and can take no moral stand. That leads to mutual terrorism. And oh, when we still used to sleep together, lying awake at night and finding one's only consolation in imagining in *detail* how one would go downstairs and find a *hatchet* and smash one's partner's head in and mash it into a bloody pudding on the pillow! Ah, Charles, Charles, you know nothing of these marital joys. Have some more whisky.'

'Thanks. And how's the little girl? What's her name? Angela.' This was Pamela's daughter by her previous marriage to 'Ginger' Godwin.

'She's not so little now. Oh, she's at school. At least I suppose she is, she goes somewhere every day. I ignore her, she ignores me, we never got on. I don't think Pam sees her either. Pam is drunk a lot of the time now. It's an edifying scene. Oh Charles, you're so lucky to have escaped bloody scot free from all those frightful wounding traps where one's blood flows and one yells with pain and watches oneself becoming a devil. You're so out of it all, God, you're clever. You're such a smooth clean bugger, Charles, your face is so clean and so smooth and pink like a girl's, I bet you only shave once a month, and your hands are so clean and your bloody nails are clean (look at mine) and you've got away with everything, scot free, scot bloody free. Yes, yes, I must get on with getting the bloody divorce, but that means communicating with Pamela and I *can't* – I can't face sitting down with her, or trying to sit down, we don't sit down any more in each other's presence, and trying to make a rational plan to rid each other of each other. Maybe she doesn't want it anyway! It may suit her to live here and use this house as a base for whatever she's doing! I pay a pretty large amount into her bank every month –'

'Can't she get a job or –'

'Job? Pam? Laissez-moi rire! Pam was never an actress, she was a starlet. She can't *do* anything. She's lived on men all her life. She lived on Ginger and she lived on some other poor American fish before that and God knows who before that. Ginger still pays her fantastic sums in alimony. And of course she'll only consent to leave me if I agree to do the same. And do you know, I'm still paying alimony to Rosina, though she's earning five times what I am. *Suis-je un homme, ou une omelette?* Sometimes I wonder. I was so bloody fed up and anxious to get rid of her I signed everything. God, if you would only remove Pamela too! You're a lucky dog. Good clean fun every time and then you ditch them. Christ, you even got away from Clement. Why did I never learn?'

'If you think I had a joy-ride with Clement –'

'The trouble with you, Charles, is that basically you despise women, whereas I, in spite of some appearances to the contrary, do not.'

'I don't despise women. I was in love with all Shakespeare's heroines before I was twelve.'

'But they don't exist, dear man, that's the point. They live in the never-never land of art, all tricked out in Shakespeare's wit and wisdom, and mock us from there, filling us with false hopes and empty dreams. The real thing is spite and lies and arguments about money.'

It might seem from this account that Perry was doing all the talking, and indeed by the end of the evening he was. He is endowed with an Irish flow of words, and when thoroughly drunk is difficult to interrupt. I was in any case in a mood to incite him rather than to talk myself. I was soothed by his eloquent lamentations and I must confess rather cheered up by his troubles. I am afraid that I was pleased rather than otherwise that his second marriage had failed; I should have felt a certain chagrin had I been the involuntary cause of his being happy *en deuxième noces.* Such feelings do me no credit; but they are not uncommon ones.

We were sitting in the rather large and handsome dining room of Peregrine's flat. A white tablecloth, much stained with wine, covered the table and looked as if it had been there for some time. Perry had moved his divan bed into this room, and had even installed an electric kettle and an electric cooking ring (on which I had cooked the curry) so as to be able to leave the rest of the flat to Pamela. The ring stood on a square of newspaper which was covered with food droppings. The charwoman had left after being insulted by Pam. The room was very dusty and smelt of burnt saucepans and dirty linen. However, as Perry said, the door could be closed and locked.

Peregrine Arbelow has, as I think I said earlier, just about the largest face that I have ever seen on a human being; though when he was young, in his 'playboy' days, this did not prevent him from looking handsome. He has a large round face, now rather fat and flabby, framed (with the help of science) by short thick chestnut brown curls. (It was he who advised me about the rescue operation on my own hair.) His large eyes have retained a look of innocence or perhaps simply puzzlement.

He is a big stout man, always dressed, even in hot weather, in tweedy suits with waistcoats. He has a watch and chain. He speaks with a light touch of the accent of his native Ulster, which of course disappears absolutely on the stage, unlike Gilbert Opian's lisp. He is an excellent comic, though not as good as Wilfred, but then nobody is.

I thought it was time to get off the dangerous topic of women. 'Been to Ireland lately?' This always set Perry off and was a guaranteed subject-changer.

'Ireland! There's another bitch. Christ, the Irish are stupid! As Pushkin said about the Poles, their history is and ought to be a disaster. At least the Poles suffer tragically, the Jews suffer intelligently, even wittily, the Irish suffer stupidly, like a bawling cow in a bog. I can't think how the English tolerate that island, there ought to have been a final solution years ago, well they did try. Cromwell, where are you now when we really need you? Belfast has been kicked to pieces. Nobody cares. The pain of it, Charles, the pain of it, the bloody suffering, the degradation, the bloody tit for tat. Why can't they let the thing stop somewhere, like Christ did? Could a hundred saints save that island, could a thousand? And I can't just forget it, it's like the shirt of what's his name, it's *on* me, it's crawling on my flesh. The only thing I get out of it is sometimes, in some moods, I can actually feel *pleased* that other people are worse off than me, that their beloved husband or son or wife has been shot down before their eyes, or that they've got to sit in a wheelchair for the rest of their life. That's how vile I am! I live Ireland, I breathe Ireland, and Christ how I loathe it, I wish I were a bloody Scot, *that's* how bloody awful it is being Irish! I think I hate Ireland more than I hate the theatre, and that's saying something!'

At that moment the door opened and Pamela put her head round it. Then, swinging on the door, she half stepped half fell into the room and gazed at us glassily. She was wearing a coat and had evidently just come in. She was still handsome, with a lot of tumbling wavy grey hair, now rather bedraggled. Her smudged scarlet mouth turned down at the corners in an aggressive unhappy sneer. She stared at me, screwing up her eyes, ignoring Perry. I said,

'Hello, Pam.'

She turned round laboriously, still holding on to the door, and started to go out, then turned about, with her face wrinkled up in a pout and her lips working, and having assembled enough saliva in her mouth, spat onto the floor, leaned forward to inspect the spit, and reeled away leaving the door open.

Peregrine leapt to his feet, rushed to kick the door violently shut, then picked up his glass and hurled it into the fireplace. It failed to break. He ran round the table literally foaming at the mouth, lifted it high with a cry of '*Aaaagh!*', a sound like a spitting cat only with the volume of a lion. I rose and took the glass out of his hand and put it on the table. He then walked slowly towards the door, looked at the place where Pamela had spat, tore a piece off one of the filthy newspapers and carefully laid it over the spittle. Then he returned to his seat. 'Drink up, Charles, dear chap. You aren't drinking. You're sober. Drink up.'

'You were saying about the theatre.'

'You were so right not to publish your plays, they were nothing, nothing, froth, but at least they didn't pretend to be anything else. Now you're offended, vanity, vanity. Yes, I hate the theatre.' Perry meant the London West End theatre. 'Lies, lies, almost all art is lies. Hell itself it turns to favour and to prettiness. *Muck.* Real suffering is – is – Christ, I'm drunk – it's so – different. Oh Charles, if you could see my native city – And that spitting bitch – How can human beings live like that, how can they do it to each other? If we could only keep our mouths shut. Drama, tragedy, belong to the stage, not to life, that's the trouble. It's the soul that's missing. All art disfigures life, misrepresents it, theatre most of all because it seems so like, you see real walking and talking people. God! How is it when you turn on the radio you can always tell if it's an actor talking? It's the vulgarity, the vulgarity, the theatre is the temple of vulgarity. It's a living proof that we don't want to talk about serious things and probably can't. Everything, everything, the saddest, the most sacred, even the funniest, is turned into a vulgar trick. You're quite right, Charles, I remember your saying about old Shakespeare that he was the – he was the – only one. Him and some Greek chap no one can understand anyway. The rest is a foul stinking sea of complacent vulgarity. Wilfred felt that. Sometimes I remember he looked so sad, after he'd had them laughing themselves sick. Oh Charles, if only there was a God, but there isn't, there isn't, at all –' Perry's big round brown eyes were filling with tears. He fumbled for a handkerchief, then used the tablecloth. After a moment he added, 'I wish I'd stayed at Queen's and become a doctor. As it is I crawl on every day towards the tomb. When I wake in the morning I think first of death, do you?'

'No.'

'No. You still have the *joie de vivre* of a young man. In your case it is nothing to do with goodness. You are ungood. It is just a natural endowment, a gift of nature, like your figure and your girlish complexion. But remember and beware – there are those who live in hell.'

I said, 'Do you ever hit Pamela? Did you ever hit Rosina?' I must have been drunker than Perry thought.

This question seemed to cheer him up a little. 'Funny you should ask that, Charles, I was thinking about it just today and wondering why I never do, I never did. No. Never raised my hand to anybody. It's the inanimate world that gets it. Glasses, plates, anything I can kick and smash. I think – you know – that's something to do with Ireland, something I do for Ireland, in a funny way. Doesn't help the bitch of course. But — you know — as soon as — anybody hits anybody, instead of screaming or — or spitting or — there's a barrier passed — perhaps it's the last barrier of civilization — and after that — it's machine guns and shooting people's knee caps off. God, why did I agree to play in that bloody TV series, it's *muck*. They hit me of course, Pam and Rosina, no inhibitions there —'

'A scratched face?'

'Scratch be damned, they punch. Well, I deserve it. I'm a skunk — a — skunk. Yes. Yes. Drink up.'

As Perry was again applying the tablecloth to his eyes the door opened and a tall thin boy with a crew cut and a black leather jacket clumped in, ignored us, went across to the cupboard, opened it, took out a bottle, and walked out again closing the door.

'Who on earth was that boy?'

'Ah that's no boy, Charles dear, that's my stepdaughter Angela, she's sixteen.'

'God. Last time I saw her she was a little thing with golden ringlets.'

'She is no longer a little thing with golden ringlets. Do you know that she shaved her head last month? It's just beginning to grow again. Her father has given her a motor bike. And when I say a motor bike I don't mean *a put-put-put* on which you sit as on a chair, I mean a long thick brutal thing which you bestride like a charger and which makes a noise like AAAARRGRR. I remember when you were being sentimental about wanting a son I told you what hell it would be. I think a daughter is worse. Thank God I haven't got any children of my own. Children — innocence — God! You should hear the language Angie uses, and she's made herself so ugly, so grotesque — Pamela doesn't care, she's — well, you saw Pamela just now, didn't you — she did come in, didn't she or did I dream it? Angie, yes. She wears climbing boots and leather everything. And she drinks. They all do. Christ, Charles, you're lucky. No family. The family, the seat of love. And to think that I not only persuaded myself I loved those two women, I really did love them – that is, if I'm capable of love. Am I? I don't know. And I loved – oh – earlier – other women – other people – lost now, lost, gone forever – but it would have been no good – skunks and rotters and cads can't be happy, so there's some justice in the world after all.'

I had reached the stage where it was very difficult to leave, very difficult to do anything except go on and on drinking whisky; and I was beginning to be stupidly affected by Peregrine's tears. 'Perry, who was your first love?'

'Don't call me "Perry", fuck you. Well, I'll tell you – it's not what you'd – it was my Uncle Peregrine – yes. Uncle Peregrine. God rest his dear soul, he was a good good man. And if there's ever a Judgment Day all my fucking family will be kneeling down behind Uncle Peregrine and hoping that he'll say the good word and save them from the fire. And I'll be lying on the ground waiting for him to raise me up, and he will raise me up. He was a sweet man. I don't know why I'm calling him good, what did I know about it, I was a child. He used to hold my hand and hold me on his knee. He *loved* me, the bugger. My parents never fondled me, they never hugged me and kissed me, I think honestly they didn't like me much, they liked my bloody sister, not me. But Uncle Peregrine liked me. He used to hug me and kiss me. And do you know, I've never had better kisses from women, though it was only – it wasn't like you think – it was so innocent and sweet – and he only did it when we were alone. That taught me something, I understood. And we talked about everything, as if we were the same age, and I longed for his company, as if he nourished me. Then one day – my parents must have seen, or maybe they decided there was something funny about Uncle Peregrine, and they just *banished* him. I never saw him again. Never.'

'What happened to him?'

'I don't know. I heard much later on that he'd committed suicide. When I became an actor I took his name, partly out of piety, partly to spite my family. I was christened William. Well, that was my first love. What was yours?'

'I forget. Thank you for telling me about your uncle. I liked hearing about him.'

'I'm sorry I told you already. You'll start making psychology. And psychology is bunk.'

'I know psychology is bunk! I must go, Peregrine.'

'Don't go. I'll tell you Freud's favourite joke, if I can remember it. The king meets his double and says, "Did your mother work in the palace?" and the double says, "No, but my father did." Ha ha ha, that's a good joke!'

'I must go.'

'Charles, you haven't understood the joke. Listen, the king meets this chap who looks just like him and the king says –'

'I have understood the joke.'

'Charles, for Christ's sake don't go, there's another bottle. "No, but my father did" !'

'I really must go –'

'That's right, sod off just when consciousness is becoming bearable, and the light of understanding has dawned. I have got a great deal more to say to you. Oh all right, sod off then! I think I'll come down to see you at your place by the sea, I'll come at Whitsun if the weather's decent, and we'll get drunk again –'

'Goodbye, Peregrine. I'm sorry about Ireland.'

'You're drunk after all. Fuck off.' As I went out of the door I heard him murmuring, 'So clean, so bloody clean,' as his head slowly drooped towards the wine-stained tablecloth.

*

When I had finished writing the above, which brought my novel-diary up to date, I packed my suitcase and left my muddled awful little London flat, where I had not had the heart to so much as move a chair or unpack a cup. I had had my lunch (I finished up the macaroni cheese) and imagined that a blank uneventful interval now divided me from my evening train home (I was wrong). I decided to spend some of the time at a picture gallery. I am not very knowledgeable about pictures, but they give me a certain calm pleasure, and I like the atmosphere of galleries, whereas I detest the atmosphere of concert halls. I must confess too that I derive a lot of sheer erotic satisfaction from pictures of women. The painters obviously did after all, so why not me?

After some indecision I decided to go to the Wallace Collection, where I had not been for some time. My father, who knew even less about pictures than I do, had taken me there once as a boy to see Frans Hals's 'Laughing Cavalier' on one of our rare visits to London, and I associated the place with him. I think my father liked the gallery because it was so quiet and there was so much furniture as well as pictures, so it seemed like a palatial private house. He was particularly pleased by the many clocks (he liked clocks) which all, not quite at the same time and with varied chimes, struck the hour while we were there. The place, when I arrived, was almost empty, and I started wandering about in a sort of daze, looking at the pictures and thinking about Hartley. I was feeling a bit unreal as a result of the serious hangover which I had been fighting all the morning. The trouble with good wine is that it is very alcoholic but you cannot publicly pour water into it. In spite of aspirins with my lunch I still had a headache. A sort of brown fuzz and some very volatile darting black spots intermittently marred my field of vision. I felt unsteady and somewhat oddly related to the ground, as if I had suddenly become extremely tall.

Then it began to seem that so many of my women were there; only not Hartley. She was a vast absence, a pale partly disembodied being, her face hanging always just above my field of vision like an elusive moon. I had always run to women as to a refuge. What indeed are women *but* refuges? And sometimes it had seemed that to be held close in a woman's arms was the only and perfect defence against any horror. Yes, they had, so many of them, been perfect to me, and yet ... after a while ... one leaves a refuge. Hartley was different, she travelled with me, I had never seen her as a place of safety. She had come inside the circle of myself and was within me, a pure substance of my being, like nerves, like blood. But the others, as I walked about, gliding and blinking and uncertainly related to the ground, they were there: Lizzie by Terborch, Jeanne by Nicolaes Maes, Rita by Domenichino, Rosina by Rubens, a perfectly delightful study by Greuze of Clement as she was when I first met her ... Darling beautiful Clement, how she hated growing old. There was even a picture of my mother by Reynolds, a bit flattering but a likeness. Yes, I looked for Hartley. Some could have rendered her, Campin perhaps, Memling or Van Eyck. But she was not there. And then the clocks all began to strike four.

Some workmen were doing something or other downstairs, hammering a lot, flashing lights swarmed and receded, blending with my headache. I found myself searching my mind for something that it was important to remember, to do with that night when I had lain out on the rocks and seen the ultimate cavern of the stars when the universe seemed to be turning inside out, and at the time this had reminded me of something, only I could not make out what; only now, as I seemed to see again that vast slowly changing infinitely deep dome of luminously golden stars, stars behind stars behind stars, did I recall what it was that I had been put in mind of. It was the changing lights in the Odeon cinema where I used to go with Hartley as a child!

I was in the big central gallery where my father had taken me to see the 'Laughing Cavalier', and the light seemed a little hazy and chunky and sort of granulated and brownish, even though the sun was shining outside, or perhaps it was just my hangover. The gallery was empty. Then I noticed something that seemed odd, a sort of resonant coincidence. I was gazing in a dazed way at Titian's picture of Perseus and Andromeda, and I had been admiring the graceful naked figure of the girl, whose almost dancing pose as she struggles with her chains makes her seem as airborne as her rescuer, when I seemed to notice suddenly, though I had seen it many times before, the terrible fanged open mouth of the sea dragon, upon which Perseus was flying down head first. The sea dragon did not quite resemble my sea monster, but the mouth was very like, and the memory of that hallucination, or whatever it was, was suddenly more disquieting than it had ever been since the first shock of its appearance. I turned quickly away and found myself face to face with, directly opposite, Rembrandt's picture of Titus. So Titus was here too. Titus and the sea monster and the stars and holding Hartley's hand in the cinema over forty years ago.

I began to walk away down the long room and as I did so the hammering of the workmen down below seemed to be becoming more rhythmic, clearer, faster, more insistent, like the sound of those wooden clappers, which the Japanese call *hyoshigi,* and which are used to create suspense or announce doom in the Japanese theatre, and which I often used to use myself in my own plays. I began to walk away down the gallery and as I went my hangover seemed to be turning into a sort of fainting fit. When I reached the door at the end I stopped and turned round. A man had come into the room by the other door at the far end and was standing looking at me through the curiously brownish murky air. I reached out and put one hand on the wall. Of course I recognized him at once. He was my cousin James.

*

'Feeling better?'

'Yes, that stuff has worked a miracle, some old Tibetan hangover remedy no doubt.'

It was five o'clock and I was sitting in James's flat in Pimlico. James's flat resembles some chaotic oriental emporium, and I used to despise it accordingly until I realized that a great many of those tall-hatted Buddhas and curvaceous Shivas which I had taken to be made of brass were in fact made of gold. I recalled Toby Ellesmere once telling me that my cousin was a very rich man. (I have often wondered why I never managed to become rich.) He must have inherited plenty from his parents. Probably Ellesmere invested it for him. A lot of the stuff in the flat now does appear to me to be valuable, although as a collector or connoisseur I do not rate cousin James very high. He seems to have no conception of how to sort or arrange his possessions, they are dumped and piled rather than arranged, and elegant *objets d'art* are juxtaposed with the merest oddments of the bazaar. Sentimentality, unworldliness, despair?

The scene is such that it must be listed rather than described. James's rooms are full of what I can only call, though I daresay he would dislike the word *fetishes*: oddly shaped stones, sticks, shells, to which other things such as feathers have been (why, by whom?) tied or stuck, uneven bits of wood carved with crude faces, large teeth and even bones with strange marks (writing?) upon them. The walls are entirely covered either with books or with embroideries, or rather brilliant blue hangings, upon which have been fixed various far from reassuring masks. A lot of necklaces (rosaries?) lie about, tangled in bowls or hanging down in front of scrolls or mandala-pictures or photos of a place picturesquely called Kumbum. There are also a number of very exquisite have-worthy jade animals which I used to feel tempted to pocket, and plates and bowls of that heavenly Chinese grey sea-green colour wherein, beneath the deep glaze, when you have mopped the dust off with your handkerchief, you can descry lurking lotuses and chrysanthemums. On little lacquer altars, as I presume they are, stand, or sit, the Buddhas, what I take to be prayer wheels, and also miniature pagodas and curious boxes with complicated towers on top of them, some studded with coral and turquoise and other semi-precious stones. There is also, perched upon a bracket, an ornate pagoda-shaped wooden casket which James says is like the ones in which lamas are accustomed to keep demons prisoner. (When I asked if there was a demon in that one James just laughed.) Bejewelled too are the sheaths and handles of daggers, one of which (it is usually on James's desk) has a long curving golden handle. I once saw it lying on his bed. I sometimes think there is something rather childish about my cousin.

The flat has an odd unique sweetish smell which I attribute to incense, though when I once asked James about it he said 'mice', which was I suppose a joke. Odd intermittent tinkling sounds are caused (I think) by pendant glass ornaments hanging in the recesses of the rather long and obscure hallway. These sounds reminded me of the faint clicking of my bead curtain at Shruff End; and it gave me a weird feeling to think of my 'funny house' all empty and silent (at least I hope so!) except for the tap-tap of that curtain swaying gently in the moving air. James's flat is situated in one of those long Pimlico streets leading down to the river, which used to be so shabby but are now becoming so smart. It is a large flat, but unusually dark because of a lot of dusky and rather randomly placed painted screens, and of James's habit of keeping the curtains half drawn by day and lighting only one lamp in each room. It took me some time to appreciate James's stuff partly because it was usually too dark to see it. The place is also of course full of books, many in languages which I cannot identify. This has been James's London base for many years, and as he has been abroad so much it is perhaps no wonder that it looks like a mere cluttered-up dumping ground.

We had been drinking tea out of little incredibly frail transparent porcelain bowls, and eating the custard cream biscuits which I remember James liking so much when he was a boy. I had no sensibility about food when I was young, but James was always choosey and faddish. He is of course a vegetarian, but was so even as a child, having made his decision, then a very odd one, entirely by himself. He was now just opening a window (the room was very stuffy and fragrant of 'mice'), to let out a fly which he had carefully caught with a tumbler and a sheet of paper which I think he kept handy for this purpose. He closed the window. I sneezed. A distant bell tinkled. I wondered how long James had been watching me in the picture gallery before I noticed him, and why indeed he had been there at all on that particular day at that particular hour.

Let me now try once more to describe my cousin's appearance. His face seems dark though he is not really swarthy. He has to shave twice a day. Sometimes he looks positively dirty. His hair, now a fairly copious untidy ruff around a little bald spot, is dark brown, like Aunt Estelle's, only very dry and floppy, whereas hers was glossy. His eyes are a murky brown, an indeterminate unspecifiable shade which seems to change, now blackish, now a dark earthy yellow. He has a thin hooked nose and thin clever-looking lips. His face is unmemorable, by which I do not mean dull, it is indeed a rather intense face, but I mean that when I picture it in absence I can only conjure up a set of features, not a coherent whole. Perhaps it is just not a very coherent face. It is as if a fuzzy cloud hangs over it, and this goes with, or perhaps is, my idea that James is rather dark or dirty. At the same time, his inane boyish square-toothed grin can often make him look almost silly. His 'muddy look' is not furtive and certainly not sinister, but just somehow occluded. I wondered once again, as I now watched him smiling slightly as he let the fly out of the window, how exactly it was that he managed to resemble Aunt Estelle. Perhaps it was some trick of expression, a glow of concentration which in Aunt Estelle's case was a kind of joy, but in James's case was something quite else.

'So your house stands there by the sea, all alone, on the rocks really?'

'Yes.'

'That's good, that's good.' James's murky eyes widened and then became for an instant vacant, as if he were voyaging elsewhere. This momentary absence was characteristic too, it never lasted more than seconds. I used to wonder if he took drugs (many of those old eastern hands do) but it may simply have been boredom. How I used to worry when I was young about whether I bored James! 'But don't you miss the bustle of the theatre? You never had any hobbies that I can remember. Whatever do you do with yourself all day? Paint the house? I am told that's what retired people do.'

James did not always, in talking to me, avoid a perhaps instinctive reversion to a slightly patronizing jokey tone which used to madden me when we were boys, especially since he was the younger. The banal phrase 'the bustle of the theatre' and the equation of me with 'retired people' seemed with an easy gesture to consign my activities past and present to unimportance. Or perhaps I was still being too sensitive.

'I am writing my memoirs.'

'Theatre chat? Anecdotes about actresses?'

'Certainly not! I want to do the deep thing, real analysis, real autobiography –'

'Not easy to do.'

'I know it's not easy to do!'

'We are such inward secret creatures, that inwardness is the most amazing thing about us, even more amazing than our reason. But we cannot just walk into the cavern and look around. Most of what we think we know about our minds is pseudo-knowledge. We are all such shocking poseurs, so good at inflating the importance of what we think we value. The heroes at Troy fought for a phantom Helen, according to Stesichorus. Vain wars for phantom goods. I hope you will allow yourself plenty of reflections on human vanity. People lie so, even we old men do. Though in a way, if there is art enough it doesn't matter, since there is another kind of truth in the art. Proust is our authority on French aristocrats. Who cares what they were really like? What does it mean even?'

'I should say it meant something simple and obvious, but then I am no philosopher! And I should say that it mattered too. It matters to the historian, it even matters to the critic.' Nor did I care for 'we old men'. Speak for yourself, cousin.

'Does it signify what really happened to Lawrence at Déraa? If even a dog's tooth is truly worshipped it glows with light. The venerated object is endowed with power, that is the simple sense of the ontological proof. And if there is art enough a lie can enlighten us as well as the truth. What is the truth anyway, that truth? As we know ourselves we are fake objects, fakes, bundles of illusions. Can you determine exactly what you felt or thought or did? We have to pretend in law courts that such things can be done, but that is just a matter of convenience. Well, well, it doesn't signify. I must come and see your seaside house and your birds. Are there gannets?'

'I don't know what gannets look like.'

James was silent, shocked.

I was beginning to have an old familiar sensation which, oddly enough, I tended to forget in the interim, a feeling of disappointment and frustrated helplessness, as if I had looked forward to talking to James and had then been deliberately excluded from some kind of treat; as if something significant which I wanted to tell him had been, inside my very soul, shrivelled, trivialized by a casual laser beam of his intelligence. James's mode of thought, his level of abstraction, was entirely unlike mine and he seemed to be sometimes almost frivolously intent upon exhibiting the impossibility of any communication between us. But of course really there was no intent, and indeed no treat, and in many ways my cousin could be seen as a bore, as an eccentric pedant with a kind of world-weariness which was simply tedious. He too after all had had his disappointments and about the most important of these I would doubtless never know. I suppose what I wanted was simply some ordinary amicable converse with James, which never happened, and which I was perhaps wrong in thinking that I could even imagine. After all, he was all that was left of my father and mother and Uncle Abel and Aunt Estelle.

'The sea, the sea, yes,' James went on. 'Did you know that Plato was descended from Poseidon on his father's side? Do you have porpoises, seals?'

'There are seals, I'm told. I haven't seen any.'

I put my little fragile tea bowl down with such force that I had to lift it up again to make sure it was not cracked. I held onto the sides of my chair. It had just occurred to me that the weird feeling I had experienced in the gallery, and which James's potion had cured, was not just a hangover, but the threatened recommencement of the hallucination induced by LSD. I quite suddenly began to have something like the same feeling again, combined with a vivid image of the open mouth of Titian's sea dragon.

'What is it, Charles? You're wrought up about something. You were distressed in the gallery. I was watching you. What is it? Are you ill?'

'Do you ever remember my mentioning a girl called Mary Hartley Smith?'

I had certainly not intended to talk to James about Hartley, I had not conceived of such a confidence. It was as if I had been driven into some corner or put under some spell where the only efficacious charm was the actual mention of her name.

James, reverting to his bored air, reflected, 'No, I can't say that I do.'

In fact I was pretty sure that I had been careful never to mention Hartley to James.

'Who is she then?'

'She was the first girl I ever loved, and I don't think I've ever really loved anyone else. She loved me too. We were at school together. Then she went off and married another man and disappeared. I never stopped thinking about her and caring about her, and that's why I never got married. Well, I've just come across her again, she's there, down there by the sea, living in the village with her husband, I've seen her, I've talked to her. It's incredible, and all that old love is still there, stretched out right from the beginning of my life till now –'

'You relieve my mind,' said James, 'I thought you might be sickening for the 'flu, and I'm *very* anxious not to catch it myself just now.'

'I've met her husband. He's nothing, a little ignorant bullying fellow. But she – oh she was so glad to see me, she still loves me – I can't help feeling it's a sign, a new beginning –'

'Is it the same man?'

'How do you mean – oh yes, it's the same man.'

'Have they children?'

'A boy, eighteen or something, he's adopted, but he's run away and they don't know where he is, he's lost –'

'Lost – that must be sad for them.'

'But oh – Hartley, of course she's changed, and yet she hasn't changed – and I mean what incredible luck to meet her again like that, it's the hand of destiny. And she's had such an unhappy life, it's as if she has prayed for me and I have come.'

'And – so –?'

'Well, so, I shall rescue her and make her happy for whatever time remains to us.' Yes, it was simple, and nothing less than that great solution would serve. I lay back in my chair.

'More tea?'

'No thanks. I think I'd like a drink now. Dry sherry.'

James began fiddling in a cupboard. He poured out a glass for me. He seemed in no hurry to comment on my amazing revelation, as if he had already forgotten it. He continued quietly drinking tea.

'Well,' I said after a minute, 'that's enough about me. Tell me about yourself, James, how is the army treating you these days? Off to Hong Kong or somewhere?' Two could play at that game.

'I know you want me to say something', said James, 'but I can't think what to say, I don't know what it means. This old flame turning up, I don't know how to react. I have various thoughts –'

'Tell me a few.'

'One is that you may be deluding yourself in thinking that you have really loved this woman all these years. What's the proof? And what is love anyway? Love's all over the mountains where the beautiful go to die no doubt, but I cannot attach much meaning to your idea of such a long-lasting love for someone you lost sight of so long ago. Perhaps it's something you've invented now. Though of course what follows from *that* is another matter. Another thought I have is that your rescue idea is pure imagination, pure fiction. I feel you cannot be serious. Do you really know what her marriage is like? You say she's unhappy, most people are. A long marriage is very unifying, even if it's not ideal, and those old structures must be respected. You may not think much of her husband, but he may suit her, however impressed she is by meeting you again. Has she said she wants to be rescued?'

'No, but –'

'What does the husband think of you?'

'He warned me off.'

'Well, my advice is stay warned.'

I was not completely surprised by James's line, his refusal to express a lively interest in my situation. I had noticed in the past that my cousin did not like any discussion of marriage. The subject embarrassed, perhaps depressed him.

I said, 'The voice of reason.'

'Of instinct. I feel it could all end in tears. Better to cool down. One should not come too close to what one may intuit as the misery of others.'

'Thanks for your reactions, cousin. Now tell me about yourself.'

'You mustn't miss your train. But I can order a taxi by telephone, there is quite a reliable firm at Victoria. What is his name?'

'The husband?'

'No, sorry, I meant the lost boy, the son.'

'Titus.'

'Titus,' said James thoughtfully. He went on, 'And have they searched for him? Told the police and so on, whatever one does?'

'I don't know.'

'Has he been gone long, have they no clue, no theory about where he is? Have they had a letter?'

'I don't know, I don't know –'

'It must be terrible –'

'Yes, no doubt. Now let's forget my antics. What about your plans, what's the latest in army life?'

'The army – oh – I've left the army.'

'Left the army?' I was perhaps stupidly surprised and oddly dismayed, as if the army had somehow been keeping James safe, or safely caged up, or innocuously occupied, or something. I suppose I always felt that his soldiering made it happily impossible for us ever to collide or compete. Whereas now ... 'Oh well, you've retired, of course, golden handshake and all that. So we are both retired generals!'

'Not exactly retired, no.'

'You mean —?'

'I have, as the expression goes, left the army under a cloud.'

I put my glass down and sat up straight. Now I was really amazed and upset. 'No! James, you can't — I mean —' Speculations, of a not too improbable kind, about what sort of cloud my cousin had left the army under, crowded my mind and reduced me to silence.

I looked at James's darkened face. He was sitting with his back to the lamp. The evening, through the gap in the curtains, was still brilliantly blue. James was smiling slightly, as he had smiled when he released the fly, and I saw now that he was looking at another fly which was perched on his finger. This fly was washing its front paws, then it was vigorously drawing its paws forward over its head. It stopped washing. James and the fly looked at each other.

'Not to worry however,' said James. He moved his finger and the fly flew off. 'I had effectively come to the end of my career in any case and I shall not lack occupations.'

'You can paint the house.'

James laughed. 'Would you like to see a picture of a gannet? Well, another time perhaps. A pity you aren't here tomorrow, we could go to Lord's. The Test Match is in an interesting condition. I had better telephone for your taxi. Here, take some of these biscuits, I know you like them, Aunt Marian always used to stuff some secretly into my pocket when I was leaving your place!'

After James had rung for the taxi I said, 'Who was that old man I saw here last time?' I had suddenly recalled, and felt that I had entirely forgotten in the interim, that on the last occasion in James's flat, and just as I was leaving, I had seen, through a half open door, in another room, a little oriental old man with a wispy beard, sitting quietly upon a chair.

James seemed a little surprised. 'Oh him – no one in particular – he's gone, I'm glad to say. There now, there's the bell for your taxi. I hope you'll get a decent dinner on the train.'

'But my dear Charles,' said Rosina, 'I know you are a most eccentric creature, but you *cannot* want a woman who looks eighty and has a moustache and beard!'

It was the following day. I had got back very late. The taxi was waiting at the station all right, but the run home was slow because of a thick fog. There was no dinner on the train because of a strike, so I had had to make do with the custard cream biscuits, which I felt annoyed and sad to think of my mother stuffing into James's pockets long ago. When I reached Shruff End I ate some bread and cheese. (The butter had all gone rancid.) My bed was uninvitingly damp, but I managed to find a hot water bottle and exhaustion sent me to sleep. I awoke late, feeling stiff and cold, and as I sat up my teeth began to chatter. Well might I be frightened of what I was proposing to do that day.

I put on my warmest available clothes, including the thick Irish woollen sweater which poor Doris gave me, but found myself still shuddering. Perhaps James's suspicion about the 'flu had been right after all? A thick grey-golden mist still covered the land and the sea, bringing with it a terrible blanketed silence. The sea, where it was, when I walked out, just visible, caressing the rocks, was oily-smooth. The air felt damp and chill though I suppose it was not really very cold. A shirt which I had left drying upon the lawn was soaking wet. The interior of the house on the other hand was really icy, tomb-like, with an entirely new smell of mildew, and the insides of the windows were streaming with water. I tried, and failed, to light the new paraffin heater which I had purchased at the Fishermen's Stores. I made some tea and was beginning to feel a little better when I heard a motor car hooting at the end of the causeway. I guessed rightly that it was Rosina, and felt for a few moments such intense irritation that I wanted to run out at her screaming. I also considered hiding, but I was beginning to feel hungry and did not see why I should abandon my house to a perhaps prolonged invasion. Then I conceived, an intelligent self-protective device, the idea of simply *telling* her. It was the right move.

We were sitting in the kitchen, with the Calor gas stove on, eating dried apricots and cheddar cheese. (Dried apricots eaten with cake should be soaked and simmered first, eaten with cheese they should be aboriginally dry.) I was drinking tea, Rosina was drinking brandy, which she had demanded. The fog was now so thick that the room seemed to be curtained, and I had lit two candles which seemed strangely unable to spread any of their pale little illumination through the opaque brown twilight of the room. An 'exciting light', Rosina called it. I had decided to tell her some version of the Hartley story because I could not, in my present mood, with my present terrible plan, abide the prospect of lying and fencing and perhaps having a dangerous row. To tell the truth, I was almost superstitiously afraid of Rosina's hatred. I wanted to neutralize her for the time, so as not to have to worry about her. I would soon have quite other dangers and decisions; and I had an intuitive conception, which turned out to be correct, of how she would react to my confidences.

She opened hostilities by saying (as I expected) that she had not believed a word of my recent story about having given up Lizzie, and had not believed that I was going to stay in London, and how right she had been, and if I imagined I was going to get rid of her – I cut this short by telling her, briefly and selectively, the story of the 'old flame'. How very convenient these cliché phrases are, how soothing to the pained mind, and how misleading, how concealing. Here I was, about to make a decisive move, tormented by love and fear and awful incipient jealousy, telling Rosina a bland, even humorous, story about an 'old flame' and thus, while telling the truth, deceiving her. Rosina was cool, intrigued, delighted, intelligent. She was a very different auditor from my cousin and a much more satisfactory one. In fact I found a certain relief in telling the edited tale to this clever and, as it turned out, not unsympathetic woman. What I had intuited at the start, seconds perhaps (so swift is the mind) after hearing the maddening impertinent hooting of the little red car, was that Rosina would view 'the Hartley question' in quite a different light from 'the Lizzie question'.

It is an interesting fact about jealousy (and jealousy is no doubt a major topic in this memoir) that although it is in so many respects a totally irrational as well as a totally irresistible emotion, it does show a certain limited reasonableness where temporal priority is concerned. I had taken up with Lizzie after I had met and appreciated Rosina, and it was fixed (quite erroneously) in Rosina's mind that Lizzie had somehow 'stolen me away'. Lizzie was moreover still an attractive woman. Such things made up a classical picture and evoked a typical response. But Hartley, under the 'old flame' heading, was a different matter altogether, and here Rosina's sheer intelligence did work on the side of reason. Hartley belonged to my remote past, Hartley was 'old' (that is, my age), Hartley was unattractive and undistinguished and (a not unimportant point) thoroughly married. These data quick Rosina had taken in and assembled, I could almost see the computer working behind her sparkling crooked eyes. Rosina had assessed my chances and did not rate them high. Like James, she thought it would end in tears; and my truthful narrative subtly encouraged this belief.

It was soon clear that of course Rosina could not, from any point of view, regard Hartley as a serious rival; so much was this so that she was even able to pity her, not maliciously, but with a kind of interested objectivity. What Rosina had grasped was that the encounter with Hartley had withered my interest in Lizzie. So ... when the whole foolish episode had ended in disaster ... intelligent sympathetic Rosina would be there to pick up the pieces. Of course Rosina saw my relief at talking, my gratitude for her lively clever responses; and indeed I was, just for this moment, pleased with her. And of course I did not tell her everything, least of all my immediate plans. So dedicatedly Machiavellian did I feel just then that I had no sense of treachery as I thus talked Hartley over with dangerous witty Rosina. I *led* Rosina, and, where it was necessary to me, her own inventive cleverness conveniently deceived her.

It was interesting that Rosina clearly remembered the occasion when the headlights of her car had revealed Hartley to me pinned against the rock. 'I thought I was going to squash the old bag like a beetle. Come, Charles, she is an old bag, the poor thing, you can't deny it.'

'Love doesn't think like that. All right, it's blind as a bat –'

'Bats have radar. Yours doesn't seem to be working.'

'Use your intelligence, anyone can love anyone, consider Perry's Uncle Peregrine.'

'Perry's what –?'

'Never mind –'

'I knew you were fibbing that time I drove you to London. You're a rotten actor, I can't think why you ever went into the theatre at all. I knew there was something going on, but I thought it was Lizzie.'

'I never felt like this about Lizzie.'

'Well, it had better not be Lizzie.'

'It isn't! Hasn't even this convinced you? I love this woman.' I love her, I thought, just as if I have been actually married to her all those years and have seen her gradually grow old and lose her beauty.

'Oh, come, darling, that's got to be a lie. This sudden move to the sea has unhinged you, and this ghastly pointless house. I think it's the nastiest house I've ever been in. No wonder you're having delusions.'

'What delusions do you mean?'

'I remember your talking about a first love, but these things are imaginary, they are fables. You're just suffering from the shock of seeing her, give it a fortnight. And she's got a bourgeois marriage and a son, and, Charles, she's *ordinary,* you can't do it to an ordinary woman just because you fancied her at school, it's nonsense and she wouldn't understand! Besides, you wouldn't be able to, you're not all-powerful, not in real life you aren't. You'd simply get yourself into a very unpleasant mess, just the sort of mess which you of all people hate. You'd *lose face*! Think of that! Have enough self-knowledge to see how you'd hate it, you haven't any role here, you haven't any lines. You even admit she doesn't want to talk to you!'

'That's because she's afraid, she loves me too much, and she doesn't yet know enough to trust my feelings. She *will* trust them. And then her love will simply sweep her to me.' I thought: I must let her know, I must convince her, that I love her absolutely, I must write a long letter and get it to her secretly, and once she really understands ...

In my solemn but rather general and undetailed version of the story I had mentioned Titus but had not, for some reason, said anything about his being adopted, or about his having run away. Perhaps I was still reluctant on my own account to reflect on the subject of Titus, and on how he might affect my chances. Nor did I describe my thoroughly unnerving *tête-à-tête* with Ben. Here the idea of 'losing face' could indeed find a foothold! I said that Titus was not at home and that I had had inconclusive meetings with Hartley in the village and polite conversations with her and her husband. I had not conveyed the fear and danger in the situation. Fortunately Rosina was too amused to ask really detailed questions.

'Charles, be human. She's timid, she's shy, she must feel terribly inadequate and mousy and dull, after *her* life, meeting you after *your* life.

She probably feels ashamed of her dull husband, and feels protective about him, and resentful against you. Use your imagination! And she'd bore you, darling, she'd bore you into a frenzy, and she knows it, poor old dear. She's an old-age pensioner, she wants to rest now, she wants to put her feet up and watch television, not to have disturbances and adventures. And then supposing you did carry her off and then felt bored, whatever would you do, with yourself or with her? You're used to witty unconventional women, and you're an old bachelor now anyway, you couldn't really stand living with anybody, unless it was a clever old friend like me. You couldn't start a new woman, and that's what she really is for all your touching memories of jaunts on bikes. I think you just want to break up her marriage, like you just wanted to break up mine. I'm pretty tough, but as it is you gave me a lot of misery over a long time, and I'm not going to let you off, you're going to have to pay for my tears, like people in the sagas pay. You've lived in a hedonistic dream all your life, and you've got away with behaving like a cad because you always picked on women who could look after themselves. And my God you told us the score, you never committed yourself, you never said you loved us even when you did! A cold fish with clean hands! But it was just luck really if the girls survived. You're like a man firing a machine gun into a supermarket who happens not to become a murderer. No, no, but it's different here, you must respect the poor old thing's choice, her life, her son, her dear dull old husband, her nice little new house. Leave her alone, Charles. No wonder she runs a mile when she sees you!'

'You don't understand.' How indeed could she? Much of what she said was sensible, more sensible even than she realized. But there was just one thing omitted: the absolute nature of the bond between myself and Hartley, and the certainty which, in spite of Hartley's behaviour, we both had about the continuity of that bond. Hartley was not a 'new woman', she was the oldest strongest longest thing in my life. Nor could I or would I ever try to explain to Rosina how tired I was of 'witty unconventional women', and how it was that that 'old bag' was for me the dearest of all beings and the most precious and unspoilt creature in the world and the most thrillingly attractive. I had given to Hartley my first and my only completely innocent love, before I became a 'hedonistic dreamer' and a 'cold fish'. Of course these insulting descriptions were the idle product of jealous spite; but in so far as I had been a 'cad', that in a way was Hartley's fault! I had given her my innocence to keep, which could now miraculously be reclaimed. And these ideas somehow composed themselves into a passion of possessive yearning. I felt tenderness, pity, a deep desire to *cherish* Hartley, to protect her from any more pain or any more harm, to indulge and spoil her, to give her everything that she wanted, and to make her eternally happy. I wanted, in the time that was left to us, to console her as a god consoles. But I also wanted increasingly, and with a violence which almost burnt the tenderness away, to own her, to possess her body and soul.

Ever since the recognition scene, physical passion, roused, disturbed, confused, had twisted and turned in me, my senses in dialogue with my thoughts, because, as I worked and worked to join together her youth and her age, I so much desired to desire her. To achieve this was a crucial test, a trial, a labour undergone for her. Now, I realized, it was done; and my desire was like a river which has forced its channel to the sea. She made me whole as I had never been since she left me. She summoned up my whole being, and I wanted to hold her and to overwhelm her and to lie with her forever, *jusqu'à la fin du monde*; and, yes, to amaze her humility with the forces of my love, but also to be humble myself and to let her, in the end, console me and give me back my own best self. For she held my virtue in her keeping, she had held it and kept it all these years, she was my alpha and my omega. It was not an illusion.

Rosina, watching me, was now actually chuckling. I was sitting with my arms spread out on the table, still feeling cold in spite of the Irish jersey and the brandy (to which I too had now resorted) and although the Calor gas stove was still burning, I had been about to light the fire in the little red room when Rosina interrupted me. She, perched on her chair, with one knee raised, was wearing wide blue cotton trousers, rolled up over blue canvas boots, and a casual blue and purple striped shirt pulled in at the waist by a narrow leather belt. She looked idle, practical, piratical, amazingly young. Her dark piercing crossed eyes regarded me with predatory amusement. Her thick wiry dark hair was now strained back and tied closely with a ribbon, giving her face a harsh animal intensity of expression. She had thrown off her coat, showing no sign of feeling the cold. And I thought, what's the matter with me, it can't *be* cold, after all it's summer. But I shivered all the same. And was it not equally absurd to have candles burning at eleven o'clock in the morning? The candles seemed to be giving no light so I blew them out. Perhaps the mist was dispersing a little, though the window was still obscured. Rosina was just beginning to reply to me when the door of the kitchen quietly opened and someone came in. It was a woman, and for a crazy moment I thought it must be Hartley, embodied by my thoughts. But no: it was Lizzie Scherer.

Both the women uttered a tiny cry, a sort of suppressed swallowed yelp of shock, when they saw each other. Rosina got up very fast and moved behind her chair. Lizzie stepped towards me, looking at Rosina, and threw her handbag onto the table as if it were a gage of war. I remained seated. Lizzie was wearing a light brown mackintosh and a very long yellow Indian scarf, which she now unwound and carefully folded up and placed on the table beside the bag. She was blushing extremely. (So was I.) Her hair was covered with little drops of water. Perhaps it was now actually raining outside.

Rosina lifted her chair and threw it sideways onto the slate-flagged floor. She said to me, 'You liar and you traitor!'

I said to Lizzie, 'Is it raining?'

Lizzie said, 'I don't think so.'

I said, 'Rosina is just leaving.' Then just in time I got to my feet and moved hastily round the table. Rosina's vermilion claws, making a slash at my face, just touched my neck as I got out of range. Lizzie retreated to the door. I faced Rosina's rage across the table. 'Look, I didn't lie to you. I haven't any sort of arrangement with Lizzie, she's just arrived out of the blue and she doesn't *know*.'

'Does she live here?' said Lizzie.

'No! No one lives here except me! She just dropped in, people drop in, you have dropped in. Have some tea, some brandy, some cheese, an apricot.'

'She doesn't know?' said Rosina, glaring at me but mollified. 'Then hadn't you better tell her? Or shall I?'

'Are you going to marry Rosina?' said Lizzie, stiff, hands in pockets.
'No!'

'Charles, can I speak to you alone?' said Lizzie.

'No, you can't,' said Rosina. 'My God, if it was only Lizzie and me we could fight for you, with kitchen knives.'

I felt I had another shivering fit coming on and I sat down again at the table. 'I don't feel very well.'

'Can I speak to you alone?'

'No,' said Rosina. 'Charles, I want to hear you tell her what you have just told me, I want to *hear* you –'

'Is Gilbert outside?' I asked Lizzie.

'No, I drove down by myself. All right then, if she won't go –' Lizzie, ignoring Rosina, sat down opposite to me at the table. 'I wanted to say thank you for your sweet generous letter –'

'Tell her, tell her!'

'Thank you for your sweet generous letter. You were being very kind to both of us.'

'I'm terribly sorry I didn't turn up for dinner that night, I –'

'Very kind to both of us. But it isn't necessary for you to be generous like that. I was a perfect fool. Gilbert doesn't matter. Nothing matters except that I'm yours on any terms. There's nothing to argue about. I'm just yours, and you can do what you like, I don't care if it all goes wrong, I don't care what happens or how long it lasts, well of course I want it to last forever, but you will do exactly what you want. I've come here just to say that, to give myself to you, if you still want me, like you said you did.'

'How touching!' said Rosina. 'What did you say to her, Charles, let's have the truth about that at last.' She picked up Lizzie's handbag and threw it onto the floor and kicked it.

Lizzie paid no attention, she was staring at me, her flushed ardent face blazing with emotion, her lips wet, her eyes bright with the truthfulness of her self-giving submission. I was very moved.

'Lizzie, dear – dear girl –'

'You're too late, Lizzie,' said Rosina, 'Charles is going to marry a bearded lady, aren't you, Charles, *aren't* you? And we were just discussing you, and Charles said he never really cared for you at all –'

'I didn't say that! Look, I'm going to talk to Lizzie upstairs. You stay here. I'll come back.'

'You'd better come back. I'll give you five minutes. If you two set off for London I'll follow you and smash you into the ditch.'

'I promise I'll come back. And, yes, I'll tell her. Just please don't break anything. Come, Lizzie.'

Lizzie picked up her scarf from the table and her handbag from the floor. She did not look at Rosina. I led her out of the kitchen and up the stairs. When we got to the upper landing I hesitated. The bead curtain was immobile and I decided not to pass through it. I led Lizzie into the little middle room and shut the door. The room was dark, since not much light was coming through the long window which gave on to the drawing room, either because of the fog or because I had failed to raise the blinds. It was also empty, since I had removed the table which was still lying in the rocky crevasse where I had dropped it on my way to the tower. There was a square of threadbare carpet. There was also, now suddenly conspicuous and rather sinister, the curly cast-iron lamp bracket rather high up on the wall. The carpet emitted a damp smell when trodden on.

'I'm so frightened of that woman. Charles, you aren't tied up with her, are you?'

'No, no, no, she's just persecuting me. Lizzie –'

'I don't know what she was saying, but it doesn't matter. Listen, Charles darling, I'm yours, and I must have been mad not to say so at once. I was stupidly frightened, I felt I just couldn't bear another broken heart, I thought I wanted peace, and I imagined I could check myself from running straight back into that old terrible madness, but it's no good, I've run back, I'm mad again. I felt sorry for Gilbert and I wanted time to think of a compromise but there isn't any compromise. I don't care what happens or what you do to me, I don't care if I die of it. I don't want you to be unselfish and scrupulous and generous, I want you to be the lord and the king as you've always been. I love you, Charles, and I belong to you and I'll do from this moment on forever whatever you ask of me.'

We stood staring at each other and trembling in that little dark cell-like room underneath the cast-iron lamp bracket. 'Lizzie, forgive me, it was a *mistake*. Sweet Lizzie, it's no use, we cannot ever be together, I can't take you and keep you like I thought, I can't be the king any more. I'm sorry I wrote to you. I'm very fond of you, I love you, but not like that. It was just an empty idea, an abstract idea, like you said, you were quite right, it wouldn't have worked, it wouldn't have lasted. You see, I've met someone else, no, not Rosina, a woman I knew and loved long ago, you remember I told you, the first one. So I can't ever be yours, little Lizzie, and you can't be mine. You must go back to Gilbert, make him happy, let things be as they were. Oh please believe me and please forgive me. It was a mistake.'

'A mistake,' said Lizzie, looking down at her shiny black high-heeled shoes which were wet from the grass of the causeway. 'I see.' She lifted her head and looked at me, her face crimson, her lower lip trembling, her eyes vague and terrible.

'You do remember about that girl, I told you once, well I met her again, she's here and –'

'I'll say goodbye then.'

'Lizzie, darling, don't go like that, we'll be friends, won't we, won't we, like you asked in your first letter, I'll come and see you and Gilbert –'

'I don't think I'll be with Gilbert any more. Things can't be as they were. I'm sorry. Goodbye.'

'Lizzie, just hold my hand for a moment –'

She gave me her limp hand. It felt damp and unresponsive and small and I could not continue the gesture into an embrace. She withdrew her hand and began to fiddle in her handbag. She brought out a fragment of the mirror which had been broken by Rosina's kick, then a small white handkerchief. As soon as she had the handkerchief in her hand she began very quietly to cry.

I felt so touched and sad, and yet so oddly proudly detached and somehow sentimental, as I seemed to see in a second, all rolled up into a ball and all vanishing, some life that I might have had with Lizzie, my Cherubino, my Ariel, my Puck, my son: some life we might have had together if I had been different, and she had been different. Now it was gone, whatever happened next, and the world was changed. I repeated with a kind of sad self-tormenting pleasure, 'No, Lizzie, dear heart, little brave Lizzie, it cannot be. I am so grateful to you for your – for your –'

'It's funny,' said Lizzie, speaking almost calmly through her quiet tears, 'it's funny. The drive from London, it's such a long way, I hired a car, I didn't drive Gilbert's, all the way I had a sort of marvellous love conversation with you, if only it hadn't been for that long drive, it all came to a climax, like a coronation, I was thinking how surprised and pleased you'd be to see me, and how perfectly happy we'd both be and we'd laugh and laugh like we used to, and I kept picturing it and I felt such love and such joy – even though I was saying to myself that I might end up with a broken heart and this time it would kill me – but I thought I don't care how it ends or how much I suffer, so long as he wants me and takes me in his arms – and now it's ended before it even began, and I never imagined it would all be spoilt and broken at the start – and now I've got nothing – except my love for you – all wakened up again and rejected – all wakened up again – forever and ever –'

'Lizzie, it will be quiet, it will sleep, it did sleep.'

She shook her head, gripping her handkerchief in her teeth.

'Lizzie, I'll write to you.'

Her tears had ceased. She put away the handkerchief and the broken mirror and unwound the yellow scarf. 'Don't write, Charles, it's kinder. It's funny, I thought it was the ending then, and it wasn't, it's the ending now. Please don't write to me if you want to be kind. I don't want – any more –'

She crumpled up the scarf and stuffed it in her pocket. Then she turned and quickly swung open the door, nearly running into Rosina who was standing just outside. Rosina jumped back, and Lizzie ran away down the stairs, leaning hard on the banister, her high-heeled shoes clattering and slithering. I tried to follow her, but Rosina grasped my arm, exerting quite a lot of force and bracing one of her booted feet against my foot. We reeled against the wall. 'Let her go.' The front door banged.

I stood for a moment staring at the bead curtain which was swaying and clicking. Then I walked slowly downstairs. Rosina followed me. We went into the kitchen and sat down again at the table.

'Don't worry, Charles, that lusty little animal won't break its heart.'

I was silent.

'Now I suppose you want me to discuss poor Lizzie with you?'

'No.'

'Poor old Charles, you're demoted as God.'

'OK. Please go.'

'If you ever set up with Lizzie Scherer I'll kill both of you.'

'Oh Rosina, don't be stupid, don't be vulgar. Just please go away. Well, I suppose you'd better let Lizzie get a start if you're going back to London.'

'I'm not, I'm going to the Raven Hotel to have a very good lunch alone. Then I'm going to Manchester to do some filming. I shall leave you to your thoughts and I hope they hurt. I won't interfere with your caper with the bearded lady on one condition.'

'What?'

'That you promise to tell me everything about it.'

'OK.'

'You promise?'

'Yes.'

'Get up, Charles.'

I rose mechanically to my feet. Rosina came round the table and for a moment I thought she was going to hit me. She gave me one of her wet kisses. 'Well, goodbye, I'll be back.'

The front door banged again, and a moment later I heard the departing scream of the little red car. For a moment only I hoped that Lizzie might return. Then I thought what luck it was that Lizzie had not come running to me after my first letter.

I went into the next room and tried to light the fire but failed. There was not enough kindling wood. I was feeling thoroughly disturbed by Lizzie's crying and Rosina's kiss. I was miserable about Lizzie but in rather a blank way and I was reluctant to think about her. I wanted her sympathy. I was already regretting my thoroughly vulgar conversation with Rosina. It had seemed a smart thing to do at the time, to tell her about Hartley, but now I was filled with forebodings. In effect, I had given Rosina another weapon. Then I began to wonder a little about cousin James and how he had come unstuck. Homosexuality? Or had the army decided that a crazy Buddhist was a bad security risk? My neck was beginning to hurt where Rosina's red fingernails had reached it. I wanted to take my temperature but could not find the thermometer.

There was no fog now. Twilight had just been overtaken by darkness, and a bright fierce little moon was shining, dimming the stars and pouring metallic brilliance onto the sea and animating the land with the ghostly intent presences of quiet rocks and trees. The sky was a clear blackish-blue, entertaining the abundant light of the moon but unillumined by it. The earth and its objects were a thick fuzzy brown. Shadows were strong, and the brooding identity of everything I passed so powerful that I kept nervously looking back. The silence was vast, different in quality from the foggy silence of the morning, punctured now and then by an owl's cry or the barking of a distant dog.

I did not go through the village. I walked along the coast road
in the direction of the harbour, through the defile which I called
'the Khyber Pass', where the big yellow rocks had invaded the land,
heaping themselves up against the side of the hill into a lumpy mound
in which a narrow cleft had been cut to allow the passage of the
road. The rocks in the moonlight were dark brown, but covered with
innumerable sparkling points of light where the moon caught the tiny
facets of the quartz. I went through the dark cleft and on past the
harbour to where, a little way further on, there was a footpath which
led up the hill, skirting a wood, and joined the tarmac road where it
petered out just beyond the bungalows. All this I had checked in a
daylight reconnaissance, when I had also worked out how to get into
the garden of Nibletts. This was not difficult, since the lower end of
the garden was separated only by a line of posts, joined by slack wire,
from the long sloping field, full of gorse bushes and outcrops of rock,
which bordered the mounting footpath on the village side. The main
drawback to my expedition, apart from the nightmarish possibility of
being discovered, was that when it was late enough for me to get into
the garden unobserved, it might also be late enough for the married
pair to be in bed. There was also of course the possibility that they
might be watching television in silence.

I had earlier rejected the idea of spying on Hartley and Ben, not
for moral reasons, but because it made me feel sick with emotion and
terror. A marriage is so hideously private. Whoever illicitly draws back
that curtain may well be stricken, and in some way that he can least
foresee, by an avenging deity. Some horrible and quite unexpected
revelation could persecute the miscreant henceforth forever with an
almost obscene haunting. And I had to struggle here with my own
superstitious horror of the married state, that unimaginable condition
of intimacy and mutual bondage. However, the logic of the situation

now forced this dangerous and distasteful adventure upon me. It was the next step, the attempt to answer the next question. I had to discover, in so far as I could possibly do so, what this marriage was really like and what these two were for each other.

The moon, shining from the sea, was casting the shadows of the wooden posts onto the sloping lawn of Nibletts. The grass looked as if it was covered with frost. I had already discerned, from below, that the curtained 'picture window' of the sitting room was glowing with light. I stepped over the slack wire and began to walk very quietly up the lawn in the direction of the house, listening to my practically noiseless footsteps in the already dewy grass, listening to my deep breathing and to the hurtful beating of my heart. In spite of a little rain earlier, the ground was hard after the sunny weather and I did not think I would leave noticeable footprints. At about fifteen yards from the house I stopped. Except for a small vent at the top, the window was closed. The curtains were unlined, and the light within illumined, like stained glass, a bright design of green parrots in a lemon tree. There was a narrow slit in the centre where the curtains failed to meet. I moved again, then listened. There was a sound of voices. Television? Avoiding the dangerous area of the slit, and feeling as if I were about to hurtle into space, I now nerved myself to move steadily, silently, right up to the window and to kneel, touching the brick wall, and then to sit down with my head just below the level of the low sill.

Anticipating encounters with rose bushes, though not foreseeing the dew, I was wearing a mackintosh. The moonlight had showed me the whereabouts of the various flower beds, but as I approached the house I must have been dazzled by the lighted window, or else become blind with fear, since I seemed to have sat down *on* a rose bush. There was a faint awful crackling sound and a small sharp spear pierced the calf of my leg. I sat, awkward, frozen, leaning back

against the wall, my eyes and my mouth wide open, suddenly staring
at the vast moonlit sea below me and waiting with horror for some
terrible 'Who's there?'

But the voices continued and now I could hear them quite clearly.
How easy it is to spy on unsuspecting people. The experience that
followed was so weird, and so literally maddening to me, that I will
not attempt to describe my feelings. I will simply, as in a play, give
you the dialogue. It will be clear who is speaking.

'Why did he come here then?'

'I don't know.'

'You keep saying "I don't know, I don't know", can't you say anything
else, or are you mentally deficient? Of course you know, you must
know. Do you think I'm a perfect fool? I'm not that thick.'

'You don't believe it —'

'Don't believe what?'

'You don't believe what you say —'

'What on earth do you mean, what do you *mean,* what did I say that
you think I don't believe? Am I supposed to be a liar then?'

'You say you think I knew, but you can't think that, it's insane —'

'So I'm either mad or a liar. Is that it? Is that it?'

'No, no —'

'I don't understand you, you're babbling. Why did he come here?'

'I don't know, it was an accident, it was a chance —'

'Funny sort of chance. My God, you're clever, it's the one bloody
thing that would torment me more than anything else. Sometimes
I think you want to drive me out of my mind and make me mad
enough to —'

'Darling, dear heart, dear Binkie, please don't — I'm so sorry oh
I'm so sorry —'

'It's no use saying that you're sorry or that you don't know, that's all you say over and over again. I'd like to split open your head and find out what you do know. Why don't you explain at last? Why don't you admit at last? It's been going on long enough. It'd be a relief to me if you'd only tell me –'

'There's nothing to tell!'

'You expect me to believe that?'

'You did believe it.'

'I never believed it, I just pretended to, Christ, I wanted to forget, I got tired of living with it all, I got tired of living with your dreams.'

'There weren't any dreams.'

'Oh you bloody –'

'*There weren't any dreams.*'

'Don't tell lies and don't shout at me either. Oh God, the lies you've told me! I've lived in a sort of soup of lies ever since the start. And then the boy –'

'No, no –'

'Well, I was pretty thick about it all, but I just couldn't credit –'

'*No!*'

'Christ, and when I think of other lucky men with their wives and their families and their simple decent lives and ordinary love and kindness, while here –'

'We've had ordinary love and kindness and –'

'It's only been a pretence because we were both tired, it was too exhausting to be honest. We got tired of telling each other the truth about the hellish cage we live in, we had to rest sometimes and pretend things were all right when they weren't and put up with this sham, this bloody *sham* you call a marriage. We had to stop stabbing ourselves and each other with the ghastly truth. So now we're both sunk in lies, your lies, they're everywhere like a stinking bog, we're drowning in them.

And, Jesus, I thought it might be better when we got away, when we got away to the sea, I thought at least I'd have a garden, I thought – But then lo and behold *he's* here! That's funny, isn't it?'

'Oh, darling, don't – You do like it here, you did like it here –'

'Well, don't say that to me *now*, do you want me to spit in your face? We just pretended to be nice quiet people –'

'You didn't pretend much.'

'Don't start that again.'

'Well then, don't you.'

'You'd better be careful. Another thing I've got against you is that you've made me into such a – you've made me so bad – oh Christ, why can't we get *out*? If only you'd tell the truth for once. I just want to know where I am. Why did that man come here, to this village, here to this very place?'

'You keep asking the same questions again and again. I don't know. I didn't want him here –'

'Liar. How often have you seen him?'

'Just that one time.'

'Liar. I actually saw you with him twice. And God knows how many more times you've been with him. Why do you lie to me so *stupidly*? And you put him up to calling round here.'

'I didn't!'

'Well, you're not going to see him again.'

'I don't want to!'

'It's the past, the past, the bloody past – there's never been anything for us, everything's spoilt, you've spoilt everything, you and your –'

'Darling, dear dear Binkie, don't –'

'And don't call me pet names, it's a mockery –'

'Can't you just try to be kind to me, to pity me, just try –?'

'Why can't you try! Oh God, how can you have been so cruel –'

'I'm not cruel. You're mad, you're MAD –'

'Don't scream at me, I've had enough screaming. You've screamed your way through life, and now we're nearly at the end of it. God, I wish mine had ended. That's what you've been praying for I expect, that I'll have a heart attack. Then you can go off with –'

'I'm sorry, I'm sorry, I'm sorry –'

'Just stop saying that, will you, I'm so tired of it, it means nothing, that parrot cry. Oh God, I'm so tired. It's all spoilt. It never even got started, because of you. And then that unspeakable deception, and I took it –'

'There was no deception – !'

'Oh shut up. I know we've said all this a million times before, we're like clockwork dolls – but, Christ, I'm thinking it all the time, I've got to say it now and then! I even accepted *that* lie because there seemed to be nothing else to do, and I just bloody wanted to be happy, well, not happy, I know that was impossible, but at least I wanted some peace in my rotten failed life and just to rest a bit, but oh no! You wouldn't even let me rest –'

'That's not true –'

'Be careful, be careful. I thought I hadn't any alternative but to put up with you and your lies – God, I must have been crazy – I ought to have cleared off and left you with –'

'No – !'

'You'd have cheered. And now *he* turns up as bold as brass and comes and rings my doorbell! You must have enjoyed arranging that.'

'Don't say what you don't think.'

'I do think it, what else can I think? I can see when you're lying. Do you think you can take me in? Where have you hidden his letters, eh? Where?'

'There aren't any letters.'

'Because you destroyed them. Oh, you're clever! But listen – I say *listen* –'

'I am listening.'

'Your little plan isn't going to work.'

'What little plan?'

'You want me to say "All right, clear out, I don't care where you go." You want to torment me into letting you go. That's it, isn't it?'

'No.'

'Take that bloody look off your face or I'll – Well, it's not going to be like that, see? I'm not going to let you go, I'm never going to let you go. See? You can stay here and look after me even if we never say another bloody word to each other. See? Even if I have to chain you up –'

'Forgive me, please, forgive me, don't be so angry, I can't bear it, stop being angry, it hurts so much, you frighten me so much –'

'Oh do stop crying, I'm so fed up with your tears. Why did he come here, what's it all about, that's what I want to know, Christ, can't you tell me the truth at last, I'm tired of living in a bad dream and pretending it's all right. All this bloody house we took so much trouble with, the bloody furniture, the garden, those fucking roses, pretence, pretence, pretence, I'd like to smash it all to pieces. Why can't you tell me the *truth*? Why has he turned up here, what does it mean?'

'Please, you're hurting me, please, please, I'm so sorry, I'm so sorry –'

'*What does it mean?*'

'Oh stop, I'm so sorry –'

I have written this out as I remember it, with the repetitions. I have not attempted to describe, and will not now, the tones of voice, his strident shout, her whining tearful apologies. I shall never forget it. The eavesdropper had indeed got what he came for.

I wanted to go away much sooner, but I was paralysed, partly by horror, partly by a physical cramp, since I had sat down in an awkward uncomfortable position and had not dared to move since. At last I rolled over and crawled away down the wet shorn moon-grey lawn. I got stiffly to my feet, got clear of the garden, and began to run down the footpath into the face of the sinking moon. I ran most of the way home. I drank some whisky and took a sleeping pill and went to bed and rushed headlong into sleep. I dreamt I found a new secret room at Shruff End, and a woman lying dead in it.

The next day I was like a madman. I rambled, almost ran, round the house, round the lawn, over the rocks, over the causeway, up to the tower. I ran about like a frenzied animal in a cage which batters itself painfully against the bars, executing the same pitiful leaps and turns again and again. There was a golden mist, gradually clearing, it would be a hot day. I looked with amazement on my familiar swimming places, and on the gentle crafty lapping of the calm sea against the yellow rocks. I ran back to the kitchen, but could not even make myself a cup of tea. 'What am I to do, oh what am I to do?' I kept saying to myself out loud. And the strange thing was that although I had received, full and complete and running over, exactly the evidence which I wanted, I seemed to be distracted with grief and fear and a kind of nausea now that I had it.

I had not understood the whole of the conversation. At moments I felt that I had hardly understood anything, except for what was so obscenely evident: those terrible tones of voice, and the sense that all this had happened before, again and again. The awful crying of souls in guilt and pain, loathing each other, tied to each other! The inferno of marriage. I could not, and did not try to, work out the meanings and implications of what had been said. Clearly the gentleman (I now suddenly started thinking of him as 'the gentleman') was displeased by my appearance on the scene. Well, too bad. I indulged in visions of going up to Nibletts, grabbing him by the collar when he opened the door, and pounding his face. But that would be no use. Besides, he was scarcely the 'dear dull old husband' imagined by Rosina. He might have a stiff leg, but he was a tough customer. He was, or perhaps just seemed to be, a dangerous man. He might be the classic bully who is supposed to collapse when threatened; but those who consider threatening bullies may well doubt whether this convenient type really exists. There would be no point in such an experiment. I simply had to get Hartley away and I had to *think* how to do it. Thought was difficult.

In my earlier reflections I had somehow vaguely taken it for granted that once it was clear, if it should become clear, that Hartley's marriage was a disaster, it would not be hard for me to break it up and remove her. I did not doubt that, in those circumstances, she would want to come, that to run to me at last would be a blessed joyful escape and the acting out of a long-cherished fantasy. This assumption may seem naïve, but it was not any sense of its naïvety which now set me at a loss. It was simply that, having been pressed up to the point of action, I could not think exactly how to act, and the details mattered terribly. Nibletts, its roses, its horrible new carpets, the brass ornaments, the lurid curtains, the bell, impressed me not at all, these were gauzy, visionary. As *he* had said, pretences. What impressed me was some quality of that awful conversation itself, some sense of the many many years which had passed, a sense of the strength and texture of the cage. Yet it could still be that I had only to say to Hartley 'come' and she would come. Then it remained to decide just how and when to say it, and that decision seemed to raise all the obscure difficulties again. Was it simply perhaps the case that I was afraid of Ben?

About eleven o'clock I stopped running and made some tea. There was an idea which I had received from the conversation, but for some time, although it was there, I could not chisel it out or identify it. It was an idea which the gentleman himself had given me. It was something like, supposing he really were to turn her out, supposing he could be driven to reject her? Would that not solve the problems about that cage, which I had found so hard to formulate? The gentleman had said that he never would drive her away, but the fact that he mentioned it at all showed that it was possible. Let him dement himself with his own foul temper and foul jealousy or whatever it was – for indeed I could not quite see what it was – that he was so enraged about. It was surely not just my appearance, the old school friend, now a celebrity, knocking upon the door, unwelcome as that doubtless was? If he could become sufficiently worked up, if things over there could just collapse and crumble, then she would have no refuge and she would have no cage and she would come running straight into my arms. Yet – if he became mad – if his world began to totter – might he not then maim her or murder her? This was one of the thoughts that sent me skipping round the rocks like a crazed leopard. Her cry at the end: 'Stop, stop, you're hurting me.' How often in those hateful years had that cry rung out? It was unbearable. I leapt up, upsetting my teacup, chattering aloud, and ran out again onto the grass. What was I to do? So many things were now clear, but I simply could not think out the final tactics, I could not *think* and I could not think because I could not clear my mind of that ghastly conversation, it obstructed me like thick adhesive scum. I had to rescue Hartley, and 'rescue' was indeed now at last plainly the word, the very word that I had longed for. But, now it came to it, *how*?

Later on it seemed as if Hartley herself had come to my assistance. I saw her gentle pale unhappy face looking at me, and I felt a ghostly calm, as if a waft of her presence had come. I must, I realized, before making any overt move at all, talk to her again, and if possible more than once. My impulse was to go round to that horrible bungalow straightaway and simply remove her, and in the end it might come to that. But of course I must prepare her. If it came to a swoop there must be no bungling, no mistakes. So much had been happening in my mind of which she knew nothing. I must let her know where, in it all, I was. I decided that it was no use, at present, attempting any more meetings in the village, since she would be too upset and frightened to attend properly. The vital explanations must be done by letter. I had assumed that what she feared, not yet knowing what my intentions were, was her own heart. For all she knew, I had other sentimental commitments. She had had, no doubt, enough of remorse and the quiet mourning of an old love, so foolishly rejected. Now however I could glimpse other and more urgent fears, and I felt sick uneasy anger at the idea of that little 'boyish' jealous man, sitting up there with his field glasses, and waiting for her to come home. It soon seemed plain, and this further clarification was a relief, that I must simply write her a long letter, then give her time to understand it, to respond to it, and by then ... It was a relief to my shocked frightened mind to reflect that there was now no terrible hurry, that I did not have to go up that hill today and decide exactly how to confront the jealous tyrant. There was the problem of conveying the letter to her, but that was not insoluble, and I had in fact already envisaged how it might be done.

I ate some corned beef with red cabbage and pickled walnuts, and the remainder of the apricots and cheddar cheese. I had no bread or butter or milk, as I had been too distracted to do any shopping. After that I rested. After that I wrote some of this diary, bringing it more nearly up-to-date. After that I wrote the letter to Hartley the text of which I will copy out in a little while. After that I washed a lot of clothes and put them out in the sun. After that I went swimming from the tower steps. Then I sat beside the tower and looked at the late afternoon sun making big blotchy shadows behind the spherical rocks of Raven Bay. After that, since I saw some tourists coming and I had nothing on, I got dressed and returned to the house and picked up my washing, which had dried. Then I fetched the snapshots of Hartley which I had brought from London and sat outside on my stone seat, beside my stone trough, and brooded on them slowly and intently.

Some of the snaps showed us both together. Who had taken those? I could not remember. From the browned curled surfaces, out of a sinless world, the bright soft unformed young faces gazed forth. It was an unspoilt world, a world of truly simple and pure pleasures, a happy world, since my trust in her was absolute, and since in our childish old-fashioned chastity we did not yet consider making love. Happier were we in this, I think, than the children of today. The light of pure love and of pure unanxious romance illuminated our days together, our nights apart. This is no absurd idealization of a youthful Arcadia. We were simple children in a simple world, we loved our parents and our teachers and were obedient to them. The pains of the human journey lay in the future, the terrible choices, the unavoidable crimes. We were *free* to love.

When did it begin to end? Perhaps when I ran off to London. Yet even then our love had still a time to run. And I never doubted her until the last. How long, how much, did she deceive me? Perhaps my selfish need of her was so great that I could not conceive of it not being satisfied. And as I reflected on that need it also occurred to me to think how much, in those years, Hartley had defended me against James. It seemed odd now that they knew practically nothing of each other. I scarcely ever spoke of James to Hartley, and never then of Hartley to James. She never knew how robustly her love defended me against some kind of collapse of my pride.

I shall now transcribe the letter which I wrote to Hartley, and which I had decided to find some way of delivering to her on the following day.

My dearest Hartley, my darling, I love you and I want you to come to me. This is what this letter says. But first there are things which I must tell you, things which I must explain. The chance which has brought you back to me has come like a great storm into my life. There is so much to say, so much to tell. It may seem to you that I belong now to some other world, to some 'great world' of which you know nothing, and that I must have in that world many friends, many relationships. It is not so. In many ways my life in the theatre now seems like a dream, the old days with you the only reality. I have few friends and no 'amorous ties', I am alone and free. This was what I was not able properly to tell you when we met in the village. I have had a successful career, but an empty life. That is what it comes to. I never conceived of marrying because I knew there was only one woman that I would or could marry. Hartley, think about that, believe it. I have waited for you, although I never dared to hope that I would ever see you again. And now, fleeing from worldly vanities, I have come to the sea, and to you. And I love you as I always did, my old love is there, every little fibre and tentacle and tendril of it intact and sensitive and alive. Of course I am older and it is in that sense a different man's love, and yet it is the same love. For it has kept its identity, it has travelled with me all this way, it has almost miraculously survived. Oh my dear, how many days and nights there have been, when you knew nothing of it, when perhaps you thought of me as far away in my 'grand world', when I have sat alone with an aching heart, thinking of you, remembering you, and *wondering where you were*. How is it that people can vanish so that we know not where they are? Hartley, I never stopped wanting you – I want you now.

I have come to know – never mind how, but I do *know* – that you are most unhappily married. I know that you live with a tyrannical perhaps violent man – I wonder how often in the past you may have wished to escape, and have sunk back, defeated and wretched, because there was nowhere to escape to? Hartley, I am offering you, now, my home, my name, my eternal devotion. I am still waiting for you, my only love. Will you not come, will you not escape to me, to be with me inseparably for the years that remain? Oh Hartley, I could make you so happy, I know I could! But let me also say this: if I thought that you were happy already, happy in your marriage, I would not dream of disturbing you with declarations of my persisting love, I would suffer my love silently, even perhaps dissemble it, perhaps go away. I suspect, and forgive me for glancing at this, that you may have suffered more than one hour of remorse as you thought of me living my 'exciting life' and how utterly, as it seemed, you had lost me. But if I thought that nevertheless you had even a moderately contented or reasonably endurable life, I would not meddle, I would gaze at you from afar and turn away. But knowing you to be very unhappy I cannot and will not pass by. How could I, loving you as I do, let you go on suffering? Hartley, you must and you will come to me, to the place where you ought always to have been.

Do not be upset or frightened by wondering what to do about this letter. There is no need for you to do anything immediately, even to reply. I wanted simply to tell you of my love and my readiness. It is for you to consider when and how you are to respond. Obviously I am not necessarily expecting you to come running to my house at once. But, when you have reflected, when you have got used to the idea of coming back to me – coming *back* to me, my dearest girl – then perhaps you will begin to consider how to start to do it. And then – we shall be ready to talk to each other – and we shall find the means to talk. Let us quietly take one step at a time – one step – at a time. When you can give me some sign that you are prepared to let me look after you forever, then I will think what we are to do, and I will, when you desire it, *take charge*. Do not worry, my Hartley, all will be well, you will see, all will be well.

For a day or two, or a few days, as you will, just think about what I have told you. Then – when you will – write me a letter and send it by post. That is, for the present, best. Do not worry, do not fear. I will find means of communicating with you. I will love you and cherish you and do my most devoted best to make you happy at last. Yours always, as once now, and in all the years,

Your faithful,

Charles.

PS Come to me anyway, of course there are no conditions, just let me help you and serve you, you can then decide freely and in peace where and how you want to live.

I wrote this letter quickly and passionately and without corrections. When I read it through I was at first tempted to alter it because it sounded, well, at moments a bit self-important: a little pompous, a little histrionic, perhaps? Then I thought, no, this is my voice, let her hear it. She will hardly be, as she reads this letter, in a critical mood. If I were to amend and polish it, it might sound insincere and lose its force. And as for self-centred, of course I am self-centred. Let her indeed be sure that I am pursuing my own interests here and not just altruistically hers! Let her know that she can give me happiness by giving herself freedom.

When I had written the letter and satisfied myself that it would serve, I put it in an envelope upon which I typed her name and address. I am a poor typist and I wrote the letter in longhand. I then sat and brooded and allowed myself to be almost hopeful, almost happy. Later on, as recorded above, I swam. The sea was cool about my warm limbs, coating them with its cool scales. The water undulated calmly, smooth and shining upon the surface, like the rind of a fruit. Even without my 'curtain-rope', which the playful sea has again untied, I managed to climb out easily. As I write this now it is the next day, and the letter to Hartley in its fat envelope still lies upon my sea-facing table in the drawing room. I have been writing this diary during the morning. Soon I shall have lunch: the remains of the corned beef with plain boiled onions. (Plain boiled onions are another dish fit for a king.) I finished the red cabbage last night with scrambled eggs and drank a lot of the Raven Hotel Spanish white wine. (A mistake.) I must shop soon, I crave for fruit, for buttered toast, for milk in my tea. The shop lady said there might be cherries this week.

Why am I delaying, waiting? Why am I almost pretending that life is ordinary, that it is as it once was? I am still floating in a sense of achievement, of a well-merited interim. I sought and found my crucial evidence. I have decided what to do and how to do it. I have spoken to her eloquently, definitively, although my words have not yet reached her. It is as if they are still winging their way through the air, going to her breast. Am I afraid, is that the real reason why I am waiting? To give her the letter in safety may prove hard, and the results of a bungled failure unthinkable, but it is not this obstacle I fear. The sooner I give her the letter the sooner I shall know her response. What will it be? If she says 'no' or if she does not reply I shall of course assume that she is simply inhibited by fear. But what shall I do then and how long can I wait before I move again and what on earth shall I do as

I wait? *That* interim will not be a calm one. Better then to prolong this one. I feel, since I heard that conversation, so much more, and dreadfully, involved with both of them. I have family membership; with this come hatred, jealousy, the familiar demons. And then again, suppose she simply uses me for her freedom, and then leaves me after? Is that conceivable? Could I lose her a second time, could she vanish? I should run mad. I felt bound, after reading the letter, to add that postscript, it seemed honourable to do so. But is it wise? Perhaps I had better delete it. Better that she should assume that in running to me she commits herself.

I must try to see and feel these speculations as premature and pointless. But I understand very well why I sit here and look at the letter and do not want, just yet, to deliver it.

I will now describe what happened next, much of which was entirely unexpected. I delayed in fact, after writing the above, no longer than the evening of that day. The dilatory calm which I described was quite suddenly succeeded by a frenzy of desperate impatient anxiety to know my fate at once. I then set out to put my delivery plan into operation. I put on a light mackintosh and a shabby sun hat, put the letter in my pocket, without deleting the postscript, and slung round my neck a pair of field glasses which James had given me for bird-watching when we were schoolboys. I cannot recall that I ever used them to watch birds. It was a tacit custom of our childhood that James gave me presents, often quite expensive ones, whereas I gave him none. I suppose my parents accepted this as an inescapable aspect of the patronage of the poor by the rich; and it only much later occurred to me that of course the presents were really from Uncle Abel and Aunt Estelle. These glasses were not very powerful, and not to be compared with Ben's wife-watching pair, but I thought they would serve.

I went by the inland route which I had taken before, through the marsh and round by Amorne Farm and into the village from the other side. My objective was the wood which lay beyond the field which bordered Nibletts' garden. I saw from the Ordnance Survey map that a little road leading off to the right at the entrance to the village (just before the church) circled away up the hill and through the upper part of the wood which lay above the bungalows. Thus I could make the whole circuit without at any time coming within viewing range. I climbed the hill, becoming rather hot and tired, and soon found an inviting woodland path which led seawards at a point a little, as I guessed, beyond the end of the Nibletts' road. In a few minutes I could see the open light of the field, and then was able to peer out through the tree trunks at the now moderately distant bungalow, which I kept under close observation through the glasses.

I waited for quite a long time, feeling cooler, then rather cold, although the sun was still shining. My arms and my eyes were beginning to ache. At last the gentleman came out. My temperature shot up and my heart beat a good deal faster. I was glad to note that he was carrying a garden fork. I could see his long evening shadow moving down the lawn. It gave me a certain pleasure to have Ben, all unsuspecting, in my sights, as he had had me. I have never handled a real gun, but I have handled many a stage gun, and I know what it feels like. Near to the bottom of the garden he started paying attention to one of the fussy flower beds, poking about rather aimlessly at first. Then suddenly he started hitting something with the fork. Not digging but hitting. What was he hitting? A slug, a wild flower? What was he thinking about, while with such terrible concentration he destroyed that innocent little thing? I was fascinated but there was no time to lose. I began to move up the hill under cover of the wood, observing him at intervals as I went, until I reached a point opposite the top of the road where a distance of some two hundred yards of open grass separated me from the end of the tarmac, and where Ben was about to disappear from view, divided from me by the bungalow. I reckoned that there would be two or three seconds, after I emerged into the open, during which it would be possible for him to see me. I took a last look at him. He had his back to me, now crouching beside the flower bed. I walked with long careful fast strides across the first bit of grass, then sprinted to the road and straight through the gate up the path to the front door.

Here I did not ring the bell. That sickly high-pitched ding-dong might well have carried upon the evening air. I *tapped* upon the door with my knuckles, using an old code which Hartley and I had used as children, when we used to knock softly upon the doors of each other's houses. After a short moment she opened the door. The shocked response to my tap had been, as I hoped, automatic. We stared at each other, gaping, both terrified. I saw her staring amazed frightened eyes. I thrust the letter towards her, awkwardly. I could not find her hand and it almost fell between us. Then she had it, clutched against her skirt, and I turned and ran, instinctively taking the way down the hill, down the road into the village. I had not in fact planned my retreat, as my thinking had ended with the delivery of the letter, and as I was passing the Black Lion I reflected that it might have been better to have gone back the way I came. However, as I strode along the village street and turned onto the footpath, well in the possible purview of Ben's glasses, I felt reckless and strong, so that even my recent caution seemed cowardly. Was Ben still bending over his flowerbed, or was he inside the house tearing my letter out of Hartley's hands? I almost felt I did not care, I almost felt it would be better if he were, at this very moment, reading my words and shaking with jealous rage. His reign of terror was nearing its end.

It was certainly not dark as I came towards the house, but the day had that luminous, gauzy blandness which in the midsummer season celebrates the approach of a twilight which, for a few final days, will never entirely darken. The evening star was just visible, and would now for a long further period of daylight blaze in splendour alone. The sea was as flat as I had ever seen it, quite still and held up brimming as if it were in a bowl, the tide being in. The water was the colour of very light blue enamel. Two sea birds (gannets?) flying low in the middle distance produced a hazy distorted reflection as upon a convex metal surface. As I walked along the road, past the handsome milestone which read *Nerodene one mile,* a faint air of warmth was wafted from the yellow rocks which had been basking in the sun all day.

The house by contrast felt cold and seemed to be up to some of its tricks. After the brilliant colour-bestowing light outside, the air within seemed grey and a little thick. There were faint sounds, perhaps just the bead curtain clicking in the draught from the opened door. I stood in the hall for a few moments listening. I wondered if the accursed Rosina had come back and was hiding somewhere about to scare me. I felt impelled to make a search, upstairs, downstairs, in the funny middle rooms. No one of course. As I went through the house I opened all the doors and windows wide and let the warm sea-fresh air from the encircling rocks circulate within. I threw off my disguising hat and mackintosh and pulled my shirt out of my trousers. I took a large glass of sweet sherry and bitters out onto the grass and stood there for some time, rising on my toes and falling back on my heels, and watching the bats, and wondering whether Hartley was all right and what she had done with that long letter after she had read it. Burnt it, shoved it down the lavatory, rolled it up in a pair of stockings?

I came inside and filled the large and now empty glass with white wine, and opened a tin of olives and a tin of Korean smoked clams and a packet of dry biscuits. There was no fresh food as of course I had once more omitted to shop. The house was still acting up, but

I felt by now that I was getting to know its oddities and I was more friendly towards it. It was not exactly a sinister or menacing effect, but as if the house were a sensitized plate which intermittently registered things which had happened in the past – or, it now occurred to me for the first time, were going to happen in the future. A premonition? I began to feel cold, and put on the white Irish jersey. It was now more gloomy inside, though it seemed to be getting even brighter outside, and I had to peer carefully as I washed and drained the olives and put them in a bowl and poured olive oil over them. And then someone began knocking very violently upon the front door.

Whoever it was had evidently not noticed the bell, whose brass handle had been painted black. There was also an old tarnished knocker in the form of a dolphin; and now the dolphin's heavy head was being cracked down onto the door with a force which seemed to shake the whole house. Fear immediately grasped me and jerked me to my feet. Rosina? No. Ben. The outraged husband. *He had seen the letter.* Oh God, what a fool I had been. I ran out, intending to bolt the door against him, but sheer terror confused me into a desire to confront the worst, and I opened it instead. Hartley flew into the house like a terrified bird. She was alone.

In the first seconds she seemed to be as amazed and confused as I was. Perhaps she was blinded by the sudden dark of the interior. She stood there clutching her face with her hands as if she were about to scream. I, with a crazed clumsiness, left the door wide open, then hurrying to shut it bumped into her. I felt the warmth of her thigh as I blundered past. I got the door shut, then realized that I was saying 'oh – oh – oh –' and that she too was uttering some incoherent sound. I put out a grasping searching hand and touched her shoulder. She made a gesture as if she were about to speak, but by then I had grabbed her, clumsily again but effectively enough, in my arms and gathered her into that bear hug that I had for so long been dreaming of. I lifted her off her feet and heard her gasp as almost the whole length of her body was crushed against me. Then, as I slowly let her down in the fuzzy grey-dark of the hall, with the curtain upstairs meditatively clicking, we stood perfectly quiet and silent, I with both my arms wrapped around her, she with her two hands gripping my shirt.

Relaxing at last as she sighed and fluttered her hand against my ribs, I said, 'Is he outside?'

'No.'

'Does he know you're here?'

'No.'

'Did you destroy the letter?'

'Pardon?'

'Did you destroy the letter?'

'Yes.'

'He didn't see it?'

'No.'

'Good. Come in here and sit down.' I pulled her into the kitchen and pushed her down into a chair beside the table. Then I went back and locked the front door. I tried to light a lamp in the kitchen but my hands were trembling too much and the wick flared up and went out. I lit a candle and pulled the curtains. Then I drew up a chair and sat close beside her and cradled her more gently in my arms, her knees touching my knees.

'Oh my darling, you've come, oh my precious darling.'

'Charles –'

'Don't say anything yet. I just want to know that you're here. I'm so happy.'

'Listen, I –'

'Please, darling, oh please don't talk – and please don't push me away like that.'

'No, but I must talk – there's so little time –'

'There's plenty of time, all the time. You did read the letter, didn't you?'

'Yes, of course –'

'And that's why you're here?'

'Yes –'

'Then that's all that matters. You're staying here. You've come, haven't you?'

'Yes, but only to explain –'

'Hartley, don't. What is there to explain? Everything is explained already. I love you. You're here. You love me, you need me. Don't resist. Let's go away to London, tomorrow morning, tonight. Never mind about clothes. I'll buy you clothes. You're my wife now.'

I held her at arm's length, gripping her shoulder with one hand, while with the other I moved the candle so that it illuminated her face. The eyes were thickly encased in wrinkles, the eyelids were brown and pitted as if stained, the cheeks were flabby and soft, not rounded, and faintly pink, perhaps with hastily-applied powder. Her short grey undulating hair was dry and brittle-looking, no doubt from years and years of absent-minded visits to inept hairdressers. Now she was past caring about it, and a forgotten slide hung down from the end of one twisted tress. The face was dry, dry, save where her tongue now moistened her unpainted lips, and where her blue eyes, those strangely timeless pools, were moist and now suddenly full of unshed tears. She moved her shoulder, pulling weakly away, and I released her. It was the first time since our reunion that I had really studied her face, and I felt with a deep triumphant joy how really unchanged that dear face was, and how little it mattered to my love that she was old.

Now too I saw in her face, though it looked both anxious and sad, something of the animation of youth. I recognized, and realized how much I had forgotten, the shape of her mouth, so much prettier without the lipstick. I kissed her gently, briefly, on the familiar mouth, as we used to kiss; and there was an intelligence in her quiet negative reception of the kiss which was itself a communication.

She said, 'I've changed so much, I'm a different person, you were so kind in your letter, but it can't be like that – you care about old times, but that's not me –'

'It is you. I recognized you in the kiss.' It was true. The kiss had transfigured her, like a kiss in a fairy tale. I remembered the feel, the texture, the movement of her mouth; and all that awkwardness was gone, that sense which I had had in the church of the impossibility of holding her. Our bodies were suddenly in tension in the same space, moved by the same forces. When I felt this I wanted to shout with joy, but I kept a quiet tone, wanting to coax her into speech, not wanting to affright her. 'Hartley, it's a miracle, I gave up the theatre, I came here to solitude, and I found you – I came here *for* you, I realize it now –'

'But you didn't know I was here –'

'No, yet I'd been searching for you, I've always been searching for you.'

She said, 'It can't be like that,' and lifted up her hand as if to conceal her face. Then she put her hand on the table where I covered it firmly with mine. 'Charles, listen, I must talk to you, there's so little time.' With the back of her other hand she touched her eyes, and caused the unshed tears to fall. Then she said, 'Oh Charles, my dear, my dear,' and bowed her head and thrust it towards me with a doglike movement. I stroked the dry brittle hair, I gently undid the hanging slide and put it in the pocket of my trousers.

'You'll stay with me forever now, Hartley.'

She raised her head and mopped her eyes again, this time with the sleeve of the green cotton coat which she was wearing over the yellow dress which I had seen before.

'Hartley, take off your coat, I want to see you, I want to touch you, take it off.'

'No, it's cold here.'

I pulled at the coat and she took it off. There was an intense charm in these movements, as if they were the merest innocent spiritual symbol of undressing a woman, something that angels might play at without quite understanding. I touched her breasts where they pressed warmly, firmly against the yellow stuff of the round-necked dress. I was delighted by the absence of any attempt to attract. This was a novelty in my life. The face powder was a careless habit, the dress was sloppy, nothing. The new unpainted lips were, I felt, alone a tribute to me. A woman who has long stopped working on her appearance cannot suddenly become smart and sleek. I was delighted that Hartley, as she was, attracted me. I felt proud, possessive, relieved, as if some life-long terror had been removed. And I thought: I'll buy her such lovely clothes – not flashy-smart, but just right for her. I'll *look after* her.

'Charles, I must just talk to you quickly, I just came to talk, after your letter, before he comes back –'

'Where is he?' I had forgotten his existence.

'He's at his woodwork.'

'Woodwork?'

'Yes, his woodwork class. It's a boat-building class really, only they do woodwork, I don't think he'll ever build a boat. It's shelves this week. It's the only evening he's out so I had to come now. They go on till quite late, I think they drink beer afterwards.'

'I don't want to talk about him,' I said. And I thought, if only I had a car and could drive, I'd take her right away now, this *instant*.

'Charles, listen, please, I haven't come to you like you think, like you said in the letter you wanted, that isn't possible. I've just come to tell you some things and – oh Charles – it's so extraordinary to see you. I thought it could never be, that it was a sort of impossibility of the world, that we two could ever be together again. I never thought I ever would – see you again and touch you – it's like a dream.'

'That's better. Only it's not a dream. Your life without me has been a dream. You are awaking from a dream, a nightmare. Oh why did you ever leave me, how could you have done, I nearly died of grief –'

'We can't talk about that now –'

'Yes we can, I want to talk about the old days, I want us to remember everything, to understand everything, to relive everything, to establish ourselves together as one being, one being that ought never to have been divided. Why did you leave me, Hartley, why did you run away?'

'I don't know, I can't remember –'

'You must remember. It's like a riddle. You've got to remember.'

'I can't, I can't –'

'Hartley, you've got to. You said that I wouldn't be faithful to you. Was it really that? You can't have thought that, you knew how much I loved you!'

'You went to London.'

'Yes, but I had to, I wasn't leaving you, I thought about you all the time, you know that, I wrote to you every day. It wasn't anyone else, was it? It wasn't *him*?' Strangely enough this terrible thought had only just this moment come to me.

'No.'

'Hartley, did you know him then, did you know him before you left me?'

'I can't remember.'

'Of course you can remember!'

'Please stop, please.'

The way she spoke these words, almost mechanically, with a kind of evasive animal instinct, words so like those which I had overheard her say so recently, made me want to cry out with pain and rage and a sort of awful pity for her.

'Did you know him then?'

'It doesn't matter.'

'It does matter, every little tiny thing matters and must be found again and must be picked up and must be redeemed, we've got to relive the past and clarify it and purify it, we've got to save each other at last, to make each other whole again, don't you see —'

'I didn't know him then, he was sort of engaged to one of my cousins, to Edna, you remember, well, no, you won't, and then she dropped him and I felt sorry for him —'

'But where did you meet him, was it after you ran away?'

'Yes, I went away to one of my aunties at Stoke-on-Trent, where Edna was. I didn't know him when we were together. It wasn't that, it wasn't anything, I didn't want you to be an actor, it wasn't anything, please don't.'

'But, Hartley, do be calm and answer my questions, I'm not angry with you and it is important. You didn't want me to be an actor! You never said so.'

'I did, I wanted you to go to the university.'

'But, Hartley, it can't have been just that.'

'It wasn't *just* anything, oh don't upset me so, we were too much like brother and sister and you were so sort of bossy and I decided I didn't want to.' Some tears spilled again. 'Have you got a hand-kerchief?'

I brought her a clean tea towel and she wearily wiped her eyes, her face, her neck. A button had come off the tight yellow dress at her breast. I had an impulse to grab her and tear the dress.

I sat down again. 'Hartley, if you had all these misgivings why didn't you utter them? We could have done something about it. It was so terrible to go away without a word, it was wicked.'

'I'm sorry, I'm sorry. I had to go like that, it was the only way, it wasn't easy. Oh it's cold, it's so cold, I must put my coat on again.' She put it on and pulled it round her, turning up the collar.

'How can it have happened, you can't simply have decided, there must be something else, something you haven't told me. Do you remember that day –'

'Charles, there isn't time, and I really can't remember. It's so long ago, it's a lifetime ago.'

'To me it's yesterday. I've been living with it ever since, reliving it and recalling it and going over and over it and wondering what went wrong and what happened to you and where you were. I think I've wondered where you were every day of my life. And I've been alone all this time, I've stayed in freedom, because of you. It's yesterday, Hartley. That was the only real time I ever lived through.'

'Alone. I'm sorry.'

It took me a moment to realize that she was not being sarcastic. Alone? Well, yes. Her tone suggested that she had not imagined, not speculated.

'You say you just decided you didn't want me, but that isn't an explanation, I want to know –'

'Oh stop – it just didn't happen. If I'd loved you enough I would have married you, if you'd loved me enough you would have married me. There aren't any reasons.'

'You say if I'd loved you enough – Don't drive me mad! I loved you to the limit, I still do, I tried to the limit, I didn't run away, I didn't marry anyone else, it was all your fault, you'll drive me crazy if you start –'

'We mustn't talk of these things – we're just sort of – plunging about – and it doesn't mean anything now. Look, I must *tell you certain things* only you won't *listen* –'

I thought, I mustn't go mad with emotion, I must stop questioning her now, though I *will* find out, I *will*. 'Hartley, have some wine.' I poured out a glass of the Spanish wine and she began mechanically to sip it. 'Have an olive.'

'I don't like olives, they're sour. Please listen to me –'

'I'm sorry it's so cold here, this house manages to be cold even when – All right, you tell me things. But just remember, you're here and you *stay* – whatever happened or didn't happen in the past you belong to me now. But tell me one thing, that night when you were on the road here and that car shone its lights on you, were you coming to see me then, that night?'

'No – but I – I just wanted to look at your house. It was a woodwork night, you see.'

'You wanted to look at my house. To stand in the road and look at the lighted windows. Oh my dear, you do love me, you can't help it.'

'Charles, it doesn't matter –'

'What do you mean, you'll make me mad again!'

'There isn't any place, any possibility, any sort of – structure – everything's broken down, you'll understand when I've told you – what I came to tell you –'

'All right, I'll listen now, but first let me kiss you. Then everything will be well. The kiss of peace.' I leaned over and very gently but persistingly let my dry lips touch her wet lips. How different different kisses are. This was a sort of holy kiss. We both closed our eyes. 'OK, now go on.' I filled up her wineglass. My hand was shaking and the wine splashed on the table.

She said again, 'There's so little time, and we've spent some of it.' Then she said, 'Oh God, I haven't got my watch with me, what time is it?'

I looked at my watch. It was a quarter to ten. I said, 'It's ten past nine.'

'Charles, it's about Titus.'

'Titus?' Titus? I had given no serious thought to Titus, and I felt dismayed.

'Yes, now I want to tell you. Oh God I feel drunk already, I'm not used to wine. I must tell you. I've sometimes thought, since I saw you in the village, that perhaps you could help somehow, but really you can only help by keeping away, by keeping right away –'

'That's nonsense –'

'You see, I told you Titus was adopted –'

'Yes, yes –'

'We hoped for a child, Ben wanted one, so did I, and we waited. And then I wanted to adopt and he didn't, he kept hoping. And I began to be so anxious because of the time limit, they only let you adopt if you're under a certain age, even then I had to lie about my age. Ben's younger than me and with him it was –'

'Is he? I thought he was in the war.'

'He was, but only in the later part –'

'What did he do in the war?'

'He was in the infantry. He doesn't talk about it much. He was captured, he was in a prisoner of war camp.'

'I was in ENSA –'

'I think he quite enjoyed the war, he saw himself as a soldier. He kept his army revolver, he was so fond of it, he wasn't supposed to. He never really settled down in civilian life. Sometimes he says, "Roll on the next war." '

'But you were married then, when he was a prisoner? Where were you?'

'I was living in Leicester, on a housing estate. I worked as a clerk in the ration book office. It was a lonely time.'

It was a lonely time. So when I was frigging around with Clement and travelling the counties in a bus to bring theatre to the war effort, Hartley was unhappy and *alone*. Christ, I even went to Leicester. 'Oh my God −'

'But listen, about Titus − you see, I did at last, at the last moment as it were, persuade Ben that we should adopt. He didn't really want to, but he did it because, I suppose, he saw what a state I was in − I was nearly − I was nearly − I was very upset − and really I arranged it all, I did it all, all the formalities, all the papers and so on, and Ben just signed the things without looking, he did it in a dream, he didn't want to know. I could see he was unhappy about it, but I thought that − when the little baby was there − he'd love it − everything would be different − and we'd all be happy −'.

'Don't cry, Hartley darling, here, let me hold your hand, I'll look after you now −'

'Titus was such a poor little mite, with a harelip, they had to operate −'

'Yes, yes, stop crying and get on with the story, if you must tell it.'

'Now I made a great mistake −'

'Hartley, don't grieve so, I can't bear it, have some more wine −'

'I made a terrible terrible mistake − and I have paid for it terribly − I ought to have known better −'

'Well, what *was* it?'

'I never told Ben about you. I mean, I didn't at the start tell him, and then later on it seemed more and more impossible to tell him −'

'Never told him how we'd grown up together, loving each other −?'

'Never told him how things were. When he asked had there been anybody, I said no. And of course he didn't know anything about it, my cousins didn't know, you remember how we were so sort of secretive, when we were children −'

'Yes. It was so precious, Hartley. Of course we were secretive. It was precious and secret and holy.'

'So there was really no danger that anyone else would tell him —'

'Danger? But why did it matter? After all you'd left me.'

'Ben was so jealous, he's such a terribly jealous person — and at first I didn't understand about jealousy, I mean I didn't understand it could be like *madness*.'

Yes, like madness. I understood that all right.

'And before we got married he used — almost to threaten me. If I annoyed him he'd say, "I'll pay you out when we're married!", and I was never sure if it was a joke. And it was usually about jealousy things. If I looked at another man, I mean just literally looked, he got so angry — and that went on and on after we got married — And then at last I just got frightened and lost my head and told him.'

'Told him you had loved me, and I had loved you?'

'Told him, sort of. I didn't want to make it seem important, but of course the fact I hadn't told him earlier made it look so terribly serious —'

'It was important, it was serious!'

'If only I had had the sense and the nerve either to tell him at the start or never to tell him at all. But you see, when I saw how jealous Ben was, what an angry jealous man he was, I began to be terrified in case one day — you would turn up —'

'And I have!'

'And I had to protect myself by at least having mentioned you before. You see, I was afraid someone might say something or that you'd find out where I was — I tried so hard not to let anyone know, anyone who could tell you, I cut off all the connections, and my parents had moved, I thought you might try to find me and —'

'You cut the connections all right! But, Hartley, if you were so frightened of him at the very start, why did you marry the blighter?'

'I always thought it would get better later on.'

'You were never frightened of me, were you?'

'No, no. But I was afraid that you would find out where I was and write to me. He always looked at my letters. For years and years I always got up first and ran down every morning so as to find the post first in case there was a letter from you.'

'Oh *God*.'

'I did this after I told him too, I was always terrified of the post, in case there was anything he could pick on and misunderstand. Anyway I felt it was too awful living with the risk of his finding out, so I did tell him – and it was – terrible.'

'He was furious, jealous?'

'It was terrible. You see, he couldn't believe it was innocent.'

'Hartley,' I said, 'it was innocent, but it was *serious*, something happened to us forever in those years. So in a way Ben was right to be impressed, you were telling him something which made everything different. I can understand that.'

'He wouldn't believe we hadn't been lovers, he thought I'd lied when I said I was a virgin. It was so especially terrible because what he thought wasn't true and I could never convince him, though I told him again and again. Sometimes he'd try to trap me by saying he'd forgive me if only I'd admit it, but I knew he wouldn't. He kept asking and pressing me and asking again and again and again, he just couldn't believe it.'

'My darling, we *were* lovers, though not in *that* sense –'

'He kept asking and asking, every day, sometimes every hour. And he'd ask the same question in the same words over and over and over, whatever answer I gave him. And of course the more angry he got the more clumsy and stupid and wretched I got so that it must have sounded as if I was lying –'

'I'd like to kill that man.'

She had drunk some more wine and was now sitting shivering, no longer crying, her wide eyes darkened, the pupils expanded, staring at the candle, with the tea towel unconsciously held up to her face, pressing it against her cheekbone like a veil. Her large brow, which looked white in the candlelight, was puckered and pitted with little shadows, but the way she had turned up the collar of her green cotton coat behind her hair gave her a girlish look. Perhaps that was what she used to do with her mackintosh collar in the days when we went bicycling. And even as I was listening intently to her words I was all the time gazing with a kind of creative passion at her candlelit face, like some god reassembling her beauty for my own purposes.

'Wait, Hartley, it's all right,' for she had suddenly looked up in alarm, 'I'm just going to light more candles, I want to look at you.' It was getting darker outside. I rattled out a box of candles and lit four more, dripping the wax into teacups and standing them upright. I ranged them round her like lights at an altar. Then I went and sat opposite to her, not near but looking. I so much wanted to see her smile. That would help the process of re-creation.

'Hartley, take away that veil. Won't you smile at me?'

She lowered the tea towel and I saw the wet drooping wretchedness of her mouth. 'Charles, what's the time?'

It was twenty-five past ten. 'Oh, half past nine, earlier. Look, Hartley, dearest, none of this matters, it's all *over,* don't you see? All right, he was a jealous stupid man, a horrible man who deserves to be punished, only it doesn't *matter* now, you don't have to go back into that hell. But what has all this got to do with Titus? You were going to tell me something about Titus.'

'He thinks Titus is your son.'

'What?'

'He thinks Titus is your son.'

Hartley had laid her hands flat on the table. Brightly lit by the candles she looked now like an interrogated prisoner.

I sat up very straight, blushing with amazement and shock, and found that I had put my hands flat on the table too. We stared at each other. 'Hartley, you can't be serious, he can't be serious! How could Titus be my son? Your husband isn't insane, is he? He knew Titus was adopted, he knew where he came from –'

'No, that's the point – he *didn't* know where Titus came from. I was the one who brought Titus into our lives, it was my idea, I arranged it all. Ben was in a state of shock throughout the whole business, he never did anything but sign papers without reading them. Once, somebody from the adoption people came to the house and saw Ben, but I did all the talking. Ben was like a zombie.'

'But Hartley, wait a minute, he knew I was a thing of the past, you didn't adopt Titus until years and years after you left me.'

'He thought we'd kept up. He thought we met secretly.' Hartley, tearless and staring-eyed, was almost, with her glare of misery and her pale pitted forehead, accusing.

'Hartley, darling, people can't believe things which are totally crazy and for which there is absolutely no evidence. He must have known you hadn't been seeing me.'

'How could he *know*? I was alone all day, sometimes all night. He had to go away travelling.'

'All right – let's stay sane about this – let's say it was extremely improbable! Besides – oh, how could he not believe you, how could he torture you with such mad imagined invented things!'

'It didn't happen all at once,' said Hartley. She gulped some more wine. 'He took against Titus from the start, perhaps because the adoption was the only thing I'd ever forced him to do against his will and he resented it and somehow deeply wanted it to fail. You see, he'd gone on and on up to that time saying that of course you had been my lover and you probably still were, and I'd gone on and on denying it till I was tired, I think we were both tired, I used to try to think about something else when he was talking about you. I thought at first he didn't really believe I'd kept up with you but only said it to spite me, and perhaps at first he didn't believe that, but I'm sure he thought we'd been lovers. And of course we couldn't forget you because you were always in the papers and then later on we saw you on telly –'

'God –'

'And this had gone on sort of festering in his mind, and then suddenly, it was as if he had worked it out, it was like a sort of revelation, he connected you with Titus. There were two bad things in his life and he went on brooding on them until he felt they must connect, they *must* connect, and they were both my fault.'

'But how old was Titus then and what sort of evidence –?'

'I can't remember how old Titus was, and perhaps it didn't happen all that suddenly. He was always harsh with Titus even when he was a tiny child, and later on it was worse. He may have said it just as a crazy thing to hurt me, and then when I was so upset he began to think about it and to see everything I said as a proof of guilt.'

'But, Hartley, this is madness, he must be mad, clinically mad –'

'He isn't mad.'

'That's what mad people do, see everything as evidence for what they want to believe.'

'He says that Titus resembles you –'

'Well, there you are.'

'And the funny thing is that he does look a bit like you.'

'He looks like you because you brought him up, and you look like me because we gazed and gazed at each other for so many years. Loving couples come to resemble each other.'

'Really? Perhaps you're right. It did seem odd, uncanny almost.' This idea seemed to strike Hartley more than anything I had said, even for a moment to please her.

'Besides, there must have been independent proof of Titus's birth and his parentage.'

'That was part of the trouble. You see, when I got Titus I simply didn't want to know who his parents were, I didn't want to think he was not entirely mine. The adoption society gave me a lot of stuff, they even gave me a letter from his mother, but I didn't read any of it, I destroyed it at once. I didn't want to give any part of my thoughts to his real parents. I didn't want to remember anything connected with Titus before I carried him home with me, and I didn't remember, I blotted it out of my mind. So when Ben became so interested and so suspicious and began to question me I didn't know how to answer, at first I couldn't even properly remember the name of the adoption society. It must all have sounded so bad, so like a lie –'

'But there are records, aren't there, official records?'

'There are now, but things were less formal then, and there wasn't any law about children having the right to know who their parents were. Of course there must have been records I suppose, but by the time Ben wanted to know the details the adoption society had ceased to exist, and I think a lot of papers had been destroyed in a fire, so someone said anyway. Ben never believed any of it, and no one would answer letters. I did try to find out, I went to London, he wouldn't come, and I stayed in a hotel –'

'Oh Hartley, Hartley –' I was picturing this journey, and the return home.

'I did try, but I couldn't find out, and somehow even then I didn't want to.'

'But I still don't understand, what did he think had happened? What did he think we'd been doing?'

'He thought we'd been going on seeing each other, perhaps not all the time, but on and off, secretly. He thought I'd become pregnant and –'

'But he was living with you!'

'That was another odd thing. Just before the adoption was finally fixed up I was away for quite a long time, it was about the only time I was away. I went to my father who was ill, he died then – and in this time away Ben thought the baby had come. I wasn't slim any more at all, I could have been pregnant, you see it all fitted in. And he thought I had invented all the adoption business so as to bring your child into his house.'

'But he saw the papers –'

'Well, I could have got hold of the papers somehow, he didn't read them anyway. And the visitor from the society could have been an accomplice.'

'Your husband is a most ingenious man. A vile hateful cruel half-mad ingenious *torturer*.'

Hartley, staring now at the candle flames, simply shook her head.

'But Titus himself, he didn't know, I suppose, I mean what Ben thought?'

'Well, he did know,' she said, 'later on, I mean when he was about nine or ten. Of course we'd always told him that he was an adopted child, like you're supposed to. But then Ben started telling him that he was the child of his mother's lover and that his mother was a whore.'

'What perfectly monstrous wickedness –'

'Ben did go through a phase of knocking Titus about. Some neighbours called the prevention of cruelty people. I couldn't do anything,

I couldn't defend him, I had to sort of take Ben's side, it was an awful time, everything was broken, as if one could still stand up but all one's bones were broken, all the bones and the little joints were broken, one wasn't whole any more, one wasn't a person any more.' Slow tears came and still staring at the candles she blindly felt about on the table for the towel. I pushed it towards her.

'But why couldn't you defend him – oh, stupid question. Hartley, I can't bear this –'

'He felt it was all my fault, and it *was* all my fault, I ought to have told him at the start, he asked me if there had ever been anyone else, and I lied really because there had been you although we weren't lovers, and later on when I told it, it sounded so mysterious and big. And I married him because I was sorry for him and I wanted to make him happy – and then – and then –'

'Oh Hartley, stop.'

'And I somehow got into a kind of fatal way of getting everything wrong, doing everything wrong, and hurting him, as if I were doing exactly the thing that would make him angry. One night when he was out at an evening class I accidentally put the chain on the door and went to bed and slept and he couldn't get in till I woke up at three and it was raining and then he started hitting me and wouldn't let me go to sleep –'

'Hartley, don't tell me any more of these *horrors* please. I don't want to hear them and anyway it's all over.'

'Oh I've been so stupid, so stupid, and of course Titus never settled down at school and everything went wrong, everything, and I'm not even sure that Ben believed it all at the start or that he always really believed it later, only everything I did seemed to make things worse, it was as if he hypnotized me into acting as if I was guilty. And I'm not sure what Titus believed or what he believes. Titus used to sit there hearing Ben saying one thing and me saying the other, it was like a sort of litany, an awful poem – and I don't know whether he knew what the truth was or whether there was any truth, it was all a kind of fog of awful senseless argument and row. It all got ravelled up into a nightmare and in the end he blamed me for it and in a way he was right, sometimes I think he blamed me and resented me more than he did Ben. Of course when Titus was small he was frightened all the time and he kept quiet and he'd sit all the evening on his little chair against the wall, all white and tense and quiet, dreadfully quiet. Later on when he was about fifteen he used to pretend sometimes that he was your child, and once or twice he told Ben that I'd told him he was. But I think he did this just to spite Ben when Titus was too big for Ben to hit him any more.'

'Hartley, *stop*. Just tell me more about Titus now. When did he go away? Where do you think he is?'

'When he left school he went into the poly, you know, the polytechnic, where we used to live, he had a student grant, he was studying electricity. He lived at home, but he sort of ignored us, he sent us to Coventry. I sometimes felt he really hated us, both of us. And he could never forgive me for not protecting him when he was small. Then just before we moved down here he went into digs, and then he just vanished. He left the digs and never let us know or sent an address. I went round there and asked about him but no one seemed to know or care where he'd gone, and he never wrote. He knew we were coming here. I think he went to look for his real parents, he always said he would. He went on and on about them sometimes and how perhaps they were rich. Anyway, he's gone now. Gone.'

'Don't be so tragic, Hartley, he'll turn up again. He knows where you live, doesn't he? He'll turn up. He'll come home when he's short of money, they always do.'

She shook her head. 'Sometimes I don't want him to come back. Sometimes I believe he's dead. Sometimes I almost wish he *were* dead, and that I could hear that he was dead, so that the anguish of the hope and the fear and the dread could just stop, and we could be at peace. If he came back – it could be – terrible –'

'You mean?'

'Terrible.' The slow tears were coming and she kept drooping her eyelids to make them slide down her cheeks. She said, 'I wish we'd never adopted a child, it was my fault, Ben was quite right, we were better without. I could have managed then and Ben would have been – like I wanted –'

In spite of the pain and horror of her story my mind was leaping ahead into a bright land, into all sorts of almost detailed vistas of sudden hope. I would take Hartley away and together we would find Titus. In some strange metaphysical sense it was true, I would make it true: Titus was my son, the offspring of our old love!

'Hartley, my little one, stop crying, you've had your orgy of horrors, now stop it. You're mine now and I'm going to look after you and protect you –'

She began shaking her head again. 'And I married him to make him happy! But you mustn't think it's been all bad, it hasn't. What I've told you is the bad part, but I've probably given you a quite wrong impression.'

'Now you're going to tell me you've had a happy marriage!'

'No, but it's not been all bad, Ben wasn't always awful with Titus. Ben's a bit of a Jekyll and Hyde, perhaps all men are. It was just that you kept cropping up and that always set him off, and we couldn't just forget you because you were so famous, but we've had better times too –'

'What were they like?'

'Oh just ordinary times, you might think it was dull, we had a quiet life –'

'A quiet life!'

'Ben didn't much like his job but he liked doing things about the house, he likes DIY.'

'DIY?'

'Do It Yourself. We went to London once to the exhibition at Olympia. He used to go to evening classes.'

'What was he learning at the class on that quiet evening when you left the chain on the door?'

'He was learning to rivet china.'

'Oh – Lord – ! Hartley, what did you do all the time? Did you entertain, have friends?'

'Well, Ben didn't like social life. I didn't mind. We don't really know anybody here either.'

'And did you go to evening classes too?'

'I once started German, but he didn't like me to go out in the evening and the classes were different nights.'

'Oh – Hartley – And in all those years was he faithful to you, did he ever have anyone else?'

For a moment she seemed not to understand. 'No, of course not!'

'I wonder how you can be so sure. And you, did you ever have anyone else?'

'No, *of course* I didn't!'

'Well, I suppose it would have been as much as your life would have been worth.'

'You see really we were very wrapped up in each other, we are very –'

'Wrapped up! Yes! I can see it all.'

'No, you can't see it all,' she said, suddenly turning towards me, blinking and drawing her fingers across her eyes and her mouth.

'You can't see it, nobody can understand a marriage. I've prayed and prayed to go on loving Ben –'

'It's a travesty, Hartley. Don't you see now *at last* that the situation is intolerable, impossible? Stop playing Jesus Christ to that torturer, if that's what you're doing.'

'He suffers too and I can be – oh so unkind. It's not his fault, and it was my fault in the beginning.'

'You gorge me full of these awful stories and then expect me to sympathize with *him*! Why did you come here, why did you come to me, why did you tell me these things at all?'

Hartley, still staring at me, seemed to reflect. She said slowly, 'Perhaps because I had *sometime,* and I've always known this, to tell someone, to say it, to say these blasphemies, what you call these horrors to someone. And, as I told you, I've never really had any friends, Ben and I have lived so much together, so much on our own, so sort of secretly, a kind of hidden life, like criminals. I never had anyone to talk to, even if I had wanted to talk.'

'So it turns out I'm your only friend!'

'Yes, I suppose you are the only person I could inflict this on –'

'Inflict it – you want me to share the pain –'

'Well, in a way you were responsible –'

'For your ruined life? Just as you were responsible for mine! So this is your revenge? No, no, I'm not serious –'

'I didn't mean that, just that Ben's ideas about you have been like – like demons in our lives. But of course it wasn't just wanting to tell someone. You know, when I saw you in the village for the first time I nearly fainted. I had just come round the corner from the bungalows and you were just going into the pub, and my knees gave way and I had to go a bit up the hill and sit on the grass. Then I thought I must be dreaming, I thought I must be mad, I didn't know what to do. Then the next day I heard somebody talking about you in the shop, saying you'd retired and come here to live. And I wondered for a bit whether I'd tell Ben, because he mightn't have been able to recognize you, you don't look quite like your pictures, but then I thought he's bound to hear anyway, someone at the boat-building class will know, so I told him I'd seen you and he was in a frenzy and said we must sell the house at once and go away, and of course he believed, or said he believed, that you'd come on purpose because of me, and of course it *was* very odd –'

'But is he selling the house?'

'I don't know, he said he'd see the house agent, he may have done, I didn't ask. But really I came here tonight because I wanted to tell you about Titus and about what Ben imagines and to ask your help –'

'My help! My dearest girl, I've been telling you, I am all help! Let's go, let's just *go,* we can go to London tomorrow, even tonight if there's a train –'

'No, no, no. You see, I can't decide, I've kept swinging to and fro. I thought first I'd simply ask you to go away, to sell your house and go away. If once you understood how much it mattered to me and Ben, how *awful,* what a nightmare it was that you're here, you would go at once.'

'Hartley, *we* are going, you and I are going, *that* is the answer.'

'I thought I'd write you a letter asking you to go, but it would have been so hard to explain it all in a letter.'

'Hartley, will you come, tonight, tomorrow? You will?'

'And then I thought – but perhaps this really is mad – that you could somehow persuade Ben, make him *see,* that I've been telling the truth all these years, impress him somehow –'

'How?'

'Oh, I don't know, swear on something sacred or with a notary or –'

The word 'notary' seemed to gather round it some of the sheer insanity of what she was saying. So now we were to be involved with notaries! I could imagine how much that would impress Ben. At the same time, in the swift way of thought, I was making realistic plans. Of course I still hoped that, when it came to it, Hartley would decide to stay with me now, tonight. However it was possible that she would not, and even if she did there might be some terrible revulsion of feeling afterwards. Such shock tactics might do more harm than good. Better perhaps to let her reflect quietly upon her reunion with me and draw her own conclusions. She seemed to me to be still in a dream, a woman *locked up* inside her own nightmare. She would emerge, but it might be slowly. I might even have a long work to do, to give her back hope and life and stir in her the instinct of freedom, which it still seemed to me was so natural to her. Meanwhile I must find ways of keeping contact with her and of making *her* plan, making *her* construct futures which contained me. Surely, once she conceived of happiness she would spring towards it. But for the moment it might be wise to humour her lunatic idea that I might 'persuade' Ben. If she just, bleakly, blankly, asked me to go away my task would be much harder, though it was still certain to be successful in the end. Hartley was a sick woman.

I said, 'I think your idea about Ben is a good one, I might be able to solve that problem anyway, to make him see and believe the truth about what happened or rather didn't happen in the old days, we must consult about how it could be done. But, Hartley, listen, the important thing is this. You are going to leave Ben and come to me, for good, forever –'

Hartley, who had been sitting entranced, absorbed in her own unusual eloquence, looked suddenly terrified. She jerked back her head and began to stare about the room. 'Charles, what *is* the time?'

It was nearly eleven o'clock. I said, 'Oh, it's about ten to ten. Darling, why not stay here now, *please*?'

'It can't be as early as that. It will take me thirty-five minutes to get home, and Ben usually gets back about eleven.' She got up and said, 'I feel drunk, I'm not used to wine, I must go.' She turned, then made a sudden pounce towards my hand and peered at my watch, then uttered a high-pitched wailing cry. 'It's eleven, it's eleven! Oh why did you do it! Why did I believe you! Why didn't I bring my watch! What shall I do, oh what shall I do! What shall I tell him, he's sure to know where I've been! Oh I've been so careful and I haven't told him lies and now he'll think – It's as bad as can be, oh I am stupid, stupid, whatever can I do?'

'Stay here, you don't have to go back!'

I was shaken and a bit ashamed when I saw her grief and terror, but I also thought: let there be disaster upon disaster, crisis on crisis, let it all break down quickly into a shambles. That will benefit me. And then I thought too: unless he kills her. And then I thought: I must keep her here. That settles it, it must all be achieved *now*. I must not let her go home.

'I can't go back, I can't stay. I shall have to tell him I've been with you, but how can I, it'll be like those nights, oh I shall die, I shall die, I want to be dead, why do I have to suffer and suffer like this. Oh what *can* I do, what *can* I do?'

'Hartley, stop being hysterical. Just make up your mind to stay here.'

'I can't stay, I must run, run. But it's no good. He must be home now, and he'll be so worried and so angry. I can't do it, I can't go back, oh why have I been so thoughtless and so foolish, it's like what I always do, making things worse and worse, I should have known the time –'

'Don't blame yourself, think of it this way, you left your watch behind on purpose so as to commit yourself to me and if you've now made it impossible to go back, so much the better!'

'I shouldn't have come here, I shouldn't have told you those things, he'll know I've told you, he'll make me tell him everything I said.'

'You came here to see an old friend, there's nothing wrong in that, and I am your friend, you said so, and I'm so glad you did, and friends help each other –'

'Oh if only I'd gone an hour ago everything would have been all right! I must run, I must get out of here –'

'Hartley, be calm! If you insist on going I will walk along with you –'

'No, you must leave me alone, we must never meet again! Oh how I wish I were dead!'

'Stop this wailing, I can't stand it!'

As she was crying out Hartley had been running to and fro in the kitchen like a demented animal, taking a few little rushing steps towards the door, then a few steps back to the table. In her agitation she even picked up the tea towel and stuffed it into her pocket. The spectacle of this frightened anguish was beginning to appal me and I was now feeling frightened too. To allay my own fear I ran to her and seized her in my arms. 'Oh my darling, don't be so afraid, *stop it, stay here,* I love you, I'll look after you –'

She then began to fight me, silently, violently, and with a surprising strength, kicking my ankles, writhing her body about, one hand pinching my arm, the other pressed hard against my neck. I caught a glimpse of her open mouth and of her glistening frothy teeth. I tried to lift her and to capture one of her hands, and then it became too dreadful and too hard to attempt to crush this pinching, kicking animal into submission and I abruptly let her go, and with the impetus staggered backwards, banged into the table and upset the candles. In that instant Hartley was gone, rushing out of the kitchen, not towards the front door but out of the back door straight onto the grass and onto the rocks.

I ought to have rushed after her like a flash, like a faithful dog. I ought to have dragged her back and kept her in the house by force. Instead some stupid instinct made me pause to pick up the candles.

Then, leaving them fallen awry in their teacups, I ran out into the blue almost-darkness and the silent emptiness of the rocky shore. After looking at the bright candles I could at first see nothing, and it struck me in an odd way that while I was talking to Hartley I had forgotten about the sea, forgotten it was there and now felt confounded and at a loss to find myself half blind among those terrible rocks.

There was no sign of Hartley, she must immediately have clambered and sprung with the agility of a girl somewhere over the ring of rocks which surrounded my small lawn. I called out 'Hartley!' and the sound was dreadful, *dangerous*. Which way had she gone? There was no easy way back to the road in either direction, either on the village side or on the tower side. There was nothing in that blue dimness all round about but wrinkled, folded rocks and slippery pools and deep sudden crevasses. I stood there and listened, hoping to hear her call me or to hear the sound of her scrambling.

What had seemed to be silence now revealed itself as a medley of small sounds, though no sound could tell me which way Hartley had gone. There was a faint lapping and sucking of the wavelets touching the foot of the little cliff, and then retreating and then touching again. There was the very distant murmur of a car on the road near the Raven Hotel. There was a scarcely audible humming which was perhaps, as a result of the wine I had drunk, inside my head. And there was a rhythmical hissing noise followed by a muted echoing report which was the sound produced by the water retreating from Minn's cauldron.

The thought of the cauldron now shocked me into another awful fear: could Hartley swim? I had not till now formulated the thought that she might have run straight out of the house to hurl herself into the sea. She had cried out, 'I want to die.' Had she, in those years, contemplated suicide, indeed how could she not? A strong swimmer would scarcely cast himself into a calm sea hoping for death, but to a non-swimmer the sea might be the very image of restful death itself. *Could* she swim? She had never learnt in the old days, when the sea was for both of us a far-off dream. It had never occurred to us to venture together into the black canal, although I had become a diffident swimmer at the age of fourteen, when I went to Wales with Mr McDowell. In our first talk at the bungalow she had said Ben could not swim, but had said nothing about herself. Had she now run straight from my arms and from my deception into the easeful peace of the drowning sea?

As I was thinking this I was climbing over the rocks towards the right, in the direction of the village, since if she was running home she would instinctively turn in this direction. The easier way back to the road was by way of the tower, because of a deep gulley between the road and the rocks on the village side, not too hard to negotiate by daylight, but very hazardous in the dark. Hartley might not know this however. I clambered and slithered, now calling again and able to see a little more in the diffused half-darkness. The evening star was present, perhaps other stars, a blanched moon. I thought and I prayed: let her just fall and sprain her ankle and I will carry her back to the house and keep her and let that devil do what he will.

It was extremely difficult to keep up any pace over the rocks since they were so unpredictable and devoid of reason. Their *senselessness* had never so much impressed me. I kept trying to get near to the edge of the sea but the rocks kept defeating me, not by malign interest but by sheer muddle, and I kept slipping down slopes into seaweedy pools and confronting black clefts and holes and smooth unclimbable surfaces. I had an intuition of light over the sea and I wanted to be able to look there and be sure there was not somewhere the dark head of a drowning woman and her desperate arms breaking the calm surface. I moaned softly as I clutched and skipped, hallooing her name at intervals like an owl's call, and at last I came unexpectedly over the smooth dome of a tall rock and found myself just above the water. I stood up on the highest point of the dome and looked out to sea. There was nothing upon the luminous faintly-wrinkled expanse except wavery yellow replicas of the evening star and the low crouching moon. The sky was still a dimmed glowing blue, not yet sunk into the blackish blue of night. One or two pin-point stars were just visible beyond the big jagged lamp of the evening star. I turned to look inland. I was conscious now of the warm air, the warm rocks, after the strange chill of my house. The rocks stretched away, visible as almost colourless lumps above black hollows. Beyond was the road, and some scattered distant lights of the village and of Amorne Farm. I shouted out more loudly now, 'Hartley! Hartley! Call to me and I'll come to you.' Call and I'll come: that was it indeed. But there was no answer, only the silence made up of little noises.

I wondered what to do next. Had Hartley managed to get across the gulley onto the road? Possibly she knew those rocks better than I did. Possibly she and Ben used to come and have picnics here. It was true that marriages were secret places. What was it like in there, and were Hartley's out-pourings the exaggerated half-dreams of a hysterical woman? What did Ben really believe? I decided to get back onto the road and return towards the tower. It took me about five minutes of cautious scrambling to cross the gulley, and then I ran back, calling out, until I had passed the house and reached the turn in the road from which I could see the lights of the Raven Hotel. Nothing, no one. By now it was getting really dark and it seemed pointless to do any more rock scrambling. Was Hartley home by now – or was she lying unconscious in one of those dark clefts in the rocks – or worse? What was I to do next? One thing I clearly could not do was to go back to Shruff End and blow out the candles and go to bed.

It was obvious by now that I would have to go to Nibletts, either to assure myself by eavesdropping that Hartley was back there, or – I was not sure what the alternative was. I set off briskly walking back again towards the village. I realized I was still wearing the Irish jersey and by now felt very hot, so I pulled the jersey off and stuffed it down behind the *Nerodene* milestone and went on, almost running, and tucking my shirt in. I had intended at first to go the longer, safer way round by the harbour and up beside the wood, approaching the house by the back way, but my anxiety was too extreme and I took the usual diagonal path towards the village. Three yellow street lamps shone upon an empty scene as I ran past the silent darkened shop and under the hanging sign of the rampant Black Lion. The pub too was shut, few windows were lit, the villagers were early bedders. My running footsteps echoed the sound of urgency and fear. I reached the church and turned panting up the hill. There were no lights here and the road lay dark under the shadow of the hanging woodland beyond. I slowed to a walk and realized that I had almost reached my objective. There were the lights of Nibletts, the door of the bungalow wide open, and there, standing at the gate and gazing down the road towards me, was Ben.

It was too late to hide and in any case I now had no desire to do so. The pettiness of concealment seemed out of place and was, I suddenly hoped, now in any case a thing of the past. I hurried on towards Ben, who had come out of the gate to peer at me. Perhaps in the dark he thought that the approaching figure might be his wife.

'Is Hartley back?'

Ben stared at me and I thought, how idiotic, he calls her Mary, he has probably never heard her real name.

I said, 'Is Mary back?'

'No. Where is she?'

The light from the front window and from the open door showed Ben's cropped boyish bullet head and the blue colour of the military style jacket of blue denim which he was wearing. He looked worried and young and for a second I saw him, not as the 'devil' of Hartley's awful stories, but as an anxious young husband wondering if his wife has met with an accident.

'I met her in the village and asked her back for a drink, but she only stayed a short while and then she said she'd take a short cut home across the rocks and after she'd gone I suddenly wondered if she might have fallen and sprained her ankle.' It sounded so feeble and false.

'A short cut across the rocks?' This was an almost senseless conception, but Ben seemed too worried to challenge it or even to exhibit hostility. 'You mean the rocks near your house? She could have fallen there. We'd better go and look, or — I'll get a torch —' As he went into the house I turned from the window and the lighted path and looked away down the road. After a moment I saw a dark figure. It was Hartley, slowly coming towards me up the hill. I had a large number of instant thoughts. One was that it had been crazy of me to come here as now I had ruined whatever lying excuse for her absence Hartley might meanwhile have invented. I also thought that I must instantly warn her that I had told Ben of her visit. I also thought that I must somehow now stay with them so as to protect her against him. I also thought with anguish that this was impossible. I also thought, well why not just run down the hill, seize her by the hand, and pull her away with me, run away, anywhere, through the village, out into the fields. Spend the night at Amorne Farm and go to London by train tomorrow. Or get a lift on a lorry going anywhere: Manchester, York, Bristol, Cardiff, Glasgow, Carlisle. This seemed impossible too, for reasons which I could not quite work out. (I had no money, Ben would follow us, she would be too frightened to come etc. etc.) I also thought, let it crash, let them have the awfullest beastliest row they've ever had. She ran to me once. *She will run to me again.* I have only to wait.

By the time I had thought all this in about four seconds I had run down the hill as fast as I could and met Hartley. I did not touch her; I said very quickly, but distinctly, in a low voice, 'I'm sorry, I got worried, I told him we met accidentally in the village and I asked you for a drink, and then you set off home over the rocks. I can't stay now, but come to me soon. Come soon and come forever. You must not continue your life here. I shall be waiting for you every day.'

I could not see Hartley's face, but her whole figure expressed not fear so much as a total dejected resigned misery which had passed beyond fear. She had an air of being dripping wet as if she had in truth been drowned and this was her ghost.

Ben was back at the gate now, and I called to him, 'She's here!' and Hartley and I walked on to meet him.

Ben came out onto the pavement. As we approached he said 'OK then. OK. Goodnight.' Then he turned and went back into the house, not waiting to see if Hartley would follow. I held the gate open. She passed me with her blind dripping drowned head.

I had an impulse to follow, to push after her into the house, to sit down, make conversation, demand coffee. But it was impossible, it would only make things worse for her. Everything had gone amiss. The door banged.

I had no wish now to eavesdrop, indeed I had almost no curiosity left, so strongly did my mind shy away in horror from the interior of that house and of that marriage. I felt disgust with myself, with him, even with her.

I walked home, neither fast nor slowly. I remembered to pick up my jersey, which was now wet with dew. I found the house in darkness. The candles had fallen over again and burnt themselves out on the wooden top of the table, making long dark burns which remained there ever after to remind me of that terrible night.

HISTORY

FOUR

W HAT follows this, and also what directly precedes it, has been written at a much later date. What I have now written is therefore more deeply reflected and more systematically remembered than it would be if I were continuing to write a diary. Events, as it happened, did not subsequently leave me much time for diary-writing, although what immediately follows has something of the air of an interlude (perhaps a comic one). This novelistic memoir, as it has now become, is however, as far as its facts are concerned (though, as James would say, what indeed are facts?), accurate and truthful. I have in particular, and this may be a professional attribute, an extremely good memory for dialogue, and I am sure that a tape-recording of my candlelit conversation with Hartley would differ but little from what I have transcribed. My account is curtailed, but omits nothing of substance and faithfully narrates the actual words spoken. How very deeply indeed many of the conversations, past and to come, recorded in this book, are engraved upon my mind and my heart!

After my return on the evening described I had had enough and I went to bed and to sleep. (I did not eat the Korean clams; later on I threw them away.) I awoke after nine the next morning and it was raining. The English weather had put on another of its transformation scenes. The sea was covered by a clear grey light together with a thick rain curtain. The rain was exhibited in the light as if it were an illuminated grille, and as if each raindrop were separately visible like the beads upon my bead curtain. There it hung, faintly vibrating in the brilliant grey air, while the house hummed like a machine with the steady sound of pattering. I got up and staggered around in the kitchen making myself tea and lowering my head like a sullen beast against any urgency of reflection. I did not wonder what had happened at Nibletts after I left. All that would soon be past history. Then as I sat in the little red room, with my head still sullenly lowered against the light of the rainy morning, I made it out that perhaps I had achieved something by thrusting the situation on into an area of crisis. Really I need not at present do anything at all but wait. Surely she *would* come. And ... if she did not ... there were other plans which I was already quietly making. I would not be without resources. I would wait. And with that I settled into a weird uneasy sort of peace.

A little later, I mean a day or two later in my condition of *sursis,* like a half-expected apparition Gilbert Opian made his appearance. Why was I not really surprised when a timid brief tinkle of the mid-morning bell revealed a nervously smiling Gilbert, and beyond him at the end of the causeway his yellow car? Oddly enough I had already made a sort of plan which included someone like Gilbert, and he would certainly do. Fate was co-operating for once. 'Lizzie?' 'No.' Just as well. It was still raining.

I put on a show of surprise and annoyance.

'What is it then?'

'May I come in, king of shadows? The rain is running down my neck.'

I led the way back into the kitchen where I had been eating chocolate digestive biscuits and drinking Ovaltine. A feature of my interim condition was that, from ten thirty in the morning onwards, I had to have regular treats and snacks all day long. A wood fire was blazing in the little red room, its lively mobile structures showing bright through the open door, and casting a flickering glow into the rain-curtained kitchen.

Gilbert was dripping.

'Well?'

'My dear, Lizzie has left me.'

'So?'

'So I decided to come here, I felt the urge. I wanted to tell you about Lizzie, I somehow felt I ought to. She's sick, you know, I mean in her mind. She's madly in love with you again, it's the old disease, I was afraid it would come back. And one of the symptoms is she can't stand me. Well, I suppose our cohabitation was a sort of precarious miracle. Anyway it's all over now, our idyll is over, our little house is smashed. I'm bombed out. She's gone. I don't even know where she is.'

'She's not here, if that's what you imagine.'

'Oh I don't –'

'I suppose you think it's my fault, is that what you came to say?'

'No, no, I accuse no one. Destiny, God perhaps, myself. The battle of life and how to fight it. Whoever conscripted me made a big mistake. Now she's gone, it seems incredible she could have cared for me and made that house with me, we chose things together like real people. No, I just thought I'd come. You've always been a magnet to me, and now I'm getting old I don't care what people think or how much they snub me, it's always worth trying, I only wish I'd been more forward when I was young. You know how I feel about you, all right you hate

that bit, you despise it, it disgusts you, though actually anybody's lucky
to be loved by anybody and ought to be grateful, well anyway as I
haven't a job at present I thought I'd come and see you and maybe you
would let me stay for a while and be useful, I can't bear being alone
at home without her where everything reminds me —'

'Useful?'

'Yes, I could cook or clean up, do odd jobs, why not? I've always
felt I ought to belong to somebody, I mean really legally as a sort of
possession, just a chattel, not anything troublesome, not with *rights*, I
mean. I often think I have the soul of a slave. Perhaps I was a Russian
house-serf in a previous incarnation, I should like to think I was, all cosy
and protected with simple things to do, kissing my master's shoulder
and sleeping on the stove —'

'Do you want to be my house-serf?'

'Yes, please, guv'nor. I'll live in that dog kennel if you like.'

'OK, you're engaged.'

Thus began an odd little period of my life to which strangely enough
I look back with a certain sad nostalgia, perhaps simply because it was
such a dead calm before such a terrible storm. I even became rather
fond of Gilbert in his role as serf. In the past, although his servility
had inhibited my regard, yet his devotion to me had proved that he
had some sound ideas. And he was, even at this stage, useful; later on
he was essential. My standard of living rose. Gilbert cleaned the house,
he even got the stains off the bath. I let him cook in a style which was
a compromise between his own and mine. I could not bring him up
to my level of simplicity and it would have been cruelty to attempt it.
Grilled sardines on toast and bananas and cream were not Gilbert's idea
of a good lunch, and equally I had no use for his thick over-rich Gallic
messes. We ate exquisitely dressed green salads and new potatoes, a
favourite dish of mine. (The shop now had lettuces and young spuds.)

I let him concoct vegetarian soups and stews and I taught him to make fritters in the Japanese style, which he was at once able to do better than me. I also let him bake cakes. He shopped for me in the village and fetched Spanish wine from the Raven Hotel, where he amused himself by posing as my butler. At night he slept on the big broken-bellied sofa in the middle room downstairs, among the driftwood. The sofa was damp, but I let him have the hot water bottle.

I swam every day, sometimes in the sun, sometimes in the rain, and began to feel soaked in the sea as if it were penetrating my skin. When the sun shone I spent time out on the rocks. Gilbert kept watch over the front door and went out to look for letters, only no one called and Hartley did not write. I returned to my obsessive task of collecting stones, picking them out of tide-washed crannies and rock pools and carrying them back to the lawn, where Gilbert helped me with my border round the edge of the grass. The stones, so close-textured, so variously decorated, so individual, so handy, pleased me as if they were a small harmless tribe which I had discovered. Some of them were beautiful with a simple wit beyond that of any artist: light grey with thin pink traceries, black with elaborate white crosses, brown with purple ellipses, spotted and blotched and striped, and their exquisitely smooth forms lightly dinted and creased by the millennial work of the sea. More and more of them now found their way into the house, to lie upon the rosewood table or on my bedroom window ledge.

Gilbert would have liked to collect stones too, and to pick flowers, but as soon as he ventured onto the rocks in his leather-soled London shoes he immediately fell. He bought some plimsolls at the Fishermen's Stores, but still tumbled. He never, of course, ventured into the sea. However he sawed wood and carried it into the house and this activity, which he felt to be in some way symbolic, gave him much satisfaction.

He continued to be busy all day long with self-invented serf activities. He washed the bead curtain with Vim, making it shine and removing the slightly sticky filthy surface to which I had become accustomed. Thus, for a brief time, we lived together, each absorbed in his own illusions, and together we regressed into a life of primal simplicity and almost fetishistic private obsession.

When I grew tired of hunting for stones I used to sit for long periods upon the rocky archway bridge beneath which the angry tide raced in and out of Minn's cauldron, dangling my bare feet over the edge and letting them bathe in the flying rainbow of the spray. It gave me a gloomy fatalistic pleasure to observe the waves, as they rushed into that deep and mysteriously smooth round hole, destroy themselves in a boiling fury of opposing waters and frenzied creaming foam. Then when the tide was receding the cauldron became an equally furious sucking whirlpool as the water churned itself into a circling froth in its desperate haste to escape through the narrow outlet under the arch, and as it met head-on the whipping power of the sea wind. The wind blew continually during those days and when it was strong the waves slapped the rocks and wailed and sucked in and out of the crannies with a noise which in my tense fretful state I was beginning to find tiring. I would never have imagined that I would dislike the sound of the sea, but sometimes, and especially at night, it was a burden to the spirit.

In the evenings I sat beside the wood fire in the little red room. Sometimes Gilbert sat in the kitchen, enjoying himself being a servant. (I suspect he would have liked to dress as a housemaid, but was right in assuming that this would not please me.) Sometimes he sat with me, in silence like a dog, gazing at me and rolling his eyes about in that disconcerting manner. Sometimes we talked a little. In the lamplight now and then he came to look uncannily like Wilfred Dunning, a resemblance of course created by Gilbert's unconscious acquisition of his hero's facial mannerisms. Yet to my vulnerable attentive nerves, it seemed more than that, something more like a real visitation. If so, it did Gilbert credit that he should be the vehicle. We talked about the past, about Wilfred and Clement and the old days. A shared past, that is something. And I thought about Clement. In a way, if there were justice, it was Clement who spanned my life and made me, and about whom this book should be written. But in such matters there is no justice, or rather justice is cruel.

'Charles, darling.'

'Yes.'

'You don't mind my asking? Did you really love Clement or was it just that Clement loved you? People often wondered.'

'Of course I loved Clement.'

Well, I came to love her. Did I love her at first? I loved her beauty, her fame, her talent, her flattery, her help. Would I have found Hartley if I had not become Clement's possession? Clement stretched over the years, she was the one permanent thing, only removed by death. I had been her boy lover, her creation, her business partner, the nearest thing she ever had to a husband, finally her middle-aged never-estranged son. The transformation of my love for Clement, its metamorphoses, had been one of the main tasks and achievements of my life: that love which so often almost failed but never quite failed. Would I ever sit by the fire with Hartley and tell her about Clement? Would she understand, would she want to know? How important it seems to continue one's life by explaining oneself to people, by justifying oneself, by memorializing one's loves.

'Charles.'

'Yes.'

'I heard something funny in the pub today.'

'Oh.'

'That chauffeur you had, Freddie Arkwright, he's the brother of the pub man, he's coming to stay at Whitsun.'

'Oh.' Shame, guilt, another demon trail.

'Funny isn't it, the way people come back into one's life.'

'Yes.'

'Charles, darling.'

'Yes.'

'If you lived with Lizzie I could be the butler. Would you like a drink?'

'No, thanks.'

'Mind if I do? I wish I could give up drink, it's a symbol of depravity, a proof that one's a slave. Being in love, that's another slavery, stupid when you come to think of it, mad really. You make another person into God. That can't be right. Thank heavens I'm out of that trap. Real love is free and sane. Obsession, romance, does one grow out of them? Lizzie and I used to talk about that. Real love is like in a marriage when the glamour is gone. Or love when you're older, like love I feel for you, darling, only you don't want to know. It's good to feel how different it is from the old craving. Not exactly that I don't want anything for myself, but going that way. Love. God, how often we uttered that word in the theatre and how little we ever thought about it.'

'Freddie's coming to stay at the pub?'

'No, at Amorne Farm, that's where the other Arkwrights live. Such a nice boy. Did you know he was queer?'

'No.'

'God, it was such hell being queer when I was young.'

And of course all the time, whether I was talking to Gilbert or remembering Clement or watching the waves destroying themselves in the cauldron, I was thinking about Hartley and waiting for her and wondering how soon my nerve would break. I had already decided in general outline what my next move would be should she make none, but I was superstitiously reluctant to make detailed plans before I felt the time had come to change the world by force. I was continually conscious of Hartley, as of her real presence, and she was with me as Jesus used to be with me when I was a child. And I thought about her intensely, and yet, again superstitiously, deliberately, in a respectfully abstract way. I let memories from the far past come and go as they would. But about the terrible present and the gulf of those suffering years my imagination was squeamish and discreet. I did not want to become simply obsessed with her misery. I did not want to waste my energy on hating that man. It would soon be irrelevant. So I reverted to the past when she was the unspoilt focus of my innocent love, seeing her as she had been when she seemed my future, my whole life, that life which had been taken from me and yet still seemed to exist somewhere as a packaged stolen possibility.

However, in the event, before I had time to decide to move upon my waiting and upon the fact of her silence, something else, quite unexpected and extraordinary, took place.

I may have described the period of my odd quiet *tête-à-tête* with Gilbert as if it could have covered weeks, but in fact it covered days. Upon the last of these days, the one on which the *tête-à-tête* came to an abrupt end, I felt, in the morning, an exceptional restlessness. Avoiding Gilbert, I went out onto the rocks with my field glasses hung round my neck, intending to look at birds. I also had it in mind that I might see a seal, since Gilbert said that he thought he had seen one. However, once I was out there, upon the top of my minuscule cliff, I was assailed by a kind of fear which seemed familiar. To begin with I felt giddy, as if the sea were a hundred feet below me, instead of being, at that state of the tide, about twelve feet, and I had to sit down. Then I felt a nervous need to scan the surface of the sea carefully with the glasses: but not looking for seals.

Of course, with every day that passed, I knew that something which frightened me was coming nearer, the need to initiate what I must think of as a rescue; or at any rate to initiate something in response to Hartley's dreadful silence, the causes of which I did not yet want to reflect upon. When you rush the house to rescue the hostage from the gunman how will the gunman behave, how will the hostage behave? It may have been this fear which had now decided to inhabit the huge empty scene. It was a sunny day, cool, with a certain wind. The sea was a choppy dark blue, the sky pale, with a smooth gleaming buff-coloured cloud just above the horizon like a long tatter of silk. I was wearing Doris's Irish jersey. I began to study the sea through the glasses. I searched the restless white-flecked surface with an increasing anxiety, realizing that what I was now looking for and expecting momently to behold was my snake-necked sea monster. I put the glasses down and found that my heart was beating fast, thumping with an accelerating sound like that of the *hyoshigi* which I had last heard in that sombre vaporous gallery in the Wallace Collection.

With deliberation and to calm myself by the discovery that there was of course nothing to see I began again to study the jumping waters. One or two thick darker patches I identified as floating seaweed, there was a piece of wood which kept lifting its end up jerkily, some floating glassy-eyed gulls, a cormorant which passed suddenly through the bright circle of vision. Then, for no particular reason, I shifted so that my charmed and magnified gaze could move from the sea to the land. I could see the waves breaking on the yellow rocks at the foot of the tower, the foaming water spilling back from folds and crevices. The wet rocks, then the dry rocks, then some patches of the fleshy cactus-like grass, then a wind-blown clump of the papery white campion. Then the level grass beside the tower. Then the base of the tower itself, the big cut stones blotched with ochre-coloured lichen, patched with black crannies. Then, part way up the tower, a human foot encased in a shabby gym shoe.

At the sight of that foot I dropped the glasses, and looking with dazzled eyes and shading my brow I could see quite clearly half way up the tower a figure straddled frog-like against the stones, clawing for handholds, dabbling for footholds, descending. In fact, for an agile person, the tower was not an impossibly difficult climb, but I felt an immediate pang of fear which made me seize the glasses and raise them again. In that interval the climber had descended further and now leapt the remaining distance to the ground, and when I had again focused upon him had turned round, leaning back against the tower, with his hands spread out on either side, and looking straight towards me, reminding me suddenly of a figure caught in the head-lights of a car and pinned against a rock. My climbing intruder, now gazing into the lifted glasses, was a boy, or rather a being in the full yet indeterminate efflorescence of earliest manhood. He was wearing brown trousers rolled up almost to the knee, and a white round-necked tee shirt with something written upon it. His face was bony, with a freckled pallor which brought out the rather sugary pinkness of his parted lips. His fairish faintly reddish brown hair, tangled rather than curly, fell to his shoulders, some of it actually spread out upon the rough stone behind him and adhering to it. He was staring back towards me with a marked attention. There was nothing so very unusual about a trespasser on my little promontory. But this was no ordinary trespasser.

I got up hastily and began to move across the rocks. It was somehow clear that I was to come to him, not he to me. The glasses impeded my progress, so I paused to perch them on top of a rock and clambered on, now losing the boy to sight. I crossed Minn's bridge. The final climb, up from a gully to the level above, required all my strength, and I was breathless when I got up onto the grass and stood there, breathing deeply and resisting an impulse to sit down. The boy had moved and was standing near to the further edge of the grass with the sea behind him.

I spoke first. 'Is it – by any chance – is your name Titus?'

'Yes, sir.'

Amid the whole surprise that 'sir' was a separate little shock. Then I sat down, and he, approaching me, sat down too, kneeling and looking at me. I could see his quick breathing, the dirty tee shirt with the legend *Leeds University,* the moist pinkness of his lips, the stubble growing in the scar. He had put one hand, with a gesture of unconscious grace, upon his heart.

'Are you – Mr Arrowby – Charles Arrowby?'

'Yes.'

His eyes were long rather than large, narrow, a wet grey-blue, like stones. His freckled mobile brow was puckered with anxiety. I had of course, in the first instant, apprehended a resemblance to Hartley, a ghostly resemblance which hung upon him or about him, as the resemblance to Wilfred Dunning hung upon Gilbert. And I had seen the harelip.

The next thing he said was, 'Are you my father?'

I was sitting holding my knees, with my feet tucked sideways. I felt now the desire to leap up again, to beat my breast, to make some absolute declaration of emotion, as if this question should be celebrated rather than answered. I also felt a distinct impulse to say *Yes,* and a stronger clearer veto on any lie, to this boy, ever. But why had I not thought about just this, this apparition, this question, why had I not expected it? I was confused, taken by surprise, and did not know how to address him.

'No, I'm not.' The words were weak and I could see his face unchanged, still frowning. I knew that it was very important to convince him at once. Any muddle here could breed horrors. I moved into a kneeling position so that I faced him level. 'No. Believe me. *No*.'

He looked down and his lips pouted and trembled. There was a momentary childish look. He drew his lower lip in and clasped it with his teeth. Then with a quick movement which startled me he stood up, and I stood up too. We were now close to each other. He was slightly taller than me. Enormous vistas of thought were unrolling in my mind.

He was frowning again now, looking stern, his head thrown back, stretching his long thin neck. 'I'm sorry. I mean, I'm sorry I troubled you.'

'Oh, Titus, I'm so glad you've come!' This was the most immediate of a great number of things which I wanted to say to him and which I was already inhibiting and placing in order in my mind. I held out my hand to him.

With a little air of dignified surprise he shook my hand rather formally and then took a step backward. 'I'm sorry. It was a stupid question. And perhaps – impertinent.'

Something about the slight hesitation conveyed, in the odd way that speech so quickly can, an impression of intelligence. I had also noticed his clear almost reflective articulation, although he spoke with the flattened Liverpool-style voice which was now the tribal accent of the young, and which I had found my novice actors so reluctant to abandon.

I said, 'No, not – at all –' And then, 'So you are a student? You are at Leeds University?'

He frowned again, scratching his scar and narrowing his eyes and lips. 'No, I'm not at any university. I just bought this. You can buy them in shops, you don't have to be what it says.' He continued in an explanatory tone, 'They have American ones too, Florida and – California and – Anyone can buy them.'

'I see.' The whirl of my thoughts then brought up the obvious, the uncomfortable, question. 'You've been with them?'

'Them?'

'Your father and mother.'

He reddened, his face and neck flushing quickly. 'You mean Mr and Mrs Fitch?'

'Yes.' I was terrified, the awkwardness, the vulnerability, terrified of hurting him as if he were a little helpless bird.

'They are not my father and mother.'

'Yes, I know, they adopted you –'

'I have been looking for my parents. But I was unlucky – there are no records. There should be records, I have a right to know. But there are none. Then I rather hoped that –'

'That I was your father?'

He said, with a look of sternness and formality, 'That I could clear the matter up somehow. But I never really imagined –'

'Have you been with them, over there, at the bungalow, where they live?'

He gave me his cold wet-stone stare, withdrawn and stiff. 'No. I only came here to see you. I'm going now.'

I kept my head against a wave of panic. The boy could vanish, be lost, never seen again. 'Aren't you going to see them, to tell them you're here? They are very worried about you, they'll be glad to see you.'

'No. I'm sorry I bothered you.'

'How did you know where I lived?'

'I saw it in a magazine I take – a music magazine.' He added, 'You're famous, people know.'

'Tell me about yourself. What are you doing now?'

'Nothing. I'm on the dole. Unemployed. Like everyone else.'

'But did you finish your training – electricity, was it?'

'No. The college was closed down. I couldn't get into another. Well, I didn't try. I took the dole. Like everyone else.'

'How did you get here?'

'Hitch-hike. I'm sorry I've bothered you, taken up your time. I'm going now.'

'Oh, I hope not. I'll go with you to the road, it's easier this way. But first, would you mind fetching my field glasses? They're over there on that rock.'

Titus seemed pleased to be asked this. In a second he had slithered down the steep incline which I had so laboriously ascended, and was leaping goat-like from rock to rock in the direction of the bridge. I wanted a short interval in which to think. Oh, he was slippery, slippery, touchy, proud. I must hold him, I must be tactful, careful, gentle, firm, I must understand how. Everything, everything, I felt, now depended on Titus, he was the centre of the world, he was the *key*. I was filled with painful and joyful emotions and the absolute need to conceal them. I could so easily, here, alarm, offend, disgust.

He was back but too soon, coming up the steep rock in a precarious scrabbling run, handing me the glasses with the first smile I had seen on that reserved suspicious still half-childish face. 'Here. Did you know there's quite a good table lying over there in the rocks?'

I had forgotten the table. 'Oh yes, thanks. Maybe you could help me with it later. Look, don't go away, I'd like to talk to you. Won't you stay to lunch? You must be hungry. Aren't you hungry?'

It was at once evident that he was hungry. I felt a rush of concern and pity, of all those dangerously joyously strong emotions which were biding their luxurious secret moment.

He hesitated. 'Thank you. Well, OK, I'll stay for a quick bite. I have to be – somewhere else –'

I did not believe too much in that somewhere else.

By this time, by the easy route, we had almost reached the road. We climbed up the last bit and stood a moment looking out over Raven Bay where the calmer shallower sea was the colour of turquoise.

'Lovely country, isn't it. Do you know this part of the world?'

'No.' He said, suddenly stretching out his hands, 'Oh, the sea, the sea – it's so wonderful.'

'I know. I feel that too. I grew up in the middle of England. So did you, I think?'

'Yes.' He turned to me. 'Look –'

'Yes?'

'Why did you – I mean – did you come here for my mother?'

There was so much to discover, so much to explain, and it must be done so carefully and in the right order. I said, 'I'm glad you call her your mother. She is, you know, even if you are adopted. There's a kind of reality, a kind of truth. They are your real parents, it would be unjust to deny it.'

'Yes, I understand about that. But there are – other things –'

'Won't you tell me –?' This was a mistake, too much, too soon.

He frowned, repeating his question. 'You came here for my mother, after her, or what?' The tone was austere, accusing.

I faced him, resisting an urge to take him by the shoulders –

'No, believe me, I didn't come, as you put it, after her. My coming here was pure chance. It was the oddest coincidence. I didn't know she was here. I didn't know where she was. I lost touch with your mother completely a very long time ago. I was absolutely – stunned, amazed – to meet her again – it was the purest accident.'

'A funny sort of accident –'

'Don't you believe me?'

'Yes. I think so. Yes. All right. Anyway, it's none of my business.'

'I've told you the truth.'

'OK, OK. It doesn't matter. They don't matter.'

'They –?'

'Ben and Mary. They don't matter. You very kindly offered me food. Perhaps I could just have some cheese or a sandwich. Then I must push off.'

Ben and Mary was a shock too. We began to walk slowly back towards the house. Titus picked up two plastic bags which were lying on a roadside rock.

'Your worldly goods?'

'Not quite all.'

As we turned onto the causeway Gilbert came out of the front door, and stopped in amazement. It occurred to me that I had never mentioned Titus's existence to either Lizzie or Gilbert. Gilbert knew what Lizzie had told him about the 'old flame', but I had checked his eager attempts to pursue the matter. Titus had not appeared to be part of the story; and what a ghost he had seemed in Hartley's own mentions of him. Whereas now …

As we neared I said to Gilbert in my ringing tones, 'Oh, hello, this is young Titus Fitch, the son of Mr and Mrs Fitch, you know, my friends in the village. And this is Mr Opian who helps me in the house.' The tone and the description were designed to establish Gilbert, for the present at any rate, as being beyond some unspecified barrier. Gilbert's eyes had already taken on a dazed and gauzy look. I did not want any trouble of that sort; and, to tell the truth, I was already feeling rather possessive about Titus.

'Come along,' I said. As I hustled Titus through the door I gave Gilbert a kick on the ankle by way of ambiguous warning. 'Gilbert, could you set lunch for me and Titus in the red room? Titus, a drink?'

He drank beer and I drank white wine while Gilbert, who had now donned his apron, quickly and discreetly laid out and then served luncheon for two on the bamboo table. I think Gilbert would have been glad to serve me thus every day, only he feared to annoy me by suggesting it. His studied and meticulous 'butler' would have graced any drawing-room comedy. At one point, catching my eye over Titus's head, he winked. I gazed coldly back. We had ham cooked in brown sugar to a recipe of Gilbert's, with a salad of Italian tinned tomatoes and herbs. (These excellent tomatoes are best eaten cold. They may be warmed, but *never* boiled as this destroys the distinctive flavour.) Then cherries with Gilbert's little lemon sponge cakes. Then double Gloucester cheese with very hard biscuits which Gilbert had rebaked in the oven. Our butler, instructed by telepathy, soon made himself scarce. We drank white wine with the meal. Titus ate ravenously.

I made a little polite conversation by way of introduction, and while Gilbert was still in evidence. 'I expect you're very left-wing, like most of the young.'

'Oh no.'

'Interested in politics?'

'Party politics? No.'

'But some kind of politics?'

He admitted to being interested in the preservation of whales. We discussed that. 'And I'm against pollution, I think the problem of nuclear waste is *terrible*.' We discussed that too.

At the next pause I said, 'So you didn't come here to see *them*?'

'No, I came to see you.'

'To ask me that question?'

'Yes. Thanks for answering it. Needless to say I won't bother you again.'

'Oh, don't say that. But – so – you aren't going to call on them, to let them know you're here?'

'No.'

'Oughtn't you to? Of course I quite understand you mightn't want to. Now I had a very happy relation with my parents, but –'

'I had a very unhappy one with mine.'

Drink had loosened his tongue. I had been doing a lot of urgent thinking. A plan, *the* plan, was emerging. 'With both of them?'

'Yes. Well, it wasn't her fault so much. He took against me. She went along with him. I suppose she had to.'

'She was frightened.'

'Well, it was a bad scene. He stopped her from talking to me. And she always felt she had to tell him lies, little lies just so as to make life easier. I hated that.'

'You mustn't blame her.' That was important.

'I suppose he wasn't a bad chap. But he couldn't succeed at anything and that was depressing and maybe made him a bit spiteful, and he took it out on us. She couldn't do a thing. Well, I do exaggerate. There were good times or goodish times, only the bad ones were so – crucial.' Again the hesitation. Perhaps the tone of someone else's voice? Whose?

'I understand.'

'You never knew when it was going to start again. You had to be careful what you said.'

The bruising and breaking of that child's pride must have been something appalling, unspeakable. I recalled Hartley's picture of the white-faced silent boy. Poor Hartley! She was the helpless witness of it all. 'Your mother must have suffered very much, for you and with you.'

He gave me one of his quick suspicious frowning stares, but did not pursue the point. On closer inspection he seemed less handsome, or perhaps just more dirty and untidy. He had the pale complexion of a redhead, but his long unkempt hair was greasy and in need of a wash. His face was thin and a little wolfish, the cheeks almost sunken. The eyes had a bright cold blue-grey glint (they were a little spotted and mottled like one of my stones) but always narrowed. Perhaps he was short-sighted. He had a small pretty mouth, the lips scarcely disfigured, and a firm straight little nose, such as a girl might have envied. He was decently shaved, his beard showing in bright points of reddish gold, but the unusually dark stubble growing inaccessibly in the scar looked like a tiny lopsided moustache. He was obviously self-conscious about the scar and kept touching it. His hands were very dirty and the nails bitten.

'And then there was this business about me.' I did not speak portentously, but I wanted to keep him on the subject.

'Oh well, yes, it came up now and then. But I don't want you to get the idea –'

'I expect you know that I loved your mother very much when we were young. I haven't seen her since then, till we suddenly met here –'

'She must have changed a bit!'

'I still love her. But we never had a love affair.'

'That's nothing to me. Sorry, that's not the phrase I want, I must be getting drunk. I mean, don't tell me things like that, I'm not – I'm not interested. I believe you that you're not my father, that's finished. All the same, I can't quite understand about your being here. Do you see them, or what?'

'Oh, occasionally.'

'If you don't mind, I'd rather you didn't tell them —'

'About you? No, all right. As I say, I'm still very attached to your mother, very concerned about her. I'd like to help her. I don't think she's had much of a life.'

'Well, a life is a life.'

'What does that mean?'

'One never knows. I daresay most lives are rotten. It's only when one's young one expects otherwise. She's a bit of an imaginer, a fantasist, I suppose most women are. I must go now. Thanks for the grub.'

'Oh I'm not going to let you go yet!' I said, laughing.'I want to hear much more about you. You said your college closed down. But what would you like to do if you could choose?'

'I used to think I'd like to work somehow with animals, I like animals.'

'You don't want to go back to electricity?'

'Oh, that was just to get away from home, I got a grant and cleared out. No, I think if I could choose now I'd like to be an actor.'

Here was a stroke of luck. I could have shouted with joy. 'An *actor*? Why then I can help you.'

He said, quickly flushing and with an aggressive precision, 'I did not come here for that. I did not come for your help or to cadge· or anything. I just came to ask. It wasn't easy. You're a celebrity. I thought about it for a long time. I hoped I'd solve it the other way, by finding the adoption people, but that didn't work out. I don't want your help or to push my way into your life. I wouldn't want that even if you were my dad.'

He got up with an air of departure and I rose too. I wanted to throw my arms around him. 'All right. But don't go yet. Wouldn't you like to have a swim?'

'A swim? Oh – *yes*.'

'Well, repose for a while, we can swim later, then have some tea –'

'I'd like to swim now.'

We walked out onto the grass, ignoring Gilbert who rose respectfully as we passed through the kitchen, and then climbed the rocks towards the sea and came out on top of the little cliff. The tide had come in further and the water was now little more than ten feet below us. It was calmer than it had been in the morning and the semi-transparent water was a rich bottle-green in the bright sunlight.

'Do you swim here? It looks marvellous. And one can dive. I hate not diving in.'

It was not a moment for dreary warnings. I was not going to admit to Titus any difficulties, any fear of the sea. 'Yes, this is the best place.'

Titus was in a frenzy to get into the water. 'I haven't any swimming things.'

'Oh, that doesn't matter, no one can see us, I never wear anything.'

Titus had already torn off the Leeds University tee shirt, revealing a lot of curly, red-golden hair. He was hopping, dragging off his trousers. Wanting suddenly to laugh with pleasure I began to undress with equal haste, but was still unbuttoning my shirt when the splash of his perfect dive blotted the glittering rock at my feet. In a moment I followed him, gasped at the coldness of the water, and seconds later began to feel warm and wildly elated.

My man Opian had come out bearing towels. He seemed to retire discreetly, but then I could see him peeping over a nearby rock, watching Titus perform. The boy, showing off of course, swam like a dolphin, graceful, playful, a white swift flashing curving form, giving glimpses of sudden hands and heels, active shoulders, pale buttocks, and a wet exuberant laughing face framed in clinging seaweed hair. His sea-darkened hair certainly changed his appearance, became dark and straight, adhering to his neck and shoulders, plastering his face, making him look like a girl. Aware of the effect, he charmingly tossed his head and drew the heavy sopping locks back out of his eyes and off his brow. He had the effortless crawl which I have never mastered, and in his marine joy kept diving vertically under, vanishing and reappearing somewhere else with a triumphant yell. Equal mad delight possessed me, and the sea was joyful and the taste of the salt water was the taste of hope and joy. I kept laughing, gurgling water, spouting, whirling. Meeting my sea-dervish companion I shouted, 'Now aren't you glad you came to me?' 'Yes, yes, yes!'

Of course he had no difficulty climbing up the little steep cliff. After all, had I not first seen him like a fly upon that tower? I had a slight difficulty myself and a bad moment, but concealed it from him. It was rather too early to start losing face and seeming old. I wanted him to accept me as a comrade. After that, in the shade of a rock, he slept. After that we had a substantial tea. And after that he agreed to stay the night, just the night and leave early the next day. I had meanwhile confiscated and hidden his two plastic bags in case he should suddenly take it into his head to slip away. I looked into the bags, there was precious little in them: shaving things, underwear, a decent striped shirt, a tie, shoes, a much creased and folded cotton jacket. Some expensive cuff links in a velvet box. The love poems of Dante, in Italian and English, in a de luxe edition with *risqué* engravings. The last two items made me think a bit.

Of course Gilbert, now fully aware of our visitor's identity, was in a scarcely controllable state of excitement and curiosity. 'What are you going to *do* with him?' 'Wait and see.' 'I know what I'd like to do!' 'For God's sake just keep out of our way.' 'All right, I know my place!'

At my suggestion Titus had rinsed his hair in fresh water. Dried and combed it became fluffy, a thick mass of spiralling red-brown tendrils, and much improved his appearance. In the evening he put on the cleanish shirt, but not the cuff links. Gilbert surreptitiously washed the Leeds University tee shirt.

We dined, Titus and I, by candlelight. He said suddenly, 'It's so romantic!' We both laughed wildly.

Titus now looked curiously at Gilbert and Gilbert's too impeccable performance, but asked no questions. I vaguely volunteered, 'He's an old actor, down on his luck' and that seemed to account for him sufficiently for the present.

At dinner we talked of theatre and television. He seemed to have seen a remarkable number of London plays and knew the names of a great many actors. He described how he had directed *The Admirable Crichton* at school. He was modest, diffident about his ambition. 'It's just an idea.' I did not press him, about this or about anything. We laughed a good deal.

He went to bed early, sleeping on cushions among my books in the front room downstairs. He expressed great interest in the books, but blew his candle out early. (I was watching from the stairs.) At breakfast, he agreed to stay to lunch. I allowed the obsequious Gilbert to join us for general conversation at breakfast time. I did not want Gilbert to become an interesting mystery.

After breakfast I turned Titus loose to swim and explore the rocks, indicating that I would be busy with my 'writing'. I thought it better not to crowd him with my company and in any case I wanted time to think. Titus seemed very happy, playing boyishly by himself. I watched his agile appearances and disappearances from the window with a piercing mixture of affection and envy. He returned at last bearing the errant table ostentatiously raised with one arm above his head. He put the table on the grass, then suggested that we should eat outside, but I vetoed this. (I agree with Mr Knightley about *al fresco* meals.) Gilbert meanwhile had been out shopping and had made, under my direction, a decent kedgeree with frozen coley.

At lunch, where Titus and I were again *tête-à-tête,* I decided it was time to speak seriously. I had had enough of gaining his confidence and refraining from scaring him. In any case my nerve was giving out and I wanted to know my fate.

'Titus, listen, there's something important I want to say to you.' He looked alarmed and put one hand flat on the table as if ready to leap up and bolt.

'I want you to stay here, for a time at any rate. I'll explain why. I want you to see your mother.'

The eyes narrowed further, the pretty lips almost sneered. 'I'm not going over there.'

'I'm not suggesting you should. She will come over here.'

'So you've told them. You said you wouldn't.'

'I haven't told them. I'm just suggesting, asking you. If your mother knows you're here she'll come. There's no need to tell him.'

'She'll tell him. She always does.'

'She won't this time, I'll persuade her not to. I just want her to visit you here. Anyway, what can he do, even if he does know? He's got to pretend to be pleased. There's nothing to be afraid of.'

'I'm not afraid!'

This was a bad start, I was fumbling and confused, and even as I spoke I imagined Ben snarling at the door.

Titus said thoughtfully, 'I'm sorry for him in a way. He hasn't had much of a life either, to use your phrase.'

'A life is a life, to use yours. If you're sorry for him you should all the more be sorry for her. She has grieved about you so much. Won't you see her and make her happy?'

'Nothing could make her happy. Nothing. Ever.' The bland finality of the reply was dreadful.

'Well, you can try!' I said with exasperation. 'It can't be very nice for her not knowing what's happened to you.'

'OK then, you can tell her you saw me.'

'That's not enough. You must see her yourself. She must come here.'

Titus was looking handsomer again today, his cheeks lightly touched by the sun, his brighter softer hair framing the bony lumpiness of his face. The horrible tee shirt was already dry, but he was again wearing the striped shirt with the collar open.

'Look, you said you saw them "occasionally". That sounds odd to me. You were the bogy man for years, the devil himself. I can remember the desperate look in her eyes when your name came up. They can't have *forgiven* you? All right, you haven't done anything, but you know what I mean. Do you go round and play bridge or what?'

'No, of course not. He still detests me, I imagine, and God knows what he really believes. Maybe he doesn't know himself. But I'm beginning to think he doesn't matter much.'

'Why, pray?'

'Because I think your mother is going to leave him.'

'She never would. Never. No way.'

'I think she would under certain circumstances. I think she would if she could only conceive of it as possible. If she saw it as possible she would see it as easy.'

'But where would she go to?'

'To me.'

'You mean – you want her?'

'Yes.'

'And so you want me to persuade my mother to leave my father? You've got to be joking! That's a lot to expect in return for lunch and dinner.'

'And breakfast and tea.'

'You're a cool one.'

I was not feeling cool. Everything in this conversation was going wrong, being crudely, grossly presented. I was anxious not to drive him to any sudden reaction by striking too portentous a note. At the same time he must appreciate my seriousness. The maddening fact was that I now had all the pieces for a solution, but would I be allowed to fit them together? 'My dear Titus, of course I don't want you to persuade your mother of anything. I want you to see her because I know this would very profoundly relieve her mind. And I want you to see her here because it would only be possible here.'

'I'm to be a lure – a kind of – hostage –'

This was dreadfully near the truth, but I had left out something very important which I now saw I ought to have mentioned at the start. 'No, no. Just listen carefully. I want to tell you something else. Why do you think I persuaded you to stay here instead of letting you go away?'

'I'm beginning to think it's because you want my mother to come to you because of me.'

The wording of this went so far that I could scarcely say again: no. It was true in a way, but true in a harmless way, an innocuous way, even a wonderful way. As we stared at each other I hoped that he might suddenly, in this light, see it. But he kept, rather deliberately perhaps, his hard suspicious mask. I said, holding his eyes and frowning with intent, 'Yes, I do want that. But I want it also because of you, through you, for you, you're part of it, you're part of everything now. You're essential.'

'What do you mean?'

'I persuaded you to stay here because I like you.'

'Oh, thanks a lot!'

'And you stayed because you like me.'

'And the food. And the swimming. OK!'

'Put it this way, and for the moment as hypothetically as you please. You are searching for a father. I am searching for a son. Why don't we make a deal?'

He refused to be impressed or startled. 'I suspect you've just thought of this son idea. Anyway, I'm looking for my real father, and not because I need one or want one, but just to kill a devil of miserable biting curiosity that I've lived with all my life.'

No, he was not at all what I had expected, though I could not now think why I had expected a dullard. Something in Hartley's rather desperate account of him had suggested this perhaps. He was a clever attractive boy and I was going to do my damnedest to get hold of him. To get hold of him and then of his mother.

'Well, think it over. It's a proposition, and as far as I'm concerned it's a deeply serious one. You see – in a curious way – because of my old relation to your mother – I am cast in the role of your father. I know this is nonsense, but you're clever enough to understand nonsense. You might have been my son. I'm not just anybody. Fate has brought us together. And I could help you a lot –'

'I don't want your money or your bloody influence, I didn't come here for that!'

'So you said, and we passed that stage some time ago, so shut up about it now. I want to take your mother away, and I want at last to make her happy, which you think is impossible and I don't. And I want you to be in the picture too. For her sake. For my sake. In the picture. I'm not suggesting more than that. You can work it for as much or as little as you like.'

'You mean you'd take us both away and we'd all three live together in a villa in the south of France?'

'Yes. If you'd like! Why not?'

He uttered an explosive yelp, then with a theatrical gesture spread out his hands, which were cleaner now. 'You love her?'

'Yes.'

'But you don't know her.'

'The odd thing is, my dear boy, that I do know her.'

'Well,' said Titus, and there was at last a look of admiration, 'let's just suppose ... that you did ... ask her to come and see me ...'

I was lying in tall luscious green grass which was just coming out into pink feathery flower. The grass was cool and very dry and squeaked slightly as I moved. I was lying on the edge of the wood, on the far side of the footpath, just level with the garden of Nibletts. I was holding a pocket mirror. Hartley had just come out into the garden.

Titus had promised, for the future, nothing. He had treated the matter with an affected cynicism and had allowed me no glimpse of the emotions which were certainly there behind it. He pretended to treat the whole thing almost as a joke, a game, at any rate as something which he was prepared to do simply to oblige me, for the hell of it, to 'see what happened'. He had agreed to stay on, 'since he had nothing better to do', and to 'say hello' to his mother. Though he added, with a slightly grimmer note, that he was pretty sure she would not come.

That remained to be seen; and it was also unclear to me how exactly, after all those years during which she 'went along' with Ben because she 'had to', he felt about her. Where and how did forgiveness figure in that scene? Mercy, loyalty, love? Was I not perhaps meddling with something dreadful? Unpredictable it certainly was. What kept me more boldly on was an optimism which Titus himself had rather crazily engendered with that image of the three of us living together in the south of France! If *he* would stick to me, and *she* would come out, there would be, for all of us, some tremendous spiritual release, like the sudden ecstasy which Titus and I had experienced in the sea. I *would* make her happy, I would. And I would make him happy and successful and free.

Another matter had come up between us after Titus had agreed, as he again cynically put it, to be a 'hostage'. After he had agreed to stay on, if I wished it, 'for a while', I had said casually, boldly, 'You haven't anyone waiting for you then anywhere? I mean a girl or anything?'

He said rather stiffly, 'No. There was somebody. But that's over.'

I wondered: did he then come to me in loneliness, in desperation? And if so would this not make him all the more ready to accept – my overtures – my love?

It was the evening of the same day. There seemed no point in waiting longer. I had even told Gilbert the outline of the plan, though part of it I still concealed, even from Titus. Gilbert, who was now to play the key part which I had envisaged earlier, was enjoying the whole drama disgracefully. I had waited, hidden in the wood, for nearly an hour when Hartley appeared. There was no sign of the gentleman.

I watched her for a moment quietly. She was wearing the yellow dress with the brown flower pattern, and over it a loose blue overall. She walked a little awkwardly, her shoulders hunched, her head down, her hands deep in the pockets of the overall. She came down to the end of the garden and stood there for a while, like an animal, staring dully at the grass. Then she lifted her head and started looking at the sea, image of an inaccessible freedom. Then she removed one hand from her pocket and touched her face. She must be crying. I could scarcely bear it.

Cautiously I uncovered the pocket mirror and leaning forward tilted it to catch the sun. The little running bright reflection, like a tiny live creature, appeared at once upon the hillside just below the garden. I was careful to keep it well away from the house. I brought the brilliant little patch of light slowly up the hill towards her feet; and in a moment I knew that she had noticed it, and that she realized what it meant. This was a trick which we used to play on each other in summers when we were children. I sent the flash up for a moment to her face, and then began to lead it away, making a line across the grass in the direction of the wood.

Hartley stood staring towards me. I rose to a kneeling position and gently stirred the creamy-flowering branch of an elder bush. Hartley made a gesture, lifting her hand to her throat. Then she turned and moved back towards the house. I nearly called out with vexation, but then realized that she was probably going to check on Ben's activity and whereabouts. Perhaps he was riveting china. I waited for an anxious minute, and then she came out again, minus the overall, ran to the fence, stooped through the wire, and came running across the grass towards me.

I retreated a bit into a little glade underneath an ash tree. A large branch had been wrenched from the tree by some winter gale, and through the gap the sun shone down upon a wild rose bush in pallid flower and a mass of fading cow parsley and buttercups. I stood beside the ash tree whose dense-textured grey smooth trunk brought back some elusive childhood memory connected with Hartley. I could now see her thrusting aside the big flat flower-heads of the elder. In a moment she had come to me, and I noticed how she instinctively avoided the patch of sunlight.

I put my arms around her and she consented to be held, a little stiff, bowing her head. I drew my hand down her back, pressing her against me; feeling her soft warmth, my knee touching her knee. She sighed and turned her head sideways but her hands still hung limply. The warmth of her body beneath the frail dress made me close my eyes and almost forget my plan and its urgency.

'Oh, Hartley, my darling, my own.'

'You shouldn't have come.'

'I love you.' I sat down at the foot of the tree, leaning against it, and drew her down beside me. I wanted her to lie relaxed with her head on my breast. 'Come. We were often like this, weren't we. Remember?' But she would not. I saw her in the sunny shady light, her breasts straining the buttons of her dress, as so much lovelier, so much like her old self, as if some woodland magic had made her young again.

She knelt beside me, clasping one of my hands, and staring at me with her big darkened eyes. Then, suddenly, and tenderly, she lifted my hand and kissed it.

This gesture moved and upset me so much that it actually served to bring me to my senses. The urgent matter was to get the girl away, and I had not even started my argument.

'Hartley, my little one, you do love me, oh, I'm so glad! But listen, I've got something to tell you. Where is he?'

'He's out. I just went to make sure. But, oh you shouldn't have come like this –'

'Where to, how long?'

'He's gone to see a man about a dog. He'll be some time.'

'A dog?'

'Yes. It's quite a long way, over at Amorne Farm. And as it's such nice weather he decided to walk.'

'Walk? I thought he was crippled – had a bad leg –'

'His leg's stiff, it slows him down, but he likes walking, and the exercise does him good. You see, there was an advertisement in the shop, they were going to have a dog put down if they couldn't find an owner, it's a Welsh collie, a grown-up dog, not a puppy. It's not good with the sheep. And we thought we'd look at it. We rang up and they sounded very nice, some people called Arkwright.'

'Oh – Arkwright. But you didn't go – you decided to stay here in case I came –'

'Ben thought I'd better not be there, I would get all excited about the dog and he'd rather decide by himself. It's always a risk taking a grown-up dog –'

'Hartley, listen. Titus is back. He's at my house.'

She toppled sideways into the grass, releasing my hand. '*No* –'

'Yes. He doesn't want to see *him* – only you – he very much wants to see you. Come, come quickly.'

'Titus – but why did he come to you –? Oh how strange, *how awful* –'

'I thought you'd be glad!'

'But that he should come to *you* – oh dear, what shall I do, what shall *I do* –' She was suddenly a whimpering distracted child.

'Come and see him, come on, *get up*.' I pulled her up. 'What's the matter, don't you want to see your son, isn't it wonderful that he's back?'

'Yes, wonderful – but I must stay here – tell him to come here. He mustn't say he was with you –'

'He won't come here, that's the point! Come on, Hartley, stop behaving like a sleepwalker, move, act! He'll never come here, you know that. Come along, he's waiting for us. There'll be plenty of time to see him before Ben gets back. I've got a car waiting at the bottom of the hill.' I began to pull her back towards the meadow and the footpath, but she resisted, maddeningly sitting down again on the ground.

'But tell me, Titus – is he –?'

'Oh hurry! If you want Titus not to say he saw me you'd better come along and tell him yourself!'

This argument, vague enough, seemed to impress her, at any rate touched her through her panic. 'All right, but I'll only stay a few minutes, and you must bring me back at once!'

'Yes, yes, yes' – I pulled her to her feet again.

'And we must stay in the wood, someone might see us –'

'I thought you didn't know anybody here! Now do hurry –'

We went down by the woodland path. It was overgrown in places and rather dark and we stumbled along, whipped by twigs, clung to by brambles, and constantly impeded by little saplings growing in the middle of the pathway. The sheer stupid awkwardness of our progress made me want to scream. Hartley's body moving beside me was jerky and clumsy, it was like conducting a log of wood.

We came out bedraggled and panting, onto the coast road. Gilbert had drawn the Volkswagen up onto the grass verge. When he saw us emerging he started the engine and backed towards us.

A few days of seaside holiday had transformed Gilbert. He looked younger, fitter, even his white curls were looser and more natural. He had been to the Fishermen's Stores and kitted himself out with plimsolls and light canvas trousers and a big loose cotton jersey which he now wore over a white shirt. He had left off the deplorable make-up. These were fine times for Gilbert. He was a necessary man. He was helping me to acquire a woman other than Lizzie, and he was engaged in an adventure which featured a charming boy. His eyes blazed with vitality and curiosity. I handed Hartley into the back of the car and got in after, suddenly trying to see each of them through the eyes of the other. Gilbert appeared as a handsome well-fed rather wealthy-looking holiday gentleman. The butler act was switched off. Now he was playing a man who owned a yacht. But no, I could not imagine how Gilbert saw my darling, or what he had expected the 'one love' to be like.

'This is my friend Mr Opian. Mrs Fitch. Step on it, Gilbert.'

Hartley turned to me as the car sped along the coast road, but she said nothing. She clutched, perhaps unconsciously, the sleeve of my jacket with one hand. I sat relaxed, content to feel the touch of her fingers and of her knee. Her eyes had their violet tint and her face the strained fey expression which when she was young had made her look so desirably wild. Now it made her look almost mad. I found myself smiling with joy at the enclosed safe feeling of the car, at its speed. The sense of a successful escape was overwhelming. I smiled at her crazily.

When the car stopped at the causeway she was reluctant to get out. 'Does he know I'm coming? Couldn't he come out here to the car?'

'Hartley, darling, do what you're told!'

When I had got her out Gilbert, as instructed, drove the car on. It disappeared round the corner in the direction of the Raven Hotel.

I had told Titus to stay in the kitchen, but when we were half way across the causeway he opened the front door.

I had been so absorbed in my mind with the mechanical detail of my plan that I had not really reflected upon what this meeting would be like. My intentions had far overleapt it and my hopes were assembling a much less awkward future. Now however I was jerked back into the present and an alarmed confused sense of what I had brought about.

As soon as she saw Titus, Hartley stopped and an almost terrible change came over her face. Her mouth opened and drooped in an ugly way as if she might cry and her eyes half closed and her forehead had the 'pitted' appearance which I had seen before; only what all this expressed was not shock or some sad overwhelming joy, but guilt and supplication. At the same time she quite unconsciously spread out her hands wide on either side of her, again not for an embrace but as a petition.

I took all this in quickly and was so instantly *hurt* by it I wanted to cry out, stop, stop! I wanted to interfere mercifully as between two unequal combatants. But I was already excluded from the scene. Titus came forward, frowning, manly, with screwed-up eyes, determined to be hard and calm and display no emotion. He could not however conceal, for it showed in his every gesture, even in the way he walked, that he was bent on raising a suppliant. He came to Hartley and somehow gruffly gathered her, hustling her towards the door. I saw him push her in through the doorway, his hands in the middle of her back. I hastened to follow.

When I got in they were already conversing, standing in the hall, and I felt: it's not like mother and son. And yet why not? Family relations are all awkward, funny. Or had Hartley never managed to *become* his mother, never been allowed to? What *would* they say?

'We didn't know where you were, where you'd gone, we tried and tried to find out, we did try, we did ask —' This as if Titus were accusing her of having failed to find him.

'Yes, yes, I'm all right, I'm perfectly all right, I'm fine,' answering a question not put yet.

'And you are well and have your work or are you still — where are you living?'

'I'm unemployed and I'm not living anywhere.'

'We left our address with the people in case you'd lost it, in case you came back. And I wrote a letter –'

'It's all right, Mary, it's all right –'

To check this conversation which I found somehow awful (I could not bear to hear him reassuring her and calling her 'Mary') I said, 'Why don't you go through to the kitchen? Would you like a drink?' I needed one, and in their situation I would have been frantic for one, but neither of them seemed to feel the necessity and in fact they ignored the question.

Titus went through into the kitchen and Hartley followed and they stood beside the table, holding on to it, and looking at each other with stricken glaring faces. Hartley's look expressed timid supplication and fear, his a kind of shamed disgusted pity. There was so much pain in the room, it was like a physical barrier. I stood watching them, wanting to help, to interrupt. 'Won't you have some supper? Let's have some supper, shall we? Let's talk –'

Titus said, 'Of course I never lost your address.'

Hartley said, 'I mustn't stay. Would you like to come over to our place? But you mustn't say you've been here. Would you like –?'

Titus shook his head.

She went on, 'Ben doesn't know you've come, he's gone out, walked over to a farm to ask about a dog.'

'About a dog?' said Titus.

'Yes, we're thinking of having a dog.'

'What kind?'

'A Welsh collie.'

'Will he bring the dog back with him?'

'I don't know.'

At least this was something like a topic of conversation.

I was tired of being invisible and inaudible, so I *shouted*, 'Have a drink, have some supper!'

Titus, without looking at me, waggled his hand in my direction, then said to Hartley, 'Come in here.' She followed him into the little red room and he shut the door in my face.

I now decided, none too soon, that I had better leave them alone. Besides, now that Hartley was here, I had to work out in more detail the dangerous and decisive next steps. I stood for a moment thinking in the hall. Then I ran upstairs to the drawing room and pulled out some writing paper. I had found in a drawer some embossed *Shruff End* paper which must have belonged to Mrs Chorney, and on a glossy sheet of this stuff I wrote:

Dear Mr Fitch,
    Just to say that Mary is over here with me, and Titus too.
        Yours sincerely,
            Charles Arrowby.

I pushed this into an envelope and ran out of the house.

I was somewhat surprised to find a warm summer evening in progress. Perhaps the house was cold, perhaps I had been feeling cold, perhaps I felt that ordinary time ought to have stopped. The grass on the other side of the road was a pullulating emerald green, the rocks that grew here and there among the grass were almost dazzlingly alight with little diamonds. The warm air met me in a wave, thick with land smells of earth and growth and flowers.

I ran across the causeway and then along the road in the tower and Raven direction, and then around the corner to where the bay was visible. Here, obedient to my orders, Gilbert had parked the car. I wanted it out of sight in case I had to tell Hartley some lie about it later.

Gilbert was sitting on a rock, looking at the brilliantly lit blue water. He jumped up and ran to me.

'Gilbert, could you take this letter now and deliver it at Nibletts, at the bungalow, you know, it's the last one in the road.'

'OK, boss. How are things in there?'

'All right. Go now, there's a good chap. And then come back again and wait here.'

'What about my supper? Can't I come into the house?' Gilbert, bursting with curiosity, was longing to busybody around.

I would not have it. 'No, not yet. You'd better buy yourself a sandwich at the Black Lion, and then come back here. I don't quite know what's going to happen.'

'Nothing violent, I hope?'

'So do I. Hurry, now.'

'But, guv'nor –'

'Go.'

'I can stay for a drink at the pub, can't I, I'm dying for a drink –'

'Yes, but not long, four minutes.'

Looking at Gilbert's disgruntled face I was unpleasantly reminded of Freddie Arkwright. And now there were Arkwrights everywhere, and they had got hold of Ben.

I ran back, and the car passed me at the causeway. I went into the house (which *was* cold) and on into the kitchen and poured myself out half a tumbler of dry sherry. I did not listen at the door of the red room. I went out onto the grass and climbed a little way up onto one of the rocks whence I could see the sea and began to sip the sherry.

So far so good. But how would Hartley behave when I began to put the screw on? And what would Ben do when he got my note? *When* would he get it? If he walked both ways to Amorne Farm and back, and allowing half an hour for the dog, he should be back at Nibletts about nine-thirty. It was now a little after eight. I remembered that I was hungry. The sherry was making me light-headed. However if the bloody Arkwrights ran him home in the car he might be back soon after eight-thirty. On the other hand, if he walked back *with* the dog he might not be there till nearer ten. What did he suddenly want a dog for anyway? Did he want to programme the animal to attack me?

I decided on reflection that it did not too much matter what time Ben got back, as he would probably make no move tonight. He would *wait,* at first expecting Hartley and Titus to turn up, and then grinding his teeth. I imagined him even finding a dark satisfaction in his own mounting rage. Not a nice man.

I finished the sherry and went inside. The murmur of voices in the little red room continued. I thought then that really the longer they talked the better. Every minute that passed could bind them closer to each other, and also would use up more of the dangerous time. When they got hungry they might come out. But more likely they were too agitated to feel hunger.

In spite of my fears I was not. I sat for a while eating biscuits and olives, then I scraped the remains of the kedgeree onto a plate and took it outside again, together with a glass of white wine, and resumed my sea view. I felt very odd, excited, nervous, a bit drunk, but clear in the head.

Almost at once however I heard Titus shouting. He evidently could not bring himself to shout either 'Charles!' or 'Mr Arrowby!' but called out several times, 'Hello there!' followed by various urgent owl hoots.

I considered ignoring these cries, but decided I had better not, even though it was far too early to expect Ben. I returned precariously to the lawn with my plate and glass.

Titus and Hartley were standing outside by the door, she wearing that distraught frightened look which I now knew so well.

Titus said, 'Look, Mary thinks she'd better go. I've told her there's lots of time but she wants to go now, OK?'

Hartley said, 'Could I have the car *at once,* please?' She spoke in a hard almost angry tone.

Titus said, 'I looked out the front, I couldn't see it. She's getting very bothered.'

'Nothing to bother about,' I said. I went into the kitchen and they followed me. 'Won't you have some supper?'

'I *must go,*' said Hartley. Her moment, whatever it had been, with Titus, was now over, and the cruel husband-dominated time whose slave she was had driven even Titus out of her head. The old panic was back. How I detested that fierce almost relentless look of fear upon her face. It made her ugly. While in the wood, when she kissed my hand, she had looked beautiful.

Titus said, 'Come on, where's the car, she's got to go home.'

Titus had evidently forgotten that his task was to keep Hartley at Shruff End. Or more likely, he had been infected by her fear. I had been too tactful in my explanations to Titus, too vague. I had not told him everything that I had in mind, partly because I did not know how he would react. I had told him that my idea was that Hartley would want to stay, and that he should add his persuasions. But I now saw that I ought to have been more explicit.

'There's no need to go,' I said.

'I've stayed much longer than I meant to already,' said Hartley. 'He said he'd be back about half past nine, but he could be sooner. So *please* I must go now, this very minute.'

'There's no need to. I've sent Opian round with a note saying you're here with Titus, so he won't worry, he'll come here. Then Gilbert can run you all back.'

Titus whistled. He saw at once the enormity of what I had done. Hartley was a moment taking it in. 'You mean – you mean you've *told* him, deliberately *told* him – oh, you wicked – oh, you fool – you don't know – you don't know –' Tears of rage and despair sprang into her eyes and her face blazed at me. I stepped back.

I said, pursuing the role that I had adopted, but also speaking sincerely, 'Hartley, you mustn't be so frightened of him! I'm absolutely fed up with your attitude to that bloody man. Why should you feel you have to lie to him all the time? Why the hell shouldn't you be here with Titus, it's perfectly natural and proper!'

Titus looked at Hartley with interested concern and at me quizzically. 'And did you *invite* him here? Jesus!' He added, 'Of course he won't have seen the letter yet because he won't be home.'

Hartley, looking at her watch, had just realized this too. 'Oh yes, he mustn't see it, he mustn't see it! If we go at once there'll be time to get it before he sees it. Then everything will be all right. He just mustn't see the letter. Please, we must go at once, the car, the car!'

I said, with a maddening air of calm, 'I'm terribly sorry, but the car isn't here. It's gone on to the garage by the Raven Hotel, there's a fault in the engine.'

'When will it be back?' said Titus.

'I don't know, oh soon, I daresay.'

'We could ring them up.'

'I haven't got a telephone.'

Hartley cried, 'I must go, I must go, I must go, if I *run* I can get there in time –'

'I'll run for you,' said Titus.

'No, you won't,' I said, glaring at him. 'Now, Hartley, just sit down here at the table and stop behaving like a mad person. The car will probably be back any moment. But listen, I don't want you to go back there, back to him, back to his house. I want you to stay here, to stay here *with Titus and me.*' I gave Titus another meaningful look. I felt as if I were *sifting* the sense into her head.

Hartley sat down. She looked from me to Titus and back like a frightened animal. I sat down beside her. She was trembling, and I saw some dawning of understanding in her terrified eyes. There was a sudden atmosphere of crisis.

Titus said, 'She wants to go back. And I'll go back with her. I've decided to.'

I said, still trying to gain time, 'No, no, both of you stay here. Hartley, my dear, he'll know where you are, he won't think you've drowned. He can come and see Titus here. Titus stays here, he lives here. Titus, you don't really want to go over there, do you?'

Titus, visibly distressed, said again, 'She wants to go back. She doesn't want him to see the letter. There's still time. I could run over there in twenty minutes. It's just beyond the village, isn't it?'

'Oh go, please, please,' cried Hartley, 'go now, the door isn't locked, you can just –'

'Or should I run to the hotel? Which is nearer?'

I said to Titus, 'I want him to see the letter. And you are both to stay here. Are we that man's slaves? I want to let your mother out of that cage.'

Hartley gave a cry of woe.

'Why do you want him to see the letter?' said Titus. 'I don't understand all this, it's like some sort of plot. I know you said you hoped she'd want to see me here, and that. But I didn't think you meant to pull the whole bag of tricks down on her head.'

'That is exactly what I do want to do,' I said, 'to pull the whole bag of tricks down on her head.'

'No, no!' Hartley leapt up and made a dash for the door.

I blundered after her, and reaching for her shoulder grabbed the neck of the dress, which tore a little. When she felt it tear she stopped. Then she came back to the table and sat down with her face in her hands.

Titus said, 'Look, I don't like this. You can't keep her here against her will.'

'I want her to be able to decide freely.'

'Freely? She can't,' said Titus. 'She's forgotten about freedom long ago. Besides, if you keep her here she'll be far too frightened to think. You don't know what this is like, she might go mad. I'm afraid I misunderstood. You didn't say so, but I thought you had some sort of understanding with her. I thought she was sort of prepared. But you can't suddenly make someone leave someone they've lived with for years.'

'Why not? When people do leave people they've lived with for years they usually do it suddenly because that's the only possible way. I'm helping her to do what she really wants to do but without help can't. Isn't that clear?'

'Not awfully.'

'She'll calm down, she'll be able to think, soon, tomorrow.'

'Tomorrow? *Here?*'

'Yes.'

'You're going to keep her all night?'

'Yes.'

'Suppose he comes?'

'I don't think he will. To answer your earlier question, I did not invite him.'

'Oh, Jesus. What'll he think?'

'I don't care a fuck what he thinks,' I said, 'in fact, the worse he thinks the better. Let him think anything his foul imagination can beget.'

'That's part of – pulling everything down?'

'Yes.'

'My God,' said Titus. Then he said, 'I think it's obscene. And I don't like this talking about her as if she were a child or mental patient. I'm going to swim.'

'Titus – don't think too ill of me – you see –'

'Oh I don't think ill of you, in a way I'm quite breathless with admiration. I just couldn't do it myself.'

'You're not going to run over there for the letter?'

'No. I expect it's too late anyway.'

'And you won't run away from me?'

'I won't run away from you.' He went out of the back door.

Outside it was a hazier later evening and the shadows of the rocks were long, long on the grass. I did not look at my watch. I sat down beside Hartley.

She had taken her hands from her face and was sitting limp, staring at the table. Where I had dragged at her dress there was a little triangular tear. I could see the deep reddish streak of sunburn that led downward from her throat. I could see her brassiere and the roundness of her contained breasts. The quick almost panting movement of her breath.

It was indeed obscene. I had, from the inception of this plan in my mind, intended to keep Hartley here, by force if necessary; but I had not imagined the details, and I had somehow hoped that as soon as she saw Titus in my house she would make the great mental leap, the intuition, the necessary conjecture: she would *see* her freedom and the possibility of living with Titus and me. And once she had grasped her freedom I had the strong and reasonable hope that she would come to me, even though Titus was an unknown quantity and had his own freedom to dispose of. But perhaps I had indeed, inspired by the boy's providential appearance, tried to move too fast. The horrors of the last half hour had shaken my resolution so that I nearly conceived of, after all, taking her home. Yet could I, now? He was almost certainly back and had read that letter and – my plan had succeeded so well that it had trapped me also. I did now look at my watch. It was twenty-five past nine.

I took her hands and put them neatly one on top of the other, and my hand above them. Then I turned her face round to look at me. She had not been crying. To my unspeakable relief I received, not the harsh anxious glare that I so much dreaded, but a new quiet look, gentle and reflective; and although she looked so sad yet she seemed younger, more like her old self, and also more alive, less apathetic, more intelligent. My confidence returned. Perhaps, after all, her freedom was stirring. Perhaps my plan had been right. It was a question of a cure, a psychological cure. And in the instant I decided that it would now be fatal to show any weakness. I must be absolute, I must be to the full the being who had made Titus breathless with admiration.

'I'm not going to let you go, Hartley. Not tonight, not ever. You can't go back tonight anyway. It's too late to get that letter. *He's* got it now. Let him think what he pleases. Why should you fear him and lie to him? That hurts me so. I can't bear it, Titus can't bear it. Titus wants you, but he doesn't want him. Doesn't that suggest anything to your mind? I like Titus, Titus likes me. Why shouldn't Titus be my son, why shouldn't you be my wife? It's fate, Hartley, it's fate. Why should Titus turn up just *now,* why should he come to *me*? Why should I be here at all? You must see how extraordinarily it's all worked out. Titus so much wanted to be with you, but he would never have gone over there, never. And you were glad to see him, weren't you? And you were able to talk to him. What did you talk about?'

'The dogs –'

'The dogs?'

'He was remembering the dogs we had when he was little, he likes animals.'

'Oh – good. Hartley, just relax, let it go, let it *drop*.'

'Let what drop?'

'You know – this burden, this useless fruitless loyalty, this pointless sacrifice. You're making *his* life a misery too, let it go, let *him* go. You're like a half-dead person.'

'Yes,' she said thoughtfully. 'I've felt half dead – yes – often. I think quite a lot of people do. But you can live on half dead and even have pleasures in your life.'

The reflective tone of her voice made me want to sing out with joy. I was reaching her. She was speaking of it, of *it*. I was waking up my sleeping princess. 'You must be hungry. Have some wine. Have some kedgeree, there's a bit left.'

'I'll just have some wine. And some of that bread.'

'And cheese. And olives.'

'I don't like olives, I told you before.'

She ate a few mouthfuls of bread and cheese, then thrust it aside. She drank some wine. I drank a little too. I could not eat.

'Hartley, do you know, I think you've crossed the Rubicon. And what's on the other side? Freedom, happiness.'

'Something has certainly happened,' she said, and she gave me her calmer face, deliberately smoothing out her brow with her hand. Then she smoothed her cheeks, moulding her face and making it calm and open. There was a capability, a capacity there which heartened me. I saw again the way her 'wildness' was also a kind of serenity. 'But it's not what you think. It isn't anything to do with happiness. I'm not going to struggle with you, dear Charles, I mean to struggle physically, to try to rush away, and to weep and scream when I can't, though that is just what I am doing now in my mind, weeping and screaming. There are moments, I've learnt, when one has to fold one's hands. I can see what you want to do and why. You want to make my marriage crash, explode. But it won't. It's indestructible.'

'You speak as if it were a prison.'

'People live in prisons.'

'Not if they can get out.'

'Then too, sometimes. But – oh you don't understand. You can only make things worse. And you have done so tonight.'

Her words, her tone, now sounded terrible, like a calm judge pronouncing a fatal sentence. Yet I thought, if she desperately, absolutely wanted to go she *would* weep and scream, and could reasonably believe that this would make me give in. So, since she was, though tragically, calm she must be a little bit glad to be forced to stay. No doubt her feelings were wretchedly mixed, positively minced up.

It was getting a little darker in the kitchen now. Titus came in through the outside door and went over to the stove. He did not look at us. He found the plate with the remains of the kedgeree. I was suddenly reminded of Gilbert who would still be at his post outside. I called after Titus, who was disappearing into the hall with the kedgeree, 'Go and tell Gilbert to come in. He's up by the tower with the car. Then lock the front door.'

I gave her some more wine. There was now something almost alarming about her resigned quietness. Did she expect I would suddenly take her home after all? Perhaps it was her dread of just this prospect which made her so quiet?

I did not immediately follow up what she said. I got up and locked the outside door and pocketed the key. I was faintly sure Ben would not turn up tonight. I was feeling so strong now that I hardly cared whether he did or not. I heard Gilbert coming in, complaining loudly to Titus, and I heard the key turn in the front door. I lit a candle and pulled the curtains although it was still light outside with a huge dull moon the colour of Wensleydale cheese. It was the first time I had been with Hartley without an urgent time limit. The sense of solitude with her, of the extension of time, was uncanny. I felt both exultant and unreal. I drank some more wine.

'Hartley, I don't think I've been perfectly happy – at all – since you went away. You can't conceive how I suffered then. But we were happy, weren't we? When we were on our bikes. That was youth, like it ought to be, joyous, perfect. I've never loved anybody else. That is why, really, you must excuse me if I now go to some lengths –' I adopted a light tone, hoping to entice her into some gentleness of response. And I thought, oh God, if only I'd found her during the war, if only I'd run into her in the street in Leicester! And with the speed of the cinema-reeling imagination I saw how I might have met her, how she would have told me her marriage was a failure, or better still Ben would already have met a hero's death, and … I even got as far as composing my explanation to Clement before Hartley spoke again.

'You think it odd I'm so quiet. It's like a sort of peace. Sometimes I feel I haven't much further to go.'

'What do you mean by that?'

'Sometimes I wish he would –'

'Would what? Has he threatened you?'

'No, no – that wasn't what I was going to say.'

'What do you mean then? Look, you *can't* go back to him, I won't let you, even if you don't want to stay with me.' But what did I think I would do then, set her up in a flower shop?

'Hartley, you've got to stay with me and Titus, it's your place. Apart from anything else, Titus having come to me will confirm Ben's idea that he is my son.'

'Have you only just thought of that?'

'Oh, Hartley, darling, be gentle with me, don't be so sort of remote. Admit it, say it, you've never really loved anybody but me, you've come home at last. That night when I saw you in the car headlights you had come *here*, you had to come. Say that you love me, say that it will be all right, that we'll be happy. Christ, don't you want to be happy at last and live with a man who loves you and is kind to you and believes what you say? Hartley, look at me. No, come in here, I don't know why we're sitting at this stupid table.'

I picked up the candle and pulled her into the little red room and drew the curtains. I sat in the armchair and wanted to take her on my knee, but she slipped to the floor at my feet and held on to my hand. I began very slowly and carefully to kiss her, then to caress her breasts. We were like children, adolescents. I felt for her a desire which was marvellously indistinguishable from pure love, reverent, strong, consumingly protective. And my desire was also that of a boy, incompetent, unskilled and humble. I did not know how to hold her or how to make her dry lips respond. Finally I got down on the floor too, manoeuvred her to lie full length beside me, and clasped her, peering awkwardly into her face.

'Hartley, you love me, don't you, don't you?'

'Oh – yes – but what does it mean?'

'We're close, we know each other.'

'Yes, it's strange, but in a way I do know you, and there isn't anyone else who's near me like that. I suppose it's just because we were young, and later you can't know people, or I couldn't.'

'You know me. I know you.'

'I've felt as if I didn't exist, as if I were invisible, miles away from the world, miles away. You can't imagine how much alone I've been all my life. It wasn't anybody's fault. It was my fault.'

'I can see you, Hartley, you exist, you're here. I love you, Titus loves you. We'll all be together.'

'Titus stopped loving me long ago.'

'Don't cry. He loves you, I know he does, he told me so. All will be well now that you've got away from that hateful man.'

I kept touching the quiet tears upon her cheek, and at last, half thrusting me away, she began to caress my face. 'Oh, Charles – Charles – so strange.'

'We're like we used to be, lying in the woods – Hartley, will you be with me tonight please at last, just to be together quietly? We don't have to lie here like this all night, do we?'

She became rigid, then sat up. 'It's the wine – I'm not used to it – I must be drunk – drunk –'

'Well, don't ask me to take you back now! It's much too late, from every possible point of view!'

She got to her knees, then stiffly to her feet. I rose and faced her, gently touching her elbows with my fingertips.

'Charles, you don't know what you've done. Of course I shall go back tomorrow. I must sleep now, I just want to sleep now, by myself, I wish I could die in my sleep, I wish I could run out and fall into the sea.'

'What rubbish. Can you swim?'

'No.'

'Let's go upstairs, promise me you won't run away in the night.'

'Tomorrow I must go back there. This is just more of my stupidity, oh I am so stupid, always stupid, I should never have left the house. I'm not angry with you. It's my fault, everything is my fault. Yes, I suppose I love you, I've never forgotten you, and when I saw you I felt it all again, but it's something childish, it isn't part of the real world. There was never any place for our love in the world. If there had been it would have won and we wouldn't have parted. It wasn't just me, it was you, you went away, you can't remember how it was – and there isn't any place for this love in the world now, it's pointless, it's irrelevant, it's a dream, we're in a dream place and tomorrow we must leave it. You say it was fated, perhaps it is but not like you think. It's an evil fate, it's *my* fate, I made it happen somehow, this muddle, this horror. Why did you come here? I somehow made you come, like people are lured to destruction, not for any good but just for disaster and death. That's what I've been making all my life, not a home, not a child, but just horrors.'

I recalled Titus's words, 'She's a bit of a fantasist.' And no doubt she was indeed quite drunk. There was certainly no point in arguing now with the madness of her words. I hugged her hard. 'Stop it, old thing, darling little Hartley. I did not go away from you, not like that, you know you're only making excuses! Our love will make its place in the world, you'll see, now that you're here, it's all very simple really. Just wait till the morning and the daylight and then you'll feel brave. Come along upstairs with me and you shall sleep where you like.'

I led her out through the kitchen, carrying the candle. As we came to the stairs I saw a faint light under the door of the front room where Titus was sleeping, and I heard the murmur of voices. At the thought of Titus and Gilbert sitting on the floor on those cushions by candlelight I felt a quick spasm of jealousy. Hartley and I went upstairs.

I showed her the bathroom. I waited for her. I led her up and into my bedroom, but it was quite clear that she would not sleep with me. It was in any case better now to leave her alone. A kind of superstitious terror had taken hold of her, which took the form of a frenzied desire for unconsciousness. 'I want to sleep, I must sleep, only sleep matters, sleep, I will sleep.' I had had the sense to anticipate this situation and had made up a bed on the floor of the little centre room upstairs, with the mattress off my divan. I had also provided a candle, matches, even a chamber pot. I offered her a pair of pyjamas, but she lay down at once in her dress and pulled the blanket up over her head as if she were a corpse covering itself. And she did seem then to go to sleep instantly: the quick flight into oblivion of the chronically unhappy person.

I withdrew and left her. I closed the door and quietly locked it on the outside. I would never now lose that nightmare image of a distraught woman rushing to drown herself in the sea. I went to my room and kicked my shoes off and crawled into bed. I was completely exhausted, but imagined I would be too excited to sleep. I was wrong. I was fast asleep in seconds.

The next morning I woke to a sense of an utterly changed and perhaps dreadful world, like on the first day of a war. Joy, hope, came too, but fear first, and a black sense of confusion as if the deep logic of the universe had suddenly gone wrong. What was it that I had been so certain of, so confident about? What exactly was I up to? Had I done something mad and frightful yesterday, like a crime committed when drunk, remembered sober? There was also, to be expected, a visit from Ben.

The presence of Hartley in the house was itself like a dream, her sheer survival overnight now something urgently in question. I felt like a child who rushes to the cage of its new pet fearing to find only a lifeless body. With a sick stomach and a pounding heart I ran out into the corridor, beat my way through the bead curtain, softly unlocked her door and tapped. No response. Had she died in the night like a captured animal, had she somehow escaped and drowned herself? I opened the door and peered in. She was there and awake. She had pushed the pillows up against the wall and lay upon the mattress with her head propped, the blanket pulled up over her mouth. Her eyes stared at me under drooped lids. Her head kept moving slightly and I saw she was shivering.

'Hartley, darling, are you all right, did you sleep? Were you warm enough?'

She lowered the blanket a little and her mouth moved.

'Hartley, you're going to stay with me forever. This is the first day of our new world – isn't it? Oh, Hartley –'

She began very awkwardly to pull herself up, leaning her back against the wall, still hiding behind the blanket.

She said in a mumbling, gabbling tone, not looking at me, 'I must go home.'

'Don't start that again.'

'I came without my bag, without anything, I've got no make-up or anything.'

'God, as if that mattered!'

I could see that, for her, it might matter however. In the bleak drained morning light which filtered in from the window which gave onto the drawing room she looked terrible. Her face was puffy and greasy, her brow corrugated, lines of haggardness outlined her mouth. Her tangled hair, dry and frizzy, looked like an old wig. As I gazed at her I felt a kind of new strength composed of pity and tenderness. And as I thought to show her how little I minded her shabby helplessness, my titanic love could even have wished for greater odds.

'Come on, old thing,' I said, 'get up. Come on down and we'll have breakfast. Then I'll send Gilbert over to Nibletts for all your things. It's perfectly simple.' Or at least I hoped it would seem so to her.

She pulled herself up slowly, and then got onto all fours and rose laboriously to her feet. Her yellow dress was horribly hopelessly crumpled and she pulled at it ineffectually. Her whole body expressed the slightly ashamed awkwardness of the very afflicted person.

'Look, I'll lend you my dressing gown, I've got such a nice one.' I ran to my bedroom and brought her my best black silk dressing gown with the red rosettes. She stood at the door of her room staring at the bead curtain.

'What's that?'

'Well may you ask. A bead curtain. Now put this on. There's the bathroom, you remember.'

She let me help her into the dressing gown, then walked slowly down to the bathroom. I waited, sitting on the stairs. When she emerged she climbed back up towards her room, moving heavily like an old woman.

'Wait then, I'll get you a comb, or you can come and use the mirror in my room, would you like, it's brighter in there.'

She went on back into her own room. I fetched the comb and a hand mirror. She combed her hair, not looking into the glass, then sat down again on the mattress. There was indeed no other furniture, since the table which Titus had retrieved from the rocks was still downstairs.

'Won't you come down?'

'No, I'll stay here.'

'I'll bring you something.'

'I feel sick, the wine has made me sick.'

'Would you like tea, coffee?'

'I feel sick.' She lay down again and pulled up the blanket.

I looked at her with despair, then went out. I closed and locked the door. I did not exclude the possibility that after this show of apathy she might suddenly run for it, rushing out of the house and disappearing among the rocks, hurling herself into the sea.

I went downstairs and found Gilbert sitting at the kitchen table. He rose respectfully as I entered. Titus was at the stove, which he had mastered, cooking eggs. He seemed now to be completely at home in the house. At this I felt both pleasure and displeasure.

'Morning, guv'nor,' said Gilbert.

'Hello, dad.'

I did not care for this pleasantry from Titus.

'If you must be familiar, my name is Charles.'

'Sorry, Mr Arrowby. How is my mother this morning?'

'Oh, Titus, Titus —'

'Have a fried egg,' said Gilbert.

'I'll take her up some tea. Does she take milk, sugar?'

'I can't remember.'

I made up a little tray with tea, milk and sugar, bread, butter, marmalade. I carried it up, balanced it, unlocked the door. Hartley was still lying under the blanket.

'Lovely breakfast. Look.'

She stared at me with almost theatrical misery.

'Wait. I'll get a table and chair.' I ran downstairs and came back with the little table and a chair. I unpacked the tray onto the table. 'Come, darling, don't let your tea get cold. And look, I've brought you such a lovely present, a stone, the most beautiful stone on the shore.' I laid down beside her plate the elliptical stone, my very first one, the prize of my collection, hand-sized, a mottled pink, irregularly criss-crossed with white bars in a design before which Klee and Mondrian would have bowed to the ground.

Hartley came slowly, crawling then rising, and stood by the table, pulling the dressing gown round her. She did not look at the stone or touch it. I put my arms round her for a moment and kissed her wig-like hair. Then I kissed her warm silk-clad shoulder. Then I left her and locked the door. At any rate she had said no more about going back. No doubt she was afraid; and if she feared to think of returning now, then every hour which kept her here would help to gain my point. But her air of apathetic misery appalled me. Later I was not surprised to find that she had drunk a little tea but eaten nothing.

I looked at my watch. It was still not eight o'clock. I wondered when, and how, Ben would arrive. I remembered uneasily what Hartley had said about his having kept his army revolver. I went down to the kitchen to issue orders.

Gilbert was eating fried eggs, fried bread, grilled tomatoes.

'Where's the boy?'

'He's gone to swim. How's Hartley?'

'Oh – terrible. I mean, all right. Listen, Gilbert, could you go outside and keep watch? All right, finish your breakfast first, you're doing well, aren't you!'

'What do you mean, keep watch?' said Gilbert suspiciously.

'Just stand, or if you like sit, on the road, at the end of the causeway, and come in and tell me when you see *him* coming.'

'How am I to know him? By his horsewhip?'

'He's unmistakable.' I described Ben minutely.

'Suppose he creeps up on me or something? He can't be feeling very pleased. You said he was a tough, a sort of thug. I love you, darling, but I'm not going to fight.'

'Nobody is going to fight.' I hope.

'I don't mind sitting in the car,' said Gilbert. 'I'll sit in the car with the doors locked and watch the road. Then if I see him I'll hoot the horn.'

This seemed a good idea. 'All right, but make it snappy.'

I went out of the back and across the grass and climbed over the rocks as far as the little cliff in time to see Titus's long pale legs elevated to heaven as he dived under the green water. He reminded me of Breughel's Icarus. *Absit omen.*

I had not the heart to swim, and anyway I did not want Ben to find me trouserless; and there was enough of a swell on for me to see that I might have difficulty getting out. Titus would be all right of course. I must remember to fix another 'rope' at the steps.

The sun was already high and the sea was a lucid green nearer to the rocks, a glittering azure farther out, shifting and flashing as if large plates of white were floating on the surface. The horizon was a line of gold. A surge of rather large but very smooth slow waves was coming in towards me and silently frothing up among the rocks; there was a quiet menace in the graceful yet machine-like power of their strong regular motions.

I waited rather impatiently for young Titus to finish his swim. He had no business to be diverting himself at a moment of crisis. He saw me, waved, but was clearly in no hurry. He shouted to me to come in but I shook my head.

I urgently wanted Titus on the land, partly because I wanted to efface the rather raw impression of our stupid exchanges in the kitchen. Also I wanted Titus beside me, clothed and efficient and in his right mind, when the gentleman turned up. I did not really imagine that Ben would come round and murder us all, but unless there was some show of strength he might possibly wish to punch my head; and while I am athletic and fairly strong, the arts of aggression have never been among my accomplishments. I often wondered during the war how it was that men were able to face other men and kill them. Training helped and I suppose fear. I was glad that it had not been my lot.

It also then occurred to me, as I dourly watched Titus's dolphin antics, that I did not really know how *he* would react. He had fairly indicated that he detested his adoptive father. But the young mind is mysterious. Confronted with him he might be cowed, or else moved by sudden sympathy. Or by old deep resistless filial emotions. *Could Titus change sides?* Did Titus himself know?

At last he swam back to the steep rock, and clinging with fingers and toes easily levered his naked body up out of the strong rising and falling surge. He crawled up, swung over the edge and lay panting.

'Titus, dear boy, get dressed, quick, here's your towel.'

He obeyed, eyeing me. 'What's the matter? Are we going somewhere?'

'No, but I'm afraid your father may arrive any moment.'

'Looking for my mother. Well, I suppose he may. What will you do?'

'I don't know. What will he do? Listen, Titus, and please forgive my clumsy haste, there's so much I want to say to you. Titus, we must hold on to each other, you and me –'

'Oh yes, I'm a very important property, I'm the decoy duck, I'm the hostage!'

'No, this is exactly my point. This is what I came out here to say to you. Not for that. For you. I mean I want *you,* I want to be your father, I want you to be my son, whatever happens. I mean even if your mother won't stay with me – but I hope and believe she will – but even if she weren't to, I still want you to accept me as your father.'

'It's a funny action,' he said, 'accepting somebody as your father, when you're grown up. I'm not sure how it's done.'

'Time will show us how it's done. You must just have the will, the intent. Please. I feel there is a real bond between us, it will grow stronger, naturally. Don't think I'm just using you, I'm not. I feel love for you. Excuse the clumsy awkwardness of what I say, I haven't time to think of a graceful speech. I feel that fate or God or something has given us to each other. Let us not stupidly miss this chance. Don't let idiotic pride or suspicion or failure of imagination or failure of hope spoil this thing for us. Let us now and henceforth belong together. Never mind what it means exactly or what it will involve, we can't see that yet. But will you accept, will you try?'

I had not prepared or anticipated quite such passionate pleading. I stared at him anxiously, hoping I had made some impression.

He was clothed by now, and we stood together on the high rock above the water. He looked at me frowning and screwing up his eyes. Then he looked away. 'All right – I suppose – yes – OK. I'm in fact, well, a little overwhelmed, actually. I'm glad you said that about wanting me for me. I wasn't sure. I believe you – I think. It's funny, I've been thinking about you so much of my life, and I always knew I'd have to come and look at you one day, but I kept putting it off because I was afraid. I thought that if you rejected me – I mean, thought I was a sort of lying scrounger, just wanting money and that – and, well, why shouldn't you have thought so, it's all so odd – it would have been a sort of crippling blow. I can't see how I would have recovered, I'd have felt so dishonoured and awful, I'd have been saddled with it somehow forever after. There was so much at stake.'

'So much, yes, but all is well, here at least. We won't misunderstand each other. We won't lose each other.'

'It's all happened so fast.'

'It's happened fast because it's right, it's easy because it's right.'

'Well then, I'll try, as you say God knows what it means, but I accept, at least I'll try.'

He held out his hand and I grasped it and for a moment we stood there, moved and embarrassed.

Then I heard, from the roadway, the loud urgent hooting of Gilbert's horn.

'That's him!' I jumped up and began to scramble towards the house. Titus passed me and raced on before me over the grass. When I reached the kitchen door Gilbert was holding on to Titus.

'He's here, he came walking along the road, he stopped at the causeway but when he saw me in the car and when I started hooting he walked on.'

'Walked on past the house?'

'Yes. Maybe he's going to come round the back over the rocks.' Gilbert seemed to be really frightened.

I ran through the hall and out onto the causeway and up to the road. There was no sign of Ben. I noticed that Gilbert, no doubt to secure his own retreat, had parked the car right across the end of the causeway as if it were intended as a barricade. That no doubt was why Ben had walked on. As I was still hesitating and staring about I heard Titus shouting from the other side of the house.

I passed Gilbert, who was gabbling something or other, at the door and rushed out again through the kitchen. Titus was standing up on top of one of the highest rocks, and pointing. 'He's there! There! I can see him. He's coming along from the tower.'

By now I felt no more doubt about whose side Titus was on. Thank goodness for that.

I called to Titus, 'You wait there, I'll go and meet him. If I want you I'll shout.'

I began to climb over the rocks keeping the tower in view, and in a moment I saw Ben, also clambering, with an impressive agility, in the direction of the house.

The place where our two paths converged, and indeed the only fairly easy way from the house to the tower, was Minn's bridge, the rocky arch under which the sea entered the cauldron. Towards this natural meeting place we both scrambled and slid until we came onto the bridge and faced each other some ten feet apart. I wondered quickly and a bit anxiously whether we were, as I hoped, still within the view of Titus upon his high rock. I looked quickly round. We were not.

Ben was wearing blackish corduroy trousers, rubbed bald at the knees, probably from the Fishermen's Stores, and a white shirt. No jacket, though the morning was still chilly. Had he donned this stripped gear to assure me he was carrying no weapon, or was he simply dressed for fighting? He looked burly, a bit tight for his trousers, but compact and business-like. He appeared to have shaved, which I had not. He had shaved alone over there in that suddenly empty house with God knows what thoughts in his mind as he faced himself in the mirror. His cropped mousy hair, his big boyish head, broad shoulders and short build were reminiscent of a little ram or other smallish but aggressive male animal. By contrast with his thick heavy look I felt positively willowy, loose, untidy, with uncombed hair and, I suddenly realized, my striped pyjama jacket still on over my trousers.

I advanced a little onto the bridge and so did he. The tide was coming in and the strong large waves were crowding in and washing hungrily round inside the deep smooth space of the cauldron. There was a low sibilant roar, not loud enough to impede a parley. I stood, checking on my pyjama buttons, and waiting for him to begin. The roaring sound comforted me. I hoped it disconcerted Ben. Noise has always been my friend.

I was now seeing Ben's face closely in a good light for the first time. He was rather better-looking than I had imagined earlier. He had long brown eyes with long lashes, and a large well-formed and, though perhaps only now, slightly sneering and fastidious mouth.

His chin receded into his thick neck. I was at once aware that he was, and I was relieved to see it, extremely nervous, though also extremely angry. Was *he* perhaps a bit frightened of *me*? Guilt? Guilt makes fear.

'Where is my wife?'

'Here, in my house, where she wants to stay. And Titus too, he wasn't my son, as you perfectly well know, but he is now, I've adopted him.'

'What?'

'Yes!'

'What did you say?'

I realized with further satisfaction that Ben was a bit deaf, deafer than me at any rate, and the noise was bothering him. I had rather gabbled my statement it is true. I said, with loud insulting clarity, 'She is – here. Titus is – here. They stay – here.'

'I've come to take her home.'

'Look, you don't really believe that Titus is my son, do you? I assure you he isn't.'

'I want my wife.'

'I'm telling you something that ought to interest you. Titus is not my son.'

'I don't care about that story any more, it's over, I want Mary.'

'She wants to stay here.'

'I don't believe you – you are keeping her by force. You kidnapped her. I *know* she wouldn't stay of her own free will, I *know*.'

'She came to me, she *ran* to me, like she did before, that evening when you were at your woodwork class. Do you imagine that I could or would remove her from your house by force?'

'She left her handbag behind.'

'You don't love her, she doesn't love you, she's terrified of you, why not admit it to yourselves? Why go on living this horrible lie?'

'Release Mary, or I shall go to the police.'

'They'd laugh at you. You know quite well the police wouldn't interfere in a case of this sort.'

'I want my wife.'

'She doesn't want to go back to you, she's had enough. I'm going to send the car round for her things.'

'What lies has she told you?'

'That's your line now is it? Vilify her, put the blame on her! How splendidly you give yourself away!'

'She's a hysterical person who imagines a lot of things, she isn't well.'

'She certainly imagines she's had enough of your cruelty. Go on, just try the police, see what happens!'

'You don't know what you're meddling with, you don't understand. She's my wife and I love her and I'm going to take her back to her home, where she belongs and where she wants to be. Why have you suddenly come interfering in our lives, why did you decide to come and live here and pester us, we didn't want you, we don't want you. I know what sort of person you are, I've read about you, you're a rotten man, a shit, a destroyer, you're *filth*. Mary isn't one of your show-business whores, she's a decent woman, like you aren't worthy to touch. Leave us alone, if you don't want to get very hurt. I'm warning you. Leave us alone.'

Ben, incoherently searching for words to match his anger, his big bull head thrust forward, was showing his strong teeth, wet with spittle. The rhythmic hissing roar of the powerful mechanical waves entranced me for a moment, as without looking down I could sense their churning movement in the rocky pit below. I thought to myself quite clearly, with a precision which involved my whole body, I have only to step quickly forward and pitch that hateful thug over the edge. He may be stronger, but I am more agile. He cannot swim; and even a good swimmer would die at once in that boiling cauldron. No one sees us. I can say he attacked me. I have only to push him in and all my troubles are over.

As I thought this I was fixing Ben with my eyes. I felt an embryonic movement of my body, though no doubt in reality I did not visibly stir. My eyes were enough, however, and I had the certainty that he had read my intention, if indeed it could be called an intention, for of course I would never have carried it out. He retreated to the far end of the bridge and I unclenched my hands and lowered my eyes. I retreated too.

'Bring her back!' he said, raising his voice, as the din of the water rose like a wall between us. 'Bring her back this morning. Or else I'll go every possible way to destroy you. I'm telling you. I mean that.'

I said nothing.

He said, as if suddenly confused and with a catch in his voice, 'Consider *her*. She wants to come home. I know she does. You don't understand. Don't let this go on. It's worse for her. She'll have to come home in the end. Don't you see?'

I said, inaudibly, 'Fuck off.'

He began to move away. Then he turned back and called out, 'Tell her I brought the dog back last night. I thought she'd be so pleased.'

I watched him as, more slowly, and seeming now at last like a cripple, he climbed over the rocks, appearing and disappearing, until he had nearly reached the road. I shook myself out of my trance and began to make my way back to the house as fast as I could. I wanted to be sure he was really going away.

Titus, who was still sitting on his high rock, jumped up and followed. Gilbert was on the lawn. They both immediately started to question me, but I ran past them. They ran after me and we emerged all three onto the causeway and advanced as far as Gilbert's car, which was still in position. We stood in a row behind the car. Ben was walking along the road towards us. Titus gazed at him for a moment, then turned round and stood there with his back to the road. The gesture was impressive. Ben passed us by, grim-faced, without a word, without a look, and walked onward unhurried in the direction of the village.

'What happened?' said Titus, now looking shaken, frightened.

'Nothing.'

'How, nothing?'

'He said what he had to say.'

'What did he say?'.

'Lies. He said she was hysterical and imagined things.'

'Hysterical all right,' said Titus. 'She could be in hysterics for an hour. It was frightening, it was meant to be.'

'If you've decided he's your father after all you can go home with him now, I'm not stopping you.'

'Don't talk to me like that. I'm just so bloody sorry for her.'

'Won't you come up and see her?'

'No – not while she's – no.'

'Oh – !' I felt violent homicidal exasperation. I ran back into the house and up the stairs and unlocked Hartley's door.

She was sitting on the mattress with her back against the wall and her knees up, draped in the black dressing gown. She looked at me with heavy swollen eyes and started speaking in a droning voice before I was through the door. 'Please let me go home, I want to go home, I've got to go there, there isn't anywhere else to go, let me go home, please.'

'This is home, with me is home, you are home!'

'Let me go now. How can you be so unkind to me? The longer I stay the worse it will be.'

'Why do you want to go back to that hateful place? Are you hypnotized or what?'

'I wish I was dead, I think I'm going to die soon, I feel it. Sometimes I felt I would die by wishing it when I went to sleep but I always woke up again and found I was still there. Every morning finding I'm still me, that's hell.'

'Well, get out of hell then! The gate's open and I'm holding it!'

'I can't. I'm hell, myself.'

'Oh, Hartley, *get up*! Come on down and sit in the sun, talk to me, talk to Titus. You're not a prisoner. Stop being so bloody miserable, you'll drive me mad! I'm offering you freedom, happiness, I want to take you and Titus to – to Paris, to Athens, to New York, anywhere you want to go!'

'I want to go home.'

'What's the matter with you? You weren't like this yesterday.'

'I think I'm going to die, I feel it.'

Her eyes, which refused to meet mine, had the defensive coldness of those who are determined to lose hope.

There followed some of the strangest days I can ever remember. Hartley refused to come downstairs. She stayed hid in her room like a sick animal. I locked her door in case she should drown herself, I left her no candle and matches in case she should burn herself. I feared for her safety and her well-being at every moment, and yet I did not dare to remain with her all the time or even most of it, indeed I scarcely knew how to be with her at all. I left her alone at night, and the nights were long, as she retired early, and slept soon (I could hear her snoring). She spent a great deal of time sleeping, both in the night and in the afternoon. That oblivion at least was her prompt friend. Meanwhile I watched and waited, calculating upon some deep unstatable theory the right intervals for my appearances. I escorted her in silence to the bathroom. I spent long vigils sitting outside in the corridor. I put some cushions into the empty alcove, the place where I had dreamt there was a secret door through which Mrs Chorney would emerge to reclaim possession of her house. I sat on the cushions watching the door of Hartley's room and listening. Sometimes as she snored I dozed.

Of course I often sat in the room with her, talking with her or attempting to, or else in silence. I knelt beside her, stroking her hands and her hair and caressing her as one might caress a small bird. Her legs and feet were bare, but she would persist in wearing my dressing gown over her dress. Yet with small contacts I made acquaintance surreptitiously with her body; the weight and mass of it, her magnificent round breasts, her plump shoulders, her thighs; and I would gladly have lain with her, only she resisted, by the slightest of signs, my slightest of efforts to undress her. She fretted about having no make-up and I sent Gilbert to the village to purchase what she wanted, and then in my presence she made up her face. This little concession to vanity seemed to me a hopeful portent. But I remained afraid of her and for her. My quiet relentless refusal to let her go was violence enough. I feared that any further pressure might produce some frenzy of hostility or some more extreme withdrawal which would render me as mad as she was; for I did at moments think of her as mad. Thus we existed together in a sort of crazy mysterious precarious mutual toleration. At intervals she repeated that she wanted to go home, but she accepted my firm refusals passively, and this was encouraging. Of course with every hour that passed her fear of returning must increase, and this in itself gave me hope. Surely a moment must come when the *amount* of her fear would automatically make her mine?

We did in fact, inconsequentially and at odd intervals, manage to converse. When I tried to remind her of old times she did not always fail to respond; and at moments in my 'treatment' of her I felt, loving her and pitying her so intensely, that I was making a little progress. Once, quite out of the blue, she asked, 'What happened to Aunt Estelle?' I could not remember having spoken to her about Aunt Estelle, so much had I made my uncle's family into a taboo subject. Another time she said, 'Philip never liked you.' Philip was her brother. 'What's Philip doing now?' 'He was killed in the war.' She added, 'You were my brother really.' She never asked me anything about my life in the theatre and I did not try to tell her anything. I think she was really without curiosity about it. It had in any case by now dawned on me that she felt little or no regret at having failed to marry a famous man. She did ask once or twice if I had met this or that well-known actor, but she clearly knew very little about the theatre and did not pursue anything that I said. Once she asked, 'Did you ever know an actress called Clement Makin?' After a moment's reflection I said, 'Yes, I knew her well, she loved me, we lived together for a bit.' 'You mean —?' 'She was my mistress.' 'But she must have been years and years older than you.' 'Yes, but that didn't seem to matter much.' 'She must have been an old woman.' A little while after this Hartley began to cry and let me put my arms round her. She did not speak of Clement again. That was one of the moments when hope itself seemed to come to me out of the pity and the love. And I reflected upon the mystery that Hartley had as large a consciousness and as long a history as I had myself and I would never know, never have access to, that interior being. Of course I was impatient. I had expected her, after despair, to be in such need that she would have to turn to me completely, having no other recourse. It was indeed her failure to break down that now left me so terribly at a loss.

Herein I did expect Titus to help me, but he was unwilling to, perhaps unable to. He seemed almost frightened of Hartley, frightened of her

situation, her captivity, her awful helplessness, what he imagined of her
mind. He hated her humiliation. He did not want to be involved in it.
He seemed to feel, about the whole business, my 'device' or 'game'
as he had called it, a mixture of disgust and complicit guilt. And no
doubt, at least vicariously, he was afraid of Ben. He complained of the
smell in Hartley's room and said he could not breathe there, and yet
he was too embarrassed to exert himself to persuade her to emerge.
He begged me to stay with him when he talked to her, and if I left him
alone with her he soon ran out. I suppose the difficulty was that they
were unable to talk about Ben and there were so few subjects which
did not relate to that gentleman. Also, I had already noted that Titus
was inclined to be secretive about what he had been doing since he
left home; he had been very unwilling to answer questions which I had
put to him on the subject, and this evasiveness cut out another possible
topic of conversation. In fact Hartley did not show any urgent curiosity
about his doings. They talked, indeed, almost *politely*. At least they did
on the first day. After that Titus was increasingly unwilling to see her,
and she being more distraught I was more reluctant to ask him to.

I could not get used to hearing him call her 'Mary'.

'Mary, why not come out in the sun, it's cold in here.'

'No, thank you.'

'Are you feeling better?' The convention that she was ill had usefully
arrived from somewhere. With an appearance of banal complacency
they discussed the bungalow. But perhaps they scarcely knew what
they were saying.

'And there's a nice garden? We didn't have a proper garden at number
thirty-four, did we? More like a yard.'

'Yes, more like a yard at number thirty-four.'

'I always remember the old mangle in the shed there. Remember
the old mangle?'

'Yes –'

'So now you can grow roses. You always wanted that, didn't you?'

'Yes, lots of roses, all colours.'

'And you can see the sea right out of the window like we used to say would be so nice?'

I could not make out what this did for Hartley. I realized I had been naïve in imagining that mother and son would clasp each other and at once discover a language of love. Well, perhaps this was a language of love. Love was there, I have no doubt, but the two of them remained amazingly awkward and tongue-tied with each other. The dialogue was forced clumsily along mainly by Titus. They soon exhausted the charms of the bungalow, to my relief. Their most successful conversations then consisted of childishly simple reminiscence concerning pointless details of houses and gardens in Titus's childhood.

'Remember the hole in the fence I used to look through when we lived at number sixty-seven?'

'Yes –'

'I stood on a box, didn't I?'

'Yes, on a box.'

Why could they not talk? Had her sympathy with Titus been really broken in those years, and his with her? A dreadful thought. Later I saw that of course it was the whole situation which made them speechless; and it was I who created and who maintained that situation.

This time of Hartley's incarceration stretches out in my memory as if it contained a whole history of mental drama, vast developments, changes, checks, surprises, progresses, revulsions, crises. In fact it was a period of only four to five days. History, drama, change it did indeed contain. It is odd that after the first day I stopped worrying terribly about Ben. Of course I did not forget him, of course I expected him. I locked the doors carefully at night. It did occur to me that he might try to set fire to the house, and this haunted me a bit; after all he was a sort of professional fireman. But I ceased being obsessed with him, perhaps because I had by now succeeded in imprisoning myself mentally as well, and the danger of Ben seemed less real. Why did he not move? Was he making an elaborate plan or did he just prefer to torment himself by waiting and thus feed his rage? Was it possible that he was afraid of Titus? I soon ceased to wonder.

As for Titus and Gilbert, as soon as they could get away from Hartley and me they behaved as if they were on holiday. Titus did not want to discuss his mother or his father. He had opted out of these problems. He swam every day, always from the little cliff, sometimes twice or three times a day. He covered himself in suntan lotion and lay about naked on the rocks. Any scruples about 'cadging' now seemed to be completely gone. He accepted my hospitality as of right and gave nothing in return, no help, no warmth. Of course this is an unfair judgment. I cannot blame Titus for 'not wanting to know' what was going on upstairs. I think he did not even speculate; and indeed it would have been difficult to do so. Moreover, I gave him very little of my time and he may have resented this rather crucial neglect. I had decided by now that Titus was a simpler character than I had imagined at first; or perhaps, faced with horrors, he had chosen simplicity.

Gilbert was a good deal more curious and also good-naturedly anxious to help (he even wanted to put flowers in Hartley's room), only I kept him well out of it. He remained essential of course. He cooked. He shopped while Titus sunbathed. But I did not let him come to the upper landing. A curious feature of the time and one which can still terribly bring it back to me was that Gilbert and Titus discovered that they were both singers. Gilbert was quite a good baritone, Titus turned out to be a tolerable tenor, and could also sing falsetto. What was more, they seemed to possess an extremely large common repertoire. Until I ordered them fiercely to go out onto the rocks they made the house ring with their noise. Of course they would have liked to have me as an audience to show off to (all singers are vain), and of course they would have liked to sit up half the night carolling and drinking my wine. (They both drank a good deal and I had to send Gilbert to the Raven Hotel for more.) Even from outside and at a distance they were audible, so loud were their voices and so pleased were they with the mutual exhibition of their talents. (Hartley never mentioned the singing; perhaps she was beyond caring or perhaps like her husband she was a bit deaf.) They roared out pieces from operas and musical comedies, madrigals, pop songs, folk songs, rounds, lewd ballads and love ditties in English, French and Italian. I think they became positively drunk with their music during this time; perhaps it was a natural reaction to the tension inside the house.

I have just said that I now found Titus simpler than I had thought at first. This was so in relation to his mother and to my own problems. (Perhaps by 'simpler' I just mean 'vaguer', 'less attentive'.) But it was certainly noteworthy, and Gilbert noticed it too, that Titus was in superficial ways more cultivated than one would expect a boy to be who had left school early to 'do electricity' at a polytechnic. Where had Titus been during the last year or two? This remained mysterious. I remembered the cuff links and the book of Dante's love poems. My own hypothesis was that he had been living with an older woman. He was just now about the age which I had been when I was kidnapped by Clement; baby-snatching, as everybody called it. Had someone snatched Titus – and then, and lately, discarded him? Gilbert's theory, not surprisingly, was that Titus had been living with a man. Titus himself remained, on this subject, silent. (Perhaps this is the place to say that Perry was of course wrong about the nature of my relations with Fritzie Eitel.)

I have spoken of histories and changes. And indeed in a way later on it seemed to me that what I was doing in those days was reliving the whole history of my love for Hartley, not only the old times, but all the intermediate times as well. Every day, every hour, I remembered more. On about the evening of the second day Hartley became for a while more talkative and had the air of having been reflecting, the talk being the fruit of the reflection. This led to a dialogue which had a most distressing conclusion.

We were sitting on the floor, she on the mattress, I on the bare boards, with our legs outstretched, and facing the long high-up window which gave onto the drawing room. The middle room, usually darkish, was now in twilight, though the evening glow communicated a dim warm illumination. I touched Hartley's hand. I felt from head to foot connected with her.

'Darling, my silk dressing gown suits you, but won't you take it off sometimes?'

'I'm cold.'

'Aren't you beginning to feel that you live here?'

'You think the important thing is that I made a mistake in not marrying you.'

'There was a mistake. What's more important is to undo it now.'

'You just want someone to remember things with.'

'That's very unfair, when I want so much to talk of the future, only you won't!'

'You feel resentment against me because I went away.'

'So you admit you went away?'

'I suppose so, it's so long ago.'

'You said I'd be unfaithful.'

'Did I? I can't remember.' I had lived my life on her words, and now she could not even recall them! 'I suppose I must have gone away because I can remember feeling guilty.'

'Guilty about hurting me?'

'Yes. Really I did always feel guilty and thought you blamed me. And in a funny way I had to protect myself from you by the idea that you hated me.'

'How on earth would that "protect" you?'

'When I saw you in the village I thought you had seen me and pretended not to because you hated me.'

'But I never hated you, darling, never for a second!'

'I had to think so.'

'But why?'

'So that I could be sure that you had really gone, that it was really over. To make it sort of dead in my mind.'

'Oh, Hartley. For me it was never over, never dead in my mind. So you wanted me, you missed me, you were afraid to think about me? Doesn't that prove that you love me?'

'I think you did hate me, though, you feel resentment.'

'You mean now? You're dotty.'

'It's resentment really, otherwise you wouldn't be so unkind.'

'Hartley, don't torment me, you reason like a mad person.'

'Or it's curiosity, like a tourist, you're visiting me, visiting my life and feeling superior.'

'Hartley, stop, will you! Or are you just trying to hurt me? You are the one who's unkind. There is an eternal bond between us, you know there is, it's the clearest thing in the world, clearer than Jesus. I want you to be my wife at last, I want you to rest in me. I want to look after you forever, until I drop dead.'

'I wish I could drop dead.'

'Oh shut up —'

'I wish it could be all over, I have *had* my life. I wish someone would kill me —'

'So he *has* threatened your life?'

'No, no, it's all in my mind —'

'You can't go back now, I won't let you, even if you don't want me. It's so simple, only you complicate things so.'

'You want to make things complicated in *your* way, you twist and turn, you're like an eel, I remember that about you.'

'So now I'm like an eel! I never twisted and turned where you were concerned. I always wanted you and no one else. I am the faithful one. *I* never got married.'

'Yes, but you lived with women, you lived with that old actress.'

'All right, but I couldn't find you! You were the one I wanted! I tried and tried to find you, I searched and searched and somehow I never really gave up hope — and perhaps that's why I've found you now.'

'I've been unjust to Ben.'

'Oh God, can't we forget Ben, Ben's over.'

'He suffered so much about Titus, when Titus disappeared, it was like a penance.'

'Maybe he did, but he deserved to suffer, he drove Titus away. I expect he was glad really.'

'No, no, he wasn't so bad to Titus, not as much as I said. He was severe —'

'He was violent. And to you. Don't try to defend him. Oh don't let's talk about that bloody man.'

'The protection of children people never came, I said they did but they didn't.'

'Oh damn the protection of children people, what do I care whether they came or not?'

'But I said they did, and they didn't.'

'Even if they didn't come, they ought to have come.'

'But it wasn't true.'

'Why are you trying to whitewash that vile cruel man? Titus hates him. Isn't that evidence enough? It is for me.'

'Ben hasn't anyone in the world but me. He hasn't any *thing* in the world.'

'He'll survive. What about me? Why not be sorry for me for a change? I've waited long enough. There's nothing so derelict as an old actor. What have I got now but my memories? I've stripped myself of all the power and all the glamour – for something – and the something, although I didn't know it, was you. You can't let me down now.'

'Do you believe in God?'

'No.'

'I think I believe in Jesus Christ. You've got to believe in something and hold on to something. People would go mad without God, wouldn't they. We used to talk about that, didn't we.'

'I'm glad you haven't forgotten those talks. You remember when we were confirmed? It meant a lot, didn't it? *Come, Holy Ghost, our souls inspire ...*'

'I think I believe in the remission of sins.'

'We all need a spot of that.'

'Love redeems, that means something, doesn't it?'

'Well don't tell me you propose to redeem Ben by love! I'm getting sick of Ben. What about redeeming me?'

'No one else will redeem him, no one else will love him.'

'Jesus will love him.'

'No, you see, for Ben, I've got to be Jesus.'

'This is mad talk, darling, really mad. Just try to think a bit. Doesn't it occur to you that Ben would heave a sigh of relief if you left him?

Damn it, you've left him already. You aren't all that necessary. He mightn't want to send you off, but he'll be jolly pleased now you've bolted.'

'You want to make him unreal, but he's real.'

'Real things become unreal when you enter into the truth.'

'Our love wasn't real, it was childish, it was like a game, we were like brother and sister, we didn't know what love was then.'

'Hartley, you know that we loved each other —'

'Yes, but we didn't make love properly, I wish we had.'

'I thought you didn't want to, I wanted to all right — Oh, *Christ*!'

'We were children. You never became part of my real life.'

'What you call your real life appears to have been hell on earth! Damn it, you said so yourself. A happy woman doesn't talk about death.'

'I wish I hadn't told you things, I'll regret having told you things. Of course it's a muddle, but it's my muddle, it's where I live and what I am. I can't run out of it and leave it behind all jagged and loose like a broken shell.'

'That's exactly what you can do! Escape, run, leave it all behind! See that the pain can stop!'

'Can it? Can the pain stop?'

As she now stared at me, wide-eyed with a sudden pausing puzzlement, I wondered, is she mad, is her mind totally astray, is she just a poor wreck, or has she become some sort of fey spiritual being, refined by suffering? Had that strange wild look of her youthful beauty which I had loved so and worshipped been the first prophetic flush of a weird spirituality? There are secret saints with strange destinies. Yet no, she was a wreck, a poor broken twig, her integrity, her last identity, destroyed by the cruel force which had made her abandon Titus. But whatever she was I loved her and was committed to her and had always been, here and out beyond the stars, those stars behind stars behind stars which I had seen that night when I lay on the rocks and the golden sky slowly turned the universe inside out.

'Yes, my darling, my queen, my angel, it can stop.'

Oh if only I could touch and liberate her mind! I wanted to see her hoping, to see some dawn of hope or desire, the desire for cherishing, for a happy life. But she frowned now in her puzzlement and reverted to Ben.

'I've never been good enough to him.'

'I'm sure you've been a saint, a long-suffering saint!'

'No, I've been bad.'

'Oh all right, call it bad if you want to! Whatever it is, it's finished.'

I saw her then as innocent, as men in the past used to see cloistered girls and think: 'We are beasts, but they are angels, pure, not soiled like us.' I saw her as beautifully innocent, simple-minded, silly, understanding nothing: a reproach to me who had lived my life among vain egoistic men and pert, knowing women. Yet also I saw her guilt as real guilt for real failures. How could it be otherwise? And I remembered Peregrine's words: the partner who feels guilty, however irrationally, becomes the slave of the other and can take no moral stand. She had taken upon herself, as well as her peccadilloes, *his* guilt. She felt herself guilty of his sins against her, against Titus. I could see it all. And as she took up the guilt, appropriated it as her own, she revered the guilty one and held him as holy. Oh, if only I could release her from that maiming crippling guilt and from that empty reverence! God, she even felt guilty about me and had to *console* herself by thinking I hated her! She was spellbound, bound by a self-protective magic, which she had developed over the years to defend herself against the horrible pain of having married a foul insanely jealous bullying maniac. She had been brainwashed through fear of him, brainwashed by hearing the same things repeated to her again and again and again: that it was *her* fault, always *her* fault. No wonder Titus wanted to go and sing on the rocks rather than be reminded of those scenes.

She had cried a little. The tears of age are not the tears of youth. 'Stop crying, Hartley, you look like the pig-baby in *Alice*, like you used to.'

'I know I'm ugly, horrible –'

'Oh, my dear, come out of it, come right out of it, come out of the nightmare –'

She dabbed her eyes with my handkerchief, let me hold her hand for a moment, began again to reflect.

'But what makes you think my marriage is so unhappy?' She was gazing at me now with an almost cunning look, as if she were about to produce a devastating refutation of anything I might say in answer.

'Hartley, darling, you're in a muddle. You admitted you were unhappy, you spoke just now about the pain of it!'

'Pain is different, in any marriage there is pain, life is pain – but perhaps for you – it all just passed you by.'

'Perhaps it did, thank God.'

'You know, so many nights quietly at home I used to think of people in labour camps –'

'If you had to cheer yourself up by thinking that at least you weren't in a labour camp you can't have been very happy!'

'But what makes you think my marriage is so bad, how can you judge? You can't see, you can't understand –'

'I can judge. I *know*.'

'But how can you know, it's just an idea, you don't understand about marriage, you've just lived with women, it's different, you haven't any evidence.'

'About you and him – I have, yes, evidence.'

'You can't have. You've only just met us, you don't know anyone who knows us, well, like that, no one knows us, you can't have evidence.'

'Yes, I have, I've heard you talking to each other, the way you talk to each other –' I said this in a final burst of exasperation and I have to confess with some desire to hurt. The calm obstinate persistence and now that superior cunning expression was driving me wild.

'What do you mean?'

'I listened, I hid outside the window and listened to you and him talking, I heard his coarse voice, his brutal bullying manner, the way he shouted at you, the way he made you say over and over again "I'm sorry, I'm so sorry." I wish I'd broken the window, I wish I'd broken his bloody neck. I'll *kill* that man. I wish I'd pushed him into the sea.'

'You *listened* – you *heard* – when?'

'Oh, I can't remember, a week ago, two weeks – I'm so upset I've lost all count of time – so you see you can't pretend any more, you can't whitewash him and tell me you're happily married, because I know the truth!'

'The *truth* – oh, you don't understand! You *listened* – how long?'

'Oh, ages, an hour, no, I can't remember – you were shouting at each other, it was perfectly horrible, at least he was shouting and you were whining, it was *disgusting* –'

'How can you – you don't know what you've done – how could you push in, spy on us like that – it was nothing to do with you – how could you intrude into secret things which you couldn't possibly understand – it's the wickedest vilest most hurtful thing anybody's ever done to me –'

'Hartley, darling, you know I only did it to help, I mean because I had to know, I had to be sure, to be certain –'

'As if you could *know* anything – oh, you've hurt me so much, I'll never forgive you, never, it's like, it's like a murder, a killing – you don't understand – Oh, it hurts so much, so *much* –'

'Darling, I'm sorry, I'm so sorry, I didn't imagine –'

Sitting bolt upright against the wall she was now crying as I have never seen any woman cry (and I have seen many). Tears seemed to shoot out of her eyes in torrents, then her wet mouth opened in a sort of strangled shout, an animal cry of tortured pain. Then she gave a low shuddering wail, and fell over sideways, grasping at her neck, pulling at the dressing gown as if she were suffocating. The wail was followed by a shuddering gasp, and in a moment she was in hysterics.

I jumped up and watched her, appalled. Well then did I understand what Titus had said about it: it is frightening and it is meant to be. I felt that the most violent assault was being made on my spirit, on my sanity. I had witnessed hysterical screaming before, but nothing like this. I knelt again and tried to hold her, to shake her, but she seemed suddenly so strong and I so weak, and also to touch her had become terrible. She was shuddering rigidly with a dreadful damaging electricity. Her face was red, wild with tears, her mouth dribbling. Her voice, raucous, piercing, shrieked out, like a terrified angry person shrieking an obscenity, a frenzied panic noise, a prolonged *'aaah'*, which turned into a sobbing wail of quick 'oh – oh – oh', with a long descending 'ooooh' sound ending almost softly, and then the scream again: this continuing mechanically, automatically, on and on as if the human creature were possessed by an alien demonic machine. I felt horror, fear, a sort of disgusted shame, shame for myself, shame for her. I did not want Titus and Gilbert to hear this ghastly rhythmical noise, this attack of aggressive mourning. I hoped they were far away on the rocks singing their songs. I *shouted* 'Stop, stop, stop!' I felt I should go violently mad if it went on for another minute, I felt I wanted to silence her even if it meant killing her, I shook her again and yelled at her, ran to the door, ran back again. I shall never forget the awful image of that face, that mask, and the relentless cruel rhythmical quality of that sound ...

It ceased at last, as everything dreadful has to cease, even if it ceases only by death. My presence, my cries, had no effect on her, I doubt if, in a sense, she knew I was there, although also, in a sense, the performance was for me, its violence directed at me. She became exhausted, stopped suddenly and fell back as in a faint. I seized her hand. It was cold. I became panic-stricken and would have run out and shouted for a doctor, only I was too frightened to leave her and too exhausted to make any decision. I lay down beside her and embraced her, uttering her name again and again. Her breathing became deep, regular, as if she were sleeping. Then I looked at her and saw her eyes open. She was looking at me again with that strange cunning look, as if now she were actually estimating the effect of her 'fit'. And when, later on, she began to talk again she sounded quite sane, quite rational, indeed more so than she had been earlier on.

'Oh, Charles – darling – I'm so sorry –'

'I'm sorry – I'm a fool, an insensitive idiot.'

'No, no – I'm sorry I got so upset and made such a nasty noise – I suppose I'm in a state of shock.'

'I'm very sorry, sweetheart.'

'That's all right. Tell me – how long have I been here, in this house?'

'Two days.'

'Has he been here, my husband? Or has he written me a letter?' This was the first time she had asked this.

'He hasn't sent a letter, I would have given it to you. He came, on that morning after you arrived.'

'What did he say?'

'He wanted you to come home, and —'

'And what?'

I was feeling so chastened and confused I went stupidly on, 'He said he'd brought the dog back with him.'

'Oh — the dog — the dog — I'd forgotten —' Some more tears welled up and ran over her cheeks which were so bloated with crying that she was almost unrecognizable, but she controlled herself. 'Oh dear — oh dear — I do wish I'd been there when the dog came.'

'Look, Hartley,' I said, 'you don't seem to be capable of thinking about this business, so let me think for you. We can't go on like this. I'm beginning to feel like a terrorist. You've put me in a position where I have to play the bully, which is the role I detest most of all. All right, I don't know what your marriage was like and maybe it wasn't all that awful and *he* wasn't all that awful, but it obviously wasn't a success and I don't see why you should put up with a violent and unpleasant man any longer when you don't have to. You can walk out. I daresay you would have walked out before if you had had anywhere to walk to. Now you have. Let's go to London. This situation here is driving me mad. I'm letting it go on because I don't want to force you, I don't want you to say later that you didn't decide for yourself. I don't want to be forced to force you. Have some consideration for me, and for Titus. I'm very fond of Titus, I regard him as my son, yes I do. And he hates that man, and if you go back to *him* you'll never see Titus again. You're not just choosing between me and your ghastly failed marriage — please forgive my language — there's Titus in the scales as well. Let's go to London, all three of us, and then away somewhere, anywhere. We're a family now. What I've never had since I left my parents' home. Let's go away together anywhere you like and chase after some happiness. Wouldn't you like to see Titus happy? He wants to be an actor, I can help him. Don't you want to *see* him happy?'

She listened to me, but towards the end of the speech began shaking her head. She said, 'Please, please don't force me to go anywhere, you'd kill me. I have got to go home. You know I have got to go, and you know I don't want to stay here. There isn't going to be any – any – what you want – it would be like a miracle in my mind.'

'Oh yes, Hartley, my sweetheart, wait for that miracle, wait for it, its name is love.'

'No, that is not its name, and it hasn't come and it won't come. Don't you see you are working to destroy me? Now he will never believe me, never. And that is your doing, your crime. It's like a murder. Never, never, never.'

Soon after this she said she was very tired and would sleep, and I left her.

I awoke suddenly. The moon was shining into my bedroom, where I had omitted to pull down the blind. I could hear the splash of the sea and a very faint rattle of the stones which the waves were gently clawing as they withdrew from the cauldron. It must be low tide. I could hear also, or sense, a vast void, a dome of silence, within which my heart was beating exceedingly fast. I felt suffocated and had to sit up abruptly and gasp for breath. I remembered, as I now did whenever I awoke, with a pang of anguish and love and fear, that Hartley was in the house. At the same time I felt the most terrible dread, a premonition of some catastrophe, some horror, or indeed the certainty that it had already occurred. I began to get out of bed, trembling violently, and fumbled for my candle. I lit it and then stood up and listened. The void dark house was ominously quiet. I very quickly opened my bedroom door and looked down the landing. There seemed to be a dim light coming from the alcove, but perhaps it was a trick of the moon. I listened and seemed to hear a beating sound, a heavy noise, deep and accelerating, very very far away. I moved slowly forward, putting each foot down carefully so as not to make the boards creak. I could now see quite clearly Hartley's door and the key in the lock. I wanted to reach it, to put my hand onto the key, but I was afraid to hurry, afraid to enter that terrible room. I got the key into my hand and turned it and stepped in through the doorway holding my candle. The mattress on the floor, at which I always looked on entering, was empty, the bedclothes disordered. Hartley was gone – I stared about, ready to cry out with panic fear. And then I saw her – she was standing in the corner. I thought, how odd I had forgotten how tall she is. Then I thought she is standing on something, how odd, she must be up on the chair or the table. Then I saw that she was suspended from the lamp bracket. She had hanged herself.

I woke up. The lightning flash of thought which showed me the dream showed me at the same moment that it was a dream. I was lying in my bed. I had not been to Hartley's room and found her dead, having hanged herself with one of her stockings from the cast-iron lamp bracket, climbing up onto the table and casting herself off. I felt intense violent relief: and then the thought, but supposing it is true? Sick and trembling I got up, lit my candle, and quietly opened my bedroom door. The candlelight illumined the barrier of the bead curtain but nothing beyond. The curtain was clicking softly, no doubt as a result of the draught from the door. I carefully plucked the bead strings apart and glided on to Hartley's room and turned the key very quietly. I leaned through the doorway and peered in.

There she was, in the light of my candle, lying curled up on the mattress, covered by a blanket, her hand over her face. I watched and heard her steady quiet breathing. Then I silently withdrew and locked the door again. I went back through the bead curtain, trying not to agitate it too much, and in sheer distraction went into the drawing room. I had, since Hartley's incarceration, kept out of the drawing room, out of a sort of sense of propriety, because of the long window which gave onto Hartley's room. I went in now, vaguely with the idea of making sure there was no one there, and of course there was not. I stood, holding my candle, and looking at the long inner window which was now like a glossy black mirror; and it occurred to me that I was shunning the drawing room not out of propriety but because of the appalling possibility that I might see Hartley actually looking out. And then I suddenly remembered the face which I had seen looking at me through the dark glass; and I thought, that face was *too high up*. It could not have been the face of someone standing on the floor. It was just at the level at which Hartley's face would have been if she had really hanged herself.

Then I thought, my candle is shining into her room, making a faint ghostly light in her room. What dreads and fears did she have, poor captive, if she woke in the night? Did she climb on a chair to peer into the dim empty moonlit drawing room? Did she very quietly try the locked door, hoping and fearing to be able to creep downstairs and run away into the dark night? I hurriedly returned to my bedroom and closed the door. I sat on my bed shuddering and looked at my watch. It was half-past two. What was I doing, or rather what was happening to me? I held my head in my hands. I was totally vulnerable and helpless. I had lost control of my life and of the lives with which I was meddling. I felt dread and a terrible fatalism; and bitter grief, grief such as I had never felt in my life since Hartley had left me so many years ago. I had wakened some sleeping demon, set going some deadly machine; and what would be would be.

*

The next morning something did happen, which was that Rosina turned up.

I had, after my horrible night interlude, managed to sleep. Perhaps sheer fatalism sent me to sleep. Let Ben come, let him set fire to the house, let him kill me. I deserved to die. I felt a good deal less fatalistic and more anxious when I woke up in the morning. It seemed urgently necessary to make a decision, but there was no material, no data, no evidence on which a decision could be made. I passionately wanted to take Hartley away, to London, to anywhere, or rather I wanted to want it enough to be able to do it now. But against her will, should I, could I? Could I pull a resisting, screaming woman into Gilbert's car and have her driven off? Could I deceive her into thinking she was going home? Would Gilbert let me? Would Titus let me? If I took her away by force, it might harden her against me, and impede that precious movement of her will for which I was so impatiently waiting.

Yet *could* the situation go on? And if not what else could possibly come of it? I felt it absolutely unthinkable to let Hartley go back to that man, especially after what she had said yesterday about how he would never, never believe her now. Suppose I let her go back and he killed her? I would have murdered her. Could I imagine myself opening the door and saying, all right, I give up, you can go home? *No.* The only piece of rational discourse which I could hang on to, and it was of great value, was what Hartley had said about the miracle in her mind which had not come about. If she could even utter such words, did not this indicate that her mind was divided and that she had some grain of hope that was favourable to me, some tiny pure inclination to make herself want what I wanted? But she *must* want to be free and happy, everybody did. She must, somewhere in her tormented soul, want me to take her away, out of misery, out of servitude. She must be moved by the idea of Titus, and the redemption of her love for him, a new family, a new world. She had only to open her eyes and stretch out her hand and say yes. There were vast liberating forces pent up somewhere which were bound to break out. It was just a matter of waiting and keeping her here and letting time enlighten her will.

I had given her breakfast and tried to talk to her and to *explain* what I have just written here, only she kept saying that she wanted to go home. Her ringed eyes and puffy face and the unnerving languor of her bearing made me wonder if she were not really ill, and whether I should call a doctor. Then, more exasperated than pitying, I wondered if I could not better serve my cause by being brusque, and I left her rather abruptly, and then was sorry. I was standing beside the bead curtain and touching it, uncertain what to do next, when I heard a sudden loud outburst of laughter from down below, followed by some part-singing with a female voice.

I ran down to the kitchen. Rosina was sitting on the table swinging her legs and being (there is no other word for it) worshipped by Gilbert and Titus. She was wearing a dark grey very fine check, very smart lightweight coat and skirt and a white silk blouse and very long wrinkled white high-heeled boots. Her glossy glowing dark hair had been cut or piled by a clever hairdresser into a rounded segmented composition which looked both complex and casual. (Horace would have liked it.) Her intense animal face was blazing with health and vitality and feral curiosity. She was entirely in control of a situation where the other two, perhaps as a result of prolonged strain, had now broken down into helpless crazy giggling and *fou rire*. My appearance provoked another outburst of slightly hysterical laughter, and they all spontaneously broke into song again. They sang in round, and showed no sign of stopping, an Italian catch whose words I can remember since Titus and Gilbert had been singing it obsessively in the preceding days. Titus taught it to Gilbert and now Rosina had got it too. It went

*Eravamo tredici, siamo rimasti dodici, sei facevano rima, e sei facevan' pima-
poma-pima-poma.* God knows what it was supposed to be about. Singing
is of course a form of aggression. The wet open mouths and glistening
teeth of the singers are ardent to devour the victim—hearer. Singers crave
hearers as animals crave their prey. Intoxicated by their own voices they
now roared it out, round and round, Gilbert's fruity baritone, Titus's
pseudo-Neapolitan tenor and Rosina's strong rather harsh contralto.
I shouted, 'Stop! Stop! Stop that bloody row!' But they went on singing
at me, their bright eyes, moist with laughter, fixed upon me, waving
their arms in time to the tune; until at last they wearied, stopped, and
went off into another crazy laughing fit.

I sat on a chair and watched them.

Coherent at last, Rosina said, wiping her eyes, 'Charles, you're so
funny, you are an endless source of amusement to your friends. I hear
you've got your lady-love here, hidden away upstairs! You really are
priceless!'

'Why the hell did you have to tell her?' I said to Gilbert and Titus.

Gilbert, attempting unsuccessfully to erase the laughter-wrinkles
from his face, avoided my look. He started rolling and swinging his eyes.

Titus said rather sulkily, 'You didn't say not to tell.' Then he caught
Rosina's eye and beamed.

Gilbert had of course met Rosina before and knew her slightly. He
had hitherto regarded her with the prudish hostility which some male
homosexuals instinctively feel towards very feminine predatory women
(whereas with gentle sweet women such as Lizzie they got on very
well). However he seemed now to have suffered an instant conversion.
Titus was simply a boy absolutely thrilled to see a famous actress in
the flesh and to find that she not only noticed him but appreciated the
charms of his youth. They kept eyeing each other, he shyly, she with
bold amusement. Titus's appearance had profited, as Gilbert's had, from

sun and sea. His reddish blond hair had been burnished and enlivened into a halo of fine wire, and his shirt, scarcely buttoned, showed the glowing skin and blazing red curls of his chest. His trousers were rolled up to reveal long elegant bronzed legs. He was barefoot. The scarred lip gave a twisted male force to his pretty mouth. Rosina was at her sleekest, delighted and amused by her exercise of power. As she held court, her piercing cross-eyed glance kept moving encouragingly from one of the bemused enthralled men and back again. They seemed to be quite dazed by her attractions. It was certainly a change from the increasingly charnel house atmosphere of Shruff End.

'What do you want, Rosina?'

'What do you mean, "What do you want?" What a way to greet a visitor. "What do you want?" ' She mimicked me. 'What sort of a question is that?'

The other two roared with laughter. They seemed to find everything Rosina said vastly clever and funny.

'Why are you here?'

'Can't you make an effort to be civil to an old friend?'

'I'm not in a social mood.'

'So I see. Yet you already have two charming guests, in fact three guests, including lady-love. All right, I'm not angling for an invitation to stay. I think this is the nastiest meanest most unpleasant house I've ever entered.'

'It has bad vibes,' said Titus.

'You can say that again,' said Gilbert.

They were ganging up against me.

'But is your funny lady really upstairs? Whatever are you going to do with her? You know, you *promised* to tell me what was going on in your interesting love life, only of course I ought to know by now that you don't keep promises. Anyway I decided I'd come and see how you were getting along. I've been working hard and I thought I needed a holiday. I'm at the Raven Hotel again, I like it there, I like the bay and those extraordinary boulders. And the food is excellent, not your style.'

'I hope you have a pleasant stay at the Raven Hotel.'

'The most amazing rumours about you are circulating in London.'

'I'm sure everyone is fascinated.'

'Well, they're not actually. I had to start a few rumours myself to keep your memory a bit greenish. They've forgotten you already. You were pretty old hat when you were still with us, now you're ancient history. The young people have never heard of you, Charles. You're exploded, you're not even a myth. I can see it now, Charles dear, you're old. Where's all that charm we used to go on about? It was nothing but power really. Now you've lost your power you've lost your charm. No wonder you have to make do with a Bearded Lady.'

'Just buzz off, Rosina, will you?'

'But what's *happening*, Charles? I'm mad with curiosity. I gather from these two that she's a sort of *prisoner* here. May I go up and poke her through the bars?'

'Rosina, please —'

'But, Charles, what *are* you up to? There's a husband in the case, isn't there, if I remember? Not that husbands ever worried you much. But you can't be going to carry her off, you can't want to *marry* her! Really, you are becoming ridiculous. You were never ridiculous in the old days. You used to have dignity and style.'

Titus and Gilbert, less amused, were looking embarrassed and studying the great slate flagstones of the kitchen floor.

'I'll see you to the road, Rosina. Is your car out there?'

'Oh, I don't want to go yet. I want to sing some more. Who's pretty-boy?' She indicated Titus.

'That is my son Titus.'

Titus frowned and stroked his scarred lip. Gilbert raised his eyebrows, Rosina changed colour, shot me a quick look of piercing malignancy, then laughed. 'Well, well – All right, I'll go. My car's outside. You may escort me to it. Goodbye, you two, I enjoyed the sing-song.' She marched out of the kitchen swinging her handbag and I followed.

Rosina walked straight out of the front door and across the causeway without looking back. I followed her as far as her horrible red car.

There she turned on me, her vixen face pointed with rage. 'Is that boy really your son?'

'Well, no, I've sort of taken him on. I always wanted a son. He's *their* son, he's the adopted son – of – of Hartley and her husband.'

'I see. I might have known it was a stupid joke. For one moment I thought perhaps – what are you going to do about that woman? You can't collect a half-crazy female at this stage of her life. You can't keep her like a mad thing on a chain. Or have I got it all wrong?'

'She's not a prisoner. She loves me. She's just been brainwashed.'

'Marriage is brainwashing. Not necessarily a bad thing. Your brain could do with a wash. Oh God, I feel so tired. That bloody long drive – I think your mind's going, you're getting senile, you're living in a dream world, a rather nasty one. Shall I tell you something to wake you up?'

'No, thank you.'

'You say you "always wanted a son". That's just a sentimental lie, you didn't want trouble, you didn't want to know. You never put yourself in a situation where you could have a *real* son. Your sons are fantasies, they're easier to deal with. Do you imagine you could really "take on" that silly uneducated adolescent boy in there? He'll vanish out of your life like everything else has done, because you can't grasp the stuff of reality. He'll turn out to be a dream child too – when you touch him he'll fade and disappear –you'll see.'

'All right, you've had your say, now go.'

'I haven't started yet. I never told you this at the time, I thought I never would. You made me pregnant. I got rid of the child.'

I drew a circle in the dust on the radiator of the car. 'Why didn't you tell me?'

'Because you weren't there to tell, you'd gone, gone off with Lizzie or whoever was the next dream girl. God, the sickening casual brutality of men – the women who are left behind to make agonizing decisions alone. I made that decision alone. Christ, how I wish I hadn't done it. I was crazy. I did it partly out of hatred of you. Why the hell didn't I keep that child. He'd have been nearly grown up by now.'

'Rosina –'

'And I'd have taught him to hate you – that would have been a consolation too.'

'I'm sorry –'

'Oh, you're sorry. And I daresay I wasn't the only one. You broke up my marriage deliberately, industriously, zealously, you worked at it. Then you walk off and leave me with nothing, with less than nothing, with that horrible crime which I had to commit by myself, I cried for months – for years – about that – I've never stopped crying.' Her dark eyes filled with tears for a second, and then she seemed to magic them away. She opened the door of the car.

'Oh – Rosina –'

'I hate you, I loathe you, you've been a devil in my mind ever after –'

'Look, all right, I left you, but you drove me to it, you were responsible too. Women's lib hasn't stopped women from putting all the blame on us when it suits them. You tell me this terrible story now to –'

'Oh shut up. What's the name of that female?'

'You mean – Hartley – ?'

'Is that her surname?'

'No, her surname is Fitch.'

'Fitch. OK. Mr Fitch, here I come.'

'What on earth do you mean?'

'He lives here, doesn't he? I shall find out where he lives and I shall go and console him. It'll do him good to meet a real live woman instead of an old rag-bag. He's probably forgotten what women are like. I won't hurt him, I'll just cheer him up, I'll do him less harm than you're doing her. I've got to have some amusement on my holiday. I thought of seducing pretty-boy, but it would be too easy. The father would be a far more interesting project. After all, life is full of surprises. The only thing that's become absolutely dull, dull, dull is you, Charles. Dull. Goodbye.'

She got into the car and slammed the door. The car shot off like a red rocket in the direction of the village.

I stared after her. Soon there was nothing on the road but a cloud of dust and above it the pale blue sky. For a short while I felt that I should go mad if I reflected too much on what Rosina had told me about what happened in the past.

The rest of that day (before something else happened in the evening) passed like a feverish dream. The weather, sensing my mood, infected by it perhaps, became hotter but with that sinister breathless heat that betokens a thunderstorm. The light was darkened although the sun blazed from a cloudless sky. I felt weak and shivery as if I were developing the 'flu. My impression increased that perhaps Hartley was ill. Her eyes glittered, her hands were hot. Her stuffy smelly room had become that of an invalid. She was rational, not frenzied, she actually argued with me. I begged her to come downstairs, to come outside into the sun and air, but she lay back as if exhausted at the very thought. Even her rationality had something unnerving about it, as if it were the reasoning of a quiet maniac or an exercise undertaken simply for its own sake. She constantly said she wanted to go home, that there was no alternative, and so on and so on, but she seemed to me to lack the final real will to go. I kept on trying to regard this absence of will as a hopeful factor, but somehow now it was beginning to frighten me.

And Ben's silence was getting me down. What did it mean? Had he decided on reflection that he did not want Hartley back? Was he settling down to a happy bachelor life with the dog? Or had he some secret girlfriend to whom in relief he had now run away? Was he making complex plans either to rescue her or to take some terrible revenge on me? Had he summoned some roughs, old army friends perhaps, who would arrive any moment to beat me up? Had he gone to a lawyer? Or was he just playing a subtle game, waiting for my nerve to break, waiting for *me* to come to *him*? Or perhaps he too had fallen into some kind of entranced nervous apathy, unsure of what he wanted, unsure of what to do? I myself felt at some moment that to be forced to act, even by the police, would be preferable to this empty echoing space of attentive possibilities.

I was now trying very hard to steel myself to take Hartley to London, to drag her to the car, to delude her by telling her she was going home. I felt the time had come to do this, although I was far from sure that it was the right move. Shruff End might have 'bad vibes' as Titus put it, but it was my home, I was used to it. And here I could communicate quietly with Hartley, there was a thin pure stream of communication, especially when we talked about the past. In an odd way we were at ease together. Surely there must soon be some break-through, some dialectical change. What on earth would I do in London with a distraught weeping Hartley in that awful little flat with the chairs piled on the table and the china not unpacked? To *whom* could we go in London? I did not want to exhibit Hartley to people who, however helpful, would secretly mock her. The fact was I wanted, perhaps we both wanted, someone to look after us, at least someone to be there as a sort of protection and guarantee of ordinariness. Titus and Gilbert might be of little use but simply their presence made the situation more bearable.

However, since Rosina's visit, Titus and Gilbert had been in a state of subdued revolt, they were mutinous. I think Ben's silence was upsetting them too, in different ways. They wanted a showdown, a dénouement. They wanted an end to the situation which would relieve their minds. Gilbert was simply frightened of Ben, afraid of fights and thuggery. What Titus felt I was unsure. Sometimes I felt terrified of what Titus might be thinking. Since Hartley's arrival I had not talked to him properly. I ought to have done, I wanted to do so, but I had not. It was possible that Titus was in an agony of tension and indecision, wanting and yet not wanting to run to his father, to be reconciled, or even to suffer punishment, to escape from his mother, to escape from me. The possibility of anything so awful in the boy's state of mind made me afraid to probe him when I had so much else to envisage and decide. Meanwhile he had withdrawn, a little sulky, wanting to be wooed. I would woo him, but at present had not the wit or the strength. And I was disappointed in him. I needed his help, his loving support, with Hartley, his ingenuity, his commitment. But he showed plainly that he had, at any rate in this weird context, given up the problem of his mother. He preferred not to reflect upon the obscene embarrassment of her incarceration. He did not want to associate himself with me as a fellow gaoler. This was understandable. But he annoyed me by seeming to enjoy himself. He swam, he sang, he sat on the rocks with Gilbert drinking white wine and blackcurrant juice (their latest drink). He behaved like the scrounger he had so proudly denied himself to be. As Gilbert now declared that he was afraid to go shopping by himself, Titus went with him and they bought quantities of expensive food and drink with my money. They did not run into Ben. Perhaps Ben had gone away? Where to? Whom to? These mysteries did me no good.

One form taken by the mutiny of Gilbert and Titus was that they began to suggest that I should do something about Ben. At least Gilbert made the suggestions, but Titus was certainly associated with them. *What* I was to do was not so clear, but they wanted an initiative. There was by now a little less singing, a little more sitting in the kitchen and plotting; and even in the midst of my other preoccupations and miseries I felt jealousy, stupid blank jealousy, when I saw those two heads together, and they fell nervously silent as I came in. They ran out all the time to look for letters. Gilbert even bought a large square basket which he mounted on stones inside the dog kennel to be sure that any letters which came would not get wet or blow away. I avoided discussion, since I so much feared to hear Titus announce that he would go over to Nibletts to spy out the land. What if Titus went to Nibletts and did not return? Of course I did not tell the others about Rosina's crazy boast, which I decided on reflection was intended simply to annoy me. Nor had I stopped thinking about what else she had told me, although I was trying hard to dismiss her from my mind. I hoped she had gone back to London.

Towards the evening of that day I got as far as concluding that if Ben made no move I would do *something* on the next day: something clarificatory, something decisive; although I could not yet see quite what this liberating move would be. Most probably I would take Hartley and Titus to London. I had waited long enough upon Hartley's will, and I was beginning to believe that she wanted me to force her. When I felt that I was nearly desperate enough to decide, I felt some relief. But the

tomorrow upon which I was to make my decision never, in the form
in which I had envisaged it, arrived.

Towards six-thirty in the evening the thick blue air seemed to be
getting darker and more stifling, although the sun was bravely shining
and the sky was unflecked. It was as if the sun were shining through
a mist, but a mist made out of the dark blue globules of the sky
itself. I remember the lurid impression of that evening, the vivid
dark light, the brilliant vibrating colours of the rocks, of the grass
on the other side of the road, of Gilbert's yellow car. There was
no breath of wind, not the softest breeze. The sea was menacingly
quiet, utterly smooth, glassy, glossy, oily, a uniform azure. Then there
were silent flashes, extraordinary lightings up of the whole horizon,
like vast distant fireworks or some weird atomic experiment. Not a
cloud, not a sound of thunder, just these huge displays of quick silent
yellowish-white light.

I had been talking to Hartley, talking about the past, enjoying that
thin pure line of easy communication with her which I could persuade
myself was becoming deeper and wider. It was true that, so far as we did
communicate, the ease of it was exceptional, the flavour unique. Here I
could post the banner of my love, hope gradually to convince. Loving her
took at this time so intensely the form of pity, compassion, an absolute
desire to cherish, to cure; to stir the desire for happiness and to make
it grow where it had not been before. To this end I tried cunningly to
exclude the idea of a return home, picturing it casually as something
now impossible; and meanwhile let Hartley continue to calm herself by
an illusion of a return which she would soon see as unthinkable and
as something which she no longer wanted. Surreptitiously I increased
the pressure and the emphasis. My policy of gradualism had been right
and would shortly be confirmed as successful. Hartley went on saying

that she must go back to her husband, but she said it fairly calmly and it seemed to me less often and the words sounded emptier.

I left her at last. I did not now bother to lock her door during the day. Her desire to hide, to hide from Gilbert and above all from Titus would keep her effectively enclosed by day. In any case, how far could she run undiscovered? The night despairs were another matter. The front doorbell rang. As I came down into the hall I saw the wire quivering just before I heard the bland clangour of the bell in the kitchen. I thought: Ben. And I wondered: alone? I moved to the door quickly and incautiously to forestall my fear. I did not put the door on the chain but opened it wide at once. The man standing outside was my cousin James.

James was smiling, with the calm inane self-satisfied smile which he sometimes put on. He was carrying a suitcase. I could see his Bentley on the road parked next to Gilbert's Volkswagen.

'James! What on earth are you doing here!'

'Have you forgotten? It's Whit weekend. You invited me.'

'You invited yourself. And of course I've forgotten.'

'Do you want me to go away?'

'No – no – come in – for a moment anyway.'

I felt confused, exasperated, profoundly startled. My cousin was always an unnerving portent. His presence in the house would change everything, even the kettle. I could not tolerate or manage James here, I could not continue to run my life with him upon the scene.

He walked in and put down his suitcase, looking around him with curiosity. 'I like your situation. And that bay with the spherical boulders is quite extraordinary. I came by the coast road of course.'

'Of course.'

'That huge rock out in the sea covered with guillemots – you know where I mean?'

'No.'

'Haven't you seen it? It's – Well, never mind. I see there's a martello tower. Does that belong to you too?'

'Yes.'

'I see the point of this place. What's the date of the house?'

'Oh, I don't know, nineteen hundred, earlier, later. Oh God.'

'What's the matter? Look, I'm sorry, I ought to have written to warn you. I tried to ring up but I gather you're not on the phone. I don't have to stay here, I passed quite a nice-looking hotel a mile or two back – Are you all right, Charles?'

'Come into the kitchen.'

Because of the weird light it was rather dark in the kitchen. Just as we entered, Gilbert and Titus came in from outside, the strange silent midsummer lightning signalling behind them.

Introductions were inescapable. 'Oh hello. This is my cousin James who's just dropped by. Gilbert Opian. And this is a young friend of mine, Titus. There's no one else here, this is our complement.' As I said this I laid my finger as if by accident upon my lips. I hoped it was not too dark for them to see.

'Titus,' said James, 'so you've come, good.'

'What do you mean?' I said to James. 'You don't *know* him, do you?'

I saw that Titus was staring at James almost as if he recognized him.

'No, but you mentioned his name to me – remember?'

'Oh yes – Well, have a drink, James? Before you go.'

'Thanks, anything. That white wine that's open.'

'We drink it with blackcurrant,' said Titus.

'Are you his maternal cousin or his paternal cousin?' asked Gilbert, who liked to get such things straight.

'Our fathers were brothers.'

'Charles always pretends to have no family. He's so secretive,' Gilbert, affably rolling his eyes, poured out four glasses of wine. He seemed to have lost some weight climbing about on the rocks in his new plimsolls. He looked younger and more relaxed. Titus added the dash of blackcurrant. He was smiling. It was clear that both of them were glad of this diversion, glad to have another person, an untainted outsider, present to talk to, to dilute the atmosphere; glad too perhaps to have an extra fighting man.

'Yes, you've got a very odd and interesting house,' said James.

'You don't feel any bad vibrations?'

James looked at me. 'Who owned it before?'

'A Mrs Chorney. I don't know anything about her.'

'Can you see the sea from the upper windows?'

'Yes, but the view's better from the rocks. I'll show you if you can spare a minute. What sort of shoes have you got on? It's a great place for breaking your ankle.'

I wanted to get James out of the house. I hustled him quickly out onto the grass and he followed me a short way over the rocks until we could sit on a warm summit with the sea view. The sea had now changed colour and was a slightly greyish glittering pale azure, crepitating with little movements.

'How stuffy it is. James, I hope you don't mind going to that hotel, it's called the Raven Hotel, and it's got a lovely outlook over that bay you liked. And you could drive down the coast and look at those seagulls and things. The fact is, I can't have you because there isn't another bed. We're full up. As it is, Titus is sleeping on the floor.'

'I quite understand the situation.'

You don't, old cock, thank God, I thought. And I thought, in a minute I'll take him back to his car.

I looked at my cousin, now vividly revealed in the bright dark light which delineated everything with a fearful clarity. James had carried his glass of wine with him over the rocks and was sipping it with a maddening air of contented repose, looking out over the sea. He was wearing lightweight black trousers with an open-necked mauve shirt and a white summer jacket. He was a careless dresser but could be foppish in his own way. His hawk-nosed face was dark with the irrepressible beard and with the curious cloud, perhaps the effect of his obscure brown eyes, which always seemed to hang over it. His brown hair was jaggedly untidy.

I suddenly thought, if he's no longer in the army, why does he have to come and see me at a holiday weekend when the roads are full of traffic?

'Are you doing anything?' I said. 'I mean, have you got another job or anything?'

'No, gentleman of leisure.'

That was odd. It then came to me in a flash that of course James had not really left the army at all. He had gone underground. He was preparing for some top-secret mission, perhaps involving a return to Tibet. Why had he seemed so annoyed that I had seen that strange oriental figure in his rooms? My cousin had become a secret agent!

I was trying to think of some subtle tactful way of letting him know that I had guessed when he spoke again.

'And what has happened about Mary Hartley Smith?'

'Mary Hartley Smith?'

'Yes. Your first love. You told me she was living here with her husband. That boy is her son. I asked you his name. Titus. Have you forgotten that too?'

The strange thing was that I had forgotten, I had completely forgotten telling James that story. Why had James wanted to know Titus's name? 'I must be mad,' I said, 'I had forgotten, but I remember now. You gave me some good advice.'

'Did you take it?'

'Yes. You were right of course. I was just imagining things. The shock of seeing her set off a lot of old memories. I've recovered now and of course I'm not in love with her, it wouldn't make sense. Anyway she's just a boring old hag now. The boy drops in occasionally. He's a bit of a bore too.'

'I see. So all's well that ends well.'

'Have you got a tie?'

'A tie? Yes.'

'You'll need one to get into the dining room at the Raven Hotel. I'll just see you to your car.'

I escorted him round by the side of the house so as to avoid further conversation in the kitchen.

'Nice car. New one?'

'Yes, it goes well. Where can I turn?'

'Just beyond that rock. How dark it is. You almost need headlights.'

'Yes, it's a funny day. Looks like a storm. Well, thanks for the drink, look after yourself.' He handed me his empty wineglass.

'Goodbye, drive carefully.'

The black Bentley moved, swung round, then shot off down the road. James waved, vanished round the corner. Would he come back? I did not think so.

I walked slowly across the causeway and into the house and shut the door. How odd that I had forgotten telling him those things. I must have been drunk. Well, tomorrow was destiny day. I was going to act tomorrow. I thought, I will take Hartley to London. This place is bedevilled somehow.

I stood in the hall for a while. I wanted to be by myself. I put James's wineglass down on the stairs. I could hear the low conspiratorial voices of Gilbert and Titus who were talking in the kitchen. Tomorrow I would speak to Titus. Titus and Hartley and I would be alone together, in another place. My act, my will would create a new family.

I heard a faint straining scraping sound. I looked up and saw the wire from the front doorbell quivering. Then I heard the resonant incoherent clamour. Ben? I turned round quickly and flung the door open.

Peregrine Arbelow was standing outside holding a suitcase.

'Hello, Charles, what a funny place.'

'Perry!'

'I *wish* you'd call me "Peregrine". How many times have I said that to you? A thousand?'

'What on earth are you doing here?'

'What on earth am I doing here, he says. You issued an invitation, I accepted it. It's Whit weekend, remember? I have had a very long and tiring drive. I have been looking forward to open arms and cries of joy for the last hundred miles.'

I could now see Peregrine's white Alfa Romeo parked where James's Bentley had lately stood.

'Peregrine, I'm terribly sorry, you can't stay here, there aren't any beds and –'

'Look, may I just push my way in?' He did so.

Peregrine's loud voice had alerted the conspirators in the kitchen.

'Peregrine!'

'Gilbert! What a pleasant surprise. Charles, I can have Gilbert's bed.'

'You bloody won't, I shall defend my sofa.'

'Introduce your charming boyfriend, Gilbert.'

'This is Titus Fitch. Not my property alas.'

'Hello, Titus. I am Peregrine Arbelow. Gilbert, get me a drink, will you, there's a good fellow.'

'OK, but there's nothing but wine and sherry here, you know. Charles doesn't drink spirits.'

'Oh, fuck, I'd forgotten, I should have brought a bottle.'

'Peregrine,' I said, 'you won't be happy here. There's nothing for you to drink and nowhere for you to sleep. I'm sorry I forgot the date and I don't actually think I invited you at all. There's an excellent hotel just down the road —'

At that moment the front doorbell ran again. Peregrine turned to open the door and over his shoulder I could see my cousin James.

'Hello,' said Peregrine, 'welcome to Hospitality Hall, proprietor Charles Arrowby, there's nothing to drink and nowhere to sleep but —'

'Hello,' said James. 'I'm sorry to come back, Charles, but the Raven Hotel is full up, and I wondered —'

'I imagine that's the place where he wanted to park me,' said Peregrine.

'Let's go into the kitchen,' said Gilbert.

Gilbert went first, then Titus, then Perry, then James. I stood for a moment, then picked up the wineglass from the stairs and followed.

'I am Peregrine Arbelow.'

'I think I've heard of you,' said James.

'Oh *goodie* —'

'This is my cousin, General Arrowby,' I said.

'You never said he was a general,' said Gilbert.

'I never knew you had a cousin,' said Peregrine. 'Hello, sir.'

I took James by the sleeve of his immaculate white coat and pulled him back into the hall. 'Look, you can't stay here, I suggest you —'

At that moment I saw James's eyes widen, looking behind me, and I realized that Hartley was standing on the stairs.

At our sudden silence the other three emerged. We all stood there looking up at Hartley.

She was still wearing my black silk dressing gown with the red rosettes. It reached to her feet and with the collar turned up to frame her hair it had something of the effect of an evening dress. Her eyes, startled and large, had their violet tint; and although, with her disordered grey hair she looked old and mad, she seemed in that arrested moment like a queen.

I recovered in a second or two and made for the stairs. As she saw me move Hartley turned and fled. I saw the flash of a bare ankle, a bare foot. I caught her at the curve of the stairs and hurried her towards the upper landing.

We almost ran together along the landing and I pushed her in through the door of her room. She went at once and sat down on the mattress, like an obedient dog. I do not think that in the whole period of her incarceration I ever saw her sit upon the chair.

'Hartley, darling, where were you going? Were you coming down to look for me? Or did you think that Ben had come? Or were you going to run away?'

She pulled the dressing gown closer about her and simply shook her head several times. She was breathless with agitation. Then she peered up at me with a sad timid sweet look which suddenly reminded me of my father.

'Oh, Hartley, I love you so much!' I sat down on the chair and lifted my hands to my face. I grimaced into my hands. I felt so helplessly, vulnerably close to my childhood. 'Hartley, don't leave me. I don't know what I'd do if you went away.'

Hartley said, 'Who was that man?'

'What man?'

'The man you were with when I was on the stairs?'

'My cousin James.'

'Oh yes – Aunt Estelle's son.'

This unexpected exhibition of memory made me sick with shock.

Down below in the kitchen I could hear a lively murmur of voices. Gilbert and Titus, feeling released by Hartley's apparition from any necessity to be discreet, were doubtless telling all they knew and more to James and Peregrine.

I groaned into my hands.

That night we slept as follows: I slept in my bedroom, Hartley slept in the middle room, Gilbert slept on his sofa, Peregrine slept on the cushions in the bookroom, James slept on a couple of chairs in the little red room, and Titus slept out on the lawn. It was a very hot night but there was no storm.

The next morning there was a holiday atmosphere among my guests. Titus swam from the cliff as usual. James, after exploring the tower and uttering various historical conjectures about it, swam from the tower steps. (I had still forgotten to fix a rope, but it was high tide.) Peregrine, a great white blob, lay half-naked sunbathing upon the grass and got thoroughly burnt. Gilbert drove into the village and came back with a mass of foodstuffs and several bottles of whisky which he put down to my account at the shop. Later James drove to the village to get *The Times* and failed. There was general amazement at my ability to live without 'news'. 'Who's dead, who's hijacked, who's on strike,' as Perry summed it up. He had brought a transistor set with him, but I told him to keep it out of my way. James pioneered a popular plan to go to the Raven Hotel to watch the Test Match on television, only Gilbert, again despatched to shop, this time for sunburn lotion for Peregrine, reported that electrical disturbances had put the local TV out of order. Gilbert and Titus, hoping to find recruits for their choir, succeeded with Perry who sang a gruff and shaggy bass, but failed with James, who could not sing a note. I had managed on the previous evening to warn Titus and Gilbert not to tell Peregrine about Rosina's visit. This was just as well, since in the morning I was almost incapable of rational thought. I felt as if something had snapped inside my head, a brain tumour had burst or something.

My desperate state was caused partly by the presence of James, who seemed to be a centre of magnetic attraction to the other three. Each of them separately told me how much he liked James. No doubt they expected to please me by this information. Titus said, 'It's funny, I feel as if I'd met him before, and yet I know I haven't. Perhaps I saw him in a dream.' The other thing which drove me half mad was a sudden change in Hartley's tone. She had been saying that she must go home, but she had lately said it almost listlessly as if she knew it was becoming impossible. Now she began to say it as if she meant it, and to back it up with almost-rational arguments.

'I know that you think you're being kind to me –'

'Kind! I love you.'

'I know you think it's for the best and I'm grateful –'

'Grateful! Oh good!'

'But it's all a nonsense, an accident, an incident – we can't stay together, it doesn't make sense.'

'I love you. You love me.'

'I do care for you –'

'Don't use that whimsy language. You love me.'

'All right, but in an unreal way, in a dream, in a might-have-been. Really, all this was over long ago and we're dreaming it.'

'Hartley, have you no sense of the present tense, can't you *live* in the present? Wake up and try it!'

'I live in long-times, not in sudden present moments, don't you see – I'm married, I've got to go back to where I *am*. If you took me to London like you just said I'd have to run away from you. You make everything worse and worse, you won't understand –'

'OK, you're married, so what? You haven't been happy.'

'It doesn't matter –'

'I should say it matters a lot. I can't think of anything that matters more.'

'I can –'

'You *admit* you love me.'

'One can love a dream. You think that makes a sort of push to action –'

'A motive, yes!'

'No, because it is a dream. It's made of lies.'

'Hartley, we have futures. That means we can make things true.'

'I have to go back.'

'He'll kill you.'

'I have to go through that door, it's the only way for me.'

'I won't let you.'

'*Please* –'

'What about Titus? He'll be with me. Don't you want to be with Titus?'

'Charles, I must go home.'

'Oh stop, can't you just think of something better and want it?'

'One can't do that to one's mind. You don't understand people like me, like us, the other ones. You're like a bird that flies in the air, a fish that swims in the sea. You move, you look about you, you want things. There are others who live on earth and move just a little and don't look –'

'Hartley, trust me, come with me, ride on my back. You too can move about and look at things –'

'*I want to go home.*'

I left her and locked the door and rushed out of the house. I climbed over a rock or two and saw my cousin standing on the bridge over the cauldron. He waved and called to me and I went to join him.

'Charles, just look at the force of that water, isn't it fantastic, isn't it terrifying?' I could just hear his voice above the roar of the outgoing tide.

'Yes.'

'It's sublime, yes, in the strict sense, sublime. Kant would love it. Leonardo would love it. Hokusai would love it.'

'I daresay.'

'And the birds – just look at those shags –'

'I thought they were cormorants.'

'They're shags. And I saw some choughs, and oyster-catchers. And I heard a curlew round in the bay.'

'When are you leaving?'

'I say, I like your friends.'

'They like you.'

'The boy seems good.'

'Yes –'

'My hat, look at that water, what it's doing now!'

We began to walk back towards the house. It was nearly time for lunch, if such conventions still existed.

James, who had evidently brought his seaside holiday outfit, had on some very old cotton khaki trousers, rolled up, and a clean but ancient blue shirt which he wore loose and unbuttoned, revealing the upper part of his thin scantily-haired pink body. He was also wearing sandals which exposed his skinny white feet with long prehensile bony toes which used to appal me when I was young. ('James has feet like hands' I told my mother, as if discovering a secret deformity.)

As we neared the house, he said, 'What are you going to do?'

'About what?'

'About her.'

'I don't know. When are you leaving?'

'May I stay till tomorrow?'

'All right.'

We came into the kitchen and I automatically picked up the tray which Gilbert had put out for Hartley. I carried it upstairs, unlocked the door, and went in and put the tray on the table as usual.

She was crying and would say nothing to me.

'Oh, Hartley, don't destroy me with this grief, you don't know what you're doing to me.'

She said nothing and made no sign, just continued to cry, leaning back against the wall and gazing in front of her, mopping the slow tears occasionally with the back of her hand.

I sat with her for a little while in silence. I sat on the chair and looked about me as if so ordinary an occupation could bring her comfort. I noted a damp patch on the ceiling, a crack in one of the panes of the long window. Purple fluff on the floor, doubtless from Mrs Chorney's furniture. At last I got up, touched her shoulder gently and went away. I never stayed to see her eat. I locked the door.

When I came back to the kitchen I found all four of them there, standing round the table where Gilbert had laid out a lunch of ham and tongue with green salad and new potatoes, and hard-boiled eggs for James. By now of course I took no interest in their food and very little in my own. Two open bottles of white wine were cooling in the sink. Peregrine, improved by being clothed, was drinking whisky and listening to the cricket on his transistor. They fell silent when I entered. Perry switched off the radio. There was an air of expectancy.

I poured myself out a glass of wine and picked up a slice of ham. 'You carry on. I'm going to eat outside.'

'Don't rush away, we want to talk to you,' said Peregrine.

'Well, I don't want to talk to you.'

'We want to help you,' said Gilbert.

'Oh, fuck off.'

'Please stay a minute,' said James. 'Titus has something to say to you. Haven't you, Titus?'

Titus, red in the face, not looking at me, mumbled, 'I think you ought to let my mother go home.'

'This is her home.'

'But seriously, old man –' said Peregrine.

'I don't want your advice. I didn't ask you to come here, any of you.'

James sat down, and the other three followed suit. I remained standing.

'We don't want to intrude –' said James.

'Don't then.'

'And we don't in fact want to force any advice on you. *We* can't see what this situation is, how could we? My impression is that you hardly understand it yourself. We don't want to persuade you –'

'Then why did you put Titus up to saying what he just said?'

'Because it's part of the evidence. It's something that Titus thinks, but which he was afraid to tell you.'

'Oh bosh.'

'You have got a difficult and, as far as I can see, fairly urgent decision to make and if you would only consent to talk to us we could help you to make it in a rational way, and we could also help you to *carry it out* in a rational way. You must see that you need help, you *need* it.'

'I need a chauffeur. Nothing else.'

'You need support. I am your only relation. Gilbert and Peregrine are your close friends.'

'They aren't.'

'Titus says he regards you as his father.'

'You all seem to have had a jolly good talk about me.'

'Don't be angry, Charles,' said Peregrine. 'We didn't expect to be landed in this soup. We came here for a holiday. But we see you in trouble and we want to back you up.'

'There's nothing you can do for me.'

'There is,' said James. 'I think it would help you a great deal to discuss the whole business with us, not necessarily the details, but the sort of strategy of it. You could do this without disloyalty. Now roughly there are two possible courses of action: you keep her or you return her. OK? Well, let's consider first what happens if you return her –'

'I'm not going to return her, as you put it. She's not a bottle.'

'I gather from Titus that one of your reasons for not taking her back, even if she wants to go –'

'She doesn't.'

'Is that you fear that her husband may be violent to her.'

'That's one reason, there are about a hundred others.'

'But supposing his violence depended on a misunderstanding, and supposing that that misunderstanding could be removed –'

'James, don't be a fool, you know perfectly well that there isn't any explanation or any excuse for what I have done, *whatever* it may be. And I advise you to be careful what you say to me.'

'Look,' said James, 'I'm saying two things. First, that if you are going to take her back it must be done intelligently. We should all go with you, as a show of force, but also to back up your statement.'

'My statement?!'

'And secondly, that if fear of violence is one of your reasons for *not* returning her, and if that fear can be reduced, this could be relevant to what you decide to do.'

'Do you see what he means?' said Peregrine.

'Yes! But as James admits, you cannot understand the situation! You speak of explaining or making statements – you might as well try to explain to a bison. In any case this whole argument is beside the point since there are not two possibilities. I do not admit her return to her husband as possible.'

'Well, then let us consider the other course –' said James.

'We will consider nothing! I don't want you lot tramping around over this problem. You are being impertinent, and I resent it extremely! But since the matter has come up I should like to ask Titus why he thinks I ought to let his mother go home.'

Titus, who had been staring at the ham (perhaps he was hungry) all this time, seemed reluctant to answer, blushed and would not look up. He said, 'Well – you see – I feel I may be to blame –'

'Why on earth?'

'It's so difficult, one has so many sort of – emotions, and sort of – prejudices, about fathers and mothers. I feel I may have made you think it was awfuller than it was, though it *was* awful. And she does exaggerate, she has fantasies and ideas in her head. I don't know. Maybe she does prefer to be with him, and I'm against forcing people, I think they should be free. You're in a hurry to fix it all at once. But if she wants to come to you she can come better later on when she's had time to think it over.'

'Well said, Titus,' said James.

Titus gave James a look which stirred my ever-vigilant jealousy. Peregrine said, 'You don't understand marriage, Charles, you've never been in it, it's deep. You think a tiff means shipwreck, the end, it's not so.'

I said, 'To begin with, "free" doesn't apply here, we're dealing with a frightened person, a prisoner. She has to be pulled out, she'll never walk. So it's got to be fixed now. If she goes back she'll never leave him, she'll never escape.'

James said, 'Well, isn't that significant too? Isn't that to admit that she ought to go back? That she'll choose to stay there? Oftener than you might think what human beings actually do is what they want to do.'

'She may stay. But "choose"? This isn't a matter of a "tiff", to use Perry's ludicrous word which shows that he has no idea what this is all about. She's a bullied terrorized woman who has never been happy with that man, she told me so herself.'

'Her marriage may not have been happy, but it has survived a long time. You think too much about happiness, Charles. It's not all that important.'

'That's what she said.'

'There you are.'

'Titus,' I said, 'is happiness important?'

'Yes, of course it is,' he said, and looked at me at last.

'There you are,' I said to James.

'A young man's reply,' said James. 'Now let me make a further point —'

'Your trouble, Charles,' said Peregrine, who was still drinking whisky, 'as I said before, is that you despise women, you regard them as chattels. You regard this woman as a chattel —'

'A further point. This drama has been developing very fast and it's a whirling mass of emotions and ideas. You say you've kept this image

of a pure first love beside you all these years. You may even have come
to think of it as a supreme value, a standard by which all other loves
have failed –'

'Yes.'

'But should you not criticize this guiding idea? I won't call it a fiction.
Let us call it a dream. Of course we live in dreams and by dreams, and
even in a disciplined spiritual life, in some ways especially there, it is
hard to distinguish dream from reality. In ordinary human affairs humble
common sense comes to one's aid. For most people common sense *is*
moral sense. But you seem to have deliberately excluded this modest
source of light. Ask yourself, what really happened between whom
all those years ago? You've made it into a story, and stories are false.'

(At this point Titus, who could bear it no longer, surreptitiously
seized a piece of ham and some bread.)

'And you are using this thing from the far past as a guide to important
and irrevocable moves which you propose to make in the future. You
are making a dangerous induction, and induction is shaky at the best
of times, consider Russell's chicken –'

'Russell's chicken?'

'The farmer's wife comes out every day and feeds the chicken, but
one day she comes out and wrings its neck.'

'I don't understand, let's leave this chicken out.'

'I mean, you are assuming on as far as I can see very insubstantial
evidence, your memory of some idyllic times at school and so on, that
if you were to carry her off you would be able to love her and make
her happy, and she would be able to love you and make you happy. Such
situations are in fact fairly rare and hard of achievement. Further, as a
matter inseparable from the happiness you prize so much, you assume
that it is morally right thus to rescue her, even in the apparent absence
of her consent. Now should you not –'

'James, please just stop insulting me with your pompous speculations will you? I wonder if you realize how insupportable you are? As you said, this business has developed fast and it's a first-class muddle. And, all right, I made the muddle. But inside it there isn't any perfect morality any more. That's what ordinary human life is like. Perhaps cloistered soldiers don't know about such things.'

James smiled. 'I like "cloistered soldiers". So you admit you aren't sure that this rescue would be a good thing?'

'I'm not sure, how can I be? But you're trying to force me to have an argument which isn't *the* argument of the situation. What you are saying is all at the side, it's a sort of abstract commentary. You're the one who's "telling a story". I'm in the place where the real things happen.'

'Well, what is *the* argument of the situation?'

'That I love her. She loves me. She says so. And love doesn't rely on "evidence" and "induction". Love *knows*. She's been very unhappy and I'm not going to let her return to a bully who will henceforth be even more cruel to her. It will be worse. OK, I made it so, but the fact remains. For his cruelty we have a witness here, though the witness seems unwilling to testify.'

'That's not an argument,' said James. 'It's a rather confused statement of intention.'

'Well, it's what I propose to act upon. I can't think why I let myself be drawn into this perfectly ridiculous discussion at all.'

'All right. What I personally think has probably emerged already, and of course needn't be a matter of any interest to you. But I'd like to add this: that if you do decide, unwisely in my view, to take her away, we would all want to help you as much as we can. That's so, isn't it?'

'Yes,' said Peregrine.

'I think I agree with Charles in some ways,' said Gilbert.

'For instance, where will you take her? The details have to be considered. What will she do all day?'

'That question alone,' said Peregrine, 'is enough to deter any man from getting married.'

'Charles, please don't think me impertinent and above all don't think me unkind. I can't just stand by and see you make a mucker of this business. It calls for a joint operation. I wonder if you'd let me talk to her, just once very briefly?'

'*You? Talk to her?* You must be mad!'

At that moment I heard a terrible sound, a sound which in fact I had been dreading ever since I embarked upon my perilous adventure. Hartley upstairs had suddenly started screaming and banging the door. *'Let me out, let me out!'*

I ran out of the kitchen, slamming the door behind me, and up the stairs. When I reached Hartley's door she was still screaming and kicking at the panels. She had never done anything like this before. *'Let me out! Let me out!'*

I wanted to scream myself. I pounded the door frenziedly with my fist. 'Oh stop it! Stop it! Shut up! Stop shouting, will you?'

Silence.

I ran downstairs again. There was silence in the kitchen too. I ran out of the front door and across the causeway and started walking along the road towards the tower.

Later on that day, towards evening, sitting on the rocks with James, I had begun to agree to things which had by now begun to seem inevitable.

'Charles, it's a terrible situation. That's one reason why you've got to end it. And there is only one way to end it. You do see that now?'

'Yes.'

'And you'll write the letter?'

'Yes.'

'I think the letter is important. You can explain things clearly in the letter.'

'He won't read it. He'll tear it up and stamp on it.'

'Well – or may keep it as evidence against you, but I think that risk is worth taking. I believe he'll read it out of curiosity.'

'He's below the level of curiosity.'

'And you agree that we should come?'

'I agree that *you* should come.'

'I think the more the better.'

'But not Titus of course.'

'Yes, Titus too. It might help her, and it could help Titus, if he could be polite to his father for five minutes.'

'*Polite?* It sounds like a tea party.'

'The liker it is to a tea party the better.'

'Titus wouldn't agree.'

'He has agreed.'

'Oh.'

'Then it's OK that Peregrine can go into the village now and make that telephone call?'

I hesitated. It was the last moment. If I said yes now the whole situation would slide out of my control. I would be sanctioning a totally new and unpredictable future. 'Yes.'

'Good. You stay here. I'll go and brief Peregrine.'

In the afternoon I had talked with Hartley. I did not admit it to James, but his 'discussion' had helped me to see certain things more clearly, or had battered certain ideas into my head; or else I had in any case reached a certain decisive point of despair. That terrible 'let me out, let me out' had cracked my faith and my hope. I asked her if she really wanted to go home. She said she did. I said all right. I did not make any more appeals or offer any more arguments. And as we looked at each other, silently, neither venturing to add to the words firmly spoken, I felt a fresh barrier rise between us. Before, I had thought our communication difficult. Now I realized how close we *had* been.

The plan was that Peregrine should go to the village and telephone Ben and say that Mr Arrowby and his friends would be bringing 'Mary' back. Would Ben say, 'Go to hell, I don't want her now'? No. Very unlikely. Whatever he ultimately wanted he would not oblige me by that move. But perhaps he would be away, perhaps he would have disappeared, perhaps when it came to it Hartley would change her mind ... But by now anything was better than hope.

James was reappearing, leaping over the rocks.

My heart beat violently, sadly.

'It's all right, he says bring her round, but he says tomorrow morning, not tonight.'

'That's odd. Why not tonight?' His woodwork class perhaps!

'He wants to pretend he doesn't care. It's an available insult. He wants to make it clear we come at *his* convenience. It's just as well. It gives you more time to write that letter. It might be as well to deliver the letter *before* we all arrive, he'll be more likely to read it.'

'Oh, James —'

'Not to worry. *Sic biscuitus disintegrat.*

'What?'

'That's the way the cookie crumbles.'

Dear Mr Fitch,

This is not a very easy letter to write. I just want to make a number of things quite clear. The main thing is that I brought your wife to my house and kept her there *against her will*. The fact that she did not even take her handbag with her is proof, if proof be needed, that she was not 'running away'. (Forgive me if I say the obvious, I want this letter to be a final and definitive account of what has happened.) I decoyed her into my car by telling her that Titus was at my house, which he was. When she arrived I locked her up. So you were right to charge me with having 'kidnapped' her. She has not ceased to ask to go home. It goes without saying that I have had no 'relations' with her. She has throughout resolutely resisted all my proposals and plans and has desired simply to be allowed to return to you. She is therefore *totally blameless* in this matter. My friends Mr Opian and Mr Arbelow, and my cousin General Arrowby, who have been here with me in the house throughout, will vouch for the truth of what I say.

There is no point in apologies and little point in further explanations. I have been in a state of illusion and caused much fruitless distress to your wife and to yourself, which I regret. I did not act out of malice, but out of the promptings of an old romantic affection which I now see to have nothing to do with what exists at present. And perhaps at this point I should add (again something obvious) that of course I have not seen or communicated with your wife in any way since she was a young girl, and our recent meeting was completely accidental.

I trust and assume that since you are a reasonable and just man you will take no reprisal against your wife who is completely innocent. This is a matter of deep concern to me, my cousin and my friends. She has been perfectly loyal to you in word and deed and deserves your respect and gratitude. As for myself, I trust you will feel that I have suffered enough humiliation, not least in consciousness of my folly,

Yours truly,
Charles Arrowby.

It was just as well that I had the extra time since it took me all the evening to compose this letter. It was indeed a difficult letter to write and I was far from satisfied with the final result. My first version was considerably more bellicose, but as James, to whom I showed it, pointed out, if I accused Ben of being a bully and a tyrant this would at once suggest that Hartley had said so. I could not justify my proceedings on that ground without casting an aspersion upon the 'perfect loyalty' which I had perjured myself by swearing that Hartley had exhibited. This omission of course left my self-defence almost non-existent, and I was well aware, without having it mentioned to me by James, that in another age both Ben and I would have been forced by convention and our own honourable consciences to fight each other to the death. In another age, and, in the case of a man like Ben, perhaps in this one too. My slender 'apologies' were also difficult to word, since I had to crawl sufficiently to propitiate, should Ben be disposed to forgive, but not so much as to seem negligible should he prefer to fight. I could only hope that Ben's own sense of guilt would weaken his aggressive instincts. The pompous reference to 'my cousin and my friends' was James's idea, though the false assertion that they had been present 'throughout' Hartley's sojourn was mine. James thought that the vague presence of a more disinterested, more formidable, group of persons might make Ben feel that his proceedings had an audience, and might thus temper the violence of his reactions. I did not believe this. His behaviour might be a matter of 'deep concern' to all sorts of worthy persons other than myself, but once the front door was closed upon the married pair Ben would do as he pleased. James did not repeat his request to be allowed to talk to Hartley. It was in any case too late. Gilbert dropped my missive through the letter box at Nibletts at about ten o'clock that evening.

I spent a little time with Hartley. It was very odd. I told her that she was going home tomorrow. She nodded, blinking her eyes intelligently.

I asked her if she wanted to come down and have supper with the others. She declined, to my relief. I did not ask her again if she was content to go. We sat on the floor and played cards, a form of 'snap' which we had invented for ourselves when we were children. Everyone in the house went to bed early.

HISTORY

FIVE

THE next day was one of the worst days of my life, perhaps the worst. I awoke as for execution. No one except Titus had any interest in breakfast. The hot stuffy weather continued, with a few distant grumblings of thunder now.

Hartley looked terrible. She had made up her face with especial care and this made her look pathetically older. Her yellow dress was dirty, crumpled and torn. I could not send her back to her husband in my dressing gown. I searched among my clothes and found a sort of blue unisex beach coat which I made her put on. I also found a light scarf to put over her head. It was like dressing a child. We did not dare to say much to each other. By now I wanted the whole thing to be over. I could scarcely endure the idea that she might even now say 'I don't think I want to go after all'; and the impulse to cry out 'Stop!' was a pain which I urgently wanted to be without. Perhaps she felt much the same. And I thought at one moment: why, it's just like it was *then*. I've done everything I can for her, everything. And she's just leaving me.

I put into a plastic bag her make-up and the mottled pink stone with the white bars which I had given her (and which she had apparently not looked at since). She said nothing, but she watched me put the stone into the bag. Gilbert shouted up that the car was ready.

While Hartley was in the bathroom I went on downstairs carrying the bag and waited in the hall. They had decided that what Peregrine called 'the delegation' should be carried in Peregrine's white Alfa Romeo. James and Perry and Titus were already outside. Gilbert came out of the kitchen. He said to me, 'Charles, a funny thing, last night, I didn't tell you.'

'What?'

'When I delivered that letter at his place I thought I heard a woman talking inside.'

'It was TV.'

'I don't think so. Charles, there won't be a fight, will there? I mean his asking us not to come till today. Perhaps he's mustered all his pals to beat us up.'

This idea had occurred to me too. 'He has no pals.' The woodwork class?

Hartley began to come down the stairs. I pushed Gilbert and he went out. She walked slowly, clutching the banister, as if walking were difficult. She was wearing the scarf over her head, as I had intended her to, and her face was shadowed. I would have liked her to wear a veil. It was our last moment, our last second, alone together. I took her hand and pressed it and kissed her cheek and said, as if it were something quite ordinary, 'It's not goodbye. You will come to me. I shall be waiting.' She squeezed my hand but said nothing. She was not tearful. Her eyes looked far away. We went out together onto the causeway. The others were waiting by the car. It was curiously like the emergence of a bride and bridegroom.

All eyes were averted as we approached the car. I had not arranged the seating. Titus opened the rear door and I hustled Hartley in and followed her, and Titus got in next to me. The other three squashed up in the front. Hartley drew her scarf forward to veil her face. The three in front did not look round.

Peregrine, who was driving, said, 'It's straight on and then right?'

Gilbert said, 'It's through the village, I'll direct you.'

Hartley was crushed against me. She was stiff, stiff. Titus was stiff too, his eyes staring and unseeing, his pink mouth slightly open. I could feel his fast breathing. Everyone was gazing straight ahead. I folded my hands together. The sun was shining. It was a bright day for the wedding.

We were just approaching the big rocks through which the road passed in a narrow defile, the place which I called the Khyber Pass, when a stone struck the windscreen with amazing force. Everyone in the car came abruptly out of whatever trance he was in. Then another stone struck the car and then another. Peregrine stopped. Another driver might have accelerated, but not Perry. 'What the hell is going on? Somebody's throwing stones at us, they're throwing on purpose.' He got out of the car.

We were now inside the defile with yellow rocks towering up on either side. James was saying something to Peregrine, perhaps telling him to get back into the car. I had time to think: Ben has arranged a brilliant ambush, he has chosen just the right place. Then the windscreen suddenly shattered. A sizable rock, pushed over the edge from above, had fallen directly upon it. With a sizzling report the glass became white, crackled and opaque. The rock rebounded on the radiator, dinting it, and scudded onto the road. Peregrine uttered a cry of rage.

Titus had jumped out of the car and I followed him. Gilbert stayed where he was. James moved into the driver's seat and, with a handkerchief wrapped around his hand, punched a hole in the glass. Then he too got out.

'There! There!' Peregrine was shouting and pointing upward.

A stone flew past my head. I looked up and outlined against the blue sky I saw Rosina. She was kneeling on one knee on top of one of the highest rocks and had evidently provided herself beforehand with an arsenal of missiles. She was black, a black witch, wearing something that looked like a peasant woman's shawl. I saw her snarling mouth and her teeth. It soon too became apparent that her main target was Peregrine. A stone struck him on the chest, another on the shoulder.

Instead of seeking cover he began, still bellowing, to return the fire. Stones were flying round Rosina's head, but I think none of them hit her.

'Who is this lady?' said James in his rather fastidious tone.

'Peregrine's former wife.'

'Need she detain us?'

'Perry, get back in the car, *get back in the car!*' I grabbed his coat tail. He pulled himself angrily away and stooped to pick up more ammunition.

A stone struck me painfully upon the hand and I returned hastily towards the car.

'Rosina! Rosina!' It was Titus, shouting, waving. It was like a war cry. He gesticulated and danced. I pulled him back with me. James got hold of Perry. In a moment we were all back inside and Peregrine was accelerating violently. The car flashed onward and round the curve to where the village road forked inland.

Here Peregrine stopped the car with a jerk, went round to the boot and came back with a jack with which he violently knocked out the rest of the windscreen, showering us all with white fragments of glass. He inspected the dint on the radiator. 'What the hell is that bloody bitch doing here?' he said, but not in a tone that seemed to require an answer. A little later he said thoughtfully, 'She used to play cricket at school.'

The bizarre violence of the incident had left me dazed, and I returned with a sick shock to my acute consciousness of Hartley who, during the whole of the episode, had not moved, and seemed not to have noticed what was happening. Then I suddenly remembered what Gilbert had said about hearing a woman talking in the bungalow last night. Had Rosina carried out her obscene threat of going to 'console' Ben, and if so had that been why Ben was not ready to receive Hartley last night? How else had Rosina known we were coming? This thought filled me with confused helpless anger.

By now we had passed through the village, past the church where I had talked so shyly with Hartley so long ago, and turned up the hill towards the bungalows. Peregrine, driving savagely, was red in the face, and remained so completely absorbed in his own thoughts that he took no further active part in the proceedings and seemed scarcely to know what was going on.

When I had imagined Hartley going home I had not imagined opening the car door and ushering her out and unlatching the gate and walking up the path, at any moment of which proceedings I could have cried out 'No! No more!' and seized her hand and dragged her away. I did not do so. I did not touch her. She slipped off the scarf and the blue coat and slithered quickly out of the car. I opened the gate for her and followed her up the path. James followed me, then Titus looking frightened, Gilbert also looking frightened, then Peregrine in some kind of private rage.

Hartley rang the bell. Its sweet chime had scarcely sounded when there was a volley of fierce barks, followed by the sound of human cursing. A door banged and the barking was less audible. Then Ben opened the door. I think he would have liked to let her in and shut it again, only in accordance with orders issued by James I went in quickly on her heels and the others came after me.

I had, equally, not imagined the scene inside the house, or in so far as I had imagined it I had pictured either an instant *fracas* or else a solemn council, with Hartley somehow featuring in both. As it was, no sooner was Hartley inside the door than she vanished. In a second she had slipped away like a mouse and gone into the bedroom and shut the door. (The main bedroom that is, not the little room where I had talked to Ben.)

The dog, which seemed to be a rather large animal, went on barking as an accompaniment to what was going on in the hall. Ben had retreated to the sitting-room door, Gilbert was leaning against the now closed front door, Peregrine was angrily inspecting the picture of the knight in armour, James was looking at Ben with an air of interest, and Ben and Titus were staring at each other.

Ben spoke first, 'Well, Titus, then.'

'Hello.'

'You coming home with mummy, you going to stay here now?' Titus was silent, trembling and biting his lip.

'Going to stay here now, eh? Eh?'

Titus shook his head. He said in a strangled whisper, 'No – I think I'll stay – away.'

I said, 'Titus is not my son, but I propose to adopt him.' My voice quavered with nervousness and the words sounded unconvincing, almost frivolous. Ben ignored them. Still staring at Titus he made a violent throwing-away movement. Titus winced.

Ben was the shortest man present, but physically the most formidable. His bull neck and big shoulders seemed to be bursting the old khaki shirt which was now too small for them. His black belt was pulled in tight under a slight pot-belly, but he looked in good condition. He glowed with sunburn, his short mousy hair stood up like fur, he had recently shaved. His hands hung by his sides and he kept waggling his fingers and rising slightly on his toes as if about to perform some physical feat. The hall was stuffy as I remembered it, but the smell was different, nastier. I noticed several bowls full of dead roses. The dog had now fallen silent.

I said, 'Did you read my letter?'

Ben paid no attention to me. He was now looking at James and James was looking at him. James was frowning thoughtfully. Then he said, 'Staff-Sergeant Fitch.'

'Yes, that's right.'

'Royal Engineers.'

'That's right.'

'You were the chap in that show in the Ardennes.'

'That's right.'

'You did well,' said James.

Ben's face hardened, perhaps to inhibit some show of emotion, even some fleeting gleam of gratification. 'You his cousin?'

'Yes.'

'Are you still serving?'

'Yes. Just retired actually.'

'Wish I'd stayed in.'

There was a moment's silence as if they were both thinking about the past and likely to break out into reminiscence. Then James said hastily, 'I'm sorry about this business now. I – er, it wasn't her fault at all, she's completely innocent, and nothing happened, I give you my word of honour.'

Ben said expressionlessly, 'OK.' He made a movement of his head and shoulders indicative of dismissal.

James turned to me, rather blandly, like a chairman tacitly asking a distinguished speaker if he has anything further to say. I did not respond to his look, but turned to go. Gilbert opened the door, Peregrine marched out, then Gilbert, then Titus, then me, then James. The door closed softly behind us.

Before I reached the car I realized that I was still carrying the plastic bag containing Hartley's make-up and the stone which I had given her. I automatically turned back. James tried to catch hold of me, but I dodged him and walked steadily back up the path. It was an almost superstitiously stringent necessity to leave that bag with Hartley, not to take it away, not to take it back to Shruff End to be a sort of unlucky token and collect the filth of demons. It only occurred to me afterwards that I could have left it on the doorstep. I rang the ding-dong bell and waited. The savage barking started up again. Ben shouted, 'Shut up, you devil!'

After a moment or two he opened the door. The expressionless mask was gone. He grimaced with hatred. I felt there was a kind of levity about what I was doing, and yet it had to be done. I was also aware of interrupting the next scene. The bedroom door was open.

I held out the bag. 'These are hers. Sorry I forgot to leave them.'

Ben seized the bag and hurled it away behind him into the hall where it bumped and clattered. He thrust his grimacing snarling head out at me and I stepped back. 'Keep away or I'll kill you. And tell that vile brat to keep away too. *I'll kill you!*'

The door slammed with a violence which set the bell vibrating. The dog was now almost screaming. I came back down the path and crossed to the car, where Ben's words would not have been audible.

Gilbert and Titus were sitting in the back. The seat was covered with opaque white stones like huge pearls. 'What's this stuff?' I said.

'The windscreen broke, remember?' said James. 'Now let's go home. Peregrine?'

THE SEA, THE SEA

The car started, roared up the hill, turned, roared down the hill, going very fast. The air blew fiercely in through the open front window. No one spoke.

When we were getting near to the junction with the coast road Titus said, 'Would you mind stopping? I'd like to walk from here.'

Peregrine stopped with an abruptness which sent us all flying forward. Titus began to get out.

'Titus, you're not going back there?' I cried to him and grabbed at his shirt.

'No!' He slipped out, and said as he turned away, 'I'm going to be sick, if you want to know.' He started walking in the direction of the harbour. Peregrine set off again, driving violently.

Gilbert said to James, 'What was that thing in the Ardennes that you were saying about?'

James was looking alert and rather pleased. The meeting with Ben seemed to have put him in a good mood. He said, 'It was an odd business. That chap Fitch was a prisoner of war in a camp in the Ardennes, he must have been captured in 1944. There weren't any officers in the camp, I suppose he was the senior NCO, anyway he was the leading figure. In May 1945 when the Germans were going to evacuate the camp before our lot arrived he staged a private war of his own. He managed to impose himself on everybody. He had a group of toughs among the prisoners, well everybody joined in, it was well organized, quite a classic piece of planning, and they sabotaged the transport, I think they even nobbled a train. They got hold of arms and started shooting up the Germans. It was rather a savage business, possibly some personal vendetta was involved. Anyway when our troops arrived the surviving Germans were the prisoners and young Fitch had got the entire camp under his control and was standing at the gate to welcome us in. It was a neat exercise of personal bravery and initiative. There was a bit of fuss about "unnecessary brutality", but that soon blew over. He got a Military Medal.'

'Were you there?' said Gilbert.

'No, I was somewhere else, but it was my outfit that relieved the camp and someone told me about it. I remember seeing a picture of the chap, he hasn't changed. And I recalled his name, and it all somehow remained in my memory, it appealed to my imagination. He was a brave man. How odd coming across him like that!'

'A rather unattractive sort of courage,' I said.

'There was a rather unattractive sort of war on,' said James.

'The man's a killer.'

'Some people are better at killing than others, it needn't mean a vicious character. He behaved like an able soldier.'

We had reached the house. Peregrine scraped the car on a rock and it stopped with a jolt. We all got out. I looked at my watch. It was ten o'clock. The day lay ahead.

I went into the house, passed automatically through the kitchen and out onto the lawn. James, who had followed on my heels, was standing at the kitchen door looking at me. I said to him, 'Thank you for your help. Now you've finished your job here I expect you'll want to be off.'

He said, 'Well, if you don't mind, I think I'll stay till tomorrow.'

'Please yourself.'

I went away across the rocks in the direction of the tower, passing over Minn's bridge. I found a place down on the edge of the water where I could see into Raven Bay. A hot wind was blowing in from the sea and there was a slightly menacing swell, but the atmosphere was less thundery. Perhaps the storms had passed by.

My hand was hurting where it had been struck by Rosina's stone. A bruise was appearing. I found that I had been sweating profusely. The hot wind was drying my shirt and denim jacket, both of which had been sticking to my back. I pulled the jacket off and loosened the shirt. There was a haze over the bay, the water was pale blue, fringed by a pretty lace of breaking waves. The big round boulders looked hot, as if the stored-up heat which they were exuding were shimmering visibly. They had a solemn, almost religious look. The dark yellow seaweed stains upon them looked like hieroglyphs. Beyond the other arm of the bay the sea was spotted with purple. I sat with my feet almost within reach of the strongly rising and falling water which was spattering the yellow rocks with a quick-drying foam. I felt that I had made a fool of myself in the recent scene and felt sad to think that in relation to anything so awful I should look ridiculous.

I heard a soft footfall and saw a shadow and James came and sat down beside me. I paid no attention to him and we sat for a while in silence.

James started fingering around in the rocks, finding small stones and tossing them into the water. He said at last, 'Don't worry too much, I think she'll be all right, I'm sure she will.'

'Why?'

'My general assessment of the situation.'

'I see.'

'And also that odd episode.'

'You think Staff-Sergeant Fitch's respect for General Arrowby will be such –?'

'Not exactly. But it's as if something passed between us.'

'Military telepathy.'

'Sort of. I think – it's hard to put – some vein of honour is touched –'

'Oh rubbish,' I said. 'It's funny, James, but whenever you start talking soldiery you seem to me to become utterly stupid. Military vanity, I suppose.'

We were silent for a bit longer. I found a few stones myself and dropped them in, after examining each one to see if it was worth keeping. I imagined Ben would soon throw away that pretty stone in the plastic bag. Perhaps he would throw it at the dog. I felt sorry for that dog.

James said, 'I hope you don't feel that I've influenced you in any way against your better judgment?'

'No.' I was not going to argue that point. Of course he had influenced me. But what was my judgment, let alone my better judgment?

'What are you going to do about Titus?'

'What?'

'What are you going to do about Titus?'

'I don't know. He'll probably clear off.'

'He won't if you hold on to him, but you'll have to hold. He says he wants to be an actor.'

'He told me that, oddly enough.'

'Can you get him into an acting school?'

'Maybe.'

'Titus will be an occupation for you.'

'Thanks for thinking about my occupations.'

'I suppose you'll leave this house now?'

'Why the hell should I?'

'Well, wouldn't it be better —?'

'This is my home. I like it here.'

'Uh-huh —'

We threw a few more stones.

'Can I go on talking, Charles?'

'Yes.'

'I've been thinking — Are you sure you don't mind?'

'Oh go on, what does it matter.'

'Time can divorce us from the reality of people, it can separate us from people and turn them into ghosts. Or rather it is we who turn them into ghosts or demons. Some kinds of fruitless preoccupations with the past can create such simulacra, and they can exercise power, like those heroes at Troy fighting for a phantom Helen.'

'You think I'm fighting for a phantom Helen?'

'Yes.'

'She is real to me. More real than you are. How can you insult an unhappy suffering person by calling her a ghost?'

'I'm not calling *her* a ghost. She is real, as human creatures are, but what reality she has is elsewhere. She does not coincide with your dream figure. You were not able to transform her. You must admit you tried and failed.'

I said nothing to this. I had certainly tried and failed to do something. But what, and what did this failure prove?

'So having tried, can you not now set your mind at rest? Don't torment yourself any more with this business. All right, you had to try, but now it's over and I'm sure you've done her no lasting harm. Think of other things now. There's a crime in the Army called deliberately making oneself unfit for duty. Don't do that. Think about Titus.'

'Why keep dragging Titus in?'

'Sorry. But seriously, look at it this way. Your love for this girl, when she was a girl, was put by shock into a state of suspended animation. Now the shock of meeting her again has led you to re-enact all your old feelings for her. It's a mental charade, a necessary one perhaps, it has its own necessity, but not like what you think. Of course you can't get over it at once. But in a few weeks or a few months you'll have run through it all, looked at it all again and felt it all again and got rid of it. It's not an eternal thing, nothing human is eternal. For us, eternity is an illusion. It's like in a fairy tale. When the clock strikes twelve it will all crumble to pieces and vanish. And you'll find you are free of her, free of her forever, and you can let the poor ghost go. What will remain will be ordinary obligations and ordinary interests. And you'll feel relief, you'll feel free. At present you're just obsessed, hypnotized.'

While James was speaking he was leaning down over the water and skimming some of the flatter stones so that they leapt upon the surface; only there was too much of a swell for them to jump very far. Watching the skimming stones I was filled with anguish because I remembered playing just that game with Hartley on an old pond near our house. She did it better than I did.

I replied, 'What you say sounds clever but it's empty. Love makes nonsense of that sort of mean psychology. You seem unable to imagine that love can endure. But just that endurance belongs to its miraculous nature. Perhaps you've never loved anybody all that much.'

As I said this I recalled something that Toby Ellesmere had said to me in some context where I was wondering whether James was homosexual. Toby had told me that James had had a great affection for some soldier servant in India, a Nepalese Sherpa, who had died somehow on a mountain. Of course one never knows about other people's loves, and I would certainly never know about James's. To cover my crude remark I went on, 'You seem to think the past is unreal, a pit full of ghosts. But to me the past is in some ways the most real thing of all, and loyalty to it the most important thing of all. It isn't just a case of sentimentality about an old flame. It's a principle of life, it's a project.'

'You mean you still believe in your idea after trying it, after having to admit that she wanted to go home and that she had better go home?'

'Yes. That's why I've got to stay here. I've got to wait. I've got to be at my post. She'll *know* that I'll wait, that I'll be here. She has got her uncertainties too. She had to go back now because it was all happening too quickly. But after this she'll *think,* and she'll find the chain has been broken after all. She'll come to me here, sooner or later, I know she will. She came before. She will come again.'

'And if she doesn't come?'

'I'll stay forever, it's my duty, it's my post, I'll stay till the end. Or rather – I'll wait – and then – I'll simply start the whole thing over again from the beginning.'

'You mean the rescue plan?'

'Yes. And do stop throwing those stones.'

'Sorry,' said James. 'We used to do that, remember, on that pond near Shaxton when you came over with Uncle Adam and Aunt Marian.'

'I've got to wait. She'll come to me here. She's part of me, it's not a caprice or a dream. When you've known someone from childhood, when you can't remember when they weren't there, that's not an illusion. She's woven into me. Don't you understand how one can be absolutely connected with somebody like that?'

'Yes,' said James. 'Well, I must go. I've got to go along with Peregrine to the garage and drive him back. See you at lunch. I suppose there will be lunch.'

There was lunch, though it was not a very cordial affair. We had fresh mackerel which Gilbert had procured from somewhere. He had also found some wild fennel. He cooked of course. No one ate much except Titus. I was very relieved when he turned up, returned like a dog to prove where its home is. Yes, I would help him, I would cherish him, would make of him an occupation and a preoccupation; only at present we avoided each other's eyes. A kind of shame hung on us both. He felt ashamed of his parents, of his unhappy ageing mother, of his stupid brutish father. I felt ashamed of having failed to keep Hartley, of having been forced to let her go back, indeed to take her back, to that matrimonial hell. Yes, I was forced to do it, I thought, somehow by James, and not only by James, but by Gilbert, by Peregrine, even by Titus. If only I had been left alone I would have had faith and I would have succeeded, would have kept her. I had been demoralized by all these spectators.

Peregrine had recovered, or feigned to have recovered, his usual aggressive equanimity. He and Gilbert kept up some sort of chatter. Gilbert exuded the secret satisfaction of one who has come unscathed through a fascinating adventure which he looks forward to gossiping about in another context. James was gently abstracted, perhaps melancholy. Titus was ashamed and resentful. I asked the other three when they would be going and expressed the wish that it might be soon, the show being over. There was general agreement that tomorrow would be departure day. Perry's car would be ready then. James would drive him to the garage. Gilbert rather reluctantly agreed to go too, though cheered by the prospect of bringing news of me to London. After that I would be alone with Titus.

After lunch I made out, at his intelligent suggestion, a longish shopping list for Gilbert so that he could stock me up with food and drink while I still had a car available. He then went off again to the village. Titus went to swim from the cliff. Peregrine, now lobster-coloured and shining with suntan lotion, lay on the grass beside the tower. James settled in the bookroom on the floor, combing through my books and reading here and there. Gilbert came back with a loaded car and the report, which he had heard in the shop, that Freddie Arkwright had arrived at Amorne Farm for his holidays. Peregrine staggered back to the house with a blinding headache and went to lie down in the bookroom with the curtains pulled. James emerged onto the lawn and began taking the stones out of the trough and arranging them on the grass in a complicated circular design. The afternoon advanced, very hot, with renewed grumblings of distant thunder. The sea was like liquid jelly, rising and falling with a thick smooth dense movement. Then some time after Titus returned from his swim it began to change its mood. A brisk wind started to blow. The smooth swell became more powerful, the waves higher and stronger. I could hear them roaring into the cauldron. There was a long line of puffy clouds low on the horizon, but the sun was descending through a blue celebration of cloudless light. Gilbert and Titus were now over by the tower, sitting in the shadow which it cast upon the grass. I could hear them singing *Eravamo tredici*.

I had deliberately declared, for my maddened wounded mind, an interim. It was indeed clear that what had happened had been engineered against my will by James. If I had kept my nerve, if I had persevered, if I had only had the sense to take her right away at the start, Hartley would have abandoned herself to me. She would have given up, she would have given in, at first with the weak despair of one in whom the hope of happiness had simply been killed. It was my task and my privilege to *teach* her the desire to live, and I would yet do so. I, and I only, could revive her; I was the destined prince. Perhaps in a way, I reflected, it was just as well to let her go back, this time, for a short period. My shock tactics would not after all have proved useless, she would have time to reflect, to compare two men and evolve a concept of a different future. The lessons I had tried to teach her would not be lost. A dose of Ben, after having been with me, after having had the seeds of liberty sown in her mind, might very well wake her up to the possibility, then the compelling desirability, of escape. A dose of Ben would make her concentrate at last. It would in fact be better thus, because she would make her own clear decision, not simply acquiesce in mine. If she could feel a little less frightened, a little less trapped, she would reflect and she would decide to come. My mistake had been to act so suddenly and so relentlessly. I ought never to have locked her up, I saw that now. I could easily have kept her, for a short time, by strong persuasions. Then I could have touched her reason. As it was she was too shocked to take it all in. I had given her the role of prisoner and victim, and this in itself had numbed her powers of reflection. Now at least, at 'home' in that horrible den, she would be able to *think*. He could not always batter her mind and supervise her body. I would wait. She would come. I would not leave the house. She might come at any hour of the day or night. And, I thought, with a final twist, yes, and if she does not come I shall do what I said to James, I shall simply start the whole thing again from the beginning.

Evening approached. Titus and Gilbert came in to make tea, then went off in Gilbert's car to the Black Lion. Peregrine emerged to dose his headache with whisky, then retired again. James wandered off in search of more stones for his mandala or whatever it was. Thinking these thoughts about Hartley and feeling slightly less desperate because of them, I clambered a little way over the rocks in the village direction. I could see the spray from the increasingly wild waves thrown up from the sea's edge in a rainbow, and the droplets were reaching me in a fine rain. I slithered into a long cleft, a secret place I had discovered earlier, where the tall rocks made a deep V-shape. Part of the floor of the cleft was occupied by a narrow pool, the other part by a rivulet of pebbles. The smooth rocks were very hot and the warmth in the enclosed space comforted my body. I sat down on the pebbles. I turned some of them over. They were damp underneath. I sat still and tried to silence my mind. A pebble came rolling down the rock into my rivulet and I looked at it idly. A moment or two later another pebble rolled down. Then another. I looked up. A head, framed by two clinging hands, gazed down on me from the crest above. A tendril or two of frizzy brown hair, tugged by the wind, had also come over the top of the rock. Two bright light-brown eyes peered short-sightedly down at me, half laughing, half afraid.

'Lizzie!'

Lizzie levered herself up onto the sharp rocky crest, got one brown leg, already grazed and bleeding slightly, over the top, then, impeded by the full skirt of her blue dress, swung the other leg over, lost her balance and slid down the long smooth surface into the pool.

'Oh, Lizzie!'

I pulled her out and hugged her, laughing with that agonized laughter which is so close to a mixture of wild exasperation and tears.

Now Lizzie, laughing too, was squeezing out the wet hem of her dress.

'You've cut yourself.'

'It's nothing.'

'You've lost a shoe.'

'It's in the pool. Can I have that one, or are you collecting my shoes? Oh Charles – you don't mind my coming?'

'You know Gilbert's here?'

'Yes, he wrote to me, he couldn't help boasting that he was staying with you.'

'Did he ask you to come?'

'No, no, I think he wanted to have you to himself. But I suddenly so much wanted to come and I thought, why not?'

'You thought "why not", did you, little Lizzie. Did you drive?'

'No, I came by train, then taxi.'

'Just as well. There soon won't be any more parking space left out there. Come on inside and get dry. Don't slip again, these rocks are tricky.'

I led her back towards the house, onto the lawn.

'What are those stones?'

'Oh just a sort of design someone's making. You're thinner.'

'I've been slimming. Oh Charles – dear – are you all right?'

'Why shouldn't I be?'

'Well, I don't know –'

We went into the kitchen. 'Here's a towel.' I was not going to enquire what vulgar impertinent travesty of the facts had been offered by Gilbert in his letter. The thought of how the story would be told would have tormented me if I had not had greater troubles.

Lizzie was wearing a peacock blue summer dress made out of some light bubbly material with a low V-neck and a wide skirt. She was indeed thinner. Her curling hair, wind-tangled, blown into long gingery corkscrews, strayed about on the brilliant blue collar. Her pale brown eyes, moist and shining with the wind, with tenderness, with relief, gazed up at me. She looked absurdly young, radioactive with vitality and unpredictable gaiety, while at the same time she looked at me so attentively, so humbly, like a dog reading his master's tiniest movements. I could not help seeing how different this alert healthy being was from the heavy confused creature whom I had allowed to be carried away from my house veiled and silent. Yet love seeks its own ends and discerns, even invents, its own charms. If necessary I would have to explain this to Lizzie.

Lizzie, sitting on a chair, had thrown off her sandals and crossed one bare leg over the other, hitching up the wide trailing blue skirt, half darkened with sea water, and was drying one foot.

James came in and stopped amazed.

I said to him, 'Another visitor. This is a theatre friend, Lizzie Scherer. This is a cousin of mine, James Arrowby.'

They said hello.

The front doorbell jangled.

I ran out, already seeing Hartley on the step, wind-tormented, distraught, falling into my arms.

A man with a cap stood there. 'Laundry.'

'Laundry?'

'Laundry. You wanted the laundry to call. I'm it.'

'Oh God, yes, nothing at the moment, thank you, call again could you, next week or –'

I ran back to the kitchen. Peregrine had arrived. He of course knew Lizzie, though not well. They were still exchanging greetings when Gilbert came in with Titus.

'Darling!'

'Gilbert!'

'Is this your suitcase? We found it outside.'

The front doorbell rang again. Would it be Hartley now? Oh let it be.

'Telephone?'

'You wanted a telephone. I've come to install it.'

By the time I had settled where the telephone was to be the company in the kitchen were all singing *Cherry Ripe*.

And they went on singing. And we got drunk. And Gilbert had made a great salad and set out bread and cheese and cherries. And Titus was looking so happy, sitting in the midst with Lizzie perched on the table near him and feeding him cherries. And I thought of that stuffy room on the other side of the village where Hartley was hiding her face and saying again and again and again, 'I'm sorry, I'm sorry, I'm so sorry.' I took some more wine. There was plenty of it, purchased by Gilbert at my expense. Then when it was getting dark, and they had moved on from *Abide with me* to *The day Thou gavest, Lord, is ended*, we all went out onto the lawn. James's stone-design had already been disordered by people tripping over it. I wanted to get Lizzie to myself and explain things to her. I led her a little way across the rocks and we sat down, hidden from the house. At once she gave me one of her chaste drying clinging kisses.

'Lizzie –'

'Darling, sweetheart, you're drunk!'

'Lizzie, you're my friend, aren't you?'

'Yes, forever and ever.'

'Why did you come to me, what do you want?'

'I want to be with you always.'

'Lizzie, it can never be, you know that, it can never be.'

'You did ask me – you asked me something – have you forgotten?'

'I forget so many things. I forgot the windscreen got broken.'

'The –?'

'Oh never mind. Listen. Listen, Lizzie. Listen –'

'I'm listening!'

'Lizzie, it cannot be. I am committed to this very unhappy person. She is going to come back to me. Did Gilbert tell you?'

'Gilbert wrote something. You tell me.'

'I can't remember what you know.'

'Rosina said you were going to marry a bearded lady, and you said that you'd met this woman from the past and that what you'd said to me was a *mistake* –'

'Lizzie, I do feel love for you, but not like that. I'm bound to her, *bound*, it's – it's absolute.'

'But she's married.'

'She's going to leave her husband and come to me. He's a vile man and she hates him.'

'And she loves you?'

'Yes –'

'And is she really so ugly?'

'She's – Lizzie, she's beautiful. I wonder if you know what it's like when you have to *guard* somebody, to guard them in your heart against all damage and all darkness, and to sort of renew them as if you were God –'

'Even if it's all – not true – like in a dream?'

'There's a way in which it must be true, it can't be a dream, pure love *makes* it true.'

'I know – you pity her –'

'It's not pity – it's something much greater, much purer. Oh Lizzie – my heart could break with it –' I dropped my head onto my knees.

'Oh my dear –' Lizzie touched my hair, stroking it very gently, very tenderly, as one might touch a child or a small quiet pet.

'Lizzie darling, are you crying? Don't cry. I do love you. Let us two love each other whatever happens.'

'You want everything, don't you, Charles.'

'Yes, but not like that. Let's love in a free open way, like you said in your letter, free and separate and not holding on like crazy –'

'It was a stupid letter. I think holding on like crazy is the only thing I understand –'

'But with her, with Hartley – it's like something eternal that's always existed, something far greater than either of us. She will come to me, she has got to. She has always been with me and she is coming home to herself. I feel in such an odd way that my retiring, my coming here, was all a sort of giving up the world just for her. I gave her the meaning of my life long ago, I gave it to her and she still has it. Even if she doesn't know she has it, she has it.'

'Just like even if she's ugly she's beautiful and even if she doesn't love you she loves you –'

'But she does –'

'Charles, either this is very fine, very noble, or else you're mad.'

'Dear Lizzie – I feel so full of love tonight because of her.'

'You've got it to give away.'

'Yes. but not to anybody. When you feel full to the brim with your own life, committed, given, complete, it makes you feel so free too. I don't know what the future holds, Lizzie. I just know it's all to do with her. But that makes other love in a way all the more real if it exists at all, because it's pure, it's unselfish, it's for nothing. Will you love me for nothing, Lizzie, asking nothing, going, nowhere, just because we're us?'

'Either this is wisdom or you're cheating. You're certainly drunk.'

'Will you, Lizzie dear?'

'Yes.' She took my hands and began kissing them.

'Lizzie, Lizzie, where are you?' The voice of Gilbert.

It had become almost dark, though there was still a little light over the sea where the sunken sun was still illuminating the line of white clouds which shone like pale lamps over the waves which were racing landward. The tide was rising.

'Lizzie, come back, we want you to sing *Voi che sapete.*'

She was away from me in a moment, a long bare leg stretched. I could see Gilbert now, reaching his hand down to her from above. I stayed where I was.

What a weird uncanny simulacrum of happiness the evening was, like a masque put on by the spirit of melancholy. Would I be able not to go to that house, not to *know* what was happening, not to burst into their lives like a storm, like rain beating upon them, like thunder?

After a little while I came back towards Shruff End. It seemed to be unusually illuminated and looked like a doll's house. Gilbert must have bought several more lamps at my expense. Some light fell onto the lawn. As I drew near to it Lizzie was still singing solo. Her true truthful small voice wandered in the air patterning it high up, making utterly still the group of men surrounding her. Perry, who was very drunk, was standing with folded arms near the kitchen door. He checked occasional swaying movements. Gilbert, smiling sentimentally, was sitting cross-legged. Titus was kneeling, his lips apart, his face concentrated with emotion and pleasure, his eyes wide. At first I could not see James. Then I discerned him just below me reclining on the grass. A family party.

Voi che sapete had been over for some time and Lizzie was now singing *Roses in Picardy*. This was a song which Aunt Estelle used to sing, accompanying herself on the piano in the drawing room at Ramsdens. There came to me, with the peculiar pain of that memory, the idea that James might have asked Lizzie to sing it. Then I remembered that I had told Lizzie I liked it, but not why. Lizzie was singing it for me.

Roses in Picardy was a bit much. As I climbed down onto the lawn James, sensing me, sat up. I sat down near him but would not look at him, though he was now looking at me. After a moment he reached out and touched me, and I murmured 'Yes, yes.' The song ended.

After that, and until the terrible thing happened, the evening seemed quietly to break up, or to become diffused and gently chaotic like the later stages of a good party. Or perhaps it is all just confused in my memory. There was some light over the rocks, though I do not recall where it came from. Perhaps the clouds were still giving off light. A moon had made its appearance, randomly shaped and spotty, large and pale as a cloud itself. The fierce foam at the edge of the sea seemed luminous. I wandered looking for Lizzie, who had vanished. Everyone seemed to be walking about on the rocks, precariously holding glasses in their hands. An owl was hooting somewhere inland and the intermittent voices of my guests sounded equally distant, equally frail and hollow. I also wanted to find James, because I felt that perhaps I had been rude to him. I wanted to say something to him, I was not sure what, about

Aunt Estelle. She had shone somehow upon my childhood. *Che cosa è amor* indeed. I went to the cliff and watched the waves pounding it. There was a soft growling of thunder. I could see the glowing whitenesses of the wave-crests out to sea. Gilbert's babbling baritone started up not far off. *Stay dainty nymphs and speak, shall we play barley-break, tra la la?* Then later on, in another quarter, Titus also by himself could be heard rendering *Jock of Hazeldean*. There was something absurd and touching about the solipsistic self-absorption and self-satisfaction of these drunken singers. Then at last I heard Lizzie's voice distantly singing *Full Fathom Five*. I listened carefully but could get no sense of direction, so loud was the accompaniment of the restless rushing sea. Then I thought, how strangely her voice echoes. It seems almost amplified. She must be singing inside the tower.

I was still fairly near the house and I set off through what was now a somewhat darker scene. The luminous clouds had been quenched, the moon was smaller and a little brighter, not yet quite radiant, in a near-midsummer sky which still had inklings of light. I could hear Lizzie's voice singing, calling me, over and over again. *Ding dong ding dong bell, ding dong ding dong bell*. . . I stumbled along through the rocks, making the little detours which I now knew so well. I reached the bridge over Minn's cauldron and paused there, as I always did, to look down into the smooth pit where the waves of the incoming tide were lashing themselves in a foaming self-destructive fury. A light seemed to rise here in the spray out of the sea itself. I looked down and it was like looking into a deep dark green glass. And then – suddenly – somebody came up behind me and pushed me in.

As I am writing this story it will be evident that I survived, and I cannot hope to convey what the experience was like, how *long* it was, how terrible, how hopeless: a primal experience of a total loss of hope.

Falling, what the child fears, what the man dreads, is itself the image of death, of the defencelessness of the body, of its frailty and mortality, its absolute subjection to alien causes. Even in a harmless fall in the road there is a little moment of horror when the faller realizes that he *cannot help himself*; he has been taken over by a relentless mechanism and must continue with it to the end and be subject to the consequences. 'There is nothing more I can do.' How long, how infinitely expansible, a second is when it contains this thought, which is an effigy of death. A complete fall into the void, something which I had often imagined on aeroplanes, is of course the most terrible thing of all. Hands, feet, muscles, all the familiar protective mechanisms of the body are suddenly useless. The enmity of matter is unleashed against the frail breakable crushable animal form, always perhaps an alien in this hard mineral gravitational scene.

It was as if each part of the body experienced its separate despair. My back and waist felt the dreadful imprint of the hands which with great sudden violence and indubitable intent propelled me over the edge. My hands reached out in vain for something to clasp. My feet, still touching the rock with which they were parting company, jerked in a weak useless spasm, a last ghostly attempt to retain balance. Then they were jerking in empty space and I was falling head downward, as if my head and shoulders were made of lead. At the same time I felt, or thought as a kind of final thought, the fragility of my head and even knew that my hands were now trying to protect it. My trunk twisted sickeningly, trying in vain to make sense of its position. I actually saw, in the diffused midsummer darkness-light, the creamy curling waves just below me, and the particular spiral of their movement in the confined space. Then I was in the water whose intense cold surprised me with a separate shock, and I made the instinctive swimmer's movement of trying to right myself; but my body was aware that no swimming could take place in that vortex. I felt as if my neck were breaking as I looked up to see a dome of dark faintly translucent green, the wave above me. I was choking and swallowing water, absorbed in the one task of getting another breath. At the same time I was able to think: this is the end. I fought, my whole body fought, now flailing senselessly in a maelstrom of powers which seemed about to dismember me. Then my head struck violently against the smooth rock and I lost consciousness.

I was lying on my back on the rocks. I opened my eyes and saw a star. I had been having an odd familiar dream, and yet I had never had that dream before. I dreamt that cousin James was kissing me on the mouth. I was aware of the star and of a marvel: that I was breathing. I apprehended my breath as a great thing, a sort of cosmic movement, natural and yet miraculous. Slowly, gently, deeply, decisively, I was breathing. Somewhere beneath me there was a dull steady uproar, and I lay in the cup of it and looked at the star. I felt pain and yet I felt at ease, detached from it. I lay relaxed as if I had woken from some golden sleep and would now perhaps sleep again. I closed my eyes. I breathed.

Mingled with the noise, then separated from it, I heard other sounds, discerned voices, and I knew where I was. I was lying on the flat piece of rock that led to the bridge. I was also aware, but in an entirely detached way, of what had happened to me. I heard someone groan, perhaps Perry, someone sob, perhaps Titus or Lizzie. James's voice said, 'Keep back, don't crowd.' Another voice said, 'I think he's breathing.' I thought, I suppose I ought to tell them I'm all right. Am I all right? I composed a sentence which I thought I might utter soon: I am perfectly all right, what is this fuss about? I felt curiously unwilling to speak, it seemed so difficult. I realized that my mouth was open. I made an effort of will and closed my mouth, then opened it again and began 'I'm –', and could go no further. Some sort of sound had emerged.

I made a convulsive movement, an embryonic attempt to rise. I went on breathing.

Someone said, 'Thank God.'

The voices went on talking.

'I think we could move him now.'

'But suppose some bones are broken?'

'We must keep him warm, he can't stay here.'

This argument went on for some time. Then they argued about whether they could improvise a stretcher and which was the best way to go. At last they carried me, or hauled me, with what seemed extreme roughness, in a blanket. The journey over the rocks was a nightmare. I tried to say I could walk but (as I gathered later) produced only unintelligible moaning. All my pains had now located themselves. My head was very painful and the movement made lights flash in my eyes. There was a terrible pain like toothache in my arm. I wondered if my arm was broken and the bone was beginning to break through the skin. There was a plate of anguish in my back. My bearers were fantastically inefficient and confused, constantly quarrelling about the route, and slipping and banging me against the rocks.

At last they got me into the kitchen and, with indescribable clumsiness, pulled all my clothes off and pummelled me with towels and pulled other clothes on and had arguments about whether I should be given soup, brandy, aspirins. When they had the bright idea of lighting a fire they could not find any dry wood, then could not find the matches. At last I was lying on cushions on the floor in front of the fire in the little red room. As I became warm I felt less pain, and when I was lying undisturbed I relaxed and began to feel sleepy. I felt relief and something of the strange ease which I had felt as I looked up at the star. And only then, just before I slept, did I remember that it was not an accident. Somebody pushed me.

*

I must here record something which I only remembered later and
which I was then half disposed to think was a dream. I was lying on
the floor, underneath a pile of blankets, alone, seeing the room by
the flickering light of the fire. I had the urgent feeling that there was
something I must do quickly before someone came back, and especially
before I should *forget* some fact of the utmost importance which was
about to vanish from my mind. I had to record this important thing,
to catch it and hold it before it disappeared. I got up on my knees and
reached a pen and paper from the table where I sometimes worked,
and I wrote down what it was that I absolutely had to remember.
What I wrote covered perhaps half a page or less. I wrote quickly but
even then was not sure that I had remembered everything. I carefully
folded up the paper and *hid it* somewhere in the room. All this, that I
had written something and hidden it, I recalled rather dreamily upon
the following morning. But – I could not remember what the thing
was which I had thought so important or what I had written about
it, and I could not, though I searched the room minutely, find the
writing. An atmosphere of extreme and crucial emotion surrounded
'the thing'; but although I constantly peered at it in my mind I could
not discern what it was. And of the paper there was no trace. Possibly
I had dreamt the whole episode. I had, of course, little doubt what
the writing, if it existed, must concern: it concerned the identity of
my would-be assassin.

'But how on earth did I get out?' I asked Lizzie. I was sitting up in an
armchair in the little red room drinking tea and eating anchovy toast.

A rather exasperated doctor had arrived about two o'clock in the
morning and woken me up and pulled me about and pronounced me

sound. He said I had no broken bones and was suffering concussion and shock. I was to rest, keep warm and in future not wander about the rocks at night when I had had too much to drink. This was the first point at which it entered my confused mind that of course no one, except the assassin and me, knew that it was not an accident.

It was now about ten o'clock in the morning. It was very hot again with sounds of thunder, louder, nearer. The lightning flashes came like scarcely visible shocks. I had been visited, asked how I was, congratulated on my narrow escape. There was a slightly brusque air about these felicitations, perhaps because my friends felt they had been quite emotional enough about me last night and now felt more curt, or because they shared the doctor's view of the matter. There was in fact a slight feeling that I had caused a lot of trouble by my stupidity. An instinct which I had not yet had time to examine advised me not, or not yet, to reveal that my fall was not accidental.

In a little while I would have to decide what to do. I was sorry I could not find my precious piece of paper. But of course I had no doubt about the identity of the murderer.

'James thinks a freak wave lifted you up,' said Lizzie.

Lizzie was looking radiant, her long frizzy hair tangled and bushy, growing like a healthy plant. She was wearing a striped shirt and lineny pants roughly cut off at the knee. Even after slimming she was a little too plump for this gear, but I did not object. Her skin shone with health. Only the tiny tight wrinkles round her eyes would have enabled one to guess her age. She shared none of the vague annoyance of the male contingent at my exploit. She was prepared to enjoy the drama in retrospect, since it had had a happy ending, and my survival had in some way increased her sense of owning me.

'It can't have done,' I said, 'the hole is too deep. Who actually pulled me out?'

'Oh everybody did. When we heard you shout we all converged, only I got there last. By then Titus and James were pulling you off the bridge towards that flat rock, and Gilbert and Peregrine were helping.'

'I can imagine how helpful they were. Funny, I can't remember shouting.'

'The doctor said you might not remember things which happened just before and just after the accident. It's an effect of concussion. The brain doesn't process it or something.'

'Will the memory come back?'

'I don't know, he didn't say.'

'I remember being carried back to the house. I think I got as many bruises then as in the water. God, I'm bruised!'

'Yes, that was awful, you were like a great dark dripping sack, so *heavy*, and we nearly dropped you down a crevasse. But that was much later.'

'How, later?'

'You don't remember James giving you the kiss of life?'

'Ah – well – sort of –'

'You see, we thought you were drowned. He had to go on for about twenty minutes before you began to breathe properly. It was *terrible* –'

'Poor Lizzie. Anyway, here I still am, ready to make more trouble for all concerned. Where did you all sleep last night? This place is getting like the Raven Hotel.'

'I slept on the sofa in the middle room here, James has got your bed, Perry is in the bookroom and Gilbert is in the dining room and Titus slept outside. There's just enough cushions and things to go round!'

'Fancy old James bagging my bed.'

'They felt they couldn't get you up the stairs, and anyway the fire could be lit here –'

'James hasn't been to see me yet.'

'I think he's still asleep, he was rather knocked out.'

'Well, I'm sorry my misadventure spoilt the party. I can remember you singing *Voi che sapete*.'

'I hoped you'd be able to hear it. Oh Charles —'

'Now, Lizzie, don't please —'

'Will you marry me?'

'Lizzie, do stop —'

'I can cook and drive a car and I love you and I'm very good-tempered and not a bit neurotic and if you want a nurse I'll be a nurse —'

'That was a joke.'

'You did care about me when you wrote —'

'I was dreaming. I told you, I love somebody else.'

'Isn't *that* the dream?'

'No.'

'She's gone.'

'Yes — but now — Lizzie — I've just been given a strange marvellous sign — and the way is suddenly — open.'

'Look, it's beginning to rain.'

'Let us just love each other in a free way like I was saying yesterday.'

'If you go to her, you will never want to see me again.'

It suddenly came home to me that this was true. If I came to possess Hartley I would take her *right away*. I would hide her, I would hide with her.

We would not go away together, not to Paris or Rome or New York, these were unreal visions. I could not introduce Hartley to Sidney Ashe or Fritzie Eitel or smart Jeanne who now styled herself a princess. I could not even take her out to dinner with Lizzie or Peregrine or Gilbert. She was in this splendid sense *insortable*. Hartley and I would live alone, secretly, incognito, somewhere in England, in the country, in a little house by the sea. And she would sew and go shopping and I would do the garden and paint the hall and have all the things which I had missed in my life. And we would gently cherish each other and there would be a vast plain goodness and a sort of space and quiet, unspoilt and uncorrupted. And I would join the ordinary people and be an ordinary person, and *rest*, my God how much I wanted to rest; and this would connect my end with my beginning in a way that was destined and proper. This, just this, was what all my instincts were seeking when I amazed everybody by giving up my work and coming here, *here*. Hartley and I would be alone together and see almost nobody and our faithfulness to each other would be remade and the old early innocent world would quietly reassemble itself round about us.

Lizzie, to whom I uttered none of the above, went away at last. I could see that she was sustained by hope; whatever I said she could not altogether believe in Hartley. The others looked in, at least Peregrine, Gilbert and Titus did. No one now talked of departure. It looked as if the holiday was to continue. What other joys would it provide? I asked for James but Gilbert told me that James was still resting upstairs, in my bed, suffering from total exhaustion. He had perhaps got a chill out on the rocks, leaning over my dripping and apparently lifeless body.

The rain came down, straight and silvery, like a punishment of steel rods. It clattered onto the house and onto the rocks and pitted the sea. The thunder made some sounds like grand pianos falling downstairs, then settled to a softer continuous rumble, which was almost drowned by the sound of the rain. The flashes of lightning joined into long illuminations which made the grass a lurid green, the rocks a blazing ochre yellow, as yellow as Gilbert's car. Tension and excitement and a kind of fear filled the house, the aftermath of my mishap now somehow being enacted by the elements. I rose from my armchair and said I would go to see James, but was told he was sleeping. Gilbert reported that the rain was coming down the stairs into the bathroom. I got as far as the kitchen and then felt giddy. My body was horribly bruised and deeply deeply cold, and I returned to the fire. As it appeared to be lunch time I ate some soup and then said I wanted to be alone and to rest. I sat in my armchair covered in blankets and began to think. The rain made so much noise that I could not hear the sea.

My assailant was of course Ben, there could be no possible doubt of that. His last words to me had been 'I'll kill you.' What made me the more certain was that I had myself drawn Ben's attention to this particular spot as an excellent place for a murder. I had myself felt the impulse to push him in and he had certainly perceived my thought. There was even a certain element of nemesis involved. And that he should act *now* was a psychological probability. He had put up with a humiliating assault which, when he reflected upon it afterwards, his pride could not tolerate or endure. Was the act premeditated? Had he waited, hidden beside the bridge? Or had he come snooping to indulge his private hate, and then seen this irresistible opportunity? Whichever it was, he must have felt certain of doing the job properly. My survival was a truly amazing fluke, and, for him, a sickening portent.

But what next? What do you do in a civilized society when someone tries to kill you? I could not involve the law, and not only because there was no proof. I could not accuse Hartley's husband in a law court or let the law's vulgarities touch this situation. Neither would I consider going round with my friends and doing Ben a mischief. I wanted somehow to confront him, but the confrontation by itself would be merely a luxury, much as I should enjoy effacing the servile impression which I had made in my last interview with Ben. I must do something with what I knew, and with what I now *was*: a survivor with a moral fury and a motive. That was what I had meant when I had spoken to Lizzie of a strange marvellous sign. The gods who preserved me had opened a door and intended me to go through it.

The problem was the same, only the light was different. I must get Hartley away, get her *to myself,* and awaken her, make her quiver and twitch with a sense of possible freedom. Yes, aloneness was the key, I understood that now. I must be alone with her soon, and then thereafter, forever. When she had been my prisoner how humiliated she must have been by the presence of other people in the house. *There must be no more witnesses.* I would tell her that. She did not have to join my grand intimidating alien world. To wed his beggar maid the king would, and how gladly, become a beggar too. The vision of that healing humility would henceforth be my guide. This was indeed the very condition of her freedom, why had I not seen this before? I would at last see her face changing. It was, I found, a part of my thought of the future that when she was with me Hartley would actually regain much of her old beauty: like a prisoner released from a labour camp who at first looks old, but then with freedom and rest and good food soon becomes young again. The pain and anxiety would leave her face and she would be calm and beautiful; and I saw that rejuvenated face shining like a lamp out of the future. When I had left the theatre I had desired a solitude: now it was set before me in the very form of my Beatrice. Only here was happiness for me an innocent and permissible goal, even an ideal. Everywhere else where I had pursued it it had proved either a will-o'-the-wisp or a form of corruption. To find one's true mate is to find the one person with whom happiness is purely innocent.

The immediate question however was a technical one. How to get her away? A long wait was now out of the question, since I must use my new power over Ben while it was still fresh. What I was beginning to envisage this time was not a kidnap but a bombardment. First of all

I would write Hartley a letter. Then I would call with Titus. Why would Ben let us in? Because he would be guilty and frightened. He would want to see what we were up to. How was he to know that there was no proof? How was he to know there had been no *witness*? On this I paused. Well, why should there not have been a witness? I could tell him there had been a witness! I could even ask somebody (Gilbert? Perry?) to say that he had seen what happened. After all, anyone might have done, and very nearly did! That would scare him completely. Why should I not *blackmail* Ben into letting Hartley go? If I could only make him say: go then. How near was he in any case to saying this? Did his long silence after the kidnap perhaps mean that he was in two minds about wanting her back? If he could only consent, the chains would fall and my angel would step out free. Or if she could see him revealed as a murderer, that might bring her the blessing of a total revulsion: horror, disgust, fear, in a more effectively violent form. If only there was some genuine *clue*. What on earth had I written on that piece of paper which I had so cleverly hidden from myself?

Yes, it was vital to act soon, before Ben should have time to recover. He must be in a state of considerable shock; although unfortunately he would by now know, from the silence of his radio and television sets, that he had failed to kill famous Charles Arrowby. However, and this was now plain, I could not proceed farther than my letter to Hartley while Lizzie and James were in the house. It would be unfair to Lizzie to expect her to witness or even assist the rescue of her rival. And James: well, James made moral judgments and confused me. So I would have to get rid of those two. Gilbert and Peregrine might be useful for a little while longer. And of course Titus ...

At this point I began to reflect and to wonder if I had not, in relation to Hartley, seriously misconceived Titus's role. Would Titus fit into the paradise *à deux* which I had lately been envisaging? No. That need not matter of course. People often had to separate conjugal and filial relationships. I would have a quite separate connection with Titus; and indeed he had already indicated that that was what he wanted. But still I had assumed that Hartley would *want* Titus in the picture somehow. Was this a wrong assumption? And at about that moment the young man himself came through the door.

I had not had a peaceful serious talk with Titus for some time, and I blamed myself. Quite apart from my concern with Hartley, I was absolutely committed to the boy, he was literally a 'godsend'. It remained to be seen how far I could, with him, make sense of the role of 'father'. I had by now been made aware that Gilbert, and even Peregrine, saw my relation with Titus in quite another light!

During my reflections the rain had stopped and between lumpy dark grey leaden clouds the sun was managing to shine upon an extremely wet world. The lawn was waterlogged, the rocks contrived to look like sponges. Upstairs I could hear Gilbert and Lizzie shouting to each other, the former up in the attics inspecting the roof, the latter in the bathroom mopping up the flood. When Titus appeared I decided to go outside to avoid interruption and ensure privacy. I was a bit stronger and the giddiness had not returned. But as he helped me slowly over the rocks I felt like an old person; and when we reached Minn's bridge I could hardly bring myself to cross it. *How* had I survived that deep pit, those smooth walls, that ferocious water?

The rocks were beginning to steam in the sun. It was as if there were hot springs everywhere. We sat down on towels which sensible Titus had brought from the kitchen, on a rock overlooking Raven Bay, not far from where I had sat with James. The sea, although it looked calm because it was so exceedingly glossy and smooth after the rain, was in a quietly dangerously violent mood, coming in in large sleek humpbacked waves which showed no trace of foam until they met the rocks in a creamy swirl. The sun continued to shine although a grey sheet of rain now obscured the horizon. A rainbow joined the land and the sea. Raven Bay was a bottle-green colour which I had never seen it wear before. I wondered for a moment where Rosina was.

We had made our climb in silence and a kind of silence held us still. I kept looking at him and he kept gazing at the bay. His handsome face had an expression of discontent, the sulky shapeless look of youth was upon his mouth. The harelip scar was deepening, seeming to pulsate, opening and closing a little with some perhaps unconscious lifelong habitual movement. His hair was extremely tangled and untidy.

'Titus.'

'Yes.'

'Can you call me "Charles"? Could you get used to it? I feel it would help us both.'

'OK, Charles.'

'Titus – I – You are very important to me and I need you –'

Titus worked at his scar, then put a finger on it to stop its little quivering. It only then occurred to me that Titus might have been reflecting on those ambiguities in our relationship which struck Gilbert so much, might indeed have been put in mind of them by some crude jest of Gilbert's. I had not thought of this fairly obvious idea before partly because I had been distracted from Titus, partly because I had somehow spread over him a canopy of innocence which derived from the suffering Hartley.

'Don't misunderstand me,' I added.

Titus's moist discontented mouth twitched in a smile or sneer.

I went on, 'I want to tell you something.' I had suddenly decided that I must tell Titus about Ben's attempt to kill me.

'If it's about Mary –'

'Yes —' I had not talked to Titus since the awful scene at Nibletts when the 'delegation' brought the erring wife back to the hateful husband.

'All that makes me sick. I'm sorry, forgive me. But I just don't want to be involved. I left home so as not to be *bothered* with muddles like that, I *hate* muddles, and I've had them all my life with those two, muddle, muddle, muddle. They're not bad people really, they've just got no sense of how to live a human life.'

'*She's* not a bad person, I agree —'

'I can't tell you how sick I felt when we went over to their place in the car, I wish to God I hadn't come and seen it all, now I'll never forget it. I felt so humiliated. Mary was being treated like a bit of property or a child. You mustn't interfere in other people's lives, especially married people. That's in a way why marriage is so *awful,* I can't think how anyone dares to do it. You've got to leave them alone. They've got their own way of hating each other and hurting each other, they enjoy it.'

'If it's so awful one *ought* to interfere. You mustn't be so cynical and pessimistic'

'I'm *not* cynical and pessimistic, that's the *point,* I don't *care,* you think I think about it, I don't, I don't want to *see,* I don't want to *know,* I don't care a fuck about their bloody misery!'

'Well, I do, and I'm going to get your mother out of it, I'm going to get her right *out.*'

'You tried, and she just squealed to go home. I'd have let her walk. Sorry, I don't mean that. You made a *mistake,* that's all, now forget it. Honestly, I can't understand why you should want her, I mean I can't see it, is it sentimental or Salvation Army or something — you can't want someone like that, I don't see it, I don't get the point. There's that woman Lizzie Scherer who seems to like you a lot, and Rosina Vamburgh —'

'I happen to love your mother.'

'Oh – love – you mean –'

'You may be too young to understand.'

'I suppose it's natural for me to be interested in girls in a normal way. When you're old I daresay it may be different.'

I was stiff and bruised. It had been foolish to come so far. I was feeling tired, weak and exasperated. Titus's sheer youth, his unspoilt youthful hopeful strength annoyed me to the point of screaming. His long bare brown legs, covered with reddish hairs, emerging from his roughly rolled-up trousers annoyed me. I felt I was losing touch with him, might be sharp with him and then be reduced to making an appeal.

'I'm sorry it all upsets you so. I partly understand. But I do want your help, well, your support. And I want to tell you something rather important about your father.'

'About Ben. Not my father. God knows who my father is. I'll never know. Look, don't let's talk about Ben, he bores me. I'm not happy about this thing –'

'What thing are we onto now?'

'This thing between you and me. Let's forget about them. Let's talk about you and me.'

'OK. I want to talk about that too. Titus, I'm not trying to kidnap *you*.'

'Yes, I know –'

'We're free, we two, in relation to each other. There's no need to define things.'

' "Father" is a definition, I should think!'

'It's an idea. Let's just be friends if you prefer it. Let's wait and see. You know there's nothing sort of – sinister – here – you know what I mean –'

'Oh I know *that*!'

'I just want to feel that there's a bond, a special relationship, a special connection.'

'I don't see why,' said Titus. 'Sorry, I'm being ungrateful – and I've been here and eaten your food and drunk your drink I *know* – but I've been thinking – after all, why should you bother about me? If you'd been my real father, great, though even then – well, anyway what I wanted to say was this. I've enjoyed meeting you, I've enjoyed being here, in spite of the horrors. Later on I'll maybe think: that was a good time, yes, good. But I want to earn my own living and lead my own life and I want to do it in the theatre. I'm not a silly stage-struck kid, I don't imagine I'll be a star, I don't even know yet if I'll be any good at acting, but I want to work with theatre people, I guess that's my scene. This place is fine for a holiday, but I want to get back to London where the real things happen.'

'Don't real things happen here?'

'Oh – you know what I mean. Where does your cousin live?'

'In London.' Again the bite of the serpent of jealousy. Had James got Titus on a lead? There had seemed to be a bond between them from the start. I said quickly, 'Please don't talk to any of the others about, you know –'

'Of course not, not a word, you don't have to say that, for Christ's sake!'

'Good –'

'The thing is, I don't want you to feel any special obligation to me. If you have obligations I'll have to have obligations. I don't want to live here at your expense any longer, I want to get cracking. I don't mind your helping me a bit if you like. Maybe you could help me get into an acting school. If I could get a place in a school I could get a grant and I'd be independent. Maybe it's a bit of a fiddle to ask you to get me in, but I don't mind fiddling that much. Then I can be on my own and we can be friends or whatever you want, but I've got to be on my own, see?'

How weak and helpless I felt before that brutal innocent free power. He would wriggle away before I had even learnt how to love him or learnt the trick of holding him.

'Yes, I'll help you into an acting school, but we'll have to think about it. I'll come with you to London later on. Meanwhile maybe you can help me here. But I want to tell you something about Ben, something that you ought to know. You say he's not a bad person, but he is. He's a wicked violent man. He tried to kill me.' I wanted to impress Titus and to shake his appalling detachment.

'To kill you? How?'

'He pushed me in. I didn't fall accidentally into that sea hole. He pushed me.'

Titus showed little emotion. He leaned forward scratching an insect bite on his ankle. 'Did you see him?'

'No, but I felt him!'

'How do you know it was him?'

'Who else could it have been? He said he'd kill me the last time we met!'

'I can't imagine him doing that, it's not in character, it's most unlikely,' said Titus in a maddeningly bovine manner.

'I was pushed! Someone pushed me in the back!'

'Are you sure? You could have fallen backward on a rock and then slipped into the water and it would feel like being pushed. You'd had some drinks, you know. And the doctor said you might be a bit confused about the whole business afterwards.'

I felt too tired and wretched to go on. It was foolish to have walked so far. 'All right, Titus, let's leave it there. Don't repeat what I've said to anyone.'

Titus looked at me out of his narrowed stone-coloured eyes. 'You see it's not so much fun as you expected, playing at fathers and sons.' This was the kindest thing he had said.

I said, 'I'll help you about acting school. We'll talk of that later. Now bugger off, will you.'

He got up. 'I must help you back.'

'I can manage.'

'You can't. Besides it's beginning to rain.'

He held out his hand. I took it and he pulled me up, and then still held me. He said, 'We'll get to know each other one day. There's time.'

'There's time.'

Hartley, dearest, listen to me. I want to say several things. First, that I am sorry I took you away like that and kept you with me. It was an act of love, but I now see that it was foolish. I frightened you and confused you. Forgive me. It was at least a demonstration that I care absolutely and am in earnest about taking you away. You belong to me and I am not going to give you up. So you will be seeing me again soon!

I expect you have been thinking things over since you got back and may now see them a little bit more from my point of view. After all, my darling, why stay in the land of unhappiness? It isn't as if I were a stranger offering you someone and something you know nothing of. You said yourself I was your only friend! And you seemed, when you were here, almost ready to say 'yes' – only you were frightened of *him*. Fear is a habit after all. But do you not feel in your heart now that you are changing? One day soon you'll be able to do what you've wanted to do for years – walk out of the door!

And listen – I want to tell you this. I don't want to take you into some grand glamorous world full of actors and famous people. I don't live in that sort of world anyway. You said you liked a quiet life. Well, so do I. That's why I came here, after all! We'll go away, just the two of us, and live simply in a little house in a little place, in England in the country, near the sea if you like, and we'll make each other happy in simple ways. That's the life I've always wanted and now I'm free of the theatre I can have it at last, with you. We'll live quietly, Hartley, and enjoy simple things. Can you not *want* that sufficiently to walk out of a house where you are bullied and unloved? And of course we shall help Titus and he will come to us in freedom and all those old scars will heal. We shall care for him. But what will always matter most is you and me.

Now I want to tell you something else, something rather terrible. Two nights ago Ben tried to kill me. He pushed me off the rocks in the dark into a frightful tide race. God knows how I managed to survive it. I've got concussion and am generally knocked about. I've been seeing the doctor. (But don't worry, I am all right.) Attempted murder is not the sort of thing which one can quietly ignore and carry on as if nothing had happened. I have not yet been to the police. Whether I go to them or not depends on Ben. I should add, a very material point, that there was a witness of what happened.

However I am not concerned about revenge. I want simply to take you away. Apart from anything else, you surely cannot want to stay with a man who has proved himself capable of murder. Just stop wanting to suffer, will you? And please start sorting out your things, deciding what clothes to take with you, and so on. I'm not going to hurry you. But now I am going to be *around the place*, I'm going to be a regular intruder, I shall tramp in and out! If Ben objects he can either consent to your departure or force me to go to the police. This isn't blackmail, it's a fair field at last!

No need to tell Ben about this, unless you want to. I'll be along pretty soon on the heels of this letter and I'll tell him myself! As my death hasn't been announced he will know by

now that he is not a murderer. Relax, darling, and don't worry,
and now leave it all to me. Sort out those clothes. I love you.
We'll be together, dear one.

    C.

I had considered writing directly to Ben, but it seemed better to
prepare Hartley first. The difficulty was, once more, how to get it
to her. I did not want to risk spoiling my entrance by delivering it
myself. I did not like to ask Titus to go, and Gilbert, whom I sounded,
said he was afraid. And I did not want James or Lizzie, or Peregrine
for that matter, to know anything about it. I thought of sending it
by post in a typed envelope, but of course he opened all her letters.
Perhaps it did not matter too much if he opened this one. The game
was nearing its end.

It was the following day and I had written my letter in the morning,
but was still undecided about what to do with it. It remained now
to get rid of James and Lizzie. I could simply ask James to go. Lizzie
might have to be told some lie.

James was, rather surprisingly, still in bed. He had slept, on and
off, for many hours. Whereas I, who had had the real ordeal, was now
feeling better. I went up to see him.

'James, you slug. Are you all right? Touch of the old malaria?'

James was lying back in my bed, propped up in a cunningly arranged
nest of pillows, his arms stretched out straight over the blankets. He
had not been reading. He looked alert, as if he had been thinking.
Yet his body looked floppy with relaxation. He had some growth of
beard which changed his face, making him look Spanish, an ecclesi-
astic, perhaps an ascetic warrior. Then he smiled cheerfully, and I
remembered how much that inane smile used to irritate me, how it

had seemed to betoken a facile superiority. There was quietness in the room and the sound of the sea was dulled.

'I'm all right. Must have caught a chill. I'll get up soon. How are you feeling?'

'Fine. Can I get you anything?'

'No, thanks, I don't want to eat. Lizzie brought me some tea.'

I frowned.

'Where's Titus?' said James.

'I've no idea.'

'Keep an eye on him.'

'He can look after himself.'

There was silence for a moment. 'Sit down,' said James, 'don't look as if you're going.'

I sat down. James's relaxation seemed to have affected me. I stretched out my legs and felt as if I might sleep myself, even though I was sitting in an upright chair. I felt my shoulders and arms become soft and heavy. Of course I was very exhausted.

'You're not still wanting Titus to go back to Ben, are you?' I said.

'Did I say that?'

'You implied it.'

'He does in a way belong with them.'

'With *them*? Soon, very soon, there would be no more "them".'

James, following this, said, 'Are you still dreaming of that rescue?'

'Yes.'

There was another silence as if we were both going to sleep. Then James went on, 'After all, he is in a real and deep sense their child. My impression was that that relationship was not beyond salvage.'

I was irritated by his 'impression'. What could it be based on? The horrible answer occurred to me: conversations with Titus. I had come up to see James in order to hasten his departure, and I had decided not to say anything to him about Ben's crime. This revelation would be too interesting. But now I felt tempted to shake his complacency. While I reflected on this I said, 'I am going to adopt Titus.'

'Adopt him, legally, can you?'

'Yes.' In fact I did not know. 'I am going to make his career. And I shall leave him my money.'

'It's not so easy.'

'What isn't?'

'To establish relationships, you can't just elect people, it can't be done by thinking and willing.'

I was tempted to reply, I daresay *you* don't find it easy! Then I recalled Titus's voice saying 'Where does your cousin live?' And I remembered what Toby Ellesmere had told me about the Sherpa whom James was fond of who died on the mountain, and I felt a momentary nervous urge to ask him about this 'attachment'. But it would have been a dangerous impertinence. I was never unaware that James retained the power to hurt me very much. How odd it was that even now my fear was an ingredient of our converse! *Cousinage, dangereux voisinage.* I felt annoyance with him all the same, he was making me feel awkward and incompetent, and I wanted to stir up his sleepy calm. I could not decide whether or not to tell him about Ben. If I told him would that delay his departure? Yet I very much wanted to tell him. It is indeed awe-inspiring to think that every tiny action has its consequences, and can mark a parting of ways which lead to vastly separate destinations.

James said, pursuing the topic, 'Most real relationships are involuntary.'

'As in a family, what you were saying about Titus?'

'Yes. Or sometimes they just seem destined. A Buddhist would say you had met in a previous life.'

'Would you say you were a superstitious man? And don't say it depends what you mean by superstition.'

'In that case I can't answer you.'

'Do you believe in reincarnation? Do you think that if one hasn't done well one will be reborn as a – as a – hamster – or a – woodlouse?'

'These are images. The truth lies beyond.'

'It seems to me a creepy doctrine.'

'Other people's religions often seem creepy. Think how creepy Christianity must seem to an outsider.'

'It seems so to me,' I said, though I had never thought this before. 'Do Buddhists believe in life after death?'

'It depends –'

'Oh all right!'

'Some Tibetans,' said James, 'believe –' He corrected himself. He now always spoke of that country in the past tense as a vanished civilization. 'Believed that the souls of the dead, while waiting to be reborn, wander in a sort of limbo, not unlike the Homeric Hades. They called it *bardo*. It can be rather unpleasant. You meet all kinds of demons there.'

'So it's a place of punishment?'

'Yes, but a just automatic sort of punishment. The learned ones regard these figures as subjective visions, which depend on the sort of life the dead man has led.'

' "For in that sleep of death what dreams may come" ...'

'Yes.'

'But what about God, or the gods? Can't a soul go to them?'

'The gods? The gods themselves are dreams. They too are merely subjective visions.'

'Well, at least one might hope for some happy illusions hereafter!'

'Just possibly,' said James, with a judicious air, as if he were discussing the likelihood of catching a train. 'But very few people ... are without ... attendant demons ...'

'And does everybody go to *bardo*?'

'I don't know. They say that you have a chance at the moment of death.'

'A chance?'

'To become free. At the moment of death you are given a total vision of all reality which comes to you in a flash. To most of us this would be – well – just a violent flash, like an atom bomb, something terrifying and dazzling and incomprehensible. But if you can comprehend and grasp it then you are free.'

'So it's useful to know you're going. You mean free to –?'

'Just free – Nirvana – out of the Wheel.'

'The wheel of reincarnation?'

'The Wheel, yes, of attachments, cravings, desires, what chains us to an unreal world.'

'Attachments? You mean – even love?'

'What we call love.'

'And do we then exist somewhere else?'

'These are images,' said James. 'Some say Nirvana is and can only be here and now. Images to explain images, pictures to explain pictures.'

'The truth lies beyond!'

We were silent then for a little time. James's eyelids dropped but I could still see the glint of his eyes. I asked jocosely, 'Are you meditating?'

'No. If I were really meditating I would be invisible. We notice each other because we are centres of restless mental activity. A meditating sage is not seen.'

'Yes, distinctly creepy!' I could not make out whether James was serious. I presumed he was not. The conversation was making me feel thoroughly uncomfortable. I said, 'When do you plan to leave? Tomorrow, I imagine? Apart from anything else I want my bed back!'

James said, 'Yes, I'm sorry, you can have the bed tonight. I'll push off tomorrow. I've got a lot of things to do in London. I have to prepare for a journey.'

So my guess had been right! James had not really left the Army, he was going secretly back to Tibet! I wanted to indicate tactfully to him that I knew. 'Oh, a journey, of course! I think I can imagine – however, I ask no questions – !'

James was silent, now looking at me out of his dark unshaven face and his dark eyes. I glanced quickly at him and looked away. I decided to tell him about Ben. 'You know – James – about my falling into that hole –'

'Minn's cauldron. Yes.'

'I didn't fall accidentally, I was pushed.'

James considered. 'Who pushed you?'

'Ben.'

'You saw him?'

'No, but somebody pushed me and it must have been him.'

James looked at me thoughtfully. Then he said, not at once, 'Are you certain? Are you sure (a) that you were pushed and (b) that it was Ben?'

I was not going to be (a)d and (b)d by James. Nothing seemed to touch him, not even attempted murder. 'I just thought I'd tell you. OK, forget it. So you're going tomorrow, that's fine.'

At that moment I heard a sound which I shall never forget. I sometimes hear it still in daylight hallucinations. It tore into my consciousness with its own immediate evidence of some frightful event, and the room was filled with fear as with fog. It was Lizzie's voice. She shrieked somewhere out in front of the house. Then she shrieked again.

James and I stared at each other. James said, 'Oh no –' I rushed out, got entangled in the bead curtain and began to tumble down the stairs. I ran panting across the hall and then at the front doorway nearly fell as if a dense cloud of weariness and despair had met me and all but made me faint. I could hear James running down the stairs behind me.

Something extraordinary seemed to be happening on the road. The first person I saw was Peregrine, who was standing beside Gilbert's car and looking along the road in the direction of the tower. Then I saw Lizzie, leaning on Gilbert's arm, walking slowly back towards the house. Up near the tower there was a car and a group of people standing looking down at something on the ground. I thought, there's been a road accident.

Peregrine turned and I shouted at him, 'What's happened?'

Instead of replying he came forward and tried to grasp my arm and detain me, but I shook him off.

James was now at my heels. He was wearing my silk dressing gown, the one that Hartley had worn. He too said to Perry, 'What's happened?'

I paused. Peregrine said, to James, not to me, 'It's Titus.'

James went up to the yellow Volkswagen and leaned against it. He mumbled something like, 'I should have held on –' Then he sat down on the ground.

Peregrine was saying something to me but I ran on towards the corner, passing Lizzie who was now sitting on a rock, with Gilbert kneeling beside her.

I reached the group of people. They were strangers, and they were looking down at Titus who was lying on the grass verge. But he had not been hit by a car. He was drowned.

I cannot bear to describe what happened next in detail. Titus was already dead, there can be no doubt of that, although I did not want to believe it at once. He looked so whole, so beautiful, lying there limp and naked and dripping, his hair dark with water, someone had drawn it away from his face, and his eyes were almost closed. He was lying on his side showing the tender fold of his stomach and the bedraggled wet hair of his front. His mouth was slightly open showing his teeth and I remember noticing the harelip. Then I saw a dark mark on the side of his forehead, as if he had been struck.

I ran back towards the house shouting for James. James was still sitting on the ground beside the car. He got up slowly. 'James, James, come, come!' James had revived me. Surely he could revive Titus.

James looked dazed and ghostly. Peregrine had to assist him to walk. 'Oh quick, quick, help him!'

By the time James reached the corner one of the strangers, they were tourists, was already attempting to do something. He had turned Titus over onto his front and was rather ineffectively pressing his shoulders.

Peregrine said, as if speaking for James, 'Kiss of life is better.'

James knelt down, he seemed unable to speak, and motioned that Titus should be turned over again. There was a moment of confusion, several people talking at once, then the sound of a police siren. It turned out later that a car on the way to the Raven Hotel had taken the news on and the hotel had rung the police.

A brisk efficient policeman took charge, told us to stand back, began himself to attempt mouth to mouth respiration. An ambulance arrived.

James went away and sat down on the grass. A policeman began to ask Peregrine and me if we knew who Titus was. Peregrine answered his questions.

It appeared that the tourists, going to bathe from the rocks in Raven Bay, had seen Titus's body being carried by the tide round the corner from the tower, and they had swum out and pulled it ashore.

There was nothing anyone could do. Men put Titus on a stretcher and slid him into the ambulance. Several cars had stopped. The police car went away, to go to Nibletts to inform the parents. The verdict of the inquest was death by misadventure. Titus died from drowning after a blow on the head. It was assumed that a wave had dashed him against a rock. What exactly had happened was never clarified.

However by then it had become dazzlingly clear to me that Titus had been murdered. We had to do with a homicidal madman. The hand that had failed to strike me down had succeeded in striking him. But I spoke of this, for the time, to no one.

Titus's body was conveyed to a hospital in a town many miles away, and was there received into the merciful anonymity of cremation.

HISTORY

SIX

IT was a short time later. Time had passed for me in a haze of misery and bitter remorse and the resolutions of hatred.

Gilbert had to go back to London to act in a television play. Lizzie stayed, and I got used to her unhappy face, reddened with crying. Peregrine stayed, but boorishly, almost angrily; dressed in tweed trousers, shirt and braces, he walked inland every day into the country near Amorne Farm, and arrived back hot and irritable. He was obviously wretched but seemed unable to drag himself away. Once or twice he drove Lizzie to the village for shopping. James stayed but was very withdrawn. He was gentle and considerate to me, but had little to say. We remained together, though we could not talk to each other, out of some sense of mutual protection. Of course they did not want to leave me alone. Perhaps each intended to be the last to go. It was as if we were all waiting for something.

Lizzie did the cooking. We lived on pasta and cheese. It was impossible to return to the ordinary feasts and festivals of human life, the meals to which people look forward and which they enjoy. We all, except James, drank a lot.

On the day which I shall now describe I woke up in the early morning and realized I had had a terrible terrible nightmare. I had dreamt that Titus was drowned. I experienced the relief of the awaking dreamer. And then remembered ...

I got up and went to the window. It was about six o'clock and the sun had been up for some time. Cool summer weather had come back with a misty sky and a calm sea. The water was a very pale luminous grey-blue, almost white, the same colour as the sky, shifting with a quick small dancing movement, and scattered by the misted sun with little explosions of metallic pale-gold light. It had the look of a happy sea and I felt I was seeing it through Titus's eyes.

I had returned to my own bedroom. The other three, though I disliked their proximity to each other, slept downstairs. I had decided that today I would tell them all to go. I felt strong enough now to do this, and although in a way I dreaded to be alone, my plans demanded solitude. I dressed quickly and went downstairs to the kitchen. Peregrine was there shaving. He ignored me and I went through onto the lawn. James was just climbing down from the rocks. A moment later I could hear Lizzie talking to Peregrine. We were all early risers on that day.

James sat down on the natural seat beside the trough where I put the stones I collected, or rather used to collect. Someone, perhaps Titus, had picked up the scattered stones from the lawn after the destruction of James's 'mandala' on the night of the party. My stone 'border' was comparatively undisturbed. I went and sat down too. The rocks were already warm.

James had shaved; his face, reddened and browned by the sun, was very smooth above the dark stippling of his beard. He seemed somehow clearer and more visible than usual, or perhaps it was just that the light was better. His murky brown eyes were displaying their ochre-coloured streaks, his thin clever lips were finely textured, ruddy, his dark hair more vital and glossy, hiding his bald spot. The mysterious mask-resemblance to Aunt Estelle was more present than usual, though he was not smiling.

'James, I want you to go, I want you all to go. Tomorrow. OK?'

James frowned. 'Only if you come too. Come and stay with me in London.'

'No, I must stay here.'

'Why?'

'I've got things to do.'

'What?'

'Oh this and that, things about the house, maybe I'll sell it after all. I want to be by myself now. I'm all right.'

James picked up a stone from the trough, a golden-brown one with two light blue lines running round it. 'I like your collection of stones. Can I have this one?'

'Yes, of course. So that's settled, is it? I'll tell the others.'

'What are you going to do about Ben and Hartley?'

'Nothing. That's over.'

'I don't believe you.'

I shrugged my shoulders and was about to get up only James held the sleeve of my shirt.

'Charles. *Tell me* what you think you are going to do. I know you are planning to do something.'

What indeed was I planning to do? I was in a state which I well knew was close to a sort of madness, and yet I was not mad. Some kinds of obsession, of which being in love is one, paralyse the ordinary free-wheeling of the mind, its natural open interested curious mode of being, which is sometimes persuasively defined as rationality. I was sane enough to know that I was in a state of total obsession and that I *could only* think, over and over again, certain agonizing thoughts, *could only* run continually along the same rat-paths of fantasy and intent. But I was not sane enough to interrupt this mechanical movement or even to desire to do so. I wanted to kill Ben.

When I say that I wanted to kill him I do not mean that I had yet a definite plan or a definite programme with a date. That would come to me, and come soon, once I was alone. The necessary period of sheer miserable brooding was over, and I would soon be able to make decisions. Ben had attempted to kill me; and it now amazed me in retrospect that I had been able so far to overlook or 'forgive' this crime, this insult, as not to feel compelled to punish it as such. My late and now outdated plan to besiege Hartley by 'tramping in and out' had had as its end her rescue, not his chastisement. I had proposed to intimidate him simply in order to get her away; to destroy him had not been my prime object. But now the situation was entirely different. I could not 'overlook' the murder of Titus or let it go unavenged. Because I had failed to die, Ben had struck Titus on the head and drowned him. He had killed the boy out of pure hideous spite against me; and that he could be crazy enough to do so I could well believe as I considered how crazy I now was myself. In truth the basis of my madness was sheer grief, the loss of that precious precious child, the horror of his sudden death, together with a sense of having been the victim of a wanton wickedness. The only balm for Titus's death was hatred and the immediate transformation of misery into revengeful purposeful rage. As in a civil war, further killing was the only consolation; and, as it seemed to me then, to survive the murder of Titus I had to become a terrorist.

During the last days, as I allowed myself to be quietly watched by James and Lizzie, and as I played my part of simple mourning, I had filled out in imagination how terribly Ben, with his mad beliefs, must have hated me, and because of me, Titus, throughout the miserable years of Titus's childhood. The connection between me and Titus in his mind must have become a dynamic obsessional pattern. The boy, continually before him, was (as he thought) the visible symbol of his wife's inconstancy and of the jaunty unpunished escape of the hated rival, whose jeering image he so regularly saw in the newspapers and on the television screen. Ben was a naturally violent man, a destroyer, a killer. How he must have loathed me and my changeling brat, and torn his own entrails with that loathing. Punishing the wife and the boy could never be enough while the prime culprit ran scot free and laughing. Sheer hatred can be a commanding form of madness. Many and many a time, in all those years, Ben must have killed me in his imagination.

When we at last met he was soon to see that his own violence and anger were matched by equally fierce emotions in me. He knew perfectly well of my impulse to push him in, on that occasion when we faced each other on the rocky bridge. He knew that I wanted him out of my way, and may have conjectured how very far I might, in the end, be prepared to go. He could even argue that he had tried to kill me in self-defence. Then when I had so disobligingly failed to die and was still there, taunting him with my free existence and brazenly protecting as my 'son' the hated bratling, what could be more natural than that Ben's mad rage should turn against me through the boy, bringing about perhaps an even more satisfying act of vengeance? I recalled Ben's last words to me, wherein a curse on the 'vile brat' was joined with 'I'll kill you.'

Could I now walk away into the world and 'get over' this act, this fact? It was unthinkable. Act must match act. But how? In all these thoughts I was just sane enough to try to steady myself by the image of Hartley. I tried to see her face looking at me, wistful and calm, beautiful as it had once been and perhaps would be again. Later, I would move to her and embrace her and we would console each other at last. What I could not really get myself to see or feel however was just how the path through the destruction of Ben led to Hartley or what exactly the destruction of Ben would be like. Now that I felt free to destroy him I sometimes felt that I hated him even more obsessively than I loved her; at least I knew, watching my obsession, that I was not now wanting to remove him simply because of her. The removal had become an end in itself.

Concerning what I was actually going to do I had evolved a number of quite different plans, which were still more or less at the stage of being fantasies. When I was alone I would have the concentration necessary to convert one of these into a practical proposition. I thought of going to the police. Someone had attempted to kill me and an explanation of all the circumstances would point an unambiguous finger at Ben; and it would, I guessed, be in Ben's character to answer a formal, or even hinted, accusation with a defiant avowal of guilt. This indeed might be the simplest easiest way to catch him: to open a big net and let him run straight into it. I saw Ben as a simple aggressive man who would be made uneasy by the subtleties of the law and would then scorn the refinements of lying. I played with this fantasy so much that the whole thing began to seem as good as done. On the other hand, if Ben did consistently deny the charge, I was certainly short of proof.

I also, and equally, considered various mixtures of guile and violence. If I could lure him to the house and push him into Minn's cauldron that would be the justest thing of all, but of course he would be too cautious to come. I considered other ways of drowning him. None was easy. I was more attracted by some straightforward sort of violence, which however could not be too straightforward since Ben was a strong dangerous man, and if he were to do me a serious damage while I was trying to damage him I really would go mad with chagrin. An accomplice would help, but I had vowed to act without one. I had not forgotten what Hartley said about Ben having kept his army revolver. I had no doubt that he kept it oiled and polished but he might have no ammunition. I possessed, but in London, a beautiful replica automatic, property of the theatre. Suppose I were to hold him up with that, make him turn round, then hit him with a hammer! And then? Tell the whole story to the police? Get Hartley to testify that I did it in self-defence? As it was at every moment possible that Ben might make another attempt to kill me, my fantasy actions did in fact begin to look to me more and more like self-defence.

Those who are caught in mental cages can often picture freedom, it just has no attractive power. I also knew, in the midst of it all, that some unexamined guilt of my own was driving me further into hatred; but this was no moment to be confused by guilt. As I moved like a ghost, performing in the house and its environs a sort of ritual dance under the eyes of James and Lizzie and Perry, I thought about Hartley and I pictured peace with her, in that little house where we would hide forever after. Yet if I did what I so intensely desired and consoled myself by desiring, if I destroyed Ben, if I killed him or crippled him or damaged his mind or got him sent to prison, could I then walk away with Hartley in peace? What would that peace be like? What would the idea of justice be able to do for me afterwards? Was it not, under all these disguises, my own death that I was planning?

I said to James, pulling away my sleeve which he was still holding, 'I am not going to do anything. I just feel all smashed up by misery.'

'Come to London with me.'

'No.'

'I can see you're scheming. Your eyes are full of awful visions.'

'Sea serpents.'

'Charles, tell me.'

These particular words brought back to me how extremely difficult I had found it to mislead James when I was a boy. He had a way of worming things out of one, as if the intended lie turned into truth on one's very lips. I was not going to tell now however. How could I reveal to anyone the horrors that now crowded my mind? 'James, go to London. I'll come later, soon. I'll come and sort out my flat. Don't torment me now. I just want a day or two of peace here by myself, that's all.'

'You've got some awful idea.'

'I have no idea, my mind is empty.'

'You said something to me before about imagining that Ben pushed you into the cauldron.'

'Yes.'

'But of course you don't really think that.'

'I do, but it's not important any more.'

James was looking at me in a calculating way. Lizzie called from the kitchen that breakfast was ready. The sun shone calm and bright on the grass, refreshed by the rain, on the border of pretty stones, on the sparkling yellow rocks. It was a caricature of a happy scene.

'It is important,' said James. 'I don't want to leave you behind here with that totally false notion in your head.'

'Let's have breakfast.'

'It *is* false, Charles.'

'You sound quite passionate! That's your view, and I have mine. Come on.'

'Wait, wait, it's not just a view, I *know*. I *know* it wasn't Ben.'

I stared at him. 'James, you can't know. Did you see it happen?'

'No, I didn't, but –'

'Did someone else see it?'

'No –'

'Then how can you know?'

'I just do. Charles, please, will you trust me? Surely you can trust me. Just don't ask any questions. Accept my statement that Ben didn't do it. Ben did not do it.'

We stared at each other. The intensity of James's tone, his eyes, his fierce face, carried conviction into my resisting mind. But I could not believe him. How could he *know* this? Unless – unless – James himself had pushed me in? What after all lay behind that Red Indian mask? We had always been rivals for the world, I the more successful one. A childhood hatred, like a childhood love, can last a lifetime. James was an odd card, a funny man with a funny mind. He was in a ruthless profession. I recalled his respectful remarks about Ben. It might even be that he had tried to remove me simply because he knew I had guessed that he was a secret agent and was returning to Tibet. I put my hands to my head.

I said however, 'Listen, James, and stop trying to impress me. Not only did Ben try to kill me. Ben killed Titus.'

'Oh – Lord –' said James. He turned away with an air of distracted hopelessness, then said, 'What's your evidence for his having killed Titus? Did you see him?'

'No, but it's obvious. No one examined that blow on the head. Titus was a strong swimmer. And when Ben had tried to murder me –'

'Yes, *that's* your "evidence". But I know it isn't so.'

'James, you can't know! I understand this man and how much he can hate. You were just gratified to see a fellow soldier. What I see is an able killer and a man absolutely consumed, *mad,* with jealous spite, with a whole history of it. And I know what jealous spite is like.'

'That's what I'm afraid of,' said James, *'your* spite. What can I swear upon that will satisfy you? I swear by our childhood, by the memory of our parents, by our cousinhood, that Ben did not do this thing. Will you not please just accept this and ask no more? Oh let it all go now, let it go. Come to London, let's get out of this place.'

'How can I "accept" it? I notice you argue that it wasn't Ben, but not that I imagined it all! Would *you* just "accept" the fact that some person unknown had tried to kill you? And you can't be sure it wasn't Ben. Unless by any chance it was you?'

'It wasn't me,' said James frowning, 'don't be absurd.'

I felt a ridiculous degree of relief. Had I then for a moment seriously entertained the idea that my cousin was filled with murderous hate against me? Of course I believed him at once, and of course it was absurd. But if it was not James, or as he argued, Ben, who was it? I was impressed by his solemn oath, though I could not believe him. Gilbert, mad with secret jealousy because of Lizzie? Rosina mourning for her lost child? Perhaps there were quite a lot of people with motives to murder me. Freddie Arkwright? Why not? He hated me, he was now at Amorne Farm where Ben had been to get the dog. Suppose Ben had hired Freddie to kill or perhaps just maim me, and it had ended with that dreadful fall?

James could see me speculating and he made a hopeless gesture.

'I'm no good at guessing games,' I said. 'I thought it was Ben and I still think so.'

'Come inside then,' said James, and he rose.

We came into the kitchen. Lizzie was standing at the stove. She had pinned her hair back and was wearing a very short check overall over a very short dress. She looked ridiculously young and had an anxious silly schoolgirl look which she sometimes wore. Perry was sitting at the table with his legs stretched beneath it and his elbows upon it. His big face was already greasy with sweat and his eyes were glazed. He might even have been drunk.

James just said, 'Peregrine.'

Peregrine said, without moving, his glazed eyes still staring ahead, 'If you've been discussing who killed Charles or failed to kill Charles, it was me.'

'Perry —'

'My name is Peregrine.'

'But, Peregrine, why on earth – did you really – why?'

Lizzie moved, without surprise, sat down to watch. She evidently already knew.

'You ask why?' said Peregrine, without looking at me. 'Just think why, just think.'

'You mean – good heavens, you mean *Rosina*?'

'Yes, oddly enough, I do. You deliberately smashed my marriage, you took away my wife whom I adored, you did it carefully, cold-bloodedly, you *worked* at it. Then when you had got her away from me you dropped her. You didn't even want her for yourself, you just wanted to steal her from me to satisfy the beastly impulses of your possessiveness and your jealousy! Then when they were satisfied, when my marriage was broken forever, you went jaunting off somewhere else. And what is more you expected me to tolerate this and to go on liking you! Why? Because you thought everybody always went on liking you whatever rotten things you did because you were wonderful wonderful Charles Arrowby.'

'But, Peregrine, you yourself *said* to me, more than once, that you were glad to be rid of the bitch –'

'OK, but why did you believe me? And don't use that foul language please. Of course everyone knows you regard women as trash. But what bugged me was that you wrecked my life and my happiness and you just didn't seem to care at all, you were so bloody perky.'

'I don't believe you were happy – you just say so now –'

'Oh for Christ's sake! You took her out of sheer spiteful jealousy. OK, I can be jealous too.'

'But you yourself encouraged me to feel it was all right! Why did you bother to pretend, and mislead me? You can't blame me now – If you had looked more stricken I would have felt more guilty. But you were so nice to me, so friendly – you always seemed so pleased to see me –'

'I am an actor. And perhaps I was pleased to see you. We sometimes like to see people whom we hate and despise so that we can stir them up to further demonstrations of how odious they are.'

'So you've been waiting all these years for revenge!'

'No, not like that. I enjoyed leading you on and just looking at you and gloating and thinking how surprised you'd be if you knew what I really felt. You've been a bad dream to me all these years, you've been with me like a demon, like a cancer.'

'Oh my God. I'm sorry —'

'If you imagine I want to hear you apologizing *now* —'

'I may have behaved badly to you, but I didn't deserve to die for it.'

'No, all right, I admit it was an impulse and I was drunk. I just pushed you and walked on. I didn't really see what happened and I didn't care.'

'But you said you were non-violent, you said you never —'

'OK, you were a special case. The last straw was seeing bloody Rosina suddenly sitting on top of that rock like a black witch. I thought you must still be carrying on with her, well obviously you are —'

'I'm not.'

'I don't care —'

'I wondered why you stopped talking about her. You were planning to kill me.'

'I don't care, I don't want to know, I don't believe anything you say, I think you're a worthless person. I just couldn't stand seeing her there, and the windscreen getting broken, I couldn't stand it, it was a shock, it made me feel mad, it made a sort of hole in me, and all the old stored-up hate came pouring out and all the green-eyed jealousy, as fresh as ever. I had to do something to you. I really just wanted to push you into the sea. I daresay I was pretty drunk. I didn't choose that spot, I didn't think it was that awful whirlpool or whatever you call it —'

'Then you were lucky, weren't you. I might be dead.'

'Oh I don't care,' said Peregrine, 'I wish you were dead. I thought of pulling you out, only then I thought you might kill me instead, because you drink less than I do. I suppose honour is satisfied now anyway, and I won't have to offer you any more drinks, thank God, and I won't even want to tell you what a four-letter man you are. You're an exploded myth. And you still think you're Genghis Khan! *Laissez-moi rire.* I can't think why I let you haunt me all these years, I suppose it was just your power and the endless spectacle of you doing well and flourishing like the green bay tree. Now you're old and done for, you'll wither away like Prospero did when he went back to Milan, you'll get pathetic and senile, and kind girls like Lizzie will visit you to cheer you up. At least they will for a while. You never did anything for mankind, you never did a damn thing for anybody except yourself. If Clement hadn't fancied you no one would ever have heard of you, your work wasn't any bloody good, it was just a pack of pretentious tricks, as everyone can see now that they aren't mesmerized any more, so the glitter's fading fast and you'll find yourself alone and you won't even be a monster in anybody's mind any more and they'll all heave a sigh of relief and feel sorry for you and forget you.'

There was a moment's silence.

I said, 'But if you're so pleased about it, why tell? You only had to keep quiet – or did you want me to know?'

'I don't care what you know or don't know. Your cousin got it out of me by one of his interrogation techniques. He said you thought it was Ben and you were working yourself up.'

'You pretend you always detested me, it isn't true. You aren't all that good an actor. You told me about your Uncle Peregrine.'

'I have no Uncle Peregrine.'

I felt totally confused. I said, 'But what about Titus?'

'What do you mean?' said James.

'What happened to Titus? Who killed Titus? I mean – I thought – surely Ben killed him?'

Lizzie answered this after a moment. She said, 'Charles, it was an accident, no one killed him.'

Peregrine got up. He said, 'Well, that's that, that's sorted that out, and I hope the General is satisfied. I'm going back to London. Goodbye Lizzie, nice to have seen you.' He marched out and I could hear him collecting his things. Then there was the sound of the Alfa Romeo backing violently onto the causeway, and then its diminishing roar.

James had got up and was looking out of the window. Lizzie, soundlessly crying, was filling the kettle at the tap. She put it on the stove and turned the gas up.

I said to James, 'You said you didn't want to leave me behind here with a false notion in my head. Well, now it's gone, so there's nothing to detain you.'

James turned round. 'Won't you come to London?'

'No.'

'But what are you going to do about *them*?'

'Nothing. It's over. *It's over.*'

But of course that was not true.

That day and the next day passed in a sick trance, a period of time which seemed like the peace of resignation and hopeless quiet mourning, but was really full of fear and venom. I passionately wanted James to go, his appearance, his company, his obtrusive unseen presence irritated me into torments. Lizzie irritated me too, partly by her frequent tears, which she seemed unable to control, and partly by a silly beseeching sympathetic expression which she put on when I looked at her, and which made me suddenly see the picture which Peregrine had sketched of me as an ageing powerless ex-magician for whom people were sorry.

I could understand why Lizzie refused to go. She wanted to be in at the kill. She was waiting for the moment when I could stand no more and would turn to her helplessly to be seized and carried off. Why James wanted to hang around was less clear. He certainly believed what I told him, that I no longer regarded Ben as a murderer. He might suspect that I had not given up my idea of rescuing Hartley, but after all he could not go on watching me forever. It was quite plain that I was not proposing to return to London in his Bentley. A little tact, and he was not usually deficient in tact, might have prompted him now to leave me and Lizzie alone. He did not even seem to want to talk to me any more. It was as if he was staying on for some purpose of his own. I guessed that he was brooding on Titus and somehow blaming himself, as I blamed myself, for not having attended more to what the boy was doing. At this time I avoided the rocks and the sea, but James was always out there, walking about on the cliff, standing on Minn's bridge, and climbing up to the tower, almost as if he were measuring the distances involved.

On several afternoons Lizzie and I walked inland, past the place where in a previous existence I had intended to put my herb garden, into the country which I had never explored. The region just beyond the road was bog, full of outcrops of rock and gorse and little black pools. There was some scrappy heather and a lot of those tiny yellow plants that catch flies, and purple and white flowers that looked like miniature orchids. Two pairs of buzzards inhabited the blue air. After the bog there was ordinary farm land, sheep-scattered hillsides, distant mustard fields catching the sunlight with their huge patches of glowing yellow. There were many ruined stone cottages, roofless and full of willow-herb and wild buddleia and butterflies, and we came on the ruin of a big house, with the box hedges of the formal garden grown into a forest and covered with rambler roses. I record these details, which

I recall so clearly, because they are the very image of sorrow; things seen which might have given pleasure, but could not.

I saw through a black veil of misery and remorse and indecision and fear; and there was a feeling as if I carried a small leaden coffin in the place of my heart. Lizzie, walking with me, had wept her fill for Titus, and was still often weeping, but now more privately and self-indulgently; with a woman's economy in grief, I could feel her tentacles clasping me. Lizzie was not going to perish, not for anyone, if she could help it. If I had fallen dead she would soon have been crying in someone else's arms. These are unkind words; but I felt a special localized bitterness against Lizzie then because I knew how temporary her affliction was, and how soon, if I required her sympathy, it could turn into a possessive triumph. Lizzie is one of those very sweet, very kind kittenish women whom men love for their sympathetic gentleness, but who have a truly relentless power of self-preservation. Well, why not? We spoke little as we walked and I could see Lizzie looking at me now and then and she was thinking to herself: it is a relief to him to walk with me thus in silence. My presence, my silence is healing him. With no one else could he quietly walk and walk like this. (This last belief was probably justified.) Of course guilt too had fed my rage. My responsibility for Titus's death, which now so largely occupied my mind, amounted to this: I had never warned him about the sea. Why had I not done so? *Out of vanity.* I recalled now very clearly that first day when Titus and I had dived in off the cliff. I had wanted to show him that I too was strong and fearless. It would have spoilt the charm of that moment if I had said, 'It's rather dangerous' or 'It's not easy to get out' or 'I don't think I'll swim here.' I had to dive in with him and conceal the difficulties I knew so well. I never stressed the impossibility of climbing out in other places. I never recommended the tower steps; in fact I had not renewed the rope there, and with a strong sea running the steps would be as dangerous as the cliff. I never, for Titus, *watched* the sea. I acted out of vanity, and out of a silly vicarious pride in his youth and his strength, in the agility which I had seen him display upon the tower on the first day. Of course he always wanted to dive in. No young boy climbs cautiously into the sea if he can dive. I did not want to spoil my picture of Titus or Titus's picture of me by any mean prudence.

I went over and over and over these things in my mind, thinking of what I might have done and what I should have done, just as James was perhaps doing as he paced it all out upon those rocks which I now could not bear to look upon. And my misery about Titus, my sobbing grasping sense of the loss from my life of what might have become its greatest blessing was the more intense now that my obsessive belief about Ben had been taken away. It had indeed been a consolation, and Ben had carried my guilt. That madness was gone, but did not leave behind a saner or purer mourning. My burden of sin and despair was constant and had simply been redistributed. New aspects of grief were opened to me. I had killed Hartley's child, I had wantonly entered her life and taken away *her* blessing, which was hers in a way that it could never be mine. I did not dare to imagine her sorrow and how it might affect her feelings about me. Would she now see *me* as a murderer? Sometimes I felt that, in an odd way, it would not *occur* to her to blame me, she would not be capable of such a thought, of seeing me simply as a wanton wandering cause. And sometimes I felt that our grief for Titus might actually, excluding Ben, draw us together. For the moment I could only wait. I even felt that it was now likely that she would give me a sign. And in thinking this I was, as it turned out, right.

And so, waiting, watching, brooding, mourning, Lizzie and I walked the countryside. And then we began to talk about the old days, about Wilfred and about Clement, and Lizzie said how jealous she had been of Clement even when I was no longer living with her. 'I always felt that, whatever happened, Clement owned you.' We talked about the theatre and how wonderful it was and how awful it was and how glad Lizzie was to be out of it. Lizzie asked me about Jeanne and I told her a little and regretted it because it clearly hurt her so much. Lizzie on these walks, sweating, puffing, wearing crumpled faded dresses, her face shiny and red with sunburn and with sudden tears, looked her age. She was a woman whose appearance varied immensely. She could still look childish, in the mysterious way that old and young can mingle in a woman's looks. But she had lost her radiance, or else my vision of her was dulled. She was faithful and sweet and she tried so hard to console me, always speaking of peripheral things, not of the centre. 'Of course Perry didn't hate you, he never did, he just said that. He loved you, he was devoted to you, he always spoke of you with such admiration.'

One afternoon we came back by a road which led unexpectedly past Amorne Farm, which I had usually tried to avoid. We passed quickly by to a chorus of yapping collies, and I was just feeling relieved when suddenly the Black Lion man, Bob Arkwright, came round the corner out of a side lane. He approached us, with the quiet intent look of a dog who approaches silently, about to snarl and bite.

'That was a bad business, Mr Arrowby.'

'Yes.'

'I warned you about the sea, didn't I.'

'Yes.'

'He couldn't get out, that was it.'

'Perhaps.'

'I seen him, just the day before, I was up near the tower and I seen him trying and trying to get up that sheer rock near your house, and he kept falling back. It was mad crazy to swim with the waves like that. Then he managed to get up somehow, but he was dead beat. When he got up the top he just flopped. What must have happened he tired himself out and then the waves threw him against the rocks. That was what happened, I bet. He shouldn't have been let swim there. That sea's a killer, I told you, didn't I, didn't I?'

'Yes. It shouldn't have happened.' I moved on. He called after me. 'My brother Freddie knows you. He knows you.'

I did not turn round. Lizzie and I were silent all the way home. I decided I would tell James to go tomorrow, and I would despatch Lizzie the following day. I could not cashier them together because I did not want James to give Lizzie a lift to London. I felt I no longer needed her, and I could certainly dispense with him, and it was beginning to be intolerable to have them as witnesses of what I increasingly felt to be the punishing horror of my degradation.

I entered the house resolved to seek my cousin out and tell him to leave the next morning, when I heard a most extraordinary rhythmical shrieking sound. It took me a moment to realize that it was the telephone, whose presence I had forgotten. This was the first time that it had rung, and I immediately thought that it might be Hartley. Then of course I could not find the thing, could not remember which room it was in. I located it at last in the bookroom and ran to it with desperate hope.

It was Rosina's voice.

'Charles. It's me.'

'Hello.'

'I say, I'm sorry about that wretched boy.'

'Yes.'

'Very sorry. Well, what can one say? But listen, Charles, I want to ask you something.'

'What?'

'Is it true that Peregrine tried to kill you?'

'He pushed me into the sea. He wasn't trying to kill me.'

'But he pushed you into that awful hole where the sea churns about.'

'Yes.'

'Good heavens.'

'Where are you?'

'At the Raven Hotel. I've got a bit of news.'

'What?'

'You know that monster epic film of the *Odyssey* that Fritzie Eitel is going to make?'

'Yes.'

'Well, he's offered me the part of Calypso!'

'That should suit you.'

'Isn't it marvellous? I don't know when I've felt so delighted and so happy.'

'Good. Just leave me alone, will you, Rosina?'

'I am leaving you alone.' She rang off.

As I came out of the bookroom I could now hear Lizzie talking to James in the kitchen. The door was shut, but something about the tone of the conversation struck me as odd. I paused, then went and opened the kitchen door. James, looking at me over Lizzie's shoulder, said, 'Charles.'

Prophetic terror pounces quickly. My heart became fast, my mouth dry.

'Yes?"

They came out into the hall. Lizzie was red-faced, frightened.

'Charles, Lizzie and I want to tell you something.'

Very fast does the human mind rush towards the most precise visions of disaster. I lived in two seconds through a long experience of mental torture. I said, 'I know what you are going to say.'

'You don't,' said James.

'You are going to say that you have become very attached to each other and feel that you must tell me so. OK.'

'No,' said James, 'Lizzie is attached to you, not to me. That is the point, and that is why I have got to tell you something which I ought to have told you long ago.'

'What?'

'Lizzie and I have known each other for a long time, only we decided not to tell you because you would be sure to be irrationally jealous. That is the matter in a nutshell.'

I stared at James. He looked as I had I think never seen him look in all his life. He looked not exactly guilty but somehow confused and at a loss. I turned round for a moment and opened the front door wide.

'You see –' said Lizzie, near to tears.

'Let me do this,' said James.

'I don't think you need to say anything more,' I said.

'You are leaping to conclusions,' said James.

'What do you expect me to do?'

'Listen to the truth. I met Lizzie a long time ago at a party which you gave for a first night. I happened to be in London, I happened to come.'

'For once I think I can even remember the occasion.'

'Lizzie remembered me simply because I was your cousin. Then at a later time, after you'd left her and when she was unhappy, she rang me up to ask if I knew your address in Japan – that was when you were working in Tokyo.'

'I wanted to write to you, I felt I had to,' said Lizzie in a choked voice. 'It was my idea, I pushed him into it –'

'But you met each other,' I said, 'you didn't just talk on the telephone.'

'Yes, we did meet, but very very rarely, perhaps in all those years six times.'

'Do you expect me to believe that?'

'He was sorry for me,' said Lizzie.

'You bet he was! So you met to discuss me.'

'Yes, but only in what I might call a business-like way.'

'Oh, very business-like!'

'I mean, Lizzie just wanted to know where you were, how you were. We never otherwise discussed you. Our acquaintance was slight and it was impersonal and unemotional.'

'That cannot be true.'

'It was entirely concerned with you, not with Lizzie and me. And as I say, we scarcely ever met or indeed communicated in any way.'

'He told me to stop bothering him,' said Lizzie, 'but sometimes I so much wanted to know how you were –'

'James is the last person who ever knew how I was!'

'Of course,' said James, 'we ought to have told you long ago that we knew each other slightly. But the nature of the acquaintance was likely to irritate you. I know, if you will forgive my saying so, what an insanely jealous disposition you have.'

'You have been at pains to make clear that I had left Lizzie at the time your acquaintance ripened –'

'It never ripened. And *la jalousie naît avec l'amour ...*'

'That's true enough.'

'What does it mean?' said Lizzie, who was still looking red and frightened and miserable.

'Jealousy is born with love, but does not always die with love.'

'But why tell me now?' I asked James. 'You could both have gone on fooling me forever.'

'I should have told you earlier,' he repeated, 'it should not have happened at all. Any lie is morally dangerous.'

'You mean you may be found out!'

'It has been a barrier. And a – and a –' he found the word judiciously, 'a *flaw*.'

'In your conception of yourself.'

'In our – our –' he searched again, 'friendship, and – yes – in me.'

'Friendship! Whatever it is between you and me it certainly isn't friendship!'

'And earlier I felt I must protect Lizzie.'

'Of course!'

'But now – lately – it becomes necessary to tell you, for Lizzie's sake, so that there may be no impediment.'

'Impediment to what, for God's sake?'

'To her loving you, to your loving her. Secrets are almost always a mistake and a source of corruption.'

'And then there was Toby,' blurted Lizzie.

'*Toby?* Christ in heaven, how does Toby come into this? You don't mean Toby Ellesmere, do you?' I asked Lizzie.

'He saw me and Lizzie in a bar together,' said James. He hated this bit.

'Talking about me of course!'

'Yes.'

'And as you were afraid he'd tell me you felt you had to! Otherwise you'd have gone on and on lying.'

'We would have told you anyway,' said Lizzie. 'We felt we had to. It was beginning to be a nightmare, at least it was to me. It seemed such a little thing to begin with, there was so little to it, and it just seemed sensible, not to tell you, knowing what you're like. And you must understand, we only met sort of every other year for five minutes. And I very very occasionally rang him up to ask about you. Usually he wasn't there anyway –'

'Too bad. You were both spying on me. At least that's how it started –'

'It wasn't like that,' said James, 'but of course if one starts lying one deserves what one gets.'

'And when you met here you pretended not to have met each other – that's a scene I shall remember!'

'We didn't tell you because we knew you'd be determined to misunderstand,' said Lizzie, 'and you are determined to misunderstand.'

'So I suppose you both think it's all my fault for being, as you put it, insanely jealous!'

'The fault is mine,' said James.

'No, no, it's my fault,' said Lizzie. 'I forced it on him, I *knew* he hated it –'

'Perhaps I know James better than you do after all,' I said to Lizzie. 'He is a man on whom no one ever forced anything he hated.'

'It isn't his fault –'

'This argument does not interest me,' I said. 'You can continue it elsewhere and I am sure you will both enjoy it very much.'

'I told you he'd be like that,' said Lizzie to James, 'I told you he wouldn't understand –'

'Well,' said James, 'there it is. It's not a very attractive confession, but I hope you can see, or will see when you calm down –'

'What do you mean, calm down?'

'That it's not, from your point of view, a matter of world-shaking importance. Naturally it irritates you. But you will see on reflection that it does not damage your relation with Lizzie, nor, I hope, your relation with me. It's obvious how and why it happened, OK, it shouldn't have happened, and I'm sorry –'

'Do you imagine that I believe you?'

'Yes,' said James. He looked at me frowning but his face expressed an almost absurd sort of distress at a loss of dignity, at a loss, for once, of the initiative.

'Well, I don't. Why should I? How can I? It's mean, it's horrible. You admit you only told me because Toby saw you secretly meeting

Lizzie in a bar. Am I supposed to be pleased that you've been meeting for years —'

'Very very infrequently.'

'And talking about me?'

'You don't see what it was *like*,' said Lizzie, with tears in her eyes. 'It wasn't an all-the-time sort of thing at all, and it wasn't like you think a relationship, it was just that we did happen to have met accidentally at that party —'

'The moral is, never give parties.'

'And we couldn't undo that, and I did ask James sometimes how you were and where you were, because I *loved* you, and it was my only connection with you, all the time you were with Jeanne and — and that time when you were in Japan and in Australia and — I was thinking about you — and there wasn't anyone but James I could —'

'There wasn't anyone but James, a very adequate substitute I daresay. Can't you see how *wickedly* hurtful this is?'

'She's right,' said James, 'it isn't like what you are thinking at all. However —'

'I can just see you holding hands and talking about me!'

'We *never* held hands!' said Lizzie.

'*Christ!* Do I care whether you held hands or not? Or whatever else you did which you will never confess? You've been telephoning and meeting and looking into each other's eyes — I expect you've known each other forever, I daresay you knew Lizzie before I ever met her, you were there first, you were there before me, as you were with — as you were with — with Aunt Estelle and — and with Titus — you'd met Titus before, he said he'd seen you in a dream. I expect you were the person he was living with for those two years, no wonder he wouldn't say! And you made Lizzie sing that special song of Aunt Estelle's. I'm sure Lizzie dreams about you every night, you're everywhere, spoiling everything in my life, you'd spoil Hartley if you could, only you can't get at her, she's the only thing that's absolutely mine!'

'Charles!'

'You've been everywhere before me and you'll be everywhere after me, when I'm dead you and Lizzie will be sitting in a bar discussing me, only then it won't matter who sees you.'

'Charles, Charles —'

'I'm disappointed in you,' I said to James. 'I didn't ever think you'd do anything mean or treacherous, I didn't ever believe you'd put yourself into this sort of squalid muddle. It's a kind of ordinary sly human stupidity which I was foolish enough to imagine you didn't suffer from. You've behaved like ordinary people do who can't imagine consequences. And one of the consequences is that, I don't believe you, I *can't* believe you. There could be anything between you and Lizzie. Ordinary mediocre people think that if they confess one tenth of the truth they're in the clear. You've made all your words into lies, you've devalued your speech and — and in a moment you've spoilt the past — and there's nothing to rely on any more.'

'Perhaps it was a mistake to tell you in this way,' said James. He seemed to be getting annoyed though he was also very upset. 'Of course you were bound to hate it whenever it emerged, we never underestimated that. I hope and believe that you will appreciate later that the thing concealed was *trivial,* though the fact of the concealment was not. I realize that all this has been an affront to your dignity —'

'Dignity? *My* dignity?'

'Well, an affront. I am heartily sorry for it. But given the mistake, the fault, you can hardly have wished it to continue. This truth-telling is something painful which we do for your sake. Lizzie felt that she could not be as she wished for you with the lie unconfessed. She wanted there to be, especially now, no barrier of untruth between you.'

'Why "especially now"? What's special about now?'

'Please,' began Lizzie, '*please* —'

'Don't worry, I'm not excited, I'm not even angry, this isn't anger.' I had not raised my voice at all.

'Then it's all right,' she said. 'It's all all right?'

'What you say in your devalued words may even be true, as true as such words can make it —'

'Then it's all right — Charles darling —?'

'It's just that it's brought this to an end.'

'Brought what to an end?' said James.

'I want you both to go now. I want you to take Lizzie back to London.'

'I was proposing to go and leave Lizzie here,' said James. 'Now I've told you surely I can go and leave her. That was the point of telling you. That was what I waited for.'

'You thought I might blame you and let her off because I needed her so much? I don't need her all that much, I can tell you!'

'Charles, don't destroy yourself,' said James. 'Why are you always so intent on breaking everything that surrounds and supports you?'

'Go please. *Go together.*'

I suddenly seized Lizzie's hand, and for a moment it clasped mine, then it became dead. I seized James's hand and I forced their two hands together. The hands struggled in mine like small captive animals trying to escape.

James wrenched himself away and went into the bookroom. I could hear him throwing things into his suitcase.

I said to Lizzie, 'Go and pack,' and she reached out towards me, then turned away with a sob.

I went out onto the causeway and walked on until I reached James's Bentley. It was big and black and expectant, a little dusty, in the lazy afternoon sunshine. I opened the door. The interior had an opulent quietness like the interior of a grand mansion or a rich silent shrine. The polished wood glowed, the brown leather gave off a fresh rare smell. The gear nestled in a soft crumpled skin. The carpet was thick, spotless. The silence, the intimacy of the car invited a privileged habitation. And in this sacred interior I was about to enclose James and Lizzie and despatch them forever, just as surely as if I were shutting them in a sealed casket and drowning them in the sea.

As I turned back towards the house I looked automatically at the stone dog kennel, where Gilbert had so carefully installed the basket to keep the mail out of the rainwater. I saw there was a letter in the basket. I went and picked it up. It was from Hartley. I put it in my pocket.

Lizzie came out first, carrying her handbag and crying. She started to say something to me but I held the car door open and ushered her into the passenger seat and closed the door on her with a soft final sound.

James came out, carrying his case and Lizzie's, and stopped on the causeway wanting me to come to him, but I would not. I went round and opened the other door and stood by it. James came on and put the cases in the boot. He came round to the door.

I said, 'I don't want to see either of you ever again. You have spoilt each other for me with an effectiveness which I shall soon begin to see as malignant.'

'Do not see it so. Don't be a fool. What happened was accidental and forgivable. Just stop driving yourself mad with jealousy.'

'I mean what I say. I don't want to see you again, James, or you again, Lizzie, ever, between now and the end of the world. I shall destroy your letters unread, I shall close the door in your face, I shall cut you in the street. Don't either of you come near me again. This may seem harsh, but you will soon see that there is a kind of automatic justice about it. You spoke about automatic justice, James, well this is it. You have, between you, made a machine and this is how it works. If you feel upset, I am sure you will soon console each other. I want you to be together. I shall think of you together. You don't have to wait till I'm dead after all, you can hold hands now. As James is such a good driver you can hold hands all the way to London. Goodbye.'

'Charles —' said James.

I walked back to the causeway and began to cross it. I heard the door of the Bentley close quietly and the engine begin to purr. The car was moving away and the sound rose in pitch, then began to fade as it turned the corner. Then there was silence. I entered the empty house with my fingertips upon Hartley's letter in my pocket.

I did not open the letter at once. Its presence there in my pocket was an absolute comfort. At any rate, I would feel it so for a time and banish fear. I wanted it to remain, for the moment, a thing, a simple object, a talisman, a magic stone, a sacred ring, a precious relic, something entirely protective and tender and pure. For now I had nothing left in the world but Hartley and her unspoilt separated being. Yes, James had always spoilt things for me. He had spoilt Aunt Estelle. Had I said something to him just now about Aunt Estelle? I could not clearly remember what I had said. My head boiled with feelings. My fingers touched the precious letter. My God, I needed salvation and I needed it now.

Yet even as I let Hartley's healing and her peace stream into me in a race of therapeutic particles I was thinking in another part of my mind that in a little while I would be suffering the most frightful regret and remorse at having sent James and Lizzie off together. Why had I been such a perfect fool? It had been an 'inevitable' impulse of sheer destructiveness, the self-destructiveness of which James had accused me. I could have dismissed James, kept Lizzie, then dismissed her. Half an hour would have done it. I did not have to press them into each other's arms like that. But I wanted to make what was terrible so much worse so as to be sure that it was fatal; like Hartley protecting herself by thinking I must hate her. I had sent them off together so as to make sure that I would never relent; and I had insured myself yet further. James would never never forgive such an enforced loss of face. Lizzie and James had, for me, destroyed each other, as in a suicide pact. I even suddenly pictured James with his revolver against Lizzie's brow, then against his own. What truly demonic arrangement of fate had brought just those two together? Whatever might or might not have happened between them in the past, and I would never know, Lizzie's hair would be spread out on James's shoulder long before they got to London. What a trap I was in. But really I had been wise. The only cure here was death. They were both gone out of my life.

The house was curiously weirdly silent. I realized that for a long time now I had not been alone in it. What a lot of visitors I had had. Gilbert, Lizzie, Perry, James. Titus. His little plastic bag with his treasures, his tie and the cuff links and the love poems of Dante, was still lying in a corner of the bookroom like an abandoned dog. I recalled Bob Arkwright's words. Titus had refused to be beaten by the cliff. He had tried again and again to get a hold on it and each time the strong quiet waves had simply pulled him off. Then when he was desperate and weary a yet stronger wave had dashed him against the rock. I went into the kitchen and poured out some of Perry's whisky. A breeze was blowing in from the sea through the open door and I could hear the bead curtain clicking on the upper landing. I drank the whisky. Now everything in the world depended on Hartley's letter. I sat down at the table. I looked at my watch. It was nearly six o'clock. James and Lizzie would stop for dinner on the way. James was sure to know a good restaurant. They would turn off the motorway. They would sit in the bar and study the menu. They would recover from their shock and feel liberated. No more secrecy now. It doesn't matter who sees them holding hands. Oh God, if I had only told Titus, don't swim there, it's dangerous. If there's any swell you can't get out. Never swim in a rough sea, dear boy, this sea's a killer. But the past refused to come back, as it did in dreams, to be remade. Titus walked in my dreams in the brightness of his youth, which was now made eternal. Or else I dreamed that he was dead and felt joy on waking. I took Hartley's letter out and pressed it to my brow and prayed to her that she would save me out of the desolation and the wreck.

I looked at the envelope. I had not received a letter from Hartley, it occurred to me, for over forty years. Yet of course I had recognized the writing at once. It was much the same, a little smaller and less neat. I had kept all her old letters for a long time, then destroyed them all in a mood when it upset me (or perhaps exasperated me) too much to see them, then regretted this. I had of course already invented dozens of possible letters which she might have written to me. *Charles, goodbye, I can never see you again.* Or *Ben has gone, whatever shall I do?* Or *Darling, I shall come to you, have a car ready tomorrow.* I had already checked the number of the local taxi and placed it beside the telephone. I had felt the envelope and decided it was a short letter. Was that a good sign? At any rate it was not an incoherent inconclusive unburdening of the heart. *I love you, but I cannot leave him, etc. etc.* for pages and pages. Not that anyway. Had Hartley really made up her mind? What would we say, what could we say, when we met, about Titus? This was the overwhelming thing, this would perhaps decide all. How strange, how terrible, of fate to bring him to me and then to drown him. Would I ever mourn for him *with* Hartley? Whatever would this mourning be like, and whatever would it do to us? So I put off opening the letter. But of all the things I imagined, not one was what she had actually written.

In fact not a very long time passed. I stopped drinking whisky. I hate
the stuff really. I walked all round the house, entering every room. I even
climbed up to the attics and looked at the hole in the roof. The place
was still very damp up there. Lizzie and Gilbert had put two buckets
under the hole. These were both brimming full. I left them there.
I searched the house as if I were looking for something, and all the time
now I was holding Hartley's letter in my hand. At last I threw myself
down on my bed and began to open the letter as if I were a child and
this were some strange treat which I had carried off to enjoy at last
in secret. What spurred me to end the play of hopes was the thought
that if I were to carry Hartley off effectively I had better book the taxi
at once. And at the very last moment I fell into a frenzy because it
occurred to me that I might already have delayed too long. Then real
absolute panic came. My teeth were chattering, my trembling clumsy
fingers tore the envelope, tore the letter, spread it out. Then I had to
get up and run to the window for a better light.

Dear Charles,
    We would be very glad if you would come and see us for tea.
Four o'clock on Friday would suit and we will expect you then
unless you write otherwise. I hope that you can come.
            Yours truly,
            Mary Fitch.

This letter stunned me partly because I could not think or feel how to
react to it. Was it good or bad? It asked for a meeting, but with 'us'.
If Hartley simply wanted me to do nothing, her best course was to do
nothing herself. But here was a letter. What did it mean, what was its
deep meaning? Friday was tomorrow.

I stared at the letter blushing and trembling and tried to understand it. I was not very bright. It even took me a little time to realize that it was not a real letter from Hartley at all. It was signed 'Mary Fitch'. She had written it but not composed it. It was a letter written for the eye of her husband, even perhaps under his dictation. But then what did *that* mean? Had she perhaps cunningly put it into his head to agree to my visit? But how had she done it and what did she want to happen? Had Hartley, in order to see me, perhaps simply to see my face, argued Ben into inviting me? And would she, when I arrived, give me some cue? Or was it perhaps a trap, a dreadful revenge plan with which she had been forced to co-operate? If Ben blamed me for Titus's death he might now be half mad with his own remorse and resentment against me. *Now* he would feel how much he loved Titus, and the only relief might be to feel how much he hated me. Just as I had sought relief from Titus's death in blaming Ben. Well, even if it was a trap, I would walk straight in.

I kept looking at the letter and turning it over and over and even holding it up to the light in case there was some hidden message. The *time* of the appointment had been changed. What had originally been written was six o'clock, but this had been altered to four o'clock. This could be made sense of. Under Ben's dictation, under his eye, she had written six, then hastily just as she was putting it into the envelope she had changed it to four, knowing that at four Ben would be absent. Perhaps away fetching somebody or something for the trap? So perhaps she would be alone after all? And she would throw herself into my arms as she had done on that night, the night when she had run away onto the rocks because she was so afraid of Ben, afraid of returning to him, afraid of staying with me. She *had* come to me then of her own accord. That was a piece of evidence, in fact the chief one.

I then thought, supposing she is alone then and supposing she says: *take me away.* I must have a car. I reflected rather desperately and miserably on this, hope fighting with fear, as I imagined how awful it would be to have the car and no Hartley: the symbol of escape but not the princess. I decided however that I must trust hope and plan for it, so I rang up the taxi man and asked for the taxi to be waiting outside the village church from four o'clock onward tomorrow. After I had done this I felt very much better, as if I had actually improved my chances.

By this time it was after nine o'clock and I decided to go to bed. I drank some wine and ate some bread and honey and then took a sleeping pill. As I lay down I remembered that I had lost James. And as it seemed to me then I had lost him not so much because of his sin, the 'flaw' he had spoken of, but simply because he had gone away in his big black car with Lizzie. Gone to perdition, by my doing. There was no getting back to my cousin now ever, through the barrier which he and I between us had so ingeniously erected. We were eternally divided. And it somehow seemed strange to me that this had not happened earlier, so dangerous were we to each other.

The next day was simply a problem of filling the time until four. At first I thought the problem insoluble and that I should run screaming mad with anxiety. However, I managed to pass the time without excessive anguish by busying myself continually with little tasks which had to do with Hartley. I paid some attention to my appearance, though there was an element of pretence in this, since I could not imagine Hartley cared about the details of my looks, and anyway I was quite sufficiently presentable when shabby and untidy, perhaps more so. I washed one of my better shirts and dried it in the sun. I got out my light black jacket and clean socks, and chose a smart pretty tie. I washed my hair and made it fair and fluffy. I had given up swimming, but it was still a bit stiff and salty. I decided it would be wise to pack a small suitcase, ready for possible instant flight, and I did so with a fast beating heart. At lunch time I ate sufficiently, not with appetite but out of a sense of duty, and drank no alcohol.

After lunch I went round the house carefully closing and fixing all the windows. I emptied the water out of the buckets in the attic and replaced them under the hole in the roof. As I came downstairs and into the little red room I suddenly saw, lying on the table and partially concealed by blotting paper, the envelope which contained the long letter which I had written to Hartley before Titus died and which I had never managed to deliver: the letter about how Ben had tried to kill me and about 'tramping in and out' and about the little quiet secret life we were going to lead together. Much of this had been made horribly out of date by Perry's confession and Titus's death, and I saw it with pain and was about to destroy it but decided to read it first. That I should actually reconsider this letter belonged somehow to the macabre economy of that day. It seemed a pity to waste the eloquence of the early part and the important explanation which it contained, so I destroyed only the last two pages which referred to Titus and Ben. Then I wrote on a separate sheet: *I wrote this letter to you earlier but never delivered it. Read it carefully. I love you and we will be together.* I also added my telephone number. I sealed it all up in a new envelope and put it in my pocket.

I set off early for the village, carrying my suitcase, and changed a cheque at the shop. I bought, together with razor blades, some cream and face powder of the kind which Hartley used. It was still not yet half past three, and I walked down towards the church. I was feeling sick with fear and hope, ready to vomit, ready to faint. The taxi was already waiting since the taxi man, as he told me, had nothing else to do. I told him to wait until I came. He said laughingly, 'Three hours?' I said, 'If necessary.' I went into the churchyard and looked at Dummy's grave and remembered how I had meant to show it to Titus. I went inside the church and sat there panting and then suddenly thought I was going to be late and ran out and hurried up the hill. It was a warm day, but with plenty of sea breeze.

I came up as far as the house and stopped to get my breath with my hand on the blue wooden gate with the complicated latch. The blaze of big garish roses, every possible colour, flickered in the sun. I found that I was still carrying my suitcase, which I had intended to leave in the taxi, and Hartley's make-up in a paper bag, which I had intended to put in the suitcase. Then I heard something awful, horrible, which chilled my blood and made me gasp with emotion. Inside the house a treble recorder and an alto recorder were in unison playing *Greensleeves*.

It was not simply that a recorder duet was the last thing I now expected to hear. *Greensleeves* had been, for Hartley and me, in the old days, our signature tune. I had had a recorder on which I laboriously rendered it, and we used to pick it out on her parents' old piano. We sang it to each other. It was our theme song, our love song. If I had heard it played now on *one* recorder I would have taken it instantly as a secret message of hope. But on two recorders ... was it possible that it was a deliberate insult, an intentional desecration of the past? No. *She had simply forgotten.*

All this passed through my mind during the time it took my fingers to undo the gate. I stepped slowly onto the path. The music ceased and a dog began to bark hysterically. I walked up to the door controlling my mind and already having fresh thoughts. The *Greensleeves* sacrilege meant nothing. Perhaps he liked the song and she had not been able to prevent its becoming a favourite. The recorder playing meant nothing. Obviously if she were intending to run she would be careful to behave

as usual. Or perhaps the tune really had been intended as a sign to
me? It was however already obvious that she was not alone. I rang the
bell though the dog had made this unnecessary and his frenzied noise
drowned the sound.

Hartley opened the door. She had her head thrown back in a way
which gave her a proud air, but she was probably just agitated. She
stared at me unsmiling, her lips parted, and I stared back, blushing
hotly and feeling that my eyes were as round as saucers. I could
somehow perceive that Ben was behind her at the open door of the
sitting room. Even if I had planned some private communication for
this moment it would have been impossible, we were both paralysed.
The dog, a slinky black and white collie with a long nose, was now at
Hartley's feet, still barking.

Against the din I said, 'Good afternoon' and Hartley said, 'Kind of
you to come.'

I moved in. The smell of the roses, of which there were several vases
even in the hall, mingled with the stuffy stench of the house, a sweetish
sickly fussy interior smell like the smell of a very old woman's room.

Hartley said 'Be quiet!' to the dog who finished its barking in its
own time and then began to sniff me and wag its tail. Ben said from
the sitting room, 'Come in.'

I walked on in. The picture window displayed the sloping meadow
and the rise of the blue sea receding into a heat haze and never had a
pretty view looked so sinister. The two recorders lay on the wide white
window sill, beside the field glasses.

'Sit you down,' said Hartley. I noticed she was almost smart today.
She had had her hair waved into a respectable mop, and was wearing
a straight plain blue shift dress over a blue and white striped blouse.
She looked younger and healthier. She said, 'Would you like to sit
there, or there?'

I sat down in a low chair with wooden arms, avoiding the tub chair I had got stuck into before.

An elaborate tea had been laid out on a little round table and on a plate stand. There was bread and butter, scones, jam, some kind of sandwiches and an iced cake.

'I'll wet the tea,' said Hartley and disappeared into the kitchen, leaving me with Ben.

Ben, still standing, busied himself with the dog. 'Chuffey!' This was evidently the animal's name. '*Chuffey,* come here. Good dog. Now sit down. *Sit.*' Chuffey sat, and Ben then seated himself, by which time Hartley had returned with the tea and Chuffey had got up again.

'Let it mash a bit,' said Ben.

Hartley shook the teapot and said, 'It's all right,' and to me, 'milk, sugar?'

'Thanks, yes, both.'

'You don't mind milk in first? A sandwich? Or something with jam? The cake's home-made but not in this home, I'm afraid!' Hartley poured out the tea.

'Sandwich, thanks. I love your view.' This remark was totally automatic, I was almost unconscious with emotion.

'Yes, it's fine,' said Ben. He added, 'Fine.' Then to Chuffey, 'Sit! Good boy.' He gave him a piece of sandwich.

'You spoil him!' said Hartley.

'That's the dog from Amorne Farm, isn't it?' I said, the automatic machinery still working. I then wondered if I was supposed to know that, then thought, it doesn't matter.

'Yes, they breed them,' said Ben. 'Good little chaps, Welsh collies. This fellow never cottoned on, though, no good with the sheep, were you, Chuff? You weren't going to waste your time with those silly sheep, were you, boy?'

Chuffey sprang up again wagging his tail.

I had placed my suitcase on the floor beside me and on top of it the paper bag with Hartley's make-up and my razor blades. I put down my cup, opened the case, put the bag inside and closed the case. I was afraid that Ben would somehow see or intuit what was in the bag. Ben and Hartley watched me.

'I was interested to meet your army brother,' said Ben.

Hartley could not have discussed my family situation in any detail. Monsters do not have families.

'He's my cousin.'

'Oh yes, cousin. What's he in?'

'King's Royal Rifle Corps.'

'Green Jackets.'

'I mean Green Jackets.'

'Is he still staying with you?'

'No, he's gone back to London.'

'I wish I'd become a regular soldier,' said Ben.

'It might be rather dull in peace time,' said Hartley.

'I wish I'd done that,' said Ben. 'You really know people in the army. You get around. Still it's nice to be at home too.'

'Very nice.'

'How's your house?'

'Rain got in.'

'It *did* rain, didn't it.'

'Have another sandwich,' said Hartley. 'Oh, you haven't eaten that one.'

I clutched the sandwich. I crushed it and some cucumber sped out onto the floor. I started to put the sandwich in my pocket. I said, 'I am so sorry – I am so sorry about – about –'

'About Titus,' said Ben. 'Yes. So are we.' He paused, then added, 'It was one of those things.'

'It was a tragedy,' said Hartley. She spoke as if this was some sort of definitive description.

I went on desperately. I wanted to drag us all down into some common pool of feeling, I wanted to stop this conventional machine of awful insincere politeness. But I could not find suitable words. I said, 'I feel it was my fault – I can't – I shall never –'

'Of course it wasn't your fault,' said Hartley.

'It certainly wasn't your fault,' said Ben judiciously. 'It's more likely to have been *his* fault.'

'I can't bear it, I can't believe it, I –'

'We have to bear it and believe it,' said Hartley. 'It has happened. It's no use talking.'

'No, it's no use talking,' said Ben. 'Like in the war. Something happens, you go on. You got to, eh?'

Hartley was sitting with her hands on her lap. She did not look at me as she spoke. She shifted self-consciously and patted her soft orderly bush of hair. She was wearing no lipstick and her tanned face showed no sign of make-up. She had unbuttoned the neck of her striped blouse to reveal her sunburnt neck and collarbones. She looked sleeker, cleaner and better cared-for than at any time since our reunion.

Ben too I noticed had an almost prosperous air. He was wearing a clean shirt with a wide stripe and a matching tie. He had a loose brown summer jacket with lighter brown trousers and new-looking white canvas shoes. His shirt-clad stomach bulged comfortably over his tight leather belt. His short schoolboy hair was smoothly combed and he was cleanly-shaven. He had a curious expression of distant calmness on his face. His eyelids drooped a little and his short upper lip was tensed, drawn up in a kind of poised fastidious manner. He too did not look at me. He had eaten several sandwiches during the previous exchanges.

'I suppose so,' I said, in answer to Ben's question.

'Let me give you a serviette,' said Hartley, 'you've got your hands all sticky.' She took a paper one from a drawer and handed it to me.

'You going to spend the winter here?' said Ben.

They had evidently finished with the subject of Titus.

I could not blame them. Why should they display their emotions to me? They had to recover from that death in their own way. They were relieved that the subject had been mentioned between us and could now be dropped. Possibly that was the point of the meeting.

'Yes. I live here.'

'I thought you might go to France or Madeira or somewhere in the winter like rich folks do.'

'Certainly not. Anyway I'm not rich.'

'It's bloody cold here, I can tell you.'

'Look at him, look at the way he's sitting!' said Hartley, indicating Chuffey who was now sitting with his front paws neatly curled in and his back legs stretched out at full length. The dog looked up, pleased with itself.

'You're a funny dog, aren't you?' said Ben. Chuffey wagged his tail in agreement.

'Are you going to get a dog?' said Hartley to me.

'No, I don't think so.'

'Cat man, eh?' said Ben.

'What?'

'Cat man?'

'Oh – er – no.'

'It's a bore about the quarantine,' said Ben. 'Six months, like here.'

'The – quarantine?'

'Yes,' said Ben. 'We're off to Australia. No more English winters for us. We didn't know it was so long when we got Chuff, but we can't leave you behind, can we, boy?'

'*To Australia*, you mean – for good?'

'Yes.'

I looked at Hartley. She met my glance with her wide open calm violet eyes and with a sort of smile, then got up and took the teapot out into the kitchen.

'*To Australia?*'

'Yes, I can't think why everybody doesn't go. Lovely climate, cheaper grub, cheaper housing. God, I wish I was young again, I'd have a go out there.'

'Ben can draw his pension in Australia,' said Hartley, coming back with the teapot.

'Ever been there?' said Ben.

'Yes,' I said, 'I've been several times. It's a marvellous country.'

'Sydney harbour, Sydney opera house, cheap wine, kangaroos, koala bears, the lot, I can't wait.'

'When are you going?' I said, looking at Hartley, who was busied with Ben's cup.

'Oh not at once, be five or six weeks. Got a lot of things to fix up, see my sister and that. We've been planning it a long time, but with the boy gone it's easier.'

'But – so you were always going to do this?' I tried to catch Hartley's eye. 'I mean, it takes some time to plan to go to Australia – I didn't know you were meaning to leave here – I'm rather surprised you didn't tell me.' I said this to Hartley.

'I could hardly believe it,' she said, smiling vaguely. 'It seemed like a dream.'

'You'll believe it when you see that opera house,' said Ben, 'smiling like a great shell on the blue water.'

If they were leaving in five or six weeks the Australian plan could surely not have been made since I last saw Hartley. Why did she not tell me? What an extraordinary thing to do, not to tell me. Then I thought, maybe she didn't believe it would happen. And if she was trying to make up her mind to bolt with me she would not tell me, that is just what she would do, not tell. I kept staring at her, but after the vague smile she looked elsewhere.

She said to Ben, 'Do you think Chuffey will know us after all that time in quarantine?'

''Course he will! Won't you, Chuff, eh, eh?'

'Have some more tea?' said Hartley to me. 'Have a scone, some cake?'

I gulped some down and handed over my cup. I ate the piece of smashed sandwich which I had failed to put in my pocket. I felt completely confused, utterly at a loss, like a man in a strange country who is the victim of some quiet impenetrable charade. I could not understand.

'I see you're off somewhere too,' said Ben, indicating my suitcase.

'Oh – just a night in London – I'll be back directly, I'll be here –'

'I can't stand London,' said Ben. 'All that noise, all those people, bloody foreigners come to do a bit of shop-lifting.'

'Yes,' I said, 'it is rather full of tourists at this time of year.' I drank up my tea.

'Well,' said Ben in a tone which clearly implied the end of my visit, 'maybe we'll see you again before we go, but if not cheerio.'

'Oh I'm sure we'll meet again,' I said. 'I'll be back in the village tomorrow. I'll be at home all the time, no travel plans. Well, I must be off now. Thank you for the tea.'

I got up. Idiotic Chuffey began to bark at once. I gave a vague wave to Ben, picked up my case and made for the door. Hartley followed me. Ben shouted at Chuffey, then closed the sitting-room door after us to stop the dog from rushing out. I was alone with Hartley for a few seconds at the front door.

'Hartley, you're not going to Australia, you're *not?*' The dog's loud barking covered my words.

She shook her head, waved a hand, opened her mouth, seeming to indicate that it was impossible to talk in this noise.

'Hartley, you can't go. Come away with me now. I've got a taxi waiting at the bottom of the hill. Come, now, run, run with me, we'll go to London, anywhere you like – look, I wrote you this letter, it explains everything.' I hardly knew what I was doing. I took the 'quiet life' letter out of my pocket and thrust it into a pocket in the skirt of her blue dress.

Ben opened the sitting-room door and slipped out. Chuffey was still barking and I could hear his claws clicking on the inside of the door. Ben glanced towards us, then went into the kitchen leaving the door open.

I took a step backward, taking Hartley's bare arm and trying to pull her after me. She had rolled up the sleeve of her blouse and her arm was soft and warm, like the arm of a young girl, it had not yet grown old. We were both now just outside the door.

'Hartley, darling, love, my own love, come with me now, *now*, we'll run down the hill to the taxi.'

She shook her head, and drew her arm away. She said something that sounded like 'I can't.' The damn dog was still barking.

'You're not going to Australia, I won't let you. Let him go, you stay. Look, the taxi's down beside the church. I'll be there in the church, I'll wait an hour, two hours, make an excuse and come down, we can get away at once. It doesn't matter about packing, just come. Hartley, don't stay here with that man. Choose happiness, come to me.' I took her arm again.

She looked at me as if she were about to cry, but there were no tears. She moved a step back and I released her. 'Hartley, *speak* to me –'

She said, but I could scarcely hear her, 'You haven't understood –'

'Hartley, darling, come to me. I'll be waiting for you, I'll wait two hours in the church. Or I'll expect you tomorrow. I'm not going away anywhere, I'll be at home. You love me, you came to me that night, you told me those things. You must come, it isn't too late, it's never too late –'

The sun, the roses, dazzled my eyes. Ben had come back into the hall and I could see him in the shadows beyond Hartley's head. One moment her face seemed a mask of pain, then, but perhaps it had not really changed, it looked empty, blank. Her big tearless eyes were blank.

Ben said loudly, over Chuffey's barking, 'Well, cheerio then.'

I stepped backward, then turned and walked to the gate. After I had gone through the gate I looked back. They were both standing at the door waving. I waved too and began to walk down the hill.

I sat in the church for more than two hours but she did not come. I paid off the taxi man and walked home.

So, I had five weeks. I was not beaten yet. What after all could Hartley say to me, with Ben behind her listening in the kitchen? What had she actually said, what had I said? Already it was fading. At any rate she had the letter, and the letter was *clear*. It would make a focus for her thoughts.

What on earth was the purpose of that invitation to tea? It had obviously been Ben's idea. Perhaps Ben had more sense and more subtlety than I had credited him with. He had set a scene where Hartley could see me, quietly and in his presence, for the last time and take a dignified and final farewell. The idea was intelligent and could even be considered humane. It was however an irrelevant device. It was plain that Hartley did not want to go to Australia, that was Ben's plan. When had he made it? When he first knew that I was in the village, or earlier?

Anyway, Hartley would not go. She would jump, at the last moment, into the rescue boat.

I had taken to drinking in the evenings. At any rate, four days had passed and I had been drunk four evenings, on wine of course. I sat long long with the bottle in the kitchen, thinking, until the late midsummer daylight had entirely gone. Again, it was a time to wait, to wait and to reflect. Of course nothing had happened, no telephone call, no letter, nothing. But there would be a sign; Hartley or the gods would give me one.

The weather continued warm. The sea had regained its bejewelled purplish look, inlaid with spotted lines of emerald. It glittered at me as it had done on the first day. There were a few clouds, big lazy chryselephantine clouds that loafed around over the water exuding light. I gazed at them and wondered at myself for being too obsessed to be able to admire the marvels that surrounded me. But knowing how blind I was did not make me see. I sometimes looked for seals, but there were none. I had no heart to go swimming and wondered if I would ever swim again.

I tried not to think about Titus. Perhaps it was just this effort that drove me to drinking. I persistently directed my thought away from him, or busily thought of him in other contexts and relations, as part of other and still living problems. I anxiously and meanly thrust him away and let myself hope that if I could only *put him off* a little longer I would find that, after all, I had re-entered the callous world of those who have recovered from bereavement. I had my own troubles and I had to survive. Now was no moment to have my mind laid waste by guilt and the torments of loss. So I did not think of *him* and that he was dead. There was a sort of grey dripping figure that kept trying to rise up in my mind and which I ruthlessly violently banished. At moments I almost felt afraid as if he were still somewhere, calling my thought, attracting my attention, and resenting my refusal to mourn. I busied my quick thought with other matters. But the dripping figure remained somehow present to me.

I thought about James and Lizzie. Which of those two had decided to tell me and why? I guessed that, especially after the sordid encounter with Toby Ellesmere, Lizzie's nerve had broken, chiefly because there was by then too much at stake. She had let her old love for me take possession and she had reason to think that the quarry was weary and near to dropping. Her love was impatient, hungry. I would soon turn to her entirely, she thought, and she wanted to be *safe*. A nagging guilty anxiety made cause with her honesty to make her take the risk of telling. She was, in the long orbit of her love for me, at the nearest point. She wanted, for the great moment that was coming, to be in the clear, to be made by confession pure, to have no haunting revelation left to fear. She was perhaps not to know how searingly destructive was her combination with James. He knew. But by then the curious situation was beyond his control, and he had to play the gentleman, both by denying that it had originally been her idea (which I was inclined to believe) and by, when it came to it, letting her speak. Such can be the awful consequences of a prudent lie. Lizzie had feared to tell about James as Hartley had feared to tell about me; well, the women had all lied, it was their nature: Hartley, Lizzie, Rosina, Rita, Jeanne, Clement ... God knows how many lies Clement must have told me. I would never know.

And I thought about the far past, sitting there in the kitchen in the warm summer twilight, drinking wine until my head reeled, with no lamp and no candle, and the form of the wine bottle outlined against the faint rectangle of the open door and a sky which was never to become entirely dark. And I heard the voice of Aunt Estelle, and not of Lizzie, singing *Roses in Picardy,* and I recalled the brilliant radiance of her presence and all the joy and all the pain she caused me once. God, how the young and beautiful vanish and are no more seen.

And I thought of Hartley on her bicycle and of her pure truthful face as it was then, so strangely like and unlike her worn old face which had suffered and sinned away all those years when I was somewhere else with Clement and Rosina and Jeanne and Fritzie. *Alas, my love, you do me wrong to cast me off discourteously, for I have loved you so long, delighting in your company.* I had invested so much, as the years went by, in my belief in Hartley's goodness. Yet had I always cherished this icon? The young too are ruthless and must survive. After I had lost all hope of her return, all hope of finding her, I had lived for a time on my resentment, on the relief of: let her go then! And I recalled now, dredged up out of the deep sea caves of memory, a conversation I had had about her with Clement. Yes, I had told Clement about Hartley. And Clement had said, 'Put her away in your old toy cupboard now, dear boy.' My God, I could *hear* Clement's powerful resonant voice saying those words now, as if she were uttering them in the dark room. And I had put Hartley away, for a time. I had certainly, after those early days, never talked of her to Clement again. It would have been bad form, and Clement did not forgive bad form. Possibly Clement forgot her. But I did not forget, and Hartley lay like a seed in my heart, and grew again, purified as of old.

It was only now clear to me how very much I had *made* that image, and yet I could not feel that it was anything like a fiction. It was more like a special sort of truth, almost a touchstone; as if a thought of mine could become a thing, and at the same time be truth. It was the dismissive resentment, the 'let her go then', which was a lie. My odd almost mad faithfulness had become its own reward in the end. I had smoothed Hartley's brow and unclouded her lovely eyes as the years went by, and the ambiguous tormenting image had become gentle and a source of light.

But what had happened now? I conjured up that weird scene in the sitting room at Nibletts with the scones and the cucumber sandwiches and the iced cake and Ben and Hartley looking so clean and well. (After they had waved me off, did Ben go back and cut himself a large slice of cake?) There had been a kind of creepy peacefulness. It was indeed like a primitive picture, the virtuous and happy couple in their pretty little house complete with collie dog. They were 'plumped out' in my memory, as art plumps out its subjects, making them fatter and smoother than life and more absolutely there. They looked better, healthier, handsomer than I had seen them before. Why? What had given them that calm satisfied look? The terrible answer came to me: Titus's death.

I recalled what Hartley had said on the day that she ran to me and told me of her unhappiness, and so much filled me with the hope of delivering her, the day which I had told her was 'evidence'. She had said that she was broken, her inner structure cracked, her integrity destroyed, by having through the years been forced to side with Ben against Titus. And I had wondered, was she a suffering redeemer or just a wreck? 'Everything was broken, as if one could still stand up but all one's bones were broken, all the bones and the little joints were broken, one wasn't whole any more, one wasn't a person any more.' It could be that those awful years had really destroyed her sympathy with Titus. She had suffered too much for him. I recalled her words, 'Sometimes I felt he hated us ... sometimes I almost wish he were dead.' The burden of guilt was too great to sustain without slow deep resentment. Titus, that fatal bundle that she herself had wantonly sought, and carried one day into the house, had ruined her marriage and ruined her life. But now it was as if Titus himself was the redeemer, he had vanished taking her guilt with him. The accusing consciousness was gone. Ben would be quietly relieved, and more secretly still she would join him, secretly, instinctively, blindly joining in his relief. The murder over, they would both feel better. Now the guilt would begin to fade. So in a way the death of Titus was fated; and in a way Ben had really killed him after all.

Of course these were rambling drunken thoughts, but I could not help thinking that I was right to see an awful relief as well as an awful resignation in their acceptance of that death. And of course in trying to see it as so weirdly falling into the pattern of their lives, I knew that I was surreptitiously attempting to ease my own remorse and guilt. How soon we cover up the horror of death and loss, if we can, with almost any sort of explanation, as if we had to justify the very fate which had maimed us.

The flight to Australia could now also be envisaged with a clear conscience. How *could* Hartley have accepted the idea of leaving England with Titus still lost? *Had* she accepted it? Perhaps not. Perhaps that was why it had to seem to her 'like a dream'. I was certain that she had not, in her awkward innocent little conversations with Titus, told him about the Australian plan. After all, she had not told me. This omission now seemed to me a good omen. She had not told me because she was already making up her mind to stay.

Titus had said of her that she was a 'fantasist'. As I went on thinking, the probable proportion of falsehood in what she had told me seemed to grow. Her structure cracked, like broken bones that would never knit, broken by Ben, by Titus, she had lost her way, her sense of direction to the truth. So where was my ideal now? The strange thing was that there was still a source of light, as if Hartley herself shed light upon Hartley. I could take it all, I could embrace it all, whatever she was like it was her I loved. It had happened so in my life that I had only one place where blameless love was taught and only one teacher. Thus people can be light sources, without ever knowing, for years in the lives of others, while their own lives take different and hidden courses. Equally one can be, and I recalled Peregrine's words, a monster, a cancer, in the mind of someone whom one has half forgotten or even never met.

But supposing it should turn out in the end that such a love should lose its object, *could* it, whatever happened, lose its object? Some loves are not defeated by death, although it is not as easy as we think to love the dead. But there are pains and devices which defeat love more ingeniously. Would I at last absolutely lose Hartley because of a treachery or desertion on her part which should turn my love into hate? Could I begin to see her as cold, heartless, uncanny, a witch, a sorceress? I felt that this could never be, and I felt it as an achievement, almost as a mode of possession. As James said, 'If even a dog's tooth is truly worshipped it glows with light.' My love for Hartley was very nearly an end in itself. Twist and turn as she might, whatever happened she could not escape me now.

My reflections did not always maintain this high level. A passing thought of Rosina brought me back to the image of Ben looking so curiously prosperous, as Fritzie Eitel would say so 'bright-eyed and bushy-tailed'. Was that only the result of an awful death endured and accepted as a way to freedom, the prospect of the opera house reflected in the waves? Where had Rosina spent the night before that hideous day when we took Hartley back? I recalled what Gilbert had said about hearing a woman talking in the house, when he came to deliver the letter, Rosina had declared she was going to 'console' Ben. This could have been just a spiteful jest. On the other hand, Rosina was *capable de tout*. If something had 'happened' between Ben and Rosina this might account not only for his curious air of satisfaction but also for his more liberal attitude to Hartley, his tolerance of my visit, of a doorstep discussion lasting almost a minute and so on. Perhaps Rosina had done Hartley a good turn, either by giving Ben a little something to conceal and feel guilty about, or by making him realize how much his funny old wife was to be preferred to a flashy show-business bitch. These were, in fact, however I turned them about, unsavoury thoughts. But at the level of a vulgar curiosity they were at times a relief from the intensity of higher longings.

It then occurred to me that Rosina might still be at the Raven Hotel and that I could simply walk along and ask her, and even if she lied I might learn something.

I was of course reluctant to leave the house because I was, from one moment to the next, expecting Hartley or her 'sign', but I decided to risk it, and left a note on the door saying *H. Wait. Back very soon.* I decided not to telephone the hotel beforehand, as I wanted a little advantage from surprise. If I rang, Rosina would have time to invent an elaborate falsehood. I also wanted the tiny consolation of seeing her sudden pleasure at seeing me. For I had to admit that I wanted from Rosina not only information relative to my case, but also some touch of the comfort which an affectionate woman can give, even if she is a bitch. The walk, the objective, was in itself a distraction, a *task,* in a period of time when inactive waiting and thinking were already becoming a burden. If Hartley gave no sign I would soon act again. Meanwhile the investigation of Rosina might even turn out to be useful.

It was a warm cloudy day and a little wind was tossing bits of white foam off the many-capped wavelets in Raven Bay. The sea was in a restless fussy mood, dark blue in colour, that grim cold northern blue which even in summertime can convey a wintry menace. The sky too had its northern look, a pallid cool blue between compact and very white fast-moving clouds. The sunlight came and went as I walked along the familiar road, and the big round boulders of the bay leapt out into a surprising variety of grotesque stony shapes, pitted with shadows and blotched with old seaweed stains and eyes of brilliant yellow lichen, then quietly faded again as the light was dipped.

I reached the hotel. I had not been there since the day when I was expelled from the dining room for not wearing a tie. The sun was shining into the cheerful comfortably furnished front hall as I went in, and it occurred to me how clean and tidy and pleasant it was after the filth and squalor of Shruff End, where I had no heart to embellish any more. There were bright chintzy armchairs and a huge vase full of wild buddleia and fuchsia and willow-herb and some of the mauve mallow which was growing among the rocks. A not too sneering servitor came forward to enquire my business. I was wearing dirty cotton trousers slightly rolled up and a straying blue shirt, but this could pass muster in the morning, even in the presence of chintz armchairs.

I said, 'Excuse me, but is Miss Vamburgh still staying in the hotel?'

The man gave me a slightly funny look and replied, 'Mr and Mrs Arbelow are in the lounge, sir.'

My God! I walked to the door he indicated. The big lounge, with a huge view of the bay, was empty except for two people seated by the window and looking out. They turned as I came in.

'Charles!'

'Why it's our favourite fun person! Charles, old man, we were just hoping you'd come, weren't we, Rose?'

Two faces were turned towards me, blazing with amused malice.

'Hello,' I said. 'How nice to see you two together again. May I buy you a drink?'

'No, no,' cried Peregrine, 'drinks are on us! Waiter, waiter! A bottle of that champagne we had yesterday, please, and three glasses.'

'Did you go back to London,' I asked Peregrine, 'or did you come straight here?'

'No,' he said, 'I just stopped to drown my sorrow and there the old cross-eyed bitch was.'

'And you fell into each other's arms.'

'Not at once,' said Rosina. 'We had a sort of jolly row to begin with. Peregrine was rather aggressive. He seemed to be chiefly annoyed about his windscreen.'

'The windscreen bugged me,' said Peregrine, 'but it was mainly symbolic. Thank you, waiter.'

'Let me open it,' cried Rosina. 'I love opening bottles of champagne.' The cork flew, the golden stuff foamed. 'Charles!'

'Thank you. Your health, Mr and Mrs Arbelow.'

'We can hardly believe it, actually,' said Rosina. 'We're happy. At least I'm happy. Are you happy, Peregrine?'

'This unfamiliar sensation I identify unerringly as happiness. Charles, the best to you. Is your macabre military cousin still around?'

'No, he's gone.'

'So you languish with the ever-faithful Liz?'

'No, she's gone too.'

'All alone?' said Rosina. 'What about the bearded lady?'

'Oh, they're going away. Anyhow I've given up the Quest of the Bearded Lady. It was a brief mental aberration.'

'That was the general view,' said Peregrine. 'We congratulate you.'

'Are you going back to London?'

'Tomorrow. Though it's lovely here and the food is excellent. I've got a TV thing. May we drive you?'

'No, thanks. And are you really joining forces again?'

'Yes,' said Rosina. 'Everything has sprung back into place. We never got over each other and now we shall never have to. It's as simple as that. But do you know, Charles, what made me suddenly see the truth?'

'What?'

'Peregrine murdering you!'

'Well, trying to,' said Peregrine. 'I must be modest.'

'Why was that so endearing?' I asked.

'Oh I don't know, it was splendid. After all, you deserved to be murdered. For what you did to us, if for nothing else.'

'Let's not talk of that,' I said.

'Oh, don't worry, we won't list your sins, we're feeling far too cheerful. But it was so sort of sporting and splendid of Peregrine to push you into that hole. I always hated the idea that he'd forgiven you. I only wish you'd drowned, it would have been more aesthetic.'

'I can't think why you didn't,' said Perry.

'It was a piece of thoroughly picturesque and proper violence. I like a violent man really, a man who's a bit of a brute in a decent straightforward way. You are an awful crook, Charles, but basically you're soft. I can't imagine why I got so attached to you. I think it was your own illusions of power that fascinated people, not personal magnetism. We were just duped by your conceit. As a man, you're a softie, I can see that now.'

'I like being nice and soft, like a squashy toy. But are you actually going to marry again? Surely you won't go that far? I thought you said marriage was hell, Peregrine, you said it was brainwashing.'

'Not when you marry the same person for the second time. Everyone should do it.'

'But what about Pamela?'

'Oh, haven't you heard? Pam's gone off with Marcus Henty. You know he's become a gentleman farmer. The manor-house life should suit Pam down to the ground.'

'So I thought I'd better grab Peregrine before he started making passes at Angie!'

'God!' said Peregrine. They laughed crazily, Perry's big wrinkled face red with the sun and the champagne. Rosina as usual was perched, now on the arm of Peregrine's chair, swinging long bare legs, her white dress hitched up. She leaned over him, brushing his hair with her nose. They both twinkled at me, then regarded each other solemnly and went off into another fit.

'I hope there's a part for Peregrine in Fritzie's *Odyssey*,' I said. 'Perhaps he could enact the old dog.'

'Oh, that's off,' said Rosina.

'Fritzie's changed his mind?'

'No, I've changed mine.'

'We're going to Ireland,' said Peregrine.

'To *Ireland*?'

'Yes, to Londonderry. We've had enough of West End show business. We're going to bring theatre to the people.'

'Oh my God!'

'Don't you mock, Charles. This is going to be the beginning of something great –'

'So you're giving up the Calypso part, Rosina?'

'Yes,' she said.

I said, 'You've impressed me, at last.'

'The beginning of something great,' said Peregrine. 'We're going to write the plays ourselves and get local people to act them. The Irish are natural actors, and there's a darling little theatre that's only a bit bombed –'

'I'm not mocking,' I said. 'I think you're brave, both of you, I wish you the best of luck. No, no more champagne, thanks, it's made me drunk already.'

'Charles never had a head for drink,' said Peregrine, pouring himself some more.

'I'm not a monster in your mind any more, I hope?' I said to him.

'No,' he said. 'I killed the monster when I pushed you into the sea. I'm glad you survived, really. All's well that ends well.'

'Ah, but when is the end? I must be off. Thanks for the champers.'

'I'll see you to the door,' said Rosina. She skipped out, and I saluted Peregrine and followed.

Rosina's white dress turned out to be a sort of shapeless prophetess's robe made of some very light fabric which practically floated on the air all round her. She held out her arms and flapped it, then drew it closely about her. We came out and stood a moment in the sun on the stony verge of the road. Rosina's feet were bare.

'So you think this'll work, I mean you and Peregrine?'

'I don't see why not,' she said. 'There was never anything the matter between us except jealousy.'

'A big matter. And ubiquitous.'

'Well, it's a sign of love. Peregrine was simply obsessed about you, then he married that Pam simply to annoy me. And, you know, I couldn't bear Peregrine being so passive about your stealing me away, I always wanted him to fight for me.'

'The Helen of Troy complex. It's fairly common.'

'And when I heard he'd killed you ...'

'He boasted of it?'

'Naturally —'

'Well, good luck to you. Tell me, Rosina, that day when you went off and said you were going to see Ben, did you go?'

Rosina peered up at me with her intense crossing eyes. She chuckled and hugged the white robe more closely around her. 'Yes.'

'And what happened?'

'Oh nothing *happened*. We had a tremendous talk.'

'I would call that a happening. What about?'

'Charles, you ask too many questions,' said Rosina, 'and you want something for nothing, you always did. But I can assure you of one thing — your bearded lady is a lucky woman. That man is *extremely attractive*.'

'Oh – !' I turned away with a wave. I would have given a lot for a tape-recording of that 'tremendous talk' – if it really took place. It then occurred to me for the first time to wonder, had Ben and Hartley come together through *sexual attraction*?

'Charles!' Rosina had run a little way after me, padding on the grass verge with her bare feet, her white robe fluttering free.

I waited.

'Charles, darling, tell me, I must know. When you came here today were you going to offer yourself to me?'

'You ask too many questions,' I said.

I could hear her laughing merrily as I walked on. Her having given up that film part, that had the hard touch of reality all right.

That evening the clouds gathered, the sun vanished, and it began to rain. The madcap English weather which had been putting on a passable imitation of June now decided to play March. A cold wind blew from the sea and brought the rain in aggressive irregular patterings, like flung pebbles against the back windows. The house was full of odd sounds of straining and creaking and the bead curtain kept up an irregular prattle of sudden flurried clicks. I looked for the Irish jersey and finally found it among the bedclothes and cushions which still lay on the floor of the bookroom. I tried to light the fire in the little red room, but my indoors store was exhausted and the outdoor wood was wet. I drank a lot of red wine after my lentil soup and went to bed early with a hot water bottle.

The next morning it was still raining a little but the wind had dropped and it was less cold. A thick clammy pearly-grey mist surrounded the house, it was impossible to see the end of the causeway. I carried the dustbins, which had not been cleared for some time, out to the road, and stood there for a while listening. The invisible countryside was a vast silence. I came in again, wet with fog and drizzle, and treated myself to a long breakfast of porridge with tinned cream and brown sugar, poached eggs, biscuits and honey (I had run out of bread) and several pots of hot tea. Sitting afterwards with a rug over my knees, my hand encountered in my pocket an object which my fingers were unable to 'read'. I drew it forth and it turned out to be Hartley's slide, which I had pocketed on the night when she 'ran to me'. I stared at the almost senseless little thing and tried to grasp it as an omen, but it just looked pathetic and filled me with sadness and I put it away in a drawer in the red room.

I resumed my rug and began to review the situation.

One consoling and clarifying thought which kept returning to me as I tried to imagine Hartley's state of mind, was that she might decide to wait until the last moment before making a dash for it. Let Ben go to Australia. It was certainly his wish, his idea, not hers. She could perhaps actually brush him off forever by slipping away just as he was about to sail. Then she would leap, like Lord Jim, down into my boat. Ben's impetus would be greatest when he was all set to go, and he might then very well say: to hell with her. This view of the matter was ingenious and plausible. But could I rely on it sufficiently to remain inactive, and could I and dare I endure that much inactivity without a firm assurance from Hartley?

I decided I could afford to allow a span of two or three days more for Hartley to reflect upon the letter which I had left with her. I was glad she had that letter and I imagined it working upon her on my behalf like a little resident imp. I recalled too that I had had the wit to give her my telephone number. Doubtless by now the woodwork class would know Ben no more, but he would surely have to leave the house sometimes to go somewhere, to pick up tickets, visas, money; and even though he might take Hartley with him he could not supervise her every move. Surely she could get away to a telephone and ring me up. Very few words would be necessary: *Wait, I will come.* Imagining those words carried me over one or two bad patches. And the constant possibility of the telephone call made endurable the short period of sheer waiting which I had decreed for myself.

But supposing nothing happened . . . and nothing happened . . .? Then of course I must contrive to see Hartley, by some method yet to be invented, and even if it were to involve some sort of 'showdown' with Ben. There must be no more charades. The prospect of this perhaps decisive showdown filled me with a mixture of fear and pleasurable excitement, as I saw *this* as the final barrier beyond which I could, if I knocked it down, see my prize secure. The 'knocking down' image was not altogether a reassuring one however. At the very least I must be prepared to use force in self-defence. Ben was a more violent man by nature, which was psychologically a considerable advantage. He probably *liked* hitting people. He was younger than me, a burly strong fellow, but now getting fat and a little out of condition, whereas I was fit and agile. The theatre demands physical fitness and I had always responded to this demand with the scrupulous keenness of an athlete.

With a view to self-defence I searched Shruff End for a suitable blunt instrument. At any moment I might, after all, receive a visit not from Hartley but from Ben. The idea of killing Ben had not entirely left my mind. It was as if, contrary to reason and more calm reflection, a deep trace had been left in my mind, like a memory trace, only this was concerned with the future. It was a sort of 'intention trace', or like what might exist in the mind of someone who could 'remember' the future as we remember the past. I am aware that this scarcely makes sense, but what I felt here was neither a rational intention nor a premonition nor even a prediction. It was just a sort of mental scar which I had received and had to reckon with. I refrained, as yet, from planning. I vaguely envisaged the moment of 'battering through' as a scene of legitimate self-defence. And I searched for a blunt instrument.

It was now late in the evening of the day following my meeting with Perry and Rosina. A bit earlier I had felt a distinct temptation to walk along to the Raven Hotel and follow Peregrine's example of drowning my sorrows in the bar. I felt a need simply to see a few ordinary human beings who were living ordinary human lives, having holidays, honeymoons, quarrels, trouble with their motor cars, trouble with their mortgages. However I feared to discover the Arbelows still there and I felt I could now do with a long interval before encountering that pair again. Perhaps I would go one day to visit the darling little theatre in Londonderry, but I thought it more likely that I would not. I did not want to go to the Black Lion because of the painful proximity to Hartley and because of the inquisitive dangerous hostility of the clientele and because I might run into Freddie Arkwright. Besides I had to stay near the telephone. Looking for a weapon was at least an occupation.

Mrs Chorney had left various things behind in the attics, which I had searched by daylight and in vain. I had found, lying behind the bath, a long piece of metal, perhaps for use as a crowbar, but it was too heavy and too large to be carried in, as I envisaged the matter, a mackintosh pocket. I had of course reviewed my own tools, but these were ridiculously scanty: screwdrivers but no chisel, and only a sort of little 'lady's hammer'. Now in the dark late twilight, I was searching with the help of a candle a space I had discovered under the sink which seemed to be a hiding place of various items. Probing, amidst damp rotting wood and a colony of woodlice, I found a thick heavy piece of metal which turned out to be a hammer head. The shank or handle, or whatever the wooden shaft is called that propels the head, was lying separately and I placed both items on the table.

It was now almost dark outside, the mist, more like a cloud descended, obscuring whatever light the twilit sky might still have offered. A small rain was falling, and although the wind was not strong the house seemed to be moving, shaking itself and twitching, jerking and creaking and stretching like a wooden ship. I could hear the window frames shifting, the bead curtain clicking, the front door rattling, and a little very high tinny vibration which I had, after some search, detected as coming from the front doorbell which hung in the kitchen. I was also startled by a sound coming from outside, from across the sea, a prolonged repeated booming, not unlike a ship's foghorn. I had never heard a foghorn before upon our strangely unfrequented sea; perhaps it was a ship that had lost its way and would, after an interval of silence, suddenly crunch upon my rocks with a most unimaginable din? The foghorn noise, if it was one, had ceased for a time; but now there was another sound, the peculiar regular slapping boom which was produced by the water racing into Minn's cauldron and being abruptly forced out again. I put the candle on the table between the hammer head and the wooden handle which looked, oddly separated from each other, like ritual instruments belonging to some unfamiliar cult. I listened to the loud hollow regular noise from the cauldron and the force of it seemed to enter my body, it began to seem like a strong beating heart, like the strong beating of my own heart, and then like the menacing accelerating sound of the wooden clappers used in the Japanese theatre.

I felt suddenly very uneasy and decided to lock the door onto the lawn. As I moved to it, with my back to the candle, I could see the scene outside dimly through the window. I stopped with a sharp pang of fright, seeing a dark figure standing near to the door, between the house and the rocks. Then the next second I somehow realized that it was James. We looked at each other through the glass. Instead of opening the door I turned back, picked up the candle, and went out into the hall to find one of the oil lamps. I lit the lamp, blew out the candle, and came back with the lamp into the kitchen. James had come inside in the dark and was sitting at the table. I put the lamp down, turned up the wick, and said, 'Oh, it's you,' as if I had not seen him before or perhaps expected it to be somebody else.

'You don't mind my turning up?'

'No.'

I sat down and started fiddling with the hammer. James rose, took off his jacket which was spotted with rain, shook it, hung it over the back of his chair, folded back his shirt cuffs, and sat down again with his elbows on the table and watched me.

'What are you doing?'

'Mending this hammer.' The problem was that the head fitted onto the handle all right, but loosely, so that it would come off in use.

'The head's loose,' said James.

'I have noticed that!'

'You need a wedge.'

'A wedge?'

'Put a chip of wood in to keep it tight.'

I found a chip of wood (the house was littered with chips of wood for some reason), balanced it inside the metal hole and drove the shaft in, keeping the chip in place. I swung the hammer. The head held firmly.

'What do you want it for?' said James.

'To crush a black-beetle.'

'You like black-beetles, at least you did when we were young.'

I got up and found a litre bottle of Spanish red wine, opened it and put it on the table with two glasses. The room was cold so I lit the Calor gas stove.

'What larks we had,' said James.

'When?'

'When we were young.'

I could not recall any larks I had had with James. I poured out the wine and we sat in silence.

James, not looking at me, was making patterns on the table with his finger. Possibly he was embarrassed; and at the idea that he might feel himself for once in the position of a suppliant I felt embarrassed too. However I was in no mood to help him out. The silence continued. This was getting like a Quaker meeting.

James said, 'Can you hear the sea?'

'That was Keats's favourite quotation from Shakespeare.' I listened. The beating sound had stopped and been succeeded by a kind of regular wailing hiss as the large methodical waves climbed the rocks and drenched them and fell back. The wind must have increased. 'Yes.'

After another pause he said, 'Anything to eat?'

'Vegetable protein stew.'

'Oh good, I'm sick of eggs.'

We sat on drinking for a while. James poured water into his wine and I followed suit. Then I got up to heat the stew. (I had thrown it together that morning as an emergency ration, it keeps well.) As I did so I reflected that the machine which I had ingeniously constructed to separate myself from my cousin forever did not seem to be working very well.

'Bread?'

'Yes, please.'

'Hell, there's no bread, only biscuits.'

'OK, anything.'

We settled down to the stew.

'When are you coming back to London?' he asked.

'I don't know.'

'What about Hartley?'

'What about her?'

'Any news, views?'

'No.'

'You've given up?'

'No.'

'Seen her?'

'I had tea with her and Ben.'

'What was it like?'

'Polite. More wine?'

'Thank you.'

I was afraid that James was going to pester me with more questions, but he did not, he seemed to have lost interest. With an air now of generalizing he said, 'I think you're nearly through, out of it. You've built a cage of needs and installed her in an empty space in the middle. The strong feelings are all around her — vanity, jealousy, revenge, your love for your youth — they aren't focused on her, they don't touch her. She seems to be their prisoner, but really you don't harm her at all. You are using her image, a doll, a simulacrum, it's an exorcism. Soon you will start seeing her as a wicked enchantress. Then you will have nothing to do except forgive her and that will be within your capacity.'

'Thank you — but as it happens I don't love her image, I love her, even what's awful.'

'Her preferring him to you? That would be a feat.'

'No, wreckage, carnage, what's in her mind.'

'Well, what is in her mind? Perhaps she was simply bound to your memory by a sense of guilt. When you released her from it she was grateful, but then her own resentment was set free, her memories of how tiresome you were perhaps, and after that she could revert to a state of indifference. Any cheese?'

'James, you understand absolutely nothing here. And I have not given up, nor am I nearly, as you put it, out or through!'

'It may even be your destiny to live alone and be everybody's uncle like a celibate priest, there are worse ends. Any cheese?'

'I'm not ending just yet I hope! Yes, there is cheese.' I set out the cheese and opened another bottle of wine.

'By the way,' said James, 'I hope you believed what I said to you about Lizzie?'

I filled our glasses. 'I can believe it was all her idea and you had to be a gent about it.'

James sat for a moment concentrating. I guessed that he was wondering whether to start again on details about how often they had met and so on. I decided it didn't matter. I believed him. 'It doesn't matter. I believe you.'

'I'm sorry it happened,' he said. It was not exactly an apology.

'OK. OK now.'

James returned to making patterns on the table and I felt embarrassed again. I said rather awkwardly, 'Well, tell me about yourself, what are you up to?'

'I'm going away —'

'Aha, so you said, you said you were going on a journey. To where there are mountains maybe, and snow maybe, and demons in and out of boxes maybe?'

'Who knows? You're a sea man. I'm a mountain man.'

'The sea is clean. The mountains are high. I think I am becoming drunk.'

'The sea is not all that clean,' said James. 'Did you know that dolphins sometimes commit suicide by leaping onto the land because they're so tormented by parasites?'

'I wish you hadn't told me that. Dolphins are such good beasts. So even they have their attendant demons. Well, you're off are you, let me know when you're back.'

'I'll do that thing.'

'I can't understand your attitude to Tibet.'

'To Tibet?'

'Yes, oddly enough! Surely it was just a primitive superstitious mediaeval tyranny.'

'Of course it was a primitive superstitious mediaeval tyranny,' said James, 'who's disputing that?'

'You seem to be. You seem to regard it as a lost Buddhist paradise.' I had never ventured to say anything like this to James before, it must have been the drink.

'I don't regard it as a Buddhist paradise. Tibetan Buddhism was in many ways thoroughly corrupt. It was a wonderful human relic, a last living link with the ancient world, an extraordinary untouched country with a unique texture of religion and folklore. All this has been destroyed deliberately, ruthlessly and unselectively. Such a quick thoughtless destruction of the past must always be a matter of regret whatever the subsequent advantages.'

'So you speak as an antiquarian?'

James shrugged his shoulders. He was examining several moths which were circling about the lamp. 'You have some splendid moths here. I haven't seen an Oak Eggar for ages. Oh dear, I think that poor fellow's had it. Do you mind if I close the window? Then they won't come in.' He deftly caught two of the moths and put them outside, together with the corpse of their handsome companion, and closed the window. I noticed that it had stopped raining and the air was clearer. The wind had blown the mist away.

'But then you were just keen on studying the superstition?' I said. I felt that this evening, in spite of our embarrassments, my cousin was more open to me than I had ever known him.

'What after all is superstition?' said James, pouring some more wine into both glasses. 'What is religion? Where does the one end and the other begin? How could one answer that question about Christianity?'

'But I mean you were just a student of – not a –' What did I mean? I could not get my question clear.

'Of course,' said James, on whom the wine seemed simply to have the effect of speeding his utterance, 'you are right to keep using the word "superstition", the concept is essential. I asked where does the one end and the other begin. I suppose almost all religion is superstition really. Religion is power, it has to be, the power for instance to change oneself, even to destroy oneself. But that is also its bane. The exercise of power is a dangerous delight. The short path is the only path but it is very steep.'

'I thought religious people felt weak and worshipped something strong.'

'That's what they think. The worshipper endows the worshipped object with power, real power not imaginary power, that is the sense of the ontological proof, one of the most ambiguous ideas clever men ever thought of. But this power is dreadful stuff. Our lusts and attachments compose our god. And when one attachment is cast off another arrives by way of consolation. We never give up a pleasure absolutely, we only barter it for another. All spirituality tends to degenerate into magic, and the use of magic has an automatic nemesis even when the mind has been purified of grosser habits. White magic is black magic. And a less than perfect meddling in the spiritual world can breed monsters for other people. Demons used for good can hang around and make mischief afterwards. The last achievement is the absolute surrender of magic itself, the end of what you call superstition. Yet how does it happen? Goodness is giving up power and acting upon the world negatively. The good are unimaginable.'

Perhaps James was drunk after all. I said, 'Well, I don't understand the half of what you say. Maybe I'm just an old-fashioned ex-Christian, but I always thought that goodness was to do with loving people, and isn't that an attachment?'

'Oh, yes,' said James, rather I thought too casually, 'yes –' He poured himself out some more wine. We had opened another bottle.

'All this giving up of attachments doesn't sound to me like salvation and freedom, it sounds like death.'

'Well, Socrates said we must practise dying –' James was now beginning to sound flippant.

'But you yourself,' I said, for I wanted to hold on to him and bring all this airy metaphysic down to earth, and also to satisfy my curiosity when for once he was in a talkative mood, 'you yourself have loved people, and after all why not, though God knows who they are, since you're so damn secretive. You've never introduced me to any of your friends from the east.'

'They never visit me.'

'Yes, they do. There was that thin bearded chap I saw in your flat once, sitting in a back room.'

'Oh him,' said James, 'he was just a tulpa.'

'Some sort of inferior tribesman I suppose! And talking of tulpas, what about that Sherpa that Toby Ellesmere said you were so keen on, the one that died on the mountain?'

James was silent for a while and I began to think that I had gone too far, but I let the silence continue. The sea was audible but quieter.

'Oh well,' he said at last, 'oh well –', and then was silent again, but was clearly going to tell something, so I waited.

'There's not much to that story,' he said, rather disappointingly, 'at any rate it's soon told. You know that some Buddhists believe that any earthly attachment, if it persists until death, ties you to the Wheel and prevents you from attaining liberation.'

'Oh yes, that wheel –'

'Of spiritual causality. But that's by the way.'

'I remember I asked you if you believed in reincarnation and you said –'

'The Sherpa in question,' said James, 'was called Milarepa. Well, that wasn't his real name, I called him that after a – after a poet I rather admire. He was my servant. We had to go on a journey together. It was winter and the high passes were full of snow, it was a pretty impossible journey really –'

'Was it a military journey?'

'We had to get through this pass. Now you know that in India and Tibet and such places there are tricks people can learn, almost anybody can learn them if they're well taught and try hard enough –'

'Tricks?'

'Yes, you know, like – like the Indian rope trick – anything –'

'Oh, just that sort of trick.'

'Well, what is that sort of trick? As I say, all sorts of people can do them, they can be jolly tiring but – you know they have nothing to do with – with –'

'With what?'

'One of these tricks is raising one's bodily warmth by mental concentration.'

'How's it done?'

'It's useful in a primitive country, like being able to go on walking for forty-eight hours at five miles an hour without eating or drinking or stopping.'

'No one could do that.'

'And to be able to keep oneself warm by mental power is obviously handy on a winter journey.'

'Like good King Wenceslas!'

'I had to cross this pass and I decided to take Milarepa with me. It would involve spending a night in the snow. I didn't have to take him. But I reckoned I could generate enough heat to keep us both alive.'

'Wait a minute! You mean *you* can do this thing of generating bodily heat by mental concentration?'

'I told you it's a *trick*,' said James impatiently. 'It's got nothing to do with anything important, like goodness or anything like that.'

'And then –?'

'We got up to the top of the pass and got caught in a blizzard. I thought we'd be all right. But we weren't. There wasn't enough heat for two. Milarepa died in the night, he died in my arms.'

I said, 'Oh God.' I couldn't think what further to say. My mind was confused and I was beginning to feel very drunk and sleepy. I heard James's voice continuing to speak and it seemed to come from very far away. 'He trusted me ... It was my vanity that killed him ... The payment for a fault is automatic ... They can get to work on any flaw ... I relaxed my hold on him ... I lost my grip ... The Wheel is just ...' By this time my head was down on the table and I was falling quietly asleep.

I awoke and it was day. A clear grey light of dawn, the sun not yet risen, illuminated the kitchen, showing the wine-stained table, the used dishes, the crumbled cheese. The wind had dropped and the sea was silent. James had gone.

I leapt up and called, running out onto the lawn. Then I ran back into the house, calling again, and then through and out of the front door onto the causeway. The blank grey silent light revealed the rocks, the road, and James just getting into his car. The car door closed. I called and waved. James saw me and lowered the window, he waved back but he had already started the engine and the car was moving.

'Let me know when you're back!'

'Yes. Goodbye!' He waved cheerily and the Bentley sped off and turned the corner and its sound fell into the silence. I returned slowly to the house.

I walked back over the causeway, aware now of a dreadful headache and a swinging sensation in the head: not surprising, since, as I established later, James and I had drunk between us nearly five litre bottles of wine. There was also a rapid sliding crowding curtain of spots before the eyes. I got inside, reached the kitchen and sat down again at the table, resting my head in my hands. I carefully worked out where I could find a glass of water and some aspirins and I got up and found them and sat down again and dozed. The sun came up.

I woke again, sitting at the table with my head lolling about and a violent pain in my neck. I recalled that I had had a curious dream about freezing to death in a snow-storm. Then I remembered that James had told me some very odd story about a journey in Tibet. And I half remembered a lot of other strange things that James had been saying. I got up, feeling horribly giddy and climbed upstairs and lay down on my bed and fell into a sort of sleep coma. I woke later on, not sure if it was morning or afternoon and feeling less giddy but rather mad. I went down to the kitchen and ate some cheese, then went back to bed again.

After that things became yet more confused. I must have stayed in bed quite a lot of that day. I remember waking during the night and seeing the moon shining. The next morning I came downstairs early and was suddenly persuaded, or perhaps I had had the idea in the night, that since I had given up swimming it was time that I had a bath. I did not fancy the labour of carrying hot water up to the bathroom. This time however I succeeded in lugging Mrs Chorney's old hip bath out of its refuge under the stairs and started to boil saucepans of water on the gas stove. Half way through this proceeding I felt a sharp pain in the chest and began to feel faint. I gave up the bath idea and made some tea, but could eat nothing. I felt a bit sick and decided to go back to bed. I was now sure that I had a temperature but possessed no thermometer. I stayed in bed. My bed felt rather like a hammock in a storm-tossed ship. I had coloured cloudy thoughts, or visions and was never sure if my eyes were shut or open. I wondered if I was seriously ill. Now I had a telephone but no doctor. I did not fancy summoning the one who had seen me at two a.m. after my 'mishap', anyway I never knew his name. I considered telephoning my London doctor and describing my symptoms, but decided not to since the symptoms would sound uninteresting and it was hard at the best of times to interest my London doctor. I comforted myself by reflecting that no doubt I had caught the 'flu or whatever it was that James had suffered from after I had survived my sea ordeal, and that James's ailment had not lasted long.

Mine lasted I think longer. At any rate some days passed during which I remained prostrate, reluctant to move, unable to eat. No one called, no one telephoned. I crawled out to the dog kennel but no one had written either. Perhaps there was a prolonged bank holiday or a postal strike. I was not too worried at the lack of news. I was entirely occupied with my illness. For the time it absorbed me, as if it were something that I was working at. I even ceased to worry about it; and generally, as I had anticipated, it began to go away. I could walk downstairs once more without resting on every step, and I was comforted by sensations of hunger. I ate a few biscuits and enjoyed them.

That day, or perhaps the next day, as I remember I was feeling stronger and more normal, the telephone rang in the morning. I was now well aware what this strange sound was. I had been thinking

urgently about Hartley and when I heard the shrill dreadful bell I said
to myself at once, *This is it.* I ran, falling over my feet, to the bookroom.
I grabbed the phone, dropped it, picked it up. 'Hello.'

'Hello, Charles!' It was Lizzie.

I said, 'Hello, wait a minute.'

I put the instrument down on some books and sat there trying to
calm myself and collect my wits. I had a misery-pain in the stomach
about Hartley which I knew would now not go away. Everything now
was *urgent*.

'Sorry, Lizzie, I was just turning off the gas.'

'Charles, are you all right?'

'Yes, why shouldn't I be? Well, I've been having 'flu, but I'm better.
Are you all right?'

'Yes, I'm at the Black Lion. Can I come and see you?'

'No. Stay there. I'll come and see you. What's the time? My watch
stopped days ago.'

'Oh about ten or something.'

'Are they open?'

'Who? Oh, the pub. No, but they will be by the time you come.'

'I'll be along.'

At the sound of Lizzie's voice I felt a sudden frantic desire to get
out of the house. I ran into the kitchen and looked at myself in the
little mirror above the sink. I had not shaved during my illness and
had developed a repulsive reddish beard. I shaved, cutting myself, and
combed my hair. I found my very crumpled jacket and my wallet.
A watery sun was shining but the air was cold. I ran out of the house
and over the causeway and turned towards the village. I soon stopped
running however as a sort of cloud of weakness enveloped my body and
twirled it about. I walked on rather slowly, breathing carefully; and only
then did it occur to me to wonder whether James had tipped Lizzie off

to come and see me. I was glad to find that I did not care, and I stopped thinking about it. When I turned into the village street the first thing I saw was Gilbert's yellow Volkswagen parked outside the Black Lion.

'Charles!'

Lizzie saw me coming and ran to me. I could see Gilbert smirking at the door of the pub. What was my role in this play? I felt myself being relaxed and smiling like a man in a dream who cannot remember his lines but knows he can manage impromptu.

'Why, Lizzie, hello there, and Gilbert too, how nice!'

'Charles, you're looking all thin and pale.'

'I am gratified to hear it, I've been ill.'

'Ought you to be still in bed?'

'No, I'm fine. What a nice surprise to see you two here.'

'Hello, *dear* Charles,' said Gilbert coming forward. His handsome self-conscious much-wrinkled face wore a dog-like look of nervous guilty imminent delight. If patted he would jump, bark.

'Charles looks quite ill.'

'Not still infectious I hope?'

'No, no.'

'We've been sitting outside,' said Lizzie. 'It's quite warm in the sun.'

'How nice.'

'What'll I get you, Charles?' said Gilbert. 'No, no, you sit down, you're the invalid, I'll get it. What about some of that cider, or is it too sweet for you?'

'Yes, fine, thanks. Well, Lizzie, what a treat to see you and how delightful you're looking.'

Some women, and as I said before Lizzie was one, vary in appearance amazingly on the scale from really ugly to really beautiful. Lizzie was up the beautiful end today, looking young and bright, like a plump principal boy, her hair blown into little screwy curls by the wind. She was wearing a long blue and green striped shirt over black trousers. Her face expressed something of the same Gilbertian dog-like uncertainty, with in her case an added air of apologetic impish confidence.

We sat down on the wooden bench outside the pub and looked at each other, I vaguely beaming and she intent and shining-eyed. I felt as never before exposed to the citizenry, but there were very few of them about.

I said, 'It was kind of you to ring me. Are you just passing through? Forgive me if I don't ask you to stay, I'm not feeling up to visitors at present.'

'No, no, we've got to get back to the motorway, Gilbert's going to see somebody in Edinburgh. There's this play coming on at the Festival –'

'Don't tell me.'

'Oh Charles, darling, darling, you do forgive me, don't you?'

'Whatever for, Lizzie?'

'Well, you do, don't you?'

'Yes, if it's necessary, but I'm quite in the dark. What a little mystery-monger you are! Ah here's dear Gilbert with the drink.'

Lizzie and Gilbert had come simply to be let off. They sat staring at me and smiling, like two children wanting to be given a certificate of forgiveness which they could rush off with, capering and flourishing it in the air. They wanted me to love them and to remove a blot on their happiness. How carefully they must have discussed the matter before coming to me almost formally like this. They were like children to me now and I suddenly felt old, and perhaps I had significantly aged in the time since I came to the sea.

I had lost Lizzie but when, how? Perhaps I should have grasped her at the start. Or perhaps she really did like Gilbert or life with Gilbert better. Or perhaps in some deep way when I sent her off with James I had frightened her too much. Lizzie was opting for ease and happiness and no more frights, I could not blame her. And I knew that James had made a barrier between us. Although with James there really had been 'nothing there', that 'nothing' was more than enough. That had always been the way with James. He could spoil anything for me by touching it with his little finger. Perhaps my childish idea was indelible, the idea that James must always be preferred. Of course James had intended no ill. But the lie itself was indeed a fatal flaw. I had probably not lost James but I had lost Lizzie, I had effectively 'strayed' her, as I had wanted to earlier on. And, I found myself almost laboriously remembering, I had wanted to stray Lizzie because of Hartley. And I had come running out of the house this morning finding it intolerable to stay there for a second longer, because of Hartley. My illness had marked the span of waiting time and it was now over. Lizzie's telephone call had been an unwitting signal, a summons to action. For me and for Hartley the hour had come.

And meanwhile I sat there beaming at Lizzie; and smile as we might – and perhaps she smiled innocently, hopefully, not realizing what had happened and imagining that she could still hold me and not hold me, have me and not have me, and all manner of thing would be well – the bond was broken. I recalled what James had said about it being my destiny to live alone and be everybody's uncle. I said, 'So you're glad to see your Uncle Charles?'

They laughed and I laughed and we all laughed and Lizzie squeezed my hand. I had given them the licence to be happy and I could see how pleased and grateful they were. Everyone seemed to be bright-eyed and bushy-tailed except me.

The cider was too sweet and rather strong and it was beginning to have its effect. My air of joviality was becoming easier, when the thought of Titus came to me almost solemnly as if someone had brought in a severed head upon a dish. James had been saying something about

Titus which I could not remember. Causality kills. The wheel is just.
I remembered Lizzie's scream on that day. Perhaps somehow after all
I had lost Lizzie because of Titus, because she blamed me, because it
was all *too much*. How tightly it was woven, the web of causes. Lizzie
was screaming with pleasure now. Well, she had to survive, we all had
to survive. Titus was a stranger who had not sojourned with us long.

We talked for a while, chatting easily as old friends do. Gilbert had
a good part in a TV series which seemed likely to run forever. They
were going to have the house redecorated. Lizzie had gone back to
her part-time hospital job. I was to come to dinner. They said nothing
about Hartley and the discreet omission seemed to set the seal upon
my separation from them, although it was hard to imagine what they
could have said.

I asked the time, took my wrist-watch from my pocket and set it
right by Lizzie's. They said they had to go and I walked them to the
car. Lizzie wanted a little hugging scene but I hustled her in with a
pat. I think Gilbert wanted to kiss me. I waved them off as if they
were the end of something. Then I began to walk along the street in
the direction of the church and the road that led up to the bungalows.
I had nearly reached the corner when someone behind me touched my
shoulder, and I turned, shocked. It was a woman who at first looked
quite strange. Then I recognized the shop lady. She had run after me
to tell me that she had fresh apricots in stock at last.

As I began to climb the hill I felt very tired and heavy. Perhaps I
should have rested for another day after my illness. Perhaps I should
not have drunk all that cider. Perhaps Lizzie and Gilbert had drained
my strength away into their vitality, their ability to change the world
and to survive. They had taken away a piece of me which they would
now use for their own purposes. Perhaps I ought to feel glad that other
people could thus feed upon my substance.

I felt unprepared and undressed but the hand of inevitability was upon me. This was the meeting from which I would not be put off, begging and pleading for another chance. I felt my heaviness as that of an irresistible crushing weight. Yet I had no clear idea of what I was going to do. There was no blunt instrument and no taxi. But I had come to where I had never been before, the blessed point of sufficient desperation.

I toiled up looking at the gardens and the flowers and the garden gates. I noticed how different each house was from the other. One had an oval of stained glass in the front door, another had a porch with geraniums, another had dormer windows in the attic. I reached the Nibletts blue gate with its irritatingly complicated little latch.

The curtains were partly drawn in the front bedrooms in an unusual way. I rang the ding-dong bell. The sound was different. How soon did I realize that the house was empty? Certainly before I confirmed the fact by peering in through the curtains into the larger bedroom and seeing that all the furniture was gone.

I went back to the front door and, for some reason, tried the bell again several times, listening to it echo in the deserted house.

'Oh excuse me, were you wanting Mr and Mrs Fitch?'

'Yes,' I said to a woman in an apron who was leaning over the fence from the front garden next door.

'Oh, they've gone, emigrated to Australia,' she told me proudly.

'I knew they were going, I hoped I'd catch them.'

'They sold the house. They took their doggie with them. He'll have to go in quarantine of course.'

'When did they leave?'

She mentioned a date. The date was, I realized at once, very soon after I had seen them. So they had lied about the date of their departure.

'I've had a postcard,' said the proud woman. 'It came this morning. Would you like to see it?' She had brought it out with her to show me.

I saw, on one side, the Sydney opera house. Upon the other in Hartley's hand: *Just arrived, I think Sydney is the most beautiful city I have ever seen, we are so happy.* Ben and Hartley had both signed.

'What a lovely card.' I gave it back to her.

'Yes, isn't it, but England's good enough for me. Are you a relative?'

'A cousin.'

'I thought you looked a bit like Mrs Fitch.'

'Too bad I missed them.'

'I'm afraid I don't know their address, but there it is, when people are gone they're gone, isn't it.'

'Well, thank you so much.'

'I expect they'll write to you.'

'I expect so. Well, good day.'

She returned to her house and I moved back to the path. The roses were already looking neglected, covered with dead flowers. I noticed an unusual stone lying half covered by the earth and I picked it up. It was the mottled pink stone with the white chequering which I had given to Hartley, and brought back in a plastic bag on that awful day. I put it in my pocket.

I walked round the side of the house into the back garden, and stood on the concrete terrace outside the picture window and peered in. The curtains had been left here too, and pulled across a little, but I could see between them into the empty room. The door was open into the hall and I could see the inside of the front door and a faded place on the wallpaper where the picture of the mediaeval knight had hung. I began to feel a frenzied desire to get into the house. Perhaps Hartley had left me a message, left at least some significant trace of her presence.

The back door was locked and the sitting-room windows were securely closed, but a kitchen window moved a little. I fetched a wooden box from the otherwise empty garden shed and stood on it, as Titus had stood in order to look through the hole in the fence. 'You stood on a box, didn't you.' 'Yes, I stood on a box.' I eased the window out and got my finger into the crack. Then the window came open, not having been properly latched on the inside, and I was able to swing my leg over. A moment later, panting with emotion, I was standing in the kitchen. A terrible quietness crept in the house.

The kitchen was empty, not entirely clean, and a tap dripping. Little rolls of fluff moved around on the floor in the draught from the window. I opened the larder, where there was already a trace of mould on the shelves. I walked about the sitting room and went into the two bedrooms. There was nothing, not a handkerchief, not a pin, no memento of my love. I went into the bathroom and looked at the stain on the bath. Then at last I saw something of interest. Beyond the edge of the linoleum, where it ended against the wall, there was the tiniest line of white. I stooped and pulled. A letter had been hidden, thrust in under the linoleum. I drew it carefully out and looked at it. It was my last letter to Hartley and it was unopened. I inspected it for a moment or two, wondering if it could have been opened and then stuck itself up again as letters sometimes do. But no. It had never been opened at all.

I was about to pocket it but decided not to. I tore it across into four pieces, stuffed it well down into the lavatory pan and pulled the chain. I went back and secured the kitchen window, then let myself out of the front door. The woman next door watched disapprovingly and even opened her front window and stared after me down the hill.

When I had reached the bottom and turned to the right into the village street, I suddenly saw a familiar figure approaching me. I was aware that it was someone I knew and was not pleased to see, just before I recognized it as Freddie Arkwright. Escape was impossible. He had already seen me and was bearing down.

'Mr Arrowby!'

'Why, it's Freddie!'

'Oh Mr Arrowby, I'm so glad to see you, I've kept missing you! I knew you were here. I was down at Whitsun and I hoped I'd see you, what luck to meet you now!'

'Well, Freddie, it's been a long time. How are you, what are you up to?'

'Didn't Bob tell you? I'm an actor!'

'An actor? Good for you!'

'I always wanted to be. That's why I went after that job with you, but it was like a sort of romance, I didn't think it would ever come real. And I loved working for you, it was great, all about London, all over the place, we did whizz about, didn't we? Then when you went away, I thought "Why not?" and then when I got my Equity card, and I wasn't so young either, somehow it always helped me that I'd worked for you, you always brought me luck, Mr Arrowby. You were so kind to me in those days, you encouraged me so much. "Decide what you want and go for it, Fred, it's just a matter of will power!" I remember you saying that to me more than once.'

I did not recall saying this nor did it sound like anything which anyone would say more than once, assuming he had ever had the misfortune to say it at all, but I was glad that Freddie had such rosy memories. We walked down as far as the footpath which led to the coast road. 'My, those were good times, Mr Arrowby, Savoy, Connaught, Ritz, Carlton, you name it, we were there! The old Carlton's gone of course, but London's still the best city in the world, and I've seen a few now. Paris, Rome, Madrid, I been there on jobs. I was in a film in Dublin a while ago, did we drink!'

'What's your stage name?'

'Oh, I kept my name, Freddie Arkwright, it seemed to be me. Can't say I've ever had any great parts, but I've loved every moment. All along of you, you were so kind to me, you encouraged me so much, and then everyone was saying, "Oh, you're a friend of Charles Arrowby, aren't you", well, I wasn't going to say no and it helped a packet. My, it's good to see you, Mr Arrowby, and you don't look a day older. Fancy your coming to live here, I came from here, you know, I was born at Amorne Farm, my uncle and auntie still live there. You're retired now, aren't you?'

'Yes.'

'I can't imagine ever retiring from the theatre. "No people like show people", you can say that again! But you still come to London, maybe we could get together? I'd love you to meet my friend I live with, Melbourne Pavitt, ever heard of him? No? Well, you will. He's a stage designer.'

'I expect we'll meet again around here –'

'Sorry, I've been talking my head off, why not let's go to the Black Lion and have drinks on the house?'

'No, I must hurry back, here's my turning. It's been very nice to see you, Freddie, and I'm glad you're doing so well.'

'I'll get my agent to send you some cuttings.'

'Do that, and the best of luck.'

'God bless you, Mr Arrowby, and thanks a million.'

I went away down the footpath, waving cordially. I might stride as a demon in the dreams of some, but in the mind of Freddie Arkwright I evidently figured, quite undeservedly, as a beneficent deity.

When I reached the house it was not yet two o'clock. I tried a little cold jellied consommé straight out of the tin, but soon gave that up.

I took two aspirins and went upstairs and lay down on my bed and fully expected, as one sometimes does in acute unhappiness and shock, to become quickly unconscious, but instead I drifted away into some sort of hell.

If there is any fruitless mental torment which is greater than that of jealousy it is perhaps remorse. Even the pains of loss may be less searching; and often of course these agonies combine, as now they did for me. I say remorse not repentance. I doubt if I have ever experienced repentance in a pure form; perhaps it does not exist in a pure form. Remorse contains guilt, but helpless hopeless guilt which knows of no cure for the painful bite.

I could not really think about Hartley, or not yet. The shock had been too great, or I may have been already surreptitiously guarding myself against too much suffering. And it was too as if, with a blandness which belonged to her youth, almost with a gesture, she had stood aside. She was constantly present to me, as if she hummed in my consciousness, but I did not concentrate upon her. I had sometimes felt, in my final struggle with her, that I wanted to rest; and now, quite suddenly, she had made me idle. But into the gap created by the finality of her disappearance came Titus, returning to me for his portion of my guilt and my grief.

The horrors of remorse abound in unfulfilled conditionals. I could not abate the proliferation of sturdy visions of happiness which knew not of their own futility. I would take Titus to London, he would go to acting school, he would come bounding in to see me with his friends, I would take him for long wonderful holidays, I would love him and look after him. Why had I not seen *at once* that this, the possession of Titus, my anxious fumbling responsible fatherhood of him, was somehow the point, the pure gift, that which the gods had really sent me, along with so much irrelevant packaging? That was what I should have grasped, that and not the chimera. I recalled Rosina's prophetic words about

Titus: he too will prove a dream child, he will fade away and vanish. Why had I not seized him and made a reality between us, given him my whole attention and taken him away from the ruthless unchilding sea? Of course Gilbert and the others would have laughed their cynical laughs, but they would have been wrong. The sacred relation of paternity can come into being, even as strangely as, that, and holy moral bonds would have made me Titus's protector, his mentor, his servant, with no demands made for myself. Perhaps this was an ideal picture. I might have been tyrannical, I might have been jealous, but I can recognize an absolute when I see one and I would have kept faith with Titus. But amid these thoughts as they rambled on there was always the picture, with its bright sea-light, of Titus lying dead, limp, dripping, with his half-open eyes and the hare-scar upon his lip.

I experienced his eternal absence as something almost impossible to comprehend. He had been with me such a short time; and he had come to me as to his death, as to his executioner. By what strange path of accidents, alive with so many other possibilities, had he made his way to the base of that sheer rock where he had tried again and again to pull himself out of the moving teasing killing sea? I ought to have warned him, I ought never to have dived in with him on that first day; I had destroyed him because I so rejoiced in his youth and because I had to pretend to be young too. He died because he trusted me. My vanity destroyed him. It is a matter of causality. The payment for faults is automatic. I relaxed my hold and he lay dead. Such thoughts as these carried me at last into a wretched comatose slumber; and when I awoke I had forgotten that Hartley was gone and I started at once on my old activity of planning what I would do to get her back.

My watch had stopped again, but the sky had an evening look with a lot of orange clouds pierced by holes of very cold very pale blue. I went downstairs and made some tea and then began drinking wine.

I began to think about Hartley but cautiously, as if trying out the thoughts to see whether they would drive me mad with pain. They had to be thought, I had to take it in. I had seen the empty house, the postcard from Sydney. I contemplated her, seeing her young bland face looking at me, now removed as if behind a gauze curtain. She quietly invited me to suffer. There was a great space now, a great silent hall in which this suffering could take place. There was no urgency now, nothing to plan, nothing to achieve. What shall I do with it, I asked her, what shall I do now with my love for you which you so terribly revived by reappearing in my life? Why did you come back, if you could not content me? What can I do now with the great useless machine of my love which has no wholesome work to do? I can do nothing for you any more, my darling. I wondered if I would be fated to live with this love, making of it a shrine which could not now be desecrated. Perhaps when I was living alone and being everyone's uncle like a celibate priest I would keep this fruitless love as my secret chapel. Could I then learn to love uselessly and unpossessively and would this prove to be the monastic mysticism which I had hoped to attain when I came away to the sea?

It began to grow dark and I lit the lamp. I closed the window to keep the moths out. It dawned on me with a vague wonderment that it had not at any point occurred to me to take a plane to Sydney. I could not remember whether Ben had said they would be living in Sydney, but Australia was not all that large and I had friends there who would be delighted to join a hunt for a girl. I could search, enquire, advertise. It would be an occupation. But it was somehow clear that I would not do so, I had given up. Follow her humbly at a distance, simply keep letting her know that I was still there? How like a frightful ghost I might become then. No, I had given up and, as it now seemed, I had done so prophetically just before her awful final flight. Why, after that unspeakable tea party, had I simply sat around waiting, imagining she would ring up? Did I really think she would ring up? Did I really imagine that she would leap, at the last moment, down into my boat? Surely I must have known by then that she was incapable of leaping. And I thought, rolling my head to and fro between my hands in anguish, oh if only it could have worked somehow for us two. If only Hartley had been my sister, I could have looked after her so happily and cared for her so tenderly.

I could not decide to eat anything. I had no desire for food or any sense that I would ever want to eat again. I went upstairs at last feeling drunk and sick. The bead curtain was jangling in some sea wind which was getting in somehow. There was a small moon racing through ragged clouds and the speed of it made me feel giddy. Perhaps she had to love Ben, hers was a loving nature and she had no alternative, no other possible object. She had wanted to love Titus but Ben had destroyed her love for Titus and in doing so destroyed her. What I had seen was a shell, a husk, a dead woman, a dead thing. Yet this was just the thing which I had so dearly wished to inhabit, to reanimate, to cherish. I took three sleeping pills. As I was falling asleep I wondered, why did she keep the letter, even though she did not read it? Why did she put the stone in the garden where I would be sure to see it? Were these, after all, *hopeful* signs?

I woke rather late the next morning and established from the telephone that it was nine-thirty. I had a headache. I went into the kitchen and fell over the hip bath which was still standing there half full of water. I managed to empty the bath, half over the slates and half onto the lawn, and to put it back under the stairs. I tried to eat some biscuits but they had become soft and curiously wet. There was no bread and no butter and no milk. In any case I was not hungry. I thought of going shopping but I was not sure what day it was. I thought I heard distant church bells so, it might be Sunday. In a rather abstract way I wondered if I should not go to London. However I had no particular motive for going there. There was no one I wanted to see and nothing I wanted to do.

I walked out to the road to look at the weather. It was warmer and more blue. I noticed some letters in Gilbert's clever basket. The strike or holiday or whatever it was was evidently over. Of course there was no letter from Hartley, but there was one from Lizzie. I took the letters into the little red room and sat at the table.

My dear, I am unhappy about our meeting. You were generous and sweet but I wish I had seen you alone. All that laughing was somehow awful. What were you really thinking? I feel I am somehow in the wrong, but you must put me in the right. Love me, Charles, love me *enough*. Since your letter I have been reliving my love for you like an inoculation, not to be 'cured', never that, but so that I can love you properly at last, and not just be stupidly 'in love'. Love matters, not 'in love'. Let there be no more partings now, Charles, no more mean possessive passions and scheming. Let there be peace between us now forever, we are no longer young. Please, my darling.
    Lizzie.
    PS Come and see us soon in London.

What a touching letter, ending with an invitation from 'us'! And 'I am in the wrong but you must put me in the right.' Typical Lizzie. I opened another letter. It was from Rosemary Ashe.

Dearest Charles,
    This is just to bring you the sad news that Sidney and I have split up. He wants a divorce. We are being peaceful about it all for the sake of the children and they don't seem to mind

too much. It's a younger actress of course, our occupational hazard – that, and the transatlantic atmosphere which seems to have driven Sidney mad. Perhaps it's temporary, I haven't given up hope, only hoping is so painful. I'm coming home and I long to see you. May I visit you in your lovely peaceful house by the sea? That's just what I need.

    Much love,
        Rosemary.

So much for the ideal marriage. I had better start polishing up my celibate uncle role. I opened another letter and for some time could not think who it was from, even though I could easily read the signature, Angela Godwin.

Dear Charles,

    Listen, it's me. And listen carefully. You don't have to put up with the old ones, why should you? Maybe you thought you couldn't get a young one? But you don't look your age, you know. You don't have to have old bags like Lizzie Scherer and Rosina Vamburgh, why should you when you can have ME? I do rather like Rosina, though, at least she's clever, and things are decenter at home since Pam went so don't think I regard you as an escape route, I don't! I've been thinking a lot these last months and I think I've changed a lot and come to terms with myself at last. I've been thinking about my identity. I don't yet know what I'm going to do with my life, *not* acting, so you needn't think I'm after that either! I'm good at maths and I think I may become a physicist, I'm doing the Cambridge exam in the autumn. Anyhow I shall jolly well be *somebody*. The reason for this letter? I have had an idea of genius. That night you came to see Peregrine I was (of course) listening at the door and I heard him say how you wanted a son, or maybe you said it, I forget, but anyway it stayed in my mind. Now comes the idea. *Why shouldn't I give you one?* He could be yours, I wouldn't want to hog him. I mean I'd visit him and that. I don't see myself tied with a child just yet, we could have a nurse. Besides I shall be jolly busy at Cambridge. And of course I'm *not* proposing marriage. I think I shall marry much later on or not at all. But why not simply *have what you want?* People don't enough, which is what is the matter with our civilization, I don't mean like people starving, but like not having the courage to grab their heart's desire even when it's in front of their noses. About me, I am seventeen, and in perfect health. I'm a virgin and I want someone special to take me over that border, *you* in fact. I enclose a photograph, and you can see how I have changed. What about it, Charles? I am serious. Not least in saying that I love you, and am if and when you want me yours,

Angela Godwin.

I pulled the photograph out of the envelope and inspected a coloured picture of a rather pretty intelligent-looking girl with large eyes and a bright tender diffident unformed face. I crumpled this missive up and thrust it into the soft ash of the woodfire. There were various other letters, but I felt I had had enough of letters for the moment.

I went out to see what the horrible sea was up to. It was calm and slippery, sliding in among the rocks like oil. I went as far as Minn's cauldron and stood on the bridge. The tide was going out and the cauldron was emptying in a whirling gushing frenzy of hasty bubbling waters whose white flux was absorbed by the calmer sea beyond. I looked down. How deep it was, how steep and smooth the sides. Surely no power on earth could have got me out of that hole. Yet I had got out, I

was alive, and poor swimming holidaying Titus was dead. I went on over
the rocks as far as the tower and climbed down to the steps. The sleek
water was rising and falling, but not too violently, the tide was right,
the iron banister reaching down as far as the waves. I felt in my body,
as if scarcely yet in my mind, a flicker of life, the old familiar semi-
sexual twitch of fear, such as I used to feel on those high diving boards
in California or before plunging into lethally cold waters off Ireland.

Trembling with emotion I tore my clothes off and walked into the
sea. The cold shock, then the warmth, then the strong gentle lifting
motion of the quiet waves reminded me terribly of happiness. I swam
about feeling the loneliness of the sea and that particular sensation which
I now identified as a sense of death which it seemed to have always
carried into my heart. Not that I then wished to die or thought that
I might drown. My strong limbs responded to the moving water, my
breath came easily, the sky was blue above me and the sun was everywhere, and I watched the near horizon of the approaching waves, their
tops a little whipped by the breeze, and they were strong and gentle.
They toyed with me. I swam and floated until I began to feel cold; then
I climbed out and returned naked to the house carrying my clothes.

The sea had restored my hunger and when it seemed to be lunch
time I heated up the remains of the consommé and opened a tin of
frankfurters and a tin of sauerkraut. I half decided to go to London
tomorrow. I half thought of telephoning James who might after all still
be around, and I got as far as looking up his number and writing it down
on the pad beside the telephone. I half intended to ring up the taxi man
to ask him to take me to the early train. Though the sun was warm, I
was a bit chilled after the swim and I put on the white Irish jersey. I
got out a suitcase and began to pack up a few clothes. I even went into
the book room to find a book to read on the journey. It occurred to
me that although my plan for my retirement had included a regime of

reading I had not opened a book since I arrived at Shruff End. I turned the books over. James had inspected them, Titus had slept on them. I needed something a bit lurid and absorbing. It was a moment even for pornography, only I cannot really stand pornography. I eventually chose *The Wings of the Dove,* another story of death and moral smash-up.

The day seemed to be passing, the evening was arriving, and I had not telephoned either James or the taxi man. I decided it was too late to decide to go early in the morning. I would ring the taxi man tomorrow and take the later train. What I would do when I got to London I did not consider. Arrange my flat, order curtains? Such things belonged to another world. Although the evening was warm I lit the fire for company in the little red room, thus consuming Rosemary's and Angie's letters and the photo of the intelligent diffident girl. I took my supper in to the fireside and sat for a while trying to start reading *The Wings of the Dove,* but its marvellous magisterial beginning failed to grab me. It was still daylight and I could see without the lamp. I sat for a while with glazed eyes, listening to the stomp of the sea and the beating of my heart. I began to feel slightly sleepy or comatose. That swim had certainly done *something* to me. I thought about Titus. Then I began to think about myself as a drowned man and I remembered how I had slept, on the night of my resurrection from Minn's cauldron, upon the floor in this room, in front of the glowing fire, wondering gratefully why I was still alive. And I seemed to see myself lying there, moving my limbs gently in the warmth to make certain that I was whole.

My eyelids drooped a little and then I very clearly *saw* something concerning which I was not afterwards able to say whether it was a hallucination or a memory image. It certainly presented itself to me, quite suddenly, as a memory. I had been vaguely, driftingly, thinking of that awful fall into the churning pit of water, my 'knowledge' of my death, the way the water showed green above me even in the dim light. Then I remembered that, just before my head cracked against the rock and the blackness came upon me, I had seen something else. I had seen a strange small head near to mine, terrible teeth, a black arched neck. *The monstrous sea serpent had actually been in the cauldron with me.*

I opened my eyes wide and, now panting and with a violently pounding heart, looked around me. All was as usual, the fire blazing, the scattering of unopened letters upon the table, my half-drunk glass of wine. I was sure I had not been asleep. I had simply *remembered* something which I had for some reason totally forgotten. This was indeed the forgetting which the doctor had said I must expect, the result of the concussion, where memory traces are lost. But now I could recall the black coiling thing, very close, reared over me and quite unmistakable in the dim light, its head and neck for a moment outlined against the sky. I saw in memory its green luminous eyes. The sight had lasted for seconds, perhaps a second, but it had been clear and not to be doubted. Then after that second had come the blow on the head.

But no, there was something else to remember, something else had happened just before I lost consciousness. But what, what? Trembling with excitement and fear I sat holding my head and tormenting my memory. There was something there waiting agonizingly to be remembered, something very important and extraordinary, waiting just outside my range of vision, waiting for me to grasp it, only I could not. I groaned aloud, I got up and walked into the kitchen and back, I drank a little more wine, I closed my eyes, I opened them. I watched my mind, as if hardly daring to touch it in case it should shift or harden and destroy some perhaps momentary proximity. But the hidden thing would not come; and I had a terrified sense that if I did not catch it now it would disappear forever, sinking into the deep total darkness of the unconscious. Just now, for perhaps the last time, it heaved to touch the surface.

After a while I gave up straining, though I still hoped that the final, the somehow essential, memory would suddenly come. I sat down again at the table and began thinking about the sea serpent and going back over my earlier theories concerning LSD. I tried to remember whether I had felt the coiling creature as well as seen it. I had a memory vision of the animal but none of my state of mind at the time, although I could remember my 'drowning' thoughts when I was under the wave. I thought of going out to inspect the cauldron in case this would help my memory, but now it was almost dark and I dared not. I felt frightened, then positively shaken by death fear. I tried to light the lamp but for some reason could not. I lit several candles, then went and locked the front door and the back door and returned to the little red room.

As I came back into the room I saw almost straight ahead of me, as if my eyes had suddenly been switched onto a new narrow wavelength, a crack in the white wooden panelling, just below the top where, a few feet from the ground, the panelling ended in a small ledge. There were quite a lot of cracks between the panels, some of them partially covered by the paint. This crack was quite short, about six inches long, and there was something in it: something white which stuck out a little way. Suddenly breathless, giddy with memory, I went across the room and pulled out a piece of paper. It was the piece of paper upon which, when I awoke in the night after being 'drowned', I had written down that very important thing which I was on no account to forget. Even as I held the paper in my hand I could not remember what it was that I had written, though I at once assumed that it had to do with the sea serpent. I unfolded the paper, and what I read was this.

I must write this down quickly as evidence, since I am beginning to forget it even as I write. James saved me. He somehow came down right into the water. He put his hands under my armpits and I felt myself coming up as if I were in a lift. I saw him against the sheer side of the rock leaning down to me, and then I rose up and he held me against his body and we came up together. But he was not standing on anything. One moment he was against the rock as if he were clinging onto it like a bat. Then he was simply standing on the water. And then

Here the writing ended, trailing away into illegible scrawls. I sat at the table gasping and I read the thing through several times, and then the dark thing that had been touching the surface of my mind broke through and I found I could remember the scene. This memory was not like my memory of the serpent. It was like my memory of Lizzie singing or of Titus lying dead, except that it was a memory of an impossibility.

I could now recall perfectly clearly what I had tried to express by saying that he was against the sheer rock 'like a bat' and that I came up 'as in a lift'. It was after the green wave had broken over me and I remember my head came above the surface and I was spewing water from my mouth and trying to shout. Then I saw James already half way down the rock, sort of kneeling against the side of it, and coming down like some animal. The bat image was not quite right, he might have been more like a lizard, but the point was that he was not climbing down with footholds and handholds like a man, he was creeping down on the smooth surface like some sort of beast. I remember trying to reach out a hand towards him, but the water was in total control of my body and hurling me about like a cork. I had in any case swallowed so much I was nearly at the end of breathing and struggling. I particularly recall that James at that moment looked like a drowned man himself, soaked with water, the leaping sea streaming down from off his head. In so far as I had any thought then I seem to recapture a sense of: so James is drowning too. Only somehow this was not a despairing thought. Then

James, as he crept right down into the churning whirlpool, detached himself from the rock like a caterpillar. There was an effect as of something sticky and adhesive deliberately unsticking itself. He did not take the hand which I was trying to reach out to him, but leaned down over me and got his hands under my armpits, as I described in the writing. I could now recall the *feel* of his hands as he touched me, and then the extraordinary sensation which I described as rising 'in a lift'. I could not remember being pulled or dragged up, there was no sense of effort. I rose up until my head was level with James's head and my body pressed against his body. I remember a sense of warmth, and also that it was at *that* moment that I lost consciousness.

But then was I not knocked on the head, and did I not suffer from concussion? I touched the back of my head and felt a distinct and still rather tender bump there. Of course I could have knocked my head earlier without being made unconscious. And when did I see the serpent, if I saw the serpent? And did James see the serpent too? And why did my little piece of mnemonic writing contain no reference to the serpent? And what had I just been going to say when the writing ended? Of course if I struck my head on the rock just after seeing the serpent I could have already forgotten about it when I came to write, even though I could still remember James's rescue. And why had I then forgotten that too, and why should I suddenly remember it now?

I leapt up in a state of the greatest excitement. My memory of James's exploit was certainly no hallucination. After all, how *had* I got out of that churning death pit? Only today I had concluded, looking at it, that no human force could have raised me nor could the waves possibly have lifted me to the top of the rock. My cousin had rescued me by the exercise of those powers which he had so casually spoken of as 'tricks'. I thought again about the story of the Sherpa whom James had intended to preserve by such 'trickery'. Had I then doubted James's

reference to 'increase of bodily heat by mental concentration'? I had
scarcely reflected on the matter. The story could be seen in quite an
ordinary light. Two men cling together for warmth in a tent, in a bag,
in the snow, and one dies. What touched and interested me was that,
whatever it was that James thought he was going to do, he had failed.
As for the claim itself, it did not now seem to me too incredible that
some weird eastern ascetic could learn to control his body temperature.
But to creep down a sheer rock and stand upon, or (as I now recalled
it) just below the surface of, raging waves, and raise a man weighing
eleven stone upwards for a matter of sixteen to twenty feet simply by
placing one's hands in one's armpits: that was a rather different task for
the credulity of a sceptical westerner. Yet I remembered it. And there
was also the evidence of the writing. And something very odd had
certainly happened.

I sat down again at my table, trying to breathe regularly, and at the
idea that my cousin had used some strange power which he possessed
to save my life I was suddenly filled with the most piercing pure and
tender joy, as if the sky had opened and a stream of white light had
descended. I felt like Danae. When, after my last talk with James, I
had felt myself at the start of a new and more open relationship with
him, that had been the merest prophetic glimmer of what I felt now.
I also thought, in a curious ridiculous way, what *fun*! And I recalled
James's saying, 'What larks we had!' And I wanted to thank him and
in doing so to laugh.

I looked at my watch. It was only just after eleven o'clock, still not
too late to telephone. I ran out to the bookroom, carrying a candle and
choking and exclaiming with emotion. I dialled James's number. I had
no idea what I was going to say to him. I thought, I must remember
to ask him whether he saw the sea serpent. The telephone began to
ring, and as it rang and rang my excitement turned to disappointment.

Perhaps he had already gone to Tibet? Or was he perhaps simply out for the evening, dining at some club with some soldier? My God, how little I knew about his life. I decided to telephone him again in the morning, and then to get away to London.

I went back into the kitchen and unlocked and opened the back door. The cold fear which I had felt earlier had entirely gone. I went out onto the lawn. The house had been dark and cool, but there was plenty of light outside and the air was warmer. I decided to sleep out, and I went and collected some cushions from the bookroom and brought blankets and a pillow down from upstairs. I climbed over to the place beside the sea where I had slept on the previous occasion and laid out my bed. Then I went back towards the house where the candles made a friendly glow in the window of the little red room. The sky, though dim and faded, was still light enough to prevent the stars, except for the evening star which shone out jagged and enormous. The low and sinking half moon was cheese-pale.

I went into the little red room where the candles, as on an altar, flanked my wineglass and the almost empty bottle. I poured out the rest of the wine and sat and reflected. I tried to recall more things. I was sure that none of the others had noticed anything odd. Peregrine said he had pushed me and walked on. He was very drunk and may genuinely not have known exactly what happened. By the time there was a general alarm I was already lying on top of the rock with James trying to revive me. I had not questioned James properly because he had become ill immediately afterwards, he had had some sort of collapse and retired to bed. Why was he so exhausted? Because of what he had endured in rescuing me, the physical and mental energy which he had expended in that unimaginable descent. I recalled his words about 'those things that people do, they can be jolly tiring'. No wonder James was knocked out and seemed to have lost his grip. But then ... 'I relaxed my hold on him, I lost my grip.' Whom had James been speaking of as I fell asleep that night, his Sherpa or perhaps . . . Titus? How was it that Titus had come to me just then? Why had James so pointedly asked for Titus's name? A name is a road. And why had Titus said that he had seen James 'in a dream'? James had always been the finder of lost things. Had he stretched out some tentacle of his mind and found Titus and brought him here and kept him as it were under his care upon a binding thread, a thread of attention which was broken when James became so strangely ill after I had been lifted from the sea? James's reaction to Titus's death had been 'it ought not to have happened', almost as if he felt that it was his own fault. But then if it was his fault it was my fault. There is a relentless causality of sin and in a way Titus died because, all those years ago, I had taken Rosina away from Peregrine. And of course my vanity had killed Titus just as James's vanity had killed the Sherpa. In each case our weakness had destroyed the thing we loved. And now I remembered something else which James had said. White magic is black magic. A less than perfect meddling in the spiritual world can breed monsters for other people, and demons used for good can hang around and make mischief afterwards. Had one of these demons, with whose help James had saved me, taken advantage of James's collapse to seize Titus and crash his young head against the rock?

These thoughts were so mad and their implications so hideously frightening that I decided I must stop thinking and try to sleep. I felt that in spite of everything, I should sleep well. I wanted most intensely to talk to James about all these things, or, supposing he had already left, to write to him. But how could I find his address, would he have an address? I really knew nobody who knew him except Toby Ellesmere, and Toby often seemed entirely mystified or ignorant about James's doings and his way of life. Could I go to some army headquarters or to the Ministry of Defence and ask? Of course they would 'know nothing'.

I had finished the wine and the fire had sunk into a pile of ash dully smudged with red. I sighed deeply as I thought of all the years I had wasted when James and I might have been friends, instead of just awkward embarrassed relatives or something almost more like enemies. I reached out to the table and began pushing the pile of unopened letters about to see if I recognized any of the writings. Of course there was nothing from James, I would have spotted that at once. There might be one from Sidney telling his side of the 'young actress' story. I noticed, because its appearance caught my eye, a letter with a London postmark addressed to *Mr C. Arrowby,* in the hand of a writer who was clearly not quite at home with Roman letters. In a tired idle curiosity I drew it towards me and opened it. It was dated two days ago and it ran as follows:

Dear Mr Arrowby, I have to be the bearer of sad news, I am sorry. I cannot find you in the telephone. But you are at liberty to make telephone to me at the number given on the paper. My sad news is this, your cousin Mr James Arrowby has just died. I am his doctor. He left me a note that you are his cousin and his heir and that I should myself inform you of his decease. So I do this. I want also to tell something to you alone. Mr Arrowby died in much quietness. He telephoned me to come to him and was already dead when I arrived, and he had left the door open. He was sitting in his chair smiling. I must tell you this. By an accident that is no accident I came to him as his doctor. I am Indian, I come from Dehra Dun. When I first met Mr Arrowby I at once recognized him as one who knows many things. Perhaps you will understand. I had some prophetic thought about him, and when I came to him I saw what had been. In northern India I have known such deaths, and I tell it to you so that you need not be sorry too much. Mr Arrowby died in happiness achieving all. I have written for cause of death on the certificate 'heart failure', but it was not so. There are some who can freely choose their moment of death and without violence to the body can by simple will power die. It was so with him. I looked upon him with reverence and bowed before him. He has gone quietly and by the force of his own thought was consciousness extinguished. Thus it is good to go. Believe me, Sir, he was an enlightened one.

I will be at your service at the telephone number. With obedient wishes, I am yours truly,

P. R. Tsang.

I read the letter through twice and a terrible cold quietness fell upon me and I sat like a statue motionless for a long time. It did not occur to me to wonder if the strange letter was a hoax or a mistake. I had no doubt that James had gone. He had gone quietly; with just a little gentle pressure of his mind upon his body he had made the restless flickering consciousness cease forever. I felt a deep grief that crouched and stayed still as if it was afraid to move. And I felt an odd new sensation which I had never known before and which it took me a little time to recognize as loneliness. Without James I was at last alone. How very much I had somehow relied upon his presence in the world, almost as if he had been my twin brother and not my cousin.

I saw from my watch that it was nearly midnight. I would indeed go to London tomorrow. And I wondered with helpless sad confusion what had happened, what had they done with him? Was James still sitting there in his chair, dead and smiling his inane smile?

I got up to go to bed and then remembered that I had made my couch out on the rocks. I decided to go to it. Outside the night was warm and had darkened just enough to show a scattering of stars and the faint smudgy arch of the Milky Way. There was a diffused lightness in the sky however, and I recalled that it must be, give or take a day or two, midsummer. I was able to find my way not too dangerously over the rocks which I now knew so well, though at one point my foot slipped into a pool. The water in the pool was warm. I found my hard bed and lay on it in shirt and trousers, just taking off my shoes. I propped my head so that I could look at the horizon which was marked by a dark line and a silver line. The water lapped below me like ripples against a slowly moving boat.

Why had James gone, why had he decided to go now? Was there any immediate reason, such as I could understand, or was it all part of some big wheeling pattern of my cousin's existence of which I could perceive nothing. All sorts of crazy hypotheses kept coming into my head. Was it something to do with Lizzie? Impossible. Or with Titus? Was he perhaps filled with remorse about Titus, imagining himself responsible for that death? Here I even began to conjecture that James really had known Titus earlier, was perhaps himself the mysterious person who had taught Titus those little airs and graces and given him the copy of Dante's poems. But this was inconceivable, such a deception not to be seriously imagined. And as I lay there looking at the sky above the sea I saw a golden satellite begin its slow careful journey over the arch of the heavens, and it looked like a calm travelling soul. James had said he was going on a journey. Death was the journey. It was his last 'trick'.

No, I could not attach this 'casting off' to any ordinary or present cause. James's decision belonged to a different pattern of being, to some quite other history of spiritual adventure and misadventure. Whatever 'flaw' had led, as James saw it, to his Sherpa's death belonged, it might be, to some more general condition. Religion is power, it must be, and yet that is its bane. The exercise of power is a dangerous delight. Perhaps James wanted simply to lay down the burden of a mysticism that had gone wrong, a spirituality which had somehow degenerated into magic. Had he been overwhelmed with disgust because he had had to use his 'power' to save my life, was that the last straw, and was it really all my fault after all? Had I proved to be, in the end, a thankless burden and a dangerous attachment? Here, and sadly, I understood the possible meaning of James's last visit. James had come to make his peace with me, but it was for his sake, not for mine, in order to break a bond, not to perfect it. He knew it was our last talk, and that was why he was so relaxed, so open, so unprecedentedly frank and gentle. He came, not with any ordinary desire for reconciliation, but in order to rid himself of a last irritating preoccupation. Anxiety or guilt about his wretched cousin might cloud the conditions of the perfect departure upon which he had perhaps long been bent.

How did it go off, that severance, I wondered. Had he responded to the vision of 'all reality' which comes at the moment of death and by which one must instantly profit? Had he gone eagerly to that rendezvous and was he now, in what strange heaven of release, 'set free', whatever that might mean? Or else, aching and weak like the shade of Achilles, shut in some purgatory to expiate sins which I could not even imagine? Was he now wandering in a dark monster-ridden *bardo*, encountering simulacra of people he had once known and being frightened by demons? For in that sleep of death what dreams may come when we have shuffled off this mortal coil must give us pause. How did one get out of *bardo*? I could not remember what James had told me. Why had I never asked him to explain? Would he meet *me* there, in the shape of some persistent horror, a foul phantom me, the creation of his mind? If so I prayed that when he achieved his liberation he might not forget me but come, in pity and in compassion, to know the truth. Whatever that might mean.

As I lay there, listening to the soft slap of the sea, and thinking these sad and strange thoughts, more and more and more stars had gathered, obliterating the separateness of the Milky Way and filling up the whole sky. And far far away in that ocean of gold, stars were silently shooting and falling and finding their fates, among those billions and billions of merging golden lights. And curtain after curtain of gauze was quietly removed, and I saw stars behind stars behind stars, as in the magical Odeons of my youth. And I saw into the vast soft interior of the universe which was slowly and gently turning itself inside out. I went to sleep, and in my sleep I seemed to hear a sound of singing.

I woke up and it was dawn. The billion billion stars had gone and the sky was a bland misty very light blue, a huge uniform over-arching cool yet muted brightness, the sun not yet risen. The rocks were clearly revealed, still indefinably colourless. The sea was utterly calm, glossy, grey, without even ripples, marked only by the thinnest palest line at the horizon. There was a complete yet somehow conscious silence, as if the travelling planet were noiselessly breathing. I remembered that James was dead. Who is one's first love? Who indeed.

I pulled myself up, knelt, and began to shake my blankets and my pillow which were wet with dew. Then I heard, odd and frightening in that total stillness, a sound coming from the water, a sudden and quite loud splashing, as if something just below the rock were about to emerge, and crawl out perhaps onto the land. I had a moment of sheer fear as I turned and leaned towards the sea edge. Then I saw below me, their wet doggy faces looking curiously upward, four seals, swimming so close to the rock that I could almost have touched them. I looked down at their pointed noses only a few feet below, their dripping whiskers, their bright inquisitive round eyes, and the lithe and glossy grace of their wet backs. They curved and played a while, gulping and gurgling a little, looking up at me all the time. And as I watched their play I could not doubt that they were beneficent beings come to visit me and bless me.

POSTSCRIPT:

LIFE GOES ON

THAT no doubt is how the story ought to end, with the seals and the stars, explanation, resignation, reconciliation, everything picked up into some radiant bland ambiguous higher significance, in calm of mind, all passion spent. However life, unlike art, has an irritating way of bumping and limping on, undoing conversions, casting doubt on solutions, and generally illustrating the impossibility of living happily or virtuously ever after; so I thought I might continue the tale a little longer in the form once again of a diary, though I suppose that, if this is a book, it will have to end, arbitrarily enough no doubt, in quite a short while. In particular I felt I ought to go on so as to describe James's funeral, although really James's funeral was such a non-event that there is practically nothing to describe. Then I felt too that I might take this opportunity to tie up a few loose ends, only of course loose ends can never be properly tied, one is always producing new ones. Time, like the sea, unties all knots. Judgments on people are never final, they emerge from summings up which at once suggest the need of a reconsideration. Human arrangements are nothing but loose ends and hazy reckoning, whatever art may otherwise pretend in order to console us.

As I write this it is August, not the yellow Provençal August of the English imagination, but an ordinary cool London August with the wind beating down the Thames at the end of the street. For, yes, I am living in James's flat. From a legal point of view it is my flat, but of course it remains really James's. I dare not alter anything, I scarcely dare to move anything. The idols of 'superstition' surround me. I have ventured to put some of the odder 'fetishes' away in a cupboard, I hope they will not mind, and I took down the glass pendants in the hall because their tinkling disturbed my sleep. But the ornate wooden box with the captive demon inside is still perched on its bracket. (James never denied that there was a demon in it. He merely laughed when I asked him.) The innumerable Buddhas are still in their places, except for one that I gave to Toby Ellesmere because he seemed annoyed at not being mentioned in James's will. The will left everything to me and, should I predecease him, to the British Buddhist Society. I gave them a Buddha too.

Another peevish shifty letter from the house agent today. Shruff End is up for sale. I never spent another night there after the night of the stars when the seals came in the morning. While sorting out my belongings for removal I stayed at the Raven Hotel. I could see the tower from my bedroom but not the house. No one seems to want to buy the place, perhaps because of the dampness, perhaps for other reasons. The Arkwrights at Amorne Farm, who have the key, said they would get the roof mended, but according to the agent have not done so. Fortunately I do not need the money urgently since James's will has left me comfortably off.

*

I suppose I must describe James's funeral as I said I was going to. There was something curiously blank about it. I did not have to organize it, thank heaven. It was organized by a Colonel Blackthorn who appeared for this purpose and then vanished. When I got to London on the day after the doctor's letter I found Colonel Blackthorn and the doctor both actually in James's flat. The colonel explained that he had organized the funeral (a cremation) because they had been unable to get in touch with me, but that if I wished for something different ... I did not. I tried to talk to the doctor but he faded away while Blackthorn was still explaining to me how to get to the crematorium. 'James' had already mercifully been removed to the 'chapel of rest'. I did not visit him.

The cremation took place two days later at one of those huge garden places in north London. There is something comfortlessly empty about a 'garden of remembrance' after the loquacious populated feeling of a graveyard. It was a stiff graceless business, rather hurried on by the staff, who kept us waiting outside while the previous 'customer' was disposed of. Doubtless the worthy colonel's despatch in booking our 'slot' had been a prudent one. He was there, also the doctor. Toby Ellesmere came and seemed genuinely upset. I had never reflected before (and have not since) upon the nature of his relation with James, but whatever it was I imagine it belonged to the remote past. James and Toby had not only been young soldiers together, they had been schoolboys together. Perhaps Toby had simply admired him at school; such bonds can be life-long. Four other well-dressed men in smart black suits turned up, I presume they were soldiers. They showed no signs of knowing who I was, and they were unknown to Toby, with whom I exchanged a few words; indeed no one except Toby talked to me at all. The business took minutes. There was no prayer of course, only a little soft listless music and then a standing in silence, which was broken by some official noisily opening the door at the back. I wished then that there could have been a proper ceremony of some sort. But any ritual I could have devised would probably have offended James's shade. I only wish I had had the wit to demand some decent music to see him off with.

We went outside into the garden. Colonel Blackthorn shook hands with me. Everybody began to go away. Again I tried to speak to the doctor, but he said he was expected at the hospital. Perhaps he was feeling a bit nervous about that death certificate. Toby rather half-heartedly offered me a lift in his car, but I declined. I think he wanted to be alone too. I walked about for a long time in shabby sad back-streets and lost myself.

I have just found in a drawer in the kitchen the hammer which I was trying to mend on the last evening when James came to Shruff End. He must have taken the precaution of carrying it away with him. I like the kitchen. There is a large dry larder, completely empty when I arrived. There is also a view of Battersea Power Station, which in the evening looks like an Assyrian monument.

I have sold my flat in Shepherd's Bush and brought some of the furniture here. I brought back my own stuff from Shruff End, but none of Mrs Chorney's. I resisted a temptation to keep the *art nouveau* oval mirror which Rosina broke and which I never had reglazed. I have put most of my things into James's dressing room. This is now, inside James's temple, a little Charles shrine. I go there sometimes and sit. My books are still in crates in the hall. My clothes are mostly in suitcases, since I cannot yet bring myself to touch James's neatly hanging, neatly folded garments. The big wardrobe in his bedroom is like the entrance to another world. I cannot say I feel at home in the flat, but I would not think of living anywhere else. Sometimes it seems incredible that he is not here too. Last night I was so persuaded that he was in the next room that I had to go and look.

I saw Lizzie and Gilbert on Friday, at their maisonette in Golders Green. I visit them now and then and they produce their smelly messes which they have spent all day cooking. Gilbert has now become very successful as the comic hero of that ludicrous interminable television series. He is famous for the first time in his life and people come up and touch him in the street. The critics even compare him with Wilfred Dunning, which is absurd. Lizzie seems happy. She has given up her hospital job and got fatter. They both still talk of how one day they will share a house with me and I will live upstairs and they will live downstairs and be my 'staff'. We make jokes about this.

Are they beginning to treat me like an elderly invalid? They think James's flat is an appalling place to live. Of course I never invite them here. I never invite anybody here.

Am I settling into my role as a celibate uncle-priest? Yesterday I took my secretary Miss Kaufman, whom I may not have mentioned before, out to coffee and listened to a tale of woe about her aged mother. Then I took Rosemary Ashe to lunch at a pub and heard all about Sidney and Maybelle. Maybelle is twenty. Rosemary still hopes Sidney may recover. The children are loving Canada. Rosemary thinks they are too philosophical about the divorce. I was glad to find that Rosemary had a very unclear idea about what had happened at Shruff End, and I did not enlighten her. Her information seemed to be that I had been persecuted by some mad village woman and a boyfriend of Gilbert's had been drowned. Fortunately she did not want to discuss my problems.

It is late in the evening in the flat. The Buddhas seem to be looking at me, although I know that beneath their drooping eyelids they do not see the world of appearance. The place is getting rather dusty as I cannot risk having a charwoman. I have done a little superficial dusting but I do not like moving things, some of them are fragile. I am especially careful with that demon-cage up on the bracket! Is the scene beginning to look more and more like a museum as James's spirit gradually withdraws? The area which I inhabit does not increase. I eat in the kitchen, then scuttle back to this desk in the sitting room. I dress in the hall. I sleep in the larger spare bedroom. Of course I dare not sleep in James's bed. James's handsome bedroom is unused and I have closed the door.

At least I have now taken possession of the desk, and collected there my favourites from among the have-worthy jade animals. Weighing down my letters and papers (Miss Kaufman still helps, thank God) are two stones, the mottled pink chequered stone which I gave to Hartley, and the brown stone with the blue lines which I gave to James. I was glad to find that lying here when I arrived. I often handle these stones. I have also propped up two photographs, the one of Uncle Abel and Aunt Estelle dancing, and a photo of Clement when she was young in the role of Cordelia. I cannot seem to find any suitable pictures of my parents, and of course I have no recent one of James. It is clear that his preparations for his journey were extremely thorough. There were no personal papers to be found in the flat. (I wonder if Colonel Blackthorn removed anything?) There were no interesting relics at all, no old letters, photos, bills. The will was tied up in a slim package together with a statement from his bank about investments. There was no trace of James having dealt with a lawyer. The will was written in his own hand. The two witnesses appeared to be uneducated people. For some time, stupidly, I searched for a hidden letter addressed to me. I even looked into cracks in the wall.

*

Last night at a little party given by Gilbert and Lizzie I heard that Peregrine is doing well with his theatre in Londonderry and is becoming quite famous as a propagandist for peace in Ireland. Rosina is equally enthusiastic and is rumoured to have become politically conscious and power-mad. Gilbert says Fritzie's *Odyssey* is off.

Yes, I go to parties now. I go about in London, I eat and drink and gossip just as if I were an ordinary person. Well, am I not one? I wonder what happened to that precious talisman which I was going to unwrap in a lonely cave beside the sea?

Perhaps it is a sign of age that I am busy all day without really doing anything. This diary has trailed on, it is company for me, an illusion of occupation. I now feel uneasily that before I end it I ought to offer some sort of reflective summing up of – of what? I shrink from this. There is so much pain. I have not recorded the pain.

What an egoist I must seem in the preceding pages. But am I so exceptional? We must live by the light of our own self-satisfaction, through that secret vital busy inwardness which is even more remarkable than our reason. Thus we must live unless we are saints, and are there any? There are spiritual beings, perhaps James was one, but there are no saints.

Well, I will try to reflect, but not today. When this is all done, will I ever write anything else? The story of Clement? Or that book about the theatre that my friends kindly profess to think so necessary? Or shall I simply sit by the fire and read Shakespeare, coming home to the place where magic does not shrink reality and turn it into tiny things to be the toys of fairies? There may be no saints, but there is at least one proof that the light of self-satisfaction can illuminate the whole world.

A few letters have arrived for James but they are all from scholars. It appears that my cousin was quite a well-known orientalist who corresponded with learned men all over the world. I have sent the letters on to a man at the British Museum who rang me up asking about the fate of James's books. I asked the BM man round to look at the books and he came yesterday. When he saw all the stuff in the flat he nearly fainted with emotion and cupidity.

I cannot think what to do about James's poems. Yes, James's POEMS! I think I have not mentioned these before! So James did, in some sense at any rate, do what he said he would do: join the army and become a poet. There, in the otherwise bare top drawer of this desk, they were, and indeed there they are: all neatly typed out and filling several large looseleaf books. A 'personal relic' no doubt, but with no directions, no covering letter. Toby Ellesmere, who, as I think I mentioned, is now a publisher, has got wind of their existence and has rung up about them twice. Perhaps James mentioned them to him sometime. He has never seen them, and I have not shown them to him. In fact I cannot bring myself to look at them, even to glance at them, for fear that they should turn out to be embarrassingly bad! I had almost rather destroy them unread.

It occurs to me that the only lines of poetry I ever heard James quoting, and he quoted them often, were *Whatever happens we have got the Maxim gun and they have not!*

Of course this chattering diary is a façade, the literary equivalent of the everyday smiling face which hides the inward ravages of jealousy, remorse, fear and the consciousness of irretrievable moral failure. Yet such pretences are not only consolations but may even be productive of a little ersatz courage.

I have had another letter from Angie, sending another photo and repeating her kind offer.

*

Gradually autumn is taking charge of London. It is remarkable how early it seems to arrive. The leaves of the plane trees, yellow and red and brightly spotted, appear like little messages stuck upon the damp pavements. Cox's Orange Pippins are to be found in the shops. I am storing them on the top shelf of my larder. I walk down the street to the embankment every morning and evening and see the turbulent skies over the august towers of Battersea Power Station, and the eternal drama of the Thames rising and falling. I wait. Peregrine is to receive some sort of award for his services to peace. Rosina has gone to America on a job. I have had lunch with Rosemary, with Miss Kaufman, with poor old Fabian, with a frenetic young actor called Erasmus Blick. Of course I have not troubled to record that I am constantly badgered by theatre people to return to the old game. When will they realize I am not interested? I have silenced my telephone with a screw of paper. I have not entered a theatre, even to see Mr Blick's new *Hamlet,* which is supposed to be the best thing since sliced bread.

Yes, I wonder if I shall ever write that book about Clement? It is as if this book has taken up forever the space which I might have given to her. How unjust this seems now. Clement was the reality of my life, its bread and its wine. She made me, she invented me, she created me, she was my university, my partner, my teacher, my mother, later my child, my soul's mate, my absolute mistress. She, and not Hartley, was the reason why I never married. She was certainly the reason why I did not seek and find Hartley at a time when it might have been quite easy to do so. Why did I not try harder, longer? Clement stopped me. In memory I have extended the time of my frantic craving for the vanished Hartley well on into Clement's regime, but the memory must be misleading. How could Clement not have cured me? Clement when I first met her was a dazzling figure, beautiful and clever and at the top of her fame; and still young, though I thought of her as old. I was twenty. She was thirty-nine, forty. My God, she was younger than Lizzie is now. When I first met her I was a green awkward ignorant graceless boy, it is a miracle that she ever looked at me. Later on, I treated her coldly, her possessiveness irritated me, I found her love a nuisance. I went away, she went away, yet I always came back and she always came back. We never really got lost, and at the end when she was dying I drove all the others out.

Clement was a long time dying. They had the headlines set up in type for weeks. I lay on the bed beside her and stroked her face, which had become, just very lately, so much more wrinkled with pain and fear. My fingers can still remember those soft wrinkles and the tears that quietly filled them. She said she wanted to die in a storm of noise and for days we had the hi-fi turned up playing Wagner and we drank whisky and together we waited. It was the strangest waiting I ever remember for it was and it was not waiting. There was a sort of intense timelessness in the way in which we kept each other company. Our fear divided us, her fear, my fear, of *the event:* two different sharp fears which we had to overcome by a constant force of mutual attention, laying our hands upon each other's hearts. We became tired and we turned off the noise and we wept and still we waited. My God, Clement's tears, how much I had seen of them before and how much they had sickened me. Now I felt they would make a saint of me, and perhaps for a month they almost did. In the end she died when I was asleep. Every morning I had thought I might find her dead, but had then seen her breathing, the little rhythmic rising and falling of the bedclothes that covered her body which had become so shrunken and small. Then one day there was no movement and I saw her eyes open and her face changed.

That time of attentive mourning for her death was quite unlike the black blank horror of the thing itself. We had mourned together, trying to soothe each other's pain. But that shared pain was so much less than the torment of her vanishing, the terrible lived time of her eternal absence. How different each death is, and yet it leads us into the self-same country, that country which we inhabit so rarely, where we see the worthlessness of what we have long pursued and will so soon return to pursuing.

I did not intend to write about Clement's death. I have made myself wretched by doing so and am still haunted by it although several days have passed. Of course I recovered from that bereavement, probably quite quickly. She left me her money, but in the end there was nothing but debts.

Since silencing my telephone I have received fewer invitations. In any case I think people have got over the excitement of my return to London. Just lately I have been spending my evenings at home drinking wine and listening to music, almost any music, on the radio. I have a record player, but it was broken in the move. I cook myself a supper of rice or lentils or spiced cabbage. I eat Cox's Orange Pippins and go to bed early quite drunk. I don't think I have the makings of an alcoholic. I have a pain in my chest, but I think this is just something to do with Clement.

I wonder if James was mad? I have found myself thinking this for the first time. Would not this hypothesis explain many things? For instance his illusion that he lifted me up out of that whirlpool by some sort of abnormal power? But wait a moment, was not that my illusion? Perhaps I am mad? I am certainly drunk and I was dozing

just now. It is later than my bed time. The Buddhas close in. To
bed, to bed.

Thinking further about James something obvious has only just occurred
to me. He is not dead at all, he has simply gone underground! The whole
charade was organized by the intelligence service! I was too upset at the
time to see how extremely fishy it all was. I never saw James's body.
By the time I arrived the mysterious Colonel Blackthorn was already
in charge and the 'body' had been removed. I never even discovered
who was supposed to have identified it. The extremely shifty Indian
doctor was obviously also in the pay of British Intelligence. His letter
was a masterpiece of bafflement. I was so confused and impressed by
it, I was unable to reflect on the extreme oddness of what was going
on. James was in perfect health when I last saw him. The notion of
his killing himself by will power was just as absurd as the idea of his
walking on the water. It occurs to me that I have never found his
passport in the flat. Where is my cousin now? Not in purgatory or
nirvana, but seated upon an army-issue yak, proceeding to a snowy
rendezvous with some slit-eyed informer!

Since writing the above I have noticed several oriental persons hanging
around in the streets nearby. I hope they are not the *others,* who are
mistaking me for James? As for that tulpa tribesman, he was certainly
an intelligence agent, which was why James was so annoyed that I
saw him.

I have just heard the terrible shocking news that Peregrine has been
murdered by terrorists in Londonderry. I can hardly believe it. I realize
now that I regarded his activities as purely comic. Some men play their
whole lives as a comedy. Only death is not comic – but then it is not

tragic either. That blank horror touches me again, with a grief that is pure fear, but I know I am not really grieving for Perry but for other deaths, perhaps my own. Poor Perry. He was a brave man. I cannot pretend I ever really loved him, but I do admire him for trying to kill me, and if it hadn't been for that freak wave he would have succeeded too. That weird vision of James which seemed so important must have been a result of the blow on the head. It was a lucky escape.

There have been a number of tributes to Peregrine from Catholic and Protestant bishops. He is quite a martyr. They are setting up a Peregrine Arbelow Peace Foundation. Rosina, returned from California to bask in the martyr's glory, is organizing a lot of American money. Lizzie says she heard that Rosina had actually left Perry before his death with no intention of returning, but this may be just malicious gossip.

The shock of Perry's death has, in a curious way, made me a good deal less certain about James's. The theory I deployed above remains a good one, extremely plausible. I just feel less inclined to believe it. Perhaps I would prefer to think of him as dead, the spirit that disturbed me for so long at peace at last. There are no mysteries after all. James died of a heart attack. As for the 'oriental persons', I realize now that they are simply waiters from an Indian restaurant in the Vauxhall Bridge Road.

No, I do not want to believe that cousin James is alive and well and living in Tibet, any more than I want to believe that Hartley is alive and well and living in Australia; and there are times when I actually feel persuaded that she too has died.

Peregrine opened the door and fell to the ground riddled with bullets. After all, he died a hero with his boots on.

To lunch with Miss Kaufman. Sidney has arrived to talk things over with Rosemary. Rosina has spoken at a meeting in Trafalgar Square. Lizzie and I watch Gilbert on television.

Uncle Abel dancing with Aunt Estelle so lightly touches her hand, so lightly touches her shoulder, as if he were lifting her off the ground simply by the force of his love. They look intently at each other; he protectively, she with absolute trust. Were they waltzing, at that fleeting moment which the camera seized and tossed on into the future? Her feet seem scarcely to touch the dance floor.

My father was something which I was destined never to be: a gentleman. Was Uncle Abel one? Not quite. Was James one? The question is absurd.

James said I was in love with my own youth, not with Hartley. Clement stopped me from finding Hartley. The war destroyed any ordinary world in which I might have married my childhood sweetheart. There were no trains going where she was.

I have just had a drunken evening with Toby Ellesmere and feel rather ashamed of it. Toby said James was 'a bit potty' and that he was 'a sphinx without a secret'. I did not disagree. I even felt some satisfaction in hearing James belittled. Ellesmere still wants those poems but I will not give them up; nor have I looked at them, not at so much as a line. Even if James is the greatest poet of the century he must wait a little longer to be recognized. I think he will have to wait until after I am dead.

James said that I must re-enact my love for Hartley, and that then it would crumble to pieces like something in a fairy tale when the clock strikes twelve. Was it just a necessary charade and is such re-enacted love just a machinery for getting rid of an old resentment? Did I simply want to take her away from Ben, as I had wanted to take Rosina away from Perry? Of course Titus's death made Hartley impossible for me, that part at least of the cold lesson, the revelation of human vanity, has remained. And am I now actually beginning to wonder how much I really loved her even at the start? The sad fact was that Hartley was not really very intelligent. What a dull humourless pair we seem, looking back, without spirit or style or a sense of fun. All *those* things were what I learnt from Clement. Did I after all mistake dullness for goodness because my mother hated Aunt Estelle?

Why have I written down these blasphemies all of a sudden? This is late night nonsense.

How long I have put off writing about Hartley, although I have been thinking about her all the time; and perhaps now after all there is little to say. A few days ago, although I did not record it, it suddenly became 'obvious' to me that of course the story of going to Australia was simply a hoax. Why had Hartley not told me earlier that she was going to Australia? Because she was not going! Ben invented the plan at the last moment. Was it not very odd to buy a dog just when one was leaving the country? The postcard from Sydney, so promptly produced by the confederate next door, could easily have been faked with the help of an Australian friend. Ben had decided to throw me off the scent for good, even send me off on a wild-goose chase to the antipodes, and had then removed his submissive wife to Bournemouth or Lytham-St-Anne's. They might even, after a while, and having found out from the Arkwrights that I had gone, return to Nibletts. What should I do then? Go back and do some more detective work in the village? Not everyone would lie.

But the impulse to do so has gone. I have battered destructively and in vain upon the mystery of someone else's life and must cease at last. I later concluded that it really did not matter whether they had gone to Sydney or to Lytham-St-Anne's. And now the idea of such an elaborate hoax for my benefit simply seems absurd.

When did they decide to go to Australia, if they did? Did Ben really believe that I was Titus's father? If he did he behaved, for a violent man, with remarkable restraint. He may even have considered me useful as a pretext. Looking back into that causal web, it is just as well I did tell James that I thought Ben had tried to kill me, since this enabled him to perceive my murderous intentions, and thus to decide to make Perry confess. Did I ever *really* intend to kill Ben? No, those were consolation fantasies. Yet such fantasies too can cause 'accidents'.

Why did I imagine Hartley was consumed by a death wish? She was a survivor, tough as old boots.

If this diary is 'waiting' for some final clarificatory statement which I am to make about Hartley it may have to wait forever. It is not of course a full account of my doings, and events and people unconnected with what went before are omitted from it. I have also omitted the dates from this meditation. Time has passed and it is October, with bright cool sunny days and an intense blue northern sky and scattered flying memories of other autumns. It is mushroom weather, and I have been having feasts of real mushrooms, the big slimy black things, not the little tasteless buttons. Crumpets too have appeared in the shops and already one can look forward to the so familiar London winter, dark afternoons and fogs and the glitter and excitement of Christmas. And however unhappy I am I cannot help responding automatically to these stimuli, as no doubt I did in the past in other unhappy autumns.

Since writing that stuff about Clement I have been missing her. Odd that one can identify a pain as 'missing so and so'. I keep seeing Clement in the street when I am on a bus, on an escalator going up when I am going down, jumping into a taxi and disappearing. Perhaps it will be like this in *bardo*. My God, if she is there, what a time she will be having! Talk of attachments, Clement had enough torment in her head to last ten thousand years.

Of course I do not believe in those 'blasphemies' which I wrote earlier.

When did I begin to relax my hold upon Hartley, or rather upon her image, her double, the Hartley of my mind? Have I relaxed my hold, did it happen before, or is it only happening now, when I can look back over the summer and see my acts and thoughts as those of a madman? I remember Rosina saying to me that her desire for me was made of jealousy, resentment, anger, not love. Was the same true of my desire for Hartley? Was the aim of the whole operation, the whole obsession, that I should be able in the end to see her as a harpy, a semi-conscious trouble-making sorceress, unworthy of my devotion, and whom I would cast off with a relieved disgust? James said I would come to see her as a wicked enchantress and then I would forgive her. But would not forgiving her finally defeat the purpose of this psychological game I have been playing with myself? Have I indeed relived my love simply in order to explain to myself that it was a false love, compounded of resentment stored from long ago and the present promptings of mad possessive jealousy? *Was* I so resentful long ago? I cannot remember. Hartley said, so strangely, that she had to think of me as hating her in order to reduce the attractive power of my image. Now as I think about it all, trying in vain swoops to recover the far past, it seems to me that perhaps what I felt about Hartley then, at any rate after I had been captured by Clement, was a kind of guilt that I was not suffering enough, not seeking her earnestly enough. Damn it, I was in love with Clement, I must have been, though I tormented her by denying it! Was it possible that, by then, I was relieved that I could not find Hartley? I have no diary to tell me and even if I had I might not believe it. I cannot now remember the exact sequence of events in those prehistoric years. That we cannot remember such things, that our memory, which is our self, is tiny, limited and fallible, is also one of those important things about us, like our inwardness and our reason. Indeed it is the very essence of both.

Whatever the cause, it is now clear that something is over. My new, my second love for her, my second 'innings', seemed at its height a thing sublime, even without illusion, when I had seen her as so pitiful, so broken, and yet as something which I could cherish, something which I could hold and be held by, and which would be a source of light even if I were to lose her utterly, as I have indeed lost her utterly. What has become of that light now? It has gone and was at best a flickering flame seen in a marsh, and my great 'illumination' a kind of nonsense. She is gone, she is nothing, for me she no longer exists, and after all I fought for a phantom Helen. *On n'aime qu'une fois, la premiére.* What a lot of folly I have run through in aid of that stupid Gallicism!

What has changed things, simply the relentless movement of time, which so quietly and automatically changes all things? I wrote earlier that Titus's death had 'spoilt' Hartley, spoilt her just by her survival of him. Yes, but it was not that I somehow blamed her for it. Rather there was some sort of demonic filth which had gradually corroded everything, and which seemed to come, without her fault, from her, so that for her sake, for my sake, we had to part eternally. And I seem to see her now, forever disfigured by that filth, untidy, frowzy, dirty, old. How cruel and unjust. Without her fault. The only fault which I can at all measure is my own. I let loose my own demons, not least the sea serpent of jealousy. But now my brave faith which said 'Whatever she is like, it is her that I love' has failed and gone, and all has faded into triviality and self-regarding indifference; and I know that quietly I belittle her, as almost every human being intentionally belittles every other one. Even the few whom we genuinely adore we have to belittle secretly now and then, as Toby and I had to belittle James, just to feed the healthy appetite of our wondrously necessary egos.

But of course the pain remains and will remain. We are conditioned beings who salivate when the bell rings. This sheer conditioning is another of our most characteristic dooms. Anything can be tarnished by association, and if you have enough associations you can blacken the world. Whenever I hear a dog barking I see again Hartley's face as I last saw it, all wrinkled up with pain, then going strangely blank. Just as, whenever I hear the music of Wagner I remember Clement dying and weeping over her own death. In hell or in purgatory there would be no need of other or more elaborate tortures.

A busy week. Had lunch with Miss Kaufman and arranged for her mother to be packed off to a comfortable and expensive 'twilight home'. I am to pay the bills, it appears. Am I becoming saintly after all? Had a drink with Rosina. She is thinking of entering politics. She says it is so easy to influence people by making speeches. Saw Aloysius Bull and Will Boase. They want me to join their new company. Refused. Went to private view of Doris's awful paintings. Lunch with Rosemary, who says the Maybelle business may be blowing over. Got another letter from Angie. To Cambridge to visit the Bansteads, and see them showing off their happy successful marriage and their handsome clever children. Dinner with Lizzie and Gilbert. Gilbert is nominated 'show business personality of the year'. We talked of Wilfred, and Gilbert was becomingly modest, or affected to be.

I must speak of Lizzie. I have been unjust to her in the preceding pages. However, I have kept her letters to me, and the keeping of a letter is always significant. (Why on earth did Hartley keep my last letter but not read it? I suppose she just had to dispose of it quickly. A long letter cannot always be rapidly destroyed, as I have found out in my time.) I have reread Lizzie's letters, the ones recorded above. At the time they seemed to me to be mere outpourings of self-deceiving nonsense. Now they seem rather touching, even wise. (Am I, for the first time since Clement, feeling short of admirers?) Since Gilbert became so busy and famous I have been seeing a little more of Lizzie by herself. I now have lunch with her regularly and have at last persuaded her not to cook. This, in almost any friendship, is a very important step. We are quiet and cheerful together. We laugh and joke a lot, we discuss nothing serious, and it may be that Lizzie's eloquence rings more in my mind than it does in hers.

My love for you is quiet at last. I don't want it to become a roaring furnace. If I could have suffered more I would have suffered more. Receive us now as if we were your children. Tenderness and absolute trust and communication and truth matter more and more as one grows older. Somehow let us not waste love, it is rare. Can we not love each other at last in freedom, without awful possessiveness and violence and fear? Love matters, not 'in love'. Let there be no more partings now. Let there be peace between us now forever, we are no longer young. Love me, Charles, love me enough.

There is no doubt that Lizzie and Gilbert are indeed happy together as she said, and I did not believe, in her first letter. 'It's all suddenly simple and innocent.' His fame makes no difference to that. It creates chances for me to see her alone and I think this pleases him. His TV success has led to other triumphs. He was away for some time in September at the Edinburgh Festival, where Al Bull directed him in a new play. Buoyed up by the love of the British public he is a good deal less frightened of me than he used to be. So is Lizzie. Is the Lion becoming old and clawless? However that may be, I notice that without any effort, without anything being said, without personal discussion of any kind, without there being any question of sexual relations, Lizzie has become what she once was and what she said she desired to be, my child, my page, my son. So at least one person in this story has got what she wanted.

Lizzie was terrified to come back to me in case her love should make her my slave. She was afraid of that dreadful tormenting dependence of one human consciousness upon another. Am I sorry that that fear has left her? There is a wicked tyrant in me that is. How did Lizzie manage it? Perhaps she too had to re-enact her love, to suffer it all over again, in order to transform it. Only she seems to have succeeded whereas I have failed; she has perfected her love, I have simply destroyed mine. Was I the destined trial that was to purify her power to love? The speculation is rather too sublime! Perhaps the horrors of the summer simply snapped some thread, Lizzie grew tired. We are all potentially demons to each other, but some close relationships are saved from this fate. My relation with Lizzie seems to have been so saved, by some grace, without my merit, without my will. I think we are both tired, and glad to rest in each other's company.

We touch and kiss, there is no urge for more. As I said at the start, I am, unlike the modern hero, not highly sexed! I can do without it, I am doing without it, I feel fine without it. Looking back, I must make a confession which would indeed shame the modern hero. I have not had all that many love affairs, and the women I pursued successfully did not always please me in bed. Of course there have been exceptions:

Clement, who taught me. Jeanne. What would it have been like with Hartley?

Lizzie and I never speak of James and somehow this does not seem to matter. It is as if the fact that he knew her had been blotted out of both our memories. All the same, and in a sense which is perhaps harmless, James has divided me from Lizzie, he has castrated our relationship. Perhaps this is precisely the unmerited grace, the source of our peace? The demons detailed to disturb our friendship have all been killed. I do not miss them. Sometimes when Lizzie and I smile quietly at each other I wonder if she is thinking just the same thing.

I have had a recurrence of the chest pain which I first experienced on the day when I tried to have a bath in the kitchen at Shruff End. I saw my doctor but he says it is simply caused by 'viruses'.

Sometimes I sit and wonder whom I should leave my money to. Perhaps I had better start giving it away now. I have sent a cheque to the Buddhist Society and another to the Arbelow Peace Foundation, and will shortly amaze young Erasmus Blick, who is getting married, by my generosity. His *Hamlet* is still running, I still haven't seen it. I imagine I shall leave all the oriental stuff to the British Museum, in fact they can have the books now. And I shall leave James's poems to Toby. Why this anxiety to tidy up? Do I imagine I am going to die soon? Not really – yet it is as if that fall into the sea did damage me after all, not with body damage but with some sort of soul damage. Perhaps James died of soul damage? I am perfectly healthy and do not feel that I am becoming an 'elderly party', but I notice that people are beginning to treat me as if I were one, and this must be a reflection of my own sense of myself. They give me presents, potted plants and tins of jellied chicken, and ask me if I am all right. Am I all right? Rosemary has given me some pottery soup bowls.

Last night someone on a BBC quiz did not know who I was.

I must have been a bit under the weather yesterday when I wrote the above. In fact I was feeling a bit queasy after attending a so-called college 'feast' in Oxford. I must not give my money away too quickly when I am in moods like that. However I have told the British Museum that they can have the books now. I suppose that is right, though there is a kind of impiety involved in letting any of James's stuff go away. Do I then suppose he is likely to come back at any moment?

As I write I am touching with my other hand the brown stone with the blue lines on it which James selected from my collection at Shruff End. It was on the desk when I came here and perhaps he handled it a lot, so touching it is a bit like touching his hand (what sentimental nonsense). I hold the stone and play with a kind of emotion which I keep at bay. Loving people, isn't that an attachment? I do not want to suffer fruitlessly. I feel regret, remorse, that I never got to know him better. We were never really friends and I spent a lot of my life stupidly envying him, nervously watching him, and exerting myself in a competition which he probably never knew existed. In so far as he did not succeed I was glad, and I valued my own success because it seemed that I outshone him. My awareness of him was fear, anxiety, envy, desire to impress. Could such an awareness contain or compose love? We missed each other because of lack of confidence, courage, generosity, because of misplaced dignity and English taciturnity. I feel now as if something of me went with James's death, like part of a bridge carried away in a flood.

A completely new view of Hartley's second defection, and indeed of her first, has just occurred to me. I think something like it was suggested to me by James. When Hartley said she had to 'protect herself' by thinking I hated her and blamed her, she added that she 'always felt guilty'. When she said she had to feel sure it was all over and to 'make it dead in her mind', I imagined that this angry hostile image of me was designed to numb her old love and the attraction which I might still exercise, because such an attraction would be too painful for her to live with. But perhaps the fundamental bond was not love at all, but guilt? Obsessive guilt can survive through the years and animate the ghost of the offended one. Could such guilt even simulate a buried love? Perhaps Hartley herself, in that long interim, did not know what it was that she was so painfully feeling about me. It must have been a terrible and a difficult action to escape from me, to betray our unseparated lives and our devoted vows. 'I had to go like that, it was the only way, it wasn't easy.' Had the shock of that betrayal gone on reverberating in her mind, like the original explosion of the universe? While there was no occasion to define it, how could she know exactly what she felt, whether it was shock, or guilt, or love?

Then I reappeared and made it, quite suddenly, abundantly clear to her that I did not hate her or blame her, that I had gone on loving her without resentment. Her first feeling was one of gratitude, and with this relief came a sense of a love revived. Perhaps this was what she felt on the night when she came to me about Titus. As I learnt in the case of myself and Peregrine, one often feels guilt not because one has sinned but because one has been accused! The withdrawal of the imagined accusation caused Hartley to feel gratitude, affection, at first. But as the guilt, and the vibrating explosive intensity which it had brought into our relationship, began to fade, the more deeply buried reality of her feelings for me became apparent. After all, it had been very hard to leave me and she must have had very compelling motives. It had required great courage to run away to her auntie at Stoke-on-Trent. Why did she go? Because I was in love and she was not; because she simply did not like me enough, because I was too selfish, too dominating, as she put it 'so sort of bossy'. I had deluded myself throughout by the idea of reviving a secret love which did not exist at all. After her liberation from the tie of guilt, that old saving resentment returned to her, she regained that sheer basic indifference to my company which in the past had enabled her to go away, and take her hopes for life elsewhere. And perhaps in that elsewhere she had soon met with a sexual awakening which I had been unable to give her.

But these speculations are too nightmarish. Better to feel 'I shall never know.'

The people from the British Museum have come and removed all the oriental books. They looked longingly at the other stuff. One even wanted to examine the demon-casket, but I ran forward with a cry. James's other books, which now conspicuously remain, are mainly history, and poetry in European languages. (I cannot find the works of Milarepa. Is he an Italian poet?) No novels. I have unpacked some of my own books, but they have an unhappy frivolous look and will never fill those empty spaces. Will the place be gradually dismantled, like Aladdin's palace?

A letter from Jeanne who wants me to visit her in Iran where her husband, a Kurd or something, is some sort of princeling. I may yet be the victim of a *crime passionnel*.

Shruff End has been sold at last, thank God, to a Dr and Mrs Schwarzkopf. I hope they will have better luck than I did with whatever it is there.

The latest gossip about Rosina is that she is living in a canyon in Los Angeles with a woman psychiatrist. I hear that idiot Will Boase has been knighted. I never coveted such 'honours', I am glad to say.

I dreamt last night that Hartley was dead, that she was drowned. Another letter from Angie.

I have talked with Lizzie about Hartley and though nothing important was said my heart feels eased, as if it has been gently prised open. I accused Hartley of being a 'fantasist', or perhaps that was Titus's word, but what a 'fantasist' I have been myself. I was the dreamer, I the magician. How much, I see as I look back, I read into it all, reading my own dream text and not looking at the reality. Hartley had been right when she said of our love that it was not part of the real world. It had no place. But what strikes me now is that at some point, in order to ease things for myself, I decided, almost surreptitiously, to regard her as a liar. In order to release myself from the burden of my tormented attachment I began, with the half-conscious cunning so characteristic of the self-protective human ego, to see her as a poor hysterical shrew; and this debased pity, which I tried to imagine was some kind of spiritual compassion, was the half-way house to my escape. I could not bear the spectacle of that whimpering captive victim in that awful windowless room which I still see in nightmares. My love's imagination gave up the real Hartley and consoled itself with high abstract ideas of blindly 'accepting it all'. That was the exit.

Lizzie said when we talked, 'Of course a marriage can look terrible but be perfectly all right.' Yes, yes. But had I not evidence? Of course I never told Lizzie about my eavesdropping, and how I heard Hartley saying again and again, 'I'm sorry, I'm sorry, I'm sorry.' Ben never settled down in civilian life. He got a medal for killing a lot of men in a prison camp in the Ardennes. There was talk of unnecessary brutality. Some people are better at killing than others. Hartley said she had lied about Ben's violence, but perhaps that was a lie, uttered out of loyalty, out of irrational fear? Can one not recognize the smell of fear? Where can such speculations lead and under what light can they even attempt to be just? The door is closed against the imagination of love. The fallibility of memory and its feeble range make perfect reconciliations impossible. But there is no doubt that Hartley was afflicted, and no doubt that she did, as I thought at first, sometimes feel sorry that she had lost me. She came to me, she ran to me, that was no dream. That was no phantom that I embraced on that night. And on that night she said that she loved me. My idea of her return to an 'original resentment' is too ingenious. One can be too ingenious in trying to search out the truth. Sometimes one must simply respect its veiled face. Of course this is a love story. She was not able to be my Beatrice nor was I able to be saved by her, but the idea was not senseless or unworthy. My pity for her need not be a device or an impertinence, it can survive after all as a blank ignorant quiet unpossessive souvenir, not now a major part of my life, but a persisting one. The past buries the past and must end in silence, but it can be a conscious silence that rests open-eyed. Perhaps this is the final forgiveness that James spoke of.

Last night I dreamt I heard a boy's voice singing *Eravamo tredici*. When I awoke I still seemed to hear that ridiculous *pima-poma-pima-poma* chorus still ringing in the flat. How differently I would feel about all these possessions if Titus were still alive. Unpacking some more of my books I came across his *de luxe* edition of Dante's love poems.

What innumerable chains of fatal causes one's vanity, one's jealousy, one's cupidity, one's cowardice have laid upon the earth to be traps for others. It is strange to think that when I went to the sea I imagined that I was giving up the world. But one surrenders power in one form, and grasps it in another. Perhaps in a way James and I had the same problem?

I keep trying to remember things which James said, but I seem to be forgetting them at an unusual rate. The flat looks dreary without his books. I think it is going to be rather cold here in the winter. Already the days are blank and yellow. I must try to learn how to raise my bodily temperature by mental concentration!

I have been to my doctor again and he can still find nothing wrong with me. I was beginning to wonder whether all this 'wisdom' was a preliminary to physical collapse! It has been raining all day and I have stayed at home. On my present stores of rice and lentils and Cox's Orange Pippins I could last the winter. I am still silencing the telephone bell. Am I after all alone now, as I intended to be, and without attachments? Is history over?

Can one change oneself? I doubt it. Or if there is any change it must be measured as the millionth part of a millimetre. When the poor ghosts have gone, what remains are ordinary obligations and ordinary interests. One can live quietly and try to do tiny good things and harm no one. I cannot think of any tiny good thing to do at the moment, but perhaps I shall think of one tomorrow.

It is very foggy today. The other side of the Thames was invisible when I went down this morning. The cold weather is making me feel better. The shops are already preparing for Christmas. I walked to Piccadilly and bought a lot of cheese. Came back to find a long effusive cable from Fritzie, who is on his way to London. He wants me to direct something he calls 'neo-ballet'. The *Odyssey* is on again.

Took Miss Kaufman to *Hamlet* and enjoyed it. Have had a very tempting invitation to Japan.

Decided to release the telephone bell and instantly Angie was on the line. Arranged to have lunch with her on Friday. Fritzie arrives tomorrow.

Yes of course I was in love with my own youth. Aunt Estelle? Not really. Who is one's first love?

My God, that bloody casket has fallen on the floor! Some people were hammering in the next flat and it fell off its bracket. The lid has come off and whatever was inside it has certainly got out. Upon the demon-ridden pilgrimage of human life, what next I wonder?

VINTAGE CLASSICS

Vintage launched in the United Kingdom in 1990, and was originally the paperback home for the Random House Group's literary authors. Now, Vintage is comprised of some of London's oldest and most prestigious literary houses, including Chatto & Windus (1855), Hogarth (1917), Jonathan Cape (1921) and Secker & Warburg (1935), alongside the newer or relaunched hardback and paperback imprints: The Bodley Head, Harvill Secker, Yellow Jersey, Square Peg, Vintage Paperbacks and Vintage Classics.

From Angela Carter, Graham Greene and Aldous Huxley to Toni Morrison, Haruki Murakami and Virginia Woolf, Vintage Classics is renowned for publishing some of the greatest writers and thinkers from around the world and across the ages – all complemented by our beautiful, stylish approach to design. Vintage Classics' authors have won many of the world's most revered literary prizes, including the Nobel, the Man Booker, the Prix Goncourt and the Pulitzer, and through their writing they continue to capture imaginations, inspire new perspectives and incite curiosity.

In 2007 Vintage Classics introduced its distinctive red spine design, and in 2012 Vintage Children's Classics was launched to include the much-loved authors of our childhood. Random House joined forces with the Penguin Group in 2013 to become Penguin Random House, making it the largest trade publisher in the United Kingdom.

@vintagebooks

penguin.co.uk/vintage-classics